THE CLONED STRANGERS

Not everyone would envy young Lord Miles Naismith Vorkosigan, even though he had formed his own mercenary fleet *before* attending the naval academy, and even though his mother was the beautiful Cordelia, the ship captain who has taught the Lords of Barrayar much about the perils of sexism. Even the fact that Miles is third in line to the throne and personally owns a major chunk of his home planet would not tempt any normal person to change places with him.

When assassins came to rid the world of his father, his mother, pregnant with Miles, was in the line of fire, and Miles was but an egg for the omelet in an all too literal sense. Thanks to heroic medical intervention, Miles survived his near fatal brush with war gas—as a pain-filled dwarf with bones as weak and brittle as some malign composite of chalk and glass. Miles is often mistaken for a mutant by his mutant-loathing countrymen.

But there is one who does envy him, who wants to be him: his brother, his cloned stranger formed from tissue stolen from Miles when he was a child. For Mark Vorkosigan was created and raised up for only one purpose: to *become* Miles, to murder and replace him. In *Brothers in Arms* that conspiracy was routed and Mark made more or less compliant to his new Miles-less fate. But in the intervening years Mark has learned that without Miles he is . . . nothing. The new and better Mark doesn't really *want* to kill his brother, but still it may come to that: Mark to stay, Miles to go. . . .

BAEN BOOKS by LOIS McMASTER BUJOLD

The Vorkosigan Saga:

Cordelia's Honor

The Warrior's Apprentice

The Vor Game

Young Miles

Cetaganda

Borders of Infinity

Brothers in Arms

Mirror Dance

Memory

Komarr

A Civil Campaign

Ethan of Athos

Falling Free

The Spirit Ring

LOIS McMASTER BUJOLD

MIRROR DANCE

This is a work of fiction. All the characters and events portrayed in this book are fictional, and any resemblance to real people or incidents is purely coincidental.

A Baen Books Original

Baen Publishing Enterprises
P.O. Box 1403
Riverdale, NY 10471
www.baen.com

ISBN: 0-671-87646-5

Cover art by Gary Ruddell

First mass market printing, March 1995
Fourth printing, June 2001

Distributed by Simon & Schuster
1230 Avenue of the Americas
New York, NY 10020

Library of Congress Cataloging-in-Publication Number 93-39663

Printed in the United States of America

For Patricia Collins Wrede,
for literary midwifery above and beyond
the long-distance call of duty

For Patricia Collins Wrede
for literary midwifery above and beyond
the long-distance call of duty

CHAPTER ONE

The row of comconsole booths lining the passenger concourse of Escobar's largest commercial orbital transfer station had mirrored doors, divided into diagonal sections by rainbow-colored lines of lights. Doubtless someone's idea of decor. The mirror-sections were deliberately set slightly out of alignment, fragmenting their reflections. The short man in the grey and white military uniform scowled at his divided self framed therein.

His image scowled back. The insignia-less mercenary officer's undress kit—pocketed jacket, loose trousers tucked into ankle-topping boots—was correct in every detail. He studied the body under the uniform. A stretched-out dwarf with a twisted spine, short-necked, big-headed. Subtly deformed, and robbed by his short stature of any chance of the disturbing near-rightness passing unnoticed. His dark hair was neatly trimmed. Beneath black brows, the grey eyes' glower deepened. The body, too, was correct in every detail. He hated it.

The mirrored door slid up at last, and a woman exited the booth. She wore a soft wrap tunic and flowing trousers. A fashionable bandolier of expensive electronic equipment hanging decoratively on a jeweled chain across her torso advertised her status. Her beginning stride was arrested at the sight of him, and she recoiled, buffeted by his black and hollow stare, then went carefully around him with a mumbled, "Excuse me . . . I'm sorry. . . ."

He belatedly twisted up his mouth in an imitation smile, and muttered something half-inaudible, conveying enough allegiance to the social proprieties for him to pass by. He hit the keypad to lower the door again, sealing himself from sight. Alone at last, for one last moment, if only in the narrow confines of a commercial comm booth. The woman's perfume lingered cloyingly in the air, along with a *frisson* of station odors; recycled air, food, bodies, stress, plastics and metals and cleaning compounds. He exhaled, and sat, and laid his hands out flat on the small countertop to still their trembling.

Not quite alone. There was another damned mirror in here, for the convenience of patrons wishing to check their appearance before transmitting it by holovid. His dark-ringed eyes flashed back at him malevolently, then he ignored the image. He emptied his pockets out onto the countertop. All his worldly resources fit neatly into a space little larger than his two spread palms. One last inventory. As if counting it again might change the sum . . .

A credit chit with about three hundred Betan dollars remaining upon it: one might live well for a week upon this orbital space station for that much, or for a couple of lean months on the planet turning below, if it were carefully managed. Three false identification chits, none for the man he was now. None for the man he was. Whoever he was. An ordinary plastic pocket comb. A data cube. That was all. He returned all but the credit chit to various pockets upon and in the jacket, gravely sorting them individually. He ran out of objects before he ran out of pockets, and snorted. *You might at least have brought your own toothbrush* . . . too late now.

And getting later. Horrors happened, proceeding unchecked, while he sat struggling for nerve. *Come on. You've done this before. You can do it now.* He jammed the credit card into the slot, and keyed in the carefully memorized code number. Compulsively, he glanced one last time into the mirror, and tried to smooth his features into something approaching a neutral expression. For all his practice, he did not think he could manage the grin just now. He despised that grin anyway.

The vid plate hissed to life, and a woman's visage formed above it. She wore grey-and-whites like his own, but with proper rank insignia and name patch. She recited crisply, "Comm Officer Hereld, *Triumph*, Dendarii Free . . . Corporation." In Escobaran space, a mercenary fleet sealed its weapons at the Outside jumppoint station under the watchful eyes of the Escobaran military inspectors, and submitted proof of its purely commercial intentions, before it was even allowed to pass. The polite fiction was maintained, apparently, in Escobar orbit.

He moistened his lips, and said evenly, "Connect me with the officer of the watch, please."

"Admiral Naismith, sir! You're back!" Even over the holovid a blast of pleasure and excitement washed out from her straightened posture and beaming face. It struck him like a blow. "What's up? Are we going to be moving out soon?"

"In good time, Lieutenant . . . Hereld." An apt name for a communications officer. He managed to twitch a smile. Admiral Naismith would smile, yes. "You'll learn in good time. In the meanwhile, I want a pick-up at the orbital transfer station."

"Yes, sir. I can get that for you. Is Captain Quinn with you?"

"Uh . . . no."

"When will she be following?"

". . . Later."

"Right, sir. Let me just get clearance for—are we loading any equipment?"

"No. Just myself."

"Clearance from the Escobarans for a personnel pod, then . . ." she turned aside for a few moments. "I can have someone at docking bay E17 in about twenty minutes."

"Very well." It would take him almost that long to get from this concourse to that arm of the station. Ought he to add some personal word for Lieutenant Hereld? She knew him; how well did she know him? Every sentence that fell from his lips from this point on packed risk, risk of the unknown, risk of a mistake. Mistakes were punished. Was his Betan accent really right? He hated this, with a stomach-churning terror. "I want to be transferred directly to the *Ariel*."

"Right, sir. Do you wish me to notify Captain Thorne?"

Was Admiral Naismith often in the habit of springing surprise inspections? Well, not this time. "Yes, do. Tell them to make ready to break orbit."

"Only the *Ariel*?" Her brows rose.

"Yes, Lieutenant." This, in quite a perfect bored Betan drawl. He congratulated himself as she grew palpably prim. The undertone had suggested just the right hint of criticism of a breach of security, or manners, or both, to suppress further dangerous questions.

"Will do, Admiral."

"Naismith out." He cut the comm. She vanished in a haze of sparkles, and he let out a long breath. Admiral Naismith. Miles Naismith. He had to get used to responding to that name again, even in his sleep. Leave the Lord Vorkosigan part completely out of it, for now; it was difficult enough just being the Naismith half of the man. Drill. What is your name? Miles. Miles. Miles.

Lord Vorkosigan pretended to be Admiral Naismith. And so did he. What, after all, was the difference?

But what is your name really?

His vision darkened in a rush of despair, and rage. He blinked it back, controlling his breathing. *My name is what I will. And right now I will it to be Miles Naismith.*

He exited the booth and strode down the concourse, short legs pumping, both riveting and repelling the sideways stares of startled strangers. *See Miles. See*

Miles run. See Miles get what he deserves. He marched head-down, and no one got in his way.

He ducked into the personnel pod, a tiny four-man shuttle, as soon as the hatch seal sensors blinked green and the door dilated. He hit the keypad for it to close again behind him immediately. The pod was too little to maintain a grav field. He floated over the seats and pulled himself carefully down into the one beside the lone pilot, a man in Dendarii grey tech coveralls.

"All right. Let's go."

The pilot grinned and sketched him a salute as he strapped in. Otherwise appearing to be a sensible adult male, he had the same look on his face as the comm officer, Hereld; excited, breathless, watching eagerly, as if his passenger were about to pull treats from his pockets.

He glanced over his shoulder as the pod obediently broke free of the docking clamps and turned. They swooped away from the skin of the station into clear space. The traffic control patterns made a maze of colored lights on the navigation console, through which the pilot swiftly threaded them.

"Good to see you back, Admiral," said the pilot as soon as the tangle grew less thick. "What's happening?"

The edge of formality in the pilot's tone was reassuring. Just a comrade in arms, not one of the Dear Old Friends, or worse, Dear Old Lovers. He essayed an evasion. "When you need to know, you'll be told." He made his tone affable, but avoided names or ranks.

The pilot vented an intrigued "*Hm,*" and smirked, apparently contented.

He settled back with a tight smile. The huge transfer station fell away silently behind them, shrinking into a mad child's toy, then into a few glints of light. "Excuse me. I'm a little tired." He settled down further into his seat and closed his eyes. "Wake me up when we dock, if I fall asleep."

"Yes, sir," said the pilot respectfully. "You look like you could use it."

He acknowledged this with a tired wave of his hand, and pretended to doze.

He could always tell, instantly, when someone he met thought they were facing "Naismith." They all had that same stupid hyper-alert *glow* in their faces. They weren't all worshipful; he'd met some of Naismith's enemies once, but worshipful or homicidal, they reacted. As if they suddenly switched on, and became ten times more alive than ever before. How the hell did he do it? Make people light up like that? Granted, Naismith was a goddamn hyperactive, but how did he make it so freaking contagious?

Strangers who met him as himself did not greet *him* like that. They were blank and courteous, or blank and rude, or just blank, closed and indifferent. Covertly uncomfortable with his slight deformities, and his obviously abnormal four-foot-nine-inch height. Wary.

His resentment boiled up behind his eyes like sinus pain. All this bloody hero-worship, or whatever it was. All for Naismith. *For Naismith, and not for me . . . never for me. . . .*

He stifled a twinge of dread, knowing what he was about to face. Bel Thorne, the *Ariel's* captain, would be another one. Friend, officer, fellow Betan, yes, a tough test, well enough. But Thorne also knew of the existence of the clone, from that chaotic encounter two years ago on Earth. They had never met face to face. But a mistake that another Dendarii might dismiss in confusion could trigger in Thorne the suspicion, the wild surmise. . . .

Even *that* distinction Naismith had stolen from him. The mercenary admiral, publicly and falsely, now claimed to be a clone himself. A superior cover, concealing his other identity, his other life. *You have two lives,* he thought to his absent enemy. *I have none. I'm the real clone, damn it. Couldn't I have even that uniqueness? Did you have to take it all?*

No. Keep his thoughts positive. He could handle Thorne. As long as he could avoid the terrifying Quinn, the bodyguard, the lover, Quinn. He *had* met Quinn face to face on Earth, and fooled her once, for a whole morning. Not twice, he didn't think. But Quinn was with the real Miles Naismith, stuck like glue; he was safe from her. No old lovers this trip.

He'd never had a lover, not yet. It was perhaps not quite fair to blame Naismith for that as well. For the first twenty years of his life he had been in effect a prisoner, though he hadn't always realized it. For the last two . . . the last two years had been one continuous disaster, he decided bitterly. This was his last chance. He refused to think beyond. No more. This had to be made to work.

The pilot stirred beside him, and he slitted open his eyes as the deceleration pressed him against his seat straps. They were coming up on the *Ariel*. It grew from a dot to a model to a ship. The Illyrican-built light cruiser carried a crew of twenty, plus room for supercargo and a commando squad. Heavily powered for its size, an energy profile typical of warships. It looked swift, almost rakish. A good courier ship; a good ship to run like hell in. Perfect. Despite his black mood, his lips curled up, as he studied that ship. *Now I take, and you give, Naismith.*

The pilot, clearly quite conscious that he was conveying his admiral, brought the personnel pod into its docking clamps with a bare click, neat and smooth as humanly possible. "Shall I wait,sir?"

"No. I shouldn't be needing you again."

The pilot hurried to adjust the tube seals while his

passenger was still unbuckling, and saluted him out with another idiot, broad, proud smile. He twitched a returning smile and salute, then grasped the handlebars above the hatch and swung himself into the *Ariel*'s gravity field.

He dropped neatly to his feet in a small loading bay. Behind him, the pod pilot was already re-sealing the hatch to return himself and his pod to its vessel of origin, probably the flagship *Triumph*. He looked up—always, up—into the face of the waiting Dendarii officer, a face he had studied before this only in a holovid.

Captain Bel Thorne was a Betan hermaphrodite, a race that was remnant of an early experiment in human genetic and social engineering that had succeeded only in creating another minority. Thorne's beardless face was framed by soft brown hair in a short, ambiguous cut that either a man or a woman might sport. Its officer's jacket hung open, revealing the black tee shirt underneath curving over modest but distinctly feminine breasts. The gray Dendarii uniform trousers were loose enough to disguise the reciprocal bulge in the crotch. Some people found hermaphrodites enormously disturbing. He was relieved to realize he found that aspect of Thorne only slightly disconcerting. *Clones who live in glass houses shouldn't throw . . . what?* It was the radiant I-love-Naismith look on the hermaphrodite's face that really bothered him. His gut knotted, as he returned the *Ariel*'s captain's salute.

"Welcome aboard, sir!" The alto voice was vibrant with enthusiasm.

He was just managing a stiff smile, when the hermaphrodite stepped up and embraced him. His heart lurched, and he barely choked off a cry and a violent, defensive lashing-out. He endured the embrace without going rigid, grasping mentally after shattered composure and his carefully rehearsed speeches. *It's not going to kiss me, is it?!*

The hermaphrodite set him at arm's length, hands familiarly upon his shoulders, without doing so, however. He breathed relief. Thorne cocked its head, its lips twisting in puzzlement. "What's wrong, Miles?"

First names? "Sorry, Bel. I'm just a little tired. Can we get right to the briefing?"

"You look a lot tired. Right. Do you want me to assemble the whole crew?"

"No . . . you can re-brief them as needed." That was the plan, as little direct contact with as few Dendarii as possible.

"Come to my cabin, then, and you can put your feet up and drink tea while we talk."

The hermaphrodite followed him into the corridor. Not knowing which direction to turn, he wheeled and waited as if politely for Thorne to lead on. He trailed the Dendarii officer through a couple of twists and turns and up a level. The ship's internal architecture was not as cramped as he'd expected. He noted directions carefully. Naismith knew this ship well.

The *Ariel's* captain's cabin was a neat little chamber, soldierly, not revealing much on this side of the latched cupboard doors about the personality of its owner. But Thorne unlatched one to display an antique ceramic tea set and a couple of dozen small canisters of varietal teas of Earth and other planetary origins, all protected from breakage by custom-made foam packing. "What kind?" Thorne called, its hand hovering over the canisters.

"The usual," he replied, easing into a station chair clamped to the floor beside a small table.

"Might have guessed. I swear I'll train you to be more venturesome one of these days." Thorne shot a peculiar grin over its shoulder at him—was that intended to be some sort of double entendre? After a bit more rattling about, Thorne placed a delicately hand-painted porcelain cup and saucer upon the table at his elbow. He picked it up and sipped cautiously as Thorne hooked another chair into its clamps a quarter turn around the table, produced a cup for itself, and sat with a small grunt of satisfaction.

He was relieved to find the hot amber liquid pleasant, if astringent. Sugar? He dared not ask. Thorne hadn't put any out. The Dendarii surely would have, if it expected Naismith to use sugar. Thorne couldn't be making some subtle test already, could it? No sugar, then.

Tea-drinking mercenaries. The beverage didn't seem nearly poisonous enough, somehow, to go with the display, no, working arsenal, of weapons clamped to the wall: a couple of stunners, a needler, a plasma arc, a gleaming metal crossbow with an assortment of grenade-bolts in a bandolier hung with it. Thorne was supposed to be good at its job. If that was true, he didn't care what the creature drank.

"You're in a black study. I take it you've brought us a lovely one this time, eh?" Thorne prodded after another moment's silence.

"The mission assignment, yes." He certainly hoped that was what Thorne meant. The hermaphrodite nodded, and raised its brows in encouraging inquiry. "It's a pick-up. Not the biggest one we've ever attempted, by any means—"

Thorne laughed.

"But with its own complications."

"It can't possibly be any more complicated than Dagoola Four. Say on, oh do."

He rubbed his lips, a patented Naismith gesture. "We're going to knock over House Bharaputra's clone creche, on Jackson's Whole. Clean it out."

Thorne was just crossing its legs; both feet now hit the floor with a thump. "Kill them?" it said in a startled voice.

"The clones? No, rescue them! Rescue them all."

"Oh. Whew." Thorne looked distinctly relieved. "I had this horrible vision for a second—they *are* children, after all. Even if they are clones."

"Just exactly so." A real smile tugged up the corners of his mouth, surprising him. "I'm . . . glad you see it that way."

"How else?" Thorne shrugged. "The clone brain-transplant business is the most monstrous, obscene practice in Bharaputra's whole catalog of slime services. Unless there's something even worse I haven't heard about yet."

"I think so too." He settled back, concealing his startlement at this instant endorsement of his scheme. Was Thorne sincere? He knew intimately, none better, the hidden horrors behind the clone business on Jackson's Whole. He'd lived through them. He had not expected someone who had not shared his experiences to share his judgment, though.

House Bharaputra's specialty was not, strictly speaking, cloning. It was the immortality business, or at any rate, the life extension business. And a very lucrative business it was, for what price could one put on life itself? All the market would bear. The procedure Bharaputra sold was medically risky, not ideal . . . wagered only against a certainty of imminent death by customers who were wealthy, ruthless, and, he had to admit, possessed of unusual cool foresight.

The arrangement was simple, though the surgical procedure upon which it was based was fiendishly complex. A clone was grown from a customer's somatic cell, gestated in a uterine replicator and then raised to physical maturity in Bharaputra's creche, a sort of astonishingly-appointed orphanage. The clones were valuable, after all, their physical conditioning and health of supreme importance. Then, when the time was right, they were cannibalized. In an operation that claimed a total success rate of rather less than one hundred percent, the clone's progenitor's brain was transplanted from its aged or damaged body into a duplicate still in the first bloom of youth. The clone's brain was classified as medical waste.

The procedure was illegal on every planet in the wormhole nexus except Jackson's Whole. That was fine with the criminal Houses that ran the place. It gave them a nice monopoly, a steady business with lots of practice upon the stream of wealthy off-worlders to keep their surgical teams at the top of their forms. As far as he had ever been able to tell, the attitude of the rest of the worlds toward it all was "out of sight, out of mind." The spark of sympathetic, righteous anger in Thorne's eyes touched him on a level of pain so numb with use he was scarcely conscious of it any more, and he was appalled to realize he was a heartbeat away from bursting into tears. *It's probably a trick.* He blew out his breath, another Naismith-ism.

Thorne's brows drew down in intense thought. "Are you sure we should be taking the *Ariel*? Last I heard, Baron Ryoval was still alive. It's bound to get his attention."

House Ryoval was one of Bharaputra's minor rivals in the illegal medical end of things. Its specialty was manufacturing genetically-engineered or surgically sculptured humans for any purpose, including sexual, in effect slaves made-to-order; evil, he supposed, but not the killing evil that obsessed him. But what had the *Ariel* to do with Baron Ryoval? He hadn't a clue. Let Thorne worry about it. Perhaps the hermaphrodite would drop more information later. He reminded himself to seize the first opportunity to review the ship's mission logs.

"This mission has nothing to do with House Ryoval. We shall avoid them."

"So I hope," agreed Thorne fervently. It paused, thoughtfully sipping tea. "Now, despite the fact that Jackson's Whole is long overdue for a housecleaning, preferably with atomics, I presume we are not doing this just out of the goodness of our hearts. What's, ah, the mission behind the mission this time?"

He had a rehearsed answer for that one. "In fact, only one of the clones, or rather, one of its progenitors, is of interest to our employer. The rest are to be camouflage. Among them, Bharaputra's customers have a lot of enemies. They won't know which one is attacking who. It makes our employer's identity, which they very much desire to keep secret, all the more secure."

Thorne grinned smugly. "That little refinement was your idea, I take it."

He shrugged. "In a sense."

"Hadn't we better know which clone we're after, to prevent accidents, or in case we have to cut and run? If our employer wants it alive—or does it matter to them if the clone is alive or dead? If the real target is the old bugger who had it grown."

"They care. Alive. But . . . for practical purposes, let us assume that all the clones are the one we're after."

Thorne spread its hands in acquiescence. "It's all right by me." The hermaphrodite's eyes glinted with enthusiasm, and it suddenly smacked its fist into its palm with a crack that made him jump. "It's about time someone took those Jacksonian bastards on! Oh, this is going to be fun!" It bared its teeth in a most alarming grin. "How much help do we have lined up on Jackson's Whole? Safety nets?"

"Don't count on any."

"Hm. How much hindrance? Besides Bharaputra, Ryoval, and Fell, of course."

House Fell dealt mainly in weapons. What had Fell to do with any of this? "Your guess is as good as mine."

Thorne frowned; that was not the usual sort of Naismith answer, apparently.

"I have a great deal of inside information about the creche, that I can brief you on once we're en route. Look, Bel, you hardly need me to tell you how to do your job at this late date. I trust you. Take over the logistics and planning, and I'll check the finals."

Thorne's spine straightened. "Right. How many kids are we talking about?"

"Bharaputra does about one of these transplants a week, on average. Fifty a year, say, that they have coming along. The last year of the clones' lives they move them to a special facility near House headquarters, for final conditioning. I want to take the whole year's supply from that facility. Fifty or sixty kids."

"All packed aboard the *Ariel*? It'll be tight."

"Speed, Bel, speed."

"Yeah. I think you're right. Timetable?"

"As soon as possible. Every week's delay costs another innocent life." He'd measured out the last two years by that clock. *I have wasted a hundred lives so far.* The journey from Earth to Escobar alone had cost him a thousand Betan dollars and four dead clones.

"I get it," said Thorne grimly, and rose and put away its tea cup. It switched its chair to the clamps in front of its comconsole. "That kid's slated for surgery, isn't it."

"Yes. And if not that one, a creche-mate."

Thorne began tapping keypads. "What about funds? That *is* your department."

"This mission is cash on delivery. Draw your estimated needs from Fleet funds."

"Right. Put your palm over here and authorize my withdrawal, then." Thorne held out a sensor pad.

Without hesitation, he laid his palm flat upon it. To his horror, the red no-recognition code glinted in the readout. *No! It has to be right, it has to—!*

"Damn machine." Thorne tapped the sensor pad's corner sharply on the table. "Behave. Try again."

This time, he laid his palm down with a very slight twist; the computer digested the new data, and this time pronounced him cleared, accepted, blessed. Funded. His pounding heart slowed in relief.

Thorne keyed in more data, and said over its shoulder, "No question which commando squad you want to requisition for this one, eh?"

"No question," he echoed hollowly. "Go ahead." He had to get out of here, before the strain of the masquerade made him blow away his good start.

"You want your usual cabin?" Thorne inquired.

"Sure." He stood.

"Soon, I gather . . ." The hermaphrodite checked a readout in the glowing complexity of logistics displays above the comconsole vid plate. "The palm lock is still keyed for you. Get off your feet, you look beat. It's under control."

"Good."

"When will Elli Quinn be along?"

"She won't be coming on this mission."

Thorne's eyes widened in surprise. "*Really*." Its smile broadened, quite inexplicably. "That's too bad." Its voice conveyed not the least disappointment. Some rivalry, there? Over what?

"Have the *Triumph* send over my kit," he ordered. Yes, delegate that thievery too. Delegate it all. "And . . . when you get the chance, have a meal sent to my cabin."

"Will do," promised Thorne with a firm nod. "I'm glad to see you've been eating better, by the way, even if you haven't been sleeping. Good. Keep it up. We worry about you, you know."

Eating better, hell. With his stature, keeping his weight down had become a constant battle. He'd starved for three months just to get back into Naismith's uniform, that he'd stolen two years ago and now wore. Another wave of weary hatred for his progenitor washed over him. He let himself out with a casual salute that he trusted would encourage Thorne to keep working, and managed to keep from snarling under his breath till the cabin door hissed shut behind him.

There was nothing for it but to try every palm lock in the corridor till one opened. He hoped no Dendarii would come along while he was rattling doors. He found his cabin at last, directly across from the hermaphrodite captain's. The door slid open at his touch on the sensor pad without any heart-stopping glitches this time.

The cabin was a little chamber almost identical to Thorne's, only blanker. He checked cupboards. Most were bare, but in one he found a set of gray fatigues and a stained tech coverall just his size. A residue of half-used toiletries in the cabin's tiny washroom included a toothbrush, and his lips twisted in an ironical sneer. The neatly made bed which folded out of the wall looked extremely attractive, and he nearly swooned into it.

I'm on my way. I've done it. The Dendarii had accepted him, accepted his orders with the same stupid blind trust with which they followed Naismith's. Like sheep. All he had to do now was not screw it up. The hardest part was over.

He'd grabbed a quick shower and was just pulling on Naismith's trousers when his meal arrived. His undress state gave him an excuse to wave the attentive tray-bearing Dendarii out again quickly. The dinner under the covers turned out to be real food, not rations. Grilled vat steak, fresh-appearing vegetables, non-synthetic coffee, the hot food hot and the cold food cold, beautifully laid out in little portions finely calculated to Naismith's appetite. Even ice cream. He recognized his progenitor's tastes, and was daunted anew by this rush by unknown people to try to give him exactly what he wanted, even in these tiny details. Rank had its privileges, but this was insane.

Depressed, he ate it all, and was just wondering if the fuzzy green stuff arranged to fill up all the empty space on the plate was edible too, when the cabin buzzer blatted again.

This time, it was a Dendarii non-com and a float pallet with three big crates on it.

"Ah," he blinked. "My kit. Just set it there in the middle of the floor, for now."

"Yes, sir. Don't you want to assign a batman?" The non-com's inviting expression left no doubt about who was first in line to volunteer.

"Not . . . this mission. We're going to be cramped for space, later. Just leave it."

"I'd be happy to unpack it for you, sir. I packed it all up."

"Quite all right."

"If I've missed anything, just let me know, and I'll run it right over."

"*Thank* you, corporal." His exasperation leaked into his voice; fortunately, it acted as a brake upon the corporal's enthusiasm. The Dendarii heaved the crates from the float pallet and exited with a sheepish grin, as if to say, *Hey, you can't blame me for trying*.

He smiled back through set teeth, and turned his attention to the crates as soon as the door sealed. He flipped up the latches and hesitated, bemused at his own eagerness. It must be rather like getting a birthday present. He'd never had a birthday present in his life. *So, let's make up for some lost time.*

The first lid folded back to reveal clothes, more clothes than he'd ever owned before. Tech coveralls, undress kit, a dress uniform—he held up the grey velvet tunic, and raised his brows at the shimmer and the silver buttons—boots, shoes, slippers, pajamas, all regulation, all cut down to perfect fit. And civilian clothes, eight or ten sets, in various planetary and galactic styles and social levels. An Escobaran business suit in red silk, a Barrayaran quasi-military tunic and piped trousers, ship knits, a Betan sarong and sandals, a ragged jacket and shirt and pants suitable for a down-on-his-luck dockworker anywhere. Abundant underwear. Three kinds of chronos with built-in comm units, one Dendarii regulation, one very expensive commercial model, one appearing cheap and battered, which turned out to be finest military surplus underneath. And more.

He moved to the second crate, flipped up the lid, and gaped. *Space armor.* Full-bore attack unit space armor, power and life support packs fully charged, weapons loaded and locked. Just his size. It seemed to gleam with its own dark and wicked glow, nested in its packing. The smell of it hit him, incredibly military, metal and plastic, energy and chemicals . . . old sweat. He drew the helmet out and stared with wonder into the darkened mirror of its visor. He had never worn space armor,though he'd studied it in holovids till his eyes crossed. A sinister, deadly carapace . . .

He unloaded it all, and laid the pieces out in order upon the floor. Strange splashes, scars, and patches decked the gleaming surfaces here and there. What weapons, what strikes, had been powerful enough to mar that metalloy surface? What enemies had fired them? Every scar, he realized, fingering them, had been intended death. This was not pretend.

It was very disturbing. *No.* He pushed away the cold shiver of doubt. *If he can do it, I can do it.* He tried to ignore the repairs and mysterious stains on the pressure suit and its soft, absorbent underliner as he packed it all away again and stowed the crate. Blood? Shit? Burns? Oil? It was all cleaned and odorless now, anyway.

The third crate, smaller than the second, proved to contain a set of half-armor, lacking built-in weapons and not meant for space, but rather for dirtside combat under normal or near-normal pressure, temperature, and atmospheric conditions. Its most arresting feature was a command headset, a smooth duralloy helmet with built-in telemetry and a vid projector in a flange above the forehead that placed any data on the net right before the commander's eyes. Data flow was controlled by certain facial movements and voice commands. He left it out on the counter to examine more thoroughly later, and repacked the rest.

By the time he finished arranging all the clothing in the cabin's cupboards and drawers, he'd begun to regret sending the batman away so precipitously. He fell onto the bed, and dimmed the lights. When he next woke, he should be on his way to Jackson's Whole. . . .

He'd just begun to doze when the cabin comm buzzed. He lurched up to answer it, mustering a reasonably coherent "Naismith here," in a sleep-blurred voice.

"Miles?" said Thorne's voice. "The commando squad's here."

"Uh . . . good. Break orbit as soon as you're ready, then."

"Don't you want to see them?" Thorne said, sounding surprised.

Inspection. He inhaled. "Right. I'll . . . be along. Naismith out." He hurried back into his uniform trousers, taking a jacket with proper insignia this time, and quickly called up a schematic of the ship's interior layout on the cabin's comconsole. There were two locks for combat drop shuttles, port and starboard. Which one? He traced a route to both.

The operative shuttle hatch was the first one he tried. He paused a moment in shadow and silence at the curve of the corridor, before he was spotted, to take in the scene.

The loading bay was crowded with a dozen men and

women in grey camouflage flight suits, along with piles of equipment and supplies. Hand and heavy weapons were stacked in symmetrical arrays. The mercenaries sat or stood, talking noisily, loud and crude, punctuated with barks of laughter. They were all so big, generating too much energy, knocking into each other in half-horseplay, as if seeking an excuse to shout louder. They bore knives and other personal weapons on belts or in holsters or on bandoliers, an ostentatious display. Their faces were a blur, animal-like. He swallowed, straightened, and stepped among them.

The effect was instantaneous. "Heads up!" someone shouted, and without further orders they arranged themselves at rigid attention in two neat, dead silent rows, each with his or her bundle of equipment at their feet. It was almost more frightening than the previous chaos.

With a thin smile, he walked forward, and pretended to look at each one. A last heavy duffle arced out of the shuttle hatch to land with a thump on the deck, and the thirteenth commando squeezed through, stood up, and saluted him.

He stood paralyzed with panic. Whatinhell *was* it? He stared at a flashing belt buckle, then tilted his head back, straining his neck. The freaking thing was *eight feet tall*. The enormous body radiated power that he could feel almost like a wave of heat, and the face—the face was a nightmare. Tawny yellow eyes, like a wolf's, a distorted, outslung mouth with *fangs*, dammit, long white canines locked over the edges of the carmine lips. The huge hands had *claws*, thick, powerful, razor-edged—enamelled with carmine polish. . . . *What?* His gaze traveled back up to the monster's face. The eyes were outlined with shadow and gold tint, echoed by a little gold spangle glued decoratively to one high cheekbone. The mahogany-colored hair was drawn back in an elaborate braid. The belt was cinched in tightly, emphasizing a figure of sorts despite the loose-fitting multi-grey flight suit. The thing was female—?

"Sergeant Taura and the Green Squad, reporting as ordered, sir!" The baritone voice reverberated in the bay.

"Thank you—" It came out a cracked whisper, and he coughed to unlock his throat. "Thank you, that will be all, get your orders from Captain Thorne, you may all stand down." They all strained to hear him, compelling him to repeat, "Dismissed!"

They broke up in disorder, or some order known only to themselves, for the bay was cleared of equipment with astonishing speed. The monster sergeant lingered, looming over him. He locked his knees, to keep himself from sprinting from it—her. . . .

She lowered her voice. "Thanks for picking the Green Squad, Miles. I take it you've got us a real plum."

More first names? "Captain Thorne will brief you en route. It's . . . a challenging mission." And this would be the sergeant in charge of it?

"Captain Quinn have the details, as usual?" She cocked a furry eyebrow at him.

"Captain Quinn . . . will not be coming on this mission."

He swore her gold eyes widened, the pupil's dilating. Her lips drew back baring her fangs further in what took him a terrifying moment to realize was a smile. In a weird way, it reminded him of the grin with which Thorne had greeted that same news.

She glanced up; the bay had emptied of other personnel. "Aah?" Her voice rumbled, like a purr. "Well, I'll be your bodyguard any time, lover. Just give me the sign."

What sign, what the hell—

She bent, her lips rippling, carmine clawed hand grasping his shoulder—he had a flashing vision of her tearing off his head, peeling, and eating him—then her mouth closed over his. His breath stopped, and his vision darkened, and he almost passed out before she straightened and gave him a puzzled, hurt look. "Miles, what's the matter?"

That had been a *kiss*. Freaking gods. "Nothing," he gasped. "I've . . . been ill. I probably shouldn't have gotten up, but I had to inspect."

She was looking very alarmed. "I'll say you shouldn't have gotten up—you're shaking all over! You can barely stand up. Here, I'll carry you to sickbay. Crazy man!"

"No! I'm all right. That is, I've been treated. I'm just supposed to rest, and recover for a while, is all."

"Well, you go straight back to bed, then!"

"Yes."

He wheeled. She swatted him on the butt. He bit his tongue. She said, "At least you've been eating better. Take care of yourself, huh?"

He waved over his shoulder, and fled without looking back. Had that been military cameraderie? From a sergeant to an admiral? He didn't think so. That had been *intimacy. Naismith, you bug-fuck crazy bastard, what have you been doing in your spare time? I didn't think you had any spare time. You've got to be a freaking suicidal maniac, if you've been screwing that—*

He locked his cabin door behind him, and stood against it,trembling, laughing in hysterical disbelief. Dammit, he'd studied everything about Naismith, everything. This couldn't be happening. *With friends like this, who need enemies?*

He undressed and lay tensely upon his bed, contemplating Naismith/ Vorkosigan's complicated life, and wondering what other booby-traps it held for him. At last a faint change in the susurrations and creaks of the ship around him, a brief tug of shifting grav fields, made him realize the *Ariel* was breaking free of Escobar orbit. He had actually succeeded in stealing a fully armed and equipped military fast cruiser, and no one even knew it. They were on their way to Jackson's Whole. To his destiny. *His* destiny, not Naismith's. His thoughts spiraled toward sleep at last.

But if you claim your destiny, his demon voice whispered at the last, before the night's oblivion, *why can't you claim your name?*

CHAPTER TWO

They exited the flex tube from the passenger ship in step, arm in arm, Quinn with her duffle swung over her shoulder, Miles with his flight bag gripped in his free hand. In the orbital transfer station's disembarkation lounge, people's heads turned. Miles stole a smug sideways glance at his female companion as they strolled on past the men's half-averted, envious stares. *My Quinn.*

Quinn was looking particularly tough this morning—was it morning? he'd have to check Dendarii fleet time—having half-returned to her normal persona. She'd managed to make her pocketed grey uniform trousers masquerade as a fashion statement by tucking them into red suede boots (the steel caps under the pointed toes eluded notice) and topping them with a skimpy scarlet tank top. Her white skin glowed in contrast to the tank top and to her short dark curls. The surface colors distracted the eye from her athleticism, not apparent unless you knew just how much that bloody duffle weighed.

Liquid brown eyes informed her face with wit. But it was the perfect, sculptured curves and planes of the face itself that stopped men's voices in midsentence. An obviously expensive face, the work of a surgeon-artist of extraordinary genius. The casual observer might guess her face had been paid for by the little ugly man whose arm she linked with her own, and judge the woman, too, to be a purchase. The casual observer never guessed the price she'd really paid: her old face, burned away in combat off Tau Verde. Very nearly the first battle loss in Admiral Naismith's service—ten years ago, now? God. The casual observer was a twit, Miles decided.

The latest representative of the species was a wealthy executive who reminded Miles of a blond, civilian version of his cousin Ivan, and who had spent much of the two-week journey from Sergyar to Escobar under such misapprehensions about Quinn, trying to seduce her. Miles glimpsed him now, loading his luggage onto a float pallet and venting a last frustrated sigh of defeat before sloping off. Except for reminding Miles of Ivan, Miles bore him no ill-will. In fact, Miles felt almost sorry for him, as Quinn's sense of humor was as vile as her reflexes were deadly.

Miles jerked his head toward the retreating Escobaran and murmured, "So what did you finally say to get rid of him, love?"

Quinn's eyes shifted to identify the man, and crinkled, laughing. "If I told you, you'd be embarrassed."

"No, I won't. Tell me."

"I told him you could do push-ups with your tongue. He must have decided he couldn't compete."

Miles reddened.

"I wouldn't have led him on so far, except that I wasn't totally sure at first that he wasn't some kind of agent," she added apologetically.

"You sure now?"

"Yeah. Too bad. It might have been more entertaining."

"Not to me. I was ready for a little vacation."

"Yes, and you look the better for it. Rested."

"I really like this married-couple cover, for travel," he remarked. "It suits me." He took a slightly deeper breath. "So we've had the honeymoon, why don't we have the wedding to go with it?"

"You never give up, do you?" She kept her tone light. Only the slight flinch of her arm, under his, told him his words had given pain, and he silently cursed himself.

"I'm sorry. I promised I'd keep off that subject."

She shrugged her unburdened shoulder, incidentally unlinking elbows, and let her arm swing aggressively as she walked. "Trouble is, you don't want me to be Madame Naismith, Dread of the Dendarii. You want me to be Lady Vorkosigan of Barrayar. That's a downside post. I'm spacer-born. Even if I did marry a dirtsucker, go down into some gravity well and never come up again . . . Barrayar is not the pit I'd pick. Not to insult your home."

Why not? Everyone else does. "My mother likes you," he offered.

"And I admire her. I've met her, what, four times now, and every time I'm more impressed. And yet . . . the more impressed, the more outraged I am at the criminal waste Barrayar makes of her talents. She'd be Surveyor-General of the Betan Astronomical Survey by now, if she'd stayed on Beta Colony. Or any other thing she pleased."

"She pleased to be Countess Vorkosigan."

"She pleased to be stunned by your Da, whom I admit is pretty stunning. She doesn't give squat for the rest of the Vor caste." Quinn paused, before they came into the hearing of the Escobaran customs inspectors, and Miles stood with her. They both gazed down the chamber, and not at each other. "For all her flair, she's a tired woman underneath. Barrayar has sucked so much out of her. Barrayar is her cancer. Killing her slowly."

Mutely, Miles shook his head.

"Yours too. Lord Vorkosigan," Quinn added somberly. This time it was his turn to flinch.

She sensed it, and tossed her head. "Anyway, Admiral Naismith is my kind of maniac. Lord Vorkosigan is a dull and dutiful stick by contrast. I've seen you at home on Barrayar, Miles. You're like half yourself there. Damped down, muted somehow. Even your voice is lower. It's extremely weird."

"I can't . . . I have to fit in, there. Scarcely a generation ago, someone with a body as strange as mine would have been killed outright as a suspected mutant. I can't push things too far, too fast. I'm too easy to target."

"Is that why Barrayaran Imperial Security sends you on so many off-planet missions?"

"For my development as an officer. To widen my background, deepen my experience."

"And someday, they're going to hook you out of here permanently, and take you home, and squeeze all that experience back out of you in *their* service. Like a sponge."

"I'm in their service now, Elli," he reminded her softly, in a grave and level voice that she had to bend her head to hear. "Now, then, and always."

Her eyes slid away. "Right-oh . . . so when they do nail your boots to the floor back on Barrayar, I want your job. I want to be Admiral Quinn someday."

"Fine by me," he said affably. The job, yes. Time for Lord Vorkosigan and his personal wants to go back into the bag. He had to stop masochistically rerunning this stupid marriage conversation with Quinn, anyway. Quinn was Quinn; he did not want her to be not-Quinn, not even for . . . Lord Vorkosigan.

Despite this self-inflicted moment of depression, anticipation of his return to the Dendarii quickened his step as they made their way through customs and into the monster transfer station. Quinn was right. He could *feel* Naismith refilling his skin, generated from somewhere deep in his psyche right out to his fingertips. Goodbye, dull Lieutenant Miles Vorkosigan, deep cover operative for Barrayaran Imperial Security (and overdue for a promotion); hello, dashing Admiral Naismith, space mercenary and all-around soldier of fortune.

Or misfortune. He slowed as they came to a row of commercial comconsole booths lining the passenger concourse, and nodded toward their mirrored doors.

"Let's see how Red Squad is cooking, first. If they're recovered sufficiently for release, I'd like to go downside personally and spring them."

"Right-oh." Quinn dumped her duffle dangerously close to Miles's sandaled feet, swung into the nearest empty booth, jammed her card into the slot, and tapped out a code on the keypad.

Miles set down his flight bag, sat on the duffle, and watched her from outside the booth. He caught a sliced reflection of himself on the mosaic of mirror on the next booth's lowered door. The dark trousers and loose white shirt that he wore were ambiguously styled as to planetary origin, but, as fit his travel-cover, very civilian. Relaxed, casual. Not bad.

Time was he had worn uniforms like a turtle-shell of high-grade social protection over the vulnerable peculiarities of his body. An armor of belonging that said, *Don't mess with me. I have friends.* When had he stopped needing that so desperately? He was not sure.

For that matter, when had he stopped hating his body? It had been two years since his last serious injury, on the hostage rescue mission that had come right after that incredible mess with his brother on Earth. He'd been fully recovered for quite some time. He flexed his hands, full of plastic replacement bones, and found them as easily his own as before they were last crunched. As before they were ever crunched. He hadn't had an osteo-inflammatory attack in months. *I'm feeling no pain,* he realized with a dark grin. And it wasn't just Quinn's doing, though Quinn had been . . . very therapeutic. *Am I going sane in my old age?*

Enjoy it while you can. He was twenty-eight years old, and surely at some sort of physical peak. He could feel that peak, the exhilarating float of apogee. The descending arc was a fate for some future day.

Voices from the comm booth brought him back to the present moment. Quinn had Sandy Hereld on the other end, and was saying, "Hi, I'm back."

"Hi, Quinnie, I was expecting you. What can I do for you?" Sandy had been doing strange things to her hair, again, Miles noted even from his offside vantage.

"I just got off the jumpship, here at the transfer station. Planning a little detour. I want transport downside to pick up the Red Squad survivors, then back to the *Triumph*. What's their current status?"

"Hold tight, I'll have it in a second . . ." Lieutenant Hereld punched up data on a display to her left.

In the crowded concourse a man in Dendarii greys walked past. He saw Miles, and gave him a hesitant, cautious nod, perhaps uncertain if the Admiral's civilian gear indicated some sort of cover. Miles returned a reassuring wave, and the man smiled and strode on. Miles's brain kicked up unwanted data. The man's name was Travis Gray, he was a field tech currently assigned to the *Peregrine*, a six-year-man so far, expert in communications equipment, he collected classic pre-Jump music of Earth origin . . . how many such personnel files did Miles carry in his head, now? Hundreds? Thousands?

And here came more. Hereld turned back, and rattled off, "Ives was released to downside leave, and Boyd has been returned to the *Triumph* for further therapy. The Beauchene Life Center reports that Durham, Vifian, and Aziz are available for release, but they want to talk to someone in charge, first."

"Right-oh."

"Kee and Zelaski . . . they also want to talk about."

Quinn's lips tightened. "Right," she agreed flatly. Miles's belly knotted, just a little. That was not going to be a happy conversation, he suspected. "Let them know we're on our way, then," Quinn said.

"Yes, Cap'n." Hereld shuffled files on her vid display. "Will do. Which shuttle do you want?"

"The *Triumph's* smaller personnel shuttle will do, unless you have some cargo to load on at the same time from the Beauchene shuttleport."

"None from there, no."

"All right."

Hereld checked her vid. "According to Escobaran flight control, I can put Shuttle Two into docking bay J-26 in thirty minutes. You'll be cleared for immediate downside departure."

"Thanks. Pass the word—there'll be a captain and captain-owner's briefing when we get back. What time is it at Beauchene?"

Hereld glanced aside. "0906, out of a 2607 hour day."

"Morning. Great. What's the weather down there?"

"Lovely. Shirtsleeves."

"Good, I won't have to change. We'll advise when we're ready to depart Port Beauchene. Quinn out."

Miles sat on the duffle, staring down at his sandals, awash in unpleasant memories. It had been one of the Dendarii Mercenaries' sweatier smuggling adventures, putting military advisors and materiel down on Marilac in support of its continuing resistance to a Cetagandan invasion. Combat Drop Shuttle A-4 from the *Triumph* had been hit by enemy fire on the last trip up-and-out, with all of Red Squad and several important Marilacans aboard. The pilot, Lieutenant Durham, though mortally injured and in shock himself, had brought his crippled and burning shuttle into a sufficiently low-velocity crunch with the *Triumph's* docking clamps that the rescue team was able to seal on an emergency flex tube, slice through, and retrieve everyone aboard. They'd managed to jettison the damaged shuttle just before it exploded, and the *Triumph* itself broke orbit barely ahead of serious Cetagandan vengeance. And so a mission that had started out simple, smooth, and covert ended yet again in the sort of heroic chaos that Miles had come to despise. The chaos, not the heroism.

The score, after heartbreaking triage: twelve seriously injured; seven, beyond the *Triumph*'s resources for resuscitation, cryogenically frozen in hope of later help; three permanently and finally dead. Now Miles would find out how many of the second category he must move to the third. The faces, names, hundreds of unwanted facts about them, cascaded through his mind. He had originally planned to be aboard that last shuttle, but instead had gone up on an earlier flight to deal with some other forest fire. . . .

"Maybe they won't be so bad," Quinn said, reading his face. She stuck out her hand, and he pulled himself up off the duffle and gathered up his flight bag.

"I've spent so much time in hospitals myself, I can't help identifying with them," he excused his dark abstraction. One perfect mission. What he wouldn't give for just one perfect mission, where absolutely nothing went wrong. Maybe the one upcoming would finally be it.

The hospital smell hit Miles immediately when he and Quinn walked through the front doors of the Beauchene Life Center, the cryotherapy specialty clinic the Dendarii dealt with on Escobar. It wasn't a bad smell, not a stench by any means, just an odd edge to the air-conditioned atmosphere. But it was an odor so deeply associated with pain in his experience, he found his heart beating faster. *Fight or flight.* Not appropriate. He breathed deeply, stroking down the visceral throb, and looked around. The lobby was much in the current style of techno-palaces anywhere on Escobar, clean but cheaply furnished. The real money was all invested upstairs, in the cryo-equipment, regeneration laboratories, and operating theaters.

One of the clinic's senior partners, Dr. Aragones, came down to greet them and escort them upstairs to his office. Miles liked Aragones' office, crammed with the sort of clutter of info disks,charts, and journal-flimsie offprints that indicated a technocrat who thought deeply and continuously about what he was doing. He liked Aragones himself, too, a big bluff fellow with bronze skin, a noble nose, and graying hair, friendly and blunt.

Dr. Aragones was unhappy not to be reporting better results. It hurt his pride, Miles judged.

"You bring us such messes, and want miracles," he complained gently, shifting in his station chair after Miles and Quinn settled themselves. "If you want to assure miracles, you have to start at the very beginning, when my poor patients are first prepared for treatment."

Aragones never called them corpsicles, or any of the other nervous nicknames coined by the soldiers. Always *my patients*. That was another thing Miles liked about the Escobaran physician.

"In general—unfortunately—our casualties don't arrive on a scheduled, orderly, one-by-one basis," Miles half-apologized in turn. "In this case we had twenty-eight people hit sickbay, with every degree and sort of injury—extreme trauma, burns, chemical contamination—all at once. Triage got brutal, for a little while, till things sorted out. My people did their best." He hesitated. "Do you think it would be worth our while to re-certify a few of our medtechs in your latest techniques, and if so, would you be willing to lead the seminar?"

Aragones spread his hands, and looked thoughtful. "Something might be worked out . . . talk with Administrator Margara, before you go."

Quinn caught Miles's nod, and made a note on her report panel.

Aragones called up charts on his comconsole. "The

worst first. We could do nothing for your Mr. Kee or Ms. Zelaski."

"I . . . saw Kee's head injury. I'm not surprised." *Smashed like a melon.* "But we had the cryo-chamber available, so we tried."

Aragones nodded understanding. "Ms. Zelaski had a similar problem, though less externally obvious. So much of her internal cranial circulation was broken during the trauma, her blood could not be properly drained from her brain, nor the cryo-fluids properly perfused. Between the crystalline freezing and the hematomas, the neural destruction was complete. I'm sorry. Their bodies are presently stored in our morgue, waiting your instructions."

"Kee wished his body to be returned for burial to his family on his homeworld. Have your mortuary department prepare and ship him through the usual channels. We'll give you the address." He jerked his chin at Quinn, who made another note. "Zelaski listed no family or next of kin—some Dendarii just don't, or won't, and we don't insist. But she did once tell some of her squad mates how she wanted her ashes disposed of. Please have her remains cremated and returned to the *Triumph* in care of our medical department."

"Very well." Aragones signed off the charts on his vid display; they disappeared like vanishing spirits. He called up others in their place.

"Your Mr. Durham and Ms. Vifian are both presently only partially healed from their original injuries. Both are suffering from what I would call normal neural-traumatic and cryo-amnesia. Mr. Durham's memory loss is the more profound, partly because of complications due to his pilot's neural implants, which we alas had to remove."

"Will he ever be able to have another headset installed?"

"It's too early to tell. I would call both their long-term prognoses good, but neither will be fit to return to their military duties for at least a year. And then they will need extensive re-training. In both cases I highly recommend they each be returned to their home and family environments, if that is possible. Familiar surroundings will help facilitate and trigger re-establishment of their access to their own surviving memories, over time."

"Lieutenant Durham has family on Earth. We'll see he gets there. Tech Vifian is from Kline Station. We'll see what we can do."

Quinn nodded vigorously, and made more notes.

"I can release them to you today, then. We've done all we can, here, and ordinary convalescent facilities will do for the rest. Now . . . that leaves your Mr. Aziz."

"My trooper Aziz," Miles agreed to the claim. Aziz was three years in the Dendarii, had applied and been accepted for officer's training. Twenty-one years old.

"Mr. Aziz is . . . alive again. That is, his body sustains itself without artificial aids, except for a slight on-going problem with internal temperature regulation that seems to be improving on its own."

"But Aziz didn't have a head wound. What went wrong?" asked Miles. "Are you telling me he's going to be a vegetable?"

"I'm afraid Mr. Aziz was the victim of a bad prep. His blood was apparently drained hastily, and not sufficiently completely. Small freezing hemocysts riddled his brain tissue with necrotic patches. We removed them, and started new growth, which has taken hold successfully. But his personality is permanently lost."

"Everything?"

"He may perhaps retain a few frustrating fragments of memories. Dreams. But he cannot re-access his neural pathways through new routes or sub-routines, because the tissue itself is gone. The new man will start over as a near-infant. He's lost language, among other things."

"Will he recover his intelligence? In time?"

Aragones hesitated for too long before answering. "In a few years, he may be able to do enough simple tasks to be self-supporting."

"I see," Miles sighed.

"What do you want to do with him?"

"He's another one with no next of kin listed." Miles blew out his breath. "Transfer him to a long-term care facility here on Escobar. One with a good therapy department. I'll ask you to recommend one. I'll set up a small trust fund to cover the costs till he's out on his own. However long that takes."

Aragones nodded, and both he and Quinn made notes.

After settling further administrative and financial details, the conference broke up. Miles insisted on stopping to see Aziz, before picking up the other two convalescents.

"He cannot recognize you," Dr. Aragones warned as they entered the hospital room.

"That's all right."

At first glance, Aziz did not look as much like death warmed over as Miles had expected, despite the unflattering hospital gown. There was color and warmth in his face, and his natural melanin level saved him from being hospital-pale. But he lay listlessly, gaunt, twisted in his covers. The bed's sides were up, unpleasantly suggesting a crib or a coffin. Quinn stood against the wall and folded her arms. She had visceral associations about hospitals and clinics too.

"Azzie," Miles called softly bending over him. "Azzie, can you hear me?"

Aziz's eyes tracked momentarily, but then wandered again.

"I know you don't know me, but you might remember this, later. You were a good soldier, smart and strong. You stood by your mates in the crash. You had the sort of self-discipline that saves lives." *Others, not your own.* "Tomorrow, you'll go to another sort of hospital, where they'll help you keep on getting better." *Among strangers. More strangers.* "Don't worry about the money. I'm setting it up so it'll be there as long as you need it." *He doesn't know what money is.* "I'll check back on you from time to time, as I get the opportunity," Miles promised. Promised who? Aziz? Aziz was no more. Himself? His voice softened to inaudibility as he ran down.

The aural stimulation made Aziz thrash around, and emit some loud and formless moans; he had no volume control yet, apparently. Even through a filter of desperate hope, Miles could not recognize it as an attempt at communication. Animal reflexes only.

"Take care," he whispered, and withdrew, to stand a moment trembling in the hallway.

"Why do you do that to yourself?" Quinn inquired tartly. Her crossed arms, hugging herself, added silently, *And to me?*

"First, he died for me, literally, and second," he attempted to force his voice to lightness, "don't you find a certain obsessive fascination in looking in the face of what you most fear?"

"Is death what you most fear?" she asked curiously.

"No. Not death." He rubbed his forehead, hesitated. "Loss of mind. My game plan all my life has been to demand acceptance of *this*," a vague wave down the length, or shortness, of his body, "because I was a smart-ass little bastard who could think rings around the opposition, and prove it time after time. Without the brains . . ." *Without the brains I'm nothing.* He straightened against the aching tension in his belly, shrugged, and twitched a smile at her. "March on, Quinn."

✧ ✧ ✧

After Aziz, Durham and Vifian were not so hard to deal with. They could walk and talk, if haltingly, and Vifian even recognized Quinn. They took them back to the shuttleport in the rented groundcar, and Quinn tempered her usual go-to-hell style of driving in consideration of their half-healed wounds. Upon reaching the shuttle Miles sent Durham forward to sit with the pilot, a comrade, and by the time they reached the *Triumph* Durham had recalled not only the man's name, but some shuttle piloting procedures. Miles turned both convalescents over to the medtech who met them at the shuttle hatch corridor, who escorted them off to sickbay to bed down again after the exhaustion of their short journey. Miles watched them exit, and felt a little better.

"Costly," Quinn observed reflectively.

"Yes," Miles sighed. "Rehabilitation is starting to take an awfully big bite out of the medical department's budget. I may have Fleet Accounting split it off, so Medical doesn't find itself dangerously short-changed. But what would you have? My troops were loyal beyond measure; I cannot betray them. Besides," he grinned briefly, "the Barrayaran Imperium is paying."

"Your ImpSec boss was on about your bills, I thought, at your mission briefing."

"Illyan has to explain why enough cash to fund a private army keeps disappearing in his department budget every year, without ever admitting to the private army's existence. Certain Imperial accountants tend to accuse him of departmental inefficiency, which gives him great pain . . . sh."

The Dendarii shuttle pilot, having shut down his ship, ducked into the corridor and sealed the hatch. He nodded to Miles.

"While I was waiting for you at Port Beauchene, sir, I picked up a minor story on the local news net, that you might be interested in. Minor news here on Escobar, that is." The man was bouncing lightly on his toes.

"Say on, Sergeant LaJoie." Miles cocked an eyebrow up at him.

"The Cetagandans have just announced their withdrawal from Marilac. They're calling it—what was that, now—'Due to great progress in the cultural alliance, we are turning police matters over to local control.' "

Miles's fists clenched, joyously. "In other words, they're abandoning their puppet government! Ha!" He hopped from foot to foot, and pounded Quinn on the back. "You hear that, Elli! We've won! I mean, they've won, the Marilacans." *Our sacrifices are redeemed.* . . .

He regained control of his tightening throat before he burst into tears or some like foolishness. "Do me a favor, LaJoie. Pass the word through the Fleet. Tell them I said, 'You folks do good work.' Eh?"

"Yes, sir. My pleasure." The grinning pilot saluted cheerfully, and trod off up the corridor.

Miles's grin stretched his face. "See, Elli! What Simon Illyan just bought would have been cheap at a thousand times the cost. A full-bore Cetagandan planetary invasion—first impeded—then bogged—foundered—failed!" And in a fierce whisper, "*I* did it! I made the difference."

Quinn too was smiling, but one perfect eyebrow curved in a certain dry irony. "It's lovely, but if I was reading between the lines correctly, I thought what Barrayaran Imperial Security really wanted was for the Cetagandan military to be *tied up* in the guerrilla war on Marilac. Indefinitely. Draining Cetagandan attention away from Barrayaran borders and jump points."

"They didn't put that in writing." Miles's lips drew back wolfishly. "All Simon said was, 'Help the Marilacans as opportunity presents.' That was the standing order, in so many words."

"But you knew damn well what he really wanted."

"Four bloody years was enough. I have not betrayed Barrayar. Nor anyone else."

"Yeah? So if Simon Illyan is so much more Machiavellian than you are, how is it that your version prevailed? Someday, Miles, you are going to run out of hairs to split with those people. And then what will you do?"

He smiled, and shook his head, evading answer.

His elation over the news from Marilac still made him feel like he was walking in half-gravity when he arrived at his cabin aboard the *Triumph*. After a surreptitious glance to be sure the corridor was unpeopled, he embraced and kissed Quinn, a deep kiss that was going to have to last them for a long while, and she went off to her own quarters. He slipped inside, and echoed the door's closing sigh with his own. Home again.

It *was* home, for half his psyche, he reflected, tossing his flight bag onto his bed and heading directly for the shower. Ten years ago, Lord Miles Vorkosigan had invented the cover identity of Admiral Naismith out of his head in a desperate moment, and frantically faked his way to temporary control of the hastily re-named Dendarii Mercenaries. Barrayaran Imperial Security had discovered the cover to be useful . . . no. Credit where it was due. He had persuaded, schemed, demonstrated, and coerced ImpSec into finding use for this cover. *Be careful what you pretend to be. You might become it.*

When had Admiral Naismith stopped being a pretense? Gradually, surely, but mostly since his mercenary mentor Commodore Tung had retired. Or perhaps the wily Tung had recognized before Miles had that his services in propping Miles up to his prematurely exalted rank were no longer required. Colored vid arrays of Dendarii Free Mercenary Fleet organization bloomed in Miles's head as he showered.

Personnel—equipment—administration—logistics—he knew every ship, every trooper, every shuttle and piece of ordnance, now. He knew how they fit together, what had to be done first, second, third, twentieth, to place a precisely calculated force at any point on the tactical fulcrum. *This* was expertise, to be able to look at a ship like the *Triumph* and see with his mind's eye right through the walls to every engineering detail, every strength and vulnerability; to look at a commando squad, or a briefing table ringed with captains and captain-owners and know what each one would do or say before they knew it themselves. *I'm on top. Finally, I'm on top of it all. With this lever, I can move worlds.* He switched the shower to "dry," and turned in the blast of warm air. He left the bathroom still chortling under his breath. *I love it.*

His chortle died away in puzzlement when he unlatched the door to his uniform cupboard, and found it bare. Had his batman taken them all off for cleaning or repairs? His bewilderment grew as he tried other drawers, and found only a residue of the wildly assorted civilian togs he wore when he stretched the chain of his identity one link further, and played spy for the Dendarii. Plus some of his shabbier underwear. Was this some sort of practical joke? If so, he'd have the last laugh. Naked and irritated, he snapped open the locker where his space armor dwelt. Empty. That was almost shocking. *Somebody's taken it down to Engineering to re-calibrate it, or add tactics programs, or something.* His batman should have returned it by now, though. What if he needed it in a hurry?

Time. His people would be gathering. Quinn had once claimed he could carry on naked, and only make those around him feel overdressed. He was momentarily tempted to test her assertion, but overcame the mordant vision, and put the shirt and trousers and sandals he'd been wearing back on. He didn't need a uniform in order to dominate a briefing room, not any more.

On the way to the meeting, he passed Sandy Hereld in the corridor, coming off duty, and gave her a friendly nod. She wheeled and walked backward in startlement. "You're back, sir! That was quick."

He would hardly describe his several-week journey to Imperial HQ on Barrayar as quick. She must mean the trip downside. "It only took two hours."

"What?" Her nose wrinkled. She was still walking backwards, reaching the end of the corridor.

He had a briefing room full of senior officers waiting. He waved and swung down a lift tube.

The briefing room was comfortingly familiar, right down to the array of faces around the darkly shining table. Captain Auson of the *Triumph*. Elena Bothari-Jesek, recently promoted captain of the *Peregrine*. Her husband Commodore Baz Jesek, Fleet engineer and in charge, in Miles's absence, of all the repair and refit activities of the Dendarii Fleet in Escobar orbit. The couple, Barrayarans themselves, were with Quinn among the handful of Dendarii apprised of Miles's double identity. Captain Truzillo of the *Jayhawk*, and a dozen more, all tested and true. His people.

Bel Thorne of the *Ariel* was late. That was unusual. One of Thorne's driving characteristics was an insatiable curiosity; anew mission briefing was like a Winterfair gift to the Betan hermaphrodite. Miles turned to Elena Bothari-Jesek, to make small talk while they waited.

"Did you get a chance to visit your mother, downside on Escobar?"

"Yes, thanks." She smiled. "It was . . . nice, to have a little time. We had a chance to talk about some things we'd never talked about the first time we met."

It had been good for both of them, Miles judged. Some

of the permanent strain seemed gone from Elena's dark eyes. Better and better, bit by bit. "Good."

He glanced up as the doors hissed open, but it was only Quinn, blowing in with the secured files in hand. She was back in full officer's undress kit, and looking very comfortable and efficient. She handed the files to Miles, and he loaded them into the comconsole, and waited another minute. Still no Bel Thorne.

Talk died away. His officers were giving him attentive, let's-get-on-with-it looks. He'd better not stand around much longer with his thumb in his ear. Before bringing the console display to life, he inquired, "Is there some reason Captain Thorne is late?"

They looked at him, and then at each other. *There can't be something wrong with Bel, it would have been reported to me first thing.* Still, a small leaden knot materialized in the pit of his stomach. "Where is Bel Thorne?"

By eye, they elected Elena Bothari-Jesek as spokesperson. That was an extremely bad sign. "Miles," she said hesitantly, "was Bel supposed to be back before you?"

"Back? Where did Bel go?"

She was looking at him as though he'd lost his mind. "Bel left with you, in the *Ariel*, three days ago."

Quinn's head snapped up. "That's impossible."

"Three days ago, we were still en route to Escobar," Miles stated. The leaden knot was transmuting into neutron star matter. He was not dominating this room at all well. In fact, it seemed to be tilting.

"You took Green Squad with you. It was the new contract, Bel said," Elena added.

"*This* is the new contract," Miles tapped the comconsole. A hideous explanation was beginning to suggest itself to his mind, rising from the black hole in his stomach. The looks on the faces around the table were also beginning to divide into two uneven camps, appalled surmise from the minority who had been in on that mess on Earth two years ago—oh, they were right with him—total confusion from the majority, who had not been directly involved. . . .

"Where did I say I was going?" Miles inquired. His tone was, he thought, gentle, but several people flinched.

"Jackson's Whole." Elena looked him straight in the eye, with much the steady gaze of a zoologist about to dissect a specimen. A sudden lack of trust . . .

Jackson's Whole. That tears it. "Bel Thorne? The *Ariel*? Taura? With *ten jumps* of Jackson's Whole?" Miles choked. "Dear God."

"But if you're you," said Truzillo, "who was that three days ago?"

"*If* you're you," said Elena darkly. The initiate crowd were all getting that same frowning look.

"You see," Miles explained in a hollow voice to the *What-the-hell-are-they-talking-about?* portion of the room, "some people have an evil twin. I am not so lucky. What *I* have is an *idiot* twin."

"Your clone," said Elena Bothari-Jesek.

"My brother," he corrected automatically.

"Little Mark Pierre," said Quinn. "Oh . . . *shit*."

CHAPTER THREE

His stomach seemed to turn inside out, the cabin wavered, and shadow darkened his vision. The bizarre sensations of the wormhole jump were gone almost as soon as they began, but left an unpleasant somatic reverberation, as if he were a struck gong. He took a deep, calming breath. That had been the fourth jump of the voyage. Five jumps to go, on the tortuous zigzag through the wormhole nexus from Escobar to Jackson's Whole. The *Ariel* had been three days en route, almost halfway.

He glanced around Naismith's cabin. He could not continue to hide out in here much longer, pretense of illness or Naismithian black mood or not. Thorne needed every bit of data he could supply to plan the Dendarii raid on the clone-creche. He had used his hibernation well, scanning the *Ariel's* mission logs back through time, all the way past his first encounter with the Dendarii two years ago. He now knew a great deal more about the mercenaries, and the thought of casual conversation with the *Ariel's* crew was far less terrifying.

Unfortunately there was very little in the mission log to help him reconstruct what his first meeting with Naismith on Earth had looked like from the Dendarii point of view. The log had concentrated on rehabilitation and refit reports, dickerings with assorted ship's chandlers, and engineering briefings. He'd found exactly one order pertinent to his own adventures embedded in the data flow, advising all ship masters that Admiral Naismith's clone had been seen on Earth, warning that the clone might attempt to pass himself off as the Admiral, giving the (incorrect) information that the clone's legs would show up on a medical scan as normal bone and not plastic replacements, and ordering use of stunners-only in apprehending the imposter. No explanations, no later revisions or updates. All of Naismith/Vorkosigan's highest-level orders tended to be verbal and undocumented anyway, for security—from the Dendarii, not for them—a habit that had just served him well.

He leaned back in his station chair and glowered at the comconsole display. The Dendarii data named him *Mark. That's another thing you don't get to choose,* Miles Naismith Vorkosigan had said. *Mark Pierre. You are Lord Mark Pierre Vorkosigan, in your own right, on Barrayar.*

But he was not on Barrayar, nor ever would be if he could help it. *You are not my brother, and the Butcher of Komarr was never a father to me,* his thought denied for the thousandth time to his absent progenitor. *My mother was a uterine replicator.*

But the power of the suggestion had ridden him ever after, sapping his satisfaction with every pseudonym he'd ever tried,though he'd stared at lists of names till his eyes ached. Dramatic names, plain names, exotic, strange, common, silly . . . Jan Vandermark was the alias he'd used the longest, the closest sideways skittish approach to identity.

Mark! Miles had shouted, being dragged away, for all he knew, to his own death. *Your name is Mark!*

I am not Mark. I am NOT your damned brother, you maniac. The denial was hot and huge, but when its echoes died away, in the hollow chamber left inside his skull he seemed not to be anyone at all.

His head was aching, a grinding tightness that crawled up his spine through his shoulders and neck, and spread out under his scalp. He rubbed hard at his neck, but the tension just circulated around through his arms and back into his shoulders.

Not his brother. But to be strictly accurate, Naismith could not be blamed for forcing him to life in the same way as the other House Bharaputran clones' progenitors. Oh, they were genetically identical, yes. It was a matter of . . . intent, perhaps. And where the money came from.

Lord Miles Naismith Vorkosigan had been just six years old when the tissue sample from a biopsy was stolen from some clinical laboratory on Barrayar, during the last gasp of Komarran resistance to Barrayaran imperial conquest. No one, neither Barrayaran nor Komarran, was intrinsically interested in the crippled child Miles. The focus had all been on his father. Admiral Count Aral Vorkosigan, Regent of Barrayar, Conqueror (or Butcher) of Komarr. Aral Vorkosigan had supplied the will and the wit which had made Komarr into Barrayar's first off-planet conquest. And made himself the target of Komarran resistance and revenge. Hope for successful resistance had faded in time. Hope for revenge lived on in exiled bitterness. Stripped of an army, arms, support, one Komarran hate group plotted a slow, mad vengeance. To strike at the father through the son upon whom he was known to dote . . .

Like a sorcerer in an old tale, the Komarrans dealt with a devil to have a simulacrum made. A bastard clone, he thought with a silent, humorless laugh. But things went wrong. The crippled original boy, poisoned before birth by yet another murderous enemy of his father's, grew strangely, unpredictably; his genetic duplicate grew straight . . . that had been his first clue that he was different from the other clones, he reflected. When the other clones went to the doctors for treatment they came back stronger, healthier, growing ever-faster. Every time he went, and he went often, their painful treatments seemed to make him sicklier, more stunted. The braces they put on his bones, neck, back, never seemed to help much. They had *made* him into this hunchbacked dwarfling as if molding him in a press, die-cut from a cast of his progenitor. *I could have been normal, if Miles Vorkosigan had not been crippled.*

When he first began to suspect the true purpose of his fellow clones, for rumors passed among the children in wild ways even their careful handlers could not totally control, his growing somatic deformations brought him silent suppressed joy. Surely they could not use *this* body for a brain transplant. He might be discarded—he might yet escape his pleasant, smiling jailer-servants. . . .

His real escape, when his Komarran owners came to collect him at age fourteen, was like a miracle. And then the training had begun. The endless harsh tutoring, drill, indoctrination. At first a destiny, any destiny at all, seemed glorious compared to his creche-mates' end. He determinedly took up the training to replace his progenitor, and strike a blow for dear Komarr, a place he had never seen, against evil Barrayar, a place he had never seen either. But learning to be Miles Vorkosigan turned out to be like running the race in Zeno's paradox. No matter how much he learned, how frantically he drilled, how harshly his mistakes were punished, Miles learned more, faster; by the time he arrived, his quarry had always moved on, intellectually or otherwise.

The symbolic race became literal once his Komarran tutors actually moved to effect the substitution. They chased the elusive young Lord Vorkosigan halfway around the wormhole nexus, never realizing that when he vanished, he utterly ceased to exist, and Admiral Naismith appeared. The Komarrans had never found out about Admiral Naismith. Not planning but chance had finally brought them together two years ago on Earth, right back where the whole stupid race had started, in pursuit of a vengeance gone twenty years cold.

The time-delay had been critical in a way the Komarrans had not even noticed. When they first began chasing Vorkosigan, their customized clone had been at the peak of his mental conditioning, committed to the goals of the revolt, unreflectingly eager. Had they not saved him from the fate of clones? Eighteen months of watching them screw up, eighteen months of travel, observation, exposure to uncensored news, views, even a few people, had planted secret doubts in his mind. And, bluntly, one could not duplicate even an imitation of a galactic-class education like Vorkosigan's without inadvertently learning something about how to think. In the middle of it all, the surgery to replace his perfectly sound leg bones with synthetics, just because Vorkosigan had smashed his, had been stunningly painful. What if Vorkosigan broke his neck, next time? Realization had crept over him.

Stuffing his head full of Lord Vorkosigan, in bits over time, was just as much of a brain transplant as anything done with vibra-scalpels and living tissue. *He who plots revenge, must dig two graves.* But the Komarrans had dug the second grave for *him.* For the person he never had a chance to become, the man he might have been if he had not been forced at shock-stick point to continually struggle to be someone *else.*

Some days he was not sure who he hated more, House Bharaputra, the Komarrans, or Miles Naismith Vorkosigan.

He shut off the comconsole with a snort, and rose to pick out his precious data cube from the uniform pocket in which it was still hidden. Upon reflection, he cleaned up and depilated again, before donning fresh Dendarii officer's undress greys. That was as regulation as he could make himself. Let the Dendarii see only the polished surface, and not the man inside the man inside. . . .

He steeled himself, exited the cabin, stepped across

the corridor, and pressed the buzzer to the hermaphrodite captain's quarters.

No response. He pressed it again. After a short delay Thorne's blurred alto voice came, "Yes?"

"Naismith here."

"Oh! Come in, Miles." The voice sharpened with interest.

The door slid aside, and he stepped within, to realize that the reason for the delay was that he'd woken Thorne from sleep. The hermaphrodite was sitting up on one elbow in bed, brown hair tousled, its free hand falling away from the keypad which had released the door.

"Excuse me," he said, stepping backward, but the door had already sealed again.

"No, it's all right," the hermaphrodite smiled sleepily, curled its body in a C, and patted the bed invitingly in front of its sheeted . . . lap. "For you, anytime. Come sit. Would you like a back rub? You look tense." It was wearing a decidedly frilly nightgown, flowing silk with lace trim edging a plunging vee neckline that revealed the swelling pale flesh of its breasts.

He sidled to a station chair instead. Thorne's smile took on a peculiarly sardonic tinge, even while remaining perfectly relaxed. He cleared his throat. "I . . . thought it was time for that more detailed mission briefing I promised." *I should have checked the duty-roster.* Would Admiral Naismith have known the captain's sleep-cycle?

"Time and past time. I'm glad to see you come up out of the fog. What the hell have you been doing, wherever you went for the past eight weeks, Miles? Who died?"

"No one. Well, eight clones, I suppose."

"Hm." Thorne nodded wry acknowledgment. The seductive sinuosity faded from its posture, and it sat up straight, and rubbed the last of the sleep from its eyes. "Tea?"

"Sure. Or, uh, I could come back after your sleep-shift." *Or after you're dressed.*

It swung its silk-swathed legs from the bed. "No way. I'd be up in an hour anyway. I've been waiting for this. Seize the day." It padded across the cabin to do its tea-ritual again. He set up the data cube in the comconsole and paused, both polite and practical, for the captain to take its first sips of the hot black liquid, and come fully awake. He wished it would put its uniform on.

He keyed up the display as Thorne wandered close. "I have a detailed holomap of House Bharaputra's main medical complex. This data is not more than four months old. Plus guard schedules and patrol patterns—their security is much heavier than a normal civilian hospital, more like a military laboratory, but it's no fortress. Their everyday concern is more against individual local intruders intent on theft. And, of course, in preventing certain of their less voluntary patients from escaping." A significant chunk of his former fortune had gone into that map cube.

The color-coded image spread itself in lines and sheets of light above the vid plate. The complex was truly that, a vast warren of buildings, tunnels, therapy-gardens, labs, mini-manufacturing areas, flyer pads, warehouses, garages, and even two shuttle docks for direct departure to planetary orbit.

Thorne put down its cup, leaned over the comconsole, and stared with interest. It took up the remote control and turned the map-image, shrank and expanded and sliced it. "So do we want to start by capturing the shuttle bays?"

"No. The clones are all kept together over here on the west side, in this sort of hospice area. I figure if we land here in this exercise court we'll be damn near on top of their dormitory. Naturally, I'm not overly concerned about what the drop shuttle damages, coming down."

"Naturally." A brief grin flickered over the captain's face. "Timing?"

"I want to make it a night drop. Not so much for cover, because there's no way we're going to make a combat drop shuttle inconspicuous, but because that's the one time all the clones are together in a small area. In the day they're all spread out in the exercise and play areas, the swimming pool and what not."

"And classrooms?"

"No, not exactly. They don't teach 'em much beyond the minimum necessary for socialization. If a clone can count to twenty and read signs, that's all they need. Throw-away brains." That had been the other way he'd known he was different from the rest. A real human tutor had introduced him to a vast array of virtual learning programs. He'd lost himself for days at a time in the computer's patient praise. Unlike his Komarran tutors later, they repeated themselves endlessly, and never punished him, never swore or raged or struck or forced him to physical exertion till he grew sick or passed out. . . . "The clones pick up a surprising amount of information despite it all, though. A lot from their holovid games. Bright kids. Damn few of these clones have stupid progenitors, or they wouldn't have amassed a sufficient fortune to buy this form of life-extension. Ruthless, maybe, but not stupid."

Thorne's eyes narrowed as it dissected the area on the vid, taking apart the buildings layer by layer, studying the layout. "So a dozen full-kit Dendarii commandos wake fifty or sixty kids out of a sound sleep in the middle of the night . . . do they know we're coming?"

"No. By the way, make sure the troops realize they won't look exactly like kids. We're taking them in their last year of development. They're mostly ten or eleven years old, but due to the growth accelerators they will appear to have the bodies of late teenagers."

"Gawky?"

"Not really. They get great physical conditioning. Healthy as hell. That's the whole point of not just growing them in a vat till transplant time."

"Do they . . . know? Know what's going to happen to them?" Thorne asked with an introspective frown.

"They're not told, no. They're told all kinds of lies, variously. They're told they're in a special school, for security reasons, to save them from some exotic danger. That they're all some kind of prince or princess, or rich man's heir, or military scion, and someday very soon their parents or their aunts or their ambassadors are going to come and take them away to some glamorous future . . . and then, of course, at last some smiling person comes, and calls them away from their playmates, and tells them that today is the day, and they run . . ." he stopped, swallowed, "and snatch up their things, and brag to their friends. . . ."

Thorne was tapping the vid control unconsciously in its palm, and looking pale. "I get the picture."

"And walk out hand-in-hand with their murderers, eagerly."

"You can stop with the scenario-spinning, unless you're trying to make me lose my last meal."

"What, you've known for years that this was going on," he mocked. "Why get all squeamish about it now?" He bit off his bitterness. Naismith. He must be Naismith.

Thorne shot him a sharp glare. "*I* was ready to fry them from orbit the last time, as you may recall. You wouldn't let me."

What last time? No time in the last three years. He'd have to scan the mission logs back even further, dammit. He shrugged, ambiguously.

"So," said Thorne, "are these . . . big kids . . . all going to decide we're their parents' enemies, kidnapping them just before they go home? I see trouble, here."

He clenched, and spread, the fingers of his right hand. "Maybe not. Children . . . have a culture of their own. Passed down from year to year. There are rumors. Boogeyman stories. Doubts. I told you, they aren't stupid. Their adult handlers try to stamp out the stories, or make fun of them, or mix them up with other, obvious lies." And yet . . . they had not fooled him. But then, he had lived in the creche much longer than the average. He'd had time to see more clones come and go, time to see stories repeated, pseudo-biographies duplicated. Time for their handlers' tiny slips and mistakes to accumulate in his observation. "If it's the same—" *If it's the same as it was in my time*, he almost said, but saved himself, "I should be able to persuade them. Leave that part to me."

"Gladly." Thorne swung a console chair into clamps close beside his, settled down, and rapidly entered some notes on logistics and angle of attack, point-men and back-ups, and traced projected routes through the buildings. "Two dormitories?" it pointed curiously. Thorne's fingernails were cut blunt, undecorated.

"Yes. The boys are kept segregated from the girls, rather carefully. The female—usually female—customers expect to wake up in a body with the seal of virginity still on it."

"I see. So. We get all these kids loaded, by some miracle, before the Bharaputrans arrive in force—"

"Speed is of the essence, yes."

"As usual. But the Bharaputrans will be all over us if there is any little hitch or hold-up. Unlike with the Marilacans at Dagoola, you haven't had weeks and weeks to drill these kids on shuttle-loading procedures. What if, then?"

"Once the clones are loaded into the shuttle they become in effect *our* hostages. We'll be safe from lethal fire with them aboard. The Bharaputrans won't risk their investment as long as any chance of recovery remains."

"Once they decide all chance is lost, they'll seek vigorous retribution to discourage imitators, though."

"True. We must cloud their minds with doubt."

"Then their next move—if we get the shuttle airborne—must be to try to blow up the *Ariel* in orbit before we get there, cutting off our escape."

"Speed," he repeated doggedly.

"Contingencies, Miles dear. Wake up. I don't usually have to re-start your brain in the morning—do you want some more tea? No? I suggest, if we suffer dangerous delay downside, that the *Ariel* take refuge at Fell Station, and we rendezvous with it there."

"Fell Station? The orbital one?" He hesitated. "Why?"

"Baron Fell is still in a state of vendetta with Bharaputra and Ryoval, isn't he?"

Jacksonian internecine House politics; he was not as current on them as he should be. He had not even thought of looking for an ally among the other Houses. They were all criminal, all evil, tolerating or sabotaging each other in shifting patterns of power. And here was Ryoval, mentioned again. Why? He took refuge in another wordless shrug. "Getting pinned, trapped on Fell Station with fifty young clones while Bharaputra hustles for control of the jumppoint stations, would not improve our position. No Jacksonian is to be trusted. Run and jump as fast as we can is still the safest strategy."

"Bharaputra won't swing Jumpstation Five into line, it's Fell-owned."

"Yes, but I want to return to Escobar. The clones can all get safe asylum there."

"Look, Miles, the jump back on this route is held by the consortium already dominated by Bharaputra. We'll never get back out the way we jump in, unless you've got something up your sleeve—no? Then may I suggest our best escape route is via Jumppoint Five."

"Do you really see Fell as so reliable an ally?" he inquired cautiously.

"Not at all. But he is the enemy of our enemies. This trip."

"But the jump from Five leads to the Hegen Hub. We can't jump into Cetagandan territory, and the only other route out of the Hub is to Komarr via Pol."

"Roundabout, but much safer."

Not for me! That's the damned Barrayaran Empire! He swallowed a wordless shriek.

"The Hub to Pol to Komarr to Sergyar and back to Escobar," Thorne recited happily. "You know, this could really work out." It made more notes, leaning across the comconsole, its nightgown shifting and shimmering in the candy lights of the vid display. Then it put its elbows on the console and rested its chin in its hands, breasts compressing, shifting beneath the thin fabric. Its expression grew gently introspective. It glanced up at him at last with an odd, rather sad smile.

"Have any clones ever escaped?" Thorne asked softly.

"No," he answered quickly, automatically.

"Except for your own clone, of course."

A dangerous turn in the conversation. "My clone did not escape either. He was simply removed by his purchasers." He should have tried to escape . . . what life might he have led, had he succeeded?

"Fifty kids," Thorne sighed. "Y'know—I *really approve* of this mission." It waited, watching him with sharp and gleaming eyes.

Acutely uncomfortable, he suppressed an idiocy such as saying *Thank you*, but found himself with no remark to put in its place, resulting in an awkward silence.

"I suppose," said Thorne thoughtfully after the too-long moment, "it would be very difficult for anyone brought up in such an environment to really trust . . . anyone else. Anyone's word. Their good will."

"I . . . suppose." Was this casual conversation, or something more sinister? A trap . . .

Thorne, still with that weird mysterious smile, leaned across their station chairs, caught his chin in one strong, slender hand, and kissed him.

He did not know if he was supposed to recoil or respond, so did neither, in cross-eyed, panicked paralysis. Thorne's mouth was warm, and tasted of tea and bergamot, silky and perfumed. Was Naismith screwing—this—too? If so, who did what to whom? Or did they take turns? *And would it really be that bad?* His terror heightened with an undeniable stirring of arousal. *I believe I would die for a lover's touch.* He had been alone forever.

Thorne withdrew at last, to his intense relief, though only a little way, its hand still trapping his chin. After another moment of dead silence, its smile grew wry. "I shouldn't tease you, I suppose," it sighed. "There is a sort of cruelty in it, all things considered."

It released him, and stood, the sensuous languor abruptly switched off. "Back in a minute." It strode to its cabin washroom, sealing the door behind it.

He sat, unstrung and shaking. *What the hell was that all about?* And from another part of his mind, *You could lose your damned virginity this trip, I bet,* and from another, *No! Not with that!*

Had that been a test? But had he passed, or failed? Thorne had not cried out in accusation, nor called for armed back-up. Perhaps the captain was arranging his arrest right now, by comm link from the washroom. There was no place to run away, aboard a small ship in deep space. His crossed arms hugged his torso. With effort he uncrossed them, placed his hands on the console, and willed his muscles to uncoil. *They probably won't kill me.* They'd take him back to the fleet and let Naismith kill him.

But no security squad broke down the door, and soon enough Thorne returned. Nattily dressed in its uniform, at last. It plucked the data cube from the comconsole, and closed its palm over it. "I'll sit down with Sergeant Taura and this and do some serious planning, then."

"Ah, yes. It's time." He hated to let the precious cube out of his sight. But it seemed he was still Naismith in Thorne's eyes.

Thorne pursed its lips. "Now that it's time to brief the crew, don't you think it would be a good idea to put the *Ariel* on a communications blackout?"

An outstanding idea, though one he'd been afraid to suggest as too suspicious and strange. Maybe it wasn't so unusual, on these covert ops. He'd had no certain idea as to when the real Naismith was supposed to return to the Dendarii fleet, but from the mercenaries' easy acceptance of him, it had to have been expected soon. He'd lived for the past three days in fear of frantic orders arriving by tight-beam and Jump-courier from the real Admiral, telling the *Ariel* to turn around. *Give me a few more days. Just a few more days, and I'll redeem it all.* "Yes. Do so."

"Very good, sir." Thorne hesitated. "How are you feeling, now? Everybody knows these black miasmas of yours can run for weeks. But if only you'll rest properly, I trust you'll be your usual energetic self in time for the drop mission. Shall I pass the word to leave you alone?"

"I . . . would appreciate that, Bel." What luck! "But keep me informed, eh?"

"Oh, yes. You can count on me. It's a straightforward raid, except for handling that herd of kids, in which I defer to your superior expertise."

"Right." With a smile and a cheery salute, he fled across the corridor to the safe isolation of his own cabin. The pulsing combination of elation and his tension headache made him feel as if he were floating. When the door sealed behind him, he fell across his bed and gripped the coverings to hold himself in place. *It's really going to happen!*

Later, diligently scanning ship's logs on his cabin comconsole, he finally found the four-year-old records of the *Ariel*'s previous visit to Jackson's Whole. Such as they were. They started out with utterly boring details about an ordnance deal, inventory entries regarding a cargo of weapons to be loaded from House Fell's orbital transfer station. Completely without preamble, Thorne's breathless voice made a cryptic entry, "Murka's lost the Admiral. He's being held prisoner by Baron Ryoval. I'm going now to make a devil's bargain with Fell."

Then records of an emergency combat drop shuttle trip downside, followed by the *Ariel*'s abrupt departure from Fell Station with cargo only half loaded. These events were succeeded by two fascinating, unexplained conversations between Admiral Naismith, and Baron Ryoval and Baron Fell, respectively. Ryoval was raving, sputtering exotic death threats. He studied the Baron's contorted, handsome face uneasily. Even in a society that prized ruthlessness, Ryoval was a man whom other Jacksonian power-brokers stepped wide around. Admiral Naismith appeared to have stepped right in something.

Fell was more controlled, a cold anger. As usual, all the really essential information, including the reason for the visit in the first place, was lost in Naismith's verbal orders. But he did manage to gather the surprising fact that the eight-foot-tall commando, Sergeant Taura, was a product of House Bharaputra's genetics laboratories, a genetically-engineered prototype super-soldier.

It was like unexpectedly meeting someone from one's old home town. In a weird wash of homesickness, he longed to look her up and compare notes. Naismith had apparently stolen her heart, or at least stolen her away, although that did not seem to be the offense Ryoval was foaming about. It was all rather incomprehensible.

He did garner one other, unpleasant fact. Baron Fell was a would-be clone consumer. His old enemy Ryoval in a move of vendetta had apparently arranged to have Fell's clone murdered before the transplant could take place, trapping Fell in his aging body, but the intent was there. Regardless of Bel Thorne's contingency planning, he resolved he would have nothing to do with Baron Fell if he could help it.

He blew out his breath, shut down the comconsole, and went back to practicing simulations with the command headset helmet, a manufacturer's training program that happily had never been deleted from its memory. *I'm going to bring this off. Somehow.*

CHAPTER FOUR

"No reply from the *Ariel* from this courier-hop either, sir," Lieutenant Hereld reported apologetically.

Miles's fists clenched in frustration. He forced his hands flat again along his trouser seams, but the energy only flowed to his feet, and he began to pace from wall to wall in the *Triumph*'s Nav and Com room. "That's the third—third? You have been repeating the message with every courier?"

"Yes, sir."

"The third no-reply. Dammit, what's holding Bel up?"

Lieutenant Hereld shrugged helplessly at this rhetorical question.

Miles re-crossed the room, frowning fiercely. Damn the time-lag. He wanted to know what was happening *right now*. Tight-beam communications crossed a local-space region at the speed of light, but the only way to get information through a wormhole was to physically record it, put it on a jumpship, and jump it through to the next relay station, where it was beamed to the next wormhole and jumped again, if it was economically worthwhile to maintain such a service. In regions of heavy message traffic, such couriers jumped as often as every half-hour or even oftener. Between Escobar and Jackson's Whole, the couriers maintained an every-four-hours schedule. So on top of the delay from the speed of light limitation, was added this other, arbitrary human one. Such a delay could be quite useful sometimes, to people playing complex games with interstellar finances, exchange rates, and futures. Or to independent-minded subordinates wishing to conceal excess information about their activities from their superior officers—Miles had occasionally used the lag for that purpose himself. A couple of clarification requests, and their replies, could buy enough time to bring off all sorts of events. That was why he'd made certain his recall order to the *Ariel* was personal, forceful, and crystal-clear. But Bel had not returned some counterfeit-demure *What do you mean by that, sir?* Bel had not replied at all.

"It's not some fault in the courier-system, is it? Other traffic—is other traffic on the route getting their messages through?"

"Yes, sir. I checked. Information flow is normal all the way through to Jackson's Whole."

"They did file a flight plan to Jackson's Whole, they did actually jump through that exit-point—"

"Yes, sir."

Four bleeding days ago, now. He considered his mental picture of the wormhole nexus. No mapped jumps leading off this standard shortest route from Escobar to Jackson's Whole had ever been discovered to go anywhere of interest. He could not imagine Bel choosing this moment to play Betan Astronomical Survey and go exploring. There *was* the very rare ship that jumped through some perfectly standard route but never materialized on the other side . . . converted to an unrecoverable smear of quarks in the fabric of space-time by some subtle malfunction in the ship's Necklin rods or the pilot's neurological control system. The jump couriers kept track of traffic on such a heavily commercialized route as this, though, and would have reported such a disappearance promptly.

He came—was driven—to decision, and that alone heated his temper a few more degrees. He had grown unaccustomed of late to being chivvied into any action by events not under his own control. *This was not in my plans for the day, blast it.* "All right, Sandy. Call me a staff meeting. Captain Quinn, Captain Bothari-Jesek, Commodore Jesek, in the *Triumph*'s briefing room, as soon as they can assemble."

Hereld raised her brows at the list of names even as her hands moved over the comconsole interface to comply. Inner Circle all. "Serious shit, sir?"

He managed an edged smile, and tried to lighten his voice. "Seriously annoying only, Lieutenant."

Not quite. What had his idiot baby brother Mark in mind to *do* with that commando squad he'd requisitioned? A dozen fully-equipped Dendarii troopers were not trivial firepower. Yet, compared to the military resources of, say, House Bharaputra . . . *enough force to get into a hell of a lot of trouble, but not enough force to shoot their way back out.* The thought of his people—Taura, God!—blindly following the ignorant Mark into some tactical insanity, trustingly thinking it was *him*, drove him wild inside. Klaxons howled and red lights flashed in his head. *Bel, why aren't you answering?*

Miles found himself pacing in the *Triumph*'s main briefing room, too, around and around the big main tac display table, until Quinn raised her chin from her hands to growl, "Will you please *sit down*?" Quinn was not as anxious as he; she was not biting her fingernails yet. The ends remained neat, un-eclipsed half-moons. He found that faintly reassuring. He swung into a station chair. One of his booted feet began tapping on the friction matting. Quinn eyed it, frowned, opened her mouth, closed it, and shook her head. He stilled the foot and bared his teeth at her in a quick false grin. Happily, before his nervous energy could materialize into some even more irritating compulsive twitch, Baz Jesek arrived.

"Elena is podding over from the *Peregrine* right now," Baz reported, seating himself in his usual station chair, and by habit calling up the fleet engineering ops interface from the comconsole. "She should be along in just a few minutes."

"Good, thanks," Miles nodded.

The engineer had been a tall, thin, dark-haired, tensely unhappy man in his late twenties when Miles had first met him, almost a decade ago, at the birth of the Dendarii Mercenaries. The outfit had then consisted only of Miles, his Barrayaran bodyguard, his bodyguard's daughter, one obsolete freighter slated for scrap and its suicidally depressed jump pilot, and an ill-conceived get-rich-quick arms-smuggling scheme. Miles had sworn Baz in as a liege-man to Lord Vorkosigan before Admiral Naismith had even been invented. Now in his late thirties, Baz remained just as thin, with slightly less dark hair, and just as quiet, but possessed of a serene self-confidence. He reminded Miles of a heron, stalking in some reedy lake-margin, all long stillnesses and economical motions.

As promised, Elena Bothari-Jesek entered the chamber shortly thereafter, and seated herself beside her engineer-husband. Both being on duty, they limited the demonstration of their reunion to the exchange of a smile and a quick hand-touch under the table. She spared a smile for Miles, too. Secondly.

Of all the Dendarii Inner Circle who knew him as Lieutenant Lord Vorkosigan, Elena was surely the deepest inside. Her father, the late Sergeant Bothari, had been Miles's liege-sworn armsman and personal protector from the day Miles had been born. Age mates, Miles and Elena had been practically raised together, since Countess Vorkosigan had taken a maternal interest in the motherless girl. Elena knew Admiral Naismith, Lord Vorkosigan, and just-plain-Miles as thoroughly—perhaps more thoroughly—as anyone in the universe.

And had chosen to marry Baz Jesek instead . . . Miles found it comforting and useful to think of Elena as his sister. Foster-sister she nearly was in truth. She was as tall as her tall husband, with cropped ebony hair and pale ivory skin. He could still see the echo of borzoi-faced Sergeant Bothari in the aquiline bones of her features, Bothari's leaden ugliness transmuted to her golden beauty by some genetic alchemy. *Elena, I still love you, dammit* . . . he clipped off the thought. He had Quinn now. Or anyway, the Admiral Naismith half of him did.

As a Dendarii officer, Elena was his finest creation. He'd watched her grow from a shy, angry, off-balance girl, barred from military service on Barrayar by her gender, to squad leader to covert operative to staff officer to ship-master. The retired Commodore Tung had once named her his second-best military apprentice ever. Miles sometimes wondered how much of his on-going maintenance of the Dendarii Mercenaries was really service to Imperial Security, how much was the wild self-indulgence of a very questionable aspect of his own faceted—or fractured—personality, and how much was a secret gift to Elena Bothari. Bothari-Jesek. The true springs of history could be murky indeed.

"There's still no word from the *Ariel*," Miles began without preamble; no formalities required with this group. Deep insiders all, he could dare to think out loud in front of them. He could feel his mind relax, re-blending Admiral Naismith and Lord Vorkosigan. He could even let his accent waver from Naismith's strict Betan drawl, and allow a few Barrayaran gutturals to slip in with the swear words. There were going to be swear words, this staff meeting, he was fairly sure. "I want to go after them."

Quinn drummed her nails on the table, once. "I expected you would. Therefore, could little Mark be expecting it too? He's studied you. He's got your number. Could this be a trap? Remember how he diddled you the last time."

Miles winced. "I remember. The possibility that this is some kind of set-up has crossed my mind. That's one reason I didn't take off after them twenty hours ago." Right after the embarrassing, hastily-dismissed full staff meeting. He'd been in the mood for fratricide on the spot. "Assuming, as seems reasonable, that Bel was fooled at first—and I don't see why not, everybody else was—the time-lag might have given Mark a chance to slip up, and Bel to see the light. But in that case the recall order should have brought the *Ariel* back."

"Mark does do an awfully good you," Quinn observed, from personal experience. "Or at least he did two years ago. If you're not expecting the possibility of a double, he seems just like you on one of your off days. His exterior appearance was perfect."

"But Bel does know of the possibility," Elena put in.

"Yes," said Miles. "So maybe Bel hasn't been fooled. Maybe Bel's been spaced."

"Mark would need the crew, or a crew, to run the ship," said Baz. "Though he might have had a new crew waiting, farside."

"If he'd been planning such outright piracy and murder, he'd hardly have taken a Dendarii commando squad along to resist it." Reason could be very reassuring, sometimes. Sometimes. Miles took a breath. "Or maybe Bel has been suborned."

Baz raised his brows; Quinn unconsciously closed her teeth upon, but did not bite through, the little fingernail of her right hand.

"Suborned how?" said Elena. "Not by money." Her smile twisted up. "D'you figure Bel's finally given up trying to seduce you, and is looking for the next best thing?"

"That's not funny," Miles snapped. Baz converted a suspicious snort into a careful cough, and met his glare blandly, but then lost it and sniggered.

"At any rate, it's an old joke," Miles conceded wearily. "But it depends upon what Mark is up to, on Jackson's Whole. The kind of . . . hell, outright slavery, practiced by the various Jacksonian body-sculptors, is a deep offense to Bel's progressive Betan soul. If Mark is thinking of taking some kind of bite out of his old home planet, he just might talk Bel into going along with it."

"At Fleet expense?" Baz inquired.

"That does . . . verge on mutiny," Miles agreed reluctantly. "I'm not accusing, I'm just speculating. Trying to see all the possibilities."

"In that case, is it possible Mark's destination isn't Jackson's Whole at all?" said Baz. "There are four other jumps out of Jacksonian local space. Maybe the *Ariel* is just passing through."

"Physically possible, yes," said Miles. "Psychologically . . . I've studied Mark, too. And while I can't say that I have his number, I know Jackson's Whole looms large in his life. It's only a gut feeling, but it's a strong gut feeling." Like a bad case of indigestion.

"How *did* we get blindsided by Mark this time?" Elena asked. "I thought ImpSec was supposed to be keeping track of him for us."

"They are. I get regular reports from Illyan's office," Miles said. "The last report, which I read at ImpSec headquarters not three weeks ago, put Mark still on Earth. But it's the damn time-lag. If he left Earth, say, four or five weeks ago, that report is still in transit from Earth to Illyan on Barrayar and back to me. I'll bet you Betan dollars to anything you please that we get a coded message from HQ in the next few days earnestly warning us that Mark has dropped out of sight. Again."

"Again?" said Elena. "Has he dropped out of sight before?"

"A couple of times. Three, actually." Miles hesitated. "You see, every once in a while—three times in the last two years—I've tried to contact him myself. Invited him to come in, come to Barrayar, or at least to meet with me. Every time, he's panicked, gone underground and changed his identity—he's rather good at it, from all the time he spent as a prisoner of the Komarran terrorists—and it takes Illyan's people weeks or months to locate him again. Illyan's asked me not to try to contact Mark any more without his authorization." He brooded. "Mother wants him to come in so much, but she won't have Illyan order him kidnapped. At first I agreed with her, but now I wonder."

"As your clone, he—" began Baz.

"Brother," Miles corrected, instantly. "Brother. I reject the term 'clone' for Mark. I forbid it. 'Clone' implies something interchangeable. A brother is someone unique. And I assure you, Mark is unique."

"In guessing . . . Mark's next moves," Baz began again, more carefully, "can we even use reason? Is he sane?"

"If he is, it's not the Komarrans' fault." Miles rose and began pacing again around the table, despite Quinn's exasperated look. He avoided her eyes and watched his boots, grey on grey against the friction matting, instead. "After we finally discovered his existence, Illyan had his agents do every kind of background check on him they could. Partly to make up for the acute embarrassment of ImpSec's having missed him, all these years, I think. I've seen all the reports. Trying and trying to get inside Mark's mind." Around the corner, down the other side, and back.

"His life in Bharaputra's clone-creche didn't seem too bad—they coddle those bodies—but after the Komarran insurgents picked him up, I gather it got pretty nightmarish. They kept training him to be me, but every time they thought they'd got it, I'd do something unexpected and they had to start over. They kept changing and elaborating their plans. The plot dragged on for years after the time they'd first hoped to bring it off. They were a small group, operating on a shoestring anyway. Their leader, Ser Galen, was half-mad himself, I think." Around and around.

"Part of the time Galen would treat Mark like the great hope for a Komarran uprising, or pet him and set him up with the idea that they were going to make him Emperor of Barrayar in a coup. But part of the time Galen would slip a cog, and see Mark as the personal genetic representative of our father, and make him whipping-boy for all his hatred of the Vorkosigans and Barrayar. Disguising the most ferocious punishments, tortures really—from himself, and maybe even from Mark—as 'training discipline.' Illyan's agent had some of this from a rather illegal fast-penta interrogation of an ex-subordinate of Galen's, so it's flat truth." Around and around.

"For example, apparently Mark's and my metabolisms are not the same. So whenever Mark's weight exceeded my parameters, instead of doing the intelligent thing and having Mark's appetite medically adjusted, Galen would first withhold food for days, then let him gorge, and then force him at shock-stick point to exercise till he vomited. Weird stuff like that, really disturbing. Galen apparently had a hair-trigger temper, at least where Mark was concerned. Or maybe he was deliberately trying to make Mark crazy. Create a Mad Emperor Miles, to replay Mad Emperor Yuri's reign and destroy the Barrayaran government from the top down. Once—this fellow reported—Mark tried to get a night out, just a night out, and actually got away for a while, till Galen's goons brought him back. Galen went nuts, accused him of trying to escape, took his shock-stick and—" his eye caught Elena's paling face, and he hastily edited his nervous outburst, "and did some ugly things." Which couldn't have helped Mark's sexual adjustment any. It had been so bad that Galen's own goons had begged him to stop, according to the informant.

"No wonder he hated Galen," said Quinn softly.

Elena's glance was rather sharper. "There's nothing you could have done. You didn't even know Mark existed, back then."

"We should have known."

"Right. So to what extent is this retroactive guilt distorting your thinking right now, Admiral?"

"Some, I suspect," he admitted. "That's why I called you all here. I feel the need of a cross-check, on this." He paused, and forced himself to sit again. "That's not the only reason, however. Before this mess with the *Ariel* leaped out of the wormhole, I had started out to give you a real, bona fide mission assignment."

"Ah, ha," said Baz with satisfaction. "At last."

"The new contract." Despite his distractions, he smiled. "Before Mark showed up, I had it figured for a mission where nothing could possibly go wrong. An all-expenses-paid vacation."

"What, a no-combat-special?" quipped Elena. "I thought you always looked down on old Admiral Oser for those."

"I've changed." He felt, as ever, a brief flash of regret for the late Admiral Oser. "His command philosophy looks better all the time. I'm growing old, I guess."

"Or up," suggested Elena. They exchanged a dry look.

"In any case," Miles continued, "Barrayaran high command wishes to supply a certain independent deep-space transfer station with a better grade of weaponry than they presently own. Vega Station is, not coincidentally, just off one of the Cetagandan Empire's back doors. However, said vacuum-republic is in an awkward junction in the wormhole nexus. Quinn, the map, please."

Quinn keyed up a three-dimensional holovid schematic

of Vega Station and its neighbors. The jump routes were represented by sparkling jagged lines between hazy spheres of local space systems.

"Of the three jump points Vega Station commands, one leads into the Cetagandan sphere of influence via its satrapy Ola Three, one is blocked by a sometimes-Cetagandan-ally, sometimes-enemy Toranira, and the other is held by Zoave Twilight, politically neutral with respect to Cetaganda, but wary of its big neighbor." As he spoke of it, Quinn highlighted each system. "Vega Station is outright blockaded through Ola Three and Toranira against the import of any kind of major space-based offensive or defensive weapons systems. Zoave Twilight, under pressure from Cetaganda, is reluctantly cooperating with the arms embargo."

"So where do we come in?" asked Baz.

"Literally, through Toranira. We're smuggling pack-horses."

"What?" said Baz, though Elena caught the reference and suddenly smirked.

"You've never heard that story? From Barrayaran history? It goes, Count Selig Vorkosigan was at war with Lord Vorwyn of Hazelbright, during the First Bloody Century. The town of Vorkosigan Vashnoi was besieged. Twice a week Lord Vorwyn's patrols would stop this crazy, motley fellow with a train of pack horses and search his packs for contraband, food or supplies. But his packs were always filled with rubbish. They poked and prodded and emptied them—he'd always gather it carefully back up—shook him down and searched him, and finally had to let him go. After the war, one of Vorwyn's border guards met Count Selig's liegeman, no longer motley, by chance in a tavern. 'What were you smuggling?' he asked in frustration. 'We know you were smuggling something, what was it?'

"And Count Selig's liegeman replied, 'Horses.'

"We're smuggling spaceships. To wit, the *Triumph*, the *D-16*, and the *Ariel*, all fleet-owned. We enter Vega Station local space through Toranira, on a through-flight plan, bound for Illyrica. Which we really will be. We exit through Zoave, still with every trooper, but minus three aging ships. We then continue on to Illyrica, and pick up our three brand-new warships, which are being completed even as we speak in the Illyrican orbital shipyards. Our happy Winterfair gift from Emperor Gregor."

Baz blinked. "Will this work?"

"No reason it shouldn't. The spadework—permits, visas, bribes and so on—is all being completed by ImpSec agents on-site. All we have to do is waft through without alarming anybody. There's no war on, not a shot should be fired. The only problem is that one-third of my trade-inventory just left for Jackson's Whole," Miles concluded with a descending snort.

"How much time do we have to recover it?" asked Elena.

"Not as much as we need. The time-window ImpSec has set up for this smuggling scenario is flexible in terms of a few days, but not weeks. The fleet must leave Escobar before the end of this week. I'd originally scheduled it for tomorrow."

"So do we go without *Ariel*?" asked Baz.

"We're going to have to. But not empty-handed. I have an idea for a substitution. Quinn, shunt those Illyrican specs to Baz."

Quinn bent her head to the secured data cube in her comconsole interface, and released a burst of code to Baz's station. The engineer began keying through advertising displays, descriptions, specifications, and plans from the Illyrican shipbuilders. His thin face lit in a rare smile. "Father Frost is generous this Winterfair," he murmured. His lips parted with delight as the ships' power-plant specs came up, and his eyes moved avidly.

Miles let him wallow for a few minutes more. "Now," he said, when Baz self-consciously came up for air. "The next-up ship in the fleet from the *Ariel* in terms of function and firepower is Truzillo's *Jayhawk*." Unfortunately, Truzillo was a captain-owner under independent contract to the Fleet corporation, not a Fleet employee. "Do you think he could be persuaded to trade? His replacement ship would be newer and faster, but while it's definitely a step up in firepower from the *Ariel*, it's a slight step down from the *Jayhawk*. I'd meant us all to trade up, not even, when we first cooked up this deal."

Elena raised her eyebrows and grinned. "This is one of your scenarios, isn't it?"

He shrugged. "Illyan asked me to solve the arms embargo problem, yes. He accepted my solution."

"Oh," Baz purred, still awash in data, "wait'll Truzillo sees this . . . and *this* . . . and . . ."

"So do you think you can persuade him?" asked Miles.

"Yes," said Baz, with certainty. He glanced up. "So could you."

"Except I'll be headed the other way. Though if things go well, it's not impossible that I might catch up with you later. I'm putting you in charge of this mission, Baz. Quinn will give you the complete orders, all the codes and contact-people—everything Illyan gave me."

Baz nodded. "Very good, sir."

"I'm taking the *Peregrine* to go after the *Ariel*," Miles added.

Baz and Elena exchanged only one quick, sideways glance. "Very good, sir," echoed Elena, with scarcely a pause. "I shifted the *Peregrine* from twenty-four-hour to one-hour alert status yesterday. When shall I schedule our departure with Escobaran flight control?"

"In one hour." And, though no one had asked for explanations, he added, "The *Peregrine* is the next-fastest thing we have that packs significant firepower, besides the *Jayhawk* and the *Ariel* itself. I think that speed is going to be of the essence. If we can overtake the *Ariel*—well, it's a lot easier to prevent a mess than to try to clean up after one. I'm sorry now I didn't leave yesterday, but I had to give it a chance to be simple. I'm assigning Quinn to myself as floating staff because she's had valuable previous experience with intelligence-gathering on Jackson's Whole."

Quinn rubbed her arm. "House Bharaputra is damn dangerous, if that's where Mark's headed. They have heavy money, heavy shit, and a sharp memory for revenge."

"Why d'you think I avoid the place? That's another danger, that certain Jacksonians will mistake Mark for Admiral Naismith. Baron Ryoval, for example."

Baron Ryoval was a persistent danger. The Dendarii had disposed of the latest bounty-hunter Ryoval had sent seeking Admiral Naismith's scalp only three months ago; he had been the fourth to appear so far. It was shaping up to an annual event. Maybe Ryoval despatched an agent on each anniversary of their first encounter, as a memorial tribute. Ryoval did not command great powers, nor possess a long reach, but he had undergone life-extension treatments; he was patient, and could keep this up for a long, long time.

"Have you considered another possible solution to the problem?" said Quinn slowly. "Send ahead to Jackson's Whole and warn them. Have, say, House Fell arrest Mark and impound the *Ariel* till you arrive to retrieve them. Fell hates Ryoval enough to protect Mark from him for the annoyance-factor alone."

Miles sighed. "I have considered it." He traced a formless pattern on the polished tabletop with his fingertip.

"You asked for a cross-check, Miles," Elena pointed out. "What's wrong with that idea?"

"It might work. But if Mark has really convinced Bel he's me, they might resist arrest. Maybe fatally. Mark is paranoid about Jackson's Whole. Mark is paranoid, period. I don't know what he'd do in a panic."

"You are awfully tender of Mark's sensibilities," said Elena.

"I'm trying to get him to trust me. I can hardly start the process by betraying him."

"Have you considered how much this little side-jaunt is going to cost, once the bill for it arrives on Simon Illyan's desk?" Quinn asked.

"ImpSec will pay. Without question."

Quinn said, "You sure? What's Mark to ImpSec anyway, now that he's only a left-over from the exploded plot? There is no danger any more to Barrayar of him being secretly substituted for you. I thought they only watched him for us as a courtesy. A rather expensive courtesy."

Miles replied carefully, "It is ImpSec's explicit task to guard the Barrayaran Imperium. That includes not only protecting Gregor's person, and running a certain amount of galactic espionage—" a wave of his hand included the Dendarii fleet, and Illyan's far-flung, if thinly stretched, network of agents, military attaches, and informants, "but also keeping watch over Gregor's immediate heirs. Keeping watch not only to protect them, but to protect the Imperium from any little plot got up by them, or by others seeking to use them. I am acutely conscious that the question of just who is Gregor's heir is rather tangled at present. I wish to hell he'd marry and get us all off the hook soon." Miles hesitated for a long moment. "By one interpretation, Lord Mark Pierre Vorkosigan has a place as heir-claimant to the Barrayaran Imperium second only to my own. That makes him not only ImpSec's business, it makes him our *primary* business. My personal pursuit of the *Ariel* is fully justified."

"Justifiable," Quinn corrected dryly.

"Whatever."

"If Barrayar—as you have often claimed—would not accept you as Emperor because of suspicion of mutation, I should think it'd go into spasms at the thought of your clone installed in the Imperial Residence," said Baz. "Twin brother," he amended hastily as Miles opened his mouth.

"It doesn't require the probability of success at gaining the Imperium to make the possibility of an attempt to do so into an ImpSec problem." Miles snorted. "It's funny. All the time the Komarrans thought of their faux-Miles as an imposter-claimant. I don't think either they or Mark realized they'd made a *real* claimant. Well, I'd have to be dead first anyway, so from my point of view the question is moot." He rapped the table and rose. "Let's get moving, people."

On the way out the door, Elena lowered her voice to ask him, "Miles—did your mother see those horrific investigation-reports of Illyan's about Mark, too?"

He smiled bleakly. "Who d'you think ordered them done?"

CHAPTER FIVE

He began donning the half-armor. First, next to his skin, a piece of the hottest new technology on the market: a nerve-disruptor shield-net. The field-generating net was worked into the fabric of a close-fitting grey bodysuit and a hood that protected skull, neck, and forehead, leaving only his eyes, nose, and mouth peeping from the hole. And so the threat of one of the most fearsome anti-personnel weapons, the brain-killing nerve disruptor, was rendered null. As an added bonus, the suit stopped stunner-fire, too. Trust Naismith to have the best and newest, and custom-made to fit . . . was the elastic fabric supposed to be this bloody tight?

Over the net-suit went a flexible torso-armor that would stop any projectile up to small hand-missiles and down to deadly needler spines. Fortunately for his ability to breathe, its catches were adjustable. He let them out to their fullest extension, rendering the valuable protection merely comfortably and correctly snug. Over it went blessedly loose camouflage-grey fatigues, made of a combat-rated fabric that would neither melt nor burn. Then came belts and bandoliers with stunner, nerve disruptor, plasma arc, grenades, power cells, a rappel-harness and spool, emergency oxygen. On his back he shrugged the harness holding a neat, flat power pack that generated, at the first touch of enemy fire, a one-man-sized plasma arc mirror field, with so minuscule a time lag one barely had time to cook, much. It was good for absorbing thirty or forty direct hits before the power cell, and its porter, died. It seemed almost a misnomer to call it all half-armor: triple armor was more like it.

Over the nerve-disruptor net covering his feet he pulled thick socks, then Naismith's combat boots. At least the boots fit without any embarrassing adjustments. A mere week of inactivity, and his body fought him, thickening . . . Naismith was a damned anorectic, that was it. A hyperactive anorectic. He straightened. Properly distributed, the formidable array of equipment was surprisingly light.

On the countertop next to his cabin comconsole, the command helmet sat waiting. The empty shadow beneath its forehead flange made him think, for whatever morbid reason, of an empty skull. He raised the helmet in his hands, and turned it in the light, and stared hungrily at its elegant curves. His hands could control one weapon, two at most. This, through the people it commanded, controlled dozens; potentially, hundreds or even thousands. This was Naismith's real power.

The cabin buzzer blatted; he jumped, nearly dropping the helmet. He could have pitched it against the wall and not harmed it, but still he set it down carefully.

"Miles?" came Captain Thorne's voice on the intercom. "You about ready?"

"Yes, come in." He touched the keypad to release the door lock.

Thorne entered, attired identically to himself, but with hood temporarily pushed back. The formless fatigues rendered Thorne not bi-sexed, but neuter, a genderless thing, *soldier*. Thorne too bore a command helmet under its arm, of a slightly older and different make.

Thorne walked around him, eyes flicking over every weapon and belt-hook, and checking the readouts of his plasma-shield pack. "Good." Did Captain Thorne normally inspect its Admiral before combat? Was Naismith in the habit of wandering into battle with his boots unfastened, or something? Thorne nodded to the command helmet sitting on the countertop. "That's quite a machine. Sure you can handle it?"

The helmet appeared new, but not that new. He doubted Naismith supplied himself with used military surplus for his personal use, regardless of what economies he practiced in the fleet at large. "Why not?" he shrugged. "I have before."

"These things," Thorne lifted his own, "can be pretty overwhelming at first. It's not a data flow, it's a damn data flood. You have to learn to ignore everything you don't need, otherwise it can be almost better to switch the thing off. You, now . . ." Thorne hesitated, "have that same uncanny ability as old Tung did, of appearing to ignore everything as it goes by, and yet being able to remember and yank it out instantly if it's needed. Of somehow always being on the right channel at the right time. It's like your mind works on two levels. Your command-response time is incredibly fast, when your adrenalin is up. It's kind of addictive. People who work with you a lot come to expect—and rely—on it." Thorne stopped, waited.

What was it expecting him to say? He shrugged again. "I do my best."

"If you're still feeling ill, you know, you can delegate this whole raid to me."

"Do I look ill?"

"You're not yourself. You don't want to make the whole squad sick." Thorne seemed tense, almost urgent.

"I'm *fine*, now, Bel. Back off!"

"Yes, sir," Thorne sighed.

"Is everything ready out there?"

"The shuttle is fueled and armed. Green Squad is kitted up, and is doing the final loading right now. We have it timed so we come into parking orbit just at midnight, downside at Bharaputra's main medical facility. We drop instantly, no waiting around for people to start asking questions. Hit and go. The whole operation should be over in an hour, if things run to plan."

"Good." His heart was beating faster. He disguised a deep breath in a strung-out sigh. "Let's go."

"Let's . . . do our helmet communication checks first, huh?" said Thorne.

That was a good idea, here in the quiet cabin, rather than in the noise and excitement and tension of the drop shuttle. "All right," he said, and added slyly, "Take your time."

There were over a hundred channels in use in the command headset, even for this limited raid. In addition to direct voice contact with the *Ariel*, Thorne, and every trooper, there were battle computers on the ship, in the shuttle, and in the helmet itself. There were telemetry readouts of every sort, weapon power checks, logistics updates. All the troopers' helmets had vid pick-ups so he could see what they were seeing in infra-red, visual, and UV bands; full sound; their medical readouts; holovid map displays. The holomap of the clone-creche had been specially programmed in, and the plan of attack and several contingencies pre-loaded. There were channels to be dedicated, on the fly, to eavesdropping upon enemy telemetry. Thorne already had Bharaputra's security guards' comm links locked in. They could even pick up commercial entertainment broadcasts from the planet they were approaching. Tinny music filled the air momentarily as he switched past those channels.

They finished, and he found himself and Thorne staring at each other in an awkward silence. Thorne was hollow-faced, apprehensive, as if struggling with some suppressed emotion. *Guilt?* Strange perception, surely not. Thorne couldn't be on to him, or it would have called a halt to this whole operation.

"Pre-combat nerves, Bel?" he said lightly. "I thought you loved your work."

Thorne came out of its lip-sucking abstraction with a start. "Oh, I do." It took a breath. "Let's do it."

"Go!" he agreed, and led the way at last out of his isolated cabin-cave into the light of the corridor and the peopled reality his actions—*his* actions—had created.

The shuttle-hatch corridor resembled his first view of it, reversed; the hulking Dendarii commandos were filing out, not spilling in. They seemed quieter this time, not as much clowning and joking. More businesslike. They had names, now, too, all filed in his command headset, which would keep them straight for him. All wore some variety of half-armor and helmet, with an array of heavier equipment in addition to such hand-weapons as he bore.

He found himself looking at the monster sergeant with new eyes, now that he knew her history. The log had said she was only nineteen years old, though she looked older; she'd been only sixteen, four years ago when Naismith had stolen her away from House Ryoval. He squinted, trying to see her as a girl. He had been taken away at age fourteen, eight years ago. Their mutual time as genetic products and prisoners of House Bharaputra must have overlapped, though he had never met her. The genetic engineering research labs were in a different town from the main surgical facility. House Bharaputra was a vast organization, in its strange Jacksonian way almost a little government. Except Jackson's Whole didn't have governments.

Eight years . . . *No one you knew then is still alive. You know that, don't you?*

If I can't do what I want, I'll at least do what I can.

He stepped up to her. "Sergeant Taura—" she turned, and his brows climbed in startlement. "*What* is that around your neck?" Actually, he could see what it was, a large fluffy pink bow. He supposed his real question was, *why* was it around her neck?

She—smiled, he guessed that repellent grimace was, at him, and fluffed it out a bit more with a huge clawed hand. Her claw-polish was bright pink, tonight. "D'you think it'll work? I wanted something to not scare the kids."

He looked up at eight feet of half-armor, camouflage cloth, boots, bandoliers, muscle and fang. *Somehow, I don't think it'll be enough, Sergeant.* "It's . . . certainly worth a try," he choked. So, she was conscious of her extraordinary appearance. . . . *Fool! How could she not be? Are you not conscious of yours?* He was almost sorry now he had not ventured out of his cabin earlier in the voyage, and made her acquaintance. *My home-town girl.*

"What does it feel like, to be going back?" he asked suddenly; a nod in no particular direction indicated the House Bharaputra drop-zone, coming up.

"Strange," she admitted, her thick brows drawing down.

"Do you know this landing-site? Ever been there before?"

"Not that medical complex. I hardly ever left the genetics facility, except for a couple of years that I lived with hired fosterers, which was in the same town." Her head turned, her voice dropped an octave, and she barked an order about loading equipment at one of her men, who gave a half-wave and hustled to obey. She turned back to him and her voice re-softened to conscious, careful lightness. In no other way did she display any inappropriate intimacy while on duty; it seemed she and Naismith were discreet lovers, if lovers they were. The discreetness relieved him. She added, "I didn't get out much."

His own voice lowered. "Do you hate them?" *As I do?* A different kind of intimate question.

Her outslung lips twisted in thought. "I suppose . . . I was terribly manipulated by them when I was growing up, but it didn't seem like abuse to me at the time. There were a lot of uncomfortable tests, but it was all science . . . there wasn't any intent to hurt in it. It didn't really hurt till they sold me to Ryoval's, after the super-soldier project was cancelled. What Ryoval's wanted to do to me was grotesque, but that was just the nature of Ryoval's. It was Bharaputra . . . Bharaputra that didn't care. That threw me away. *That* hurt. But then *you* came . . ." She brightened. "A knight in shining armor and all that."

A familiar, surly wave of resentment washed over him. *Bugger the knight in shining armor, and the horse he rode in on.* And, *I can rescue people too, dammit!* She was looking away, fortunately, and didn't catch the spasm of anger in his face. Or perhaps she took it for anger at their former tormentors.

"But for all that," she murmured, "I would not have even existed, without House Bharaputra. They made me. I am alive, for however long . . . shall I return death for life?" Her strange distorted face grew deeply introspective.

This was not the ideal gung-ho frame of mind to inculcate in a commando on a drop mission, he realized belatedly. "Not . . . necessarily. We're here to rescue clones, not kill Bharaputran employees. We kill only if forced to, eh?"

This was good Naismithery; her head came up, and she grinned at him. "I'm so relieved you're feeling better. I was terribly worried. I wanted to see you, but Captain Thorne wouldn't allow it." Her eyes warmed like bright yellow flames.

"Yes, I was . . . very ill. Thorne did right. But . . . maybe we can talk more on the way home." When this was over. When he'd earned the right . . . *earned the right to what?*

"You got a date, Admiral." She *winked* at him, and straightened, ferociously joyous. *What have I promised?* She bounded forward, happily sergeantly again, to oversee her squad.

He followed her into the combat-drop shuttle. The light level was much lower in here, the air colder, and, of course, there was no gravity. He floated forward from hand-grip to hand-grip after Captain Thorne, mentally dividing up the floor space for his intended cargo. Twelve or fifteen rows of kids seated four across . . . there was plenty of room. This shuttle was equipped to carry two squads, plus armored hovercars or a whole field hospital. It had a first-aid station at the back, including four fold-down bunks and a portable emergency cryo-chamber. The Dendarii commando-medic was rapidly organizing his area and battening down his supplies. Everything was being fastened down, by quietly-moving fatigue-clad soldiers, with very little fuss or conversation. A place for everything and everything in its place.

The shuttle pilot was at his post. Thorne took the co-pilot's seat. He took a communication station chair just behind them. Out the front window he could see distant hard-edged stars, nearby the winking colored lights of some human activity, and, at the very edge of the field of view, the bright slice of the planet's curvature. Almost home. His belly fluttered, and not just from zero-gee. Bands of tightness throbbed around his head beneath his helmet-straps.

The pilot hit his intercom. "Gimme a body-check back there, Taura. We've got a five-minute thrust to match orbit, then we blow bolts and drop."

After a moment Sergeant Taura's voice returned, "Check. All troops tied down, hatch sealed. We are ready. Go-repeat-go."

Thorne glanced over its shoulder, and pointed. Hastily, he fastened his seat straps, and just in time. The straps bit deeply, and he lurched from side to side as the *Ariel* shuddered into its parking orbit, accelerative effects that would have been compensated for and nullified by the artificial gravity generated between the decks of the larger ship.

The pilot poised his hands, and abruptly dropped them, as if he were a musician playing some crescendo. Loud, startling clanks reverberated through the fuselage. Ululating whoops keened in response from the compartment behind the flight deck.

When they say drop, he thought wildly, *they mean it.* Stars and the planet turned, nauseatingly, in the forward window. He closed his eyes; his stomach tried to climb his esophagus. He suddenly realized a hidden advantage to full space armor. If you shit yourself with terror, going down, the suit's plumbing would take care of it, and no one would ever know.

Air began to scream over the outer hull as they hit the ionosphere. His seat straps tried to slice him like an egg. "Fun, huh?" yelled Thorne, grinning like a loon, its face distorted and lips flapping with deceleration. They were pointed straight down, or so the shuttle's nose was aimed, although his seat was attempting to eject him into the cabin ceiling with neck-breaking and skull-smashing force.

"I sure hope there's nothing in our way," the pilot yelled cheerfully. "This hasn't been cleared with anybody's flight control, y'know!"

He pictured a mid-air collision with a large commercial passenger shuttle . . . five hundred women and children aboard . . . vast yellow and black explosions and arcing bodies. . . .

They crossed the terminator into twilight. Then darkness, whipping clouds . . . bigger clouds . . . shuttle vibrating and bellowing like an insane tuba . . . still pointed straight down, he swore, though how the pilot could tell in this screaming fog he did not know.

Then, suddenly, they were level as an airshuttle, clouds above, lights of a town like jewels spilled on a carpet below. An airshuttle that was dropping like a rock. His spine began to compress, harder, harder. More hideous clanks, as the shuttle's feet extended. An array of half-lit buildings bulked below. A darkened playing-court—*Shit, that's it, that's it!* The buildings loomed up beside them, above them. *Thud-crunch-crunch.* A solid, six-legged landing. The silence stunned him.

"All *right*, let's *go*!" Thorne swung up out of its seat, face flushed, eyes lit, with blood-lust or fear or both he could not tell.

He tramped down the ramp in the wake of a dozen Dendarii. His eyes were about half dark-adapted, and there were enough lights around the complex, diffused by the cool and misty midnight air, that he had no trouble seeing, though the view was drained of color. The shadows were black and sinister. Sergeant Taura, with silent hand signals, divided her squad. No one was making noise. Silent faces were gilded by brief staccato flashes of light as their helmet vids supplied some data bit or another, projected to the side of their vision. One Dendarii, with extra 'scopes on her helmet, rolled out a personal float-bike, mounted it, and rose quietly into the darkness. Air cover.

The pilot stayed aboard, and Taura counted off four other Dendarii. Two vanished into the shadows of the perimeter, two stayed with the shuttle as rear-guard. He and Thorne had argued about that. Thorne had wanted more perimeter. His own gut-feel was that they would need as many troopers as possible at the clone-creche. The civilian hospital guards were little threat, and it would take time for their better-armed back-up to arrive. By then, the Dendarii would be gone, if they could move the clones along fast enough. He cursed himself, in retrospect, for not ordering two commando squads instead of one, back at Escobar. He could have done so, just as easily, but he'd been caught up in calculations about the *Ariel's* passenger capacity, and fancied himself conserving life support for the final escape. So many factors to balance.

His own helmet framed his vision with a colored clutter of codes,numbers, and graphs. He'd studied them all, but they flicked by too fast; by the time he'd taken one in, and interpreted it to himself, it was gone, replaced by another. He took Thorne's advice, and with a whispered word reduced the light intensity to a bare hallucinatory murmur. The helmet's audio pick-up was not so bad. No one was doing any unnecessary chatter.

He, Thorne, and the other seven Dendarii followed Taura at a trot—her stride—between two adjacent buildings. There was activity on the Bharaputran security guards' comm links, he found by keying his helmet to their audio bands. The first *What the hell. Did you hear that? Joe, check sector four,* stirrings of response. More to follow, he was sure, though he had no intention of waiting around for it.

Around a corner. *There.* A three-story, pleasant white building with lots of plants and landscaping, big windows, balconies. Not quite a hospital, not quite a dormitory, vague, ambiguous, discreet. THE LIFE HOUSE it was labelled in Jacksonian double-speak. *The death house. My dear old home.* It was terribly familiar and terribly strange. Once, it had seemed quite splendid to him. Now it seemed . . . smaller than he remembered.

Taura raised her plasma arc, adjusted its beam to *wide*, and removed the locked glass front doors in an orange, white, and blue spray of flying, spattering cullet. Dendarii bounded through, splitting right and left, before the glow of the spattered globs of glass died. One took up station patrolling the ground floor. Alarms and fire alarms went off: Dendarii killed the noisy speakers they passed with more plasma fire, on the fly, but units in more distant parts of the building kept up a muted clamor. Automatic sprinklers made steam and a mess in their trail.

He ran to catch up. A uniformed Bharaputran security guard in brown trimmed with pink lurched into the corridor ahead. Three Dendarii stunners simultaneously downed him as his own stunner beam was absorbed harmlessly by the ceiling.

Taura and two female Dendarii took the lift tube toward the third floor; another trooper passed them in hope of gaining the roof. He led Thorne and the remaining troopers out into the second floor foyer and to the left. Two unarmed adults, one a night-gowned woman pulling on a robe, were felled the instant they appeared. *There.* Through those double doors. They were locked, and someone was beating on them from the inside.

"We're going to break the door open," Thorne bellowed through it. "Back away, or you'll get hurt!" The pounding stopped. Thorne nodded. A trooper adjusted his plasma arc to narrow beam, and sliced through a metal bolt. Thorne kicked the doors wide.

A blond young man fell back a pace, and stared at Thorne with bewilderment. "You're not the firemen."

A crowd of other men, tall boys, filled the corridor behind the blond. He did not have to remind himself that these were a bunch of ten-year-olds, but he wasn't sure about the perceptions of the troopers. Every variation of height and racial mix and build was represented, much more motley than the Greek-god look one might have anticipated from their garden-and-fountain setting. Personal wealth, not personal beauty, had been the ticket for their creation. Still, each was as glowingly healthy as the particularities of his genetics permitted. They all wore uniform sleepwear, bronze-brown tunics and shorts.

"Front," Thorne hissed, and shoved him forward. "Start talking."

"Get me a head-count," he ripped out of the corner of his mouth as Thorne pulled him past.

"Right."

He'd practiced the speech for this supreme moment in his mind ten thousand times, every possible variation. The only thing he knew for certain that he was *not* going to start with was, *I'm Miles Naismith.* His heart was racing. He inhaled a huge gulp of air. "We're the Dendarii Mercenaries, and we're here to save you."

The boy's expression was repelled, scared, and scornful all mixed. "You look like a mushroom," he said blankly.

It was so . . . so *off-script.* Of his thousand rehearsed second lines, not one followed this. Actually, with the command helmet and all, he probably did look a bit like a big gray—*not* the heroic image he'd hoped to—

He tore off his helmet, ripped back his hood, and bared his teeth. The boy recoiled.

"Listen up, you clones!" he yelled. "The secret you may have heard whispered is true! Every single one of you is waiting in line to be murdered by House Bharaputra surgeons. They're gonna stick somebody else's brain in your head, and throw your brain away. That's where your friends have been going, one by one, to their deaths. We're here to take you to Escobar, where you'll be given sanctuary—"

Not all the boys had assembled in the corridor in the first place, and now ones at the rear of the mob began to break away and retreat into individual rooms. A babble started to rise from them, and yells and cries. One dark-haired boy tried to dart past them to the corridor beyond the big double doors, and a trooper grabbed him in a standard arm-lock. He screamed in pain and surprise, and the sound and shock seemed to blow the others back in a wave. The boy struggled without effect in the trooper's iron grip. The trooper looked exasperated and uncertain, and stared at him as if expecting some direction or order.

"Get your friends and follow me!" he yelled desperately to the retreating boys. The blond turned on his heel and sprinted.

"I don't think they bought us," said Thorne. The hermaphrodite's face was pale and tense. "It might actually be easier to stun them all and carry them. We can't afford to lose time in here, not with that damned thin perimeter."

"No—"

His helmet was calling him. He jammed it back on. Comm-link babble burst in his ears, but Sergeant Taura's deep voice penetrated, selectively enhanced by her channel. "Sir, we need your help up here."

"What is it?"

Her answer was lost in an override from the woman riding the float-bike. "Sir, there's three or four people climbing down the outside balconies of the building you're in. And there's a group of four Bharaputran security people approaching you from the north."

He sorted frantically through channels till he found the one out-going to the air-guard. "Don't let any get away!"

"How should I stop 'em, sir?" Her voice was edged.

"Stunner," he decided helplessly. "Wait! Don't stun any that are hanging off the balcony, wait'll they reach the ground."

"I may not have a clear shot."

"Do your best." He cut her off and found Taura again. "What do you want, Sergeant?"

"I want you to come talk to this crazy girl. *You* can convince her if anyone can."

"Things are—not quite under control down here."

Thorne rolled its eyes. The captured boy was drumming his bare heels against the Dendarii trooper's shins. Thorne set its stunner to the lightest setting, and touched it to the back of the squirming boy's neck. He convulsed and hung more limply. Still conscious, eyes blearing and wild, the boy began to cry.

In a burst of cowardice he said to Thorne, "Get them rounded up. Any way you can. I'm going to help Sergeant Taura."

"You do that," growled Thorne in a distinctly insubordinate tone. It wheeled, gathering its men. "You and you, take that side—you, take the other. Get those doors down—"

He retreated ignominiously to the sound of shattering plastic.

Upstairs, things were quieter. There were fewer girls than boys altogether, a disproportion that had also prevailed in his time. He'd often wondered why. He stepped over the stunned body of a heavy-set female security guard, and followed his vid map, projected by his helmet, to Sergeant Taura.

A dozen or so girls were seated cross-legged on the floor, their hands clasped behind their necks, under the waving threat of one Dendarii's stunner. Their sleep-tunics and shorts were pink silk, otherwise identical to the boys'. They looked frightened, but at least they sat silent. He stepped into a side room to find Taura and the other trooper confronting a tall Eurasian girl-woman, who sat at a comconsole with her arms aggressively crossed. Where the vid plate should have been was a smoking hole, hot and recent, from plasma fire.

The Eurasian girl's head turned, her long black hair swinging, from Taura to himself and back. "My lady, what a circus!" Her voice was a whip of contempt.

"She refuses to budge," said Taura. Her tone was strangely worried.

"Girl," he nodded curtly. "You are dead meat if you stay here. You are a clone. Your body is destined to be stolen by your progenitor. Your brain will be removed and destroyed. Perhaps very soon."

"*I* know that," she said scornfully, as if he were a babbling idiot.

"What?" His jaw dropped.

"I know it. I am perfectly aligned with my destiny. My lady required it to be so. I serve my lady perfectly." Her chin rose, and her eyes rested in a moment of dreamy, distant worship, of what he could not guess.

"She got a call out to House Security," reported Taura tightly, with a nod at the smoking holovid. "Described us, our gear—even reported an estimate of our numbers."

"You will not keep me from my lady," the girl affirmed with a short, cool nod. "The guards will get you, and save me. I'm very important."

What the hell had the Bharaputrans done to turn this girl's head inside-out? And could he undo it in thirty seconds or less? He didn't think so. "Sergeant," he took a deep breath, and said in a high, light voice on the outgoing sigh, "Stun her."

The Eurasian girl started to duck, but the sergeant's reflexes worked at lightning speed. The stunner beam took her precisely between the eyes as she leapt. Taura vaulted the comconsole and caught the girl's head before it could strike the floor.

"Do we have them all?" he asked.

"At least two went down the back stairs before we blocked them," Taura reported with a frown.

"They'll be stunned if they try to escape the building," he reassured her.

"But what if they hide, downstairs? It'll take time to find 'em." Her tawny eyes flicked sideways to take in some chrono display from her helmet. "We should all be on our way back to the shuttle by now."

"Just a second." Laboriously, he keyed through his channels till he found Thorne again. Off in the distance, carried thinly by the audio, someone was yelling, " 'n-of-a-bitch! You little—"

"*What?*" Thorne snapped in a harried voice. "You got those girls rounded up yet?"

"Had to stun one. Taura can carry her. Look, did you get that head-count yet?"

"Yes, took it off a comconsole in a keeper's room—thirty-eight boys and sixteen girls. We're missing four boys who apparently went over the balcony. Trooper Philippi accounted for three of them but says she didn't spot a fourth. How about you?"

"Sergeant Taura says two girls went down the back stairs. Watch for them." He glanced up, peering out of his vid display, which was swirling like an aurora. "Captain Thorne says there should be sixteen bodies here."

Taura stuck her head out into the corridor, lips moving, then returned and eyed the stunned Eurasian girl. "We're still short one. Kesterton, make a pass around this floor, check cupboards and under the beds."

"Right, Sergeant." The Dendarii trooper ran to obey.

He followed her, Thorne's voice urging in his ears, "*Move* it up there! This is a smash-and-grab, remember? We don't have *time* to round up strays!"

"*Wait*, dammit."

In the third room the trooper checked, she bent to look under a bed and said, "Ha! Got her, Sergeant!" She swooped, grabbed a couple of kicking ankles, and yanked. Her prize slid into the light, a short girl-woman in the pink crossover tunic and shorts. She emitted little helpless muted noises, distress with no hope of her cries bringing help. She had a cascade of platinum curls, but her most notable feature was a stunning bustline, huge fat globes that the strained pink silk of her tunic failed to contain. She rolled to her knees, buttocks on heels, her upraised hands vaguely pushing and cradling the heavy flesh as if it still shocked and unaccustomed to finding it there.

Ten years old. Shit. She looked twenty. And such monstrous hypertrophy couldn't be natural. The progenitor-customer must have ordered body-sculpture, prior to taking possession. That made sense, let the clone do the surgical and metabolic suffering. Tiny waist, flare of hip . . . from her exaggerated, physically mature femininity, he wondered if she might be one of the change-of-sex transfers. Almost certainly. She must have been slated for surgery very soon.

"No, go away," she was whimpering. "Go away, leave me alone . . . my mother is coming for me. My mother is coming for me *tomorrow*. Go away, leave me alone, I'm going to meet my *mother*. . . ."

Her cries, and her heaving . . . chest, would shortly make him crazy, he thought. "Stun that one too," he croaked. They'd have to carry her, but at least they wouldn't have to listen to her.

The trooper's face was flushed, as transfixed and embarrassed as he by the girl's grotesque build. "Poor doll," she whispered, and put her out of her misery with a light touch of stunner to her neck. She slumped forward, splayed on the floor.

His helmet was calling him, he wasn't sure which trooper's voice. "Sir, we just drove back a crew of House Bharaputra fire-fighters with our stunners. They didn't have anti-stun suits. But the security people who are coming on now do. They're sending new teams, carrying heavier weapons. The stunner-tag game is about over."

He keyed through helmet displays, trying to place the trooper on the map-grid. Before he could, the air-guard's breathless voice cut in. "A Bharaputran heavy-weapons team is circling around your building to the south, sir. You've got to get the hell out of there. It's about to turn real nasty out here."

He waved the Dendarii trooper and her doll-woman burden out of the bedroom ahead of him. "Sergeant

Taura," he called. "Did you pick up those outside reports?"

"Yes, sir. Let's move it."

Sergeant Taura slung the Eurasian girl over one broad shoulder and the blonde over the other, apparently without noticing their weight, and they herded the mob of frightened girls down the endstairs. Taura made them walk two-by-two, holding hands, keeping them rather better organized than he would have expected. The girls' hushed voices burbled in shock when they were directed into the boys' dormitory section. "We're not allowed down here," one tried to protest, in tears. "We'll get in *trouble*."

Thorne had six stunned boys laid out face-up on the corridor floor, and another twenty-odd lined up leaning against the wall, legs spread, arms extended, prisoner-control posture, with a couple of nervous troopers yelling at them and keeping them in their places. Some clones looked angry, some were crying, and all looked scared to death.

He looked with dismay at the pile of stunner victims. "How are we going to carry them all?"

"Have some carry the rest," Taura said. "It leaves your hands free and ties up theirs." She gently laid down her own burdens at the end of the row.

"Good," said Thorne, jerking its gaze, with difficulty, from fascinated fixation on the doll-woman. "Worley, Kesterton, let's—" its voice stopped, as the same static-laden emergency message overrode channels in both their command helmets.

It was the bike-trooper, screaming, "Sonofabitch, the shuttle—watch *out* guys, on your left—" a hot wash of static, and "—oh holy fuckin' shit—" Then a silence, filled only with the hum of an empty channel.

He keyed frantically for a readout, any readout at all, from her helmet. The locator still functioned, plotting her on the ground between two buildings in back of the play-court where the shuttle was parked. Her medical readouts were flatline blanks. Dead? Surely not, there should at least still be blood chemistry . . . the static, empty view being transmitted, upward at an angle into the night fog, at last cued him. Phillipi had lost her helmet. What else she'd lost, he could not tell.

Thorne called the shuttle pilot, over and over, alternated with the rear-guards; no replies. It swore. "*You* try."

He found empty channels too. The other two perimeter Dendarii were tied up in an exchange of fire with the Bharaputran heavy-weapons squad to the south that the bike-trooper had reported earlier.

"We gotta reconnoiter," snarled Thorne under its breath. "Sergeant Taura, take over here, get these kids ready to march. You—" This was to his address, apparently; why did Thorne no longer call him *Admiral*, or *Miles*? "Come with me. Trooper Sumner, cover us."

Thorne departed at a flat-out run; he cursed his short legs as he fell steadily farther behind. Down the lift-tube, out the still-hot front doors, around one dark building, between two others. He caught up with the hermaphrodite, who was flattened against a corner of the building at the edge of the playing-court.

The shuttle was still there, apparently undamaged—surely no hand-weapon could penetrate its combat-hardened shell. The ramp was drawn up, the door closed. A dark shape—downed Dendarii, or enemy?—slumped in the shadow beneath its wing-flanges. Thorne, whispering curses, jabbed codes into a computer control plate bound to its left forearm. The hatch slid aside, and the ramp tongued outward with a whine of servos. Still no human response.

"I'm going in," said Thorne.

"Captain, standard procedure says that's my job," said the trooper Thorne had detailed to cover them, from his vantage behind a large concrete tree-tub.

"Not this time," said Thorne grimly. Not continuing the argument, it dashed forward in a zigzag, then straight up the ramp, hurtling inside, plasma arc drawn. After a moment its voice came over the comm. "Now, Sumner."

Uninvited, he followed Trooper Sumner. The shuttle's interior was pitch-dark. They all turned on their helmet lights, white fingers darting and touching. Nothing inside appeared disturbed, but the door to the pilot's compartment was sealed.

Silently, Thorne motioned the trooper to take up a firing stance opposite him, bracketing the door in the bulkhead between fuselage and flight deck. He stood behind Thorne. Thorne punched another code into its arm control-pad. The door slid open with a tortured groan, then shuddered and jammed.

A wave of heat boiled out like the breath of a blast furnace. A soft orange explosion followed, as enough oxygen rushed into the searing compartment to re-ignite any flammables that were left. The trooper fastened his emergency oxygen mask, grabbed a chemical fire-extinguisher from a clamp on the wall, and aimed it into the flight deck. After a moment they followed in his wake.

Everything was slagged and burned. The controls were melted, communications equipment charred. The compartment stank, chokingly, of toxic oxidation products from all the synthetic materials. And one organic odor. Carbonized meat. What was left of the pilot—he turned his head, and swallowed. "Bharaputra doesn't have—isn't supposed to have heavy weapons on-site!"

Thorne hissed, beyond swearing. It pointed. "They threw a couple of our own thermal mines in here, closed the door, and ran. Pilot had to have been stunned first. One *smart* goddamn Bharaputran son-of-a-bitch . . . didn't have heavy weapons, so they just used ours. Drew off or ganged up on my guards, got in, and grounded us. Didn't even stick around to ambush us . . . they can do *that* at their leisure, now. This beast won't fly again." Thorne's face looked like a chiseled skull-mask in the white light from their helmets.

Panic clogged his throat. "What do we do now, Bel?"

"Fall back to the building. Set a perimeter. Use our hostages to negotiate some kind of surrender."

"No!"

"You got a better idea—*Miles*?" Thorne's teeth gritted. "I thought not."

The shocked trooper stared at Thorne. "Captain—" he glanced back and forth between them, "the Admiral will pull us through. We've been in tighter spots than this."

"Not this time." Thorne straightened, voice drawn with agony. "My fault—take full responsibility. . . . That's *not* the Admiral. That's his clone-brother, Mark. He set us up, but I've known for days. Tumbled to him before we dropped, before we ever made Jacksonian locals pace. I thought I could bring this off, and not get caught."

"Eh?" The trooper's brows wavered, disbelieving. A clone, going under anesthetic, might have that same stunned look on his face.

"We can't—we can't betray those children back into Bharaputra's hands," Mark grated. Begged.

Thorne dug its bare hand into the carbonized blob glued to what used to be the pilot's station chair. "Who is betrayed?" It lifted its hand, rubbed a black crumbling smear across his face from cheek to chin. "Who is betrayed?" Thorne whispered. "Do you have. A better. Idea."

He was shaking, his mind a white-out blank. The hot carbon on his face felt like a scar.

"Fall back to the building," said Thorne. "On my command."

CHAPTER SIX

"No subordinates," said Miles firmly. "I want to talk to the head man, once and done. And then get out of here."

"I'll keep trying," said Quinn. She turned back to her comconsole in the *Peregrine*'s tac room, which was presently transmitting the image of a high-ranking Bharaputran security officer, and began the argument again.

Miles sat back in his station chair, his boots flat to the deck, his hands held deliberately still along the control-studded armrests. Calm and control. That was the strategy. That was, at this point, the only strategy left to him. If only he'd been nine hours sooner . . . he'd methodically cursed every delay of the past five days, in four languages, till he'd run out of invective. They'd wasted fuel, profligately, pushing the *Peregrine* at max accelerations, and had nearly made up the *Ariel*'s lead. Nearly. The delays had given Mark just enough time to take a bad idea, and turn it into a disaster. But not Mark alone. Miles was no longer a proponent of the hero-theory of disaster. A mess this complete required the full cooperation of a cast of dozens. He very much wanted to talk privately with Bel Thorne, and very, very soon. He had not counted on Bel proving as much of a loose cannon as Mark himself.

He glanced around the tac room, taking in the latest information from the vid displays. The *Ariel* was out of it, fled under fire to dock at Fell Station under Thorne's second-in-command, Lieutenant Hart. They were now blockaded by half a dozen Bharaputran security vessels, lurking outside Fell's zone. Two more Bharaputran ships presently escorted the *Peregrine* in orbit. A token force, so far; the *Peregrine* outgunned them. That balance of power would shift when all their Bharaputran brethren arrived topside. Unless he could convince Baron Bharaputra it wasn't necessary.

He called up a view of the downside situation on his vid display, insofar as it was presently understood by the *Peregrine*'s battle computers. The exterior layout of the Bharaputran medical complex was plain even from orbit, but he lacked the details of the interiors he'd have liked if he were planning a clever attack. No clever attack. Negotiation, and bribery . . . he winced in anticipation of the upcoming costs. Bel Thorne, Mark, Green Squad, and fifty or so Bharaputran hostages were presently pinned down in a single building, separated from their damaged shuttle, and had been for the last eight hours. The shuttle pilot dead, three troopers injured. *That* would cost Bel its command, Miles swore to himself.

It would be dawn down there soon. The Bharaputrans had evacuated all the civilians from the rest of the complex, thank God, but had also brought in heavy security forces and equipment. Only the threat of harm to their valuable clones held back an overwhelming Bharaputran onslaught. He would not be negotiating from a position of strength, alas. *Cool.*

Quinn, without turning around, raised her hand and flashed him a high sign, *Get ready.* He glanced down, checking his own appearance. His officer's undress grays were borrowed from the next smallest person aboard the *Peregrine*, a five-foot-tall female from Engineering, and fit him sloppily. He only had half his proper insignia. Aggressively messy was a possible command style, but he really needed more props to bring it off. Adrenalin and suppressed rage would have to power his appearance.

If not for the biochip on his vagus nerve, his old ulcers would be perforating his stomach about now. He opened his comconsole to Quinn's communications shunt, and waited.

With a sparkle, the image of a frowning man appeared over the vid plate. His dark hair was drawn back in a tight knot held by a gold ring, emphasizing the strong bones of his face. He wore a bronze-brown silk tunic, and no other jewelry. Olive-brown skin; he looked a healthy forty or so. Appearances were deceiving. It took more than one lifetime to scheme and fight one's way to the undisputed leadership of a Jacksonian House. Vasa Luigi, Baron Bharaputra, had been wearing the body of a clone for at least twenty years. He certainly took good care of it. The vulnerable period of another brain transplant would be doubly dangerous for a man whose power so many ruthless subordinates coveted. *This man is not for playing games with,* Miles decided.

"Bharaputra here," the man in brown stated, and waited. Indeed, the man and the House were one, for practical purposes.

"Naismith here," said Miles. "Commanding, Dendarii Free Mercenary Fleet."

"Apparently not completely," said Vasa Luigi blandly.

Miles peeled back his lips on set teeth, and managed not to flush. "Just so. You do understand, this raid was not authorized by me?"

"I understand you claim so. Personally, I should not be so anxious to announce my failure of control over my subordinates."

He's baiting you. Cool. "We need to have our facts straight. I have not yet established if Captain Thorne was actually suborned, or merely taken in by my fellow-clone. In any case, it is your own product, for whatever sentimental reasons, who has returned to attempt to extract some personal revenge upon you. I'm just an innocent bystander, trying to straighten things out."

"You," Baron Bharaputra blinked, like a lizard, "are a curiosity. *We* did not manufacture you. Where did you come from?"

"Does it matter?"

"It might."

"Then it is information for sale or trade, not for free." That was good Jacksonian etiquette; the Baron nodded, unoffended. They were entering the realm of Deal, if not yet a deal between equals. Good.

The Baron did not immediately pursue Miles's family history, though. "So what is it you want from me, Admiral?"

"I wish to help you. I can, if given a free hand, extract my people from that unfortunate dilemma downside with a minimum of further damage to Bharaputran persons or property. Quiet and clean. I would even consider paying reasonable costs of physical damages thus far incurred."

"I do not require your help, Admiral."

"You do if you wish to keep your costs down."

Vasa Luigi's eyes narrowed, considering this. "Is that a threat?"

Miles shrugged. "Quite the reverse. Both our costs can be very low—or both our costs can be very high. I would prefer low."

The Baron's eyes flicked right, at some thing or person out of range of the vid pick-up. "Excuse me a moment, Admiral." His face was replaced with a holding-pattern.

Quinn drifted over. "Think we'll be able to save any of those poor clones?"

He ran his hands through his hair. "Hell, Elli, I'm still trying to get Green Squad out! I doubt it."

"That's a shame. We've come all this way."

"Look, I have crusades a lot closer to home than

Jackson's Whole, if I want 'em. A hell of a lot more than fifty kids are killed each year in the Barrayaran backcountry for suspected mutation, for starters. I can't afford to get . . . quixotic like Mark. I don't know where he picked up those ideas, it couldn't have been from the Bharaputrans. Or the Komarrans."

Quinn's brows rose; she opened her mouth, then shut it as if on some second thought, and smiled dryly. But then she said, "It's Mark I was thinking about. You keep saying you want to get him to trust you."

"Make him a gift of the clones? I wish I could. Right after I finish strangling him with my bare hands, which will be right after I finish hanging Bel Thorne. Mark is Mark, he owes me nothing, but Bel should have known better." His teeth clenched, aching. Her words shook him with galloping visions. Both ships, with every clone aboard, jumping triumphantly from Jacksonian local space . . . thumbing their noses at the bad Bharaputrans . . . Mark stammering gratitude, admiring . . . bring them all home to Mother . . . *madness.* Not possible. If he'd planned it all himself, from beginning to end, maybe. His plans certainly would not have included a midnight frontal assault with no back-up. The vid plate sparkled again, and he waved Quinn out of range. Vasa Luigi reappeared.

"Admiral Naismith," he nodded. "I have decided to allow you to order your mutinous crew to surrender to my security forces."

"I would not wish to put your security to any further trouble, Baron. They've been up all night, after all. Tired, and jumpy. I'll collect all my people myself."

"That will not be possible. But I will guarantee their lives. The individual fines for their criminal acts will be determined later."

Ransoms. He swallowed rage. "This . . . is a possibility. But the fines must be determined in advance."

"You are hardly in a position to add conditions, Admiral."

"I only wish to avoid misunderstandings, Baron."

Vasa Luigi pursed his lips. "Very well. The troopers, ten thousand Betan dollars each. Officers, twenty-five thousand. Your hermaphrodite captain, fifty thousand, unless you wish us to dispose of it ourselves—no? I do not see that you have any use for your, ah, fellow clone, so we'll retain custody of him. In return, I shall waive property damage charges." The Baron nodded in satisfaction at his own generosity.

Upwards of a quarter of a million. Miles cringed inwardly. Well, it could be done. "But I am not without interest in the clone. What . . . price do you put on his head?"

"What possible interest?" Vasa Luigi inquired, surprised.

Miles shrugged. "I'd think it was obvious. My profession is full of hazards. I am the only survivor of my clone-clutch. The one I call Mark was as much a surprise to me as I was to him, I think; neither of us knew there was a second cloning project. Where else would I find such a perfect, ah, organ-donor, and on such short notice?"

Vasa Luigi opened his hands. "We might arrange to keep him safe for you."

"If I needed him at all, I'd need him urgently. In the circumstances, I'd fear a sudden rise in the market price. Besides, accidents happen. Look at the accident that happened to poor Baron Fell's clone, in your keeping."

The temperature seemed to drop twenty degrees, and Miles cursed his tongue. That episode was apparently still classified information in these parts, or at least some kind of hot button. The Baron studied him, if not with more respect, then with increased suspicion. "If you wish another clone made for transplant purposes, Admiral, you've come to the right place. But *this* clone is not for sale."

"*This* clone does not belong to you," Miles snapped out, too quickly. No—steady on. Keep it cool, keep his real thoughts buried deep, maintain that smarmy surface persona that could actually cut a deal with Baron Bharaputra without vomiting. Cool. "Besides, there's that ten-year lead time. It's not some long-anticipated death from old age that concerns me. It's the abrupt surprise sort." After a pause, and with a heroic effort, he choked out, "You need not waive the property damage charges, of course."

"I *need* not do anything at all, Admiral," the Baron pointed out. Coolly.

Don't bet on it, you Jacksonian bastard. "Why do *you* want this particular clone, Baron? Considering how readily you could make yourself another."

"Not that readily. His medical records reveal he was quite a challenge." Vasa Luigi tapped the side of his aquiline nose with one forefinger, and smiled without much humor.

"Do you plan punishment? A warning to other malefactors?"

"He will doubtless regard it so."

So, there was a plan for Mark, or at least an idea that smelled of some profit. "Nothing in the direction of our Barrayaran progenitor, I trust. That plot is long dead. They know about us both."

"I admit, his Barrayaran connections interest me. *Your* Barrayaran connections interest me too. It is obvious from the name that you took for yourself that you've long known where you came from. Just what is your relationship with Barrayar, Admiral?"

"Queasy," he admitted. "They tolerate me, I do them a favor now and then. For a price. Beyond that, mutual avoidance. Barrayaran Imperial Security has a longer arm even than House Bharaputra. You don't want to attract their negative attention, I assure you."

Vasa Luigi's brows rose, politely skeptical. "A progenitor and two clones . . . three identical brothers. And all so short. Among you, I suppose you make a whole man."

Not to the point; the Baron was casting for something, information, presumably. "Three, but hardly identical," said Miles. "The original Lord Vorkosigan is a dull stick, I am assured. The limitations of Mark's capacities, he has just demonstrated, I fear. I was the improved model. My creators planned higher things for me, but they did their job too well, and I began planning for myself. A trick neither of my poor siblings seems to have mastered."

"I wish I could talk with your creators."

"I wish you could too. They are deceased."

The Baron favored him with a chill smile. "You're a cocky little fellow, aren't you?"

Miles stretched his lips in return, and said nothing.

The Baron sat back, tenting his fingers. "My offer stands. The clone is not for sale. But every thirty minutes, the fines will double. I advise you to close your deal quickly, Admiral. You will not get a better."

"I must have a brief consultation with my Fleet accountant," Miles temporized. "I will return your call shortly."

"How else?" Vasa Luigi murmured, with a small smile at his own wit.

Miles cut the comm abruptly, and sat. His stomach was shaking, hot red waves of shame and anger radiating outward through his whole body from the pit of his belly.

"But the Fleet accountant isn't here," Quinn pointed out, sounding slightly confused. Lieutenant Bone had indeed departed with Baz and the rest of the Dendarii from Escobar.

"I . . . don't like Baron Bharaputra's deal."

"Can't ImpSec rescue Mark later?"

"*I am* ImpSec."

Quinn could hardly disagree; she fell silent.

"I want my space armor," he growled petulantly, hunching in his station chair.

"Mark has it," said Quinn.

"I know. My half-armor. My command headset."

"Mark has those too."

"I know." His hand slapped down hard on the arm of the chair, the harsh crack in the quiet chamber making Quinn flinch. "A squad leader's helmet, then!"

"What for?" said Quinn in a flat, unencouraging tone. "No crusades here, you said."

"I'm cutting myself a better deal." He swung to his feet. His blood beat in his ears, hotter and hotter. "Come on."

The seat straps bit into his body as the drop shuttle blew its clamps and accelerated away from the side of the *Peregrine*. Miles glanced up over the pilot's shoulder for a quick check of the planet's curvature sliding across the window, and a glimpse of his two fighter-shuttles peeling away from the mothership to cover them. They were followed by the *Peregrine*'s second combat drop shuttle, the other half of his two pronged attack. His faint feint. Would the Bharaputrans take it seriously? *You hope.* He turned his attention back to the glittering global data-world supplied by his command headset.

He was not stuck with a squad leader's helmet after all. He'd commandeered Elena Bothari-Jesek's downside-team captain's gear, while she rode the tactics room back aboard the *Peregrine*. *Bring it back without any unsightly holes through it, damn you,* she'd told him, her lips pale with unexpressed anxiety. Practically everything he wore was donated. An oversized nerve-disruptor shield-net suit had its cuffs turned up and held with elastic bands at wrists and ankles. Quinn had insisted on it, and as nerve-disruptor damage was his particular nightmare, he hadn't argued. Sloppy fatigues, held ditto. The plasma-mirror field pack straps cinched the extra fabric around his body reasonably well. Two pairs of thick socks kept his borrowed boots from sliding around. It was all very annoying, but hardly his greatest concern while trying to pull together a downside raid on thirty minutes' notice.

His greatest concern was their landing site. On top of Thorne's building would have been his first choice, but the shuttle pilot claimed fears that the whole building would collapse if they tried to set the drop shuttle down on it, and anyway the roof was peaked, not flat. The next closest possible site was occupied by the *Ariel's* dead and abandoned shuttle. The third-choice site looked like it was going to be a long walk, especially on the return journey when Bharaputra's security would have had time to set up counter measures. Straight up the slot was not his preferred attack style. Well, maybe Sergeant Kimura and Yellow Squad in the second drop shuttle would give Baron Bharaputra something more urgent to think about. *Take care of your shuttle, Kimura. It's our only back-up, now. I should have brought the whole damned fleet.*

He ignored his own shuttle's clanks and screams of deceleration as they hit the atmosphere—it was an excellent hell-drop, but it couldn't go fast enough to suit him—and watched the progress of his high cover in the colored codes and patterns of his helmet data display. The startled Bharaputran fighter-shuttles that had been guarding the *Peregrine* now found their attention suddenly divided. They wasted a few futile shots against the *Peregrine* itself, wavered after Kimura, then turned to pursue Miles's attack formation. One Bharaputran was blown to bits for its attempt almost immediately, and Miles whispered a pithy commendation for his Dendarii fighter pilot into his recorder on the spot. The other Bharaputran, unnerved, broke away to await reinforcements. Well, that had been easy. It was the trip back that was going to be maximum fun. He could feel the adrenalin high starting already, stranger and sweeter than a drug-rush through his body. It would last for hours, then depart abruptly, leaving him a burnt-out husk with hollow eyes and voice. Was it worth it? *It will be if we win.*

We will win.

As they rounded the planet to line-of-sight to their target, he tried contacting Thorne again. The Bharaputrans were jamming the main command channels. He tried dropping down and broadcasting a brief query on commercial bands, but got no response. Someone should have been assigned to monitor those. Well, he'd be able to punch through once they were on-site. He called up the holoview of the medical complex, ghost images dancing before his eyes. Speaking of straight up the slot, he was briefly tempted to order his fighter-shuttles to lay down a line of fire and blast a trench from his proposed landing site to Thorne's refuge, removing those inconvenient buildings from his path. But the trench would take too long to cool, and besides, the cover might benefit his own as much as Bharaputra's forces. Not quite as much, the Bharaputrans knew the layout better. He considered the probability of tunnels, utility tunnels, and ducts. He snorted at the thought of ducts, and frowned at the thought of Taura, led blindly into this meat grinder by Mark.

The wild, jerking decelerations ended at last as buildings rose around them—*sniper vantage-points*—and the shuttle thumped to the ground. Quinn, who'd been trying to raise communication channels from the station chair opposite his, behind the co-pilot, looked up and said simply, "I've got Thorne. Try setting 6 2 j. Audio only, no vids so far."

With a flick of his eyes and a controlled blink, he keyed in his erstwhile subordinate. "Bel? We're down, and coming for you. Get ready to break out. Is anyone left alive down here?"

He didn't have to see Bel's face to sense the wince. But at least Bel didn't waste time on excuses or apologies. "Two non-walking wounded. Trooper Phillipi died about fifteen minutes ago. We packed her head in ice. If you can bring the portable cryo-chamber, we might save something."

"Will do, but we don't have much time to fool with her. Start prepping her now. We'll be there as fast as we can." He nodded to Quinn, and they both rose and exited the flight-deck. He had the pilots seal the door behind them.

Quinn passed the word to the medic on what he was going to be dealing with, and the first half of Orange Squad swarmed from the shuttle to take up defensive positions. Two small armored hovercars went up immediately behind them, to clear any vantage points of Bharaputran snipers and replace them with Dendarii. When they reported a temporary *Clear!* Miles and Quinn followed Blue Squad down the ramp into the chill, damp dawn. He left the entire second half of Orange Squad to guard the shuttle, lest the Bharaputrans try to repeat their previous successful ploy.

Morning mist roiled faintly around the shuttle's hot skin. The sky was pearly with the slow-growing light, but the medical complex's structures still loomed in blotted shadow. A float-bike soared aloft, two troopers took the point at a dead run, and Blue Squad followed. Miles concentrated, forcing his short legs to pump fast enough to keep up. He wanted no long-legged trooper to temper his stride for his sake, ever. This time at least, none did, and he grunted satisfaction under his remaining breath. A scattered roar of small-arms fire echoing all around told him his Orange Squad perimeter-people were already hard at work.

They streamed around one building, under the cover of a second's portico, then past a third, the half-squads leap-frogging and covering each other. It was all too easy. The complex reminded Miles of those carnivorous flowers with the nectar-coated spines that all faced inwards. Slipping in was simple, for little bugs like him. It was the attempt to get out that would exhaust and kill. . . .

It was therefore almost a relief when the first sonic grenade went off. The Bharaputrans weren't saving it *all* for dessert. The explosion was a couple of buildings away, and rocked and reverberated strangely around the walkways. Not Dendarii issue, its deafening timbre was a tad off. He keyed his command helmet to follow the fire fight, half-subliminally, as Orange Squad rooted out a nest of Bharaputran security. It wasn't the Bharaputrans his people could smoke out that worried him. It was the ones they overlooked. . . . He wondered if the enemy had brought in more mass-projectile weapons in addition to sonic grenades, and was coldly conscious of the missing element in his borrowed half-armor. Quinn had tried to make him take her torso-armor, but he'd convinced her its oversized loose sliding around as he moved would just make him crazy. *Crazier,* he'd thought he'd heard her mutter, but he hadn't asked for an amplification. He wasn't planning on leading any cavalry charges this trip, that was certain.

He blinked away the distracting ghostly data flow as they rounded a final corner, scared off three or four lurking Bharaputrans, and approached the clone-creche. Big blocky building, it looked like a hotel. Shattered glass doors led into a foyer where shadowy gray-camouflaged defenders moved among hastily-raised shielding, metal doors torn from hinges and propped up. A quick exchange of countersigns, and they were in. Half of Blue Squad scattered instantly to reinforce the building's weary Green Squad defenders; the other half guarded him.

The medic warped the float pallet containing the portable cryo-chamber through the doors, and was hurriedly directed down a hallway by his comrades. Intelligently, they were prepping Phillipi in a side room, out of sight of their clone hostages. Step One was to remove as much as possible of the patient's own blood; under these hasty combat conditions, without any attempt to recover and store it. Rough, ready, and extremely messy; it was not a sight for the faint-hearted, nor the unprepared mind.

"Admiral," said a quiet alto voice.

He wheeled to find himself face to face with Bel Thorne. The hermaphrodite's features were almost as gray as the shield-net hood that framed them, an oval of lined and puffy fatigue. Plus another look, one he hated seeing there despite his anger. *Defeat.* Bel looked beaten, looked like it had lost it all. *And so it has.* They did not exchange a single word of blame or defense. They didn't need to; it was all plain in Bel's face and, he suspected, his own. He nodded in acknowledgment, of Bel, of it all.

Beside Bel stood another soldier, the top of his helmet—*my helmet*—not quite level with the top of Bel's shoulder. He had half-forgotten how startling Mark was. *Do I really look like that?*

"You—" Miles's voice cracked, and he found he had to stop and swallow. "Later, you and I are going to have a long talk. There's a lot you don't seem to understand."

Mark's chin came up, defiantly. *Surely my face is not that round.* It must be an illusion, from the hood. "What about these kids?" said Mark. "These clones."

"What about them?" A couple of young men in brown silk tunics and shorts appeared to be actually helping the Dendarii defenders, scared and excited rather than surly. Another group, boys and girls mixed, sat in a plain-scared bunch on the floor under the watchful eye of a stunner-armed trooper. *Crap, they really are just kids.*

"We've—you've got to take them along. Or I'm not going." Mark's teeth were set, but Miles saw him swallow.

"Don't tempt me," snarled Miles. "Of *course* we're taking them along, how the hell else would we get out of here alive?"

Mark's face lit, torn between hope and hatred. "And then what?" he demanded suspiciously.

"Oh," Miles carolled sarcastically, "we're just going to waltz right over to Bharaputra Station and drop them off, and thank Vasa Luigi kindly for the loan. *Idiot!* What d'you think? We load up and run like hell. The only place to put them would be out the airlock, and I guarantee you'd go first!"

Mark flinched, but took a deep breath and nodded. "All right, then."

"It is not. All. Right," Miles bit out. "It is merely . . . merely . . ." he could not come up with a word to describe what it merely was, aside from the most screwed-up mess he'd ever encountered. "If you were going to try and pull a stupid stunt like this, you might at least have consulted the expert in the family!"

"You? Come to *you* for help? D'you think I'm crazy?" demanded Mark furiously.

"Yes—" They were interrupted by a staring blond clone boy, who'd walked up to them open-mouthed.

"You really *are* clones," he said in wonderment.

"No, we're twins born six years apart," snapped Miles. "Yes, we're just as much clones as you are, that's right, go back and sit down and obey orders, dammit."

The boy retreated hastily, whispering, "It's true!"

"Dammit," Mark howled under his breath, if that squeezed sotto voce could be so described, "how come they believe *you* and not *me*? It's not fair!"

Quinn's voice, through his helmet, derailed the family reunion. "If you and Don Quixote Junior are done greeting each other, Medic Norwood has Phillipi prepped and loaded, and the wounded ready to transport."

"Form up, let's get the first batch out the door, then," he responded. He called up Blue Squad's sergeant. "Framingham, take the first convoy. You ready to roll?"

"Ready. Sergeant Taura has marshalled them for me."

"Go. And don't look back."

Half a dozen Dendarii, about three times that many bewildered and exhausted clones, and the two wounded troopers on float pallets assembled in the foyer and filed out the ruined doors. Framingham did not look too happy to be using a couple of young girls as a projectile-weapon shield; his chocolate-dark face was grim. But any Bharaputran snipers were going to have to take aim very, very carefully. The Dendarii forced the kids forward, if not at a run, then at least at a steady jog. A second group followed the first within a minute. Miles ran both non-coms' helmet transmissions down either side of his peripheral vision, while his ears strained for the deadly whine of small-arms fire.

Were they going to bring this off? Sergeant Taura shepherded the final gaggle of clones into the foyer. She greeted him with a demi-salute, without even pausing to puzzle between himself and Mark. "*Glad* to see you, sir," she rumbled.

"You too, Sergeant," he replied, heart-felt. If Mark had managed to get Taura killed, he didn't know how it could ever have been made right between them. At some more convenient moment he urgently wanted to find out how Mark had managed to fool her, and how intimately. Later.

Taura moved closer, and lowered her voice. "We lost four kids, escaped back to the Bharaputrans. Makes me kinda sick. Any chance . . . ?

Regretfully, he shook his head. "No way. No miracles this time. We've got to take what we can get and go, or we'll lose it all."

She nodded, understanding the tactical situation perfectly well. Understanding didn't cure the gut-churning nausea of regret, unfortunately. He offered her a brief *I'm sorry* smile, and her long lips twisted up on one side in wry response.

The Blue Squad medic brought in the big float pallet containing the cryo-chamber, a blanket tossed over the transparent part of the gleaming cylinder to shield his comrade-and-patient's naked and cooling body from uncomprehending or horrified outsiders' eyes. Taura urged the clones to their feet.

Bel Thorne glanced around. "I hate this place," it said levelly.

"Maybe we can bomb it this time, on the way out," Miles returned, equally levelly. "Finally."

Bel nodded.

The mob of them, the fifteen or so last clones, the float pallet, the Dendarii rear-guard, Taura and Quinn, Mark and Bel, oozed out the front door. Miles glanced up, feeling like he had a bull's-eye painted on the top of his helmet, but the moving shape crossing the roof of the building opposite wore Dendarii grays. Good. The holovid on the right side of his field of view informed him Framingham and his group had made it to the shuttle without incident. Even better. He cut Framingham's helmet transmissions, squelched the second squad leader's to a bare murmur, and concentrated on the present moment.

His concentration was broken by Kimura's voice, the first he'd heard from Yellow Squad across town in their own drop zone. "Sir, resistance is soft. They're not buying us. How far should I go to make them take us seriously?"

"All the way, Kimura. You've got to draw Bharaputran

attention off us. Draw them away, but don't risk yourselves, and especially don't risk your shuttle." Miles hoped Lieutenant Kimura was too busy to reflect upon the slightly schizoid logic of that order. If—

The first sign of Bharaputran sharpshooters arrived with a bang, literally; a sonic grenade put down about fifteen meters ahead of them. It blew a hole in the walkway, which returned a few moments later in obedience to gravity as a sharp hot patter of raining fragments, startling but not very dangerous. The clone-childrens' screams were muffled, in his stunned ears.

"Gotta go, Kimura. Use your initiative, huh?"

The miss hadn't been accidental, Miles realized as plasma fire struck a potted tree to the right and a wall to the left of them, exploding both. They were being deliberately bracketed to panic the clones. It was working quite nicely, too—they were ducking, dropping, clutching each other and screaming, and showing every sign of getting ready to bolt off in all directions. There would be no rounding them up after that. A plasma arc beam hit a Dendarii square on, just to prove the Bharaputrans could do it, Miles supposed; the beam was absorbed by his mirror-field and re-emitted with the usual hellish blue snap, further terrifying the nearby kids. The more experienced troopers fired back coolly, while Miles yelled into his headset for his air cover. The Bharaputrans were above them, mostly, judging by the angle of fire.

Taura studied the hysterical clones, glanced around, raised her plasma arc, and blew apart the doors of the nearest building, a big windowless warehouse or garage-looking structure. "Inside!" she bellowed.

It was good, in that if they were going to bolt, at least it had them all bolting in the same direction. As long as they didn't *stop* inside. If they got pinned down and penned up again, there'd be no big brother to rescue *him*.

"Move!" Miles seconded the idea, "but *keep moving*. Out the other side!"

She waved an acknowledgement as the kids stampeded out of the fire-zone into what no doubt looked like safety to them. To him, it looked like a trap. But they needed to stay together. If there was anything worse than being pinned down, it was being *scattered* and pinned down. He waved the squad through and followed. A couple of Blue Squad troopers took rear guard, firing plasma arcs upward at their . . . herders, Miles feared. He figured it for keep-your-heads-down warning shots, but one trooper got lucky. His plasma arc beam hit a Bharaputran who unwisely attempted to dart along the roof-edge on the building opposite. The Bharaputran's shielding absorbed the shot, but then he unbalanced and fell, screaming. Miles tried not to hear the sound when he hit the concrete, but did not quite succeed, even with grenade-stunned ears. The screaming stopped.

Miles turned and dashed down the corridor and through some big double doors, beckoned anxiously onward by Thorne, who waited to help cover him.

"I'll take rear guard," Thorne volunteered.

Was Thorne entertaining thoughts of dying heroically, thus avoiding the inevitable court-martial? For a moment, Miles entertained thoughts of letting it do so. It would be the Vorish thing to do. The Old Vor could be a bunch of assholes, at times. "*You* get those clones to the shuttle," Miles snapped in turn. "Finish the job you took on. If I'm paying this much, I want to get what I'm paying for."

Thorne's teeth bared, but it nodded. They both galloped after the squad.

The double doors opened onto an enormous concrete-floored room, which obviously nearly filled the big building. Red- and green-painted catwalks ran around a girdered ceiling high above, festooned with looping cables of mysterious function. A few harsh pale lights shone down, casting multiple shadows. He blinked in the gloom and almost lowered his infra-red visor. It appeared to be an assembly area for large projects of some kind, though at the moment there seemed to be nothing in progress. Quinn and Mark hesitated, waiting for them to catch up despite Miles's urgent gesture for them to hurry on. "What are you stopping for?" he barked in furious fear. He skidded to a halt beside them.

"Look out!" someone yelled. Quinn spun, raising her plasma arc, seeking aim. Mark's mouth opened, the "o" foolishly echoing the circle of his gray hood around his face.

Miles saw the Bharaputran because they were looking square at each other, in that frozen moment. A team of brown-clad Bharaputran snipers, probably come up through the tunnels. They were scrambling along the girders, barely more prepared than the Dendarii they pursued. The Bharaputran had a hand-sized projectile weapon launcher of some kind pointed straight at him, its muzzle bright with flare.

Miles could not, of course, see the projectile, not even as it entered his chest. Only his chest, bursting outward like a flower, and a sound not heard but only felt, a hammer-blow launching him backward. Dark flowers bloomed too in his eyes, covering everyone.

He was astonished, not by how much he thought, for there was no time for thought, but by how much he felt, in the time it took for his last heartburst of blood to finish flowing through his brain. The chamber careening around him . . . pain beyond measure . . . rage, and outrage . . . and a vast regret, infinitesimal in duration, infinite in depth. *Wait, I haven't—*

CHAPTER SEVEN

Mark was standing so close, the report of the exploding projectile was like a silence, pressing in his ears, obliterating all other sounds. It happened too fast for understanding, too fast to close the eyes and defend the mind against the sight. The little man who had been yelling and gesturing them onward fluttered backward like a gray rag, arms outflung, face contorted. A spray of blood spattered across Mark with stinging force, part of a wide half-circle of blood and tissue-bits. Quinn's whole left side was scarlet.

So. You are not perfect, was his first absurd thought. This sudden absolute vulnerability shocked him unbearably. *I didn't think you could be hurt. Damn you, I didn't think you could be—*

Quinn was screaming, everyone was recoiling, only he stood still, paralyzed in his private, ear-stunned silence. Miles lay on the concrete with his chest blown out, open-mouthed, unmoving. *That's a dead man.* He'd seen a dead man before, there was no mistaking it.

Quinn, her face wild, fired her plasma arc at the Bharaputrans, shot after shot, till hot ceiling fragments started to fall lethally back down around them, and a Dendarii knocked her weapon aside. "Taura, get them!" Quinn pointed upward with her free hand.

The monster sergeant fired a rappel-hook upward, which wrapped around a girder. She rose upon it at full acceleration, like a mad spider. Between the lights and the shadows, Mark could scarcely follow her progress, leaping at inhuman speed along the catwalks, until broken-necked Bharaputran security personnel began raining down. All their high-tech half-armor was no protection at all against those huge, enraged clawed hands. Three men fell in a welter of their own blood, their throats torn out, an insane bombardment; one Dendarii trooper, running across the chamber, was almost smashed beneath an enemy body. Modern warfare wasn't supposed to have this much blood in it. The weapons were supposed to cook everyone neatly, like eggs in their shells.

Quinn paid no attention, scarcely seeming to care about the results of her order. She knelt by Miles's side, her shaking hands outspread, hesitating. Then they dove and pulled off Miles's command helmet. She flung her own squad leader's helmet to the floor and replaced it on her smooth gray hood with Miles's. Her lips moved, establishing contact, checking channels. The helmet was undamaged, apparently. She yelled orders to perimeter-people, queries to the drop shuttle, and one other. "Norwood, get back here, *get back here. Yes*, bring it, bring it *now*. On the double, Norwood!" Her head swivelled away from Miles only long enough to shout, "Taura, get this building secured!" From above, the sergeant in turn bellowed orders to her scurrying troopers.

Quinn pulled a vibra-knife from her belt sheath and began cutting away Miles's fatigues, ripping through belts and the nerve-disruptor shield-suit, tossing the bloody fragments aside. Mark looked up, following her glance, to see the medic with the float-pallet returning, hauling his burden across the concrete. The float-pallet counteracted gravity, but not mass; the inertia of the heavy cryo-chamber fought his attempts to run, and fought him again as he braked and lowered the pallet to the floor near his dead commander. Half a dozen confused clones followed the medic like baby ducks, clustering together and staring around in horror at the ghastly aftermath of the brief sharp firefight.

The medic looked back and forth from Miles's body to the loaded cryo-chamber. "Captain Quinn, it's no good. It won't hold two."

"The hell it's not." Quinn staggered to her feet, her voice grating like gravel. She seemed unaware of the tears running down her face, tracking pinkly through the spatter. "The hell it's not." She stared bleakly at the gleaming cryo-chamber. "Dump her."

"Quinn, I can't!"

"On my order. On my hands."

"*Quinn* . . ." The medic's voice was anguished. "Would *he* have ordered this?"

"*He* just lost his damn vote. All right." She took a deep breath. "I'll do it. You start prepping *him*."

Teeth clenched, the medic moved to obey. He flipped open a door at the end of the chamber and removed a tray of equipment. It was all in disarray, having been used once already and hastily re-packed. He rolled out some big insulated bottles.

Quinn keyed open the chamber. Its lid popped, breaking the seal, and rose. She reached within, unfastening things that Mark could not see. Did not wish to see. She hissed, as instantly-frozen skin tore from her hands, but reached again. With a grunt, she heaved a woman's greenish, empurpled nude body from the chamber and laid it on the floor. It was the smashed-up bike-trooper, Phillipi. Thorne's patrol, daring Bharaputran fire, had finally found her near her downed float-bike some two buildings away from her lost helmet. Broken back, broken limbs; she'd taken hours to die, against all the Green Squad medic's heroic efforts to save her. Quinn looked up and saw Mark staring at her. Her face was ravaged.

"You, you useless . . . *wrap* her." She pointed to Phillipi.

then hurried around the cryo-chamber to where the Blue Squad medic now knelt beside Miles.

Mark broke his paralysis at last, to scuttle around and find a thin foil heat wrap among the medical supplies. Frightened of the body, but too terrified by Quinn to disobey, he laid out the silver wrap and rolled the cold dead woman up in it. She was stiff and heavy, under his cringing touch.

He rose to hear the medic muttering, with his ungloved hands plunged deep into the gory mess that had been Miles Vorkosigan's chest, "I can't find an *end*. Where the hell's an *end*? At least the damned aorta, *something* . . ."

"It's been over four minutes," snarled Quinn, pulled out her vibra-knife again, and cut Miles's corpse's throat, two neat slashes bracketing but not touching the windpipe. Her fingers scrabbled in the cut.

The medic glanced up only to say, "Be sure you get the carotid and not the jugular."

"I'm *trying*. They're not color-coded." She found something pale and rubbery. She pulled tubing from the top of one of the insulated jugs, and jammed its plastic end-nozzle into the presumed artery. She switched the power on; the tiny pump hummed, pushing lucent greenish cryo-fluid through the transparent tubing. She pulled out a second piece of tubing from the jug and inserted it on the other side of Miles's neck. Blood began to flow from the slashed exit veins, over her hands, over everything; not spurting as from a heartbeat, but in a steady, inhuman, mechanical fashion. It spread on the floor in a shimmering pool, then began to flow away across some subtle drainage-slope, a little carmine creek. An impossible quantity of blood. The clustered clones were weeping. Mark's own head throbbed, pain so bad it darkened his vision.

Quinn kept the pumps going till what came out ran

greenish-clear. The medic meanwhile had apparently found the ends he was looking for, and attached two more tubes. More blood, mixed with cryo-fluid, welled up and spilled from the wound. The creek became a river. The medic pulled Miles's boots and socks off, and ran sensors over his paling feet. "Almost there . . . damn, we're nearly dry." He hastened to his jug, which had switched itself off and was blinking a red indicator light.

"I used all I had," said Quinn.

"It's probably enough. They were both small people. Clamp those ends—" He tossed her something glittering, which she snatched out of the air. They bent over the little body. "Into the chamber, then," said the medic. Quinn cradled the head, the medic took the torso and hips. The arms and legs dangled down. "He's light . . ." They swung their stripped burden hastily into the cryochamber, leaving the blood-soaked uniform on the floor in a sodden heap. Quinn left the medic to make the last connections and turned away blind-eyed, talking to her helmet. She did not look down at the long silver package at her feet.

Thorne appeared, crossing the chamber at a jog. Where had it been? Thorne caught Quinn's eye, and with a jerk of its head at the dead Bharaputrans reported, "They came up through the tunnels, all right. I have the exits secured, for now." Thorne glowered bleakly at the cryochamber. The hermaphrodite looked suddenly . . middle-aged. Old.

Quinn acknowledge this with a nod. "Key to Channel 9-C. We got trouble outside."

A kind of dreary curiosity winkled through Mark's numb shock. He turned his own headset back on. He'd had it helplessly and hopelessly turned off for hours, ever since Thorne had snatched back its command. He followed the captains' transmissions.

The Blue and Orange Squad perimeter teams were

under heavy pressure from beefed-up Bharaputran security forces. Quinn's delay in this building was drawing Bharaputrans like flies to carrion, with a buzzing excitement. With over two-thirds of the clones now packed aboard the shuttle, the enemy had stopped directing heavy fire toward it, but airborne reinforcements were gathering fast, hovering like vultures. Quinn and company were in imminent danger of being surrounded and cut off.

"Got to be another way," muttered Quinn. She switched channels. "Lieutenant Kimura, how's it going with you? Resistance still soft?"

"It's hardened up beautifully. I kinda got my hands full right now, Quinnie." Kimura's thin, weirdly cheerful voice came back cut by a wash of static indicating plasma fire and the activation of his plasma mirror field. "We've achieved our objective and are pulling out now. Trying to. Chat later, huh?" More static.

"Which objective? Take care of your damn shuttle, y'hear, boy? You may yet have to come for us. Report to me the second you're back in the air."

"Right." A slight pause. "Why isn't the Admiral on this channel, Quinnie?"

Quinn's eyes squeezed shut in pain. "He's . . . temporarily out of range. Move it, Kimura!"

Kimura's reply, whatever it was, broke up in another wash of static. No program regarding Kimura and his objective was loaded in Mark's helmet, but the lieutenant seemed to be transmitting from somewhere other than the medical complex. A feint? If so, Kimura wasn't drawing nearly enough enemy troops away from them. Sergeant Framingham's channel, from the drop shuttle, broke in urging Quinn to hurry, almost simultaneously with an Orange Squad perimeter team reporting themselves forced off another vantage point.

"Could the shuttle land on top of this building and

pick us up?" Quinn inquired, gazing at the girders overhead.

Thorne frowned, following her eyes. "I think it would cave in the roof."

"Hell. Other ideas?"

"Down," said Mark suddenly. Both Dendarii jerked, catching themselves from flattening to the floor as they realized what he meant. "Through the tunnels. The Bharaputrans got in, we can get back out."

"It's a blind warren," objected Quinn.

"I have a map," said Mark. "All of Green Squad does, loaded programs. Green Squad can lead."

"Why didn't you say so earlier?" snapped Quinn, illogically ignoring the fact that there had hardly been an earlier.

Thorne nodded confirmation, and began hastily tracing through its helmet's holovid map. "Can do. There's a route—puts us up inside the building beyond your shuttle, Quinn. Bharaputran defenses are thin, there, and all facing the other way. And their superior numbers won't help them, down below."

Quinn stared down. "I hate dirt. I want vacuum, and elbow room. All right, let's do it. Sergeant Taura!"

A flurry of organization, a few more doors blown away, and the little party was on the march once more, down a lift tube and into the utility tunnels. Troopers scouted ahead of the main group. Taura had half a dozen clones carry Phillipi's wrapped body, laid across three metal bars she'd torn from the catwalk railings. As if the bike-trooper still had some forlorn hope of preservation and revival.

Mark found himself pacing beside the cryo-chamber on its float pallet, tugged along by the anxious medic. He glanced from the corner of his eye through the transparent cover. His progenitor lay open-mouthed, pale and gray-lipped and still. Frost formed feathers along the seals, and a blast of waste heat flowed from the refrigeration unit's radiator. It would burn like a bonfire on an enemy's infra-red sensor 'scope. Mark shivered, and crouched in the heat. He was hungry, and terribly cold. *Damn you, Miles Vorkosigan. There was so much I wanted to say to you, and now you're not listening.*

The straight tunnel they were traversing passed under another building, giving way through double doors to a wide foyer full of multiple cross-connections; several lift tubes, emergency stairs, other tunnels, and utility closets. All the doors were opened or blown open by the point-men looking for Bharaputran resistance. The air was pungent with smoke and the harsh lingering tang from plasma arc fire. Unfortunately, at this juncture the point men found what they were looking for.

The lights went out. Dendarii helmet visors snapped shut all around Mark, as they switched to infra-red. He followed suit, and stared disoriented into a world drained of color. His helmet crackled with voice communications stepping on each other as two point-men came running backwards into the foyer from separate corridors, firing plasma arcs that blared blindingly on his heat-enhanced vision. Four half-armored Bharaputran security personnel swung out of a lift tube, cutting Quinn's column in half. So confined was the confusion, they found themselves fighting hand-to-hand. Mark was knocked down by accident by a swinging Dendarii, and crouched near the float-pallet.

"This isn't shielded," the medic groaned, slapping the cryo-chamber as arcs of fire whipped by close overhead. "One square hit, and . . ."

"Into the lift tube, then," yelled Mark at him. The medic nodded, and swung the pallet around into the nearest dark opening free of Bharaputrans. The lift-tube was switched off, or the conflicting grav fields might have blown circuits on both tube and pallet. The medic scrambled aboard the cryo-chamber as if it were a horse, and began to sink from sight. Another trooper followed, hand over hand down the emergency ladder on the tube's interior. Plasma arc fire struck Mark three times in rapid succession, as he scrambled to his feet, knocking him down again. His mirror-field shed a roar of blue crackles as he rolled toward the tube through waves of heat. He swung down the ladder after the trooper, out of the line of fire.

But not for long. A Bharaputran helmet flashed above them in the entrance, then plasma arc fire followed them downward with a glare like lightning in the tube. The trooper helped the medic yank and heave the float-pallet out of this sudden shooting gallery and through the lowest entrance, and ducked after. Mark scrambled in their wake, feeling like a human torch, netted and entwined with racketing blue incandescence. How many shots had that been? He'd lost count. How many more could his shielding take before it gave way and burned out?

The trooper took a firing stance aimed back into the lift tube, but no Bharaputran followed them. They stood in a pocket of dark and quiet, shouts and shots echoing faintly down the tube from the battle overhead. This was a much smaller foyer, with only two exits. Dim yellow emergency lighting along the floor gave a falsely cozy sense of warmth.

"Hell," said the medic, staring upward. "I think we've just cut ourselves off."

"Not necessarily," said Mark. Neither the medic nor the trooper were Green Squad, but Mark's helmet of course had Green Squad programming. He called up the holomap, found their current location, and let the helmet's computer sketch a route. "You can get there from this level, too. It's a bit more roundabout, but you're less likely to encounter Bharaputrans for that very reason."

"Let me see," demanded the medic.

Half-reluctant, half-relieved, Mark gave his helmet up to him. The medic jammed it on his head, and studied the red line snaking through the 3-D schematic grid of the medical complex, projected before his eyes. Mark risked a darting glance up the lift tube. No Bharaputrans loomed overhead, and the sounds of combat were muffled, as if growing more distant. He ducked back to find the trooper staring at him, unsettling glints of his eyes gleaming through his visor. *No. I'm not your damned Admiral. More's the pity, eh?* The trooper clearly was of the opinion that the Bharaputrans had shot the wrong short man. Mark didn't even need words to get that message. He hunched.

"Yeah," the medic decided. His jaw tightened, behind his visor.

"If you hurry, you might even get there ahead of Captain Quinn," said Mark. He still held the medic's helmet. There were no more sounds from overhead. Should he run after Quinn's moving fire-fight, or stay and try to help guide and guard the float-pallet? He was not sure if he was more afraid of Quinn, or of the Bharaputran fire her party drew. Either way he'd probably be safer with the cryo-chamber.

He took a deep breath. "You . . . keep my helmet. I'll take yours." The medic and the trooper were both glowering at him with disfavor, repellingly. "I'll go after Quinn and the clones." His clones. Would Quinn have any regard at all for their lives?

"Go, then," said the medic. He and the trooper aimed the float-pallet out the doors, and didn't look back. They obviously had him pegged as more of a liability than an asset, and felt well-rid of him.

Grimly, he climbed the ladder back up the lift tube. He peeked cautiously across the foyer floor, as it came to his eye level. A lot of property damage. A sprinkler system had added steam to the choking smoke. One brown-clad body lay prone, unmoving. The floor was wet and slippery. He swung out of the tube and darted skittishly out the corridor the Dendarii company must have taken, if they were sticking to their planned route. More plasma arc damage assured him he was on the right track.

He rounded a corner, skidded to a halt, and flung himself backward, out of sight. The Bharaputrans hadn't seen him; they'd been facing the other way. He retreated back down the corridor while awkwardly keying through the channels of the unfamiliar helmet till he made contact with Quinn.

"Captain Quinn? Uh, Mark here."

"Where the hell *are* you, where's *Norwood*?"

"He's got my helmet. He's taking the cryo-chamber through by another route. I'm behind you, but I can't close up. There are at least four Bharaputrans in full space armor between us, coming up on your rear. Watch out."

"Hell, now we're outgunned. That tears it." Quinn paused. "No. I can take care of *them*. Mark, get the hell away, follow Norwood. Run!"

"What are you going to do?"

"Drop the roof on those bastards. Lotta good space armor'll do 'em then. *Run!*"

He ran, realizing what she was planning. At the first lift tube he came to, he took to the ladder, climbing wildly, regardless of where it led. He didn't want to be any further underground than he had to when—

It was like an earthquake. He clung as the tube cracked and buckled, and the *felt* sound beat through his body. It was over in a moment, but for an echoing rumble, and he resumed his climb. Daylight ahead, reflecting silver down a tube entrance.

He came out on the ground floor of a building furnished like a fancy office. Its windows were cracked and starred. He knocked a hole in one and climbed through, and flipped up his infra-red visor. To his right, half of another building had fallen away into an enormous crater. Dust still rose in choking clouds. The Bharaputrans in their sturdy, deadly space armor were possibly still alive, under all that, but it would take an excavation crew hours to dig them out. He grinned despite his terror, panting in the daylight.

The medic's helmet did not have nearly the eavesdropping capacity of the command headset, but he found Quinn again. "All right, Norwood, keep on going," she was saying. "Go like hell! Framingham! Got that? Lock on Norwood. Start pulling in your perimeter people. Lift as soon as Norwood and Tonkin are aboard. Kimura! You in the air?" A pause; Mark could not get Kimura's reply, whoever and wherever he was. But he could fill in the sense of it from Quinn's continuation. "Well, we've just made you a new drop zone. It's a bit lumpy, but it'll do. Follow my signal, come straight down into the crater. You'll just fit. Yes,you will too, I've laser-'scoped it, you do too have clearance. You can risk the shuttle *now*, Kimura. Come on!"

He made for the crater too, scuttling along close to the side of the building, taking advantage of overhangs till the patter of falling concrete chips made him realize that the blast-damaged balcony above his head was losing its structural integrity. Stay under and get smashed, or step out in the open and get shot? Whichever he did would prove the wrong choice, he was certain. What was that line Vorkosigan's military textbooks were so fond of quoting? *No battle plan survives first contact with the enemy*. Quinn's tactics and dispositions shifted with bewildering speed. She was exploiting a quite literal new opening—the roar of a drop shuttle grew in his ears, and he sprinted out from under the balcony as the vibrations weakened it. One end gave way and fell with a crash. He kept on sprinting. Let the Bharaputran snipers try to hit a moving target. . . .

Quinn and her group ventured into the open just as the drop shuttle, feet extended like an enormous insect, felt its way carefully into the crater. A few last Bharaputrans were in position on a roof opposite to offer harrying fire. But they had only plasma arcs, and were still being careful of the clones, though one pink-clad girl screamed, caught in the backwash of a Dendarii plasma mirror field. Light burns, painful but not fatal. She was crying and panicked, but a Dendarii trooper nevertheless caught her and aimed her at the shuttle hatch, now opening and extruding a ramp.

The few Bharaputrans, hopeless of bringing the shuttle down with mere sniper's weapons, changed their tactics. They began concentrating their fire on Quinn, shot after shot pumping into her overloading mirror field. She shimmered in a haze of blue fire, staggering under the impact. Clones and Dendarii pelted up the ramp.

Command helmets draw fire. He could see no other way but to run in front of her. The air around him lit as his mirror field spilled energy, but in the brief respite Quinn regained her balance. She grabbed him by the hand and together they sprinted up the ramp, the last to board. The shuttle was lurching back into the air and the ramp withdrawing even as they fell through the hatch. The hatch sealed behind them. The silence felt like a song.

Mark rolled over on his back and lay gasping for air, lungs on fire. Quinn sat up, her face red in its circle of gray. Just a sunburn. She cried hysterically for three breaths, then clamped her mouth shut. Fearfully, her fingers touched her hot cheeks, and Mark remembered that this was the woman who had had her face burned entirely away by plasma fire, once. But not twice. Not twice.

She scrambled to her knees, and began keying through command channels on her almost-fatal headset again. She then yanked herself to her feet and ricocheted forward in the jinking accelerations of the shuttle. Mark sat up and stared around, disoriented. Sergeant Taura, Thorne, the clones, he recognized. The rest were strange Dendarii, Lieutenant Kimura's Yellow Squad presumably, some in the usual gray fatigues, some in full space armor. They looked rather the worse for wear. All four bunks for wounded in the back were folded down and filled, and a fifth man was laid out on the floor. But the attending medic moved smoothly, not frantically. Her patients were clearly stabilized, able to wait for further treatment under more favorable conditions. Yellow Squad's cryo-chamber was recently occupied, though. The prognosis was now so bad for the foil-wrapped Phillipi, Mark wondered if they would even attempt to continue freezing her, once they were back aboard the *Peregrine*. But except for the bike-trooper and the cryo-chamber, there were no more covered forms, no body bags—Kimura's squad seemed to have made it through their mission, whatever it had been, fairly lightly.

The shuttle banked; they were circling, not boosting to orbit yet. Mark moaned under his breath, and rose to follow Quinn and find out what was going on.

When he came in sight of the prisoner he stopped short. The man sat with his hands bound behind him, securely strapped into a seat and guarded by two Yellow Squad troopers, a big fellow and a thin woman who made Mark think of a snake, all sinuous muscle and unblinking beady eyes. The prisoner looked a striking forty or so years of age, and wore a torn brown silk tunic and trousers. Loose strands of dark hair escaped from a gold ring on the back of his head and fell about his face. He did not struggle, but sat calmly, waiting, with a cold patience that quite matched the snake-woman's.

Bharaputra. The Bharaputra, Baron Bharaputra, Vasa Luigi himself. The man hadn't changed a hair in the eight years since Mark had last glimpsed him.

Vasa Luigi's face rose, and his eyes widened slightly, seeing Mark. "So, Admiral," he murmured.

"Just so," Mark responded automatically with a Naismith-phrase. He swayed as the shuttle banked more sharply, concealing weak-kneed terror, concealing exhaustion. He hadn't slept the night before this mission, either. *Bharaputra, here?*

The Baron cocked an eyebrow. "Who is that on your shirt?"

Mark glanced down at himself. The bandolier of blood had not yet turned brown, and was still damp, sticky and cold. He found himself actually wanting to answer, *My brother*, for the shock value. But he wasn't sure the Baron was shockable. He fled forward, avoiding more intimate conversation. *Baron Bharaputra.* Did Quinn and company plan to ride this tiger, and how? But at least he now understood why the shuttle could circle the combat zone without apparent fear of enemy fire.

He found Quinn and Thorne both in the pilot's compartment, along with Kimura the Yellow Squad commander. Quinn had taken over the shuttle's communication station, her gray hood pushed back, sweat-soaked dark curls in disarray.

"Framingham! Report!" she was crying into the comm. "You've got to get into the air. Bharaputran airborne reinforcements are almost on top of you."

Across the flight deck at the station opposite Quinn's, Thorne monitored a tactical holovid. Two Dendarii colored dots, fighter shuttles, dove upon but failed to break up an array of enemy shuttles passing over a ghost city, astral projection of the live city turning below them. Mark glanced out the window past the pilots' shoulders, but could not spot the originals in the sunlit morning smog.

"We have a downed-man recovery in progress, ma'am," Framingham's voice returned. "One minute, till the squad gets back."

"Do you have everyone else? *Do you have Norwood?* I can't raise his helmet!"

There was a short delay. Quinn's fists clenched, opened. Her fingernails were bitten to red stumps.

Framingham's voice at last. "We've got him now, ma'am. Got everyone, the quick and the dead alike, except for Phillipi. I don't want to leave anyone for those bloody bastards if I can help it—"

"We have Phillipi."

"Thank God! Then everyone's accounted for. We have lift-off now, Captain Quinn."

"Precious cargo, Framingham," said Quinn. "We rendezvous in the *Peregrine*'s umbrella of fire. The fighter shuttles will guard your wings." In the tac display, the Dendarii dots peeled away from the lumbering enemy and left them behind.

"What about your wings?"

"We'll be right behind you. Yellow Squad bought us a first-class ticket home free. Home free is Fell Station."

"And then we head out?"

"No. The *Ariel* took some damage, earlier. We're docking. It's arranged."

"Understood. See you there."

The Dendarii formation came together at last, and began to boost upward. Mark fell into a station chair, and hung on. The fighter shuttles were more at risk from enemy fire than the drop shuttles, he realized, watching the tac display. One fighter shuttle was distinctly limping. It clung close to the Yellow Squad's craft. The formation paced itself to its wounded member. But for once, things ran to plan. Their Bharaputran harriers dropped reluctantly behind as they broke out of the atmosphere and into orbit.

Quinn rested her elbows for a weary moment on her console, and hid her red-and-white face in her hands, rubbing tender eyelids. Thorne sat pale and silent. Quinn, Thorne, himself, all bore broken segments of that arc of blood. Like a red ribbon, binding them one to another.

Fell Station was coming up at last. It was a huge structure, the largest of the orbital transfer stations circling Jackson's Whole, and House Fell's headquarters and home city. Baron Fell liked holding the high ground. In the delicate interlocking network of the Great Houses, House Fell probably held the most raw power, in terms of capacity for destruction. But raw destruction was seldom profitable, and coup was counted in coins, here. What coin were the Dendarii using to buy Fell Station's help, or at least neutrality? The person of Baron Bharaputra, now secured in the cargo bay? What kind of bargaining chips were the clones, then, small change? And to think he'd despised the *Jacksonians* for being dealers in flesh.

Fell Station was just now passing out of the planet's eclipse, the advancing line of sunlight dramatically unveiling its vast extent. They decelerated toward one arm, giving up direction to Fell's traffic controllers and some heavily armed tugs which appeared out of nowhere to escort them. And there was the *Peregrine*, coasting in. The drop shuttles and the fighter shuttles all gavotted around their mother ship, coming meekly to their docking clamps. The *Peregrine* itself eased delicately toward its assigned mooring.

With a *clank* of the portside clamps and the hiss of flex-tube seals, they were home. In the cargo bay, the Dendarii expedited removal of the wounded to the *Peregrine*'s infirmary, then turned much more slowly and wearily to tie-down and clean-up chores. Quinn shot past them, Thorne close on her heels. As if pulled by that mortal red ribbon, Mark followed.

The goal of Quinn's mad dash was the starboard side shuttle hatch, where Framingham's shuttle was coming to dock. They arrived there just as the flex-tube seals were secured, then had to stand out of the way as the wounded were rushed out first. Mark was disturbed to recognize Trooper Tonkin, who had accompanied Norwood the medic, among them. Tonkin had reversed roles, from guard to patient. His face was dark and still, unconscious, as eager hands hustled him past and shifted him onto a float pallet. *Something's very wrong, here.*

Quinn shifted impatiently from foot to foot. Other Dendarii troopers started to exit, herding clones. Quinn frowned, and shouldered upstream past them through the flex tube and into the shuttle.

Thorne and Mark went after her into free fall chaos. There were clone-youths everywhere, some crying, some violently sick—Dendarii were attempting to catch them, and get them towed to the exit. One harried trooper with a hand-vac was chasing floating globs of some child's last meal before everyone had to breathe it. The shouts and screams and babble were like a blow to the mind. Framingham's bellows were failing to speed a return to military order any faster than the terrorized clones could be removed from the cargo bay.

"Framingham!" Quinn floated over and grabbed him by the ankle. "Framingham! Where the hell's the cryo-chamber Norwood was escorting?"

He glanced down, frowning. "But you said *you* had it, Captain."

"What?"

"You said you *had* Phillipi." His lips stretched in a fierce grimace. "Goddammit, if we've left her behind I'll—"

"We have Phillipi, yes, but she's—she was no longer in the cryo-chamber. Norwood was supposed to be getting it to you, Norwood and Tonkin."

"They didn't have it when my rescue patrol pulled them out. We got them both, what was left of 'em. Norwood was killed. Hit through the eye with one of those frigging projectile spine-grenades. Blew his head apart. But I didn't leave his body, it's in the bag over there."

Command helmets draw fire, oh yes, I knew that. . . . No wonder Quinn hadn't been able to raise Norwood's comm channels.

"The cryo-chamber, Framingham!" Quinn's voice held a high pitch of anguish Mark had never heard before.

"We didn't *see* any goddamn cryo-chamber, Quinn! Norwood and Tonkin didn't have it when we got to them! What's so frigging important about the cryo-chamber if Phillipi wasn't even in it?"

Quinn released his ankle, and floated in a tightening ball, arms and legs drawing in. Her eyes were dark and huge. She bit off a string of inadequate foul words, grinding her teeth so hard her gums went white. Thorne looked like a chalk doll.

"Thorne," Quinn said, when she could speak again. "Get on the comm to Elena. I want both ships on a total security blackout, as of now. No leaves, no passes, no communications with Fell Station or anybody else that isn't cleared by me. Tell her to get Lieutenant Hart over here from the *Ariel*. I want to meet with them both at once, and *not* over comm channels. Go."

Thorne nodded, rotated in air, and launched itself forward toward the flight deck.

"What is this?" demanded Sergeant Framingham.

Quinn took a deep, slow breath. "Framingham, we left the Admiral downside."

"Have you lost your mind, he's right there—" Framingham's finger sagged in mid-point at Mark. His hand closed into a fist. "Oh." He paused. "That's the clone."

Quinn's eyes burned; Mark could feel them boring through to the back of his skull like laser-drills.

"Maybe not," Quinn said heavily. "Not as far as House Bharaputra has to know."

"Ah?" Framingham's eyes narrowed in speculation.

No! Mark screamed inside. Silently. Very silently.

CHAPTER EIGHT

It was like being trapped in a locked room with half a dozen serial killers with hangovers. Mark could hear each one's breathing from where they sat in a ring around the officer's conference table. They were in the briefing chamber off the *Peregrine*'s main tactics room. Quinn's breath was the lightest and fastest, Sergeant Taura's was the deepest and most ominous. Only Elena Bothari-Jesek at her captain's place at the head of the table, and Lieutenant Hart on her right, were shipboard-clean and natty. The rest had come as they were from the drop mission, battered and stinking: Taura, Sergeant Framingham, Lieutenant Kimura, Quinn on Bothari-Jesek's left. And himself, of course, lonely at the far end of the oblong table.

Captain Bothari-Jesek frowned, and wordlessly handed around a bottle of painkiller tablets. Sergeant Taura took six. Only Lieutenant Kimura passed. Taura handed them across to Framingham without offering any to Mark. He longed for the tablets as a thirsty man might yearn after a glass of water, poured out and sinking into desert sand. The bottle went back up the table and disappeared into the captain's pocket. Mark's eyes throbbed in time to his sinuses, and the back of his head felt tight as drying rawhide.

Bothari-Jesek spoke. "This emergency debriefing is called to deal with just two questions, and as quickly as possible. What the hell happened, and what are we going to do next? Are those helmet recorders on their way?"

"Yes, ma'am," said Sergeant Framingham. "Corporal Abromov is bringing them."

"Unfortunately, we are missing the most pertinent one," said Quinn. "Correct, Framingham?"

"I'm afraid so, ma'am. I suppose it's embedded in a wall somewhere at Bharaputra's, along with most of the rest of Norwood's helmet. Friggin' grenades."

"Hells." Quinn hunched in her seat.

The briefing room door slid open, and Corporal Abromov entered at a jog. He carried four small, clear plastic trays, stacked, and labeled "Green Squad," "Yellow Squad," "Orange Squad," and "Blue Squad." Each tray held an array of ten to sixteen tiny buttons. Helmet recorders. Each trooper's personal records of the past hours, tracking every movement, every heartbeat, every scan, shot, hit, and communication. Events that had passed too rapidly for comprehension in real-time could be slowed, analyzed, teased apart, errors of procedure detected and corrected—next time.

Abromov saluted and handed the trays to Captain Bothari-Jesek. She dismissed him with thanks, and passed the trays on to Captain Quinn, who in turn inserted them into the simulator's data slot and downloaded them. She also encoded the file top secret. Her raw-tipped fingers darted over the vid control panel.

The now-familiar ghostly three-dimensional holomap of Bharaputra's medical facility formed above the table top. "I'll jump forward to the time we were attacked in the tunnel," Quinn said. "There we are, Blue Squad, part of Green Squad . . ." A spaghetti-tangle of lines of green and blue colored light appeared deep inside a misty building. "Tonkin was Blue Squad Number Six, and kept his helmet throughout what follows." She made Tonkin's Number Six map-track yellow, for contrast. "Norwood was still wearing Blue Squad Number Ten. Mark . . ." her lips pinched, "was wearing Helmet One." That track, of course, was conspicuously missing. She made Norwood's Number Ten track pink. "At what point did you change helmets with Norwood, Mark?" She did not look at him as she asked this question.

Please, let me go. He was sure he was sick, because he was still shivering. A small muscle in the back of his neck spasmed, tiny twitches in a prickling underlayer of pain. "We went to the bottom of that lift tube." His voice came out a dry whisper. "When . . . when Helmet Ten comes back up, I'm wearing it. Norwood and Tonkin went on together, and that's the last I saw of them."

The pink line indeed crawled back up the tube and wormed after the mob of blue and green lines. The yellow track went on alone.

Quinn fast-forwarded voice contacts. Tonkin's baritone came out in a whine like an insect on amphetamines. "When I last contacted them, they were here." Quinn marked the spot with a glowing dot of light, in an interior corridor deep inside another building. She fell silent, and let the yellow line snake on. Down a lift tube, through yet another utility tunnel, under a structure, up and through yet another.

"There," said Framingham suddenly, "is the floor they were trapped on. We picked up contact with 'em *there*."

Quinn marked another dot. "Then the cryo-chamber has to be somewhere near the line of march between here and here." She pointed to the two bright dots. "It has to be." She stared, eyes narrowed. "Two buildings. Two and a half, I suppose. But there's not a damn thing on Tonkin's voice transmissions that gives me a clue." The insect-voice described Bharaputran attackers, and cried for help, over and over, but did not mention the cryo-chamber. Mark's throat contracted in synchrony. *Quinn, turn him off, please. . . .*

The program ran to its end. All the Dendarii around

the table stared at it, as if willing it to yield up something more. There was no more.

The door slid aside and Captain Thorne entered. Mark had never seen a more exhausted-looking human being. Thorne too was still dressed in dirty fatigues, only the plasma mirror pack discarded from its half armor. Its gray hood was pushed back, brown hair plastered flat to its head. A circle of grime in the middle of Thorne's pale face marked the hood opening, gray twin to the circle of red on Quinn's face from her mirror-field overload burn. Thorne's movements were hurried and jerky, will overriding a fatigue close to collapse. Thorne leaned, hands on the conference table, mouth a grim horizontal line.

"So, could you get anything at all out of Tonkin?" asked Quinn of Thorne. "What the computer has, we just saw. And I don't think it's enough."

"The medics got him waked up, briefly," reported Thorne. "He did talk. I was hoping the recorders would make sense of what he said, but . . ."

"What did he say?"

"He said when they reached this building," Thorne pointed, "they were cut off. Not yet surrounded, but blocked from a line to the shuttle, and the enemy closing the ring fast. Tonkin said, Norwood yelled he had an idea, he'd seen something "back there". He had Tonkin create a diversion with a grenade attack, and guard a particular corridor—must be that one there. Norwood took the cryo-chamber and ran back along their route. He returned a few minutes later—not more than six minutes, Tonkin said. And he told Tonkin, "It's all right now. The Admiral will get out of here even if we don't." About two minutes later, he was killed by that projectile grenade, and Tonkin was knocked loopy by the concussion."

Framingham nodded. "My crew got there not three

minutes after that. They drove off a pack of Bharaputrans who were searching the bodies—looting, looking for intelligence, or both, Corporal Abromov wasn't sure—they picked up Tonkin and Norwood's body and ran like hell. Nobody in the squad reported seeing a cryo-chamber anywhere."

Quinn chewed absently on a fingernail stump. Mark did not think she was even conscious of the gesture. "That's all?"

"Tonkin said Norwood was laughing," Thorne added.

"Laughing." Quinn grimaced. "Hell."

Captain Bothari-Jesek was sunk in her station chair. Everyone around the table appeared to digest this last tid-bit, staring at the holomap. "He did something clever," said Bothari-Jesek. "Or something that he thought was clever."

"He only had about five minutes. How clever could he be in five minutes?" Quinn complained. "Gods *damn* the clever jerk to sixteen hells for not reporting!"

"He was doubtless about to." Bothari-Jesek sighed. "I don't think we need to waste time apportioning blame. There's going to be plenty to go around."

Thorne winced, as did Framingham, Quinn, and Taura. Then they all glanced at Mark. He cringed back in his seat.

"It's only been," Quinn glanced at her chrono, "less than two hours. Whatever Norwood did, the cryo-chamber has to still be down there. It has to."

"So what do we do?" Lieutenant Kimura asked dryly. "Mount another drop mission?"

Quinn thinned her lips in non-appreciation of the weary sarcasm. "You volunteering, Kimura?" Kimura flipped up his palms in surrender and subsided.

"In the meantime," Bothari-Jesek said, "Fell Station is calling us, pretty urgently. We have to start dealing. I presume this will involve our hostage." A short nod of thanks in Kimura's direction acknowledged the only wholly successful part of the drop mission, and Kimura nodded back. "Does anyone here know what the Admiral intended to do with Baron Bharaputra?"

A circle of negative headshakes. "Don't *you* know, Quinnie?" asked Kimura, surprised.

"No. There wasn't time to chat. I'm not even sure if the Admiral seriously expected your kidnapping expedition to succeed, Kimura, or whether it was only for the diversionary value. That would be more like his strategizing, not to let the whole mission turn on one unknown outcome. I expect he planned," her voice faded in a sigh, "to use his initiative." She sat up straight. "But I sure as hell know what I intend to do. The deal this time is going to be in *our* favor. Baron Bharaputra could be the ticket out of here for all of us, and the Admiral too, but we have to work it just right."

"In that case," said Bothari-Jesek, "I don't think we should let on to House Bharaputra just how valuable a package we left downside." Bothari-Jesek, Thorne, Quinn, all of them, turned to look at Mark, coldly speculative.

"I've thought of that too," said Quinn.

"No," he whispered. "No!" His scream emerged as a croak. "You can't be serious. You can't make me be him, I don't *want* to be him any more, God! No!" He was shaking, shivering, his stomach turning and knotting. *I'm cold.*

Quinn and Bothari-Jesek glanced at each other. Bothari-Jesek nodded, some unspoken message.

Quinn said, "You are all dismissed to your duties. Except you, Captain Thorne. You are relieved of command of the *Ariel*. Lieutenant Hart will take over."

Thorne nodded, as if this were entirely expected. "Am I under arrest?"

Quinn's eyes narrowed in pain. "Hell, we don't have

the time. Or the personnel. And you're not debriefed yet, and besides, I need your experience. This . . . situation could change rapidly at any moment. Consider yourself under house arrest, and assigned to me. You can guard yourself. Take a visiting officer's cabin here on the *Peregrine*, and call it your cell if it makes you feel any better."

Thorne's face went very bleak indeed. "Yes, ma'am," it said woodenly.

Quinn frowned. "Go clean up. We'll continue this later."

Except for Quinn and Bothari-Jesek, they all filed out. Mark tried to follow them. "*Not* you," said Quinn in a voice like a death bell. He sank back into his station chair and huddled there. As the last Dendarii cleared the chamber, Quinn reached over and turned off all recording devices.

Miles's women. Elena-the-childhood-sweetheart, now Captain Bothari-Jesek, Mark had studied back when the Komarrans had tutored him to play Lord Vorkosigan. Yet she was not quite what he had expected. Quinn the Dendarii had taken the Komarran plotters by surprise. The two women had a coincidental resemblance in coloration, both with short dark hair, fine pale skin, liquid brown eyes. Or was it so coincidental? Had Vorkosigan subconsciously chosen Quinn as Bothari-Jesek's substitute, when he couldn't have the real thing? Even their first names were similar, Elli and Elena.

Bothari-Jesek was the taller by a head, with long aristocratic features, and was more cool and reserved, an effect augmented by her clean officer's undress grays. Quinn, fatigue-clad and combat-booted, was shorter, though still a head taller than himself, rounder and hotter. Both were terrifying. Mark's own taste in women, if ever he should live to exercise it, ran more to something like that little blonde clone they'd pulled from under the bed, if only she'd been the age she looked to be.

Somebody short, soft, pink, timid, somebody who wouldn't kill and eat him after they mated.

Elena Bothari-Jesek was watching him with a sort of appalled fascination. "So like him. Yet not him. Why are you shivering?"

"I'm cold," muttered Mark.

"*You're* cold!" Quinn echoed in outrage. "*You're* cold! You gods be-damned little sucker—" She turned her station chair abruptly around, and sat with her back to him.

Bothari-Jesek rose and walked around to his end of the table. Willow-wand woman. She touched his forehead, which was clammy; he flinched almost explosively. She bent and stared into his eyes. "Quinnie, back off. He's in psychological shock."

"He doesn't deserve consideration!" Quinn choked.

"He's still in shock, regardless. If you want results, you have to take it into account."

"Hell." Quinn turned back. New clean wet tracks ran down from her eyes across her red-and-white, dirt-and-dried-blood-smudged face. "You didn't see. You didn't see Miles lying there with his heart blown all over the room."

"Quinnie, he's not really dead. Is he? He's just frozen, and . . . and misplaced." Was there the faintest tinge of uncertainty, denial, in her voice?

"Oh, he's really dead all right. Very really frozen dead. And he's going to stay that way forever if we don't get him back!" The blood all over her fatigues, caked in the grooves of her hands, smeared across her face, was finally turning brown.

Bothari-Jesek took a breath. "Let's focus on the business to hand. The immediate question is, can Mark fool Baron Fell? Fell met the real Miles once."

"That's one of the reasons I didn't put Bel Thorne under close arrest. Bel was there, and can advise, I hope."

"Yes. And that's the curious thing . . ." She hitched a hip over the tabletop, and let one long booted leg swing. "Shock or no shock, Mark hasn't blown Miles's deep-cover. The name *Vorkosigan* hasn't passed his lips, has it?"

"No," Quinn admitted.

Bothari-Jesek twisted up her mouth, and studied him. "Why not?" she asked suddenly.

He crouched down a little further in his station chair, trying to escape the impact of her stare. "I don't know," he muttered. She waited implacably for more, and he mustered in an only slightly louder voice, "Habit, I guess." Mostly Ser Galen's habit of beating the shit out of him whenever he'd screwed up, back in the bad old days. "When I do the part, I do the part. M-Miles would never have slipped on that one, so I don't either."

"Who are you when you're not doing the part?" Bothari-Jesek's gaze was narrowed, calculating.

"I . . . hardly know." He swallowed, and tried again for more volume in his voice. "What's going to happen to my—to the clones?"

As Quinn began to speak, Bothari-Jesek held up her hand, stopping her. Bothari-Jesek said instead, "What do you want to have happen to them?"

"I want them to go free. To be set free somewhere safe, where House Bharaputra can't kidnap them back."

"A strange altruism. I can't help wondering, why? Why this whole mission in the first place? What did you hope to gain?"

His mouth opened, but no sound came out. He couldn't answer. He was still clammy, weak and shaking. His head ached blackly, as though draining of blood. He shook his head.

"Peh!" snorted Quinn. "What a loser. What a, a damned *anti*-Miles. Snatching defeat from the jaws of victory."

"Quinn," said Bothari-Jesek quietly. There was a

profound reproof in her voice, just in that single word, which Quinn heard and acknowledged with a shrug of her shoulder. "I don't think either one of us knows quite what we have hold of here," Bothari-Jesek continued. "But I know when I'm out of my depth. However, I know someone who wouldn't be."

"Who?"

"Countess Vorkosigan."

"Hm." Quinn sighed. "That's another thing. Who's going to tell *her* about—" A downward jerk of her thumb indicated Jackson's Whole, and the fatal events that had just passed there. "And gods help me, if I'm really in command of this outfit now, I'm gonna have to report all this to Simon Illyan." She paused. "Do you want to be in command, Elena? As senior shipmaster present, now that Bel's under quasi-arrest, and all that. I just grabbed 'cause I had to, under fire."

"You're doing fine," said Bothari-Jesek with a small smile. "I'll support you." She added, "You've been more closely involved with intelligence all along, you're the logical choice."

"Yes, I know." Quinn grimaced. "You'll tell the family, if it comes to that?"

"For that," Bothari-Jesek sighed, "I am the logical choice. I'll tell the Countess, yes."

"It's a deal." But they both looked as if they wondered who had the better, or worse, half of it.

"As for the clones," Bothari-Jesek eyed Mark again, "how would you like to *earn* their freedom?"

"Elena," said Quinn warningly, "don't make promises. We don't know what we're going to have to trade yet, to get out of here. To get—" another gesture downward, "him back."

"No," Mark whispered. "You can't. Can't send them . . . back down there, after all this."

"I traded Phillipi," said Quinn grimly. "I'd trade *you*

in a heartbeat, except that *he* . . . Do you know why we came downside on this bloody drop mission in the first place?" she demanded.

Wordlessly, he shook his head.

"It was for you, you little shit. The Admiral had a deal half-cut with Baron Bharaputra. We were going to buy out Green Squad for a quarter of a million Betan dollars. It wouldn't have cost much more than the drop mission, counting all the equipment we lost along with Thorne's shuttle. And the lives. But the Baron refused to throw you into the pot. Why he wouldn't sell you, I don't know. You're worthless to everybody else. But Miles wouldn't leave you!"

Mark stared down at his hands, which plucked at each other. He glanced up to see Bothari-Jesek studying him again as if he were some vital cryptogram.

"As the Admiral would not leave his brother," said Bothari-Jesek slowly, "so Mark will not leave the clones. Will you? Eh?"

He would have swallowed, but he'd run out of spit.

"You'll do anything to save them, eh? Anything we ask?"

His mouth opened and closed. It might have been a hollow, soundless *yes*.

"You'll play the part of the Admiral for us? We'll coach you, of course."

He half-nodded, but managed to blurt out, "What promise—?"

"We'll take all the clones with us when we go. We'll put them down somewhere House Bharaputra can't reach."

"Elena!" objected Quinn.

"I want," he did swallow this time, "I want the Barrayaran woman's word. Your word," he said to Bothari-Jesek.

Quinn sucked on her lower lip, but did not speak. After a long pause, Bothari-Jesek nodded. "All right. You have my word on it. But you give us your total cooperation, understood?"

"Your word as what?"

"Just my word."

". . . Yes. All right."

Quinn rose and stared down at him. "But is he even fit to play the part right now?"

Bothari-Jesek followed her look. "Not in that condition, no, I suppose not. Let him clean up, eat, rest. Then we'll see what can be done."

"Baron Fell may not give us time to coddle him."

"We'll tell Baron Fell he's in the shower. That'll be true enough."

A shower. *Food.* He was so ravenous as to be almost beyond hunger, numb in the belly, listless in the flesh. And cold.

"All I can say," said Quinn, "is that he's a damn poor imitation of the real Miles Vorkosigan."

Yes, that's what I've been trying to tell you.

Bothari-Jesek shook her head in, presumably, exasperated agreement. "Come on," she said to him.

She escorted him to an officer's cabin, small but thank-God private. It was disused, blank and clean, military-austere, the air a little stale. He supposed Thorne must now be similarly housed nearby.

"I'll get some clean clothes sent over for you from the *Ariel*. And send some food."

"Food first—please?"

"Sure."

"Why are you being nice to me?" His voice came out plaintive and suspicious, making him sound weak and paranoid, he feared.

Her aquiline face went introspective. "I want to know . . . who you are. What you are."

"You know. I'm a manufactured clone. Manufactured right here on Jackson's Whole."

"I don't mean your body."

He hunched in an automatic defensive posture, though he knew it emphasized his deformities.

"You are very closed," she observed. "Very alone. That's not at all like Miles. Usually."

"He's not a man, he's a mob. He's got a whole damned army trailing around after him." *Not to mention the harrowing harem.* "I suppose he likes it like that."

Her lips curved in an unexpected smile. It was the first time he'd seen her smile. It changed her face. "He does, I think." Her smile faded. "Did."

"You're doing this for him, aren't you. Treating me like this because you think he'd want it." Not in his own right, no, never, but all for Miles and his damned brother-obsession.

"Partly."

Right.

"But mostly," she said, "because someday Countess Vorkosigan will ask me what I did for her son."

"You're planning to trade Baron Bharaputra for him, aren't you?"

"Mark . . ." her eyes were dark with a strange . . . pity? irony? He could not read her eyes. "She'll mean you."

She turned on her heel and left him by himself, sealed in the cabin.

He showered in the hottest water the tiny unit would yield, and stood for long minutes in the heat of the dryer-blast, till his skin flushed red, before he stopped shivering. He was dizzy with exhaustion. When he finally emerged, he found someone had been and gone and left clothes and food. He hastily pulled on underwear, a black Dendarii T-shirt, and a pair of his progenitor's ship-knit grey trousers, and fell upon the dinner. It wasn't a dainty Naismith-special-diet this time, but rather a tray of standard ready-to-eat rations designed to keep a large and physically active trooper going strong. It was far from gourmet fare, but it was the first time he'd had enough food on his plate for weeks. He devoured it all, as if whatever fairy had delivered it might reappear and snatch it away again. Stomach aching, he rolled into bed and lay on his side. He no longer shivered as if from cold, nor felt drained and sweating and shaky from low blood sugar. Yet a kind of psychic reverberation still rolled like a black tide through his body.

At least you got the clones out.

No. Miles *got the clones out.*

Dammit, dammit, dammit . . .

This half-baked disaster was not the glorious redemption of which he'd dreamed. Yet what had he expected the aftermath to be? In all his desperate plotting, he'd planned almost nothing past his projected return to Escobar with the *Ariel*. To Escobar, grinning, with the clones under his wing. He'd imagined himself dealing with an enraged Miles then, but then it would have been too late for Miles to stop him, too late to take his victory from him. He'd half-expected to be arrested, but to go willingly, whistling. What *had* he wanted?

To be free of survivor guilt? To break that old curse? *Nobody you knew back then is still alive. . . .* That was the motive he'd thought was driving him, when he thought at all. Maybe it wasn't so simple. He'd wanted to free himself from something. . . . In the last two years, freed of Ser Galen and the Komarrans by the actions of Miles Vorkosigan, freed again altogether by Miles on a London street at dawn, he had not found the happiness he'd dreamed of during his slavery to the terrorists. Miles had broken only the physical chains that bound him; others, invisible, had cut so deep that flesh had grown around them.

What did you think? That if you were as heroic as

Miles, they'd have to treat you like Miles? That they would have to love you?

And who were *they*? The Dendarii? Miles himself? Or behind Miles, those sinister, fascinating shadows, Count and Countess Vorkosigan?

His image of Miles's parents was blurred, uncertain. The unbalanced Galen had presented them, his hated enemies, as black villains, the Butcher of Komarr and his virago wife. Yet with his other hand he'd required Mark to study them, using unedited source materials, their writings, their public speeches, private vids. Miles's parents were clearly complex people, hardly saints, but just as clearly not the foaming sadistic sodomite and murderous bitch of Galen's raving paranoias. In the vids Count Aral Vorkosigan appeared merely a grey-haired, thick-set man with oddly intent eyes in his rather heavy face, with a rich, raspy, level voice. Countess Cordelia Vorkosigan spoke less often, a tall woman with red-roan hair and notable grey eyes, too powerful to be called pretty, yet so centered and balanced as to seem beautiful even though, strictly speaking, she was not.

And now Bothari-Jesek threatened to deliver him to them. . . .

He sat up, and turned on the light. A quick tour of the cabin revealed nothing to commit suicide with. No weapons or blades—the Dendarii had disarmed him when he'd come aboard. Nothing to hang a belt or rope from. Boiling himself to death in the shower was not an option, a sealed fail-safe sensor turned it off automatically when it exceeded physiological tolerances. He went back to bed.

The image of a little, urgent, shouting man with his chest exploding outward in a carmine spray replayed in slow motion in his head. He was surprised when he began to cry. Shock, it had to be the shock that Bothari-Jesek had diagnosed. *I hated the little bugger when he was alive, why am I crying?* It was absurd. Maybe he was going insane.

Two nights without sleep had left him ringingly numb, yet he could not sleep now. He only dozed, drifting in and out of near-dreams and recent, searing memories. He half-hallucinated about being in a rubber raft on a river of blood, bailing frantically in the red torrent, so that when Quinn came to get him after only an hour's rest, it was actually a relief.

CHAPTER NINE

"Whatever you do," said Captain Thorne, "don't mention the Betan rejuvenation treatment.

Mark frowned. "What Betan rejuvenation treatment? Is there one?"

"No."

"Then why the hell would I mention it?"

"Never mind, just don't."

Mark gritted his teeth, swung around in his station chair square to the vid plate, and pressed the keypad to lower his seat till his booted feet were flat to the floor. He was fully kitted in Naismith's officer's greys. Quinn had dressed him as though he were a doll, or an idiot child. Quinn, Bothari-Jesek, and Thorne had then proceeded to fill his head with a mass of sometimes-conflicting instructions on how to play Miles in the upcoming interview. *As if I didn't know.* The three captains now each sat in station chairs out of range of the vid pick-up in the *Peregrine*'s tac room, ready to prompt him through an ear-bug. And he'd thought *Galen* was a puppet master. His ear itched, and he wriggled the bug in irritation, earning a frown from Bothari-Jesek. Quinn had never stopped scowling.

Quinn had never stopped. She still wore her blood-soaked fatigues. Her sudden inheritance of command of this debacle had allowed her no rest. Thorne had cleaned up and changed to ship greys, but obviously had not slept yet. Both their faces stood out pale in the shadows, too sharply lined. Quinn had made Mark take a stimulant when, getting him dressed, she'd found him too muzzy-mouthed for her taste, and he did not quite like its effects. His head and eyes were almost too clear, but his body felt beaten. All the edges and surfaces of the tac room seemed to stand out with unnatural clarity. Sounds and voices in his ears seemed to have a painful serrated quality, sharp and blurred at once. Quinn was on the stuff too, he realized, watching her wince at a high electronic squeal from the comm equipment.

("All right, you're on,") said Quinn through the ear-bug as the vid plate in front of him began to sparkle. They all shut up at last.

The image of Baron Fell materialized, and frowned at him too. Georish Stauber, Baron Fell of House Fell, was unusual for the leader of a Jacksonian Great House in that he still wore his original body. An old man's body. The Baron was stout, pink of face, with a shiny liver-spotted scalp fringed by white hair trimmed short. The silk tunic he wore in his House's particular shade of green made him look like a hypothyroid elf. But there was nothing elfin about his cold and penetrating eyes. Miles was not intimidated by a Jacksonian Baron's power, Mark reminded himself. Miles was not intimidated by any power backed by less than three entire planets. His father the Butcher of Komarr could eat Jacksonian Great Houses for breakfast.

He, of course, was not Miles.

Screw that. I'm Miles for the next fifteen minutes, anyway.

"So, Admiral," rumbled the Baron. "We meet again after all."

"Quite." Mark managed not to let his voice crack.

"I see you are as presumptuous as ever. And as ill-informed."

"Quite."

("Start talking, dammit,") Quinn's voice hissed in his ear.

Mark swallowed. "Baron Fell, it was not a part of my original battle plan to involve Fell Station in this raid. I am as anxious to decamp with my forces as you are to have us leave. To that end, I request your help as a go-between. You . . . know that we've kidnapped Baron Bharaputra, I trust?"

"So I'm told." One of Fell's eyelids tic'd. "You've rather over-reached your available back-up, have you not?"

"Have I?" Mark shrugged. "House Fell is in a state of vendetta with House Bharaputra, are you not?"

"Not exactly. House Fell was on the verge of *ending* the vendetta with House Bharaputra. We've found it mutually unprofitable, of late. I'm now suspected of collusion in your raid." The Baron's frown deepened.

"Uh . . ." his thought was interrupted by Thorne whispering, ("Tell him Bharaputra's alive and well.")

"Baron Bharaputra is alive and well," said Mark, "and can remain so, for all I care. As a go-between, it seems to me you would be well-placed to demonstrate your good faith to House Bharaputra by helping to get him back. I only wish to trade him—intact—for one item, and then we'll be gone."

"You are optimistic," Fell said dryly.

Mark plowed on. "A simple, advantageous trade. The Baron for my clone."

("Brother,") Thorne, Quinn, and Bothari-Jesek all corrected in unison in his ear-bug.

"—brother," Mark continued, edged. He unset his teeth. "Unfortunately, my . . . brother, was shot in the melee downside. Fortunately, he was successfully frozen in one of our emergency cryo-chambers. Um, unfortunately, the cryo-chamber was accidentally left behind in the scramble to get off. A live man for a dead one; I fail to see the difficulty."

The Baron barked a laugh, which he muffled in a cough. The three Dendarii faces across from Mark in the shadows were chill and stiff and not amused. "You've been having an interesting visit, Admiral. What do you want with a dead clone?"

("Brother,") Quinn said again. ("Miles insists, always.")

("Yes,") seconded Thorne. ("That's how I first knew you weren't Miles, back on the *Ariel*, when I called you a clone and you didn't jump down my throat.")

"Brother," Mark repeated wearily. "There was no head-wound, and the cryo-treatment was begun almost instantly. He has good hope of revival, as such things go."

("Only if we get him back,") Quinn growled.

"I have a brother," remarked Baron Fell. "He inspires no such emotions in me."

I'm right with you, Baron, Mark thought.

Thorne piped up in Mark's ear, ("He's talking about his half-brother, Baron Ryoval of House Ryoval. The original axis of this vendetta was between Fell and Ryoval. Bharaputra got dragged in later.")

I know who Ryoval is, Mark wanted to snap, but could not.

"In fact," Baron Fell went on, "my brother will be quite excited to learn you are here. After you so reduced his resources on your last visit, he is alas limited to small-scale attacks. But I suggest you watch your back."

"Oh? Do Ryoval's agents operate so freely on Fell Station?" Mark purred.

Thorne approved, ("Good one! Just like Miles.")

Fell stiffened. "Hardly."

Thorne whispered, ("Yes, remind him you helped him with his brother.")

What the hell had Miles done here, four years ago? "Baron. I helped you with your brother. You help me with mine, and we can call it square."

"Hardly that. The apples of discord you threw among us on your last departure took far too much time to sort out. Still . . . it's true you dealt Ry a better blow that I could have." Was there a tiny glint of approval in Fell's eye? He rubbed his round chin. "Therefore, I will give you one day to complete your business and depart."

"You'll act as go-between?"

"The better to keep an eye on both parties, yes."

Mark explained the Dendarii's best guess as to the approximate location of the cryo-chamber, and gave its description and serial numbers. "Tell the Bharaputrans, we think it may have been hidden or disguised in some way. Please emphasize, we wish it returned in good condition. And their Baron will be too."

("Good,") Bothari-Jesek encouraged. ("Let 'em know it's too valuable to destroy, without letting 'em guess they could hold us up for more ransom.")

Fell's lips thinned. "Admiral, you are an acute man, but I don't think you altogether understand how we do things on Jackson's Whole."

"But you do, Baron. That's why we'd like to have you on our side."

"I am not on your side. That is perhaps the first thing you don't understand."

Mark nodded, slowly; Miles would have, he thought. Fell's attitude was strange. Faintly hostile. *Yet he acts like he respects me.*

No. He respected *Miles*. Hell. "Your neutrality is all I ask."

Fell shot him a narrow glance from under his white eyebrows. "What about the other clones?"

"What about them?"

"House Bharaputra will be inquiring."

"They do not enter into this transaction. Vasa Luigi's life should be sufficient and more."

"Yes, the trade seems uneven. What is so valuable about your late clone?"

Three voices chorused in his ear, ("Brother!") Mark

yanked the ear-bug out and slapped it to the counter beside the vid plate. Quinn nearly choked.

"I cannot trade back fractions of Baron Bharaputra," snapped Mark. "Tempted as I am to start doing so."

Baron Fell raised a placating plump palm. "Calm, Admiral. I doubt it will be necessary to go so far."

"I hope not." Mark trembled. "It'd be a shame if I had to send him back without his brain. Like the clones."

Baron Fell apparently read the absolute personal sincerity of his threat, for he opened both palms. "I'll see what I can do, Admiral."

"Thank you," whispered Mark.

The Baron nodded; his image dissolved. By some trick of the holovid or the stimulant, Fell's eyes seemed to linger for one last unsettling stare. Mark sat frozen for several seconds till he was certain they were gone.

"Huh," said Bothari-Jesek, sounding surprised. "You did that rather well."

He did not bother to answer that one.

"Interesting," said Thorne. "Why didn't Fell ask for a fee or a cut?"

"Dare we trust him?" asked Bothari-Jesek.

"Not trust, exactly." Quinn ran the edge of her index finger along her white teeth, nibbling. "But we must have Fell's cooperation to exit Jumppoint Five. We dare not offend him, not for any money. I thought he would be more pleased with our bite out of Bharaputra, but the strategic situation seems to have changed since your last visit here, Bel."

Thorne sighed agreement.

Quinn continued, "I want you to see what you can find out about the current balance of power here. Anything that may affect our operations, anything we can use to help. Houses Fell, Bharaputra and Ryoval, and anything coming up on the blindside. There's something about all this that's making me feel paranoid as hell, though it may be just the drugs I'm on. But I'm too damned tired to see it right now."

"I'll see what I can do." Thorne nodded and withdrew.

When the door hissed shut behind Thorne, Bothari-Jesek asked Quinn, "Have you reported all this to Barrayar yet?"

"No."

"*Any* of it?"

"No. I don't want to send this one over any commercial comm channel, not even in code. Illyan may have a few deep cover agents here, but I don't know who they are or how to access them. Miles would have known. And . . ."

"And?" Bothari-Jesek raised an eyebrow.

"And I'd really like to have the cryo-chamber back first."

"To shove under the door along with the report? Quinnie, it wouldn't fit."

Quinn shrugged one defensive shoulder.

After a moment Bothari-Jesek offered, "I agree with you about not sending anything through the Jacksonian jump-courier system, though."

"Yes, from what Illyan's said, it's riddled with spies, and not just the Great Houses checking up on each other, either. There's nothing Barrayar could do to help us in the next day-cycle anyway."

"How long," Mark swallowed, "is that how long I have to go on playing Miles?"

"I don't know!" said Quinn sharply. She gulped back control of her voice. "A day, a week, two weeks—at least till we can deliver you and the cryo-chamber to ImpSec's galactic affairs HQ on Komarr. Then it will be out of my hands."

"How the hell do you think you're going to keep all this under wraps?" Mark asked scornfully. "Dozens of people know what really happened."

" 'Two can keep a secret, if one of them is dead'?"

Quinn grimaced. "I don't know. The troops will be all right, they have the discipline. The clones I can keep incommunicado. Anyway, we're all going to be bottled up on this ship till we reach Komarr. Later . . . I'll deal with later."

"I want to see my . . . the . . . my clones. What you've done with them," Mark demanded suddenly.

Quinn looked like she was about to explode, but Bothari-Jesek cut in, "I'll take him down, Quinnie. I want to check on my passengers too."

"Well . . . as long as you escort him back to his cabin when you're done. And put a guard on his door. We can't have him wandering around the ship."

"Will do." Bothari-Jesek chivvied him out quickly, before Quinn decided to have him bound and gagged as well.

The clones had been housed in three hastily-cleared freight storage chambers aboard the *Peregrine*, two assigned to the boys and one to the girls. Mark ducked through a door behind Bothari-Jesek into one of the boys' chambers, and looked around. Three rows of bedrolls, which must have been podded over from the *Ariel*, filled the floor space. A self-contained field latrine was strapped into one corner, and a field shower hastily connected in the other, to keep any need for the clones to move about the ship to a minimum. Half jail, half refugee camp, crowded—as he walked down a row between bedrolls the boys glowered up at him with the hollow faces of prisoners.

I freed you all, dammit. Don't you know I freed you?

It had been a rough rescue, true. During that hideous night of siege the Dendarii had been liberal with the most dire threats, to keep their charges under control. Some clones now slept, exhausted. The stunned ones were waking up sick and disoriented; a female Dendarii medic moved among them administering synergine and soothing words. Things were . . . under control. Suppressed. Silent. Not jubilant; not grateful. *If they believed our threats, why don't they believe our promises?* Even the active boys who had cooperated enthusiastically in the excitement of siege and firefight now stared at him with renewed doubt.

The blond boy was one of them. Mark stopped by his bedroll, and hunkered down. Bothari-Jesek waited, watching them. "All this," Mark waved vaguely at the chamber, "is temporary, you know. It's going to get better later. We're going to get you out of here."

The boy, propped on his elbow, shrank slightly away. He chewed on his lip. "Which one are you?" he asked suspiciously.

The live one, he thought of answering, but did not dare in front of Bothari-Jesek. She might mistake it for flippancy. "It doesn't matter. We're going to get you out of here just the same." Truth or not? He had no control over the Dendarii now, still less over the Barrayarans, if indeed as Quinn threatened that was their new destination. Dreary depression washed over him as he stood and followed Bothari-Jesek into the girls' chamber across the corridor.

The physical set-up was identical, with bedrolls and sanitary facilities, though with only fifteen girls it was slightly less crowded. A Dendarii was passing out a stack of packaged meals, which lent the chamber a moment of positive activity and interest. The trooper was Sergeant Taura, unmistakable even from the back and dressed in clean grey ship-knits and friction-slippers. She sat cross-legged to reduce her intimidating height. The girls, overcoming fear, crept up to her and even touched her with apparent fascination. Of all the Dendarii Taura had never, even in the most frantic moments, addressed the clones with anything but politely-worded requests. She now had all the air of a fairy-tale heroine trying to make pets of wild animals.

And succeeding. As Mark came up, two of the clone girls actually skittered around behind the seated sergeant, to peek at him over the protection of her broad shoulders. Taura frowned at him, and looked at Bothari-Jesek, who returned a short nod, *It's all right. He's with me.*

"S-surprised to see you here, Sergeant," Mark managed.

"I volunteered to baby-sit," rumbled Taura. "I didn't want anybody bothering them."

"Is . . . that likely to be a problem?" Fifteen beautiful virgins . . . well, maybe. *Sixteen, counting yourself*, came a tiny jeer from the back of his brain.

"Not now," said Bothari-Jesek firmly.

"Good," he said faintly.

He waffled up the row of mats for a moment. It was all as comfortable and secure as possible, under the circumstances, he supposed. He found the short platinum blonde clone asleep on her side, the soft masses of her body sculpture spilling out of her pink tunic. Embarrassed by his own arrested eye, he knelt and drew her cover up to her chin. His hand, half-unwilled, stole a touch of her fine hair in passing. Guiltily, he glanced up at Taura. "Has she had a dose of synergine?"

"Yes. We're letting her sleep it off. She should feel all right when she wakes up."

He took one of the sealed meal trays and set it down by the blonde's head, for when she did wake. Her breathing was slow and steady. There seemed not much else he could do for her. He looked up to catch the Eurasian girl watching him with knowing, malicious eyes, and he turned hastily away.

Bothari-Jesek completed her inspection and exited, and he followed in her trail. She paused to speak with the stunner-armed guard in the corridor.

"—wide dispersal," she was saying. "Shoot first and ask questions later. They're all young and healthy, you don't have to worry about hidden heart conditions with this lot, I don't think. But I doubt they'll give you much trouble."

"With one exception," Mark put in. "There's this dark-haired girl, slim, very striking—she appears to have undergone some special mental conditioning. Not . . . quite sane. Watch out for her."

"Yes, sir," said the trooper automatically, then caught himself, glancing at Bothari-Jesek, ". . . uh . . ."

"Sergeant Taura confirms the report on that one," said Bothari-Jesek. "Anyway, I don't want any of them loose on my ship. They're totally untrained. Their ignorance could be as dangerous as any hostility. This is not an ornamental guard post. Stay awake."

They exchanged parting salutes. The trooper, overcoming reflex, managed not to include Mark in his directed courtesy. Mark trotted after Bothari-Jesek's long stride.

"So," she said after a moment, "does our treatment of your clones meet with your approval?" He could not quite tell if her tone was ironic.

"It's as good as anyone could do for them, for now." He bit his tongue, but the too self-revealing outburst escaped it anyway. "Dammit, it's not fair!"

Bothari-Jesek's brows rose, as she paced along the corridor. "What's not fair?"

"I *saved* these kids—or we did, you did—and they act like we're some kind of villains, kidnappers, monsters. They're not happy at all."

"Perhaps . . . it will have to be enough for you just to have saved them. To demand that they be happy about it too may exceed your mandate . . . little hero." Her tone was unmistakably ironic now, though oddly devoid of scorn.

"You'd think there'd be a little gratitude. Belief. Acknowledgement. Something."

"Trust?" she said in a quiet voice.

"Yes, trust! At least from some of them. Can't any of them tell we're on the level?"

"They've been rather traumatized. I wouldn't expect too much if I were you, till they get a chance to see more evidence." She paused, in speech and stride, and swung to face him. "But if you ever figure it out—figure out how to make an ignorant, traumatized, paranoid stupid kid trust you—tell Miles. He urgently wants to know."

Mark stood, nonplussed. "Was that . . . directed to me?" he demanded, dry-mouthed.

She glanced over his head, around the empty corridor, and smiled a bitter, maddening smile. "You're home." She nodded pointedly toward his cabin door. "Stay there."

He slept at last, for a long time, though when Quinn came to wake him it seemed like not long enough. Mark wasn't sure if Quinn had slept at all, though she had finally cleaned up and changed back into her officer's undress greys. He'd been starting to imagine her planning to wear the bloodstained fatigues till they retrieved the cryo-chamber, as some sort of vow. Even without the fatigues she radiated an unsettling edginess, red-eyed and strained.

"Come on," she growled. "I need you to talk to Fell again. He's been giving me a run-around. I'm starting to wonder if he could be in collusion with Bharaputra. I don't understand, it doesn't add up."

She hauled him off to the tac room again, though this time she did not rely on the ear-bug, but stood aggressively at his elbow. To the outside eye, she'd ranged herself as bodyguard and chief assistant; all Mark could think of was how conveniently placed she was to grab him by the hair and slit his throat.

Captain Bothari-Jesek sat in, occupying a spare station chair as before, watching quietly. She eyed Quinn's frazzled demeanor with a look of concern, but said nothing.

When Fell's face appeared above the vid plate again, its pinkness was decidedly more irate than jolly. "Admiral Naismith, I told Captain Quinn that when I had firm information, *I* would contact *you*."

"Baron, Captain Quinn . . . serves me. Please forgive any importunity on her part. She only, ah, faithfully reflects my own anxieties." Miles's typical overflowing vocabulary filled his mouth like flour. Quinn's fingers bit into his shoulder, silent painful warning that he had better not let his invention carry him too far. "What, shall we say, less-than-firm information can you give us?"

Fell settled back, frowning but placated. "To put it bluntly, the Bharaputrans say they cannot find your cryo-chamber."

"It has to be there," hissed Quinn.

"Now, now, Quinnie." Mark patted her hand. It clamped like a vise. Her nostrils flared murderously, but she achieved a faint false smile for the holovid. Mark turned back to Fell. "Baron—in your best judgment—are the Bharaputrans lying?"

"I don't think so."

"Do you have some independent corroboration for your opinion? Agents on site, or anything of the sort?"

The Baron's lips twisted. "Really, Admiral, I cannot say."

Naturally not. He rubbed his face, a Naismith-thoughtful gesture. "Can you say anything specific about what the Bharaputrans are doing?"

"They are in fact turning their medical complex inside out right now. All the employees, and all the security forces they brought in to contain your raid, have been engaged in the search."

"Could it be an elaborate charade, to mislead us?"

The Baron paused. "No," he said flatly at last. "They're really scrambling. On all levels. Are you aware . . ." he took a decisive breath, "of what your kidnapping of Baron Bharaputra, if it should prove more than a brief interlude, could do to the balance of power among the Great Houses of Jackson's Whole?"

"No, what?"

The Baron's chin went up, and he checked Mark sharply for signs of sarcasm. The vertical lines between his eyes deepened, but he answered seriously. "You should realize, the value of your hostage may go down with time. No power-vacuum at the top of a Great House, or even a House Minor, can last long. There are always factions of younger men waiting, perhaps in secret, to rush in and fill it. Even supposing Lotus manages to get Vasa Luigi's chief loyalist lieutenant to fill and retain his place—as time goes on, it can only dawn on him that the return of his master will involve demotion as well as reward. Think of a Great House as the hydra of mythology. Chop off its head, and seven more arise on the stump of neck—and begin biting each other. Eventually, only one will survive. In the meantime, the House is weakened, and all its old alliances and deals are thrown into doubt. The turmoil expands in a widening ring to associate Houses . . . such abrupt changes are not welcomed, here. Not by anyone." Least of all by Baron Fell himself, Mark gathered.

"Except maybe by your younger colleagues," Mark suggested.

A wave of Fell's hand dismissed the concerns of his younger colleagues. If they wanted power, the wave implied, let them plot and scramble and kill for it as he had.

"Well, I have no desire to keep Baron Bharaputra till he grows old and moldy," said Mark. "I have no personal use for him at all, out of this context. Please urge House Bharaputra to speed in finding my brother, eh?"

"They need no urging." Fell regarded him coldly. "Be aware, Admiral, if this . . . situation is not brought to a satisfactory conclusion quickly, Fell Station will not be able to harbor you."

"Uh . . . define quickly."

"Very soon. Within another day-cycle."

Fell Station surely had enough force to evict the two small Dendarii ships whenever it willed. Or worse than evict. "Understood. Uh . . . what about unimpeded passage out at Jumppoint Five?" If things did not go well . . .

"That . . . you may have to deal for separately."

"Deal how?"

"If you still had your hostage . . . I would not desire that you carry Vasa Luigi out of Jacksonian local space. And I am positioned to see that you do not."

Quinn's fist slammed down beside the vid plate. "No!" she cried. "No way! Baron Bharaputra is the only card we have to get muh, get the cryo-chamber back. We will not give him up!"

Fell recoiled slightly. "Captain!" he reproved.

"We *will* take him with us if we're forced out," Quinn threatened, "and you can all hang out to dry. Or he can walk back from Jumppoint Five without a pressure suit. If we don't get that cryo-chamber—well, we have better allies than you. And with fewer inhibitions. They won't care about your profits, or your deals, or your balances. The only question they'll be asking is whether to start at the north pole, and burn down, or at the south pole, and burn up!"

Fell grimaced angrily. "Don't be absurd, Captain Quinn. You speak of a planetary force."

Quinn leaned into the vid pick-up and snarled, "Baron, I speak of a *multi*-planetary force!"

Bothari-Jesek, startled, made an urgent throat-slicing gesture across her neck, *Cut it, Quinn!*

Fell's eyes went hard and bright as glass glints. "You're bluffing," he said at last.

"I am not. You'd best believe I am not!"

"No one would do all that for one man. Still less for one corpse."

Quinn hesitated. Mark's hand closed on hers upon his shoulder and squeezed hard to say, *Control yourself, dammit*. She was on the verge of giving away what she'd practically threatened him with death not to reveal. "You may be right, Baron," she said finally. "You'd better pray you're right."

After a long moment of silence, Fell inquired mildly, "And just who is this uninhibited ally of yours, Admiral?"

After an equally long pause, Mark looked up and said sweetly, "Captain Quinn was bluffing, Baron."

Fell's lips drew back in an extremely dry smile. "All Cretans are liars," he said softly. His hand moved to cut the comm; his image faded in the usual haze of sparkles. This time it was his cold smile that seemed to linger, bodiless.

"Good job, Quinn," Mark snarled into the silence. "You've just let Baron Fell know how much he could really get for that cryo-chamber. And maybe even who from. Now we have two enemies."

Quinn was breathing hard, as though she'd been running. "He's not our enemy; he's not our friend. Fell serves Fell. Remember that, 'cause he will."

"But was Fell lying, or was he merely passing on House Bharaputra's lies?" Bothari-Jesek asked slowly. "What independent line of profit could Fell possibly have on all this?"

"Or are they both lying?" said Quinn.

"What if neither of them are?" asked Mark in irritation. "Have you thought of that? Remember what Norwood—"

A comm beeper interrupted him. Quinn leaned on her hands on the comconsole to listen.

"Quinn, this is Bel. That contact I found agrees to meet us at the *Ariel's* docking bay. If you want to be in on the interrogation, you need to pod over now."

"Yes, right, I'll be there, Quinn out." She turned, haggard, and started for the door. "Elena, see that *he*," a jerk of her thumb, "is confined to quarters."

"Yeah, well, after you talk with whatever Bel dragged in, get yourself some rest, huh, Quinnie? You're unstrung. You almost lost it back there."

Quinn's ambiguous parting wave acknowledged the truth of this, without making any promises. As Quinn exited, Bothari-Jesek turned to her station console, to order up a personnel pod to be ready for Quinn by the time she arrived at the hatch.

Mark rose and wandered around the tactics room, his hands thrust carefully into his pockets. A dozen real-time and holo-schematic display consoles sat dark and still; communication and encoding systems lay silent. He pictured the tactics nerve center fully staffed, alive and bright and chaotic, heading into battle. He imagined enemy fire peeling the ship open like a meal tray, all that life smashed and burned and spilled into the hard radiation and vacuum of space. Fire from House Fell's station at Jumppoint Five, say, as the *Peregrine* fought for escape. He shuddered, nauseated.

He paused before the sealed door to the briefing chamber. Bothari-Jesek was now engaged in some other communication, some decision having to do with the security of their Fell Station moorings. Curious, he laid his palm upon the lock-pad. Somewhat to his surprise, the door slid demurely open. Somebody had some re-programming to do, if all top-secured Dendarii facilities were keyed to admit a dead man's palm print. A lot of re-programming—Miles doubtless had it fixed so he could just waft right through anywhere in the fleet. That would be his style.

Bothari-Jesek glanced up, but said nothing. Taking that as tacit permission, Mark walked into the briefing room, and circled the table. Lights came up for him as he paced. Thorne's words, spoken here, echoed in his head. *Norwood said, The Admiral will get out of here even if we don't.* How carefully had the Dendarii examined their recordings of the drop mission? Surely someone had been over them all several times by now. What could he possibly see that they hadn't? They knew their people, their equipment. *But I know the medical complex. I know Jackson's Whole.*

He wondered how far his palm would take him. He slipped into Quinn's station chair; sure enough, files bloomed for him, opened at his touch as no woman ever had. He found the downloaded records of the drop mission. Norwood's data was lost, but Tonkin had been with him part of the time. What had Tonkin seen? Not colored lines on the map, but real-time, real-eye, real-ear? Was there such a record? The command helmet had kept such, he knew, if trooper-helmets did too then—ah, ha. Tonkin's visuals and audio came up on the console before his fascinated eyes.

Trying to follow them gave him an almost instant headache. This was no ballasted and gimballed vid pick-up, no steady pan, but rather the jerky, snatching glances of real head movements. He slowed the replay to watch himself in the lift-tube foyer, a short, agitated fellow in grey camouflage, glittering eyes in a set face. *Do I really look like that?* The deformities of his body were not so apparent as he'd imagined, under the loose uniform.

He sat behind Tonkin's eyes and walked with him through the hurried maze of Bharaputra's buildings, tunnels, and corridors, all the way to the last firefight at the end. Thorne had quoted Norwood correctly; it was right there on the vid. Though he'd been wrong on the time; Norwood was gone eleven minutes by the helmet's unsubjective clock. Norwood's flushed face reappeared,panting, the urgent laugh sounded—and, moments later, the grenade-strike, the explosion—almost ducking, Mark hastily shut off the vid, and glanced down at himself as if half-expecting to be branded with another mortal splattering of blood and brains.

If there's any clue, it has to be earlier. He started the program again from the parting in the foyer. The third time through, he slowed it down and took it step by step, examining each. The patient, finicky, self-forgetful absorption was almost pleasurable. Tiny details—you could lose yourself in tiny details, an anesthetic for brain-pain.

"*Got you,*" he whispered. It had flashed past so fast as to be subliminal, if you were running the vid in real-time. The briefest glimpse of a sign on the wall, an arrow on a cross-corridor labeled *Shipping and Receiving.*

He looked up to find Bothari-Jesek watching him. How long had she been sitting there? She slumped relaxed, long legs crossed at booted ankles, long fingers tented together. "What have you got?" she asked quietly.

He called up the holomap of the ghostly buildings with Norwood and Tonkin's line of march glowing inside. "Not here," he pointed, "but *there.*" He marked a complex well off-sides from the route the Dendarii had traveled with the cryo-chamber. "*That's* where Norwood went. Through that tunnel. I'm sure of it! I've seen that facility—been all over that building. Hell, I used to play hide and seek in it with my friends, till the babysitters made us stop. I can see it in my head as surely as if I had Norwood's helmet vid playing right here on the table. He took that cryo-chamber down to Shipping and Receiving, and he *shipped* it!"

Bothari-Jesek sat up. "Is that possible? He had so little time!"

"Not just possible. Easy! The packing equipment is fully automated. All he had to do was put the cryo-chamber in the casing machine and hit the keypad. The robots would even have delivered it to the loading dock. It's a busy place—receives supplies for the whole complex, ships everything from data disks to frozen body parts for transplants to genetically engineered fetuses to emergency equipment for search and rescue teams. Such as reconditioned cryo-chambers. All sorts of stuff! It operates around the clock, and it would have had to be evacuated in a hurry when our raid hit. While the packing equipment was running, Norwood could have been generating the shipping label on the computer. Slapped 'em together, gave it to the transport robot—and then, if he was as smart as I think, erased the file record. Then he ran like hell back to Tonkin."

"So the cryo-chamber is sitting packed on a loading dock downside! Wait'll I tell Quinn! I suppose we'd better tell the Bharaputrans where to look—"

"I . . ." he held up a restraining hand. "I think . . ."

She looked at him, and sank back into the station chair, eyes narrowing. "Think what?"

"It's been almost a full day since we lifted. It's been a half-day and more since we told the Bharaputrans to look for the cryo-chamber. If that cryo-chamber was still sitting on a loading dock, I think the Bharaputrans would have found it by now. The automated shipping system is *efficient*. I think the cryo-chamber already went out, maybe within the first hour. I think the Bharaputrans and Fell are telling the truth. They must be going insane right now. Not only is there no cryo-chamber down there, they haven't got a clue in hell where it went!"

Bothari-Jesek sat stiff. "Do we?" she asked. "My God. If you're right—it could be on its way *anywhere*. Freighted out from any of two dozen orbital transfer stations—it could have been *jumped* by now! Simon Illyan is going to have a stroke when we report this."

"No. Not anywhere," Mark corrected intently. "It could only have been addressed to somewhere that Medic Norwood knew. Someplace he could remember, even when he was surrounded and cut off and under fire."

She licked her lips, considering this. "Right," she said at last. "Almost anywhere. But at least we can start guessing by studying Norwood's personnel files." She sat back, and looked up at him with grave eyes. "You know, you do all right, alone in a quiet room. You're not stupid. I didn't see how you could be. You're just not the field-officer type."

"I'm not any kind of officer-type. I hate the military."

"Miles loves field work. He's addicted to adrenalin rushes."

"I hate them. I hate being afraid. I can't think when I'm scared. I freeze when people shout at me."

"Yet you *can* think. . . . How much of the time are you scared?"

"Most of it," he admitted grimly.

"Then why do you . . ." she hesitated, as if choosing her words very cautiously, "why do you keep trying to be Miles?"

"I'm not, you're making me play him!"

"I didn't mean now. I mean generally."

"I don't know what the hell you mean."

CHAPTER TEN

Twenty hours later, the two Dendarii ships undocked from Fell Station and maneuvered to boost toward Jumppoint Five. They were not alone. An escort of half a dozen House Fell security vessels paced and policed them. The Fell vessels were dedicated local space warships, lacking Necklin rods and wormhole jump capacity; the power thus saved was shunted into a formidable array of weapons and shielding. Muscle-ships.

The convoy was trailed at a discreet distance by a Bharaputran cruiser, more yacht than warship, prepared to accept the final transfer of Baron Bharaputra, as arranged, in space near Fell's Jumppoint Five station. Unfortunately, Miles's cryo-chamber was not aboard it.

Quinn had come close to a breakdown, before accepting the inevitable. Bothari-Jesek had literally backed her against the wall, at their last private conference in the briefing room.

"I won't leave Miles!" Quinn howled. "I'll space that Bharaputran bastard first!"

"Look," Bothari-Jesek hissed, Quinn's jacket bunched in her fist. If she'd been an animal, Mark thought, her ears would have been flat to her head. He huddled in a station chair and tried to make himself small. Smaller. "I don't like this any better than you do, but the situation has gone way beyond our capacity. Miles is clearly out of Bharaputran hands, heading God knows where. We need reinforcements: not warships, but trained intelligence agents. A pile of 'em. We need Illyan, and ImpSec, we need them bad, and we need them as fast as possible. It's time to cut and run. The faster we get out of here, the faster we can return."

"I *will* be back," Quinn swore.

"That'll be between you and Simon Illyan. I promise you, he'll be just as interested as we are in retrieving that cryo-chamber."

"Illyan's just a Barrayaran," Quinn sputtered for a word, "*bureaucrat*. He can't care the way we do."

"Don't bet on that," whispered Bothari-Jesek.

In the end, Bothari-Jesek, Quinn's downward duty to the rest of the Dendarii, and the logic of the situation had prevailed. And so Mark found himself dressing in officer's greys for what he earnestly prayed would be his last public appearance ever as Admiral Miles Naismith, observing the transfer of their hostage onto a House Fell shuttle. Whatever happened to Vasa Luigi after that would be up to Baron Fell. Mark could only hope it would be something unpleasant.

Bothari-Jesek came to escort Mark personally from his cabin-prison to the shuttle hatch corridor where the Fell ship was scheduled to clamp on. She looked cool as ever, if weary, and unlike Quinn she limited her critique of the fit of his uniform to a pass of her hand to straighten his collar insignia. The pocketed jacket was roomy, and came down far enough to cover and so disguise the tight bite of the trouser waistband, and the way his flesh was beginning to burgeon over the belt. He yanked the jacket down firmly, and followed the *Peregrine*'s captain through her ship.

"Why do I have to do this?" he asked her plaintively.

"It's our last chance to prove—for certain—to Vasa Luigi that you are Miles Naismith, and that . . . thing in the cryo-chamber is just a clone. Just in case the cryo-chamber didn't go off-planet, and just in case, by whatever chance, wherever it went, Bharaputra finds it again before we do."

They arrived at the shuttle hatch corridor at the same time as a couple of heavily-armed Dendarii techs, who took up station at the docking clamp controls. Baron Bharaputra appeared shortly thereafter, escorted by a wary Captain Quinn and two edgy Dendarii guards. The guards, Mark decided, were mainly ornamental. The real power, and the real threat, the heavy pieces on this chessboard, were Jumppoint Station Five and the House Fell ships that supported it. He pictured them, arrayed in space around the Dendarii ships. Check. Was Baron Bharaputra king? Mark felt like a pawn masquerading as a knight. Vasa Luigi ignored the guards, kept half an eye on Quinn the Red Queen, but mostly watched the shuttle hatch.

Quinn saluted Mark. "Admiral."

He returned the salute. "Captain." He stood at parade rest, as if overseeing his operation. Was he supposed to bandy words with the Baron? He waited for Vasa Luigi to open the conversation. The Baron merely waited, with a disturbingly controlled patience, as if he did not even perceive time the same way Mark did.

Regardless of how outgunned they were, the Dendarii were only minutes from escape. As soon as the transfer was complete, the *Peregrine* and the *Ariel* could jump, and the clones would be beyond House Bharaputra's lethal reach. That much he had accomplished, ass-backwards and screwed up beyond repair, but done. Small victories.

At last came the clanking of the shuttle hatch clamps grasping and positioning their prey, and the hiss of the flex-tube sealing. The Dendarii oversaw the dilation of the hatch portal, and stood to attention. On the other side of the portal a man dressed in House Fell green with captain's insignia, and flanked by two ornamental guards of his own, nodded sharply and identified himself and his vessel of origin.

He spotted Mark as the highest ranking officer present, and saluted. "Baron Fell's compliments, Admiral Naismith sir, and he is returning to you something you accidentally left behind."

Quinn went pale with hope; Mark could swear her heart stopped beating. The Fell captain stepped back from the hatch. But through it swung not the ardently-desired cryo-chamber on a float pallet, but a file of three men and two women, civilian-clothed, looking variously sheepish, angry, and grim. One man was limping, and supported by another.

Quinn's spies. The group of Dendarii volunteers she had attempted to slip onto Fell Station to continue the search. Quinn's face flushed red with chagrin. But she raised her chin and said clearly, "Tell Baron Fell we thank him for his care."

The Fell captain acknowledged the message with a salute and a sour smirk.

"Meet you all in debriefing, soonest," she breathed, and dismissed the unhappy mob with a nod. They clattered off. Bothari-Jesek went with them.

The Fell captain announced, "We are ready to board our passenger." Punctiliously, he did not set foot aboard the *Peregrine*, but waited. Equally punctiliously, the Dendarii guards and Quinn stood away from Baron Bharaputra, who raised his square chin and began to stride forward.

"My lord! Wait for me!"

The high cry from behind them made Mark's head snap around. The Baron's eyes too widened in surprise.

The Eurasian girl, her hair swinging, slipped out of a cross-corridor and ran forward. She held hands with the platinum blonde clone. She darted like an eel around the Dendarii guards, who had better sense than to draw weapons in this dicey moment, but not quite enough speed of reflex to catch her. The small-footed blonde was not so athletic, half out-of-balance with her other arm crossed under her breasts, and she was pulled along gasping for breath, blue eyes wide with fear.

Mark saw her, in his mind's eye, laid out on some operating table, light-crowned scalp peeled carefully back—the whine of a surgical saw cutting through bone, the slow teasing apart of living neurons in the brain stem, then at last the lifting-out of brain, like a gift, mind, memory, person, an offering to some dark god in the masked monster's gloved hands—

He tackled her around the knees. Her fine-boned hand jerked out of the dark-haired girl's grip, and she fell forward on the deck. She cried out, then just cried, and kicked at him, rocking and bucking and twisting onto her back. Terrified he would lose his clutch, he worked upward till he lay across her with his full weight. She squirmed beneath him, ineffectually; she didn't even know enough to try to knee him in the groin. "Stop. Stop, for God's sake, I don't want to hurt you," he mumbled in her ear around a mouthful of sweet-smelling hair.

The other girl meanwhile had succeeded in diving through the shuttle hatch. The House Fell guard captain was confused by her arrival, but not by the Dendarii; he'd drawn a nerve disruptor instantly, repelling the first reflexive lurch of Quinn's men. "Stop right there. Baron Bharaputra, what is this?"

"My lord!" the Eurasian girl cried. "Take me with you, please! I will be united with my lady. I will!"

"Stay on that side," the Baron advised her calmly. "They cannot touch you there."

"You try me—" began Quinn, starting forward, but the Baron raised a hand, fingers delicately crooked, neither fist nor obscenity yet somehow faintly insulting.

"Captain Quinn. Surely you do not wish to create an incident and delay your departure, do you? Clearly, this girl chooses of her own free will."

Quinn hesitated.

"No!" screamed Mark. He scrambled to his feet, hauled the blonde girl up, and jammed her into the grip of the biggest Dendarii guard. "*Hold* her." He wheeled to pass Baron Bharaputra.

"Admiral?" The Baron raised a faintly ironic brow.

"You're wearing a corpse," Mark snarled. "Don't talk to me." He staggered forward, hands out, to face the dark-haired girl across that little, dreadful, politically significant gap. "Girl . . ." he did not know her name. He did not know what to say. "Don't go. You don't have to go. They'll kill you."

Growing more certain of her security, though still positioned behind the Fell captain and well out of reach of any Dendarii lunge, she smiled triumphantly at Mark and tossed back her hair. Her eyes were alight. "I've saved my honor. All by myself. My honor is my lady. *You* have no honor. Pig! My life is an offering . . . greater than you can imagine being. I am a flower on her altar."

"You are frigging crazy, Flowerpot," Quinn opined bluntly.

Her chin rose, and her lips thinned. "Baron, come," she ordered coolly. She held out a theatric hand.

Baron Bharaputra shrugged as if to say, *What would you?*, and walked toward the hatch. No Dendarii raised a weapon; Quinn had not ordered them to. Mark had no weapon. He turned to her, anguished. "*Quinn . . .*"

She was breathing hard. "If we don't jump now, we could lose it all. *Stand still.*"

Vasa Luigi paused in the hatchway, hand on the seal, one foot still on the *Peregrine*'s deck, and turned back to face Mark. "In case you are wondering, Admiral—she is my wife's clone," he purred. He raised his right hand, licked his index finger, and touched it to Mark's forehead. It left a cool spot. Counting coup. "One for me. Forty-nine for you. If you ever dare to return here.

I promise you I'll even up that score in ways that will make your death something you'll beg for." He slipped the rest of the way through the shuttle hatch. "Hello, Captain, thank you for your patience . . ." The hatch seals closed on the rest of his greeting to his rival's, or ally's, guards.

The silence was broken only by the releasing clank of the clamps and the blonde clone's hopeless, abandoned weeping. The spot on Mark's forehead itched like ice. He rubbed at it with the back of his hand as if half-expecting it to shatter.

Friction-slippered footsteps were nearly silent, but these were heavy enough to vibrate the deck. Sergeant Taura pelted into the shuttle hatch corridor. She saw the blonde clone, and yelled over her shoulder, "Here's another one! Just two to go." Another trooper came panting in her wake.

"What happened, Taura?" sighed Quinn.

"That girl, that ringleader. The really smart one," said Taura, skidding to a halt. Her eyes checked the cross-corridors as she spoke. "She told all the girls some bullshit story about how we were a slave ship. She persuaded ten of them to try for a break-out at once. Stunner guard got three, the other seven scattered. We've recaptured four. Mostly just hiding, but I think that long-haired girl actually had a coherent plan to try to get to the personnel pods before we jumped from local space. I've put a guard on them to cut her off."

Quinn swore, bleakly. "Good thinking, Sergeant. Your cut-off must have succeeded, because she came up here. Unfortunately, she ran smack into Baron Bharaputra's exchange. She got out with him. We were able to grab the other one before she made it across." Quinn nodded at the blonde, whose weeping had choked down to snivels. "So you're only looking for one more."

"How did—" the sergeant's eyes flicked over the shuttle

hatch corridor, puzzled. "How did you let that happen, ma'am?"

Quinn's face was set in an expressionless mask. "I chose not to start a fire-fight over her."

The sergeant's big clawed hands twitched in bewilderment, but no verbal criticism of her superior escaped those outslung lips. "We'd better find the last one, then, before something worse happens."

"Carry on, Sergeant. You four, help her," Quinn gestured to her now-unemployed guards. "Report to me in the briefing room when you have them all re-secured, Taura."

Taura nodded, motioned the troopers down the various cross-corridors, and herself loped toward the nearest lift tube. Her nostrils flared; she seemed to be almost sniffing for her quarry.

Quinn turned on her heel, muttering, "I've got to get to the debriefing. Find out what happened to—"

"I'll . . . take her back to the clone quarters, Quinn," Mark volunteered, with a nod at the blonde.

Quinn looked doubtfully at him.

"Please. I want to."

She glanced at the hatch where the Eurasian girl had gone, and back at his face. He didn't know what his face looked like, but she inhaled. "You know, I've been over the drop records a couple of times, since we left Fell Station. I hadn't . . . had a chance to tell you. Did you realize, when you stepped in front of me when we were scrambling to board Kimura's drop shuttle, just what your plasma mirror field power was down to?"

"No. I mean, I knew I'd taken a lot of hits, in the tunnels."

"One hit. If it had absorbed one more hit, it would have failed. Two more hits and you'd have fried."

"Oh."

She frowned at him, as if still trying to decide whether

to credit him with courage or simply with stupidity. "Well. I thought it was interesting. Something you'd want to know." She hesitated longer. "My power pack was down to zero. So if you're really comparing scores with Baron Bharaputra, you can raise yours back to fifty."

He didn't know what she expected him to say. At last Quinn sighed, "All right. You can escort her. If it'll make you feel better." She strode off toward the debriefing, her own face very anxious.

He turned, and took the blonde by the arm, very gently; she flinched, blinking through big tear-sheened blue eyes. Even though he knew very well—none better—how intentionally her features and body were sculptured and designed, the effect was still overwhelming: beauty and innocence, sexuality and fear mixed in an intoxicating draught. She looked a ripe twenty, at fresh physical peak, a perfect match to his own age. And only a few centimeters taller than himself. She might have been designed to be the heroine in his drama, except that his life had dissolved into some sub-heroic puddle, chaotic and beyond control. No rewards, only more punishments.

"What's your name?" he asked with false brightness.

She looked at him suspiciously. "Maree."

Clones had no surnames. "That's pretty. Come on, Maree. I'll take you back to your, uh, dormitory. You'll feel better, when you're back with your friends."

She perforce began to walk with him.

"Sergeant Taura is all right, you know. She really wants to take care of you. You just scared her, running off like that. She was worried you'd get hurt. You're not really afraid of the sergeant, are you?"

Her lovely lips pressed closed in confusion. "I'm . . . not sure." Her walk was a dainty, swaying thing, though her steps made her breasts wobble most distractingly, half-bagged in the pink tunic. She ought to be offered reduction treatment, though he was not sure such was in the *Peregrine*'s ship's surgeon's range of expertise. And if her somatic experiences at Bharaputra's were anything like his had been, she was probably sick of surgery right now. He certainly had been, after all the bodily distortions they'd laid on him.

"We're not a slave ship," he began again earnestly. "We're taking you—" The news that their destination was the Barrayaran Empire might not be so reassuring, at that. "Our first stop will probably be Komarr. But you might not have to stay there." He had no power to make promises about her ultimate destination. None. One prisoner could not rescue another.

She coughed, and rubbed her eyes.

"Are you . . . all right?"

"I want a drink of water." Her voice was hoarse from the running and the crying.

"I'll get you one," he promised. His own cabin was just a corridor away; he led her there.

The door hissed open at the touch of his palm upon the pad."Come in. I never had a chance to talk with you. Maybe if I had . . . that girl wouldn't have fooled you." He guided her within, and settled her on the bed. She was trembling slightly. So was he.

"Did she fool you?"

"I . . . don't know, Admiral."

He snorted bitterly. "I'm not the Admiral. I'm a clone, like you. I was raised at Bharaputra's, one floor down from where you live. Lived." He went to his washroom, drew a cup of water, and carried it to her. He had half an impulse to offer it to her on his knees. She had to be made to—"I have to make you understand. Understand who you are, what's happened to you. So you won't be fooled again. You have a lot to learn, for your own protection." Indeed—in *that* body. "You'll have to go to school."

She swallowed water. "Don't want to go to school," she said, muffled into the cup.

"Didn't the Bharaputrans ever let you into the virtual learning programs? When I was there, it was the best part. Better even than the games. Though I liked the games, of course. Did you play Zylec?"

She nodded.

"That was fun. But the history, the astrography shows—the virtual instructor was the funniest program. A white-haired old geezer in Twentieth-century clothes, this jacket with patches on the elbows—I always wondered if he was based on a real person, or was a composite."

"I never saw them."

"What did you do all day?"

"We talked among ourselves. We did our hair. Swam. The proctors made us do calisthenics every day—"

"Us, too."

"—till they did this to me." She touched a breast. "Then they only made me swim."

He could see the logic of that. "Your last body-sculpture was pretty recent, I take it."

"About a month ago." She paused. "You really don't . . . think my mother was coming for me?"

"I'm sorry. You don't have a mother. Neither do I. What was coming for you . . . was a horror. Almost beyond imagining."Except he could imagine it all too vividly.

She frowned at him, obviously reluctant to part with her beloved dream-future. "We're all beautiful. If you're really a clone, why aren't you?"

"I'm glad to see you're beginning to think," he said carefully. "My body was sculpted to match my progenitor's. He was crippled."

"But if it's true—about the brain transplants—why not you?"

"I was . . . part of another plot. My purchasers took me away whole. It was only later that I learned all the truth, for sure, about Bharaputra's." He sat beside her on the bed. The smell of her—had they genetically engineered some subtle perfume into her skin? It was intoxicating. The memory of her soft body, squirming under his on the hatch corridor deck, perturbed him. He could have dissolved into it. . . . "I had friends—don't you?"

She nodded mutely.

"By the time I could do anything for them—long before I could do anything for them—they were gone. All killed. So I rescued you instead."

She stared doubtfully at him. He could not tell what she was thinking.

The cabin wavered, and a flash of nausea that had nothing to do with suppressed eroticism twisted his stomach.

"What was that?" Maree gasped, her eyes widening. Unconsciously, she grasped his hand. His hand burned at her touch.

"It's all right. It's more than all right. That was your first wormhole jump." From his vantage of, well, several wormhole jumps, he made his tone heartily reassuring. "We're away. The Jacksonians can't get us now." *Much* better than the double-cross he'd been half-anticipating, in some reserved part of his mind, from Baron Fell's forces the moment he had Vasa Luigi hostage in his own fat hands. Not the roar and rock of enemy fire. Just a nice little tame jump. "You're safe. We're all safe now." He thought of the mad Eurasian girl. *Almost all.*

He so wanted Maree to believe. The Dendarii, the Barrayarans—he'd scarcely expected them to understand. But this girl—if only he could shine in her eyes. He wanted no reward but a kiss. He swallowed. *You sure it's only a kiss you want?* There was an uncomfortable hot knot growing in his belly, beneath that ghastly constricted waistband. An embarrassing stiffening in his loins. Maybe she wouldn't notice. Understand. Judge.

"Will you . . . kiss me?" he asked humbly, very dry-mouthed. He took the cup from her, and tossed back the last trickle of water. It was not enough to unlock the tension in his throat.

"Why?" she asked, brow wrinkling.

"For . . . pretend."

That was an appeal she understood. She blinked, but, willingly enough, leaned forward and touched her lips to his. Her tunic shifted. . . .

"Oh," he breathed. His hand went round her neck, and stopped its retreat. "Please, again . . ." He drew her face to his. She neither resisted nor responded, but her mouth was amazing nonetheless. *I want, I want* . . . It couldn't hurt to touch her, just to touch her. Her hands went around his neck, automatically. He could feel each cool finger, tipped by a tiny bite of nail. Her lips parted. He melted. His head was pounding. Hot, he shrugged off his jacket.

Stop. Stop now, dammit. But she *should* have been his heroine. Miles had a damned harem full of them, he was certain. Might she let him . . . do more than kiss her? Not penetration, definitely not. Nothing to hurt her, nothing invasive. A rub between those vast breasts could not hurt her, though it would doubtless bewilder her. He might bury himself in that soft flesh and find release as effectively, more effectively, than between her thighs. She might think he was crazy, but it wouldn't hurt her. His mouth sought hers again, hungrily. He touched her skin. *More.* He slipped her tunic down off her shoulders, freeing her body to his starving hand. Her skin was velvet soft. His other hand, shaking, dove to release the strangling-tight waistband of his trousers. That was a relief. He was dreadfully, excruciatingly aroused. But he would not touch her below the waist, no. . . .

He rolled her backwards on the bed, pinning her, kissing frantically down her body. She emitted a startled gasp. His breath deepened, then, suddenly, stopped. A spasm reached deep into his lungs, as if all his bronchia had constricted at once with a snap like a trap closing.

No! Not again! It was happening again, just like the time he'd tried last year—

He rolled off her, icy sweat breaking out all over his body. He fought his locked throat. He managed one asthmatic, shuddering indrawn breath. The flashbacks of memory were almost hallucinatory in their clarity.

Galen's angry shouting. Lars and Mok, pinning him at Galen's command, pulling off his clothes, as if the beating he'd just taken at their hands was not punishment enough. They'd sent the girl away before they'd started; she'd run like a rabbit. He spat salt-and-iron blood. The shock-stick pointing, touching, there, *there*, pop and crackle. Galen going even more red-faced, accusing him of treason, worse, raving on about Aral Vorkosigan's alleged sexual proclivities, turning up the power far too high. "Flip him." Knotting terror deep in his gut, the visceral memory of pain, humiliation, burning and cramps, a weird short-circuited arousal and horribly shameful release despite it all, the stink of searing flesh. . . .

He pushed back the visions, and almost passed out before he managed to inhale and exhale one more time. Somehow he was sitting not on the bed but on the floor beside it, arms and legs spasmodically drawn up. The astonished blonde girl crouched half-naked on the rumpled mattress, staring down at him. "What's the matter with you? Why did you stop? Are you dying?"

No, just wishing I were. It wasn't *fair*. He knew exactly where this conditioned reflex came from. It wasn't a memory buried in his subconscious, more's the pity, nor from some distant, blurred childhood. It was barely four years ago. Wasn't that sort of clear insight supposed to free one from such demons of the past? Was he going to go into self-induced spasms every time he tried to have sex with a real girl? Or was it just the extreme tension of the occasion? If ever the situation was less tense, less conscience-thwarted, if ever he really had time to make love instead of a hasty, sweaty scramble, then maybe he might overcome memory and madness—*or maybe I won't . . .* he fought for another shuddering inhalation. Another. His lungs began to work again. Was he really in danger of choking to death? Presumably once he actually passed out his autonomic nervous system would take over again.

His cabin door slid open. Taura and Bothari-Jesek stood silhouetted in the aperture, peering into the dimness. What they saw made Bothari-Jesek swear, and Sergeant Taura shoulder forward.

Now, he wanted to pass out *now*. But his single-minded demon did not cooperate. He continued to breathe, curled up with his trousers around his knees.

"What are you doing?" Sergeant Taura growled. A dangerous, truly wolflike timbre; her fangs gleamed at the corners of her mouth in the soft light. He'd seen her tear men's throats out with one hand.

The little clone sat up on her knees on the bed, looking terribly worried, her hands as usual trying to cover and support her most notable features, as usual only drawing more attention to them. "I only asked for a drink of water," she whimpered. "I'm sorry."

Sergeant Taura hastily dropped her eight-foot height to one knee and turned out her palms, to indicate to the girl that she wasn't angry with *her*. Mark wasn't sure if Maree caught that subtlety.

"Then what happened?" Bothari-Jesek asked sternly.

"He made me kiss him."

Bothari-Jesek's eye raked his huddled disarray, and

glinted furiously. She was stiff and tense as a drawn bow. She wheeled to face him. Her voice went very low. "Did you just try to rape her?"

"No! I don't know. I only—"

Sergeant Taura rose, grasped him by the shirt and some skin, pulled him to his feet and beyond, and pinned him against the nearest wall. The floor was a meter beyond his stretching toes. "Answer straight, damn you," the sergeant snarled.

He closed his eyes, and took a deep breath. Not for any threat from Miles's women, no. Not for them. But for the second half of Galen's humiliation of him, in its own way a more excruciating rape than the first. When Lars and Mok, alarmed, had finally persuaded Galen to stop, Mark had been in shock so deep as to be skirting cardiac arrest. Galen had been forced to take his valuable clone to his pet physician in the middle of the night, the one he'd somehow strong-armed into supplying him with the drugs and hormones to keep Mark's body growth on track, matching Miles's. Galen had explained the burns by telling the physician that Mark had been secretly masturbating with the shock-stick, accidentally powered it up, and been unable to turn it off for the muscle spasms it caused, till his screams brought help. The doctor had actually barked a shocked laugh. Thin-voiced, Mark had concurred, too afraid to gainsay Galen even when he was alone with the physician. Yet the doctor saw his bruises, must have known there was more to the story. But said nothing. Did nothing. It was his own weak concurrence that he regretted most, in hindsight, the black laugh that burned the deepest. He could not, would not, let Maree exit bearing any such burden of proof.

In short, blunt phrases, he described exactly what he had just tried to do. It all came out sounding terribly ugly, though it had been her beauty that had overwhelmed him. He kept his eyes shut. He did not mention his panic attack, or try to explain Galen. He writhed inside, but spoke flat truth. Slowly, as he spoke, the wall bumped up his spine till his feet were on the deck again. The pressure on his shirt released, and he dared to open his eyes.

He almost closed them again, scorched by the open contempt in Bothari-Jesek's face. He'd done it now. She who had been almost sympathetic, almost kind, almost his only friend here, stood rigidly enraged, and he knew he had alienated the one person who might have spoken for him. It hurt, a killing hurt, to have so little and then lose it.

"When Taura reported she was one clone short," Bothari-Jesek bit out, "Quinn said you'd insisted on taking her. Now we know why."

"*No*. I didn't intend . . . anything. She really only wanted a drink of water." He pointed to the cup, lying on its side on the deck.

Taura turned her back on him, and knelt on one knee by the bed, and addressed the blonde in a deliberately gentle voice. "Are you hurt?"

"I'm all right," she quavered. She pulled her tunic back up over her shoulders with a shrug. "But that man was real sick." She stared at him in puzzled concern.

"Obviously," muttered Bothari-Jesek. Her chin went up, and her eyes nailed Mark, still clinging to the wall. "You're confined to quarters, mister. I'm putting the guard back on your door. Don't even try to come out."

I won't, I won't.

They marched Maree away. The door seals hissed closed like a falling guillotine blade. He rolled onto his narrow bed, shaking.

Two weeks to Komarr. He very seriously wished he were dead.

CHAPTER ELEVEN

Mark spent the first three days of his solitary confinement lying in a depressed huddle. He had meant his heroic mission to save lives, not destroy them. He added up the body count, one by one. The shuttle pilot. Phillipi. Norwood. Kimura's trooper. And the eight seriously wounded. All those people hadn't had names, back when he had first been planning this. And all the anonymous Bharaputrans, too. The average Jacksonian security guard was just a joe scrambling for a living. He wondered bleakly if any of the dead Bharaputrans were people he had once met or joked with when he'd lived in the clone creche. As ever, the little people were ground up like meat, while those with enough power to really be held responsible escaped, walking out free like Baron Bharaputra.

Did the lives of forty-nine clones outweigh four dead Dendarii? The Dendarii did not seem to think so. *Those people were not volunteers. You tricked them to their deaths.*

He was shaken by an unwelcome insight. Lives did not add as integers. They added as infinities.

I didn't mean it to come out this way.

And the clones. The blonde girl. He of all men knew she was not the mature woman her general physique and particular augmentations so stunningly advertised her as being. The sixty-year-old brain which had been planning to move in doubtless would have known how to handle such a body. But Mark had seen her so clearly, in his mind, that ten-year-old on the inside. He hadn't wanted to hurt or frighten her, yet he'd managed to do both. He'd wanted to please her, make her face light. *The way they all lit up for Miles?*, the internal voice mocked.

None of the clones could possibly respond as he so ached to have them do. He must let that fantasy go. Ten years from now, twenty years from now, they might thank him for their lives. Or not. *I did all I could. I'm sorry.*

Somewhere around the second day he became obsessed with the thought of himself as brain-transplant bait for Miles. Oddly enough, or perhaps logically enough, he did not fear it from Miles. But Miles was hardly in a position to veto the plan. What if it occurred to someone that it would be easier to transplant Miles's brain into Mark's warm and living body than to attempt the tedious repair of that gaping mortal chest wound, and all the cryo-trauma on top of it? It was so frightening a possibility that he half-wanted to volunteer, just to get it over with.

The only thing that kept him from total gibbering breakdown was the reflection that with the cryo-chamber lost, the threat was moot. Until it was found again. In the dark of his cabin, his head buried in his pillow, it came to him that the face he'd most desired to see transformed with respect for him by his daring clone-rescue was Miles's.

You've rather eliminated that possibility, haven't you?

The only surcease from his mental treadmill came with food, and sleep. Forcing down an entire field-ration tray left him blood-stunned enough to actually doze, in inadequate snatches. Desiring unconsciousness above all things, he cajoled the glowering Dendarii who shoved the trays through his door three times a day to bring him extras. Since the Dendarii apparently did not regard their disposable-container field rations as treats, they were willing enough to do so.

Another Dendarii brought, and shoved through the door, a selection of Miles's clean clothing from the stores on the *Ariel*. This time all the insignia were carefully removed. On the third day he gave up even attempting to fasten Naismith's uniform trousers, and switched to loose ship knits. At this point the inspiration struck him.

They can't make me play Miles if I don't look like Miles.

After that, things grew a little foggy, in his head. One of the Dendarii became so irritated by his repeated requests for extra rations that he lugged in a whole case, dumped it in a corner, and told Mark roughly not to pester him again. Mark was left alone with his self-rescue and cunning calculation. He had heard of prisoners tunneling out of their cells with a spoon; might not he?

Still, loony as it was, and on some level he knew that it was, it gave his life a focus. From too much time, endless hours on the multi-jump boost through to Komarr, suddenly there seemed to be not enough. He read the nutrition labels. If he maintained maximum inactivity, a single tray provided all the daily fuel he required. Everything he consumed after that must be converted directly into Not-Miles. Every four trays ought to produce a kilo of extra body mass, if he had the numbers right. Too bad they were all the same menu. . . .

There were scarcely enough days to make the project work. Still, on his body, any extra kilos had no place to hide. Toward the end, panicked at the thought of time running out, he ate continuously, till the sheer gasping pain forced him to stop, thus combining pleasure, rebellion, and punishment into one weirdly satisfying experience.

Quinn entered without knocking, flipping up the lights with brutal efficiency from pitch-dark to full illumination.

"Agh." Mark recoiled, and held his hands over his eyes. Ripped from his uncomfortable doze, he rolled over in bed. He blinked at the chrono on the wall. Quinn had come for him a half day-cycle earlier than he'd expected. The Dendarii ships must have been putting on maximum accelerations, if this meant they were about to arrive in Komarr orbit. *Oh, help.*

"Get up," said Quinn. She wrinkled her nose. "Get washed. Put on this uniform." She laid something forest-green with gold gleams across the foot of the bed. From her general air he'd have expected her to fling things; from the reverent care she bestowed, Mark deduced the uniform must be one of Miles's.

"I'll get up," said Mark. "And I'll get washed. But I won't put on the uniform, or any uniform."

"You'll do as you're told, mister."

"That's a Barrayaran officer's uniform. It represents real power, and they guard it accordingly. They *hang* people who wear fake uniforms." He tossed off the covers and sat up. He was a little dizzy.

"My *gods*," said Quinn in a choked voice. "What have you done to yourself?"

"I suppose," he allowed, "you can still try to stuff me into the uniform. But you might want to consider the effect." He staggered to the washroom.

While washing and depiliating, he inventoried the results of his escape attempt. There just hadn't been enough time. True, he'd regained the kilos he'd had to lose to play Admiral Naismith at Escobar, plus maybe a slight bonus, and in a mere fourteen days instead of the year it had taken them to creep on in the first place. A hint of a double chin. His torso was notably thickened, though, his abdomen—he moved carefully—achingly distended. *Not enough, not enough to be safe yet.*

Quinn being Quinn, she had to convince herself, and she tried the Barrayaran uniform on him anyway. He made sure to slump. The effect was . . . very unmilitary. She gave up, snarling, and let him dress himself. He chose clean ship-knit pants, soft friction-slippers, and a loose Barrayaran civilian-style tunic of Miles's with big sleeves and an embroidered sash. It took him a moment of careful consideration to decide whether it would annoy Quinn more to see the sash positioned across his rounding belly, equatorially, or under the bulge like a sling. Judging from the lemon-sucking look on her face, under it was, and he left it that way.

She sensed his fey mood. "Enjoying yourself?" she inquired sarcastically.

"It's the last fun I'll get today. Isn't it?"

Her hand opened in dry acquiescence.

"Where are you taking me? For that matter, where are we?"

"Komarr orbit. We are about to pod over, secretly, to one of the Barrayaran military space stations. There we are going to have a very private meeting with Chief of Imperial Security Captain Simon Illyan. He came by fast courier all the way from ImpSec headquarters on Barrayar on the basis of a rather ambiguous coded message I sent him, and he's going to be extremely hot to know why I've interrupted his routine. He's going to demand to know what the hell was so important. And," her voice wavered in a sigh, "I'm going to have to tell him."

She led him out of his cabin-cell through the *Peregrine*. She had evidently dismissed his door guard when she'd first come in, but in fact all the corridors seemed deserted. No, not deserted. Cleared.

They came to a personnel pod hatch, and ducked through to find Captain Bothari-Jesek herself at the controls. Bothari-Jesek and no one else. A very private party indeed.

Bothari-Jesek's usual coolness seemed particularly frigid today. When she glanced over her shoulder at him, her eyes widened, and her dark winged brows drew down in startled disapproval of his pasty, bloated appearance.

"Hell, Mark. You look like a drowned corpse that's floated to the surface after a week."

I feel like one. "Thank you," he intoned blandly.

She snorted, whether with amusement, disgust, or derision he was not sure, and turned her attention back to the pod control interface. Hatches sealed, clamps retracted, and they sped silently away from the side of the *Peregrine*. Between the zero-gee and the accelerations, he found his attention centered on his stretched stomach again, and he swallowed against the nausea.

"Why is the ImpSec head man only ranked as captain?" Mark inquired, to take his mind off his queasiness. "It can't be for secrecy, everybody knows who he is."

"Another Barrayaran tradition," Bothari-Jesek said. Her tone put a slightly bitter spin on the term *tradition*. At least she was speaking to him. "Illyan's predecessor in the post, the late great Captain Negri, never took a promotion beyond captain. That kind of ambition was apparently irrelevant to Emperor Ezar's Familiar. Everybody knew Negri spoke with the Emperor's Voice, and his orders cut across all ranks. Illyan . . . was always a little shy of promoting himself over the rank of his former boss, I guess. He's paid a vice-admiral's salary, though. Whatever poor sucker heads ImpSec next after Illyan retires is probably going to be stuck with the rank of captain forever."

They approached a mid-sized high orbital space station. Mark finally glimpsed Komarr, turning far below, shrunken by the distance to a half-moon. Bothari-Jesek kept strictly to the flight path assigned to her by an extremely laconic station traffic control. After a nervous pause while they exchanged codes and countersigns, they locked onto a docking hatch.

They were met by two silent, expressionless armed

guards, very neat and trim in Barrayaran green, who ushered them through the station and into a small windowless chamber set up as an office, with a comconsole desk, three chairs, and no other decoration.

"Thank you. Leave us," said the man behind the desk. The guards exited as silently as they had done everything else.

Alone, the man seemed to relax slightly. He nodded to Bothari-Jesek. "Hullo, Elena. It's good to see you." His light voice had an unexpected warm timbre, like an uncle greeting a favorite niece.

The rest of him seemed exactly as Mark had studied in Galen's vids. Simon Illyan was a slight, aging man, gray rising in a tide from his temples into his brown hair. A rounded face with a snub nose was too etched with faint lines to look quite youthful. He wore, on this military installation, correct officer's undress greens and insignia like the ones Quinn had tried to foist on Mark, with the Horus-eye badge of Imperial Security winking from his collar.

Mark realized Illyan was staring back at him with the most peculiar suffused look on his face. "My God, Miles, you—" he began in a strangled voice, then his eye lit with comprehension. He sat back in his chair. "Ah." His mouth twisted up on one side. "Lord Mark. Greetings from your lady mother. And I am most pleased to meet you at last." He sounded perfectly sincere.

Not for long, thought Mark hopelessly. And, *Lord Mark? He can't be serious.*

"Also pleased to know where you are again. I take it, Captain Quinn, that my department's message about Lord Mark's disappearance from Earth finally caught up with you?"

"Not yet. It's probably still chasing us from . . . our last stop."

Illyan's brows rose. "So did Lord Mark come in from

the cold on his own, or did my erstwhile subordinate send him to me?"

"Neither, sir." Quinn seemed to have trouble speaking. Bothari-Jesek wasn't even trying to.

Illyan leaned forward, growing more serious, though still tinged with a slight irony. "So what half-cocked, insubordinate, I-thought-you-wanted-me-to-use-my-initiative-sir scam has he sent you to try to con me into paying for this time?"

"No scam, sir," muttered Quinn. "But the bill is going to be huge."

The coolly amused air faded altogether as he studied her grey face. "Yes?" he said after a moment.

Quinn leaned on the desk with both hands, not for emphasis, Mark fancied, but for support. "Illyan, we have a problem. Miles is dead."

Illyan took this in with a waxen stillness. Abruptly, he turned his chair around. Mark could see only the back of his head. His hair was thin. When he turned back, the lines had sprung out on his set face like a figure-ground reversal; like scars. "That's not a problem, Quinn," he whispered. "That's a *disaster*." He laid his hands down flat, very carefully, across the smooth black surface of the desk. *So that's where Miles picked up that gesture*, Mark, who had studied it, thought irrelevantly.

"He's frozen in a cryo-chamber." Quinn licked her dry lips.

Illyan's eyes closed; his mouth moved, whether on prayers or curses Mark could not tell. But he only said, mildly, "You might have said that first. The rest would have followed as a logical supposition." His eyes opened, intent. "So what happened? How bad were his wounds—not a head wound, pray God? How well-prepped was he?"

"I helped do the prep myself. Under combat conditions. I . . . I *think* it was good. You can't know until . . . well.

He took a very bad chest wound. As far as I could tell he was untouched from the neck up."

Illyan breathed, carefully. "You're right, Captain Quinn. Not a disaster. Only a problem. I'll alert the Imperial Military Hospital at Vorbarr Sultana to expect their star patient. We can transfer the cryo-chamber from your ship to my fast courier immediately." Was the man babbling, just a little, with relief?

"Uh . . ." said Quinn. "No."

Illyan rested his forehead gingerly in his hand, as if a headache was starting just behind his eyes. "Finish, Quinn," he said in a tone of muffled dread.

"We lost the cryo-chamber."

"How could you lose a cryo-chamber?!"

"It was a portable." She intercepted his burning stare, and hurried up her report. "It was left downside in the scramble to get off. Each of the combat drop shuttles thought the other one had it. It was a mis-communication—I *checked*, I swear. It turned out the medic in charge of the cryo-chamber had been cut off from his shuttle by enemy forces. He found himself with access to a commercial shipping facility. We think he shipped the cryo-chamber from there."

"You *think*? I will ask—*what* combat drop mission, in a moment. Where did he ship it?"

"That's just it, we don't know. He was killed before he could report. The cryo-chamber could be on its way literally anywhere by now."

Illyan sat back and rubbed his lips, which were set in a thin, ghastly smile. "I see. And all this happened when? And where?"

"Two weeks and three days ago, on Jackson's Whole."

"*I* sent you all to Illyrica, via Vega Station. How the hell did you end up on Jackson's Whole?"

Quinn stood at parade rest, and took it from the top, a stiff, clipped synopsis of the events of the last four weeks from Escobar onward. "I have a complete report with all our vid records and Miles's personal log here, sir." She laid a data cube on his comconsole.

Illyan eyed it like a snake; his hand did not move toward it. "And the forty-nine clones?"

"Still aboard the *Peregrine*, sir. We'd like to off-load them."

My clones. What would Illyan do with them? Mark dared not ask.

"Miles's personal log tends to be a fairly useless document, in my experience," observed Illyan distantly. "He is quite canny about what to leave out." He grew introspective, and fell silent for a time. Then he rose, and walked from side to side across the little office. The cool facade cracked without warning; face contorted, he turned and slammed his fist into the wall with bone-crunching force, shouting, "*Damn* the boy for making a fucking farce out of his own funeral!"

He stood with his back to them; when he turned again and sat down his face was stiff and blank. When he looked up, he addressed Bothari-Jesek.

"Elena. It's clear I'm going to have to stay here at Komarr, for the moment, to coordinate the search from ImpSec's galactic affairs HQ. I can't afford to put an extra five days of travel time between myself and the action. I will, of course . . . compose the formal missing-in-action report on Lieutenant Lord Vorkosigan and forward it immediately to Count and Countess Vorkosigan. I hate to think of it delivered by some subordinate, but it will have to be. But will you, as a personal favor to me, escort Lord Mark to Vorbarr Sultana, and deliver him to their custody?"

No, no, no, Mark screamed inside.

"I . . . would rather not go to Barrayar, sir."

"The Prime Minister will have questions that only one who was on the spot can answer. You are the most ideal courier I can imagine for a matter of such . . . complex delicacy. I grant you the task will be painful."

Bothari-Jesek was looking trapped. "Sir, I'm a senior shipmaster. I'm not free to leave the *Peregrine*. And—frankly—I do not care to escort Lord Mark."

"I'll give you anything you ask, in return."

She hesitated. "Anything?"

He nodded.

She glanced at Mark. "I gave my word that all the House Bharaputra clones would be taken somewhere safe, somewhere humane, where the Jacksonians can't reach. Will you redeem my word for me?"

Illyan chewed his lip. "ImpSec can launder their identities readily enough, of course. No difficulty there. Appropriate placement might be trickier. But yes. We'll take them on."

Take them on. What did Illyan mean? For all their other flaws, the Barrayarans at least did not practice slavery.

"They're children," Mark blurted. "You have to remember they're only children." *It's hard to remember*, he wanted to add, but couldn't, under Bothari-Jesek's cold eyes.

Illyan averted his glance from Mark. "I shall seek Countess Vorkosigan's advice, then. Anything else?"

"The *Peregrine* and the *Ariel*—"

"Must remain, for the moment, in Komarr orbit and communications quarantine. My apologies to your troops, but they'll have to tough it out."

"You'll cover the costs for this mess?"

Illyan grimaced. "Alas, yes."

"And . . . and look *hard* for Miles!"

"Oh, yes," he breathed.

"Then I'll go." Her voice was faint, her face pale.

"Thank you," said Illyan quietly. "My fast courier will be at your disposal as quickly as you can make ready to depart." His eye fell reluctantly on Mark. He had been avoiding looking at Mark for the whole last half of this interview. "How many personal guards do you wish?" he asked Bothari-Jesek. "I'll make it clear to them that they are under your command till they see you safe to the Count."

"I don't want any, but I suppose I have to sleep sometime. Two," Bothari-Jesek decided.

And so he was officially made a prisoner of the Barrayaran Imperial government, Mark thought. *The end of the line.*

Bothari-Jesek rose and motioned Mark to his feet. "Come on. I want to get a few personal items from the *Peregrine*. And tell my exec he's got the command, and explain to the troops about being confined to quarters. Thirty minutes."

"Good. Captain Quinn, please remain."

"Yes, sir."

Illyan stood, to see Bothari-Jesek out. "Tell Aral and Cordelia," he began, and paused. Time stretched.

"I will," said Bothari-Jesek quietly. Mutely, Illyan nodded.

The door seals hissed open for her stride. She didn't even look back to see if Mark was following. He had to break into a run every five steps to keep up.

His cabin aboard the ImpSec fast courier proved to be even tinier and more cell-like than the one he'd occupied aboard the *Peregrine*. Bothari-Jesek locked him in and left him alone. There was not even the time marker and limited human contact of three-times-a-day ration delivery; the cabin had its own computer-controlled food dispensing system, pneumatically connected to some central store. He over-ate compulsively, no longer sure why or what it could do for him, besides provide a combination of comfort and self-destruction. But death from the complications of obesity took years, and he only had five days.

On the last day his body switched strategies, and he became violently ill. He managed to keep this fact secret until the trip downside in the personnel shuttle, where it was mistaken for zero-gravity and motion sickness by a surprisingly sympathetic ImpSec guard, who apparently suffered from some such slight weakness himself. The man promptly and cheerfully slapped an anti-nausea patch from the med kit on the wall onto the side of Mark's neck.

The patch also had some sedative power. Mark's heart rate slowed, an effect which lasted till they landed and transferred to a sealed ground-car. A guard and a driver took the front compartment, and Mark sat across from Bothari-Jesek in the rear compartment for the last leg of his nightmare journey, from the military shuttleport outside the capital into the heart of Vorbarr Sultana. The center of the Barrayaran Empire.

It wasn't until he found himself having something resembling an asthma attack that Bothari-Jesek looked up from her own glum self-absorption and noticed.

"What the hell's the matter with you?" She leaned forward and took his pulse, which was racing. He was clammy all over.

"Sick," he gasped, and then at her irritated I-could-have-figured-that-out-for-myself look, admitted, "Scared." He thought he'd been as frightened as a human being could be, under Bharaputran fire, but that was as nothing compared to this slow, trapped terror, this drawn-out suffocating helplessness to affect his destiny.

"What do you have to be afraid of?" she asked scornfully. "Nobody's going to hurt you."

"Captain, they're going to kill me."

"Who? Lord Aral and Lady Cordelia? Hardly. If for any reason we fail to get Miles back, you could be the next Count Vorkosigan. Surely you've figured on that."

At this point he satisfied a long-held curiosity. When he passed out, his breathing did indeed begin again automatically. He blinked away black fog, and fended off Bothari-Jesek's alarmed attempt to loosen his clothes and check his tongue to be sure he hadn't swallowed it. She had pocketed a couple of anti-nausea patches from the shuttle medkit, just in case, and she held one uncertainly. He motioned urgently for her to apply it. It helped.

"Who do you think these people are?" she demanded angrily, when his breathing grew less irregular.

"I don't know. But they're sure as hell going to be pissed at me."

The worst was the knowledge that it need not have been this bad. Any time before the Jackson's Whole debacle he could in theory have walked right in and said hello. But he'd wanted to meet Barrayar on his own terms. Like trying to storm heaven. His attempt to make it better had made it infinitely worse.

She sat back and regarded him with slow bemusement. "You really are scared to death, aren't you?" she said, in a tone of revelation that made him want to howl. "Mark, Lord Aral and Lady Cordelia are going to give you the benefit of every doubt. I know they will. But you have to do your part."

"What is my part?"

"I'm . . . not sure," she admitted.

"Thanks. You're such a help."

And then they were there. The ground-car swung through a set of gates and into the narrow grounds of a huge stone residence. It was the pre-electric Time-of-Isolation design that gave it such an air of fabulous age, Mark decided. The architecture he'd seen like it in London all dated back well over a millennium, though this pile was only a hundred and fifty standard years old. Vorkosigan House.

The canopy swung up, and he struggled out of the ground-car after Bothari-Jesek. This time she waited for him. She grasped him firmly by the upper arm, either worried he would collapse or fearing he would bolt. They stepped through a pleasantly-hued sunlight into the cool dimness of a large entry foyer paved in black and white stone and featuring a remarkable wide curving staircase. How many times had Miles stepped across this threshold?

Bothari-Jesek seemed an agent of some evil fairy, which had snatched away the beloved Miles and replaced him with this pallid, pudgy changeling. He choked down an hysterical giggle as the sardonic mocker in the back of his brain called out, *Hi, Mom and Dad, I'm home. . . .* Surely the evil fairy was himself.

CHAPTER TWELVE

They were met in the entry hall by a pair of liveried servants wearing Vorkosigan brown and silver. In a high Vor household even the staff played soldier. One of them directed Bothari-Jesek away to the right. Mark could have wept. She despised him, but at least she was familiar. Stripped of all support and feeling more utterly alone than when locked in the darkness of his cabin, he turned to follow the other manservant through a short arched hallway and a set of doors on the left.

He had memorized the layout of Vorkosigan House under Galen's tutelage, long ago, so he knew they were entering a room dubbed the First Parlor, an antechamber to the great library that ran from the front of the house to the back. By the standards of Vorkosigan House's public rooms he supposed it was relatively intimate, though its high ceiling seemed to lend it a cool, disapproving austerity. His consciousness of the architectural detail was instantly obliterated when he saw the woman sitting on a padded sofa, quietly awaiting him.

She was tall, neither thin nor stout, a sort of middle-aged solid in build. Red hair streaked with natural gray wound in a complex knot on the back of her head, leaving her face free to make its own statement of cheekbone, line of jaw, and clear grey eye. Her posture was contained, poised rather than resting. She wore a soft silky beige blouse, a hand-embroidered sash that he suddenly realized matched the pattern on his own stolen one, and a calf-length tan skirt and buskins. No jewelry. He had expected something more ostentatious, elaborate, intimidating, the formal icon of Countess Vorkosigan from the vids of reviewing stands and receptions. Or was her sense of power so fully encompassed that she didn't need to wear it, she *was* it? He could see no physical similarity whatsoever between her and himself. Well, maybe eye color. And the paleness of their skins. And the bridge of the nose, perhaps. The line of the jaw had a certain congruence not apparent from vids—

"Lord Mark Vorkosigan, milady," the manservant announced portentously, making Mark flinch.

"Thank you, Pym," she nodded to the middle-aged retainer, dismissing him. The Armsman's disappointed curiosity was well-concealed, except for one quick glance back before closing the doors after himself.

"Hello, Mark." Countess Vorkosigan's voice was a soft alto. "Please sit." She waved at an armchair set at a slight angle opposite her sofa. It did not appear to be hinged and sprung to snap closed upon him, and it was not too close to her; he lowered himself into it, gingerly, as instructed. Unusually, it was not too high for his feet to touch the floor. Had it been cut down for Miles?

"I am glad to meet you at last," she stated, "though I'm sorry the circumstances are so awkward."

"So am I," he mumbled. Glad, or sorry? And who were these *I's* sitting here, lying politely to each other about their gladness and sorrow? *Who are we, lady?* He looked around fearfully for the Butcher of Komarr. "Where is . . . your husband?"

"Ostensibly, greeting Elena. Actually, he funked out and sent me into the front line first. Most unlike him."

"I . . . don't understand. Ma'am." He didn't know what to call her.

"He's been drinking stomach medicine in beverage quantities for the past two days . . . you have to understand how the information has been trickling in, from our point of view. Our first hint that there was anything amiss came four days ago in the form of a courier officer from ImpSec HQ, with a brief standard message from Illyan that Miles was missing in action, details to follow. We were not at first inclined to panic. Miles has been missing before, sometimes for quite extended periods. It was not until Illyan's full transmission was relayed and decoded, several hours later, together with the news that you were on your way, that it all came clear. We've had three days to think it through."

He sat silent, struggling with the concept of the great Admiral Count Vorkosigan, the feared Butcher of Komarr, that massive, shadowy monster, even having a point of view, let alone one that low mortals such as himself were casually expected to understand.

"Illyan never uses weasel-words," the Countess continued, "but he made it through that whole report without once using the term 'dead,' 'killed,' or any of their synonyms. The medical records suggest otherwise. Correct?"

"Um . . . the cryo-treatment appeared successful." What did she want from him?

"And so we are mired in an emotional and legal limbo," she sighed. "It would be almost easier if he . . ." She frowned fiercely down into her lap. Her hands clenched, for the first time. "You understand, we're going to be talking about a lot of possible contingencies. Much revolves around you. But I won't count Miles as dead till he's dead and *rotted*."

He remembered that tide of blood on the concrete. "Um," he said helplessly.

"The fact that you could potentially play Miles has been a great distraction to some people." She looked him over bemusedly. "You say the Dendarii accepted you . . .?"

He cringed into the chair, body-conscious under her sharp grey gaze, feeling the flesh of his torso roll and bunch under Miles's shirt and sash, the tightness of the trousers. "I've . . . put on some weight since then."

"All that? In just three weeks?"

"Yes," he muttered, flushing.

One brow rose. "On purpose?"

"Sort of."

"Huh." She sat back, looking surprised. "That was *extremely* clever of you."

He gaped, realized it emphasized his doubling chin, and closed his mouth quickly.

"Your status has been the subject of much debate. I voted against any security ploy to conceal Miles's situation by having you pose as him. In the first place, it's redundant. Lieutenant Lord Vorkosigan is often gone for months at a time; his absence is more normal than not, these days. It's strategically more important to establish you as yourself, Lord Mark, if Lord Mark is indeed who you are to be."

He swallowed in a dry throat. "Do I have a choice?"

"You will, but a reasoned one, after you've had time to assimilate it all."

"You can't be serious. I'm a *clone*."

"I'm from Beta Colony, kiddo," she said tartly. "Betan law is very sensible and clear on the topic of clones. It's only Barrayaran custom that finds itself at a loss. Barrayarans!" She pronounced it like a swear word. "Barrayar lacks a long experience of dealing with all the technological variants on human reproduction. No legal precedents. And if it's not a *tradition*," she put the same sour spin on the word as had Bothari-Jesek, "they don't know how to cope."

"What am I, to you as a Betan?" he asked, nervously fascinated.

"Either my son or my son once removed," she answered promptly. "Unlicensed, but claimed by me as an heir."

"Those are actual legal categories, on your homeworld?"

"You bet. Now, if *I* had ordered you cloned from Miles, after getting an approved child-license first of course, you would be my son pure and simple. If Miles as a legal adult had done the same, he would be your legal parent and I would be your mother-once-removed, and bear claims upon you and obligations to you approximately the equivalent of a grandparent. Miles was not, of course, a legal adult at the time you were cloned, nor was your birth licensed. If you were still a minor, he and I could go before an Adjudicator, and your guardianship would be assigned according to the Adjudicator's best judgment of your welfare. You are no longer, of course, a minor in either Betan or Barrayaran law." She sighed. "The time for legal guardianship is past. Lost. The inheritance of property will mostly be tangled in the Barrayaran legal confusions. Aral will discuss Barrayaran customary law, or the lack of it, with you when the time comes. That leaves our emotional relationship."

"Do we have one?" he asked cautiously. His two greatest fears, that she would either pull out a weapon and shoot him, or else throw herself upon him in some totally inappropriate paroxysm of maternal affection, both seemed to be fading. He was left facing a level-voiced mystery.

"We do, though exactly what it is remains to be discovered. Realize this, though. Half my genes run through your body, and my selfish genome is heavily evolutionarily pre- programmed to look out for its copies. The other half is copied from the man I admire most in all the worlds and time, so my interest is doubly riveted. The artistic combination of the two, shall we say, arrests my attention."

Put like that, it actually seemed to make sense, logically

and without threat. He found his stomach un-knotting, his throat relaxing. He promptly felt hungry again, for the first time since planetary orbit.

"Now, what's between you and me has nothing to do with what's between you and Barrayar. That's Aral's department, and he'll have to speak for his own views. It's all so undecided, except for one thing. While you are here, you are yourself, Mark, Miles's six-years-younger twin brother. And not an imitation or a substitute for Miles. So the more you can establish yourself as distinct from Miles, from the very beginning, the better."

"Oh," he breathed, "please, yes."

"I suspected you'd already grasped that. Good, we agree. But just not-being-Miles is no more than the inverse of being an imitation Miles. I want to know, who is Mark?"

"Lady . . . I don't know." His prodded honesty had an edge of anguish.

She watched him, sapiently. "There is time," she said calmly. "Miles . . . wanted you to be here, you know. He talked about showing you around. Imagined teaching you to ride horseback." She gave a furtive shudder.

"Galen tried to have me taught, in London," Mark recalled. "It was terrifically expensive, and I wasn't very good at it, so he finally told me just to avoid horses, when I got here."

"Ah?" she brightened slightly. "Hm. Miles, you see, has . . . had . . . has these only-child romantic notions about siblings. Now, I have a brother, so I have no such illusions." She paused, glanced around the room, and leaned forward with a suddenly confidential air, lowering her voice. "You have an uncle, a grandmother, and two cousins on Beta Colony who are just as much your relatives as Aral and myself and your cousin Ivan here on Barrayar. Remember, you have more than one choice. I've given one son to Barrayar. And watched for twenty-eight years while Barrayar tried to destroy him. Maybe Barrayar has had its turn, eh?"

"Ivan's not here *now*, is he?" Mark asked, diverted and horrified.

"He's not staying at Vorkosigan House, no, if that's what you mean. He is in Vorbarr Sultana, assigned to Imperial Service Headquarters. Perhaps," her eye lit in speculation, "he could take you out and show you some of the things Miles wanted you to see."

"Ivan may still be angry for what I did to him in London," Mark jittered.

"He'll get over it," the Countess predicted confidently. "I have to admit, Miles would have positively enjoyed unsettling people with you."

A quirk Miles inherited from his mother, clearly.

"I've lived almost three decades on Barrayar," she mused. "We've come such a long way. And yet there is still so terribly far to go. Even Aral's will grows weary. Maybe we can't do it all in one generation. Time for the changing of the guard, in my opinion . . . ah, well."

He sat back in his chair for the first time, letting it support him, starting to watch and listen instead of just cower. An ally. It seemed he had an ally, though he was still not sure just why. Galen had not spent much time on Countess Cordelia Vorkosigan, being totally obsessed with his old enemy the Butcher. Galen, it appeared, had seriously underestimated her. She had survived twenty-nine years here . . . might he? For the first time, it seemed something humanly possible.

A brief knock sounded on the hinged double doors to the hallway. At Countess Vorkosigan's "Yes?", they swung open partway, and a man poked his head around the frame and favored her with a strained smile.

"Is it all right for me to come in now, dear Captain?"

"Yes, I think so," said Countess Vorkosigan.

He let himself through and closed the doors again.

Mark's throat locked; he swallowed and breathed, swallowed and breathed, with frighteningly fragile control. He would *not* pass out in front of this man. Or vomit. He hadn't more than a teaspoon of bile left in his belly by now anyway. It was him, unmistakably him, Prime Minister Admiral Count Aral Vorkosigan, formerly Regent of the Barrayaran Empire and de facto dictator of three worlds, conqueror of Komarr, military genius, political mastermind—accused murderer, torturer, madman, too many impossible things to be contained in that stocky form now striding toward Mark.

Mark had studied vids of him taken at every age; perhaps it was not so odd that his first coherent thought was, *He looks older than I expected.* Count Vorkosigan was ten standard years older than his Betan wife, but he looked twenty or thirty years older. His hair was a whiter shade of grey than in the vids from even two years ago. He was short for a Barrayaran, eye to eye with the Countess. His face was heavy, intense, weathered. He wore green uniform trousers but no jacket, just the cream shirt with the long sleeves rolled up and open at the round collar which, if it was an attempt at a casual look, was failing utterly. The tension in the room had risen to choking levels with his entrance.

"Elena is settled," Count Vorkosigan reported, seating himself beside the Countess. His posture was open, hands on knees, but he did not lean back comfortably. "The visit seems to be stirring up more old memories than she was ready for. She's rather disturbed."

"I'll go talk to her in a bit," promised the Countess.

"Good." The Count's eyes inventoried Mark. Puzzled? Repelled? "Well." The practiced diplomat whose job it was to talk three planets down the road to progress sat speechless, at a loss, as if unable to address Mark directly. He turned instead to his wife. "*He* passed as Miles?"

A tinge of dark amusement flashed in Countess

Vorkosigan's eyes. "He's put on weight since then," she said blandly.

"I see."

The silence stretched for excruciating seconds.

Mark blurted out, "The first thing I was supposed to do when I met you was try to kill you."

"Yes. I know." Count Vorkosigan settled back on the sofa, eyes on Mark's face at last.

"They made me practice about twenty different back-up methods, till I could do them in my sleep, but the primary was to have been a skin patch with a paralyzing toxin that left evidence on autopsy pointing to heart failure. I was to get alone with you, touch it to any part of your body I could reach. It was strangely slow, for an assassination drug. I was to wait, in your sight, for twenty minutes while you died, and never let on that I was not Miles."

The Count smiled grimly. "I see. A good revenge. Very artistic. It would have worked."

"As the new Count Vorkosigan, I was then to go on and spearhead a drive for the Imperium."

"*That* would have failed. Ser Galen expected it to. It was merely the chaos of its failure, during which Komarr was supposed to rise, that he desired. You were to be another Vorkosigan sacrifice then." He actually seemed to grow more at ease, professional, discussing these grotesque plots.

"Killing you was the entire reason for my existence. Two years ago I was all primed to do it. I endured all those years of Galen for no other purpose."

"Take heart," advised the Countess. "Most people exist for no reason at all."

The Count remarked, "ImpSec assembled a huge pile of documentation on you, after the plot came to light. It covers the time from when you were a mere mad gleam in Galen's eye, to the latest addition about your disappearance from Earth two months ago. But there's nothing in the documentation that suggests your, er, late adventure on Jackson's Whole was some sort of latent programming along the lines of my projected assassination. Was it?" A faint doubt colored his voice.

"No," said Mark firmly. "I've been programmed enough to know. It's not something you can fail to notice. Not the way Galen did it, anyway."

"I disagree," said Countess Vorkosigan unexpectedly. "You were set up for it, Mark. But not by Galen."

The Count raised his brows in startled inquiry.

"By Miles, I'm afraid," she explained. "Quite inadvertently."

"I don't see it," said the Count.

Mark felt the same way. "I was only in contact with Miles for a few days, on Earth."

"I'm not sure you're ready for this, but here goes. You had exactly three role models to learn how to be a human being from. The Jacksonian body-slavers, the Komarran terrorists—and Miles. You were *steeped* in Miles. And I'm sorry, but Miles thinks he's a knight-errant. A rational government wouldn't allow him possession of a pocket-knife, let alone a space fleet. And so, Mark, when you were finally forced to choose between two palpable evils and a lunatic—you upped and ran after the lunatic."

"I think Miles does very well," objected the Count.

"Agh." The Countess buried her face in her hands, briefly. "Love, we are discussing a young man upon whom Barrayar laid so much unbearable stress, so much pain, he created an entire other personality to escape into. He then persuaded several thousand galactic mercenaries to support his psychosis, and on top of that conned the Barrayaran Imperium into paying for it all. Admiral Naismith is one hell of a lot more than just an ImpSec cover identity, and you know it. I grant you he's a genius, but don't you dare try to tell me he's sane." She paused.

"No. That's not fair. Miles's safety valve works. I won't really begin to fear for his sanity till he's cut off from the little admiral. It's an extraordinary balancing act, in all." She glanced at Mark. "And a nearly impossible act to follow, I should think."

Mark had never thought of Miles as seriously crazed; he'd only thought of him as perfect. This was all highly unsettling.

"The Dendarii truly function as a covert operations arm of ImpSec," said the Count, looking a bit unsettled himself. "Spectacularly well, on occasion."

"Of course they do. You wouldn't let Miles keep them if they didn't, so he makes sure of it. I merely point out that their official function is not their only function. And—if Miles ever ceases to need them, it won't be a year before ImpSec finds reason to cut that tie. And you'll all earnestly believe you are acting perfectly logically."

Why weren't they blaming him . . . ? He mustered the courage to ask it aloud. "Why aren't you blaming me for killing Miles?"

With a glance, the Countess fielded the question to her husband, who nodded and answered. For them both? "Illyan's report stated Miles was shot by a Bharaputran security trooper."

"But he wouldn't have been in the line of fire if I hadn't—"

Count Vorkosigan held up an interrupting hand. "If he hadn't foolishly chosen to be. Don't attempt to camouflage your real blame by taking more than your share. I've made too many lethal errors myself to be fooled by that one." He glanced at his boots. "We have also considered the long view. While your personality and persona are clearly distinct from Miles's, any children you sire would be genetically indistinguishable. Not you, but your son, may be what Barrayar needs."

"Only to continue the Vor system," Countess

Vorkosigan put in dryly. "A dubious goal, love. Or are you picturing yourself as a grandfatherly mentor to Mark's theoretical children, as your father was to Miles?"

"God forbid," muttered the Count fervently.

"Beware your own conditioning." She turned to Mark. "The trouble is . . ." she looked away, looked back, "if we fail to recover Miles, what you will be facing is not just a relationship. It's a job. At a minimum, you'd be responsible for the welfare of a couple of million people in your District; you would be their Voice in the Council of Counts. It's a job Miles was trained for literally from birth; I'm not sure it's possible to send in a last-minute substitute."

Surely not, oh, surely not.

"I don't know," said the Count thoughtfully. "*I* was such a substitute. Until I was eleven years old I was the spare, not the heir. I admit, after my older brother was murdered, the rush of events made the shift in destinies easy for me. We were all so intent on revenge, in Mad Yuri's War. By the time I looked up and drew breath again, I'd fully assimilated the fact I would be Count someday. Though I scarcely imagined that someday would be another fifty years. It's possible you too, Mark, could have many years to study and train. But it's also possible my Countship could land in your lap tomorrow."

The man was seventy-two standard years old, middle-aged for a galactic, old for harsh Barrayar. Count Aral had used himself hard; had he used himself nearly up? His father, Count Piotr, had lived twenty years more than that, a whole other lifetime. "Would Barrayar even accept a clone as your heir?" he asked doubtfully.

"Well, it's past time to start developing laws one way or the other. Yours would be a major test case. With enough concentrated will, I could probably ram it down their throats—"

Mark didn't doubt that.

"But starting a legal war is premature, till things sort themselves out with the missing cryo-chamber. For now, the public story is that Miles is away on duty, and you are visiting for the first time. All true enough. I need scarcely emphasize that the details are classified."

Mark shook his head and nodded in agreement, feeling dizzy. "But—is this necessary? Suppose I'd never been created, and Miles was killed in the line of duty somewhere. Ivan Vorpatril would be your heir."

"Yes," said the Count, "and House Vorkosigan would come to an end, after eleven generations of direct descent."

"What's the problem with that?"

"The problem is that it is not the case. You do exist. The problem is . . . that I have always wanted Cordelia's son to be my heir. Note, we're discussing rather a lot of property, by ordinary standards."

"I thought most of your ancestral lands glowed in the dark, after the destruction of Vorkosigan Vashnoi."

The Count shrugged. "Some remain. This residence, for example. But my estate is not just property; as Cordelia puts it, it comes with a full-time job. If we allow your claim upon it, you must allow its claim upon you."

"You can keep it all," said Mark sincerely. "I'll sign anything."

The Count winced.

"Consider it orientation, Mark," said the Countess. "Some of the people you may encounter will be thinking much about these questions. You simply need to be aware of the unspoken agendas."

The Count acquired an abstracted look; he let out his breath in a slow trickle. When he looked up again his face was frighteningly serious. "That's true. And there's one agenda that is not only unspoken, it's unspeakable. You must be warned."

So unspeakable Count Vorkosigan was having trouble spitting it out himself, apparently. "What now?" asked Mark warily.

"There is a . . . false theory of descent, one of six possible lines, that puts me next in line to inherit the Barrayaran Imperium, should Emperor Gregor die without issue."

"Yes," said Mark impatiently, "of course I knew. Galen's plot turned on exploiting that legal argument. You, then Miles, then Ivan."

"Yes, well now it's me, then Miles, then you, then Ivan. And Miles is—technically—dead at the moment. That leaves only me between you, and being targeted. Not as an imitation Miles, but in your own right."

"That's *rubbish*," exploded Mark. "That's even crazier than the idea of my becoming Count Vorkosigan!"

"Hold that thought," advised the Countess. "Hold it hard, and never even hint that you could think otherwise."

I am fallen among madmen.

"If anyone approaches you with a conversation on the subject, report it to me, Cordelia, or Simon Illyan as soon as possible," the Count added.

Mark had retreated as far back into his chair as he could go. "All right. . . ."

"You're scaring him, dear," the Countess remarked.

"On *that* topic, paranoia is the key to good health," said the Count ruefully. He watched Mark silently for a moment. "You look tired. We'll show you to your room. You can wash up and rest a bit."

They all rose. Mark followed them out to the paved hallway. The Countess nodded to an archway leading straight back under the curved stairway. "I'm going to take the lift tube up and see Elena."

"Right," the Count agreed. Mark perforce followed him up the stairs. Two flights let him know how out of shape he was. By the time they reached the second landing he was breathing as heavily as the old man. The Count turned down a third floor hallway.

Mark asked in some dread, "You're not putting me in Miles's room, are you?"

"No. Though the one you're getting was mine, once, when I was a child."

Before the death of his older brother, presumably. The second son's room. That was almost as unnerving.

"It's just a guest room, now." The Count swung open another blank wooden door on hinges. Beyond it lay a sunny chamber. Obviously hand-made wooden furniture of uncertain age and enormous value included a bed and chests; a domestic console to control lighting and the mechanized windows sat incongruously beside the carved headboard.

Mark glanced back, and collided with the Count's deeply questioning stare. It was a thousand times worse than even the Dendarii's I-love-Naismith look. He clenched his hands to his head, and grated, "Miles isn't in here!"

"I know," said the Count quietly. "I was looking for . . . myself, I suppose. And Cordelia. And you."

Uncomfortably compelled, Mark looked for himself in the Count, reciprocally. He wasn't sure. Hair color, formerly; he and Miles shared the same dark hair he had seen on vids of the younger Admiral Vorkosigan. Intellectually, he'd known Aral Vorkosigan was the old General Count Piotr Vorkosigan's younger son, but that lost older brother had been dead for sixty years. He was astonished the present Count remembered with such immediacy, or made of it a connection with himself. Strange, and frightening. *I was to kill this man. I still could. He's not guarding himself at all.*

"Your ImpSec people didn't even fast-penta me. Aren't you at all worried that I might still be programmed to assassinate you?" Or did he seem so little threat?

"I thought you shot your father-figure once already. Catharsis enough." A bemused grimace curved the Count's mouth.

Mark remembered Galen's surprised look, when the nerve-disruptor beam had taken him full in the face. Whatever Aral Vorkosigan would look like, dying, Mark fancied it would not be surprised.

"You saved Miles's life then, according to his description of the affray," the Count said. "You chose your side two years ago, on Earth. Very effectively. I have many fears for you, Mark, but my death at your hand is not one of them. You're not as one-down with respect to your brother as you imagine. Even-all, by my count."

"Progenitor. Not brother," said Mark, stiff and congealed.

"Cordelia and I are your progenitors," said the Count firmly.

Denial flashed in Mark's face.

The Count shrugged. "Whatever Miles is, we made him. You are perhaps wise to approach us with caution. We may not be good for you, either."

His belly shivered with a terrible longing, restrained by a terrible fear. Progenitors. *Parents.* He was not sure he wanted parents, at this late date. They were such enormous figures. He felt obliterated in their shadow, shattered like glass, annihilated. He felt a sudden weird wish to have Miles back. Somebody his own size and age, somebody he could talk to.

The Count glanced again into the bedchamber. "Pym should have arranged your things."

"I don't have any things. Just the clothes I'm wearing . . sir." It was impossible to keep his tongue from adding that honorific.

"You must have had something more to wear!"

"What I brought from Earth, I left in a storage locker

on Escobar. The rent's up by now, it's probably confiscated."

The Count looked him over. "I'll send someone to take your measurements, and supply you with a kit. If you were visiting under more normal circumstances, we would be showing you around. Introducing you to friends and relatives. A tour of the city. Getting you aptitude tests, making arrangements for furthering your education. We'll do some of that, in any case."

A school? What kind? Assignment to a Barrayaran military academy was very close to Mark's idea of a descent into hell. Could they make him . . . ? There were ways to resist. He had successfully resisted being lent Miles's wardrobe.

"If you want anything, ring for Pym on your console," the Count instructed.

Human servants. So very strange. The physical fear that had turned him inside out was fading, to be replaced by a more formless general anxiety. "Can I get something to eat?"

"Ah. Please join Cordelia and me for lunch in one hour. Pym will show you to the Yellow Parlor."

"I can find it. Down one floor, one corridor south, third door on the right."

The Count raised an eyebrow. "Correct."

"I've studied you, you see."

"That's all right. We've studied you, too. We've all done our homework."

"So what's the test?"

"Ah, that's the trick of it. It's not a test. It's real life."

And real death. "I'm sorry," Mark blurted. For Miles? For himself? He scarcely knew.

The Count looked like he was wondering too; a brief ironic smile twitched one corner of his mouth. "Well . . . in a strange way, it's almost a relief to know that it's as bad as it can be. Before, when Miles was missing, one didn't know where he was, what he might be doing to, er, magnify the chaos. At least this time we know he can't possibly get into any worse trouble."

With a brief wave, the Count walked away, not entering the room after Mark, not crowding him in any way. Three ways to kill him flashed through Mark's mind. But that training seemed ages stale. He was too out of shape now anyway. Climbing the stairs had exhausted him. He pulled the door shut and fell onto the carved bed, shivering with reaction.

CHAPTER THIRTEEN

Ostensibly to allow Mark to recover from jump-lag, the Count and Countess set no tasks for him the first two days. Indeed, except for the rather formal mealtimes, Mark did not see Count Vorkosigan at all. He wandered the house and grounds at will, with no apparent guard but the Countess's discreet observation of him. There were uniformed guards at the gates; he did not yet have the nerve to test and discover if they were charged to keep him in as well as unauthorized persons out.

He had studied Vorkosigan House, yes, but the immediacy of actually being here took some getting used to. It all seemed subtly askew from his expectations. The place was a warren, but for all the antiques with which Vorkosigan House was cluttered, every original window had been replaced with modern high-grade armor-glass and automatic shutters, even the ones high up on the wall in the basement kitchen. It was like a shell, if a vast one, of protection, palace/fortress/prison. Could he slide into this shell?

I've been a prisoner all my life. I want to be a free man.

On the third day, his new clothing arrived. The Countess came to help him unpack it all. The morning light and cool air of early autumn streamed into his bedchamber through the window which he had, mulishly, opened wide to the mysterious, dangerous, unknown world.

He opened one bag on a hanger to reveal a garment in a disturbingly military style, a high-necked tunic and side-piped trousers in Vorkosigan brown and silver, very like the Count's armsmen's liveries, but with more glitter on the collar and epaulettes. "What's this?" he asked suspiciously.

"Ah," said the Countess. "Gaudy, isn't it? It's your uniform as a cadet lord of House Vorkosigan."

His, not Miles's. All the new clothes were computer-cut to generous fit; his heart sank as he calculated how much he'd have to eat to escape *this* one.

The Countess's lips curved up at the dismayed expression on his face. "The only two places you actually have to wear it are if you attend a session of the Council of Counts, or if you go to the Emperor's birthday ceremonies. Which you might; they're coming up in a few weeks." She hesitated, her finger tracing over the Vorkosigan logo embroidered on the tunic's collar. "Miles's birthday isn't very long after that."

Well, Miles wasn't aging at the moment, wherever he was. "Birthdays are sort of a non-concept, for me. What do you call it when you take someone out of a uterine replicator?"

"When I was taken out of *my* uterine replicator, my parents called it my birthday," she said dryly.

She was Betan. Right. "I don't even know when mine is."

"You don't? It's in your records."

"What records?"

"Your Bharaputran medical file. Haven't you ever seen it? I'll have to get you a copy. It's, um, fascinating reading, in a sort of horrifying way. Your birthday was the seventeenth of last month, in point of fact."

"I missed it anyway, then." He closed the bag and stuffed the uniform far back in his closet. "Not important."

"It's important that someone celebrate our existence," she objected amiably. "People are the only mirror we have to see ourselves in. The domain of all meaning.

All virtue, all evil, are contained only in people. There is none in the universe at large. Solitary confinement is a punishment in every human culture."

"That's . . . true," he admitted, remembering his own recent imprisonment. "Hm." The next garment he shook out suited his mood: solid black. Though on closer examination it proved to be almost the same design as the cadet lord's uniform, the logos and piping muted in black silk instead of glowing in silver thread, almost invisible against the black cloth.

"That's for funerals," commented the Countess. Her voice was suddenly rather flat.

"Oh." Taking the hint, he tucked it away behind the Vor cadet's uniform. He finally chose the least military-flavored outfit available, soft loose trousers, low boots without buckles, steel toe caps, or any other aggressive decorations, and a shirt and vest, in dark colors, blues, greens, red-browns. It felt like a costume, but it was all extremely well-made. Camouflage? Did the clothes represent the man inside, or disguise him? "Is it me?" he asked the Countess, upon emerging from the bathroom for inspection.

She half-laughed. "A profound question, to ask of one's clothing. Even I can't answer that one."

On the fourth day, Ivan Vorpatril turned up at breakfast. He wore an Imperial lieutenant's undress greens, neatly setting off his tall, physically fit frame; with his arrival the Yellow Parlor seemed suddenly crowded. Mark shrank down guiltily as his putative cousin greeted his aunt with a decorous kiss on the cheek and his uncle with a formal nod. Ivan nailed a plate from the sideboard and piled it precariously with eggs, meat, and sugared breads, juggled a mug of coffee, hooked back a chair with his foot, and slid into a place at the table opposite Mark.

"Hello, Mark," Ivan acknowledged his existence at last.

"You look like hell. When did you get so bloated?" He shoved a forkful of fried meat into his mouth and started chewing.

"Thank you, Ivan," Mark took what refuge he could in faint sarcasm. "You haven't changed, I see." Implying *no improvement*, he hoped.

Ivan's brown eyes glinted; he started to speak, but was stopped by his aunt's "Ivan" in a tone of cool reproof. Mark didn't think it was for trying to talk with his mouth full, but Ivan swallowed before replying, not to Mark but to the Countess, "My apologies, Aunt Cordelia. But I still have a problem with closets and other small, unvented dark areas because of him."

"Sorry," muttered Mark, hunching. But something in him resisted being cowed by Ivan, and he added, "I only had Galen kidnap you to fetch Miles."

"So that was *your* idea."

"It worked, too. He came right along and stuck his head in the noose for you."

Ivan's jaw tightened. "A habit he has failed to break, I understand," he returned, in a tone halfway between a purr and a snarl.

It was Mark's turn to be silent. Yet in a way, it was almost comforting. Ivan at least treated him as he deserved. A little welcome punishment. He felt himself reviving under the rain of scorn like a parched plant. Ivan's challenge almost brightened his day. "Why are you here?"

"It wasn't my idea, believe me," said Ivan. "I am to take you out. For an airing."

Mark glanced at the Countess, but she was focused on her husband. "Already?" she asked.

"It is by request," said Count Vorkosigan.

"Ah ha," she said, as if enlightened. No light dawned for Mark; it wasn't *his* request. "Good. Perhaps Ivan can show him a bit of the city on the way."

"That's the idea," said the Count. "Since Ivan is an officer, it eliminates the need for a bodyguard."

Why, so they could talk frankly? A terrible idea. And who would protect him from Ivan?

"There will be an outer perimeter, I trust," said the Countess.

"Oh, yes."

The outer perimeter was the guard no one was supposed to see, not even the principals. Mark wondered what prevented the outer perimeter people from just taking the day off, and claiming they'd been there, invisible men. You could get away with the scam for quite a long time, between crises, he suspected.

Lieutenant Lord Vorpatril had his own ground-car, Mark discovered after breakfast, a sporty model featuring lots of red enamel. Reluctantly, Mark slid in beside Ivan. "So," he said, in an uncertain voice. "Do you still want to scrag me?"

Ivan whipped the car through the residence's gates and out into Vorbarr Sultana city traffic. "Personally, yes. Practically, no. I need all the bodies I can get to stand between me, and Uncle Aral's job. I wish Miles had a dozen children. He could have, by now, if only he'd started—in a way, you are a godsend. They'd have me clamped in as heir apparent right now if not for you." He hesitated, in speech only; the ground-car he accelerated through an intersection, weaving narrowly past four other vehicles bearing down in collision courses. "How dead is Miles really? Uncle Aral was pretty vague, on the vid telling me about it. I wasn't sure if it was for security, or—I've never seen him so stiff."

The traffic was worse than London's and, if possible, even more disorderly, or ordered according to some rule involving survival of the fittest. Mark gripped the edges of his seat and replied, "I don't know. He took a needle-grenade in the chest. Almost as bad as it could be without actually blowing him in half."

Did Ivan's lips ripple in suppressed horror? If so, the breezy facade re-closed again almost instantly. "It will take a top-notch revival facility to put his torso back together right," Mark continued. "For the brain . . . you never know till revival's over." *And then it's too late.* "But that's not the problem. Or not the problem yet."

"Yeah," Ivan grimaced. "That was a real screw-up, y'know? How could you *lose* . . ." He turned so sharply he trailed an edge, which struck sparks from the pavement, and swore cheerfully at a very large hovertruck which nearly lunged through Mark's side of the ground-car. Mark crouched down and shut his mouth. Better the conversation should die than him; his life could depend on not distracting the driver. His first impression of the city of Miles's birth was that half the population was going to be killed in traffic before nightfall. Or maybe just the ones in Ivan's path. Ivan did a violent U-turn and skidded sideways into a parking space, cutting off two other ground-cars maneuvering toward it, and coming to a halt so abruptly Mark was nearly launched into the front panel.

"Vorhartung Castle," Ivan announced with a nod and a wave as the engine's whine died away. "The Council of Counts is not in session today, so the museum is open to the public. Though *we* are not the public."

"How . . . cultural," said Mark warily, peering out through the canopy. Vorhartung Castle really looked like a castle, a rambling, antiquated pile of featureless stone rising out of the trees. It perched on a bluff above the river rapids that divided Vorbarr Sultana. Its grounds were now a park; beds of cultivated flowers grew where men and horses had once dragged siege engines through icy mud in vain assaults. "What is this really?"

"You are to meet a man. And I am not to pre-discuss

it." Ivan popped the canopy and clambered out. Mark followed.

Ivan, whether by plan or perversity, really did take him to the museum, which occupied one whole wing of the castle and was devoted to the arms and armor of the Vor from the Time of Isolation. As a soldier in uniform, Ivan was admitted free, though he dutifully paid Mark's way in with a few coins. For a cover, Mark guessed, for members of the Vor caste were also admitted free, Ivan explained in a whisper. There was no sign to that effect. If you were Vor you were presumed to know.

Or maybe it was Ivan's subtle slur on Mark's Vor-ness, or lack of same. Ivan played the upper-class lout with the same cultivated thoroughness with which he played the Imperial lieutenant, or any other role his world demanded of him. The real Ivan was rather more elusive, Mark gauged; it would not do to underestimate his subtlety, or mistake him for a simpleton.

So he was to meet a man. What man? If it was another ImpSec debriefing, why couldn't he have met the man at Vorkosigan House? Was it someone in government, or Prime Minister Count Aral's Centrist Coalition party? Again, why not come to him? Ivan couldn't be setting him up for an assassination, the Vorkosigans could have had him killed in secret anytime these past two years. Maybe he was being set up to be *accused* of some staged crime? Even more arcane plot ideas twisted through his mind, all sharing the same fatal flaw of being totally lacking in motivation or logic.

He stared at a crammed array of dual sword sets in a chronological row on a wall, displaying the evolution of the Barrayaran smiths' art over two centuries, then hurried to join Ivan in front of a case of chemical-explosive-propelled projectile weapons: highly decorated large-bore muzzle loaders that had once, the card proclaimed, belonged to Emperor Vlad Vorbarra. The bullets were peculiar in being solid gold, massive spheres the size of Mark's thumbtip. At short range, it must have been like being hit by a terminal-velocity brick. At long range, they probably missed. So what poor peasant or squire had been stuck with the job of going around retrieving the misses? Or worse, the hits? Several of the bright balls in display were flattened or misshapen, and to Mark's intense bemusement, one card informed the museum patron that this very distorted blob had killed Lord Vor So-and-so during the battle of Such-and-such . . . "taken from his brain," after death, Mark presumed. Hoped. Yech. He was only surprised someone had cleaned the ancient gore from the spent bullet before mounting it, given the blood-thirsty gruesomeness of some of the other displays. The tanned and cured scalp of Mad Emperor Yuri, for instance, on loan from some Vor clan's private collection.

"Lord Vorpatril." It was not a question. The man speaking had appeared so quietly Mark was not even sure from what direction he had come. He was dressed as quietly, middle-aged, intelligent-looking; he might have been a museum administrator. "Come with me, please."

Without question or comment, Ivan fell in behind the man, gesturing Mark ahead of him. Thus sandwiched, Mark trod in his wake, torn between curiosity and nerves.

They went through a door marked "No Admittance," which the man unlocked with a mechanical key and then locked again behind them, went up two staircases, and down an echoing wood-floored corridor to a room occupying the top floor of a round tower at the building's corner. Once a guard post, it was now furnished as an office, with ordinary windows cut into the stone walls in place of arrow slits. A man waited within, perched on a stool, gazing pensively down at the grounds falling away to the river, and the sprinkling of brightly-dressed people strolling or climbing the paths.

He was a thin, dark-haired fellow in his thirties, pale skin set off by loose dark clothing entirely lacking in pseudo-military detailing. He looked up with a quick smile at their guide. "Thank you, Kevi." Both greeting and dismissal seemed combined, for the guide nodded and exited.

It wasn't until Ivan nodded and said, "Sire," that recognition clicked.

Emperor Gregor Vorbarra. Shit. The door behind Mark was blocked by Ivan. Mark controlled his surge of panic. Gregor was only a man, alone, apparently unarmed. All the rest was . . . propaganda. Hype. Illusion. His heart beat faster anyway.

"Hullo, Ivan," said the Emperor. "Thank you for coming. Why don't you go study the exhibits for a while."

"Seen 'em before," said Ivan laconically.

"Nevertheless." Gregor jerked his head doorward.

"Not to put too fine a point on it," said Ivan, "but this is not Miles, not even on a good day. And despite appearances, he *was* trained as an assassin, once. Isn't this a touch premature?"

"Well," said Gregor softly, "we'll find out, won't we? Do you want to assassinate me, Mark?"

"No," Mark croaked.

"There you have it. Take a hike, Ivan. I'll send Kevi for you in a bit."

Ivan grimaced in frustration, and Mark sensed, not a little frustrated curiosity. He departed with an ironic salaam that seemed to say, *On your head be it.*

"So, Lord Mark," said Gregor. "What do you think of Vorbarr Sultana so far?"

"It went by pretty fast," Mark said cautiously.

"Dear God, don't tell me you let *Ivan* drive."

"I didn't know I had a choice."

The Emperor laughed. "Sit down." He waved Mark into the station chair behind the comconsole desk; the little room was otherwise sparsely furnished, though the antique military prints and maps cluttering the walls might be spill-over from the nearby museum.

The Emperor's smile faded back into his initial pensive look as he studied Mark. It reminded Mark a little of the way Count Vorkosigan looked at him, that *Who are you?* look, only without the Count's ravenous intensity. A bearable wonder.

"Is this your office?" asked Mark, cautiously settling himself in the Imperial swivel-chair. The room seemed small and austere for the purpose.

"One of them. This whole complex is crammed with various offices, in some of the oddest niches. Count Vorvolk has one in the old dungeons. No head room. I use this as a private retreat when attending the Council of Counts meetings, or when I have other business here."

"Why do I qualify as business? Besides not being pleasure. Is this personal or official?"

"I can't spit without being official. On Barrayar, the two are not very separable. Miles . . . was . . ." Gregor's tongue tripped over that past tense too, "in no particular order, a peer of my caste; an officer in my service; the son of an extremely, if not supremely, important official; and a personal friend of lifelong standing. And the heir to the Countship of a District. And the Counts are the mechanism whereby one man," he touched his chest, "multiplies to sixty, and then to a multitude. The Counts are the first officers of the Imperium; I am its captain. You do understand, that *I* am not the Imperium? An empire is mere geography. The Imperium is a society. The multitude, the whole body—ultimately, down to every subject—*that* is the Imperium. Of which I am only a piece. An interchangeable part, at that—did you notice my great-uncle's scalp, downstairs?"

"Um . . . yes. It was, uh, prominently displayed."

"This *is* the home of the Council of Counts. The

fulcrum of the lever may fancy itself supreme, but it is nothing without the lever. Mad Yuri forgot that. I don't. The Count of the Vorkosigan's District is another such living piece. Also interchangeable." He paused.

"A . . . link in a chain," Mark offered carefully, to prove he was paying attention.

"A link in a chain-mail. In a web. So that one weak link is not fatal. Many must fail at once, to achieve a real disaster. Still . . . one wants as many sound, reliable links as possible, obviously."

"Obviously." *Why are you looking at me?*

"So. Tell me what happened on Jackson's Whole. As you saw it." Gregor sat up on his perch, hooking one heel and crossing his booted ankles, apparently centered and comfortable, like a raven on a branch.

"I'd have to start the story back on Earth."

"Feel free." His easy brief smile implied Mark had all the time in the world, and one hundred percent of his attention.

Haltingly, Mark began to stammer out his tale. Gregor's questions were few, only interjected when Mark hung up on the difficult bits; few but searching. Gregor was not in pursuit of mere facts, Mark quickly realized. He had obviously already seen Illyan's report. The Emperor was after something else.

"I cannot argue with your good intentions," said Gregor at one point. "The brain transplant business is a loathsome enterprise. But you do realize—your effort, your raid, is hardly going to put a dent in it. House Bharaputra will just clean up the broken glass and go on."

"It will make a permanent difference to the forty-nine clones," Mark asserted doggedly. "Everybody makes that same damned argument. 'I can't do it all, so I'm not going to do any.' And they don't. And it goes on, and on. And anyway, if I had been able to go back via Escobar as I'd planned in the first place—there would have been a big news splash. House Bharaputra might even have tried to reclaim the clones legally, and then there would *really* have been a public stink. I'd have made sure of it. Even if I'd been in Escobaran detention. Where, by the way, the House Bharaputra enforcers would have had a hard time getting at me. And maybe . . . maybe it would have interested some more people in the problem."

"Ah!" said Gregor. "A publicity stunt."

"It was not a stunt," Mark grated.

"Excuse me. I did not mean to imply your effort was trivial. Quite the reverse. But you *did* have a coherent long-range strategy after all."

"Yeah, but it went down the waste disintegrator as soon as I lost control of the Dendarii. As soon as they knew who I really was." He brooded on the memory of that helplessness.

At Gregor's prodding, Mark went on to recount Miles's death, the screw-up with the lost cryo-chamber, their aborted efforts to retrieve it, and their humiliating ejection from Jacksonian local space. He found himself revealing far more of his real thoughts than he was comfortable doing, yet . . . Gregor almost put him at his ease. How did the man do it? The soft, almost self-effacing demeanor camouflaged a consummately skillful people-handler. In a garbled rush, Mark described the incident with Maree and his half-insane time in solitary confinement, then trailed off into inarticulate silence.

Gregor frowned introspectively, and was quiet for a time. Hell, the man was quiet all the time. "It seems to me, Mark, that you devalue your strengths. You have been battle-tested, and proved your physical courage. You can take an initiative, and dare much. You do not lack brains, though sometimes . . . information. It's not a bad start on the qualities needed for a countship. Someday."

"Not any day. I don't want to be a Count of Barrayar," Mark denied emphatically.

"It could be the first step to my job," Gregor said suggestively, with a slight smile.

"No! That's even worse. They'd eat me alive. My scalp would join the collection downstairs."

"Very possibly." Gregor's smile faded. "Yes, I've often wondered where all my body parts are going to end up. And yet—I understand you were set to try it, just two years ago. Including Aral's Countship."

"Fake it, yes. Now you're talking about the real thing. Not an imitation." *I'm just an imitation, don't you know?* "I've only studied the outsides. The inner surface I can barely imagine."

"But you see," said Gregor, "we all start out that way. Faking it. The role is a simulacrum, into which we slowly grow real flesh."

"Become the machine?"

"Some do. That's the pathological version of a Count, and there are a few. Others become . . . more human. The machine, the role, then becomes a handily-worked prosthetic, which serves the man. Both types have their uses, for my goals. One must simply be sure where on the range of self-delusion the man you're talking to falls."

Yes, Countess Cordelia had surely had a hand in training this man. Mark sensed her trail, like phosphorescent foot steps in the dark. "What are your goals?"

Gregor shrugged. "Keep the peace. Keep the various factions from trying to kill each other. Make bloody sure that no galactic invader ever puts a boot on Barrayaran soil again. Foster economic progress. Lady Peace is the first hostage taken when economic discomfort rises. Here my reign is unusually blessed, with the terraforming of the second continent, and the opening of Sergyar for full colonization. Finally, now that that vile subcutaneous worm plague is under control. Settling Sergyar should absorb everyone's excess energies for several generations. I've been studying various colonial histories lately, wondering how many of the mistakes we can avoid . . . well, so."

"I still don't want to be Count Vorkosigan."

"Without Miles, you don't exactly have a choice."

"Rubbish." At least, he hoped it was rubbish. "You just said it's an interchangeable part. They could find someone else just fine if they had to. Ivan, I guess."

Gregor smiled bleakly. "I confess, I've often used the same argument. Though in my case the topic is progeny. Bad dreams about the destiny of my body parts are nothing compared to the ones I have about my theoretical future children's. And I'm not going to marry some high Vor bud whose family tree crosses mine sixteen times in the last six generations." He contained himself abruptly, with an apologetic grimace. And yet . . . the man was so controlled, Mark fancied even this glimpse of the inner Gregor served a purpose, or could be made to.

Mark was getting a headache. Without Miles . . . *With* Miles, all these Barrayaran dilemmas would be Miles's. And Mark would be free to face . . . his own dilemmas, anyway. His own demons, not these adopted ones. "This is not my . . . gift. Talent. Interest. Destiny. Something, I don't know." He rubbed his neck.

"Passion?" said Gregor.

"Yes, that'll do. A countship is not my passion."

After a moment, Gregor asked curiously, "What is your passion, Mark? If not government, or power, or wealth—you have not even mentioned wealth."

"Enough wealth to destroy House Bharaputra is so far beyond my reach, it just . . . doesn't apply. It's not a solution I can have. I . . . I . . . some men are cannibals. House Bharaputra, its customers—I want to stop the cannibals. *That* would be worth getting out of bed for."

He became aware his voice had grown louder, and slumped down again in the soft chair.

"In other words . . . you have a passion for justice. Or dare I say it, Security. A curious echo of your, um, progenitor."

"No, no!" *Well . . . maybe, in a sense.* "I suppose there are cannibals on Barrayar too, but they haven't riveted my close personal interest. I don't think in terms of law enforcement, because the transplant business isn't illegal on Jackson's Whole. So a policeman isn't the solution either. Or . . . it would have to be a damned unusual policeman." Like an ImpSec covert ops agent? Mark tried to imagine a detective-inspector bearing a letter of marque and reprisal. For some reason a vision of his progenitor kept coming up. Damn Gregor's unsettling suggestion. *Not a policeman. A knight-errant. The Countess had it dead-on.* But there was no place for knights-errant any more; the police would have to arrest them.

Gregor sat back with a faintly satisfied air. "That's very interesting." His abstracted look resembled that of a man assimilating the code-key to a safe. He slid from his stool to wander along the windows and gaze down from another angle. Face to the light, he remarked, "It seems to me your future access to your . . . passion, depends rather heavily on getting Miles back."

Mark sighed in frustration. "It's out of my hands. They'll never let me . . . what can I do that ImpSec can't? Maybe they'll turn him up. Any day now."

"In other words," said Gregor slowly, "the most important thing in your life at this moment is something you are powerless to affect. You have my profound sympathies."

Mark slipped, unwilled, into frankness. "I'm a virtual prisoner here. I can't do anything, and I can't leave!"

Gregor cocked his head. "Have you tried?"

Mark paused. "Well . . . no, not yet, actually."

"Ah." Gregor turned away from the window, and took a small plastic card from his inner jacket pocket. He handed it across the desk to Mark. "My Voice carries only to the borders of Barrayar's interests," he said. "Nevertheless . . . here is my private vidcom number. Your calls will be screened by only one person. You'll be on their list. Simply state your name, and you will be passed through."

"Uh . . . thank you," said Mark, in cautious confusion. The card bore only the code-strip: no other identification. He put it away very carefully.

Gregor touched an audiocom pin on his jacket, and spoke to Kevi. In a few moments there came a knock, and the door swung open to admit Ivan again. Mark, who had started to rock in Gregor's station chair—it did not squeak—self-consciously climbed out of it.

Gregor and Ivan exchanged farewells as laconically as they had exchanged greetings, and Ivan led Mark out of the tower room. As they rounded the corner Mark looked back at the sound of footsteps. Kevi was already ushering in the next man for his Imperial appointment.

"So how did it go?" Ivan inquired.

"I feel drained," Mark admitted.

Ivan smiled grimly. "Gregor can do that to you, when he's being Emperor."

"Being? Or playing?"

"Oh, not playing."

"He gave me his number." *And I think he got mine.*

Ivan's brows rose. "Welcome to the club. I can count the number of people who have that access without even taking both boots off."

"Was . . . Miles one of them?"

"Of course."

CHAPTER FOURTEEN

Ivan, apparently acting under orders—from the Countess, was Mark's first guess—took him out to lunch. Ivan followed a lot of orders, Mark noticed with a slight twinge of sympathy. They went to a place called the caravanserai, a stretched walking distance from Vorhartung Castle. Mark escaped another ground-car ride with Ivan by virtue of the narrowness of the streets—alleys—in the ancient district.

The caravanserai itself was a curious study in Barrayaran social evolution. Its oldest core was cleaned up, renovated, and converted into a pleasant maze of shops, cafes, and small museums, frequented by a mixture of city workers seeking lunch and obvious provincial tourists, come up to the capital to do the historic shrines.

This transformation had spread from the clusters of old government buildings like Vorhartung Castle along the river, toward the district's center; on the fringes to the south, the renovation petered out into the kind of shabby, faintly dangerous areas that had given the caravanserai its original risky reputation. On the way, Ivan proudly pointed out a building in which he claimed to have been born, during the war of Vordarian's Pretendership. It was now a shop selling overpriced hand-woven carpets and other antique crafts supposedly preserved from the Time of Isolation. From the way Ivan carried on Mark half-expected there to be a plaque on the wall commemorating the event, but there wasn't; he checked.

After lunch in one of the small cafes, Ivan, his mind

now running on his family history, was seized with the notion of taking Mark to view the spot on the pavement where his father Lord Padma Vorpatril had been murdered by Vordarian's security forces during that same war. Feeling it fit in with the general gruesome historic tenor of the rest of the morning, Mark agreed, and they set out again on foot to the south. A shift in the architecture, from the low tan stucco of the first century of the Time of Isolation to the high red brick of its last century, marked the marches of the caravanserai proper, or improper.

This time, by God, there *was* a plaque, a cast bronze square set right in the pavement; ground-cars ran past and over it as Ivan gazed down.

"You'd think they'd at least have put it on the sidewalk," said Mark.

"Accuracy," said Ivan. "M'mother insisted."

Mark waited a respectful interval to allow Ivan who-knew-what inward meditations. Eventually Ivan looked up and said brightly, "Dessert? I know this great little Keroslav District bakery around the corner. Mother always took me there after, when we came here to burn the offering each year. It's sort of a hole in the wall, but good."

Mark had not yet walked down lunch, but the place proved as delectable on the inside as it was derelict on the outside, and he somehow ended up possessed of a bag of nut rolls and traditional brillberry tarts, for later. While Ivan lingered over a selection of delicacies to be delivered to Lady Vorpatril, and possibly some sweeter negotiation with the pretty counter-girl—it was hard to tell if Ivan was serious, or just running on spinal reflex—Mark stepped outside.

Galen had placed a couple of Komarran underground spy contacts in this area once, Mark remembered. Doubtless picked up two years ago in the post-plot sweep by Barrayaran Imperial Security. Still, he wondered if he could have found them, if Galen's dreams of revenge had ever come real. Should be one street down and two over . . . Ivan was still chatting up the bakery girl. Mark took a walk.

He found the address in a couple of minutes, to his sufficient satisfaction; he decided he didn't need to check inside. He turned back and took what looked like a short cut toward the main street and the bakery. It proved to be a cul-de-sac. He turned again and started for the alley's mouth.

An old woman and a skinny youth, who had been sitting on a stoop and watched him go in, now watched him coming out. The old woman's dull eye lit with a faint hostility as he came again into her short-sighted focus.

"That's no boy. That's a *mutie*," she hissed to the youth. Grandson? She nudged him pointedly. "A mutie come on *our* street."

Thus prodded, the youth slouched to his feet and stepped in front of Mark. Mark stopped. The kid was taller than he—who wasn't?—but not much heavier, greasy-haired and pale. He spread his legs aggressively, blocking Mark's dodge. Oh, God. Natives. In all their surly glory.

"Shouldn't ought to be here, mutie." He spat, in imitation-bully-mode; Mark almost laughed.

"You're right," he agreed easily. He let his accent go mid-Atlantic Earth, non-Barrayaran. "This place is a pit."

"Offworlder!" the old woman whined in even sharper disapproval. "You can take a wormhole jump to hell, offworlder!"

"I seem to have already," Mark said dryly. Bad manners, but he was in a bad mood. If these slum-louts wanted to bait him, he would bait them right back. "Barrayarans. If there's anything worse than the Vor it's the fools under 'em. No wonder galactics despise this place for a hole."

He was surprised at how easily the suppressed rage vented, and how good it felt. Better not go too far.

"Gonna get you, mutie," the boy promised, hovering on the balls of his feet in nervous threat. The hag urged her bravo on with a rude gesture at Mark. A peculiar set-up; little old ladies and punks were normally natural enemies, but these two seemed in it together. Comrades of the Imperium, no doubt, uniting against a common foe.

"Better a mutie than a moron," Mark intoned with false cordiality.

The lout's brows wrinkled. "Hey! Is that back-chat to me? Huh?"

"Do you see any *other* morons around here?" At the boy's eye-flicker, Mark looked over his shoulder. "Oh. Excuse me. There *are* two more. I understand your confusion." His adrenalin pumped, turning his late lunch into a lump of regret in his belly. Two more youths, taller, heavier, older, but only adolescents. Possibly vicious, but untrained. Still . . . where was Ivan now? Where was that bloody invisible supposed outer perimeter guard? On break? "Aren't you late for school? Your remedial drooling class, perhaps?"

"*Funny* mutie," said one of the older ones. He wasn't laughing.

The attack was sudden, and almost took Mark by surprise; he thought etiquette demanded they exchange a few more insults first, and he was just working up some good ones. Exhilaration mixed strangely with the anticipation of pain. Or maybe it was the anticipation of pain that was exhilarating. The biggest punk tried to kick him in the groin. He caught the foot with one hand and boosted it skyward, flipping the kid onto his back on the stones with a wham that knocked the wind out of him. The second one launched a blow with his fist; Mark caught his arm. They whirled, and the punk found himself stumbling into his skinny companion. Unfortunately, now they both were between Mark and the exit.

They scrambled to their feet, looking astonished and outraged; what kind of easy pickings had they expected, for God's sake? *Easy enough.* His reflexes were two years stale, and he was already getting winded. Yet the extra weight made him harder to knock off his feet. *Three to one on a crippled-looking fat little lost stranger, eh? You like those odds? Come to me, baby cannibals.* The bakery bag was still clutched absurdly in his fist as he grinned and opened his arms in invitation.

They jumped him both together, telegraphing every move. The purely defensive *katas* continued to work charmingly; they flowed into, and out of, his momentum-gate to end up both on the ground,shaking their heads dizzily, victims of their own aggression. Mark wriggled his jaw, which had taken a clumsy blow, hard enough to sting and wake him up. The next round was not so successful; he ended up rolling out of reach, finally losing his grip on the bakery bag, which promptly got stomped. And then one of them caught up with him in a grapple, and they took some of their own back, pounding unscientific blows of clenched fists. He was getting seriously out of breath. He planned an arm-bar and a sprint to the street. It might have ended there, a good time having been had by all, if one of the idiot punks, crouching, hadn't pulled out a battered old shock-stick and jabbed it toward him.

Mark almost killed him instantly with a kick to the neck; he pulled his punch barely in time, and the blow landed slightly off-center. Even through his boot he could feel the tissues crush, a sickening sensation ricocheting up through his body. Mark recoiled in horror as the kid lay gurgling on the ground. *No, I wasn't trained to fight. I was trained to kill. Oh, shit.* He'd managed not to quite smash the larynx. He prayed the kick hadn't snapped a major internal blood vessel. The other two assailants paused in shock.

Ivan pounded around the corner. "What the hell are you doing?" he cried hoarsely.

"I don't know," Mark gasped, bent over with his hands on his knees. His nose was bleeding all over his new shirt. In delayed reaction, he was beginning to shake. "They jumped me." *I baited them. Why* the hell was he doing this? It had all happened so fast. . . .

"Is the mutie with *you*, soldier?" the skinny kid demanded in a mixture of surprise and dread.

Mark could see the struggle in Ivan's face with the urge to disavow all connection with him. "Yes," Ivan choked out at last. The big punk who was still on his feet faded backward, turned, and ran. The skinny kid was glued to the scene by the presence of the injured man and the old woman, though he looked like he wanted to run too. The hag, who had risen and hobbled over to her downed champion, screamed accusations and threats at Mark. She was the only one present who seemed undismayed by the sight of Ivan's officer's greens. Then the municipal guards arrived.

Once he was sure the injured punk was going to be taken care of, Mark shut up and let Ivan handle it. Ivan lied like a . . . trooper, to keep the name of *Vorkosigan* from ever coming up; the municipal guards in turn, realizing who Ivan was, dampened the old woman's hysteria and extricated them with speed. Mark declined to press assault charges even without Ivan's urgent advice to that effect. Thirty minutes later they were back in Ivan's ground car. This time Ivan drove much more slowly;residual terror, Mark judged, from having almost lost his charge.

"Where the hell was that outer perimeter guy who was supposed to be my guardian angel?" Mark asked, gingerly probing the contusions on his face. His nose had finally stopped bleeding. Ivan hadn't let him in his ground car until it had, and he'd made sure Mark wasn't going to throw up.

"Who d'you think called the municipal guards? The outer perimeter's *supposed* to be discreet."

"Oh." His ribs hurt, but nothing was broken, Mark decided. Unlike his progenitor, he'd never had a broken bone. *Mutie*. "Was . . . did *Miles* have to deal with this kind of crap?" All he'd done to those people was walk past them. If Miles had been dressed as he was, been alone as he was, would they have attacked *him*?

"*Miles* wouldn't have been stupid enough to wander in there by himself in the first place!"

Mark frowned. He'd gained the impression from Galen that Miles's rank made him immune to Barrayar's mutagenic prejudices. Did Miles actually have to run a constant safety-calculation in his head, editing where he could go, what he could do?

"And if he had," Ivan continued, "he'd have talked his way out of it. Slid on by. Why the hell did you mix in with three guys? If you just want somebody to beat the shit out of you, come to me. I'd be glad to."

Mark shrugged uncomfortably. Is that what he'd been secretly seeking? Punishment? Was that why things went so bad, so fast? "I thought you all were the great Vor. Why should you have to slide on by? Can't you just stomp the scum?"

Ivan groaned. "No. And am I ever glad I'm not going to be *your* permanent bodyguard."

"I'm glad too, if this is a sample of your work," Mark snarled in return. He checked his left canine tooth; his gum and lips were puffy, but it wasn't actually loose.

Ivan merely growled. Mark settled back, wondering how the kid with the damaged throat was doing. The municipal guards had taken him away for treatment. Mark should not have fought him; he'd come within a centimeter of killing him. He might have killed all three. The punks were only *little* cannibals, after all. Which was why, Mark realized, Miles would have talked and slid away; not fear, and not *noblesse oblige*, but because those people weren't up to his . . . weight class. Mark felt ill. *Barrayarans. God help me.*

Ivan swung by his apartment, which was in a tower in one of the city's better districts, not far from the entirely modern government buildings housing the Imperial Service Command headquarters. There he allowed Mark to wash up and remove the bloodstains from his clothing before his return to Vorkosigan House. Tossing Mark's shirt back to him from the dryer, Ivan remarked, "Your torso is going to be piebald tomorrow. Miles would have been in hospital for the next three weeks over that. I'd have had to cart him out of there on a board."

Mark glanced down at the red blotches, just starting to turn purple. He was stiffening up all over. Half a dozen pulled muscles protested their abuse. All that, he could conceal, but his face bore marks that were going to have to be explained. Telling the Count and Countess that he'd been in a ground-car wreck with Ivan would be perfectly believable, but he doubted they'd get away with the lie for long.

In the event, Ivan did the talking again, delivering him back to the Countess with a true but absolutely minimized account of Mark's adventure: "Aw, he wandered off and got pushed around a little by the local residents, but I caught up with him before anything much could happen. 'Bye, Aunt Cordelia . . ." Mark let him escape without impediment.

The whole report had certainly caught up with the Count and Countess by dinner. Mark sensed the cool faint tension even as he slid into his place at the table opposite Elena Bothari-Jesek, who was back at last from her lengthy and presumably grueling debriefing at ImpSec HQ.

The Count waited until the first course had been served and the human servant had departed the dining room before remarking, "I'm glad your learning experience today was not lethal, Mark."

Mark managed to swallow without gagging, and said in a subdued voice, "For him, or me?"

"Either. Do you wish a report on your, ah, victim?"

No. "Yes. Please."

"The physicians at the municipal hospital expect to release him in two days. He will be on a liquid diet for a week. He will recover his voice."

"Oh. Good." *I didn't mean to . . .* What was the point of excuses, apologies, protests? None, surely.

"I looked into picking up his medical bill, privately, only to discover that Ivan had been in ahead of me. Upon reflection, I decided to let him stand for it."

"Oh." Ought he to offer to repay Ivan, then? Did he have any money, or any right to any? Legally? Morally?

"Tomorrow," stated the Countess, "Elena will be your native guide. And Pym will accompany you."

Elena looked very much less than thrilled.

"I spoke with Gregor," Count Vorkosigan continued. "You apparently impressed him enough, somehow, that he has given his approval for my formal presentation of you as my heir, House Vorkosigan's cadet member of the Council of Counts. At a time of my discretion, if and when Miles's death is confirmed. Obviously, this step is still premature. I'm not sure myself whether it would be better to get your confirmation pushed through before the Counts get to know you, or after they have had time to get used to the idea. A swift maneuver, hit and run, or a long tedious siege. For once, I think a siege would be better. If we won, your victory would be far more secure."

"Can they reject me?" Mark asked. *Is that a light I see at the end of this tunnel?*

"They must accept and approve you by a simple majority vote for you to inherit the Countship. My personal property is a separate matter. Normally, such approval is routine for the eldest son, or, lacking a son, whatever competent male relative a Count may put forward. It doesn't even have to be a relative, technically, though it almost always is. There was the famous case of one of the Counts Vortala, back in the Time of Isolation, who had fallen out with his son. Young Lord Vortala had allied with his father-in-law in the Zidiarch Trade War. Vortala disinherited his son and somehow managed to maneuver a rump session of the Counts into approving his horse, Midnight, as his heir. Claimed the horse was just as bright and had never betrayed him."

"What . . . a hopeful precedent for me," Mark choked. "How did Count Midnight do? Compared to the average Count."

"Lord Midnight. Alas, no one found out. The horse pre-deceased the Vortala, the war petered out, and the son eventually inherited after all. But it was one of the zoological high points of the Council's varied political history, right up there with the infamous Incendiary Cat Plot." Count Vorkosigan's eye glinted with a certain skewed enthusiasm, relating all this. His eye fell on Mark and his momentary animation faded. "We've had several centuries to accumulate any precedent you please, from absurdities to horrors. And a few sound saving graces."

The Count did not make further inquiries into Mark's day, and Mark did not volunteer further details. The dinner went down like lead, and Mark escaped as soon as he decently could.

He slunk off to the library, the long room at the end of one wing of the oldest part of the house. The Countess had encouraged him to browse there. In addition to a reader accessing public databanks and a code-locked and secured government comconsole with its own dedicated comm links, the room was lined with bound books printed and even hand-calligraphied on paper from the Time of Isolation. The library reminded Mark of Vorhartung Castle, with its modern equipment and functions awkwardly stuffed into odd corners of an antique architecture that had never envisioned nor provided place for them.

As he was thinking about the museum, a large folio volume of woodcuts of arms and armor caught his eye, and he carefully pulled it from its slipcase and carried it to one of a pair of alcoves flanking the long glass doors to the back garden. The alcoves were luxuriously furnished, and a little table pulled up to a vast wing-chair provided support for the, in both senses, heavy volume. Bemused, Mark leafed through it. Fifty kinds of swords and knives, with every slight variation possessing its own name, and names for all the parts as well . . . what an absolutely fractal knowledge-base, the kind created by, and in turn creating, a closed in-group such as the Vor. . . .

The library's door swung open, and footsteps sounded across the marble and carpeting. It was Count Vorkosigan. Mark shrank back in the chair in the alcove, drawing his legs up out of sight. Maybe the man would just take something and go out again. Mark did not want to get trapped into some intimate chat, which this comfortable room so invited. He had conquered his initial terror of the Count, yet the man managed still to make him excruciatingly uncomfortable, even without saying a word.

Unfortunately, Count Vorkosigan seated himself at one of the comconsoles. Reflections of the colored lights of its display flickered on the glass of the windows Mark's chair faced. The longer he waited, Mark realized, lurking like an assassin, the more awkward it was going to be to reveal himself. *So say hello. Drop the book. Blow your nose, something.* He was just working up the courage to try a little throat-clearing and page-rustling, when the door hinges squeaked again, and lighter footsteps sounded. The Countess. Mark huddled into a ball in the wing-chair.

"Ah," said the Count. The lights reflecting in the window died away as he shut down the machine in favor of this new diversion, and swung around in his station chair. Did she lean over for some quick embrace? Fabric whispered as she seated herself.

"Well, Mark is certainly getting a crash-course about Barrayar," she remarked, effectively spiking Mark's last frantic impulse to make his presence known.

"It's what he needs," sighed the Count. "He has twenty years of catching up to do, if he is to function."

"Must he function? I mean, instantly?"

"No. Not instantly."

"Good. I thought you might be setting him an impossible task. And as we all know, the impossible takes a little longer."

The Count vented a short laugh, which faded quickly. "At least he's had a glimpse of one of our worst social traits. We must be sure he gets a thorough grounding in the history of the mutagen disasters, so he'll understand where the violence is coming from. How deeply the agony and the fear are embedded, which drive the visible anxieties and, ah, as you Betans would see it, bad manners."

"I'm not sure he'll ever be able to duplicate Miles's native ability to dance through that particular minefield."

"He seems more inclined to plow through it," murmured the Count dryly, and hesitated. "His appearance . . . Miles took enormous pains to move, act, dress, so as to draw attention away from his appearance.

To make his personality overpower the evidence of the eye. A kind of whole-body sleight-of-hand, if you will. Mark . . . almost seems to be willfully exaggerating it."

"What, the surly slump?"

"That, and . . . I confess, I find his weight gain disturbing. Particularly, judging from Elena's report, its rapidity. Perhaps we ought to have him medically checked. It can't be good for him."

The Countess snorted. "He's only twenty-two. It's not an immediate health problem. That's not what's bothering you, love."

"Perhaps . . . not entirely."

"He embarrasses you. My body-conscious Barrayaran friend."

"Mm." The Count did not deny this, Mark noticed.

"Score one for his side."

"Would you care to clarify that?"

"Mark's actions are a language. A language of desperation, mostly. They're not always easy to interpret. *That* one is obvious, though."

"Not to me. Analyze, please."

"It's a three-part problem. In the first place, there's the purely physical side. I take it you did not read the medical reports as carefully as I did."

"I read the ImpSec synopsis."

"I read the raw data. All of it. When the Jacksonian body-sculptors were cutting Mark down to match Miles's height, they did not genetically retrofit his metabolism. Instead they brewed up a concoction of time-release hormones and stimulants which they injected monthly, tinkering with the formula as needed. Cheaper, simpler, more controlled in result. Now, take Ivan as a phenotypic sample of what Miles's genotype should have resulted in, without the soltoxin poisoning. What we have in Mark is a man physically reduced to Miles's height who is genetically programmed for Ivan's weight. And when the Komarrans' treatments stopped, his body again began to try to carry out its genetic destiny. If you ever bring yourself to look at him square on, you'll notice it's not just fat. His bones and muscles are heavier too, compared to Miles or even to himself two years ago. When he finally reaches his new equilibrium, he's probably going to look rather low-slung."

You mean spherical, Mark thought, listening with horror, and intensely conscious of having overeaten at dinner. Heroically, he smothered an incipient belch.

"Like a small tank," suggested the Count, evidently entertaining a somewhat more hopeful vision.

"Perhaps. It depends on the other two aspects of his, um, body-language."

"Which are?"

"Rebellion, and fear. As for rebellion—all his life, *other* people have made free with his somatic integrity. Forcibly chosen his body-shape. Now at last it's his turn. And fear. Of Barrayar, of us, but most of all fear, frankly, of being overwhelmed by Miles, who can be pretty overwhelming even if you're not his little brother. And Mark's right. It's actually been something of a boon. The Armsmen and servants are having no trouble distinguishing him, taking him as Lord Mark. The weight ploy has that sort of half-cocked half-conscious brilliance that . . . reminds me of someone else we both know."

"But where does it stop?" The Count was now picturing something spherical too, Mark decided.

"The metabolism—when he chooses. He can march himself to a physician and have it adjusted to maintain any weight he wants. He'll choose a more average body-type when he no longer needs rebellion or feels fear."

The Count snorted. "I know Barrayar, and its paranoias. You can never be safe enough. What do we do if he decides he can never be fat enough?"

"Then we can buy him a float pallet and a couple of

muscular body-servants. *Or*—we can help him conquer his fears. Eh?"

"If Miles is dead," he began.

"If Miles is not recovered and revived," she corrected sharply.

"Then Mark is all we have left of Miles."

"No!" Her skirts rustled as she rose, stepped, turned, paced. *God, don't let her walk over this way!* "That's where you take the wrong turn, Aral. Mark is all we have left of *Mark*."

The Count hesitated. "All right. I concede the point. But if Mark is all we have—do we have the next Count Vorkosigan?"

"Can you accept him as your son even if he *isn't* the next Count Vorkosigan? Or is that the test he has to pass to get in?"

The Count was silent. The Countess's voice went low. "Do I hear an echo of your father's voice in yours? Is that him I see, looking out from behind your eyes?"

"It is . . . impossible . . . that he not be there." The Count's voice was equally low, disturbed, but defiant of apology. "On some level. Despite it all."

"I . . . yes. I understand. I'm sorry." She sat again, to Mark's frozen relief. "Although surely it isn't that hard to qualify as a Count of Barrayar. Look at some of the odd ducks who sit on the Council now. Or fail to show up, in some cases. How long did you say it's been since Count Vortienne cast a vote?"

"His son is old enough to hold down his desk now," said the Count. "To the great relief of the rest of us. The last time we had to have a unanimous vote, the Chamber's Sergeant-at-Arms had to go collect him bodily from his Residence, out of the most extraordinary scene of . . . well, he finds some unique uses for his personal guard."

"Unique qualifications, too, I understand." There was a grin in Countess Cordelia's voice.

"Where did you learn *that*?"

"Alys Vorpatril."

"I'm . . . not even going to ask how she knows."

"Wise of you. But the point is, Mark would really have to work at it to be the worst Count on the Council. They are not so elite as they pretend."

"Vortienne is an unfairly horrible example. It's only because of the extraordinary dedication of so many of the Counts that the Council functions at all. It consumes men. But—the Counts are only half the battle. The sharper edge of the sword is the District itself. Would the people accept him? The disturbed clone of the deformed original?"

"They came to accept Miles. They've even grown rather proud of him, I think. But—Miles creates that himself. He radiates enough loyalty, they can't help but reflect some of it back."

"I'm not sure what Mark radiates," mused the Count. "He seems more of a human black hole. Light goes in, nothing comes out."

"Give him time. He's still afraid of you. Guilt projection, I think, from having been your intended assassin all these years."

Mark, breathing through his mouth for silence, cringed. Did the damned woman have x-ray vision? She was a most unnerving ally, if ally she was.

"Ivan," said the Count slowly, "would certainly have no trouble with popularity in the District. And, however reluctantly, I think he would rise to the challenge of the Countship. Neither the worst nor the best, but at least average."

"That's exactly the system he's used to slide through his schooling, the Imperial Service Academy, and his career so far. The invisible average man," said the Countess.

"It's frustrating to watch. He's capable of so much more '

"Standing as close to the Imperium as he does, how brightly does he dare shine? He'd attract would-be conspirators the way a searchlight attracts bugs, looking for a figurehead for their faction. And a handsome figurehead he'd make. He only plays the fool. He may in fact be the least foolish one among us."

"It's an optimistic theory, but if Ivan is so calculating, how can he have been like this since he could walk?" the Count asked plaintively. "You'd make of him a fiendishly Machiavellian five-year-old, dear Captain."

"I don't insist on the interpretation," said the Countess comfortably. "The point is, if Mark were to choose a life on, say, Beta Colony, Barrayar would contrive to limp along somehow. Even your District would probably survive. And Mark would not be one iota less our son."

"But I wanted to leave so much more. . . . You keep coming back to that idea. Beta Colony."

"Yes. Do you wonder why?"

"No." His voice grew smaller. "But if you take him away to Beta Colony, I'll never get a chance to know him."

The Countess was silent, then her voice grew firmer. "I'd be more impressed by that complaint if you showed any signs of wanting to get to know him *now*. You've been avoiding him almost as assiduously as he's been ducking you."

"I cannot stop all government business for this personal crisis," said the Count stiffly. "As much as I might like to."

"You did for Miles, as I recall. Think back on all the time you spent with him, here, at Vorkosigan Surleau . . . you stole time like a thief to give to him, snatches here and there, an hour, a morning, a day, whatever you could arrange, all the while carrying the Regency at a dead run through about six major political and military crises. You cannot deny Mark the advantages you gave Miles, and then turn around and decry his failure to outperform Miles."

"Oh, Cordelia," the Count sighed. "I was younger then. I'm not the Da Miles had twenty years ago. That man is gone, burned up."

"I don't ask that you try to be the Da you were then; that would be ludicrous. Mark is no child. I only ask that you try to be the father you are now."

"Dear Captain . . ." His voice trailed off in exhaustion.

After a thoughtful silence, the Countess said pointedly, "You'd have more time and energy if you *retired*. Gave up the Prime Ministership, at long last."

"Now? Cordelia, think! I dare not lose control now. As Prime Minister, Illyan and ImpSec still report to me. If I step down to a mere Countship, I am out of that chain of command. I'll lose the very power to prosecute the search."

"Nonsense. Miles is an ImpSec officer. Son of the Prime Minister or not, they'll hunt for him just the same. Loyalty to their own is one of ImpSec's few charms."

"They'll search to the limits of reason. Only as Prime Minister can I compel them to go beyond reason."

"I think not. I think Simon Illyan would still turn himself inside out for you after you were dead and buried, love."

When the Count spoke again at last his voice was weary. "I was ready to step down three years ago and hand it off to Quintillan."

"Yes. I was all excited."

"If only he hadn't been killed in that stupid flyer accident. Such a pointless tragedy. It wasn't even an assassination!"

The Countess laughed blackly at him. "A *truly* wasted death, by Barrayaran standards. But seriously. It's time to stop."

"Past time," the Count agreed.

"Let *go*."

"As soon as it's safe."

She paused. "You will never be fat enough, love. Let go anyway."

Mark sat bent over, paralyzed, one leg gone pins and needles. He felt plowed and harrowed, more thoroughly worked over than by the three thugs in the alley. The Countess was a scientific fighter, there was no doubt.

The Count half-laughed. But this time he made no reply. To Mark's enormous relief, they both rose and exited the library together. As soon as the door shut he rolled out of the wing-chair onto the floor, moving his aching arms and legs and trying to restore circulation. He was shaking and shivering. His throat was clogged, and he coughed at last, over and over, blessedly, to clear his breathing. He didn't know whether to laugh or cry, felt like doing both at once, and settled for wheezing, watching his belly rise and fall. He felt obese. He felt insane. He felt as if his skin had gone transparent, and passers-by could look and point to every private organ.

What he did not feel, he realized as he caught his breath again after the coughing jag, was afraid. Not of the Count and Countess, anyway. Their public faces and their privates ones were . . . unexpectedly congruent. It seemed he could trust them, not so much not to hurt him, but to be what they were, what they appeared. He could not at first put a word to it, this sense of personal unity. Then it came to him. *Oh. So that's what integrity looks like. I didn't know.*

CHAPTER FIFTEEN

The Countess kept her promise, or threat, to send Mark touring with Elena. The ensuing few weeks were punctuated by frequent excursions all over Vorbarr Sultana and the neighboring Districts, slanted heavily to the cultural and historical, including a private tour of the Imperial Residence. Gregor was not at home that day, to Mark's relief. They must have hit every museum in town. Elena, presumably acting under orders, also dragged him over what must have been two dozen colleges, academies, and technical schools. Mark was heartened to learn that not every institution on the planet trained military officers; indeed, the largest and busiest school in the capital was the Vorbarra District Agricultural and Engineering Institute.

Elena remained a formal and impersonal factotum in Mark's presence. Whatever her own feelings upon seeing her old home for the first time in a decade, they seldom escaped the ivory mask, except for an occasional exclamation of surprise at some unexpected change: new buildings sprouted, old blocks leveled, streets re-routed. Mark suspected that the frenetic pace of the tours was just so she wouldn't have to actually talk to him; she filled the silences instead with lectures. Mark began to wish he'd buttered up Ivan more. Maybe his cousin could have sneaked him out to go pub-crawling, just for a change.

Change came one evening when the Count returned abruptly to Vorkosigan House and announced that they were all going to Vorkosigan Surleau. Within an hour Mark found himself and his things packed into a lightflyer, along with Elena, Count Vorkosigan, and Armsman Pym, arrowing south in the dark to the Vorkosigans' summer residence. The Countess did not accompany them. The conversation en route ranged from stilted to non-existent, except for an occasional laconic code between the Count and Pym, all half-sentences. The Dendarii mountain range loomed up at last, a dark blot against cloud shadows and stars. They circled a dimly glimmering lake to land halfway up a hill in front of a rambling stone house, lit up and made welcoming by yet more human servants. The Prime Minister's ImpSec guards were discreet shapes exiting a second lightflyer in their wake.

Since it was nearing midnight, the Count limited himself to giving Mark a brief orienting tour of the interior of the house, and depositing him in a second-floor guest bedroom with a view downslope to the lake. Mark, alone at last, leaned on the windowsill and stared into the darkness. Lights shimmered across the black silken waters, from the village at the end of the lake and from a few isolated estates on the farther shore. *Why have you brought me here?* he thought to the Count. Vorkosigan Surleau was the most private of the Vorkosigans' several residences, the guarded emotional heart of the Count's scattered personal realm. Had he passed some test, to be let in here? Or was Vorkosigan Surleau itself to be a test? He went to bed and fell asleep still wondering.

He woke blinking with morning sun slanting through the window he'd failed to re-shutter the night before. Some servant last night had arranged a selection of his more casual clothing in the room's closet. He found a bathroom down the hall, washed, dressed, and went in cautious search of humanity. A housekeeper in the kitchen directed him outside to find the Count without, alas, offering to feed him breakfast.

He walked along a path paved with stone chips toward a grove of carefully-planted Earth-import trees, their distinctive green leaves mottled and gilded by the beginnings of autumn color change. Big trees, very old. The Count and Elena were near the grove in a walled garden that served now as the Vorkosigan family cemetery. The stone residence had originally been a guard barracks serving the now-ruined castle at the lake's foot; its cemetery had once received the guardsmen's last stand-downs.

Mark's brows rose. The Count was a violent splash of color in his most formal military uniform, Imperial parade red-and-blues. Elena was equally, if more quietly, decorous in Dendarii dress-grey velvet set off with silver buttons and white piping. She squatted beside a shallow bronze brazier on a tripod. Little pale orange flames flickered in it, and smoke rose to wisp away in the gold-misted morning air. They were burning a death-offering, Mark realized, and paused uncertainly by the wrought-iron gate in the low stone wall. Whose? Nobody had invited him.

Elena rose; she and the Count spoke quietly together while the offering, whatever it was, burned to ash. After a moment Elena folded a cloth into a pad, picked the brazier off its tripod, and tapped out the gray and white flakes over the grave. She wiped out the bronze basin and returned it and its folding tripod to an embroidered brown and silver bag. The Count gazed over the lake, noticed Mark standing by the gate, and gave him an acknowledging nod; it did not exactly invite him in, but neither did it rebuff him.

With another word to the Count, Elena exited the walled garden. The Count saluted her. She favored Mark with a courteous nod in passing. Her face was solemn, but, Mark fancied, less tense and mask-like than he had seen since their coming to Barrayar. Now the Count definitely waved Mark inside. Feeling awkward, but curious, Mark let himself in through the gate and crunched over the gravel walks to his side.

"What's . . . up?" Mark finally managed to ask. It came out sounding too flippant, but the Count did not seem to take it in bad part.

Count Vorkosigan nodded to the grave at their feet: *Sergeant Constantine Bothari*, and the dates. *Fidelis*. "I found that Elena had never burned a death-offering for her father. He was my armsman for eighteen years, and had served under me in the space forces before that."

"Miles's bodyguard. I knew that. But he was killed before Galen started training me. Galen didn't spend much time on him."

"He should have. Sergeant Bothari was very important to Miles. And to us all. Bothari was . . . a difficult man. I don't think Elena ever was quite reconciled to that. She's needed to come to some acceptance of him, to be easy with herself."

"Difficult? Criminal, I'd heard."

"That is very . . ." The Count hesitated. *Unjust*, Mark expected him to add, or *untrue*, but the word he finally chose was ". . . incomplete."

They walked around among the graves, the Count giving Mark a tour. Relatives and retainers . . . who was Major Amor Klyeuvi? It reminded Mark of all those museums. The Vorkosigan family history since the Time of Isolation encapsulated the history of Barrayar. The Count pointed out his father, mother, brother, sister, and his Vorkosigan grandparents. Presumably anyone dying prior to their dates had been buried at the old District capital of Vorkosigan Vashnoi, and been melted down along with the city by the Cetagandan invaders.

"I mean to be buried here," commented the Count, looking over the peaceful lake and the hills beyond. The morning mist was clearing off the surface, sun-sparkle starting to glitter through. "Avoid that crowd at the Imperial Cemetery in Vorbarr Sultana. They wanted to bury my poor father there. I actually had to argue with them over that, despite the declaration of his will." He nodded to the stone, *General Count Piotr Pierre Vorkosigan*, and the dates. The Count had won the argument, apparently. The Counts.

"Some of the happiest periods of my life were spent here, when I was small. And later, my wedding and honeymoon." A twisted smile flitted across his features. "Miles was conceived here. Therefore, in a sense, so were you. Look around. This is where you came from. After breakfast, and I change clothes, I'll show you more."

"Ah. So, uh, no one's eaten yet."

"You fast, before burning a death-offering. They often tend to be dawn events for just that reason, I suspect." The Count half-smiled.

The Count could have had no other use for the glorious parade uniform here, nor Elena her Dendarii greys. They'd packed them along for that dedicated purpose. Mark glanced at the dark distorted reflection of himself in the Count's mirror-polished boots. The convex surface widened him to grotesque proportions. His future self? "Is that what we all came down here for, then? So that Elena could do this ceremony?"

"Among other things."

Ominous. Mark followed the Count back to the big stone house, feeling obscurely unsettled.

Breakfast was served by the housekeeper on a sunny patio off the end of the house, made private by landscaping and flowering bushes except for a view cut through to the lake. The Count re-appeared wearing old black fatigue trousers and a back-country style tunic, loose-cut and belted. Elena did not join them. "She wanted to take a long walk," explained the Count briefly. "So shall we." Prudently, Mark returned a third sweet roll to its covered basket.

He was glad for his restraint very shortly, as the Count led him directly up the hill. They crested it and paused to recover. The view of the long lake, winding between the hills, was very fine and worth the breath. On the other side a little valley flattened out, cradling old stone stables and pastures cultivated to Earth-green grasses. Some unemployed-looking horses idled around the pasture. The Count led Mark down to the fence, and leaned on it, looking pensive.

"That big roan over there is Miles's horse. He's been rather neglected, of late years. Miles didn't always get time to ride even when he was home. He used to come running, when Miles called. It was the damndest thing, to see that big lazy horse get up and come running." The Count paused. "You might try it."

"What? Call the horse?"

"I'd be curious to see. If the horse can tell the difference. Your voices are . . . very like, to my ear."

"I was drilled on that."

"His name is, uh, Ninny." At Mark's look he added, "A sort of pet or stable name."

Its name is Fat Ninny. You edited it. Ha. "So what do I do? Stand here and yell 'Here, Ninny, Ninny'?" He felt a fool already.

"Three times."

"What?"

"Miles always repeated the name three times."

The horse was standing across the pasture, its ears up, looking at them. Mark took a deep breath, and in his best Barrayaran accent called, "Here, Ninny, Ninny, Ninny. Here, Ninny, Ninny, Ninny!"

The horse snorted, and trotted over to the fence. It didn't exactly run, though it did kick up its heels once, bouncing, en route. It arrived with a huff that sprayed horse moisture across both Mark and the Count. It leaned against the fence, which groaned and bent. Up close, it was bloody huge. It stuck its big head over the fence. Mark ducked back hastily.

"Hello, old boy." The Count patted its neck. "Miles always gives him sugar," he advised Mark over his shoulder.

"No wonder it comes running, then!" said Mark indignantly. And he'd thought it was the I-love-Naismith effect.

"Yes, but Cordelia and I give him sugar too, and he doesn't come running for us. He just sort of ambles around in his own good time."

The horse was staring at him in, Mark swore, utter bewilderment. Yet another soul he had betrayed by not being Miles. The other two horses, in some sort of sibling rivalry, now arrived also, a massive jostling crowd determined not to miss out. Intimidated, Mark asked plaintively, "Did you bring any sugar?"

"Well, yes," said the Count. He drew half a dozen white cubes from his pocket and handed them to Mark. Cautiously, Mark put a couple into his palm and held it out as far as his arm would reach. With a squeal, Ninny laid his ears back and snapped from side to side, driving off his equine rivals, then demurely pricked them forward again and grubbed up the sugar with big rubbery lips, leaving a trail of grass-green slime in Mark's palm. Mark wiped some of it off on the fence, considered his trouser seam, and wiped the rest off on the horse's glossy neck. An old ridged scar spoiled the fur, bumpy under his hand. Ninny butted him again, and Mark retreated out of range. The Count restored order in the mob with a couple of shouts and slaps—*Ah, just like Barrayaran politics*, Mark thought irreverently—and made sure the two laggards received a share of sugar as well. He did wipe his palms on his trouser seams afterward, quite unself-consciously.

"Would you like to try riding him?" the Count offered. "Though he hasn't been worked lately, he's probably a bit fresh."

"No, thank you," choked Mark. "Some other time, maybe."

"Ah."

They walked along the fence, Ninny trailing them on the other side till its hopes were stopped by the corner. It whinnied as they walked away, a staggeringly mournful noise. Mark's shoulders hunched as from a blow. The Count smiled, but the attempt must have felt as ghastly as it looked, for the smile fell off again immediately. He looked back over his shoulder. "The old fellow is over twenty, now. Getting up there, for a horse. I'm beginning to identify with him."

They were heading toward the woods. "There's a riding trail . . . it circles around to a spot with a view back toward the house. We used to picnic there. Would you like to see it?"

A hike. Mark had no heart for a hike, but he'd already turned down the Count's obvious overture about riding the horse. He didn't dare refuse him twice, the Count would think him . . . surly. "All right." No armsmen or ImpSec bodyguards in sight. The Count had gone out of his way to create this private time. Mark cringed in anticipation. Intimate chat, incoming.

When they reached the woods' edge the first fallen leaves rustled and crackled underfoot, releasing an organic but pleasant tang. But the noise of their feet did not exactly fill the silence. The Count, for all his feigned country-casualness, was stiff and tense. Off-balance. Unnerved by him, Mark blurted, "The Countess is making you do this. Isn't she."

"Not really," said the Count, ". . . yes."

A thoroughly mixed reply and probably true.

"Will you ever forgive the Bharaputrans for shooting the wrong Admiral Naismith?"

"Probably not." The Count's tone was equable, unoffended.

"If it had been reversed—if that Bharaputran had aimed one short guy to the left—would ImpSec be hunting my cryo-chamber now?" Would Miles even have dumped Trooper Phillipi, to put Mark in her place?

"Since Miles would in that case be ImpSec in the area—I fancy the answer is yes," murmured the Count. "As I had never met you, my own interest would probably have been a little . . . academic. Your mother would have pushed all the same, though," he added thoughtfully.

"Let us by all means be honest with each other," Mark said bitterly.

"We cannot possibly build anything that will last on any other basis," said the Count dryly. Mark flushed, and grunted assent.

The trail ran first along a stream, then cut up over a rise through what was almost a gully or wash, paved with loose and sliding rock. Thankfully it then ran level for a time, branching and re-branching through the trees. A few little horse jumps made of cut logs and brush were set up deliberately here and there; the trails ran around as well as over them, optionally. Why was he certain Miles chose to ride over them? He had to admit, there was something primevally restful about the woods, with its patterns of sun and shade, tall Earth trees and native and imported brush creating an illusion of endless privacy. One could imagine that the whole planet was such a people-less wilderness, if one didn't know anything about terraforming. They turned onto a wider double track, where they could walk side by side.

The Count moistened his lips. "About that cryo-chamber."

Mark's head came up like the horse's had, sensing sugar. ImpSec wasn't talking to him, the Count hadn't been talking to him; driven half-crazy by the information vacuum, he'd finally broken down and badgered the Countess, though it made him feel ill to do so. But even she could only report negatives. ImpSec now knew over four hundred places the cryo-chamber was not. It was a start. Four hundred down, the rest of the universe to go . . . it was impossible, useless, futile—

"ImpSec has found it." The Count rubbed his face.

"What!" Mark stopped short. "They got it back? Hot damn! It's over! Where did they—why didn't you—" He bit off his words as it came to him that there was probably a very good reason the Count hadn't told him at once. And he wasn't sure he wanted to hear it. The Count's face was bleak.

"It was empty."

"Oh." What a stupid thing to say, *Oh.* Mark felt incredibly stupid, just now. "How—I don't understand." Of all the scenarios he'd pictured, he'd never pictured that. *Empty?* "Where?"

"The ImpSec agent found it in the sales inventory of a medical supply company in the Hegen Hub. Cleaned and re-conditioned."

"Are they sure it's the right one?"

"If the identifications Captain Quinn and the Dendarii gave us are correct, it is. The agent, who is one of our brighter boys, simply quietly purchased it. It's being shipped back by fast courier to ImpSec headquarters on Komarr for a thorough forensic analysis right now. Not that, apparently, there is much to analyze."

"But it's a lead, a break at last! The supply company must have records—ImpSec should be able to trace it back to—to—" To what?

"Yes, and no. The record trail breaks one step back from the supply company. The independent carrier they bought it from appears to be guilty of receiving stolen property."

"From Jackson's Whole? Surely that narrows down the search area!"

"Mm. One must remember that the Hegen Hub is a *hub*. The possibility that the cryo-chamber was routed into the Cetagandan Empire from Jackson's Whole, and back out again via the Hegen Hub, is . . . remote but real."

"No. The timing."

"The timing would be tight, but possible. Illyan has calculated it. The timing limits the search area to a mere . . . nine planets, seventeen stations, and all the ships en route between them." The Count grimaced. "I almost wish I was sure we were dealing with a Cetagandan plot. The Ghem-lords at least I could trust to know or guess the value of the package. The nightmare that makes me despair is that the cryo-chamber somehow fell into the hands of some Jacksonian petty thief, who simply dumped the contents in order to re-sell the equipment. We would have paid a ransom . . . a dozen times the value of the cryo-chamber for the dead body alone. For Miles preserved and potentially revivable—whatever they asked. It drives me mad to think that Miles is rotting somewhere by *mistake*."

Mark pressed his hands to his forehead, which was throbbing. His neck was so tight it felt like a piece of solid wood. "No . . . it's crazy, it's too crazy. We have both ends of the rope now, we're only missing the middle. It has to be connectable. Norwood—Norwood was loyal to Admiral Naismith. And smart. I met him, briefly. Of course, he hadn't planned to be killed, but he wouldn't have sent the cryo-chamber into danger, or off at random." Was he so sure? Norwood had expected to be able to pick up the cryo-chamber from its destination within a day at most. If it had arrived . . . wherever . . .

with some sort of cryptic hold-till-called-for note attached, and then no one had called for it . . . "Was it re-conditioned before or after the Hub supply company purchased it?"

"Before."

"Then there has to be some sort of medical facility hidden in the gap somewhere. Maybe a cryo-facility. Maybe . . . maybe Miles was shifted into somebody's permanent storage banks." Unidentified, and destitute? On Escobar such a charity might be possible, but on Jackson's Whole? A most forlorn hope.

"I pray so. There are only a finite number of such facilities. It's checkable. ImpSec is on it now. Yet only the . . . frozen dead require that much expertise. The mere mechanics of cleaning an emptied chamber could be done by any ship's sickbay. Or engineering section. An unmarked grave could be harder to locate. Or maybe no grave, just disintegrated like garbage. . . ." The Count stared off into the trees.

Mark bet he wasn't seeing trees. Mark bet he was seeing the same vision Mark was, a frozen little body, chest blown out—you wouldn't even need a hand-tractor to lift it—shoved carelessly, mindlessly, into some disposal unit. Would they even wonder who the little man had been? Or would it just be a repellent *thing* to them? Who was *them*, dammit?

And how long had the Count's mind been running on this same wheel of thought, and how the devil was it that he could still walk and talk at the same time? "How long have you known this?"

"The report came in yesterday afternoon. So you see . . . it becomes measurably more important that I know where you stand. In relation to Barrayar." He started again up the trail, then took a side branch that narrowed and began to rise steeply through an area of taller trees and thinner brush.

Mark toiled on his heels. "Nobody in their right mind would stand in relation to Barrayar. They would run in relation to Barrayar. Away."

The Count grinned over his shoulder. "You've been talking too much to Cordelia, I fear."

"Yes, well, she's about the only person here who will talk to me." He caught up with the Count, who had slowed.

The Count grimaced painfully. "That's been true." He paced up the steep stony trail. "I'm sorry." After a few more steps he added, with a flash of dark humor, "I wonder if the risks I used to take did this to my father. He is nobly avenged, if so." More darkness than humor, Mark gauged. "But it's more than ever necessary . . . to know . . ."

The Count stopped and sat down abruptly by the side of the trail, his back to a tree. "That's strange," he murmured. His face, which had been flushed and moist with the hill-climb and the morning's growing warmth, was suddenly pale and moist.

"What?" said Mark cautiously, panting. He rested his hands on his knees and stared at the man, so oddly reduced to his eye level. The Count had a distracted, absorbed look on his face.

"I think . . . I had better rest a moment."

"Suits me." Mark sat too, on a nearby rock. The Count did not continue the conversation at once. Extreme unease tightened Mark's stomach. *What's wrong with him? There's something wrong with him. Oh, shit. . . .* The sky had grown blue and fine, and a little breeze made the trees sigh, and a few more golden leaves flutter down. The cold chill up Mark's spine had nothing to do with the weather.

"It is not," said the Count in a distant, academic tone, "a perforated ulcer. I've had one of those, and this isn't the same." He crossed his arms over his chest. His breath was becoming shallow and rapid, not recovering its rhythm with sitting as Mark's was.

Something very wrong. A brave man trying hard not to look scared was, Mark decided, one of the most frightening sights he'd ever seen. Brave, but not stupid: the Count did not, for example, choose to pretend that nothing was the matter and go charging up the trail to prove it.

"You don't look well."

"I don't feel well."

"What do you feel?"

"Er . . . chest pain, I'm afraid," he admitted in obvious embarrassment. "More of an ache, really. A very . . . odd . . . sensation. Came up between one step and the next."

"It couldn't be indigestion, could it?" Like the kind that was boiling up acidly in Mark's belly right now?

"I'm afraid not."

"Maybe you had better call for help on your comm link," Mark suggested diffidently. There sure as hell wasn't anything *he* could do, if this was the medical emergency it looked like.

The Count laughed, a dry wheeze. It was not a comforting sound. "I left it."

"What? You're the frigging Prime Minister, you can't go around without—"

"I wanted to assure an uninterrupted, private conversation. For a change. Unpunctuated by half the under-ministers in Vorbarr Sultana calling up to ask me where they left their agendas. I used to . . . do that for Miles. Sometimes, when it got too thick. Drove everyone crazy but eventually . . . they became . . . reconciled." His voice went high and light on the last word. He lay back altogether, in the detritus and fallen leaves. "No . . . that's no improvement. . . ." He extended a hand and Mark, his own heart lumping with terror, pulled him back into the sitting position.

A paralyzing toxin . . . heart failure . . . I was to get alone with you . . . I was to wait, in your sight, for twenty minutes while you died. . . . How had he made this happen? Black magic?Maybe he *was* programmed, and part of him was doing things the rest of him didn't know anything about, like one of those split personalities. *Did I do this? Oh, God. Oh shit.*

The Count managed a pallid grin. "Don't look so scared, boy," he whispered. "Just go back to the house and get my guardsmen. It's not that far. I promise I won't move." A hoarse chuckle.

I wasn't paying any attention to the paths on the way up. I was following you. Could he possibly carry . . . ? No. Mark was no medtech, but he had a clear cold feeling that it would be a very bad idea to try to move this man. Even with his new girth he was heavily outweighed by the Count. "All right." There hadn't been that many possible wrong turns, had there? "You . . . you . . ." *Don't you dare die on me, godammit. Not now!*

Mark turned, and trotted, skidded, and flat ran back down the path. Right or left? Left, down the double track. Where the hell had they turned on to it, though? They'd pushed through some brush—there was brush all along it, and half a dozen openings. There was one of those horse-jumps they'd passed. Or was it? A lot of them looked alike. *I'm going to get lost in this frigging woods, and run around in circles for . . . twenty minutes, till he's brain-dead and rigor-stiff, and they're all going to think I did it on purpose . . .* He tripped, and bounced off a tree, and scrambled for balance and direction. He felt like a dog in a drama, running for help; when he arrived, all he'd be able to do would be bark and whine and roll on his back, and no one would understand. . . . He clung to a tree, gasping, and staring around. Wasn't moss supposed to grow on the north side of trees, or was that only on Earth? These were Earth trees, mostly.

On Jackson's Whole a sort of slimy lichen grew on the south sides of everything, including buildings, and you had to scrape it out of the door grooves . . . ah! there was the creek. But had they walked up or down stream? *Stupid, stupid, stupid.* A stitch had started in his side. He turned left and ran.

Hallelujah! A tall female shape was striding down the path ahead of him. Elena, heading back to the barn. Not only was he on the right path, he'd found help. He tried to shout. It came out a croak, but it caught her attention; she looked over her shoulder, saw him, and stopped. He staggered up to her.

"What the hell's got into you?" Her initial coldness and irritation gave way to curiosity and nascent alarm.

Mark gasped out, "The Count . . . took sick . . . in the woods. Can you get . . . his guardsmen . . . up there?"

Her brows drew down in deep suspicion. "Sick? How? He was just fine an hour ago."

"*Real* sick, pleasedammit, hurry!"

"What did you *do*—" she began, but his palpable agony overcame her wariness. "There's a comm link in the stable, it's closest. Where did you leave him?"

Mark waved vaguely backward. "Somewhere . . . I don't know what you call it. On the path to your picnic spot. Does that make sense? Don't the bloody ImpSec guards have scanners?" He found he was practically stamping his feet in frustration at her slowness. "You have longer legs. Go!"

She believed at last, and ran, with a blazing look back at him that practically flayed his skin.

I didn't do— He turned, and began to leg it back to where he'd left the Count. He wondered if he ought to be running for cover instead. If he stole a lightflyer and made it back to the capital, could he get one of the galactic embassies there to give him political asylum? *She thinks I . . . they're all going to think I* . . . hell, even *he* didn't trust himself, why should the Barrayarans? Maybe he ought to save steps, and just kill himself right now, here in these stupid woods. But he had no weapon, and rough as the terrain was, there hadn't been any cliffs high and steep enough to fling himself over and be sure of death on impact.

At first Mark thought he'd taken another wrong turn. Surely the Count couldn't have risen and walked on—no. There he was, lying down on his back beside a fallen log. He was breathing in short labored gasps, with too-long pauses in between, arms clutched in, clearly in much greater pain than when Mark had left him. But not dead. Not dead yet.

"Hello. Boy," he huffed in greeting.

"Elena's bringing help," Mark promised anxiously. He looked up and around, and listened. *But they're not here yet.*

"Good."

"Don't . . . try to talk."

This made the Count snort a laugh, an even more horrible effect against the disrupted breathing. "Only Cordelia . . . has ever succeeded . . . in shutting me up." But he fell silent after that. Mark prudently allowed him the last word, lest he try to go another round.

Live, damn you. Don't leave me here like this.

A familiar whooshing sound made Mark look up. Elena had solved the problem of getting transport through the trees with a float-bike. A green-uniformed ImpSec man rode behind her, clutching her around the waist. Elena swiftly dropped the bike through the thinner branches, which crackled. She ignored the whipping backlash that left red lines across her face. The ImpSec man dismounted while the bike was still half a meter in the air. "Get back," he snarled to Mark. At least he carried a medkit. "What did you do to him?"

Mark retreated to Elena's side. "Is he a doctor?"

"No, just a medic." Elena was out of breath too.

The medic looked up and reported, "It's the heart, but I don't know what or why. Don't have the Prime Minister's doctor come here, have him meet us in Hassadar. Without delay. I think we're going to need the facilities."

"Right." Elena snapped orders into a comm link.

Mark tried to help them get the Count temporarily positioned on the float bike, propped between Elena and the corpsman. The medic glared at Mark. "Don't touch him!"

The Count, whom Mark had thought half-conscious, opened his eyes and whispered, "Hey. The boy's all right, Jasi." Jasi the medic wilted. " 'S all right, Mark."

He's frigging dying, yet he's still thinking ahead. He's trying to clear me of suspicion.

"The aircar's meeting us in the nearest clearing," Elena pointed downslope. "Get there if you want to ride along." The bike rose slowly and carefully.

Mark took the hint, and galloped off down the hill, intensely conscious of the moving shadow just above the trees. It left him behind. He slammed faster, using tree trunks to make turns, and arrived at the double trail with palms scraped raw just as the ImpSec medic, Elena, and Armsman Pym finished laying Count Vorkosigan across the backseat of the rear compartment of a sleek black aircar. Mark tumbled in and sat next to Elena on the rear-facing seat as the canopy closed and sealed. Pym took the controls in the front compartment, and they spiraled into the air and shot away. The medic crouched on the floor by his patient and did logical things like attaching oxygen and administering a hypospray of synergine to stabilize against shock.

Mark was puffing louder than the Count, to the point that the absorbed corpsman actually glanced up at him with a medical frown, but unlike the Count, Mark caught his breath after a time. He was sweating, and shaking inside. The last time he'd felt this bad Bharaputran security troops had been firing lethal weapons at him. *Are aircars supposed to fly this fast?* Mark prayed they wouldn't suck anything bigger than a bug into the thruster intakes.

Despite the synergine the Count's eyes were going shocked and vague. He pawed at the little plastic oxygen mask, batted away the medic's worried attempt to control his hands, and motioned urgently to Mark. He so clearly wanted to say something, it was less traumatic to let him than to try and stop him. Mark slid onto his knees by the Count's head.

The Count whispered to Mark in a tone of earnest confidence, "All . . . true wealth . . . is biological."

The medic glanced wildly at Mark for interpretation; Mark could only shrug helplessly. "I think he's going out of it."

The Count only tried to speak once more, on the hurtling trip; he clawed his mask away to say, "Spit," which the medic held his head to do, a nasty hacking which cleared his throat only temporarily.

The Great Man's last words, thought Mark blackly. All that monstrous, amazing life dwindled down at the end to *Spit*. Biological indeed. He wrapped his arms around himself and sat in a huddled ball on the floor, gnawing absently on his knuckles.

When they arrived at the landing pad at Hassadar District Hospital, what seemed a small army of medical personnel descended instantly upon them, and whisked the Count away. The corpsman and the armsman were swept up; Mark and Elena were shuttled into a private waiting area, where they perforce waited.

At one point a woman with a report panel in her hand popped in to ask Mark, "Are you the next of kin?"

Mark's mouth opened, and stopped. He literally could

not reply. He was rescued by Elena, who said, "Countess Vorkosigan is flying down from Vorbarr Sultana. She should be here in just a few more minutes." It seemed to satisfy the woman, who popped out again.

Elena had it right. It wasn't another ten minutes before the corridor was enlivened by the clatter of boots. The Countess swung in trailed by two double-timing liveried armsmen. She flashed past, giving Mark and Elena a quick reassuring smile, but blasted on through the double doors without pausing. Some clueless passing doctor on the other side actually tried to stop her: "Excuse me, ma'am, no visitors beyond this point—"

Her voice overrode his, "Don't give me that crap, kid, I *own* you." His protests ended in an apologetic gurgle as he saw the armsmen's uniforms and made the correct deduction; with a "Right this way, m'lady," their voices faded into the distance.

"She meant that," Elena commented to Mark with a faint sardonic curl to her lip. "The medical network in the Vorkosigan's District has been one of her pet projects. Half the personnel here are oath-sworn to her to serve in exchange for their schooling."

Time ticked by. Mark wandered to the window and stared out over the Vorkosigan's District capital. Hassadar was a New City, heir of destroyed Vorkosigan Vashnoi; almost all its building had taken place after the end of the Time of Isolation, mostly in the last thirty years. Designed around newer methods of transportation than horse carts, it was spread out like a city on any other developed galactic world, accented by a few sky-piercing towers gleaming in the morning sun. Still only morning? It seemed a century since dawn. This hospital was indistinguishable from a similar modest one on, say, Escobar. The Count's official residence here was one of the few entirely modern villas in the Vorkosigans' household inventory. The Countess claimed to like it, yet they used it only when in Hassadar on District business; more of a hotel than a home. Curious.

The shadows of Hassadar's towers had shortened toward noon before the Countess returned to collect them. Mark searched her face anxiously as she entered. Her steps were slow, her eyes tired and strained, but her mouth was not distorted with grief. He knew the Count still lived even before she spoke.

She embraced Elena and nodded to Mark. "Aral is stabilized. They're going to transfer him to the Imperial Military Hospital in Vorbarr Sultana. His heart is badly damaged. Our man says a transplant or a mechanical is definitely indicated."

"Where were you earlier this morning?" Mark asked her.

"ImpSec Headquarters." That was logical. She eyed him. "We divided up the work load. It didn't take the both of us to ride the tight-beam decoding room. Aral did tell you the news, didn't he? He swore to me he would."

"Yes, just before he collapsed."

"What were you doing?"

Slightly better than the usual, *What did you do to him?* Haltingly, Mark tried to describe his morning.

"Stress, breakfast, running up hills," the Countess mused. "He set the pace, I'll bet."

"Militarily," Mark confirmed.

"Ha," she said darkly.

"Was it an occlusion?" asked Elena. "That's what it looked like."

"No. That's why this took me so by surprise. I knew his arteries were clean—he takes a medication for that, or his awful diet would have killed him years ago. It was an arterial aneurism, within the heart muscle. Burst blood vessel."

"Stress, eh?" said Mark, dry-mouthed. "Was his blood pressure up?"

Her eyes narrowed. "Yes, considerably, but the vessel was weakened. It would have happened sometime soon anyway."

"Was there . . . any more word come in from ImpSec?" he asked timidly. "While you were there."

"No." She paced to the window, and stared unseeing at the web and towers of Hassadar. Mark followed her. "Finding the cryo-chamber that way . . . was pretty shattering to our hopes. At least it finally goaded Aral into trying to connect with you." Pause. "Did he?"

"No . . . I don't know. He took me around, showed me things. He tried. He was trying so hard, it hurt to watch." It hurt still, a knotted ache somewhere behind his solar plexus. The soul dwelt there, according to somebody-or-other's mythology.

"Did it," she breathed.

It was all too much. The window was safely shatterproof, but his hand was not; his soul-driven fist bunched, drew back, and struck.

The Countess caught it with a quick open hand; his self-directed violence smacked into her palm and was deflected.

"Save that," she advised him coolly.

CHAPTER SIXTEEN

A large mirror in a hand-carved frame hung on the wall of the antechamber to the library. Mark, nervous, detoured to stand in front of it for one last check before his inspection by the Countess.

The brown and silver Vorkosigan cadet's uniform did little to conceal the shape of his body, old distortions or new, though when he stood up very straight he fancied it lent him a certain blunt blockiness. Unfortunately, when he slumped, so did the tunic. It fit well, which was ominous, as when it had been delivered eight weeks ago it had been a little loose. Had some ImpSec analyst calculated his weight gain against this date? He wouldn't put it past them.

Only eight weeks ago? It felt like he'd been a prisoner here forever. A gently held prisoner, true, like one of those ancient officers who, upon giving their oath of parole, were allowed the run of the fortress. Though no one had demanded his word on anything. Perhaps his word had no currency. He abandoned his repellent reflection and trudged on into the library.

The Countess was seated on the silk sofa, careful of her long dress, which was a high-necked thing in cloud-soft beige netted with ornate copper and silver embroidery which echoed the color of her hair, done up in loops on the back of her head. Not a speck of black or gray or anything that could suggest anticipation of mourning anywhere: almost arrogantly elegant. *We're just fine here*, the ensemble seemed to say, *and very Vorkosigan.* Her head turned at Mark's entry, and her absorbed look melted into a brief spontaneous smile. It drew an answering smile from him despite himself.

"You look well," she said approvingly.

"So do you," he replied, and then, because it seemed too familiar, added, "ma'am."

Her brow quirked at the addition, but she made no comment. He paced to a nearby chair but, too keyed-up to sit, only leaned on its back. He suppressed a tendency for his right boot to tap on the marble floor. "So how do you think they're going to take this tonight? Your Vor friends."

"Well, you will certainly rivet their attention," she sighed. "You can count on it." She lifted a small brown silk bag with the Vorkosigan logo embroidered in silver on it, and handed it across to Mark. It clinked interestingly from the heavy gold coins it held. "When you present this to Gregor in the taxation ceremony tonight as proxy for Aral, it will serve formal notice to all that we claim you as a legitimate son—and that you accept that claim. Step One. Many others to follow."

And at the end of that path—the countship? Mark frowned deeply.

"Whatever your own feelings—whatever the final outcome of the present crisis—don't let them see you shake," the Countess advised. "It's all in the mind, this Vor system. Conviction is contagious. So is doubt."

"You consider the Vor system an illusion?" Mark asked.

"I used to. Now I would call it a creation, which, like any living thing, must be continually re-created. I've seen the Barrayaran system be awkward, beautiful, corrupt, stupid, honorable, frustrating, insane and breathtaking. Its gets most of the work of government done most of the time, which is about average for any system."

"So . . . do you approve of it, or not?" he asked, puzzled.

"I'm not sure my approval matters. The Imperium is like a very large and disjointed symphony, composed by a committee. Over a three-hundred year period. Played by a gang of amateur volunteers. It has enormous inertia, and is fundamentally fragile. It is neither unchanging nor unchangeable. It can crush you like a blind elephant."

"What a heartening thought."

She smiled. "We aren't plunging you into total strangeness, tonight. Ivan and your Aunt Alys will be there, and young Lord and Lady Vortala. And the others you've met here in the past few weeks."

Fruit of the excruciating private dinner parties. From before the Count's collapse, there had been a select parade of visitors to Vorkosigan House to meet him. Countess Cordelia had determinedly continued the process despite the week-old medical crisis, in preparation for this night.

"I expect everyone will be trolling for inside information on Aral's condition," she added.

"What should I tell 'em?"

"Flat truth is always easiest to keep track of. Aral is at ImpMil awaiting a heart to be grown for transplant, and being a very bad patient. His physician is threatening alternately to tie him to his bed or resign if he doesn't behave. You don't need to go into all the medical details."

Details that would reveal just how badly damaged the Prime Minister was. Quite. ". . . What if they ask me about Miles?"

"Sooner or later," she took a breath, "if ImpSec doesn't find the body, sooner or later there must be a formal declaration of death. While Aral lives, I would rather it be later. No one outside of the highest echelons of ImpSec, Emperor Gregor, and a few government officials know Miles is anything but an ImpSec courier officer of modest rank. It is a perfectly true statement that he is away on duty. Most who inquire after him will be willing to accept that ImpSec hasn't confided to you where they sent him or for how long."

"Galen once said," Mark began, and stopped.

The Countess gave him a level look. "Is Galen much on your mind, tonight?"

"Somewhat," Mark admitted. "He trained me for this, too. We did all the major ceremonies of the Imperium, because he didn't know in advance just what time of year he'd drop me in. The Emperor's Birthday, the Midsummer Review, Winterfair—all of 'em. I can't do this and not think of him, and how much he hated the Imperium."

"He had his reasons."

"He said . . . Admiral Vorkosigan was a murderer."

The Countess sighed, and sat back. "Yes?"

"Was he?"

"You've had a chance to observe him for yourself. What do you think?"

"Lady . . . *I'm* a murderer. And I can't tell."

Her eyes narrowed. "Justly put. Well. His military career was long and complex—and bloody—and a matter of public record. But I imagine Galen's main focus was the Solstice Massacre, in which his sister Rebecca died."

Mark nodded mutely.

"The Barrayaran expedition's Political Officer, not Aral, ordered that atrocious event. Aral executed him for it with his own hands, when he found out. Without the formality of a court martial, unfortunately. So he evades one charge, but not the other. So yes. He is a murderer."

"Galen said it was to cover up the evidence. There'd been a verbal order, and only the Political Officer knew it."

"So how could Galen know it? Aral says otherwise. I believe Aral."

"Galen said he was a torturer."

"No," said the Countess flatly. "*That* was Ges Vorrutyer,

and Prince Serg. Their faction is now extinct." She smiled a thin, sharp smile.

"A madman."

"No one on Barrayar is sane, by Betan standards." She gave him an amused look. "Not even you and me."

Especially not me. He took a small breath. "A sodomite."

She tilted her head. "Does that matter, to you?"

"It was . . . prominent, in Galen's conditioning of me."

"I know."

"You do? Dammit . . ." Was he glass, to these people? A feelie-drama for their amusement? Except the Countess didn't seem amused. "An ImpSec report, no doubt," he said bitterly.

"They fast-penta'd one of Galen's surviving subordinates. A man named Lars, if that means anything to you."

"It does." He gritted his teeth. Not a chance at human dignity, not one shred left to him.

"Aside from Galen, does Aral's private orientation matter? To you?"

"I don't know. Truth matters."

"So it does. Well, in truth . . . I judge him to be bisexual, but subconsciously more attracted to men than to women. Or rather—to soldiers. Not to men generally, I don't think. I am, by Barrayaran standards, a rather extreme, er, tomboy, and thus became the solution to his dilemmas. The first time he met me I was in uniform, in the middle of a nasty armed encounter. He thought it was love at first sight. I've never bothered explaining to him that it was his compulsions leaping up." Her lips twitched.

"Why not? Or were your compulsions leaping up too?"

"No, it took me, oh, four or five more days to come completely unglued. Well, three days, anyway." Her eyes were alight with memory. "I wish you could have seen him then, in his forties. At the top of his form."

Mark had overheard himself verbally dissected by the Countess too, in this very library. There was something weirdly consoling in the knowledge that her scalpel was not reserved for him alone. *It's not just me. She does this to everybody. Argh.*

"You're . . . very blunt, ma'am. What did Miles think of this?"

She frowned thoughtfully. "He's never asked me anything. It's possible that unhappy period in Aral's youth has come to Miles's ears only as the garbled slander of Aral's political enemies, and been discounted."

"Why tell me?"

"You asked. You are an adult. And . . . you have a greater need to know. Because of Galen. If things are ever to be square between you and Aral, your view of him should be neither falsely exalted nor falsely low. Aral is a great man. I, a Betan, say this; but I don't confuse greatness with perfection. To be great anyhow is . . . the higher achievement." She gave him a crooked smile. "It should give you hope, eh?"

"Huh. Block me from escape, you mean. Are you saying that no matter how screwed up I was, you'd still expect me to work wonders?" *Appalling.*

She considered this. "Yes," she said serenely. "In fact, since no one is perfect, it follows that all great deeds have been accomplished out of imperfection. Yet they were accomplished, somehow, all the same."

It wasn't just his *father* who had made Miles crazy, Mark decided. "I've never heard you analyze yourself, ma'am," he said sourly. Yes, who shaved the barber?

"Me?" she smiled bleakly. "I'm a fool, boy."

She evaded the question. Or did she? "A fool for love?" he said lightly, in an effort to escape the sudden awkwardness his question had created.

"And other things." Her eyes were wintry.

✧ ✧ ✧

A wet, foggy dusk was gathering to cloak the city as the Countess and Mark were conveyed to the Imperial Residence. The splendidly liveried and painfully neat Pym drove the groundcar. Another half-dozen of the Count's armsmen accompanied them in another vehicle, more as honor guards than bodyguards, Mark sensed; they seemed to be looking forward to the party. At some comment of his to the Countess she remarked, "Yes, this is more of a night off for them than usual. ImpSec will have the Residence sewn up. There is a whole parallel sub-society of servants at these things—and it's not been totally unknown for an armsman of address to catch the eye of some junior Vor bud, and marry upward, if his military background is good enough."

They arrived at the Imperial pile, which was architecturally reminiscent of Vorkosigan House multipled by a factor of eight. They hurried out of the clinging fog into the warm, brilliantly-lit interior. Mark found the Countess formally attached to his left arm, which was both alarming and reassuring. Was he escort, or appendage? In either case, he sucked in his stomach and straightened his spine as much as he could.

Mark was startled when the first person they met in the vestibule was Simon Illyan. The security chief was dressed for the occasion in Imperial parade red-and-blues, which did not exactly render his slight form inconspicuous, though perhaps there were enough other red-and-blues present for him to blend in. Except that Illyan wore real lethal weapons at his hip, a plasma arc and a nerve disruptor in used-looking holsters, and not the blunted dual dress sword sets of the Vor officers. An oversized earbug glittered in his right ear.

"Milady," Illyan nodded, and drew them aside. "When you saw him this afternoon," he said in a low voice to the Countess, "how was he?"

No need to specify who *he* was, in this context. The

Countess glanced around, to be sure they were out of earshot of casual passers-by. "Not good, Simon. His color's bad, he's very edemic, and he tends to drift in and out of focus, which I find more frightening than all the rest put together. The surgeon wants to spare him the double stress of having a mechanical heart installed while they're waiting to bring the organic one up to size, but they may not be able to wait. He could end up in surgery for that at any moment."

"Should I see him, or not, in your estimation?"

"Not. The minute you walk in the door he'll sit up and try to do business. And the stress of trying will be as nothing compared to the stress of failing. That would agitate the hell out of him." She paused. "Unless you just popped in for a moment to, say, convey a bit of good news."

Illyan shook his head in frustration. "Sorry."

Since the Countess did not speak again immediately into the silence that followed, Mark dared to say, "I thought you were on Komarr, sir."

"I had to come back for this. The Emperor's Birthday Dinner is the security nightmare of the year. One bomb could take out practically the whole damned government. As you well know. I was en route when the news of Aral's . . . illness, reached me. If it would have made my fast courier go any faster, I would have gotten out and pushed."

"So . . . what's happening on Komarr? Who's supervising the, uh, search?"

"A trusted subordinate. Now that it appears we may be searching only for a body—" Illyan glanced at the Countess, and cut himself off. She frowned grayly.

They're dropping the priority of the search. Mark took a disturbed breath. "So how many agents do you have searching Jackson's Whole?"

"As many as can be spared. This new crisis," a jerk of

Illyan's head indicated Count Vorkosigan's dangerous illness, "is straining my resources. Do you have any idea how much unhealthy excitement the Prime Minister's condition is going to create on Cetaganda alone?"

"How many?" His voice went sharp, and too loud, but the Countess at least made no motion to quiet him. She watched with cool interest.

"Lord Mark, you are not yet in a position to request and require an audit of ImpSec's most secret dispositions!"

Not yet? Not ever, surely. "Request only, sir. But you can't pretend that this operation is not my business."

Illyan gave him an ambiguous, noncommittal nod. He touched his earbug, looked abstracted for a moment, and gave the Countess a parting salute. "You must excuse me, Milady."

"Have fun."

"You too." His grimace echoed the irony of her smile.

Mark found himself escorting the Countess up a wide staircase and into a long reception room lined with mirrors on one side and tall windows on the other. A major domo at the wide-flung doors announced them by title and name in an amplified voice.

Mark's first impression was of a faceless, ominous blur of colorful forms, like a garden of carnivorous flowers. A rainbow of Vor house uniforms, heavily sprinkled with parade red-and-blues, actually outshone the splendid dresses of the ladies. Most of the people stood in small, changing groups, talking in a babble; a few sat in spindly chairs along the walls, creating their own little courts. Servants moved smoothly among them, offering trays of food and drink. Mostly servants. All those extremely physically fit young men in the uniform of the Residence's staff were surely ImpSec agents. The tough-looking older men in the Vorbarra livery who manned the exits were the Emperor's personal armsmen.

It was only his paranoia, Mark decided, that made it

seem as if all heads turned toward him and a wave of silence crossed the crowd at their entry; but a few heads did turn, and a few nearby conversations did stop. One was Ivan Vorpatril and his mother,Lady Alys Vorpatril; she waved Countess Vorkosigan over to them at once.

"Cordelia, dear," Lady Vorpatril gave her a worried smile. "You must bring me up to date. People are asking."

"Yes, well, you know the drill," the Countess sighed.

Lady Vorpatril nodded wryly. She turned her head to direct Ivan, evidently continuing the conversation the Vorkosigan entrance had interrupted, "Do make yourself pleasant to the Vorsoisson girl this evening, if the opportunity arises. She's Violetta Vorsoisson's younger sister, perhaps you'll like her better. And Cassia Vorgorov is here. This is her first time at the Emperor's Birthday. And Irene Vortashpula, do get in at least one dance with her, later. I promised her mother. Really, Ivan, there are so many suitable girls here tonight. If only you would apply yourself a little . . ." The two older women linked arms to step away, effectively shedding Mark and Ivan from their private conversation. A firm nod from Countess Vorkosigan to Ivan placed him on notice that he was on guard duty again. Recalling the last time, Mark thought he might prefer the more formidable social protection of the Countess.

"What was that all about?" Mark asked Ivan. A servant passed with a tray of drinks; following Ivan's example, Mark snagged one too. It turned out to be a dry white wine flavored with citrus, reasonably pleasant.

"The biennial cattle drive," Ivan grimaced. "This and the Winterfair Ball are where all the high Vor heifers are trotted out for inspection."

This was an aspect of the Emperor's Birthday ceremonies Galen had never mentioned. Mark took a slightly larger gulp of his drink. He was beginning to damn Galen more for what he'd left out than for what and how he'd forced Mark to learn. "They won't be looking back at me, will they?"

"Considering some of the toads they do kiss, I don't see why not," shrugged Ivan.

Thank you, Ivan. Standing next to Ivan's tall red-and-blue glitter, he probably did look rather like a squat brown toad. He certainly felt like one. "I'm out of the running," he said firmly.

"Don't bet on it. There are only sixty Counts' heirs, but a lot more daughters to place. Hundreds, seems like. Once it gets out what happened to poor damned Miles, anything could happen."

"You mean . . . I wouldn't have to chase women? If I just stood still, they'd come to me?" Or at any rate, to his name, position, and money. A certain glum cheer came with the thought,if that wasn't a contradiction in terms. Better to be loved for his rank than not to be loved at all; the proud fools who proclaimed otherwise had never come so close to starving to death for a human touch as he had.

"It seemed to work that way for Miles," said Ivan, an inexplicable tincture of envy in his voice. "I could never get him to take advantage of it. Of course, he couldn't stand rejection. *Try again*, was my motto, but he'd just get all shattered and retreat into his shell for days. He wasn't adventurous. Or maybe he just wasn't greedy. Tended to stop at the first safe woman he came to. First Elena, and then when that fell through, Quinn. Though I suppose I can see why he might stop at Quinn." Ivan knocked back the rest of his wine, and exchanged the glass for a full one from a passing tray.

Admiral Naismith, Mark reminded himself, was Miles's *alternate* personality. Very possibly Ivan did not know everything about his cousin.

"Aw, hell," Ivan remarked, glancing over his glass rim.

"There's one of the ones on Mamere's short list, being aimed our way."

"So are you chasing women, or not?" asked Mark, confused.

"There's no point in chasing the ones *here*. It's all look-don't-touch. No chance."

By *chance* in this context, Mark gathered Ivan meant sex. Like many backward cultures still dependent on biological reproduction instead of the technology of uterine replicators, the Barrayarans divided sex into two categories: licit, inside a formal contract where any resultant progeny must be claimed, and illicit, i.e., all the rest. Mark brightened still further. Was this event, then, a sexual safety-zone? No tension, no terror?

The young woman Ivan had spotted was approaching them. She wore a long, soft pastel-green dress. Dark brown hair was wound up on her head in braids and curls, with some live flowers woven in. "So what's wrong with that one?" whispered Mark.

"Are you kidding?" murmured Ivan in return. "Cassia Vorgorov? Little shrimp kid with a face like a horse and a figure like a board . . . ?" He broke off as she came within earshot, and gave her a polite nod. "Hi, Cass." He kept almost all of the pained boredom out of his voice.

"Hello, Lord Ivan," she said breathlessly. She gave him a starry-eyed smile. True, her face was a little long, and her figure slight, but Mark decided Ivan was too picky. She had nice skin, and pretty eyes. Well, all of the women here had pretty eyes, it was the make-up. And the heady perfumes. She couldn't be more than eighteen. Her shy smile almost made him want to cry, so uselessly focused was it on Ivan. *Nobody has ever looked at me like that. Ivan, you are a filthy ingrate!*

"Are you looking forward to the dance?" she inquired of Ivan, transparently encouraging.

"Not particularly," shrugged Ivan. "It's the same every year."

She wilted. Her first time here, Mark bet. If there had been stairs, Mark would have been tempted to kick Ivan down them. He cleared his throat. Ivan's eye fell on him, and lit with inspiration.

"Cassie," Ivan purred, "have you met my new cousin, Lord Mark Vorkosigan, yet?"

She seemed to notice him for the first time. Mark gave her a tentative smile. She stared back dubiously. "No . . . I'd heard . . . I guess he doesn't look exactly like Miles, does he."

"No." said Mark. "I'm not Miles. How do you do, Lady Cassia."

Belatedly recovering her manners, she replied, "How do you do, um, Lord Mark." A nervous bob of her head made the flowers shiver.

"Why don't you two get acquainted. Excuse me, I have to see a man—" Ivan waved to a red-and-blue uniformed comrade across the room, and slithered away.

"Are you looking forward to the dance?" Mark tried. He'd been so concentrated on remembering all the formal moves of the taxation ceremony and the dinner, not to mention a Who's Who approximately three hundred names long all starting with "Vor," he'd hardly given the ensuing dance a thought.

"Um . . . sort of." Her eyes reluctantly abandoned Ivan's successful retreat, touched Mark, and flicked away.

Do you come here often? he managed not to blurt. What to say? *How do you like Barrayar?* No, that wouldn't do. *Nice fog we're having outside tonight.* Inside, too. *Give me a cue, girl! Say something, anything!*

"Are you really a *clone*?"

Anything but that. "Yes."

"Oh. My."

More silence.

"A lot of people are," he observed.

"Not here."

"True."

"Uh . . . oh!" Her face melted with relief. "Excuse me, Lord Mark. I see my mother is calling me—" She handed off a spasmodic smile like a ransom, and turned to hurry toward a Vorish dowager on the other side of the room. Mark had not seen her beckon.

Mark sighed. So much for the hopeful theory of the overpowering attraction of rank. Lady Cassia was clearly not anxious to kiss a toad. *If I were Ivan I'd do handstands for a girl who looked at me like that.*

"You look thoughtful," observed Countess Vorkosigan at his elbow. He jumped slightly.

"Ah, hello again. Yes. Ivan just introduced me to that girl. Not a girlfriend, I gather."

"Yes, I was watching the little playlet past Alys Vorpatril's shoulder. I stood so as to keep her back to it, for charity's sake."

"I . . . don't understand Ivan. She seemed like a nice enough girl to me."

Countess Vorkosigan smiled. "They're all nice girls. That's not the point."

"What is the point?"

"You don't see it? Well, maybe when you've had more time to observe. Alys Vorpatril is a truly doting mother, but she just can't overcome the temptation to try to micro-manage Ivan's future. Ivan is too agreeable, or too lazy, to resist openly. So he does whatever she begs of him—except the one thing she wants above all others, which is to settle into a marriage and give her grandchildren. Personally, I think his strategy is wrong. If he really wants to take the heat off himself, grandchildren would absolutely divert poor Alys's attention. Meanwhile her heart is in her mouth every time he takes a drive."

"I can see that," allowed Mark.

"I could slap him sometimes for his little game, except I'm not sure he's conscious of it, and anyway it's three-quarters Alys's fault."

Mark watched Lady Vorpatril catch up with Ivan, down the room. Checking his evening's progress down the short list already, Mark feared. "You seem able to maintain a reasonably hands-off maternal attitude yourself," he observed idly.

"That . . . may have been a mistake," she murmured.

He glanced up and quailed inwardly at the deathly desolation he surprised, momentarily, in the Countess's eyes. *My mouth. Shit.* The look twitched away so instantly, he didn't even dare apologize.

"Not altogether hands-off," she said lightly, attaching herself to his elbow again. "Come on, and I'll show you how they cross-net, Barrayaran style."

She steered him down the long room. "There are, as you have just seen, two agendas being pursued here tonight," the Countess lectured amiably. "The political one of the old men—an annual renewal of the forms of the Vor—and the genetic agenda of the old women. The men imagine theirs is the only one, but that's just an ego-serving self-delusion. The whole Vor system is founded on the women's game, underneath. The old men in government councils spend their lives arguing against or scheming to fund this or that bit of off-planet military hardware. Meanwhile, the uterine replicator is creeping in past their guard, and they aren't even conscious that the debate that will fundamentally alter Barrayar's future is being carried on right now among their wives and daughters. To use it, or not to use it? Too late to keep it out, it's already here. The middle classes are picking it up in droves. Every mother who loves her daughter is pressing for it, to spare her the physical dangers of biological childbearing. They're fighting not the old men, who haven't got a clue, but an old guard of their sisters who say to their daughters, in effect, '*We* had to suffer, so must you!' Look around tonight, Mark. You're witnessing the last generation of men and women on Barrayar who will dance this dance in the old way. The Vor system is about to change on its blindest side, the side that looks to—or fails to look to—its foundation. Another half generation from now, it's not going to know what hit it."

Mark almost swore her calm, academic voice concealed a savagely vengeful satisfaction. But her expression was as detached as ever.

A young man in a captain's uniform approached them, and split a nod of greeting between the Countess and Mark. "The Major of Protocol requests your presence, my lord," he murmured. The statement too seemed to hang indeterminately in the air between them. "This way, please."

They followed him out of the long reception room and up an ornately carved white marble staircase, down a corridor, and into an antechamber where half a dozen Counts or their official representatives were marshalled. Beyond a wide archway in the main chamber, Gregor was surrounded by a small constellation of men, mostly in red-and-blues, but three in dark Minister's robes.

The Emperor was seated on a plain folding stool, even less than a chair. "I was expecting a throne, somehow," Mark whispered to the Countess.

"It's a symbol," she whispered back. "And like most symbols, inherited. It's a standard-issue military officer's camp stool."

"Huh." Then he had to part from her, as the Major of Protocol herded him into his appointed place in line. The Vorkosigan's place. *This is it.* He had a moment of utter panic, thinking he'd somehow mislaid or dropped the bag of gold along the way, but it was still looped safely to his tunic. He undid the silken cords with sweaty fingers. *This is a stupid little ceremony. Why should I be nervous now?*

Turn, walk forward—his concentration was nearly shattered by an anonymous whisper from somewhere in the antechamber behind him, "My God, the Vorkosigans are really going to do it . . . !"—step up, salute, kneel on his left knee; he proffered the bag right-handed, palm correctly up, and stuttered out the formal words, feeling as if plasma arc beams were boring into his back from the gazes of the waiting witnesses behind him. Only then did he look up to meet the Emperor's eyes.

Gregor smiled, took the bag, and spoke the equally formal words of acceptance. He handed the bag aside to the Minister of Finance in his black velvet robe, but then waved the man away.

"So here you are after all—Lord Vorkosigan," murmured Gregor.

"Just Lord Mark," Mark pleaded hastily. "I'm not Lord Vorkosigan till Miles is, is . . ." the Countess's searing phrase came back to him, "dead and *rotted*. This doesn't mean anything. The Count and Countess wanted it. It didn't seem like the time to give them static."

"That's so." Gregor smiled sadly. "Thank you for that. How are you doing yourself?"

Gregor was the first person ever to ask after him instead of the Count. Mark blinked. But then, Gregor could get the real medical bulletins on his Prime Minister's condition hourly, if he wanted them. "All right, I guess," he shrugged. "Compared to everybody else, anyway."

"Mm," said Gregor. "You haven't used your comm card." At Mark's bewildered look he added gently, "I didn't give it to you for a souvenir."

"I . . . I haven't done you any favors that would allow me to presume upon you, sir."

"Your family has established a credit account with the

Imperium of nearly infinite depth. You can draw on it, you know."

"I haven't asked for anything."

"I know. Honorable, but stupid. You may fit right in here yet."

"I don't want any favors."

"Many new businesses start with borrowed capital. They pay it back later, with interest."

"I tried that once," said Mark bitterly. "I borrowed the Dendarii Mercenaries, and bankrupted myself."

"Hm." Gregor's smile twisted. He glanced up, beyond Mark, at the throng no-doubt backing up in the antechamber. "We'll talk again. Enjoy your dinner." His nod became the Emperor's formal dismissal.

Mark creaked to his feet, saluted properly, and withdrew back to where the Countess waited for him.

CHAPTER SEVENTEEN

At the conclusion of the lengthy and tedious taxation ceremony, the Residence's staff served a banquet to a thousand people, spread through several chambers according to rank. Mark found himself dining just downstream from Gregor's own table. The wine and elaborate food gave him an excuse not to chat much with his neighbors. He chewed and sipped as slowly as possible. He still managed to end up uncomfortably overfed and dizzy from alcohol poisoning, till he noticed the Countess was making it through all the toasts by merely wetting her lips. He copied her strategy. He wished he'd noticed sooner, but at least he was able to walk and not crawl from the table afterwards, and the room only spun a little.

It could have been worse. I could have had to make it through all this while simultaneously pretending to be Miles Vorkosigan.

The Countess led him to a ballroom with a polished marquetry floor, which had been cleared for dancing, though no one was dancing yet. A live human orchestra, all men in Imperial Service uniforms, was arrayed in one corner. At the moment only a half dozen of its musicians were playing, a sort of preliminary chamber music. Long doors on one side of the room opened to the cool night air of a promenade. Mark noted them for future escape purposes. It would be an unutterable relief to be alone in the dark right now. He was even beginning to miss his cabin back aboard the *Peregrine.*

"Do you dance?" he asked the Countess.

"Only once tonight."

The explanation unfolded shortly when Emperor Gregor appeared, and with his usual serious smile led Countess Vorkosigan out onto the floor to officially open the dance. On the music's first repeat other couples began to join them. The Vor dances seemed to tend to the formal and slow, with couples arranged in complex groups rather than couples alone, and with far too many precise moves to memorize. Mark found it vaguely allegorical of how things were done here.

Thus stripped of his escort and protectress, Mark fled to a side chamber where the volume of the music was filtered to background level. Buffet tables with yet more food and drink lined one wall. For a moment, he longingly considered the attraction of anesthetic drinking. Blurred oblivion . . . *Right, sure. Get publicly drunk, and then, no doubt, get publicly sick.* Just what the Countess needed. He was halfway there already.

Instead he retreated to a window embrasure. His surly presence seemed enough to claim it against all comers. He leaned against the wall in the shadows, folded his arms, and set himself grimly to endure. Maybe he could persuade the Countess to take him home early, after her one dance. But she seemed to be working the crowd. For all that she appeared relaxed, social, cheerful, he hadn't heard a single word out of her mouth tonight that didn't serve her goals. So much self-control in one so secretly strained was almost disturbing.

His grim mood darkened further, as he brooded on the meaning of that empty cryo-chamber. *ImpSec can't be everywhere,* the Countess had once said. Dammit . . . ImpSec was supposed to be all-seeing. That was the intended implication of the sinister silver Horus-eye insignia on Illyan's collar. Was ImpSec's reputation just propaganda?

One thing was certain. Miles hadn't removed *himself*

from that cryo-chamber. Whether or not Miles was rotted, disintegrated, or still frozen, a witness or witnesses must exist, somewhere. A thread, a string, a hook, a connection, a trail of bloody breadcrumbs, *something. I believe it's going to kill me if there isn't.* There had to be something.

"Lord Mark?" said a light voice.

He raised his eyes from blind contemplation of his boots to find himself facing a lovely cleavage, framed in raspberry pink gauze with white lace trim. Delicate line of collarbone, smooth swelling curves, and ivory skin made an almost abstract sculpture, a tilted topological landscape. He imagined himself shrunk to insect size, marching across those soft hills and valleys, barefoot—

"Lord Mark?" she repeated, less certainly.

He tilted his head back, hoping the shadows concealed the embarrassed flush in his cheeks, and managed at least the courtesy of eye contact. *I can't help it, it's my height. Sorry.* Her face was equally rewarding to the eye: electric blue eyes, curving lips. Short loose ash-blonde curls wreathed her head. As seemed the custom for young women, tiny pink flowers were braided into it, sacrificing their little vegetable lives for her evening's brief glory. However, her hair was too short to hold them successfully, and several were on the verge of falling out.

"Yes?" It came out sounding too abrupt. Surly. He tried again with a more encouraging, "Lady—?"

"Oh," she smiled, "I'm not Lady anything. I'm Kareen Koudelka."

His brow wrinkled. "Are you any relation to Commodore Clement Koudelka?" A name high on the list of Aral Vorkosigan's senior staff officers. Galen's list, of further assassinations if opportunity had presented.

"He's my father," she said proudly.

"Uh . . . is he here?" Mark asked nervously.

The smile disappeared in a momentary sigh. "No. He had to go to HQ tonight, at the last minute."

"Ah." To be sure. It would be a revealing study, to count the men who should have been here tonight but weren't because of the Prime Minister's condition. If Mark were actually the enemy agent he'd trained to be, in that other lifetime, it would be a fast way for him to discover who were the real key men in Aral Vorkosigan's support constellation, regardless of what the rosters said.

"You really don't look quite like Miles," she said, studying him with a critical eye—he stiffened, but decided sucking in his gut would only draw more attention to it—"your bones are heavier. It would be a treat to see you two together. Will he be back soon?"

She does not know, he realized with a kind of horror. *Doesn't know Miles is dead, doesn't know I killed him.* "No," he muttered. And then, masochistically, asked, "Were you in love with him too?"

"Me?" She laughed. "I haven't a chance. I have three older sisters, and they're *all* taller than I am. They call me the dwarf."

The top of his head was not quite level with the top of her shoulder, which meant that she was about average height for a Barrayaran woman. Her sisters must be valkyries. Just Miles's style. The perfume of her flowers, or her skin, rocked him in faint, delicate waves.

An agony of despair twisted all the way from his gut to behind his eyes. *This could have been mine. If I hadn't screwed it up, this could have been my moment.* She was friendly, open, smiling, only because she did not know what he had done. And suppose he lied, suppose he tried, suppose he found himself contrary to all reason walking in Ivan's most drunken dream with this girl, and she invited him mountain-climbing, like Miles—what then? How entertaining would it be for her, to watch him choke half to death in all his naked impotence? Hopeless, helpless, hapless—the mere anticipation of that pain and humiliation, again, made his vision darken.

His shoulders hunched. "Oh, for God's sake go away," he moaned.

Her blue eyes widened in startled doubt. "Pym warned me you were moody . . . well, all right." She shrugged, and turned, tossing her head.

A couple of the little pink flowers lost their moorings and bounced down. Spasmodically, Mark clutched at them. "Wait—!"

She turned back, still frowning. "What?"

"You dropped some of your flowers." He held them out to her in his two cupped hands, crushed pink blobs, and attempted a smile. He was afraid it came out as squashed as the blossoms.

"Oh." She took them back—long clean steady fingers, short undecorated nails, not an idle woman's hands—stared down at the blooms, and rolled up her eyes as if unsure how to reattach them. She finally stuffed them unceremoniously through a few curls on top of her head, out of order of their mates and more precarious than before. She began to turn away again.

Say something, or you'll lose your chance! "You don't wear your hair long, like the others," he blurted. Oh, no, she'd think he was criticizing—

"I don't have time to fool with it." Unconsciously compelled, her fingers raked a couple of curls, scattering more luckless vegetation.

"What do you do with your time?"

"Study, mostly." The vivacity his rebuff had so brutally suppressed began to leak back into her face. "Countess Vorkosigan has promised me, if I keep my class standing she'll send me to school on Beta Colony next year!" The light in her eyes focused to a laser-scalpel's edge. "And I can. I'll show them. If Miles can do what he does, I can do this."

"What do you know about what Miles does?" he asked alarmed.

"He made it through the Imperial Service Academy, didn't he?" Her chin rose, inspired. "When everyone said he was too puny and sickly, and it was a waste, and he'd just die young. And then after he succeeded they said it was only his father's favor. But he graduated near the top of his class, and I don't think his father had anything to do with *that.*" She nodded firmly, satisfied.

But they had the die-young part right. Clearly, she was not apprised of Miles's little private army.

"How old are you?" he asked her.

"Eighteen-standard."

"I'm, um, twenty-two."

"I know." She observed him, still interested, but more cautious. Her eye lit with sudden understanding. She lowered her voice. "You're very worried about Count Aral, aren't you?"

A most charitable explanation for his rudeness. "The Count my father," he echoed. That was Miles's one-breath phrase. "Among other things."

"Have you made any friends here?"

"I . . . don't quite know." Ivan? Gregor? His mother? Were any of them friends, exactly? "I've been too busy making relatives. I never had any relatives before, either."

Her brows went up. "Nor any friends?"

"No." It was an odd realization, strange and late. "I can't say as I missed friends. I always had more immediate problems." *Still do.*

"Miles always seems to have a lot of friends."

"I'm not Miles," Mark snapped, stung on the raw spot. No, it wasn't her fault, he was raw all over.

"I can see that . . ." She paused, as the music began again in the adjoining ballroom. "Would you like to dance?"

"I don't know any of your dances."

"That's a mirror dance. Anybody can do the mirror dance, it's not hard. You just copy everything your partner does."

He glanced through the archway, and thought of the tall doors to the promenade. "Maybe—maybe outside?"

"Why outside? You wouldn't be able to see me."

"Nobody would be able to see me, either." A suspicious thought struck him. "Did my mother ask you to do this?"

"No . . ."

"Lady Vorpatril?"

"No!" She laughed. "Why ever should they? Come on, or the music will be over!" She took him by the hand and towed him determinedly through the archway, dribbling a few more flowers in her wake. He caught a couple of buds against his tunic with his free hand, and slipped them surreptitiously into his trouser pocket. *Help, I'm being kidnapped by an enthusiast . . . !* There were worse fates. A wry half-smile twitched his lips. "You don't mind dancing with a toad?"

"What?"

"Something Ivan said."

"Oh, Ivan." She shrugged a dismissive white shoulder. "Ignore Ivan, we all do."

Lady Cassia, you are avenged. Mark brightened still further, to medium-gloomy.

The mirror dance was going on as described, with partners facing each other, dipping and swaying and moving along in time to the music. The tempo was brisker and less stately than the large group dances, and had brought more younger couples out onto the floor.

Feeling hideously conspicuous, Mark plunged in with Kareen, and began copying her motions, about half a beat behind. Just as she had promised, it took about fifteen seconds to get the hang of it. He began to smile, a little. The older couples were quite grave and elegant but some of the younger ones were more creative. One young Vor took advantage of a hand-pass to bait his lady by briefly sticking one finger up his nose and wriggling the rest at her; she broke the rule and didn't follow, but he mirrored her look of outrage perfectly. Mark laughed.

"You look quite different when you laugh," Kareen said, sounding startled. She cocked her head in bemusement.

He cocked his head back at her. "Different from what?"

"I don't know. Not so . . . funereal. You looked like you'd lost your best friend, when you were hiding back there in the corner."

If only you knew. She pirouetted; he pirouetted. He swept her an exaggerated bow; looking surprised but pleased, she swept one back at him. The view was charming.

"I'll just have to make you laugh again," she decided firmly. So, perfectly deadpan, she proceeded to tell him three dirty jokes in rapid succession; he ended up laughing at the absurdity of their juxtaposition with her maidenly airs as much as anything else.

"Where did you learn those?"

"From my big sisters, of course," she shrugged.

He was actually sorry when the music came to an end. This time he took the lead, and urged her back into the next room for something to drink, and then out onto the promenade. After the concentration of the dance was over he'd become uncomfortably conscious of just how many people were looking at him, and it wasn't paranoid dementia this time. They'd made a conspicuous couple, the beautiful Kareen and her Vorkosigan toad.

It was not as dark outside as he'd hoped. In addition to the lights spilling from the Residence windows, colored spotlights in the landscaping were diffused by the fog to a gentle general illumination. Below the stone balustrade the slope was almost woods-like with old-growth bushes and trees. Stone-paved walkways zig-zagged down, with granite benches inviting lingerers.

Still, the night was chilly enough to keep most people inside, which helped.

It was a highly romantic setting, to be wasted on him. *Why am I doing this?* What good was it to bait a hunger that could not feed? Just looking at her hurt. He moved closer anyway, more dizzy with her scent than with the wine and the dancing. Her skin was radiantly warm with the exercise; she'd light up a sniper-scope like a torch. Morbid thought. Sex and death seemed too close-connected, somewhere in the bottom of his brain. He was afraid. *Everything I touch, I destroy. I will not touch her.* He set his glass on the stone railing and shoved his hands deep into his trouser pockets. His left fingertips compulsively rotated the little flowers he'd secreted there.

"Lord Mark," she said, after a sip of wine, "you're almost a galactic. If you were married, and going to have children, would you want your wife to use a uterine replicator, or not?"

"Why would any couple not choose to use a replicator?" he asked, his head spinning with this sudden new tack in conversation.

"To, like, prove her love for him."

"Good God, how barbaric! Of course not. I'd think it would prove just the opposite, that he didn't love *her.*" He paused. "That was a strictly theoretical question, wasn't it?"

"Sort of."

"I mean, you don't know anyone who's seriously having this debate—not your sisters or anything?" he asked in worry. *Not you, surely?* Some barbarian needed his head stuck in a bucket of ice water, if so. And held under for a good long time, like till he stopped wriggling.

"Oh, none of my sisters are married yet. Though it's not for lack of offers. But Mama and Da are holding out. It's a strategy," she confided.

"Oh?"

"Lady Cordelia encouraged them, after the second of us girls came along. There was a period soon after she immigrated here, when galactic medicine was really spreading out, and there was this pill you could take to choose the sex of your child. Everyone went crazy for boys, for a while. The ratio's evened up again lately. But my sisters and I are right in the middle of the girl-drought. Any man who won't agree in the marriage contract to let his wife use a uterine replicator is having a real hard time getting married, right now. The go-betweens won't even bother dealing for him." She giggled. "Lady Cordelia's told Mama if she plays the game well, every one of her grandchildren could be born with a Vor in front of their names."

"I see," Mark blinked. "Is that an ambition of your parents?"

"Not necessarily," Kareen shrugged. "But all else being equal, that prefix does give a fellow an edge."

"That's . . . good to know. I guess." He considered his wine, and did not drink.

Ivan came out of one of the ballroom doors, saw them both, and gave them a friendly wave, but kept on going. He had not a glass but an entire bottle swinging from his hand, and he cast a slightly hunted look back over his shoulder before disappearing down the walkway. Glancing over the balustrade a few minutes later, Mark saw the top of his head pass by on a descending path.

Mark took a gulp of his drink then. "Kareen . . . am I *possible*?"

"Possible for what?" She tilted her head and smiled.

"For—for women. I mean, look at me. Square on. I really do look like a toad. All twisted up, and if I don't do something about it soon, I'm going to end up as wide as I am . . . short. And on top of it all, I'm a clone." Not to mention the little breathing problem. Summed up that way, hurling himself head-first over the balustrade seemed a completely logical act. It would save so much pain in the long run.

"Well, that's all true," she allowed judiciously.

Dammit, woman, you're supposed to deny it all, to be polite.

"But you're *Miles's* clone. You have to have his intelligence, too."

"Do brains make up for all the rest? In the female view?"

"Not to every woman, I suppose. Just to the smart ones."

"*You're* smart."

"Yes, but it would be rude of me to say so." She raked her curls and grinned.

How the hell was he to construe that? "Maybe I don't have Miles's brains," he said gloomily. "Maybe the Jacksonian body-sculptors stupified me, when they were doing all the rest, to keep me under control. That would explain a *lot*about my life." Now there was a morbid new thought to wallow in.

Kareen giggled. "I don't think so, Mark."

He smiled wryly back at her. "No excuses. No quarter."

"Now you sound like Miles."

A young woman emerged from the ballroom. Dressed in some pale blue silky stuff, she was athletically trim, glowingly blonde, and nearly as tall as Ivan. "Kareen!" she waved. "Mama wants us all."

"*Now,* Delia?" said Kareen, sounding quite put-out.

"Yes." She eyed Mark with alarmingly keen interest, but drawn by whatever daughterly duty, swung back inside.

Kareen sighed, pushed away from the stonework upon which she had been leaning, dusted futilely at a snag in her raspberry gauze, and smiled farewell. "It was nice meeting you, Lord Mark."

"It was nice talking with you too. And dancing with

you." It was true. He waved, more casually than he felt, as she vanished into the warm light of the Residence. When he was sure she was out of sight, he knelt and surreptitiously collected the last of the tiny flowers she had shed, and stuffed them into his pocket with the rest.

She smiled at me. Not at Miles. Not at Admiral Naismith. Me, myself, Mark. This was how it could have been, if he hadn't bankrupted himself at Bharaputra's.

Now that he was alone in the dark as he had wished, he discovered he didn't much care for it. He decided to go find Ivan, and struck off down the garden walkways. Unfortunately, the paths divided and re-divided, presumably to more than one destination. He passed couples who had taken to the sheltered benches despite the chill, and a few other men and women who'd just wandered down here for private talks, or to cool off. Which way had Ivan gone? Not this way, obviously; a little round balcony made a dead-end. He turned back.

Someone was following him, a tall man in red-and-blues. His face was in shadow. "Ivan?" said Mark uncertainly. He didn't think it was Ivan.

"So you're Vorkosigan's *clowne.*" Not Ivan's voice. But his skewed pronunciation made the intended insult very clear.

Mark stood square. "You've got that straight, all right," he growled. "So who in this circus are you, the dancing bear?"

"A Vor."

"I can tell that by the low, sloping forehead. Which Vor?" The hairs were rising on the back of his neck. The last time he'd felt such exhilaration combined with intense sickness to his stomach had been in the alley in the caravanserai. His heart began to pound. *But he's made no threat yet, and he's alone. Wait.*

"Offworlder. You have no concept of the honor of the Vor," the man grated.

"None whatsoever," Mark agreed cheerfully. "I think you're all insane."

"You are no soldier."

"Right again. My, we are quick tonight. I was trained strictly as a lone assassin. Death in the shadows is a sort of speciality of mine." He began counting seconds in his head.

The man, who had started to move forward, sagged back again. "So it seems," he hissed. "You've wasted no time, promoting yourself to a Countship. Not very subtle, for a trained assassin."

"I'm not a subtle man." He centered his balance, but did not move. No sudden moves. Keep bluffing.

"I can tell you this, little *clowne.*" He gave it the same insulting slur as before. "If Aral Vorkosigan dies, it won't be *you* who steps into his place."

"Well, that's just exactly right," purred Mark. "So what are you all hot about, Vor bore?" *Shit. This one knows that Miles is dead. How the hell does he know? Is he an ImpSec insider?* But no Horus-eye stared from his collar; he bore a ship insignia of some kind, which Mark could not quite make out. Active-duty type. "What, to you, is one more little spare Vor drone living off a family pension in Vorbarr Sultana? I saw a herd of them up there tonight, swilling away."

"You're very cocky."

"Consider the venue," said Mark in exasperation. "You're not going to carry out any death threats here. It would embarrass ImpSec. And I don't think you want to annoy Simon Illyan, whoever the hell you are." He kept on counting.

"I don't know what hold you think you have on ImpSec," the man began furiously.

But he was interrupted. A smiling servant in the Residence's livery walked down the path carrying a tray of glasses. He was a very physically fit young man.

"Drinks, gentlemen?" he offered.

The anonymous Vor glowered at him. "No, thank you." He turned on his heel and strode off. Shrubbery whipped in his wake, scattering droplets of dew.

"I'll take one, thanks," said Mark brightly. The servant proffered the tray with a slight bow. For his abused stomach's sake Mark stuck with the same light wine he'd been drinking most of the evening. "Eighty-five seconds. Your timing is lousy. He could have killed me three times over, but you interrupted just as the talk was getting interesting. How do you fellows pick this stuff out, real-time? You can't possibly have enough people upstairs to be following every conversation in the building. Automated key-word searches?"

"Canape, sir?" Blandly, the servant turned the tray and offered the other side.

"Thank you again. Who was that proud Vor?"

The servant glanced down the now-empty pathway. "Captain Edwin Vorventa. He's on personal leave while his ship is in orbital dock."

"He's not in ImpSec?"

"No, my lord."

"Oh? Well, tell your boss I'd like to talk to him, at his earliest convenience."

"That would be Lord Voraronberg, the castellan's food and beverage manager."

Mark grinned. "Oh, sure. Go away, I'm drunk enough."

"Very good, my lord."

"Not come morning. Ah! One more thing. You wouldn't know where I could find Ivan Vorpatril right now, would you?"

The young man stared absently over the balcony a moment, as though listening, though no earbug showed. "There is a sort of gazebo at the bottom of the next left-hand turn, my lord, near a fountain. You might try there."

"Thank you."

Mark followed his directions, through the cool night mist. In a stray ray of light, fog droplets on his uniform sleeve shone like a cloud across the little silver rivers of the embroidery. He soon heard the plash of the fountain. A petite stone building, no walls, just deeply shadowed arches, overlooked it.

It was so quiet in this pocket of the garden, he could hear the breathing of the person inside. Only one person; good, he wasn't about to diminish his already low popularity still further by interrupting a tryst. But it was strangely hoarse. "Ivan?"

There was a long pause. He was trying to decide whether to call again or tiptoe off when Ivan's voice returned an uninviting growl of, "What?"

"I just . . . wondered what you were doing."

"Nothing."

"Hiding from your mother?"

". . . Yeah."

"I, ah, won't tell her where you are."

"Good for you," was the sour reply.

"Well . . . see you later." He turned to go.

"Wait."

He waited, puzzled.

"Want a drink?" Ivan offered after a long pause.

"Uh . . . sure."

"So, come get it."

Mark ducked inside, and waited for his eyes to adjust. The usual stone bench, and Ivan a seated shadow. Ivan proffered the gleaming bottle, and Mark topped up his glass, only to find too late that Ivan wasn't drinking wine, but rather some sort of brandy. The accidental cocktail tasted vile. He sat down by the steps with his back to a stone post, and set his glass aside. Ivan had dispensed with the formality of a glass.

"Are you going to be able to make it back to your ground car?" asked Mark doubtfully.

"Don't plan to. The Residence's staff will cart me out in the morning, when they pick up the rest of the trash."

"Oh." His night vision continued to improve. He could pick out the glittery bits on Ivan's uniform, and the polished glow of his boots. The reflections of his eyes. The gleam of wet tracks down his cheeks. "Ivan, are you—" Mark bit his tongue on *crying*, and changed it in mid-sentence to, "all right?"

"I," Ivan stated firmly, "have decided to get very drunk."

"I can see that. Why?"

"Never have, at the Emperor's Birthday. It's a traditional challenge, like getting laid here."

"Do people do that?"

"Sometimes. On a dare."

"How entertaining for ImpSec."

Ivan snorted a laugh. "Yeah, there is that."

"So who dared you?"

"Nobody."

Mark felt he was running out of probing questions faster than Ivan was running out of monosyllabic replies.

But, "Miles and I," Ivan said in the dark, "used to work this party together, most every year. I was surprised . . . how much I missed the little bugger's slanderous political commentary, this time around. Used to make me laugh." Ivan laughed. It was a hollow and un-funny noise. He stopped abruptly.

"They told you about finding the empty cryo-chamber, didn't they," said Mark.

"Yeah."

"When?"

"Couple of days ago. I've been thinking about it, since. Not good."

"No." Mark hesitated. Ivan was shivering, in the dark. "Do you . . . want to go home and go to bed?" *I sure do.*

"Never make it up the hill, now," shrugged Ivan.

"I'll give you a hand. Or a shoulder."

". . . All right."

It took some doing, but he hoisted Ivan to his unsteady feet, and they navigated back up the steep garden. Mark didn't know what charitable ImpSec guardian angel passed the word, but they were met at the top not by Ivan's mother, but by his aunt.

"He's, ah . . ." Mark was not sure what to say. Ivan peered around blearily.

"So I see," said the Countess.

"Can we spare an armsman, to drive him home?" Ivan sagged, and Mark's knees buckled. "Better make it two armsmen."

"Yes." The Countess touched a decorative comm pin on her bodice. "Pym . . . ?"

Ivan was thus taken off his hands, and Mark breathed a sigh of relief. His relief grew to outright gratitude when the Countess commented that it was time for them to quit, too. In a few minutes Pym brought the Count's groundcar around to the entrance, and the night's ordeal was over.

The Countess didn't talk much, for a change, in the groundcar going back to Vorkosigan House. She leaned back against her seat and closed her eyes in exhaustion. She didn't even ask him anything.

In the black-and-white paved foyer the Countess handed off her cloak to a maid, and headed left, toward the library.

"You'll excuse me, Mark. I'm going to call ImpMil."

She looked so tired. "Surely they'd have called you, ma'am, if there was any change in the Count's condition."

"I'm going to call ImpMil," she said flatly. Her eyes were puffy slits. "Go to bed, Mark."

He didn't argue with her. He trudged wearily up the stairs to his bedroom corridor.

He paused outside the door to his room. It was very late at night. The hallway was deserted. The silence of the great house pressed on his ears. On an impulse, he turned back and stepped down the hall to Miles's room. There he paused again. In all his weeks on Barrayar, he had not ventured in here. He had not been invited. He tried the antique knob. The door was not locked.

Hesitantly, he entered, and keyed up the lights with a word. It was a spacious bedchamber, given the limits of the house's old architecture. An adjoining antechamber once meant for personal servants had long ago been converted to a private bathroom. At first glance the room seemed almost stripped, bare and neat and clean. All the clutter of childhood must have been boxed and put away in an attic, in some spasm of maturity. He suspected Vorkosigan House's attics were astonishing.

Yet a trace of the owner's personality remained. He walked slowly around the room, hands in his pockets like a patron at a museum.

Reasonably enough, the few mementos that had been retained tended heavily to reminders of successes. Miles's diploma from the Imperial Service Academy, and his officer's commission, were normal enough, though Mark wondered why a battered old Service issue weather manual was also framed and placed exactly between them. A box of old gymkhana awards going back to youth looked like they might be heading for an attic very soon. Half a wall was devoted to a massive book-disk and vid collection, thousands of titles. How many had Miles actually read? Curious, he took the hand-viewer off its hook on the wall nearby, and tried three disks at random. All had at least a few notes or glosses entered in the margin-boxes, tracks of Miles's thought. Mark gave up the survey, and passed on.

One object he knew personally; a cloissone-hilted dagger, which Miles had inherited from old General Piotr. He dared to take it down and test its heft and edge. So when in the past two years had Miles stopped carting it around, and sensibly began leaving it safely at home? He replaced it carefully on the shelf in its sheath.

One wall-hanging was ironic, personal, and obvious: an old metal leg-brace, crossed, military-museum fashion, with a Vor sword. Half-joke, half-defiance. Both obsolete. A cheap photonic reproduction of a page from an ancient book was matted and mounted in a wildly expensive silver frame. The text was all out of context, but appeared to be some sort of pre-Jump religious gibberish, all about pilgrims, and a hill, and a city in the clouds. Mark wasn't sure what that was all about; nobody had ever accused Miles of being the religious type. Yet it was clearly important to him.

Some of these things aren't prizes, Mark realized. *They are lessons.*

A holovid portfolio box rested on the bedside table. Mark sat down, and activated it. He expected Elli Quinn's face, but the first videoportrait to come up was of a tall, glowering, extraordinarily ugly man in Vorkosigan Armsmen's livery. Sergeant Bothari, Elena's father. He keyed through the contents. Quinn was next, then Bothari-Jesek. His parents, of course. Miles's horse, Ivan, Gregor: after that, a parade of faces and forms. He keyed through faster and faster, not recognizing even a third of the people. After the fiftieth face, he stopped clicking.

He rubbed his face wearily. *He's not a man, he's a mob.* Right. He sat bent and aching, face in his hands, elbows on his knees. *No. I am not Miles.*

Miles's comconsole was the secured type, in no way junior to the one in the Count's library. Mark walked over and examined it only by eye; his hands he shoved back deep into his trouser pockets. His fingertips encountered Kareen Koudelka's crumpled flowerlets.

He drew them out, and spread them on his palm. In a spasm of frustration, he smashed the blooms with his other hand, and threw them to the floor. Less than a minute later he was on his hands and knees frantically scraping the scattered bits up off the carpet again. *I think I must be insane.* He sat on his knees on the floor and began to cry.

Unlike poor Ivan, no one interrupted his misery, for which he was profoundly grateful. He sent a mental apology after his Vorpatril cousin, *Sorry, sorry* . . . though odds were even whether Ivan would remember anything about his intrusion come the morning. He gulped for control of his breath, his head aching fiercely.

Ten minutes delay downside at Bharaputra's had been all the difference. If they'd been ten minutes faster, the Dendarii would have made it back to their drop shuttle before the Bharaputrans had a chance to blow it up, and all would have unfolded into another future. Thousands of ten-minute intervals had passed in his life, unmarked and without effect. But *that* ten minutes had been all it took to transform him from would-be hero to permanent scum. And he could never recover the moment.

Was that, then, the commander's gift: to recognize those critical minutes, out of the mass of like moments, even in the chaos of their midst? To risk all to grab the golden ones? Miles had possessed that gift of timing to an extraordinary degree. Men and women followed him, laid all their trust at his feet, just for that.

Except once, Miles's timing had failed. . . .

No. He'd been screaming his lungs out for them to keep moving. *Miles's* timing had been shrewd. His feet had been fatally slowed by others' delays.

Mark climbed up off the floor, washed his face in the bathroom, and returned and sat in the comconsole's station chair. The first layer of secured functions was entered by a palm-lock. The machine did not quite like his palm-print; bone growth and subcutaneous fat deposits were beginning to distort the pattern out of the range of recognition. But not wholly, not yet; on the fourth try it took a reading that pleased it, and opened files to him. The next layer of functions required codes and accesses he did not know, but the top layer had all he needed for now: a private, if not secured, comm channel to ImpSec.

ImpSec's machine bounced him to a human receptionist almost immediately. "My name is Lord Mark Vorkosigan," he told the corporal on night-duty, whose face appeared above the vid plate. "I want to speak with Simon Illyan. I suppose he's still at the Imperial Residence."

"Is this an emergency, my lord?" the corporal asked.

"It is to me," growled Mark.

Whatever the corporal thought of that, he patched Mark on through. Mark insisted his way past two more layers of subordinates before the ImpSec chief's tired face materialized.

Mark swallowed. "Captain Illyan."

"Yes, Lord Mark, what is it?" Illyan said wearily. It had been a long night for ImpSec, too.

"I had an interesting conversation with a certain Captain Vorventa, earlier this evening."

"I am aware. You offered him some not-too-oblique threats."

And Mark had assumed that ImpSec guard/servant had been sent to protect *him* . . . ah, well.

"So I have a question for you, sir. Is Captain Vorventa on the list of people who are supposed to know about Miles?"

Illyan's eyes narrowed. "No."

"Well, he does."

"That's . . . very interesting."

"Is that helpful for you to know?"

Illyan sighed. "It gives me a new problem to worry about. Where is the internal leak? Now I'll have to find out."

"But—better to know than not."

"Oh, yes."

"Can I ask a favor in return?"

"Maybe." Illyan looked extremely non-committal. "What kind of favor?"

"I want in."

"What?"

"I want in. On ImpSec's search for Miles. I want to start by reviewing your reports, I suppose. After that, I don't know. But I can't stand being kept alone in the dark any more."

Illyan regarded him suspiciously. "No," he said at last. "I'm not turning you loose to romp through my top-secret files, thank you. Good night, Lord Mark."

"Wait, sir! You complained you were understaffed. You can't turn down a volunteer."

"What do you imagine you can do that ImpSec hasn't?" Illyan snapped.

"The point is, sir—ImpSec hasn't. You haven't found Miles. I can hardly do *less.*"

He hadn't put that quite as diplomatically as he should have, Mark realized, as Illyan's face darkened with anger. "Good *night*, Lord Mark," Illyan repeated through his teeth, and cut the link with a swipe of his hand.

Mark sat frozen in Miles's station chair. The house was so quiet the loudest sound he could hear was his own blood in his ears. He should have pointed out to Illyan how clever he'd been, how quick on the uptake; Vorventa had revealed what he knew, but in no way had Mark cross-revealed that he knew Vorventa knew. Illyan's investigation must now take the leak, whatever it was, by surprise. *Isn't that worth something? I'm not as stupid as you think I am.*

You're not as smart as I thought you were, either, Illyan. You are not . . . perfect. That was disturbing. He had expected ImpSec to be perfect, somehow; it had anchored his world to think so. And Miles, perfect. And the Count and Countess. All perfect, all unkillable. All made out of rubber. The only real pain, his own.

He thought of Ivan, crying in the shadows. Of the Count, dying in the woods. The Countess had kept her mask up better than any of them. She had to. She had more to hide. Miles himself, the man who had created a whole other personality just to escape into. . . .

The trouble, Mark decided, was that he had been trying to be Miles Vorkosigan all by himself. Even *Miles* didn't do Miles that way. He had co-opted an entire supporting cast. A cast of thousands. *No wonder I can never catch up with him.*

Slowly, curiously, Mark opened his tunic and removed Gregor's comm card from his inner breast pocket, and set it on the comconsole desk. He stared hard at the anonymous plastic chip, as if it bore some coded message for his eyes only. He rather fancied it did.

You knew. You knew, didn't you, Gregor you bastard. You've just been waiting for me to figure it out for myself.

With spasmodic decision, Mark jammed the card into the comconsole's read-slot.

No machines this time. A man in ordinary civilian clothing answered immediately, though without identifying himself. "Yes?"

"I'm Lord Mark Vorkosigan. I should be on your list. I want to talk to Gregor."

"Right now, my lord?" said the man mildly. His hand danced over a keypad array to one side.

"Yes. Now. Please."

"You are cleared." He vanished.

The vid plate remained dark, but the audio transmitted a melodious chime. It chimed for quite a long time. Mark began to panic. What if—but then it stopped. There was a mysterious clanking sound, and Gregor's voice said, "Yes?" in a bleary tone. No visuals.

"It's me. Mark Vorkosigan. Lord Mark."

"Yeah?"

"You told me to call you."

"Yes, but it's . . ." a short pause, "five in the bleeding *morning*, Mark!"

"Oh. Were you asleep?" he carolled frantically. He leaned forward and beat his head gently on the hard cool plastic of the desk. *Timing. My timing.*

"*God*, you sound just like Miles when you say that," muttered the Emperor. The vid plate activated; Gregor's image came up as he turned on a light. He was in some sort of bedroom, dim in the background, and was wearing nothing but loose black silky pajama pants. He peered at Mark, as if making sure he wasn't talking to a ghost. But the *corpus* was too corpulent to be anyone but Mark. The Emperor heaved an oxygenating sigh and blinked himself to focus. "What do you need?"

How wonderfully succinct. If he answered in full, it could take him the next six hours.

"I need to be in on ImpSec's search for Miles. Illyan won't let me. You can override him."

Gregor sat still for a minute, then barked a brief laugh. He swiped a hand through sleep-bent black hair. "Have you asked him?"

"Yes. Just now. He turned me down."

"Mm, well . . . it's his job to be cautious for me. So that my judgment may remain untrammeled."

"In your untrammeled judgment, sir. Sire. Let me in!"

Gregor studied him thoughtfully, rubbing his face. "Yes . . ." he drawled slowly after a moment. "Let's . . . see what happens." His eyes were not bleary now.

"Can you call Illyan right now, sire?"

"What is this, pent-up demand? The dam breaks?"

I am poured out like water . . . where did that quote come from? It sounded like something of the Countess's.

"He's still up. Please. Sire. And have him call me back at this console to confirm. I'll wait."

"Very well," Gregor's lips twisted up in a peculiar smile, "Lord Mark."

"Thank you, sire. Uh . . . good night."

"Good morning." Gregor cut the comm.

Mark waited. The seconds ticked by, stretched out of all recognition. His hangover was starting, but he was still slightly drunk. The worst of both worlds. He had started to doze when the comconsole chimed at last, and he nearly spasmed out of his chair.

He slapped urgently at the controls. "Yes. Sir?"

Illyan's saturnine face appeared over the vid plate. "Lord Mark." He gave Mark the barest nod. "If you come to ImpSec headquarters at the beginning of normal business hours tomorrow morning, you will be permitted to review the files we discussed."

"Thank you, sir," said Mark sincerely.

"That's two-and-one-half hours from now," Illyan mentioned with, Mark thought, an understandable hint of sadism. Illyan hadn't slept either.

"I'll be there."

Illyan acknowledged this with a shiver of his eyelids, and vanished.

Damnation through good works, or grace alone? Mark meditated on Gregor's grace. *He knew. He knew it before I did.* Lord Mark Vorkosigan was a real person.

CHAPTER EIGHTEEN

The level light of dawn turned the night's lingering mist to gold, a smoky autumnal haze that gave the city of Vorbarr Sultana an almost magical air. The Imperial Security Headquarters building stood windowless, foursquare against the light, a vast utilitarian concrete block with enormous gates and doors certainly designed to diminish any human supplicant fool enough to approach it. In his case, a redundant effect, Mark decided.

"What awful architecture," he said to Pym, beside him, chauffeuring him in the Count's ground car.

"Ugliest building in town," the armsman agreed cheerfully. "It dates back to Mad Emperor Yuri's Imperial architect, Lord Dono Vorrutyer. An uncle to the later vice-admiral. He managed to get up five major structures before Yuri was killed, and they stopped him. The Municipal Stadium runs this a close second, but we've never been able to afford to tear it down. Still stuck with it, sixty years later."

"It looks like the sort of place that has dungeons in the basement. Painted institutional green. Run by ethics-free physicians."

"It did," said Pym. The Armsman negotiated their way past the gate guards and slowed in front of a vast flight of steps.

"Pym . . . aren't those steps a bit oversized?"

"Yep," grinned the Armsman. "You'd have a cramp in your leg by the time you reached the top, if you tried to take it in one go." Pym eased the ground car forward, and stopped to let Mark off. "But if you go around the left end, here, you'll find a little door at ground level, and a lift tube foyer. That's where everybody actually goes in."

"Thank you." Pym popped the front canopy, and Mark climbed out. "Whatever happened to Lord Dono, after Mad Yuri's reign? Assassinated by the Architectural Defense League, I hope?"

"No, he retired to the country, lived off his daughter and son-in-law, and died stark mad. There's a bizarre set of towers he built on their estate, that they charge admission to see, now." With a wave, Pym lowered the canopy and pulled away.

Mark trod around to the left, as directed. So here he was, bright and early . . . or at least, early. He'd taken a long shower, donned comfortable dark civilian clothes, and tanked himself on enough painkillers, vitamins, hangover remedies, and stimulants to leave him feeling artificially normal. More artificial than normal, but he was determined not to let Illyan bully him out of his chance.

He presented himself to the ImpSec guards in the foyer. "I'm Lord Mark Vorkosigan. I'm expected."

"Hardly that," growled a voice from the lift tube. Illyan himself swung out. The guards braced; Illyan put them back at ease with an unmilitary wave. Illyan too had showered, and changed back into his usual undress greens. Mark suspected Illyan had eaten pills for breakfast too. "Thank you, Sergeant, I'll take him up."

"What a depressing building to work in," Mark commented, as he rose in the lift tube beside the ImpSec chief.

"Yes," sighed Illyan. "I visited the Investigatif Federale building on Escobar, once. Forty-five stories, all glass . . . I was never closer to emigrating. Dono Vorrutyer should have been strangled at birth. But . . . it's mine now." Illyan glanced around with a dubious possessiveness.

Illyan led him deep into the—yes, this building definitely had bowels, Mark decided. The bowels of ImpSec. Their footsteps echoed down a bare corridor lined with tiny, cubicle-like rooms. Mark glanced through a few half-open doors at highly-secured comconsoles manned by green-uniformed men. One man at least had a bank of non-regulation full spectrum lights blazing away, aimed at his station chair. There was a large coffee dispenser at the end of the corridor. He didn't think it was random chance that Illyan led him to the cubicle numbered thirteen.

"This comconsole has been loaded with every report I've received pertaining to the search for Lieutenant Vorkosigan," said Illyan coolly. "If you think you can do better with it than my trained analysts have, I invite you to try."

"Thank you, sir." Mark slid into the station chair, and powered up the vid plate. "This is unexpectedly generous."

"You should have no complaint, my lord," Illyan stated, in the tone of a directive. Gregor must have lit quite a fire under him, earlier this morning, Mark reflected, as Illyan bowed himself out with a distinctly ironic nod. Hostile? No. That was unjust. Illyan was not nearly as hostile as he had a right to be. *It's not only obedience to his Emperor*, Mark realized with a shiver. Illyan could have stood up to Gregor on a security issue like this if he'd really wanted to. *He's getting desperate.*

He took a deep breath and plunged into the files, reading, listening, and viewing. Illyan hadn't been joking about the *everything* part. There were literally hundreds of reports, generated by fifty or sixty different agents scattered throughout the near wormhole nexus. Some were brief and negative. Others were long and negative. But somebody seemed to have visited, at least once, every possible cryo-facility on Jackson's Whole, its orbital and jump point stations, and several adjoining local space systems. There were even recently-received reports tracing as far away as Escobar.

What was missing, Mark realized after quite a while, were any synopses or finished analyses. He had received raw data only, in all its mass. On the whole, he decided he preferred it that way.

Mark read till his eyes were dry and aching, and his stomach gurgled with festering coffee. *Time to break for lunch*, he thought, when a guard knocked at his door.

"Lord Mark, your driver is here," the guard informed him politely.

Hell—it was time to break for *dinner.* The guard escorted him back through the building and delivered him to Pym. It was dark outside. *My head hurts.*

Doggedly, Mark returned the next morning and started again. And the next. And the next. More reports arrived. In fact, they were arriving faster than he could read them. The harder he worked, the more he was falling behind. Halfway through the fifth day he leaned back in his station chair and thought, *This is crazy.* Illyan was burying him. From the paralysis of ignorance, he had segued with surprising speed to the paralysis of information-glut. *I've got to triage this crap, or I'll never get out of this repulsive building.*

"Lies, lies, all lies," he muttered wildly to his comconsole. It seemed to blink and hum back at him, sly and demure.

With a decisive punch, he turned off the comconsole with its endless babble of voices and fountains of data, and sat for a while in darkness and silence, till his ears stopped ringing.

ImpSec hasn't. Hasn't found Miles. He didn't need all this data. Nobody did. He just needed one piece. *Let's cut this down to size.*

Start with a few explicit assumptions. One. Miles is recoverable.

Let ImpSec look for a rotted body, unmarked grave, or disintegration record all they wanted. Such a search was no use to *him*, even if successful. Especially if successful.

Only cryo-chambers, whether permanent storage banks or other portables, were of interest. Or—less likely, and notably less common—cryo-revival facilities. But logic put an upper cap on his optimism. If Miles had been successfully revived by friendly hands, the first thing he would do would be to report in. He hadn't, ergo: he was still frozen. Or, if revived, in too bad a shape to function. Or not in friendly hands. So. Where?

The Dendarii cryo-chamber had been found in the Hegen Hub. Well . . . so what? It had been sent there after it was emptied. Sinking down into his station chair with slitted eyes, Mark thought instead about the opposite end of the trail. Were his particular obsessions luring him into believing what he wanted to believe? *No, dammit. To hell with the Hegen Hub. Miles never got off the planet.* In one stroke, that eliminated over three-fourths of the trash-data clogging his view.

We look at Jackson's Whole reports only, then. Good. Then what?

How had ImpSec checked all the remaining possible destinations? Places without known motivations or connections with House Bharaputra? For the most part, ImpSec had simply asked, concealing their own identity but offering a substantial reward. All at least four weeks after the raid. A cold trail, so to speak. Quite a lot of time for someone to think about their surprise package. Time to hide it, if they were so inclined. So that, in those cases where ImpSec did a second and more complete pass, they were even more likely to come up empty.

Miles is in a place that ImpSec has already checked

off, in the hands of someone with hidden motivations to be interested in him.

There were still hundreds of possibilities.

I need a connection. There has to be a connection.

ImpSec had torn apart Norwood's available Dendarii records down to the level of a word-by-word analysis. Nothing. But Norwood was medically trained. And he hadn't sent his beloved Admiral's cryo-chamber off at random. He'd sent it *someplace* to *someone.*

If there's a hell, Norwood, I hope you're roasting in it right now.

Mark sighed, leaned forward, and turned the comconsole back on.

A couple of hours later, Illyan stopped by Mark's cubicle, closing the soundproof door behind him. He leaned, falsely casual, on the wall and remarked, "How is it going?"

Mark ran his hands through his hair. "Despite your amiable attempt to bury me, I think I'm actually making some progress."

"Oh? What kind?" Illyan did not deny the charge, Mark noticed.

"I am absolutely convinced Miles never left Jackson's Whole."

"So how do you explain our finding the cryo-chamber in the Hegen Hub?"

"I don't. It's a diversion."

"Hm," said Illyan, non-committally.

"And it worked," Mark added cruelly.

Illyan's lips thinned.

Diplomacy, Mark reminded himself. Diplomacy, or he'd never get what he needed. "I accept that your resources are finite, sir. So put them to the point. Everything that you do have available for this, you ought to send to Jackson's Whole."

The sardonic expression on Illyan's face said it all. The man had been running ImpSec for nearly thirty years. It was going to take a lot more than diplomacy for him to accept Mark telling him how to do his job.

"What did you find out about Captain Vorventa?" Mark tried another line.

"The link was short, and not too sinister. His younger brother was my Galactic Operations supervisor's adjutant. These are not disloyal men, you understand."

"So . . . what have you done?"

"About Captain Edwin, nothing. It's too late. The information about Miles is now out on the Vorish net, as whispers and gossip. Beyond damage control. Young Vorventa has been transferred and demoted. Leaving an ugly hole in my staffing. He was good at his job." Illyan did not sound very grateful to Mark.

"Oh." Mark paused. "Vorventa thought I did something to the Count. Is that out on the gossip net too?"

"Yes."

Mark winced. "Well . . . at least *you* know better," he sighed. He glanced up at Illyan's stony face, and felt a nauseated alarm. "Don't you, sir?"

"Perhaps. Perhaps not."

"How not?! You have the medical reports!"

"Mm. The cardiac rupture certainly appeared natural. But it could have been artificially created, using a surgical hand-tractor. The subsequent damage to the cardiac region would have masked its traces."

Mark shuddered in helpless outrage. "Tricky work," he choked."Extremely precise. How did I make the Count hold still, and not notice, while I was doing this?"

"That is one problem with the scenario," Illyan agreed.

"And what did I do with the hand tractor? And the medical scanner, I'd have needed one of those, too. Two or three kilos of equipment."

"Ditched them in the woods. Or somewhere."

"Have you found them?"

"No."

"Have you looked?"

"Yes."

Mark rubbed his face hard, and clenched and unclenched his teeth. "So. You have all the men you need to quarter and re-quarter several square kilometers of woods looking for a hand tractor that isn't there, but not enough to send to Jackson's Whole to look for Miles, who is. *I* see." No. He had to keep his temper, or he'd lose everything. He wanted to howl. He wanted to beat Illyan's face in.

"A galactic operative is a highly-trained specialist with rare personal qualities," said Illyan stiffly. "Area-searches for known objects can be conducted by low-level troopers, who are more abundant."

"Yes. I'm sorry." *He* was apologizing? *Your goals. Remember your goals.* He thought of the Countess, and drew a deep, calming breath. He drew several.

"I do not hold this as a conviction," Illyan said, watching his face. "I hold it merely as a doubt."

"Thank-you-I-think," Mark snarled.

He sat for a full minute, trying to marshall his scattered thoughts, his best arguments. "Look," he said at last. "You are wasting your resources, and one of the resources you are wasting is me. Send *me* back to Jackson's Whole. I know more about the entire situation than any other agent you have. I have some training, an assassin's training only maybe, but some. Enough to lose your spies three or four times on Earth! Enough to get this far. I know Jackson's Whole, visceral stuff you can only acquire growing up there. And you wouldn't even have to pay me!" He waited, holding his breath in the courage of his terror. *Go back?* Blood sprayed through his memory. *Going to give the Bharaputrans a chance to correct their aim?*

Illyan's cool expression did not change. "Your track record so far in covert ops is not notably impressive for its successes, Lord Mark."

"So, I'm not a brilliant combat field commander. I am not Miles. We all know that by now. How many of your other agents are?"

"If you are as, ah, incompetent as you have appeared, sending you would be a further waste. But suppose you are more sly than even I think. All your thrashing around here, a mere smokescreen." Illyan could deliver the veiled insults too. Stiletto-sharp, right between the ribs. "And suppose you get to Miles before we do. What happens then?"

"What do you mean, what happens then?"

"If you return him to us as a room-temperature corpse, fit only for burying, instead of a cryo-stat hopeful—how will we know that was the way you found him? And you will inherit his name, his rank, his wealth, and his future. Tempting, Mark, to a man without an identity. Very tempting."

Mark buried his face in his hands. He sat crushed, infuriated, and wildly frustrated. "Look," he said through his fingers, "look. Either I'm the man who, by your theory, succeeded in half-assassinating Aral Vorkosigan and was so good I left no trace of proof—or I'm not. You can argue that I'm not competent enough to send. Or you can argue that I'm not trustworthy enough to send. But you can't use both arguments at once. Pick one!"

"I await more evidence." Illyan's eyes were like stones.

"I swear," Mark whispered, "excess suspicion makes us bigger fools than excess trust does." It had certainly been true in his case. He sat up suddenly. "So fast-penta me."

Illyan raised his brows. "Mm?"

"Fast-penta me. You never have. Relieve your suspicions." Fast-penta interrogations could be excruciatingly humiliating experiences, by all reports. So what. What was one more humiliation in *his* life? Warm and familiar, that was what.

"I have longed to, Lord Mark," Illyan admitted, "but your, ah, progenitor has a known idiosyncratic response to fast-penta that I assume you share. Not the usual allergy, exactly. It creates an appalling hyperactivity, a great deal of babble, but alas, no overwhelming compulsion to tell the truth. It is useless."

"In Miles." Mark seized the hope. "You assume? You don't know! My metabolism is demonstrably not like Miles's. Can't you at least check?"

"Yes," said Illyan slowly, "I can do that." He pushed himself off from the wall, and exited the cubicle, saying, "Carry on. I'll be back shortly."

Tense, Mark rose and paced the little room, two steps each way. Fear and desire pulsed in his brain. The memory of the inhuman chill of Baron Bharaputra's eyes clashed with hot rage in his throat. *If you want to find something, look where you lost it.* He'd lost it all on Jackson's Whole.

Illyan returned at last. "Sit down and roll up your left sleeve."

Mark did so. "What's that?"

"Patch test."

Mark felt a burr-like prickle, as Illyan pressed the tiny med-pad onto the underside of his forearm, then peeled it away. Illyan glanced at his chrono, and leaned on the comconsole, watching Mark's arm.

Within a minute, there was a pink spot. Within two, it was a hive. Within five, it had grown to a hard white welt surrounded by angry red streaks that ran from his wrist to his elbow.

Illyan sighed disappointment. "Lord Mark. I highly recommend that you avoid fast-penta at all costs, in your future."

"That was an allergic reaction?"

"That was a highly allergic reaction."

"Shit." Mark sat and brooded. And scratched. He rolled down his sleeve before he drew blood. "If Miles had been sitting here, reading these files, making these same arguments, would you have listened to him?"

"Lieutenant Vorkosigan has a sustained record of successes that compels my attention. Results speak for themselves. And, as you yourself have *repeatedly* pointed out, you are not Miles. You can't use both arguments at once," he added icily. "Pick one."

"Why did you even bother letting me in here, if nothing I say or do can make any difference?" Mark exploded.

Illyan shrugged. "Aside from Gregor's direct order—at least I know where you are and what you are doing."

"Like a detention cell, except that I enter it voluntarily. If you could lock me in a cell without a comconsole. you'd be even happier."

"Frankly, yes."

"Just. So." Blackly, Mark switched the comconsole back on. Illyan left him to it.

Mark jumped out of his chair, stumbled to the door, and stuck his head out. Illyan's retreating back was halfway down the corridor.

"I have my own name now, Illyan!" Mark shouted furiously.

Illyan glanced back over his shoulder, raised his brows, and walked on.

Mark tried reading another report, but it seemed to turn to gibberish somewhere between his eyes and his brain. He was too rattled to continue his analysis today. He gave up at last, and called Pym for a pick-up. It was still light out. He stared into the sunset, glimpsed between the buildings on the way home to Vorkosigan House, till his eyes burned.

✧ ✧ ✧

It was the first time that week he had returned from ImpSec in time to join the Countess for dinner. He found her and Bothari-Jesek dining casually in a ground-floor nook that looked onto a sheltered corner of the garden, densely arranged with autumn flowers and plants. Spot lighting kept the display colorful in the gathering dusk The Countess wore a fancy green jacket and long skirt a Vor matron's town wear; Bothari-Jesek wore a similar costume in blue obviously borrowed from the Countess's wardrobe. A place was set for him at the table despite the fact that he hadn't shown up for the meal for four straight days. Obscurely touched, he slid into his seat.

"How was the Count today?" he asked diffidently.

"Unchanged," the Countess sighed.

As was the Countess's custom, there was a minute of silence before they plowed in, which the Countess used for an inward prayer that Mark suspected involved more this day than calling blessings upon the bread. Bothari-Jesek and he waited politely, Bothari-Jesek meditating God-knew-what, Mark rerunning his conversation with Illyan in his head and evolving all the smarter things he should have said, too late. A servant brought food in covered dishes and departed to leave them in privacy, which was the way the Countess preferred it when not dining formally with official guests. *Family style. Huh.*

In truth, Bothari-Jesek had been lending the Countess the support of a daughter in the days since the Count's collapse, accompanying her on her frequent trips to the Imperial Military Hospital, running personal errands, acting as confidant; Mark suspected the Countess had revealed more of her real thoughts to Bothari-Jesek than to anyone else, and felt a little inexplicable envy. As their favorite Armsman's only child, Elena Bothari had been practically the Vorkosigans' foster-daughter; Vorkosigan House had been the home in which she had grown up. So if he was really Miles's brother, did that make Elena his foster-sister too? He would have to try the idea on her. And prepare to duck. Some other time.

"Captain Bothari-Jesek," Mark began, after he'd swallowed the first couple of bites, "what's going on with the Dendarii at Komarr? Or does Illyan keep you in the dark too?"

"He'd better not," said Bothari-Jesek. To be sure, Elena had allies that outranked even the ImpSec commander. "We've done a little re-shuffling. Quinn retained the chief eyewitnesses to your, um, raid—" kind of her, not to use some more forthright term, like *debacle*, "Green Squad, part of Orange and Blue Squads. She's sent everyone else off in the *Peregrine* under my second, to rejoin the fleet. People were getting itchy, cooped up in orbit with no downside leave and no duties." She looked distinctly unhappy at this temporary loss of her command.

"Is the *Ariel* still at Komarr, then?"

"Yes."

"Quinn of course . . . Captain Thorne? Sergeant Taura?"

"All still waiting."

"They must be pretty itchy themselves, by now."

"Yes," said Bothari-Jesek, and stabbed her fork so hard into a chunk of vat protein that it skittered across her plate. Itchy. Yes.

"So what have you learned this week, Mark?" the Countess asked him.

"Nothing you don't already know, I'm afraid. Doesn't Illyan pass you reports?"

"Yes, but due to the press of events I've only had time to glance at his analysts' synopses. In any case, there's only one piece of news I really want to hear."

Right. Encouraged, Mark began to detail his survey to her, including his data-triage and his growing convictions.

"You seem to have been quite thorough," she remarked.

He shrugged. "I now know roughly what ImpSec knows, if Illyan has been honest with me. But since ImpSec frankly doesn't know where Miles is, it's all futile. I swear . . ."

"Yes?" said the Countess.

"I *swear* Miles is still on Jackson's Whole. But I can't get Illyan to focus down. His attention is spread all over hell and gone. He has Cetagandans on the brain."

"There are sound historical reasons for that," said the Countess. "And current ones too, I'm afraid, though I'm sure Illyan has been cagey about confiding to you any of ImpSec's troubles not directly connected to Miles's situation. To say he's had a bad month would be a gross understatement." She hesitated too, for rather a long time. "Mark . . . you are, after all, Miles's clone-twin. As close as one human being can be to another. This conviction of yours has a passionate edge. You seem to *know*. Do you suppose . . . you really do know? On some level?"

"Do you mean, like, a psychic link?" he said. What an awful idea.

She nodded, faintly flushed. Bothari-Jesek looked appalled, and gave him a strange beseeching look, *Don't you dare mess with her mind, you—!*

This is the true measure of her desperation. "I'm sorry. I'm not psychic. Only psychotic." Bothari-Jesek relaxed. He slumped, then brightened slightly with an idea. "Though it might not hurt to let *Illyan* think that you think so."

"Illyan is too sturdy a rationalist." The Countess smiled sadly.

"The passion is only frustration, ma'am. No one will let me do anything."

"What is it that you wish to do?"

I want to run away to Beta Colony. The Countess would probably help him to.

. . . No. I am never running away again.

He took a breath, in place of a courage he did not feel. "I want to go back to Jackson's Whole and look for him. I could do as good a job as Illyan's other agents, I know I could! I tried the idea on him. He wouldn't bite. If he could, he'd like to lock me in a security cell."

"It's days like these poor Simon would sell his soul to make the world hold still for a while," the Countess admitted. "His attention isn't just spread right now, it's splintered. I have a certain sympathy for him."

"I don't. I wouldn't ask Simon Illyan for the time of day. Nor would he give it to me." Mark brooded. "Gregor would hint obliquely where I might look for a crono. You . . ." his metaphor extended itself, unbidden, "would give me a clock."

"If I had one, son, I'd give you a clock factory," the Countess sighed.

Mark chewed, swallowed, stopped, looked up. "Really?"

"R—" she began positively, then caution caught up with her. "Really what?"

"Is Lord Mark a free man? I mean, I've committed no crime within the Barrayaran Empire, have I? There being no law against stupidity. I'm not under arrest."

"No . . ."

"I could go to Jackson's Whole myself! Screw Illyan and his precious resources. If—" ah, the catch—he deflated slightly, "if I had a ticket," he ran down. His whole wealth, as far as he knew, was seventeen Imperial marks left from a twenty-five note the Countess had given him for spending money earlier in the week, now wadded up in his trouser pocket.

The Countess pushed her plate away and sat back, her face drained. "This does not strike me as a very safe idea. Speaking of stupidity."

"Bharaputra's probably got an execution contract out on you now, after what you did," Bothari-Jesek put in helpfully.

"No—it's on Admiral Naismith," Mark argued. "And I wouldn't be going back to Bharaputra's." Not that he didn't agree with the Countess. The spot on his forehead where Baron Bharaputra had counted coup burned in secret. He stared urgently at her. "Ma'am . . ."

"Are you seriously asking me to finance your risking your life?" she said.

"No—my saving it! I can't"—he waved around helplessly, at Vorkosigan House, at his whole situation—"go on like this. I'm all out of balance here, I'm all wrong."

"Balance will come to you, in time. It's just too soon," she said earnestly. "You're still very new."

"I have to go back. I have to try to undo what I did. If I can."

"And if you can't, what will you do then?" asked Bothari-Jesek coldly. "Take off, with a nice head start?"

Had the woman read his mind? Mark's shoulders bowed with the weight of her scorn. And his doubt. "I," he breathed, "don't . . ." *know.* He could not finish the sentence aloud.

The Countess laced her long fingers. "I don't doubt your heart," she said, looking at him steadily.

Hell, and she could break that heart more thoroughly with her trust than Illyan ever could with his suspicion. He crouched in his seat.

"But—you are my second chance. My new hope, all unlooked-for. I never thought I could have another child, on Barrayar. Now Jackson's Whole has eaten Miles, and you want to go down there after him? You, too?"

"Ma'am," he said desperately, "Mother—I cannot be your consolation prize."

She crossed her arms, and rested her chin in one hand, cupped over her mouth. Her eyes were grey as a winter sea.

"You of all people, have to see," Mark pleaded, "how important a second chance can be."

She pushed back her chair, and stood up. "I'll . . . have to think about this." She exited the little dining room. She'd left half her meal on her plate, Mark saw with dismay.

Bothari-Jesek saw it too. "Good job," she snarled.

I'm sorry, I'm sorry. . . .

She rose to run after the Countess.

Mark sat, abandoned and alone. And, blindly and half-consciously, proceeded to eat himself sick. He stumbled up to his room's level by the lift tube, afterward, and lay wishing for sleep more than for breath. Neither came to him.

After an interminable time his stunned headache and hot abdominal pain were just starting to recede, when there came a knock on his door. He rolled over with a muffled groan. "Who is it?"

"Elena."

He keyed on the light, and sat up in bed against the carved headboard, stuffing a pillow under his spine against some killer solid walnut acanthus leaves in high relief. He didn't want to talk to Bothari-Jesek. Or to any other human being. He refastened his shirt as loosely as it would go. "Enter," he muttered.

She came cautiously around the doorframe, her face serious and pale. "Hello. Are you feeling all right?"

"No," he admitted.

"I came to apologize," she said.

"You? Apologize to me? Why?"

"The Countess told me . . . something of what was going on with you. I'm sorry. I didn't understand."

He'd been dissected again, *in absentia.* He could tell by the horrified way Bothari-Jesek was looking at him, as if his swollen belly was laid open and spread wide in an autopsy with a cut from *here* to *there.* "Aw, hell. What did she say now?" He struggled, with difficulty, to sit up straighter.

"Miles had talked around it. But I hadn't understood how bad it really was. The Countess told me exactly. What Galen did to you. The shock-stick rape, and the, um, eating disorders. And the other disorder." She kept her eyes away from his body, onto his face, a dead give-away of the unwelcome depth of her new knowledge. She and the Countess must have been talking for two hours. "And it was all so deliberately *calculated.* That was the most diabolical part."

"I'm not so sure about the shock-stick incident being calculated," Mark said carefully. "Galen seemed out of his head, to me. Over the top. Nobody's that good an actor. Or maybe it started out calculated, and got out of hand." And then burst out, helplessly, *"Dammit!"* Bothari-Jesek jumped a foot in the air. "She has no *right* to talk about that with you! Or with anybody! What the hell am I, the best show in town?"

"No, no," Bothari-Jesek opened her hands. "You have to understand. I told her about Maree, that little blonde clone we found you with. What I thought was going on. I accused you to the Countess."

He froze, flushed with shame, and a new dismay. "I didn't realize you hadn't told her at the first." Was everything he thought he'd built with the Countess on a rotten foundation, collapsing now in ruins?

"She wanted you for a son so badly, I couldn't bring myself to. But I was so furious with you tonight, I blurted it all out."

"And then what happened?"

Bothari-Jesek shook her head in wonderment. "She's so Betan. She's so strange. She's never where you think she is, mentally. She wasn't the least surprised. And then she explained it all to me—I felt like my head was being turned inside out, and given a good wash-and-brush."

He almost laughed. "That sounds like a typical

conversation with the Countess." His choking fear began to recede. *She doesn't despise me . . . ?*

"I was wrong about you," Bothari-Jesek said sturdily.

His hands spread in exasperation. "It's nice to know I have such a defender, but you weren't wrong. What you thought was exactly what *was* going on. I would have if I could have," he said bitterly. "It wasn't my virtue that stopped me, it was my high-voltage conditioning."

"Oh, I don't mean wrong about the facts. But I was projecting a lot of my own anger, into the way I was explaining you to myself. I had no idea how much you were a product of systematic torture. And how incredibly you resisted. I think I would have gone catatonic, in your place."

"It wasn't that bad *all* the time," he said uncomfortably.

"But you have to understand," she repeated doggedly, "what was going on with *me*. About my father."

"Huh?" He felt as if his head had just been given a sharp half-twist to the left. "I know what my father has to do with this, why the hell is yours in on it?"

She walked around the room. Working up to something. When she did speak, it came out all in a rush. "My father raped my mother. That's where I came from, during the Barrayaran invasion of Escobar. I've known for some years. It's made me allergically sensitive on the subject. I can't stand it," her hands clenched, "yet it's *in* me. I can't escape it. It made it very hard for me to see you clearly. I feel like I've been looking at you through a fog for the last ten weeks. The Countess has dispelled it." Indeed, her eyes did not freeze him any more. "The Count helped me too, more than I can say."

"Oh." What was he to say? So, it hadn't been just him they'd been talking about for the past two hours. There was clearly more to her story, but *he* sure wasn't going to ask. For once, it wasn't his place to apologize. "I'm . . . not sorry you exist. However you got here."

She smiled, crookedly. "Actually, neither am I."

He felt very strange. His fury at the violation of his privacy was fading, to be replaced by a light-heartedness that astonished him. He was greatly relieved, to be unburdened of his secrets. His dread was shrunken, as if giving it away had literally diminished it. *I swear if I tell four more people, I'll be altogether free.*

He swung his legs out of the bed, grabbed her by the hand, led her to a wooden chair beside his window, climbed up and stood on it, and kissed her. "Thank you!"

She looked quite startled. "What for?" she asked on the breath of a laugh. Firmly, she repossessed her hand.

"For existing. For letting me live. *I* don't know." He grinned, exhilarated, but the grin faded in dizziness, and he climbed down more carefully, and sat.

She stared down at him, and bit her lip. "Why do you do that to yourself?"

No use to pretend he didn't know what *that* was, the physical manifestations of his compulsive gorge were obvious enough. He felt monstrous. He swiped a hand over his sweaty face. "I don't know. I do think, half of what we call madness is just some poor slob dealing with pain by a strategy that annoys the people around him."

"How is it dealing with pain to give yourself more pain?" she asked plaintively.

He half-smiled, hands on his knees, staring at the floor. "There is a kind of riveting fascination to it. Takes your mind off the real thing. Consider what a toothache does to your attention span."

She shook her head. "I'd rather not, thank you."

"Galen was only trying to screw up my relation with my father," he sighed, "but he managed to screw up my relation with everything. He knew he wouldn't be able to control me directly once he turned me loose on Barrayar, so he had to build in motivations that would last." He added lowly, "It ricocheted back on him. Because in a sense, Galen was my father too. My foster-father. First one I ever had." The Count had been alive to that one. "I was so hungry for identity, when the Komarrans picked me up on Jackson's Whole. I think I must have been like one of those baby birds that imprints on a watering pot or something, because it's the first parent-bird-sized thing it sees."

"You have a surprising talent for information analysis," she remarked. "I noticed it even back at Jackson's Whole."

"Me?" he blinked. "Certainly not!" Not a talent, surely, or he'd be getting better results. But despite all his frustrations, he had felt a kind of contentment, in his little cubicle at ImpSec this past week. The serenity of a monk's cell, combined with the absorbing challenge of that universe of data . . . in an odd way it reminded him of the peaceful times with the virtual learning programs, in his childhood back at the clone-creche. The times when no one had been hurting him.

"The Countess thinks so too. She wants to see you."

"What, now?"

"She sent me to get you. But I had to get my word in first. Before it got any later, and I lost my chance. Or my nerve."

"All right. Let me pull myself together." He was intensely grateful wine had not been served tonight. He retreated to his bathroom, washed his face in the coldest water, forced down a couple of painkiller tabs, and combed his hair. He slipped one of the back-country-style vests over his dark shirt, and followed Bothari-Jesek into the hall.

She took him to the Countess's own study, which was a serene and austere chamber overlooking the back garden, just off her bedroom. Her and her husband's bedroom. Mark glimpsed the dark interior, down a step and through an archway. The Count's absence seemed an almost palpable thing.

The Countess was at her comconsole, not a secured government model, just a very expensive commercial one. Shell flowers inlaid on black wood framed the vid plate, which was generating the image of a harried-looking man. The Countess was saying sharply, "Well, find out the arrangements, then! Yes, tonight, now. And then get back to me. Thank you." She batted the off-key, and swung around to face Mark and Bothari-Jesek.

"Are you checking on a ticket to Jackson's Whole?" he asked tremulously, hoping against hope.

"No."

"Oh." Of course not. How could she let him go? He was a fool. It was useless to suppose—

"I was checking on getting you a ship. If you're going, you'll need a lot more independent mobility than scheduled commercial transport will allow."

"*Buy* a ship?" he said, stunned. And he'd thought that line about the clock factory had been a *joke*. "Isn't that pretty expensive?"

"Lease, if I can. Buy if I have to. There seem to be three or four possibilities, in Barrayar or Komarr orbit."

"Still—how?" He didn't think even the Vorkosigans could buy a jump-ship out of pocket change.

"I can mortgage something," the Countess said rather vaguely, looking around.

"Since synthetics came in, you can't hock the family jewels any more." He followed her gaze. "Not Vorkosigan House!"

"No, it's entailed. Same problem with the District Residence at Hassadar. I can pledge Vorkosigan Surleau on my bare word, though."

The heart of the realm, oh shit . . .

"All these houses and history are all very well," she complained, raising her eyebrows at his dismayed expression, "but a bloody museum doesn't make a very liquid asset. In any case, the finances are my problem. You'll have your own worries."

"A crew?" was the first thought that popped into his head, and out of his mouth.

"A jump-pilot and engineer will come with the ship, at a minimum. As for supercargo, well, there are all those idle Dendarii, hanging in Komarr orbit. I imagine you could find a volunteer or two among them. It's obvious they can't take the *Ariel* back into Jacksonian local space."

"Quinnie has bleeding fingers by now, from scratching at the doors," Bothari-Jesek said. "Even Illyan won't be able to hold her much longer, if ImpSec doesn't get a break soon."

"Will Illyan try to hold me?" asked Mark anxiously.

"If it weren't for Aral, I'd be going myself," said the Countess. "And I sure as hell wouldn't let Illyan stop *me*. You are my proxy. I'll deal with ImpSec."

Mark bet she would. "The Dendarii I'm thinking of are highly motivated, but—I foresee problems, getting them to follow my orders. Who will be in command of this little private excursion?"

"It's the golden rule, boy. He who has the gold, makes the rules. The ship will be yours. The choice of companions will be yours. If they want a ride, they have to cooperate."

"That would last past the first wormhole jump. Then Quinn would lock me in a closet."

The Countess puffed a laugh despite herself. "Hm. That is a point." She leaned back in her station chair, and steepled her fingers together, her eyes half-closed for a minute or two. They opened wide again. "Elena," she said. "Will you take oath to Lord Vorkosigan?" The fingers of her right hand fanned at Mark.

"I'm already sworn to Lord Vorkosigan," Elena said stiffly. Meaning, to Miles.

The grey eyes went flinty. "Death releases all vows." And then glinted. "The Vor system never has been very good at catching the curve balls thrown at it by galactic technologies. Do you know, I don't think there has ever been a ruling as to the status of a voice-oath when one of the respondents is in cryo-stasis? Your word can't be your breath when you don't have any breath, after all. We shall just have to set our own precedent."

Elena paced to the window, and stared out into nothing. The reflecting lights of the room obscured any view of the night. At last, she turned decisively on her heel, went down on both knees in front of Mark, and raised her hands pressed palm to palm. Automatically, Mark enclosed her hands with his own.

"My lord," she said, "I pledge you the obedience of a liegewoman."

"Um . . ." said Mark. "Um . . . I think I may need more than that. Try this one. 'I, Elena Bothari-Jesek, do testify I am a freewoman of the District Vorkosigan. I hereby take service under Lord Mark Pierre Vorkosigan, as an Armsman—Armswoman?—simple, and will hold him as my liege commander until my death or he releases me.' "

Shocked, Bothari-Jesek stared up at him. Not very far up, true. "You can't do that! Can you?"

"Well," said the Countess, watching this playlet with her eyes alight, "there isn't actually a law saying a Count's heir can't take a female Armsman. It's just never been done. You know—*tradition.*"

Elena and the Countess exchanged a long look. Hesitantly, as if half-hypnotized, Bothari-Jesek repeated the oath.

Mark said, "I, Lord Mark Pierre Vorkosigan, vassal secundus to Emperor Gregor Vorbarra, do accept your oath, and pledge you the protection of a liege commander; this by my word as Vorkosigan." He paused. "Actually," he said aside to the Countess, "I haven't made my oath to Gregor yet, either. Would that invalidate this?"

"Details," said the Countess, waving her fingers. "You can work out the details later."

Bothari-Jesek stood up again. She looked at him like a woman waking up in bed with a hangover and a strange partner she didn't remember meeting the night before. She rubbed the backs of her hands where his skin had touched hers.

Power. Just how much Vor-power did this little charade give him? Just as much as Bothari-Jesek allowed, Mark decided, eyeing her athletic frame and shrewd face. No danger she would permit him to abuse his position. The uncertainty in her face was giving way to a suppressed pleasure that delighted his eye. *Yes. That was the right move.* No question but that he had pleased the Countess, who was grinning outright at her subversive son.

"Now," said the Countess, "how fast can we pull this together? How soon can you be ready to travel?"

"Immediately," said Bothari-Jesek.

"At your command, ma'am," said Mark. "I do feel—it's nothing psychic, you understand. It's not even the general itch. It's only logic. But I do think we could be running out of time."

"How so?" asked Bothari-Jesek. "There's nothing more static than cryo-stasis. We're all going crazy from uncertainty, sure, but that's our problem. Miles may have more time than we do."

Mark shook his head. "If Miles had fallen frozen into friendly or even neutral hands, they ought to have responded to the rumors of reward by now. But if . . . someone . . . wanted to revive him, they'd have to do the prep first. We're all very conscious right now of how long it takes to grow organs for transplant."

The Countess nodded wryly.

"If—wherever Miles is—committed to the project soon

after they got him, they could be nearly ready to attempt a revival by now."

"They might botch it," said the Countess. "They might not be careful enough." Her fingers drummed on the pretty shell inlay.

"I don't follow that," objected Bothari-Jesek. "Why would an enemy bother to revive him? What fate could be worse than death?"

"I don't know," sighed Mark. *But if there is one, I bet the Jacksonians can arrange it.*

CHAPTER NINETEEN

With breath, came pain.

He was in a hospital bed. That much he knew even before opening his eyes, from the discomfort, the chill, and the smell. That seemed right. Vaguely, if unpleasantly, familiar. He blinked, to discover that his eyes were plastered with goo. Scented, translucent, medical goo. It was like trying to see through a pane of glass covered with grease. He blinked some more, and achieved a limited focus, then had to stop and catch his breath from the effort.

There was something terribly wrong with his breathing, labored panting that didn't provide enough air at all. And it whistled. The whistling came from a plastic tube down his throat, he realized, trying to swallow. His lips were dry and cracked; the tube blocking his mouth prevented him from moistening them. He tried to move. His body sent back shooting aches and pains, burning through every bone. There were tubes going into, or perhaps out of, his arms. And his ears. And his nose.

There were too damn many tubes. That was bad, he realized dimly, though how he knew he could not have said. With a heroic effort, he tried to raise his head and see down his body. The tube in his throat shifted painfully.

Ridges of ribs. Belly gaunt and sunken. Red welts radiated all over his chest, like a long-legged spider crouched just beneath his skin, its body over his sternum. Surgical glue held together jagged incisions, multiple scarlet scars looking like a map of a major river drainage delta. He was pocked with monitor-pads. More tubes ran from places orifices ought not to be. He caught a glimpse of his genitalia, lying in a limp discolored lump; there was a tube from there, too. Pain from there would be subtly reassuring, but he couldn't feel anything at all. He couldn't feel his legs or feet, either, though he could see them. His whole body was covered thickly with the scented goo. His skin was peeling in nasty big pale flakes, stuck in the stuff. His head fell back on a pad, and black clouds boiled in his eyes. *Too many damn tubes. Bad . . .*

He was in a muzzy, half-awake state, floating between confusing dream-fragments and pain, when the woman came.

She leaned into his blurred vision. "We're taking the pacer out, now." Her voice was clear and low. The tubes had gone away from his ears, or maybe he'd dreamed them. "Your new heart will be beating and your lungs working all on their own."

She bent over his aching chest. Pretty woman, of the elegantly intellectual type. He was sorry he was dressed only in goo, in front of her, though it seemed to him that he had carried on with even less to wear, once. He could not remember where or how. She did something to the spider-body lump; he saw his skin part in a thin red slit and then be sealed again. She seemed to be cutting out his heart, like an antique priestess making sacrifice, but that could not be, for his labored breathing continued. She'd definitely taken out something, for she placed it on a tray held by her male assistant.

"There." She watched him closely.

He watched her in return, blinking away the distortions of the ointment. She had straight, silky black hair, bound in a knot—more of a wad, actually—on the back of her head. A few fine strands escaped to float around her face. Golden skin. Brown eyes with a hint of an epicanthic fold. Stubby, stubborn black lashes. The bridge of her nose was coolly arched. A pleasant, original face,not surgically altered to a mathematically perfect beauty, but enlivened by an alert tension. Not an empty face. Somebody interesting was in there. But not, alas, somebody familiar.

She was tall and slim, dressed in a pale green lab smock over other clothes. "Doc-tor," he tried to guess, but it came out a formless gurgle around the plastic in his mouth.

"I'm going to take that tube out now," she told him. She pulled something sticky from around his lips and cheeks—tape? More dead skin came with it. Gently, she drew out the throat-tube. He gagged. It was like un-swallowing a snake. The relief of being rid of it almost made him pass out again. There was still some sort of tube—oxygen?—blocking his nostrils.

He moved his jaw, and swallowed for the first time in . . . in . . . Anyway, his tongue felt thick and swollen. His chest hurt terribly. But saliva flowed; his dry mouth re-hydrated. One did not really appreciate saliva till one was forced to do without it. His heart beat fast and light, like bird wings fluttering. It did not feel right, but at least he felt something.

"What's your name?" she asked him.

The subliminal terror he had been studiously ignoring yawned black beneath him. His breath quickened in his panic. Despite the oxygen, he could not get enough air. And he could not answer her question. "Ah," he whispered. "Ag . . ." He did not know who he was, nor how he had come by this huge burden of hurt. The not-knowing frightened him far more than the hurt.

The young man in the pale-blue medical jacket snorted, "I think I'm going to win my bet. That one's coagulated behind the eyeballs. All short circuits back there." He tapped his forehead.

The woman frowned in annoyance. "Patients don't come popping up out of cryo-stasis like a meal out of a microwave. It takes just as much healing as if the original injury hadn't killed them, and more. It will be a couple of days before I can even begin to evaluate his higher neural functions."

Still, she pulled something sharp and shiny from the lapel of her jacket, and moved around him, touching him and watching a monitor readout on the wall above his head. When his right hand jerked back at a prick, she smiled. *Yeah, and when my prick jerks up at a right hand, I'll smile,* he thought dizzily.

He wanted to speak. He wanted to tell that blue fellow to take a wormhole jump to hell, and take his bet with him. All that came out of his mouth was a hollow hiss. He shuddered with frustration. He had to function, or die. That, he was bone-sure of. Be the best or be destroyed.

He didn't know where this certainty came from. Who was going to kill him? He didn't know. Them, some faceless them. No time to rest. March or die.

The medical duo left. Driven by the obscure fear, he began to try to exercise, isometrics in his bed. All he could move was his right arm. Attracted by his thrashing as reported by his monitor pads, the youth came back and sedated him. When the darkness closed in again, he wanted to howl. He had very bad dreams, after that; any content would have been welcome to his bewildered brain, but all he could remember when he woke was the badness.

An interminable time later, the doctor returned to feed him. Sort of.

She touched a control to raise the head of his bed, saying chattily, "Let's try out your new stomach, my friend."

Friend? Was he? He needed a friend, no question.

"Sixty milliliters of glucose solution—sugar water. The first meal of your life, so to speak. I wonder if you have enough basic muscle control to suck on a straw yet?"

He did, once she touched a few drops of liquid to his lips to get him started. Suck and swallow, you couldn't get much more basic than that. Except that he couldn't drink it all.

"That's all right," she rippled on. "Your stomach's not fully grown yet, you see. Neither were your heart or lungs. Lilly was in a hurry to have you awake. All your replacement organs are a bit undersized for your body, which means they're going to be working hard, and won't grow as fast as they did in the vat. You're going to be short of breath for quite a while. Still, it made it all easier to install. More elbow room for me, which I appreciated."

He wasn't quite sure if she was talking to him, or just to herself, as a lonely person might talk to a pet. She took the cup away and came back with a basin, sponges, and towels, and began washing him, section by section. Why was a surgeon doing nursing care? DR. R. DURONA, read the name on the breast pocket of her green coat. But she seemed to be doing a neurophysiological examination at the same time. Checking her work?

"You were quite a little mystery, you know. Delivered to me in a crate. Raven said you were too small to be a soldier, but I picked out enough camouflage cloth and nerve disruptor shield-netting, along with the forty-six grenade fragments, to be quite sure you weren't just a bystander. Whatever you were, that needle-grenade had your name on it. Unfortunately, not in writing." She sighed half to herself. "Who *are* you?"

She did not pause for an answer, which was just as well. The effort of swallowing the sugar water had exhausted him again. An equally pertinent question was,

Where was he, and he was peeved that she, who must surely know, didn't think to tell him. The room was an anonymous high-tech medical locale, without windows. On a planet, not a ship.

How do I know that? A vague picture of a ship, in his head, seemed to shatter at his touch. *What ship?* For that matter, what planet?

There ought to be a window. A big window, framing a high hazy city-scape with a rapid river cutting through it. And people. There were people missing, who ought by rights to be here, though he could not picture them. The mix of generic medical familiarity and particular strangeness tied his guts in knots.

The cleaning-cloths were icy, grating, but he was glad to be rid of the goo, not to mention all the disgusting crud stuck in it. He felt like a lizard, shedding his skin. When she was done, all the dead white flakes were gone. The new skin looked very raw.

She rubbed depilatory cream over his face, which seemed redundant, and stung like hell. He decided he liked the sting. He was starting to relax, and enjoy her ministrations, embarrassingly intimate though they were. She was returning him at least to the dignity of being clean, and she did not feel like an enemy. Some sort of ally, at least on the somatic level. She cleaned his face of cream, beard, and a good deal of skin, and also combed his hair, though unfortunately, like his skin, his hair too seemed to be coming out in alarming clumps.

"There," she said, sounding satisfied. She held a large hand-mirror up to his face. "See anybody you recognize?" She was watching him closely, he realized, noting his eyes focus and track.

That's me? Well . . . I suppose I can get used to it. Red skin stretched over its frame of bones. Jutting nose, a sharp chin . . . the grey eyes looked bizarrely hung-over, their whites solid scarlet. His dark hair was patchy, like a bad case of mange. He'd really been hoping for something much better-looking.

He tried to speak, to ask. His mouth moved but, like his thoughts, too disconnectedly for coherence. He puffed air and spittle. He couldn't even swear, which made him want to swear even more, which rapidly degenerated into a gurgling snarl. She hastily took the mirror away and stood staring at him in worry.

Steady on. If he kept thrashing around, they'd probably hit him with another dose of sedative, and he didn't want that. He lay back panting helplessly. She lowered the bed again, dimmed the lights, and made to leave. He managed a moan. It worked; she came back.

"Lilly called your cryo-chamber Pandora's box," she murmured reflectively. "But I thought of it as the enchanted knight's crystal coffin. I wish it *were* as easy as waking you with a kiss."

She bent over, eyelids fluttering half-closed, and touched her lips to his. He lay very still, half-pleased, half-panicked. She straightened, watched him another moment, and sighed. "Didn't think it would work. Maybe I'm just not the right princess."

You have a very strange taste in men, milady, he thought dizzily. *How fortunate for me. . . .*

Feeling hopeful of his future for the first time since recovering consciousness, he lay quietly, and let her go. Surely she would come back. Before, he had passed out, or been knocked out; this time natural sleep came to him. He didn't exactly like it—*if I should die before I wake*—but it served his body's craving, and blotted out the pain.

Slowly, he gained control of his left arm. Then he made his right leg twitch. His beautiful lady came back and fed him more sugar water, but with no more sweet kisses for dessert. By the time he compelled his left leg to twitch, she came back again, but this time there was something terribly wrong.

Dr. Durona looked ten years older, and had grown cool. Cold. Her hair was parted in the middle and hung down in two smooth wings, chopped off at jaw-length, with threads of silver gleaming in the ebony. Her hands on his body, helping him to sit up, were dryer, colder, more severe. Not caressing.

I've gone into a time-warp. No. I've been frozen again. No. I'm taking too long to recover, and she's pissed at me for making her wait. No . . . Confusion clogged his throat. He'd just lost the only friend he had, and he didn't know why. *I have destroyed our joy. . . .*

She massaged his legs, very professionally, provided him with a loose patient gown, and made him stand up. He almost passed out. She put him back to bed and left.

When she came back the next time, she'd changed her hair yet again. This time it was grown long, held back tightly bound in a silver ring on the back of her head, and flowing down in a blunt-ended horse-tail with wide silver streaks running through it. She'd aged another ten years, he swore. *What's happening to me?* Her manner was a little softened, but nothing so happy as at first. She walked him across the room and back, which drained him totally, after which he slept again.

He was deeply distressed when she returned once more in her cold, short-haired incarnation. He had to admit, she was efficient getting him up and moving. She barked at him like a drill sergeant, but he walked, and then he walked unassisted. She steered him outside of his room for the first time, to where a short hallway ended in a sliding door, and then back.

They'd just turned for another circuit when the door at the end hissed open, and Dr. Durona came through. She was in her horse-tail morph. He stared at the wing-haired Dr. Durona beside him, and almost burst into tears. *It's not fair. You're confusing me.* Dr. Durona strode up to Dr. Durona. He blinked back the water in his eyes, and focused on their name tags. Wing-hair was Dr. C. Durona. Horse-tail was Dr. P. Durona. *But where's my Dr. Durona? I want Dr. R.*

"Hi, Chrys, how's he doing?" asked Dr. P.

Dr. C. answered, "Not too badly. I've just about worn him out for this therapy-session, though."

"I should say so—" Dr. P. moved to help catch him as he collapsed. He could not make his mouth form words; they came out choked sobs. "Over-done it, I'd say."

"Not at all," said Dr. C., supporting his other side. Together they steered him back to bed. "But it looks like mental recovery is going to come after physical recovery, in this one. Which is not good. The pressure's on. Lilly's getting impatient. He has to start making connections soon, or he'll be no use to us."

"Lilly is never impatient," chided Dr. P.

"She is this time," said Dr. C. grimly.

"Will the mental recovery really follow?" She helped him lie back without falling.

"Anyone's guess. Rowan has guaranteed us the physical. Tremendous job, that. There's plenty of electrical activity in his brain, something has to be healing."

"Yes, but not instantly," came a warmly amused voice from the hallway. "What are you two doing to my poor patient?"

It was Dr. Durona. Again. She had long fine hair bunched in a messy wad on the back of her head, pure ebony dark. He peered worriedly at her name tag as she approached, smiling. *Dr. R. Durona. His* Dr. Durona. He whimpered in relief. He wasn't sure he could take much more confusion, it hurt more than the physical pain. His nerves seemed more shattered than his body. It was like being in one of his bad dreams, except that his dreams were much nastier, with more blood and dismemberment, not just a green-coated woman standing all around a room arguing with herself.

"P.T. stands for Physical Torture," Dr. C. quipped.

That explained it. . . .

"Come back and torture him again later," Dr. R. invited. "But—gently."

"How hard dare I push?" Dr. C. was intent, serious, standing with her head cocked, making notes on a report panel. "Urgent queries are coming down from above, you know."

"I know. Physical therapy no oftener than every four hours, till I give you the go-ahead. And don't run his heart rate above one-forty."

"That high?"

"An unavoidable consequence of its still being undersized."

"You have it, love." Dr. C. snapped her report panel closed and tossed it to Dr. R., then marched out; Dr. P. wafted after her.

His Dr. Durona, Dr. R., came to his side, smiled, and brushed his hair out of his eyes. "You're going to need a haircut soon. And new growth is starting on the bare patches. That's a very good sign. With all that happening on the outside of your head, I think there has to be something happening on the inside, hey?"

Only if you counted spasms of hysteria as activity . . . a tear left over from his earlier burst of terror escaped his eye at a nervous blink. She touched its track. "Oh," she murmured in sympathetic worry, which he found suddenly embarrassing. *I am not . . . I am not . . . I am not a mutant.* What?

She leaned closer. "What's your name?"

He tried. "Whzz . . . d'buh . . ." His tongue would not obey him. He knew the words, he just couldn't make them come out. "Whzz . . . yr nme?"

"Did you repeat me?" She brightened. "It's a start—"

"Ngh! Whzz *yr* nme?" He touched her jacket pocket, hoping she wouldn't think he was trying to grope her.

"What . . . ?" She glanced down. "Are you asking what's *my* name?"

"Gh! Gh!"

"My name is Dr. Durona."

He groaned, and rolled his eyes.

". . . My name is Rowan."

He fell back onto his head-pad, sighing with relief. *Rowan.* Lovely name. He wanted to tell her it was a lovely name. But what if they were all named Rowan—no, the sergeantly one had been called Chrys. It was all right. He could cut his Dr. Durona out of the herd if he had to; she was unique. His wavering hand touched her lips, then his own, but she didn't take the hint and kiss him again.

Reluctantly, only because he didn't have the strength to hold her, he let her pull her hand from his. Maybe he had dreamed that kiss. Maybe he was dreaming all of this.

A long, uncertain time passed after she left, but for a change he did not doze off. He lay awake, awash in disquieting, disconnected thought. The thought-stream carried odd bits of jetsam, an image here, what might be a memory there, but as soon as his attention turned inward to examine it, the flow of thoughts froze, and the tide of panic rose again. Well, and so. Let him occupy himself otherwise, only watching his thoughts at an angle, obliquely; let him observe himself reflected in what he knew, and play detective to his own identity. *If you can't do what you want, do what you can.* And if he couldn't answer the question, Who was he?, he might at least take a crack at *Where* was he? His monitor pads were gone; he was no longer radio-tagged.

It was very silent. He slipped out of bed and navigated to the door. It opened automatically onto the short hallway, which was dimly lit by night-strips at floor level.

Including his own, there were only four rooms off the little corridor. None had windows. Or other patients. A tiny office or monitor-station was empty—no. A beverage cup steamed on the countertop next to a switched-on console, its program on *hold.* Somebody would be back soon. He nipped past, and tried the only exit door, at the corridor's end; it too opened automatically.

Another short corridor. Two well-equipped surgeries lined it. Both were shut down, cleaned up, night-silent. And windowless. A couple of storage rooms, one locked, one not. Two palm-locked laboratories; one had a bank of small animal cages at one end, that he could glimpse dimly through the glass. It was all crammed with equipment of the medical/biochemical sort, far more than a mere treatment clinic would require. The place fairly reeked of research.

How do I know—no. Don't ask. Just keep going. A lift-tube beckoned at the corridor's end. His body ached, breathing hurt, but he had to grab his chance. *Go, go, go.*

Wherever he was, he was at the very bottom of it. The tube's floor was at his feet. It rose into dimness, lit by panels reading S-3, S-2, S-1. The tube was switched off, its safety door locked across the opening. He slid it open manually, and considered his options. He could switch the tube on, and risk lighting up some security monitor panel somewhere (why could he picture such a thing?); or he could leave it off and climb the safety-ladder in secret. He tried one rung of the ladder; his vision blackened. He backed down carefully and switched on the tube.

He rose gently to level S-1, and swung out. A tiny foyer had one door, solid and blank. It opened before him, and closed behind him. He stared around what was obviously a junk-storage chamber, and turned back. His door had vanished into a blank wall.

It took him a full minute of frightened examination to convince himself his sputtering brain wasn't playing tricks on him. The door was disguised as the wall. And he'd just locked himself out. He patted it frantically all over, but it would not re-admit him. His bare feet were freezing, on the polished concrete floor, and he was dizzy and dreadfully tired. He wanted to go back to bed. The frustration and fear were almost overwhelming, not that they were so vast, but that he was so weak.

You only want it 'cause you can't have it. Perverse. Go on, he told himself sternly. He made his way from support to support to the outer door of the storage chamber. It too was locked from the outside, he found out the hard way when it sealed behind him. *Go on.*

The storage room had opened onto another short corridor, centered around an ordinary lift-tube foyer. This level pretended to be the end of the line, Level B-2; openings marked B-1, G, 1, 2, and so on ascended out of sight. He went for the zero-point, G. G for Ground? Yes. He exited into a darkened lobby.

It was a neat little place, elegantly furnished but in the manner of a business rather than a home, with potted plants and a reception or security desk. No one around. No signs. But there were windows at last, and transparent doors. They reflected a dim replica of the interior; it was night outside. He leaned on the comconsole desk. Jackpot. Here was not only a place to sit down, but data in abundance . . . hell. It was palm-locked, and would not even turn on for him. There were ways to overcome palm-locks—how did he . . . ?—the fragmentary visions exploded like a school of minnows, eluding his grasp. He nearly cried with the uselessness of it, sitting in the station chair with his too-heavy head laid in his arms, across the blank unyielding vid plate.

He shivered. *God, I hate cold.* He wobbled over to the glass door. It was snowing outside, tiny scintillant dots whipping by slantwise through the white arc of a floodlight. They would be hard, and hiss and sting on bare skin. A weird vision of a dozen naked men standing shivering in a midnight blizzard flitted across his mind's eye, but he could attach no names to the scene, only a sensation of deep disaster. Was that how he had died, freezing in the wind and snow? Recently, nearby?

I was dead. The realization came to him for the first time, a burst of shock radiating outward from his belly. He traced the aching scars on his torso through the thin fabric of his gown. *And I'm not feeling too good now, either.* He giggled, an off-balance noise disturbing even to his own ears. He stifled his mouth with his fist. He must not have had time to be afraid, before, because the retroactive wash of terror knocked him to his knees. Then to his hands and knees. The shivering cold was making his hands shake uncontrollably. He began to crawl.

He must have triggered some sensor, because the transparent door hissed open. Oh, no, he wasn't going to make that error again, and get exiled to the outer darkness. He began to crawl away. His vision blurred, and he got turned around somehow; icy concrete instead of smooth tile beneath his hand warned him of his mistake. Something seemed to seize his head, half-shock, half-blow, with a nasty buzzing sound. Violently rebuffed, he smelled singed hair. Fluorescent patterns spun on his retinas. He tried to withdraw, but collapsed across the door-groove in a puddle of ice water and some slimy orange glop like gritty mold. *No, damn it no, I don't want to freeze again . . . !* He curled up in desperate revulsion.

Voices; shouts of alarm. Footsteps, babble, warm, oh blessed warm hands pulled him away from the deadly portal. A couple of women's voices, and one man's: "How did he get up here?" "—shouldn't have gotten out." "Call

Rowan. Wake her up—" "He looks terrible." "No," a hand held his face to the light by his hair, "that's the way he looks anyway. You can't tell."

The face belonging to the hand loomed over his, harsh and worried. It was Rowan's assistant, the young man who'd sedated him. He was a lean fellow with Eurasian features, with a definite bridge to his nose. His blue jacket said *R. Durona*, insanely enough. But it wasn't *Dr.* R. *So call him . . . Brother Durona.* The young man was saying, "—dangerous. It's incredible that he penetrated our security in that condition!"

"Na' sec'rty." Words! His mouth was making words! "Fire saf'ty." He added reflectively, "Dolt."

The young man's face jerked back in bewildered offense. "Are you talking to me, Short Circuit?"

"He's talking!" *His* Dr. Durona's face circled overhead, her voice thrilled. He recognized her even with her fine hair loose, falling all around her face in a dark cloud. *Rowan, my love.* "Raven, what did he say?"

The youth's dark brows wrinkled. "I'd swear he just said 'fire safety.' Gibberish, I guess."

Rowan smiled wildly. "Raven, all the secured doors open outward without code-locks. For escape in case of fire or chemical accident or—do you realize the level of understanding that reveals?"

"No," said Raven coldly.

That *dolt* must have stung, considering its source . . . he grinned darkly up at the hovering faces and the lobby ceiling wavering beyond them.

An older, alto voice came in from the left, restoring order, disbanding the crowd. "If you don't have a function here, get back to bed." A Dr. Durona whose short-cut hair was almost pure white, the owner of the alto voice, shuffled into his field of view, and stared thoughtfully down at him. "Dearheart, Rowan, he almost escaped, disabled as he is!"

"Hardly an escape," said Brother Raven. "Even if he'd somehow gotten through the force screen, he'd have frozen to death in twenty minutes out there tonight, dressed like that."

"How did he get out?"

An upset Dr. Durona confessed, "He must have gone past the monitor station while I was in the lav. I'm sorry!"

"Suppose he had made it this far in the daytime?" speculated the alto. "Suppose he had been seen? It could have been disastrous."

"I'll palm-lock the door to the private wing after this," the flustered Dr. Durona promised.

"I'm not sure that will be enough, considering this remarkable performance. Yesterday he couldn't even walk. Still, this fills me with hope as much as alarm. I think we have something here. We had better set a closer guard."

"Who can be spared?" asked Rowan.

Several Dr. Duronas, clad variously in robes and nightgowns, looked at the young man.

"Aw, no," Raven protested.

"Rowan may watch him in the daytime, and continue her work. You will take the night shift," the white-haired woman instructed firmly.

"Yes, ma'am," the youth sighed.

She gestured imperiously. "Take him back to his room now. You had better check him for damages, Rowan."

"I'll get a float pallet," said Rowan.

"You don't need a float pallet for him," scoffed Raven. He knelt, gathered the wanderer up in his arms, and grunted to his feet. Showing off his strength? Well . . . no. "He weighs about as much as a wet coat. Come on, Short Circuit, back to bed with you."

Muzzily indignant, he suffered himself to be carried off. Rowan hovered apprehensively at his side across the lobby, down the tube, through the storage chamber, and back into the peculiar building-under-a-building. At least, in response to his continued shivering, she set the bed's heat-bubble zone to a higher temperature this time.

Rowan examined him, with particular attention to his aching scars. "He hasn't managed to rip anything apart inside. But he seems physiologically upset. It may be from the pain."

"Do you want me to give him another two cc's of sedative?" asked Raven.

"No. Just keep the room dim and quiet. He's exhausted himself. Once he warms up I think he'll sleep on his own." She touched his cheek, then his lips, tenderly. "That was the second time today that he spoke, do you know?"

She wanted him to speak to her. But he was too tired now. And too rattled. There had been a tension among those people tonight, all those Dr. Duronas, that was more than medical fear for a patient's safety. They were very worried about something. Something to do with him? He might be a blank to himself, but they knew more and they weren't telling him.

Rowan eventually pulled her night robe more closely about herself, and left. Raven arranged two chairs, one for a seat and one for his feet, settled down, and began reading from a hand-viewer. Studying, for he occasionally re-ran screens or made notes. Learning to be a doctor, no doubt.

He lay back, drained beyond measure. His excursion tonight had nearly killed him, and what had he learned for all his pains? Not much, except this: *I am come to a very strange place.*

And I am a prisoner here.

CHAPTER TWENTY

Mark, Bothari-Jesek, and the Countess were in the library of Vorkosigan House going over ship specs the day before the scheduled departure.

"Do you think I would have time to stop and see my clones on Komarr?" Mark asked the Countess a little wistfully. "Would Illyan let me?"

ImpSec had settled on a Komarran private boarding school as the clones' initial depository, after consultation with the Countess, who had in turn kept Mark informed. ImpSec liked it because it meant they had only one location to guard. The clones liked it because they were together with their friends, the only familiarity in their sudden new situation. The teachers liked it because the clones could all be treated as one remedial class, and brought up to academic speed together. At the same time the young refugees had a chance to mingle with youths from normal, if mostly upper-class, families, and begin to get a handle on socialization. Later, when it was safer, the Countess was pushing for placement in foster-families despite the clones' awkward age and size. *How will they learn to form families themselves, later, if they have no models?* she'd argued with Illyan. Mark had listened in on that conversation with the most intense imaginable fascination, and kept his mouth tightly shut.

"Certainly, if you wish," the Countess now said to Mark. "Illyan will kick, but that's pure reflex. Except . . . I can think of one proper complaint he might have, because of your destination. If you encounter House Bharaputra again, God forbid, it might be better if you don't know everything about ImpSec's arrangements. Stopping on your way back might be more prudent." The Countess looked as if she didn't care for the flavor of her own words, but years of living with security concerns made her reasoning automatic.

If I encounter Vasa Luigi again, the clones will be the least of my worries, Mark thought wryly. What did he want of a personal visit anyway? Was he still trying to pass himself off as a hero? A hero should be more self-contained and austere. Not so desperate for praise as to pursue his—victims—begging for it. Surely he'd played the fool enough. "No," he sighed at last. "If any of them ever want to talk to me, they can find me, I guess." No heroine was going to kiss him anyway.

The Countess raised her brows at his tone, but shrugged agreement.

Led by Bothari-Jesek, they turned to more practical matters involving fuel costs and life-support system repairs. Bothari-Jesek and the Countess—who, Mark was reminded, had been a ship captain herself once—were deep into a startlingly technical discussion involving Necklin rod adjustments, when the comconsole image split, and Simon Illyan's face appeared.

"Hello, Elena." He nodded to her, in the comconsole's station chair. "I wish to speak with Cordelia, please."

Bothari-Jesek smiled, nodded, muted the outgoing audio, and slid aside. She beckoned urgently to the Countess, whispering, "Do we have trouble?"

"He's going to block us," worried Mark, agitated, as the Countess settled into the comconsole's station chair. "He's going to nail me to the floor, I know he is."

"Hush," reproved the Countess, smiling slightly. "Both of you sit over there and resist the temptation to talk. Simon is my meat." She re-opened her audio transmission mode. "Yes, Simon, what can I do for you?"

"Milady," Illyan gave her a short nod, "in a word, you

can desist. This scheme you are putting forward is unacceptable."

"To whom, Simon? Not to me. Who else gets a vote?"

"Security," Illyan growled.

"You are Security. I'll thank you to take responsibility for your own emotional responses, and not try to shift them onto some vague abstraction. Or get off the line and let me talk to Captain Security, then."

"All right. It's unacceptable to me."

"In a word—tough."

"I *request* you to desist."

"I refuse. If you want to stop me, ultimately, you'll have to generate an order for Mark's and my arrest."

"I will speak to the Count," said Illyan stiffly, with the air of a man driven to a last resort.

"He's much too ill. And I've spoken with him already."

Illyan swallowed his bluff without gagging, much. "I don't know what you think this unauthorized venture can do, besides muddy the waters, maybe risk lives, and cost you a small fortune."

"Well, that's just the point, Simon. I *don't* know what Mark will be able to do. And neither do you. The trouble with ImpSec is that you've had no competition lately. You take your monopoly for granted. A bit of hustle will be good for you."

Illyan sat with his teeth clenched for a short time. "You put House Vorkosigan at triple risk, with this," he said at last. "You are endangering your last possible back-up."

"I am aware. And I choose the risk."

"Do you have that right?"

"I have more right than you."

"The government is in the biggest uproar behind closed doors that I've seen in years," said Illyan. "The Centrist Coalition is scrambling to find a man to replace Aral. And so are three other parties."

"Excellent. I hope one of them may succeed before Aral gets back on his feet, or I'll never get him to retire."

"Is that what you see in this?" Illyan demanded. "A chance to end your husband's career? Is this *loyal* milady?"

"I see a chance to get him out of Vorbarr Sultana alive," she said icily, "an end I have often despaired of, over the years. You pick your loyalties, I'll pick mine."

"Who is capable of succeeding him?" asked Illyan plaintively.

"A number of men. Racozy, Vorhalas, or Sendorf, to name three. If not, there was something terribly wrong with Aral's leadership. One mark of a great man is the legacy of men he leaves behind him, to whom he's passed on his skills. If you think Aral so small as to have stifled all possible others around him, spreading smallness like a plague, then perhaps Barrayar is better off without him."

"You know I don't think that!"

"Good. Then your argument annihilates itself."

"You tie me in knots." Illyan rubbed his neck. "Milady, he said at last, "I didn't want to have to say this to you. But have you considered the possible *dangers* of letting Lord Mark get to Lord Miles before anyone else?"

She leaned back in her chair, smiling, her fingers lightly drumming. "No, Simon. What dangers are you thinking of?"

"The temptation to promote himself," Illyan bit out.

"Murder Miles. Say what you damn mean." Her eyes glinted dangerously. "So you'll just have to make sure your people get to Miles first. Won't you. I've no objection."

"Damn it, Cordelia," he cried, harried, "you realize, that if they get into trouble, the first thing they're going to do is cry to ImpSec for rescue!"

The Countess grinned. "You live to serve, I believe you fellows say in your oath. Don't you?"

"We'll see," snapped Illyan, and cut the comm.

"What's he going to do?" asked Mark anxiously.

"At a guess, go over my head. Since I've already cut him out with Aral, that leaves only one choice. I don't think I'll bother getting up. I expect I'll get another call here shortly."

Distracted, Mark and Bothari-Jesek attempted to carry on with the ship specs. Mark jumped when the comm chimed again.

An anonymous young man appeared, nodded to the Countess, stated, "Lady Vorkosigan. Emperor Gregor," and vanished. Gregor's face appeared in his place, looking bemused.

"Good morning, Lady Cordelia. You really ought not to stir up poor Simon that way, you know."

"He deserved it," she said equably. "I admit, he has far too much on his mind at the moment. Suppressed panic turns him into a prick every time, it's what he does instead of running in circles screaming. A way of coping, I suppose."

"While others of us cope by becoming over-analytical," Gregor murmured. The Countess's lip twitched, and Mark suddenly thought he knew who might shave the barber.

"His security concerns are legitimate," Gregor continued. "Is this Jackson's Whole venture *wise*?"

"A question that can only be answered by empirical testing. So to speak. I grant you, Simon argues sincerely. But—how do you consider *Barrayar's* concerns will best be served, Sire? That's the question you must answer."

"I'm divided in mind."

"Are you divided in heart?" Her question was a challenge. She opened her hands, half-placation, half-leading. "One way or another, you're going to be dealing with Lord Mark Vorkosigan for a long time to come. This excursion, if it does nothing else, will test the validity of all doubts. If they are not tested, they will always remain with you, an unanswered itch. And that's not fair to Mark."

"How very scientific," he breathed. They regarded each other with equal dryness.

"I thought it might appeal to you."

"Is Lord Mark with you?"

"Yes," the Countess gestured him to her side.

Mark entered the range of the vid pick-up. "Sire."

"So, Lord Mark." Gregor studied him gravely. "It seems your mother wants me to give you enough rope to hang yourself."

Mark swallowed. "Yes, Sire."

"Or save yourself . . ." Gregor nodded. "So be it. Good luck and good hunting."

"Thank you, Sire."

Gregor smiled and cut the comm.

They did not hear from Illyan again.

In the afternoon, the Countess took Mark with her to the Imperial Military Hospital on her daily visit to her husband. Mark had made that journey in her company twice before, since the Count's collapse. He didn't much care for it. For one thing, the place smelled entirely too much like the clinics that had helped make a torment of his Jacksonian youth; he found himself remembering details of early surgeries and treatments that he thought he'd altogether forgotten. For another, the Count himself still terrified Mark. Even laid low, his personality was as powerful as his life was precarious, and Mark wasn't sure which teetering aspect scared him more.

His feet slowed to a halt in the hospital corridor outside the Prime Minister's guarded room, and he stood in indecisive misery. The Countess glanced back, and stopped. "Yes?"

"I . . . really don't want to go in there."

She frowned thoughtfully. "I won't force you. But I'll predict you a prediction."

"Say on, oh seeress."

"You will never regret having done so. But you may deeply regret not having done so."

Mark digested that. "All right," he said faintly, and followed her.

They tiptoed in quietly on the deep carpeting. The drapes were open on a wide view of the Vorbarr Sultana cityscape, sweeping down to the ancient buildings and the river that bisected the capital's heart. It was a cloudy, chilly, rainy afternoon, and grey and white mists swirled around the tops of the highest modern towers. The Count's face was turned to the silver light. He looked abstracted, bored, and ill, his face puffy and greenish, only partly a reflection of the light and the green uniform pajamas that reminded all forcibly of his patient-status. He was peppered with monitor pads, and had an oxygen tube to his nostrils.

"Ah." His head turned at their entry, and he smiled. He keyed up a light at his bedside, which cast a warmer pool of illumination that nonetheless failed to improve his color. "Dear Captain. Mark." The Countess bent to his bedside, and they exchanged a longer-than-formal kiss. The Countess swung herself up on the end of his bed and perched there cross-legged, arranging her long skirt. Casually, she began to rub his bare feet, and he sighed contentedly.

Mark advanced to about a meter distance. "Good afternoon, sir. How are you feeling?"

"Hell of a deal, when you can't kiss your own wife without running out of breath," he complained. He lay back, panting heavily.

"They let me into the lab to see your new heart," the Countess commented. "It's chicken-heart sized already, and beating away cheerfully in its little vat."

The Count laughed weakly. "How grotesque."

"*I* thought it was cute."

"*You* would."

"If you really want grotesque, consider what you want to do with the old one, after," the Countess advised with a wicked grin. "The opportunities for tasteless jokes are almost irresistible."

"The mind reels," murmured the Count. He glanced up at Mark, still smiling.

Mark took a breath. "Lady Cordelia has explained to you what I intend to do, hasn't she, sir?"

"Mm." The Count's smile faded. "Yes. Watch out for your back. Nasty place, Jackson's Whole."

"Yes, I . . . know."

"So you do." He turned his head to stare out the grey window. "I wish I could send Bothari with you."

The Countess looked startled. Mark could read her thought right off her face, *Has he forgotten Bothari is dead?* But she was afraid to ask. She pasted a brighter smile on her mouth instead.

"I'm taking Bothari-Jesek, sir."

"History repeats itself." He struggled to sit up on one elbow, and added sternly, "It had better not, boy, y'hear?" He relaxed back into his pillows before the Countess could respond and make him. Her face lost its tension; he was clearly a little fogged, but he wasn't so far out of it as to have forgotten his Armsman's violent death. "Elena's smarter than her father was, I'll give her that," he sighed. The Countess finished with his feet.

He lay back, brows drawn down, apparently struggling to think of more useful advice. "I once thought—I only found this out when I grew old, understand—that there is no more terrible fate than to become the mentor. To be able to tell how, yet not to do. To send your protégé out, all bright and beautiful, to stand your fire . . . I think I've found a worse fate. To send your student out knowing damn well you haven't had a chance to teach *enough*. . . . Be smart, boy. Duck fast. Don't sell yourself to your enemy in advance, in your mind. You can only be defeated *here*." He touched his hands to his temples.

"I don't even know who the enemy is, yet," said Mark ruefully.

"They'll find you, I suppose," sighed the Count. "People give themselves to you, in their talking, and in other ways, if you are quiet and patient and let them, and not in such a damn rush to give yourself to *them* you go bat-blind and deaf. Eh?"

"I guess so. Sir," said Mark, baffled.

"Huh." The Count had run himself completely out of breath. "You'll see," he wheezed. The Countess eyed him, swung herself off the bed, and stood up.

"Well," said Mark, and nodded briefly, "goodbye." His word hung in the air, insufficient. *Cardiac conditions are not contagious, dammit. What are you scared of?* He swallowed, and cautiously went nearer the Count. He had never touched the man except the once when trying to help load him onto the float bike. Afraid, emboldened, he held out his hand.

The Count grasped it, a brief, strong grip. His hand was big and square and blunt-fingered, a hand fit for shovels and picks, swords and guns. Mark's own hand seemed small and childlike, plump and pale by contrast. They had nothing in common but the grip.

"Confusion to the enemy, boy," whispered the Count.

"Turn-about is fair play, sir."

His father snorted a laugh.

Mark made one final vid-call that evening, his last night on Barrayar. He sneaked off to use the console in Miles's room, not in secret, exactly, but in private. He stared at the blank machine for ten minutes before spasmodically punching in the code he had obtained.

A middle-aged blonde woman's image appeared over the vid plate when the chime stopped. The remains of a striking beauty made her face strong and confident. Her eyes were blue and humorous. "Commodore Koudelka's residence," she answered formally.

It's her mother. Mark choked down panic to quaver, "May I speak with Kareen Koudelka, please—ma'am?"

A blonde brow twitched. "I believe I know which one you are, but—who may I say is calling?"

"Lord Mark Vorkosigan," he got out.

"Just a moment, my lord." She left the range of the vid pick-up; he could hear her voice fading in the distance, calling "Kareen!"

There was a muffled bumping in the background, garbled voices, a shriek, and Kareen's laughing voice crying, "No, Delia, it's for me! Mother, make her go away! Mine, all mine! Out!" The sound of a door thumping closed on, presumably, flesh, a yelp, then a firmer and more final slam.

Panting and tousled, Kareen Koudelka arrived in range, and gave him a starry-eyed "Hi!"

If not *just* like the look Lady Cassia had given Ivan, it was a robust and blue near-cousin. Mark felt faint. "Hello," he said breathlessly. "I called to say goodbye." No, dammit, that was much too short—

"What?"

"Um, excuse me, that's not quite what I meant. But I'm going to be traveling off-planet soon, and I didn't want to leave without speaking to you again."

"Oh." Her smile drooped. "When will you come back?"

"I'm not sure. But when I do, I'd like to see you again."

"Well . . . sure."

Sure, she said. What a lot of joyful assumptions were embedded in that *sure*.

Her eyes narrowed. "Is there something wrong, Lord Mark?"

"No," he said hastily. "Um . . . was that your sister I heard in the background just now?"

"Yes. I had to lock her out, or she'd stand out of range and make faces at me while we talked." Her earnest air of injury was immediately spoiled when she added, "That's what I do to her, when fellows call."

He was a *fellow*. How . . . how *normal*. He led her on with one question after another, to talk about her sisters, her parents, and her life. Private schools and cherished children . . . The Commodore's family was well-to-do, but with some sort of Barrayaran-style work ethic driving a passion for education and accomplishment, an ideal of service running like an undercurrent, towing them all into their future. He went awash in her words, dreamily sharing. She was so peaceable and real. No shadow of torment, nothing spoiled or deformed. He felt like he was feeding, not his belly but his head. His brain felt warm and distended and happy, a sensation near-erotic but less threatening. Alas, after a time she became conscious of the disproportion in the conversation.

"Good heavens, I'm babbling. I'm sorry."

"No! I like listening to you talk."

"That's a first. In this family, I'm lucky to get a word in edgewise. I didn't talk till I was three. They had me tested. It turned out it was just because my sisters were answering everything for me!"

Mark laughed.

"Now they say I'm making up for lost time."

"I know about lost time," Mark said ruefully.

"Yes, I've . . . heard a little. I guess your life has been quite an adventure."

"Not an adventure," he corrected. "A disaster, maybe." He wondered what his life would look like, reflected in her eyes. Something shinier. . . . "Maybe when I get back I can tell you a bit about it." If he got back. If he brought this off.

I'm not a nice person. You should know that, before. Before what? The more over-extended their acquaintance became, the harder it would be to tell her his repellent secrets.

"Look, I . . . you have to understand." God, he sounded just like Bothari-Jesek, working up to her confession. "I'm kind of a mess, and I'm not just talking about my outsides." Hell, hell, and what had this nice young virgin to do with the arcane subtleties of psycho-programming tortures, and their erratic results? What right had he to put horrors in her head? "I don't even know what I should tell you!"

Now was too soon, he could feel that clearly. But *later* might be too late, leaving her feeling betrayed and tricked. And if he continued this conversation one more minute, he'd drift into abject-blurting mode, and lose the one bright, un-poisoned thing he'd found.

Kareen tilted her head in puzzlement. "Maybe you ought to ask the Countess."

"Do you know her well? To talk to?"

"Oh, yes. She and my mother are best friends. My mother used to be her personal bodyguard, before she retired to have us."

Mark sensed the shadowy league of grandmothers again. Powerful old women with genetic agendas. . . . He felt obscurely that there were some things a man ought to do for himself. But on Barrayar, they used go-betweens. He had in his camp an ambassadoress-extraordinary to the whole female gender. The Countess would act for his good. Yeah, like a woman holding down a screaming child to get it a painful vaccination that would save it from a deadly disease.

How much did he trust the Countess? Did he dare trust her in this?

"Kareen . . . before I come back, do me a favor. If you get a chance to talk privately to the Countess, ask her what she thinks you ought to know about me, before we get better acquainted. Tell her I asked you to."

"All right. I like to talk with Lady Cordelia. She's sort of been my mentor. She makes me think I can do anything." Kareen hesitated. "If you're back by Winterfair, will you dance with me again at the Imperial Residence Ball? And not hide in the corner this time," she added sternly.

"If I'm back by Winterfair, I won't have to hide in the corner. Yes."

"Good. I'll hold you to your word."

"My word as Vorkosigan," he said lightly.

Her blue eyes widened. "Oh. My." Her soft lips parted in a blinding smile.

He felt like a man who's gone to spit, and had a diamond pop accidentally from his lips instead. And he couldn't call it back and re-swallow it. There must be a Vorish streak in the girl, to take a man's word so seriously.

"I have to go now," he said.

"All right. Lord Mark—be careful?"

"I—why do you say that?" He hadn't said a word about where he was going or why, he swore.

"My father is a soldier. You have that same look in your eyes that he gets, when he's lying through his teeth about some difficulty he's heading into. He can never fool my mother, either."

No girl had ever told him to *be careful*, like she meant it. He was touched beyond measure. "Thank you, Kareen." Reluctantly, he cut the comm, with a gesture that was nearly a caress.

CHAPTER TWENTY-ONE

Mark and Bothari-Jesek hitched a ride from Barrayar back to Komarr on an ImpSec courier vessel very like the one they'd ridden before, the last favor, Mark swore, that he would ever ask of Simon Illyan. This resolve lasted till they arrived at Komarr orbit, where Mark found that the Dendarii had given him his Winterfair gift early. All of Medic Norwood's personal effects had finally arrived, shipped from the main Dendarii fleet.

ImpSec being ImpSec, they had opened it first. So much the better; they would hardly have let Mark touch it if they had not convinced themselves they'd already emptied it of all its secrets. With Bothari-Jesek's backing, Mark begged, bluffed, bullied and whined his way to access to it. With obvious reluctance, ImpSec admitted him under supervision to a locked room in their orbital HQ. But they admitted him.

Mark turned Bothari-Jesek loose to oversee the arrangements for the ship the Countess's agent had located. As a Dendarii shipmaster Bothari-Jesek was not only the most logical person for the logistical tasks, she was probably overkill. With barely a pang of conscience Mark dismissed her from his thoughts to plunge into his examination of his new treasure box. Alone in an empty room. Heavenly.

After his first excited pass through the material—which included old clothing, a disk library, letters, and souvenir knickknacks from Norwood's four years of Dendarii service—Mark, depressed, was inclined to allow ImpSec was right. There was nothing here of value. Nothing up any of the sleeves—ImpSec had checked; Mark set aside clothing, boots, mementos, and all the physical effects. It gave him a queer feeling to handle the old clothes, marked with the wear of a body that was gone forever. Too damn much mortality around here. He turned his attention instead to the more intellectual detritus of the medic's life and career: his library and technical notes. ImpSec had gone through this same focusing before him, he noted glumly.

He sighed, and settled back in his station chair for a long slog. He desperately wanted Norwood to yield him the clue, if only so that a man he had inadvertently led to his death might not have died so in vain. *I never want to be a combat commander again. Ever.*

He hadn't expected it to be obvious. But his connector, when he finally ran across it hours later, was just about as subliminal as they came. It was a note hand-jotted on a plastic flimsy stuck in a pile of similar notes, interspersed in a cryo-prep training manual for emergency medical technicians. All it said was, *See Dr. Durona at 0900 for laboratory materials.*

Not *the* Durona . . . ?

Mark back-pedaled to Norwood's certifications and transcripts, part of the medic's computerized records he'd already seen in the ImpSec files on Barrayar. Norwood had taken his Dendarii cryonics training at a certain Beauchene Life Center, a respected commercial cryo-revival facility on Escobar. The name "Dr. Durona" did not appear anywhere among his immediate instructors. It did not appear on a listing of the Life Center's staff. It did not, in fact, appear anywhere at all. Mark checked it all again, to be sure.

There are probably lots of people named Durona on Escobar. It's not that rare a name. He clutched the flimsy anyway. It itched in his palm.

He called Quinn, aboard the *Ariel* moored nearby.

"Ah," she said, eyeing him without favor in the vid. "You're back. Elena said you were. What do you think you're doing?"

"Never mind that. Look, is there anyone here among the Dendarii, any medics or medtechs, who were trained at the Beauchene Life Center? Preferably at the same time as Norwood? Or near his time?"

She sighed. "There were three in his group. Red Squad's medic, Norwood, and Orange Squad's medic. ImpSec has already asked us about that, Mark."

"Where are they now?"

"Red Squad's medic was killed in a shuttle crash several months ago—"

"Agh!" He ran his hands through his hair.

"Orange Squad's man is here on the *Ariel*."

"Right!" Mark crowed happily. "I have to talk to him." He almost said, *Put him on*, then remembered he was on ImpSec's private line and certainly being monitored. "Send a personnel pod to pick me up."

"One, ImpSec has already interrogated him, at great length, and two, who the hell are you to give orders?"

"Elena hasn't told you much, I see." Curious. Did Bothari-Jesek's dubious Armsman's oath then outrank her loyalties to the Dendarii? Or was she just too busy to chat? How much time had he been—he glanced at his chrono. *My God.* "I happen to be on my way to Jackson's Whole. Very soon. And if you are *very* nice to me, I *might* ask ImpSec to release you to me, and let you ride along as my guest. Maybe." He grinned breathlessly at her.

The smoldering look she gave him in return was more eloquent than the bluest string of swear words he'd ever heard. Her lips moved—counting to ten?—but no sound came out. When she did speak, her tone was clipped to a burr. "I'll have your pod at the station's hatch ring in eleven minutes."

"Thank you."

✧ ✧ ✧

The medic was surly.

"Look, I've been through this. For hours on end. We're *done.*"

"I promise I'll keep it brief," Mark assured him. "Just one question."

The medic eyed Mark malignantly, perhaps correctly identifying him as the reason why he'd been stuck shipbound in Komarr orbit for the last dozen weeks.

"When you and Norwood were taking your cryonics training at Beauchene Life Center, do you ever remember meeting a Dr. Durona? Handing out lab supplies, maybe?"

"The place was knee-deep in doctors. No. Can I go now?" The medic made to rise.

"Wait!"

"That was your one question. And the ImpSec goons asked it before you."

"And that was the answer you gave them? Wait. Let me think." Mark bit his lip anxiously. The name alone was not enough to hare off on, not even for him. There had to be more. "Do you ever remember . . . Norwood being in contact with a tall, striking woman with Eurasian features, straight black hair, brown eyes . . . extremely smart." He didn't dare to suggest an age. It could be anywhere between twenty and sixty.

The medic stared at him in astonishment. "Yeah! How did you know?"

"What was she? What was her relation with Norwood?"

"She was a student too, I think. He was chasing her for a time, playing off his military glamour to the hilt, but I don't think he caught her."

"Do you remember her name?"

"Roberta, or something like that. Rowanna. I don't remember."

"Was she from Jackson's Whole?"

"Escobaran, I thought." The medic shrugged. "The clinic had post-doc trainees from all over the planet to take residencies in cryo-revival. I never talked to her. I saw her with Norwood a couple of times. He might have figured we'd try to cut him out with her."

"So the clinic is a top place. With a wide reputation."

"We thought so."

"Wait here." Mark left the medic sitting in the *Ariel*'s little briefing room, and rushed out to find Quinn. He hadn't far to rush. She was waiting in the corridor, her boot tapping.

"Quinn, quick! I need a visual off Sergeant Taura's helmet recorder from the drop mission. Just one still."

"ImpSec confiscated the originals."

"You kept copies, surely."

She smiled sourly. "Maybe."

"*Please,* Quinn!"

"Wait here." She returned promptly, and handed him a data disk. This time she followed him into the briefing room. Since the secured console wouldn't take his palm-print any more no matter how he wriggled it, Mark perforce let her power it up. He fast-forwarded Taura's visuals to the image he wanted. A close-up of a tall, dark-haired girl, her head turning, eyes wide. Mark blurred the background of the clone-creche, in the view.

Only then did he motion the medic to look.

"Hey!"

"Is it her?"

"It's . . ." the medic peered. "She's younger. But it's her. Where did you get that?"

"Never mind. Thank you. I won't take any more of your time. You've been a great help."

The medic exited as reluctantly as he had entered, staring back over his shoulder.

"What's this all about, Mark?" Quinn demanded.

"When we're on my ship and on our way, I'll tell you.

Not before." He had ahead-start on ImpSec, and he wasn't going to give it up. If they were anything less than desperate, they'd never let him go, Countess or no Countess. It was quite fair; he didn't have any information ImpSec didn't, potentially. He'd just put it together a little differently.

"Where the hell did you get a ship?"

"My mother gave it to me." He tried not to smirk.

"The Countess? Rats! She's turning *you* loose?"

"Don't begrudge me my little ship, Quinn. After all, my parents gave my big brother a whole *fleet* of ships." His eyes gleamed. "I'll see you on board, as soon as Captain Bothari-Jesek reports it ready."

His ship. Not stolen, nothing faked or false. His by right of legitimate gift. He who'd never had a birthday present, had one now. Twenty-two years' worth.

The little yacht was a generation old, formerly owned by a Komarran oligarch in the palmy days before the Barrayaran conquest. It had been quite luxurious, once, but obviously had been neglected for the past ten years or so. This did not represent hard times for the Komarran clan, Mark understood; they were in the process of replacing it, hence the sale. The Komarrans understood business, and the Vor understood the relation between business and taxation. Business under the new regime had recovered much of its former vigor.

Mark had declared the yacht's lounge to be the mission-briefing room. He glanced around now at his invitees, draped variously over the furniture secured to the carpeted deck around a fake fireplace that ran a vid program of atavistic dancing flames, complete with infra-red radiance.

Quinn was there, of course, still in her Dendarii uniform. She had entirely overgrazed her fingernails and had taken to cheek-biting instead. Bel Thorne sat silent and reserved, a permanent bleakness emphasizing the fine lines around its eyes. Sergeant Taura loomed next to Thorne, big and puzzled and wary.

It was no strike-group. Mark wondered if he ought to have packed along more muscle . . . no. If there was one thing his first mission had taught him, it was that if you didn't have enough force to win, it was better not to engage force at all. What he *had* done was cream off the maximum expertise the Dendarii could supply on the subject of Jackson's Whole.

Captain Bothari-Jesek entered, and gave him a nod. "We're on our way. We've broken orbit, and your pilot has the comm. Twenty hours to the first jump point."

"Thank you, Captain."

Quinn made a place beside her for Bothari-Jesek; Mark sat on the fake fieldstone hearth with his back to the crackling flames, his hands clasped loosely between his knees. He took a deep breath. "Welcome aboard, and thank you all for coming. You all understand, this is not an official Dendarii expedition, and is neither authorized nor funded by ImpSec. Our expenses are being privately paid by Countess Vorkosigan. You are all listed as being on unpaid personal leave. With one exception, I have no formal authority over any of you. Nor you over me. We do have an urgent mutual interest, which demands we pool our skills and information. The first piece is the proper identity of Admiral Naismith. You've brought Captain Thorne and Sergeant Taura up to speed on that, haven't you, Quinn?"

Bel Thorne nodded. "Old Tung and I had it figured out a long time ago. Miles's secret identity isn't as secret as he hoped, I'm afraid."

"It was news to me," rumbled Sergeant Taura. "It sure explained a lot I'd wondered about, though."

"Welcome to the Inner Circle anyway," said Quinn. "Officially." She turned to Mark. "All right, what do you have? A connection, finally?"

"Oh, Quinn. I'm up to my ass in connections. It's motive I'm missing now."

"You're ahead of ImpSec, then."

"Maybe not for long. They've sent an agent to Escobar for more details on the Beauchene Life Center—they're bound to make the same connection I did. Eventually. But I planned this expedition with a primary list of twenty sites on Jackson's Whole to re-check in depth. As a result of something I found in Norwood's personal effects, I've altered the order of the list. If Miles gets revived—which is part of my hypothesis—how long d'you think it would be till he did something to draw attention to himself?"

"Not long," said Bothari-Jesek reluctantly.

Quinn nodded wryly. "Though he could well wake amnesic, for a time." *Or forever,* she did not add aloud, though Mark could see the fear in her face. "It's almost more normal than not, in cryo-revivals."

"The thing is—ImpSec and we are not the only ones looking for him. I'm getting a timing-itch. Whose attention will he draw first?"

"Mm," said Quinn glumly. Thorne and Taura exchanged a worried look.

"All right." Mark rubbed his hands through his hair. He did not rise and pace, Miles-fashion; for one thing, Quinn's disapproving glances made him feel like he was starting to waddle. "Here's what I found and here's what I think. When Norwood was on Escobar for his cryo-prep training, he met a certain Dr. Roberta or Rowanna Durona, from Jackson's Whole, who was there also taking a residency in cryo-revival. They had some positive relationship, enough, anyway, that when Norwood was cornered at Bharaputra's, he remembered her. And trusted her enough to ship her the cryo-chamber. Remember, Norwood was also under the impression at this time that House Fell was our ally. Because the Durona Group works for House Fell."

"Wait a minute," said Quinn instantly. "House Fell claims not to have the cryo-chamber!"

Mark held up a restraining hand. "Let me give you a little Jacksonian history, as far as I know it. About ninety or a hundred years ago—"

"My God, Lord Mark, how long is this story going to be?" asked Bothari-Jesek. Quinn glanced up sharply at her use of the Barrayaran honorific.

"Bear with me. You have to understand who the Durona Group is. About ninety years ago, the present Baron Ryoval's father was setting up his arcane little genetic slave-trade, the manufacture of humans to order. At some point it occurred to him: Why hire genius from outside? Grow your own. Mental properties are the most elusive to create genetically, but the old Ryoval was a genius himself. He started a project that culminated in the creation of a woman he named Lilly Durona. She was to be his medical research muse, his slave-doctor. In both senses.

"She grew, was trained, and put to work. And she was brilliant. About this time the old Baron Ryoval died, not too mysteriously, during an early attempt at a brain transplant.

"I say not too mysteriously because of the character his son and successor, the present Baron Ryoval, immediately revealed. His first project was to get rid of all his potential sibling-rivals. The old man had sired a lot of children. Ryoval's early career is something of a Jacksonian legend. The eldest and most dangerous males, he simply had assassinated. The females and some of the younger males he sent to his body-modification laboratories, and thence to his very-private bordellos, to service the customers on that side of the business. I suppose they're all dead by now. If they're lucky.

"Ryoval also, apparently, used this direct management approach on the staff he had inherited. His father had handled Lilly Durona as a cherished treasure, but the new Baron Ryoval threatened to send her after his sisters, to satisfy the biological fantasies of his customers directly, if she didn't cooperate. She began to plot her escape with a despised young half-brother of Ryoval's by the name of Georish Stauber."

"Ah! Baron Fell!" said Thorne. Thorne was looking enlightened, Taura fascinated, Quinn and Bothari-Jesek horrified.

"The same, but not yet. Lilly and young Georish escaped to the protection of House Fell. In fact, I gather that Lilly was Georish's ticket in. They both set up in service to their new masters, with considerable negotiated autonomy, at least on Lilly's part. It was the Deal. Deals are as semi-sacred as anything can be, on Jackson's Whole.

"Georish began to rise through the ranks of House Fell. And Lilly began the Durona Research Group by cloning herself. Again and again. The Durona Group, which is now up to thirty or forty cloned sisters, serves House Fell in several ways. It's sort of a family doctor for upper level Fell executives who don't want to entrust their health to outside specialist houses like Bharaputra. And since House Fell's stock in trade is weapons, they've done R&D on military poisons and biologicals. And their antidotes. The Durona Group made House Fell a small fortune on Peritaint, and a few years later made it a huge fortune on Peritaint's antidote. The Durona Group is kind of quietly famous, if you follow that sort of thing. Which ImpSec does. There was a pile of stuff on 'em even in the stripped-down files they let me see. Though most of this is common knowledge on Jackson's Whole.

"Georish, not least owing to the coup he brought House Fell in the person of Lilly, ascended to the pinnacle a few years back when he became Baron Fell. Now, enter the Dendarii Mercenaries. And now you have to tell *me* what happened." Mark nodded to Bel Thorne. "I've only caught garbled bits."

Bel whistled. "I knew some of this, but I don't think I'd ever heard the whole story. No wonder Fell and Ryoval hate each other." It glanced at Quinn: she nodded permission to proceed. "Well, about four years ago, Miles brought the Dendarii a little contract. It was for a pick-up. Our Employer—excuse me, Barrayar, I've been calling them Our Employer for so long it's a reflex."

"Keep that reflex," Mark advised.

Bel nodded. "The Imperium wanted to import a galactic geneticist. I don't quite know why." It glanced at Quinn.

"Nor do you need to," said she.

"But a certain Dr. Canaba, who was then one of House Bharaputra's top genetics people, wanted to defect. House Bharaputra takes a lethally dim view of employees departing with a head full of trade secrets, so Canaba needed help. He struck a deal with the Barrayaran Imperium to take him in."

"That's where I come from," Taura put in.

"Yes," said Thorne. "Taura was one of his pet projects. He, um, insisted on taking her along. Unfortunately, the super-soldier project had recently been canceled, and Taura sold to Baron Ryoval, who collects genetic, excuse me Sergeant, oddities. So we had to break her out of House Ryoval, in addition to breaking Canaba out of House Bharaputra. Um, Taura, you'd better say what happened next."

"The Admiral came and rescued me from Ryoval's main biologicals facility," the big woman rumbled. She heaved a large sigh, as if at some sweet memory. "In the process of escaping, we totally destroyed House Ryoval's main gene banks. A hundred-year-old tissue collection went up in smoke. Literally." She smiled, baring her fangs.

"House Ryoval lost about fifty percent of its assets that night, Baron Fell estimated," Thorne added. "At least."

Mark hooted, then sobered. "*That* explains why you all think Baron Ryoval's people will be hunting for Admiral Naismith."

"Mark," said Thorne desperately, "if Ryoval finds Miles first, he'll have him revived just so he can kill him again. And again. And again. That's why we were all so insistent that you play Miles, when we were pulling out of Jackson's Whole. Ryoval has no motive to take revenge on the clone, just on the Admiral."

"I see. Gee. Thanks. Ah, whatever happened to Dr. Canaba? If I may ask."

"He was delivered safely," said Quinn. "He has a new name, a new face, a new laboratory, and a salary that ought to keep him happy. A loyal new subject for the Imperium."

"Hm. Well, that brings me to the other cross-connection. It's not a new or secret one, though I don't know yet what to make of it. Neither does ImpSec, incidentally, though as a result of it they've sent agents to check the Durona Group twice. Baronne Lotus Bharaputra, the Baron's wife, is a Durona clone."

Taura's clawed hand flew to her lips. "That girl!"

"Yes, *that* girl. I wondered why she gave me the cold chills. I'd seen her before, in another incarnation. The clone of a clone.

"The Baronne is one of the oldest of Lilly Durona's clone daughters, or sisters, or whatever you want to call the tribe. Hive. She didn't sell herself cheaply. Lotus went renegade for one of the biggest bribes in Jacksonian history—co-control, or nearly so, of House Bharaputra. She's been Baron Bharaputra's mate for twenty years. And now it seems she's getting one other thing. The Durona Group among them have an astonishing range of bio-expertise, but they refuse to do clone-brain transplants. It was written right into Lilly Durona's foundation-deal with House Fell. But Baronne Bharaputra, who must be over sixty-standard, apparently plans to embark on her second youth very shortly. Judging from what we witnessed."

"Rats," muttered Quinn.

"So that's another cross-connection," said Mark. "In fact, it's a damned cat's cradle of cross-connections, once you get hold of the right thread. But it doesn't explain, to me at least, why the Durona Group would conceal Miles *from their own House Fell bosses*. Yet they must have done so."

"If they have him," Quinn said, gnawing on her cheek.

"If," Mark conceded. "Although," he brightened slightly, "it would explain why that incriminating cryo-chamber ended up in the Hegen Hub. The Durona Group wasn't trying to hide it from ImpSec. They were trying to hide it from other Jacksonians."

"It almost all fits," said Thorne.

Mark opened his hands and held them apart palm to palm, as if invisible threads ran back and forth between them. "Yeah. Almost." He closed his hands together. "So here we are. And there we're going. Our first trick will be to re-enter Jacksonian space past Fell's jump point station. Captain Quinn has brought along quite a kit for doctoring our identities. Coordinate your ideas with her on that one. We have ten days to play with it."

The group broke up, to study the new problems each in his, her, or its own way. Bothari-Jesek and Quinn lingered as Mark rose, and stretched his aching back. His aching brain.

"That was quite a pretty piece of analysis, Mark," said Quinn grudgingly. "If it's not all hot air."

She ought to know. "Thank you, Quinn," he said sincerely. He too prayed it wouldn't all turn out to be hallucinatory, an elaborate mistake.

"Yes . . . he's changed a bit, I think," Bothari-Jesek observed judiciously. "Grown."

"Yeah?" Quinn's gaze swept him, up and down. "True . . ."

Mark's heart warmed in hungry anticipation of a crumb of approval.

"—he's fatter."

"Let's get to work," Mark growled.

CHAPTER TWENTY-TWO

He could remember studying tongue-twisters, once. He could even picture a whole screen-list of them, black words on pale blue. Had it been for some sort of rhetoric course? Unfortunately, though he could picture the screen, he could only remember one of the actual lines. He struggled to sit upright in bed, and try it. "Sheshells . . . shsh . . . she shells she *shit!*" He took a breath, and started over. Again. Again. His tongue seemed thick as an old sock. It felt staggeringly important to recover control of his speech. As long as he kept talking like an idiot, they were going to keep treating him like one.

It could be worse. He was eating real food now, not sugar-water or soft sludge. He'd been showering and dressing on his own for two whole days. No more patient gowns. They'd given him a shirt and pants, instead. *Like ship knits.* Their grey color at first pleased him, then worried him because he could not think why it pleased him. "She. Sells. Sea. Shells. By. The. Sea. Shore. Ha!" He lay back, wheezing in triumph. He glanced up to see Dr. Rowan leaning in the doorway, watching him with a slight smile.

Still catching his breath, he waved his fingers at her in greeting. She pushed off and came to sit at his side on his bed. She wore her usual concealing green smock, and carried a sack.

"Raven said you were babbling half the night," she remarked, "but you weren't, were you. You were practicing."

"Yuh," he nodded. "Gotta talk. C'mand—" he touched his lips, and waved vaguely around the room, "obey."

"You think so, do you?" Her brows arched in amusement but her eyes, beneath them, regarded him sharply. She shifted, and swung his tray table across between them. "Sit up, my authoritarian little friend. I brought you some toys."

"Sec'on chil'hd," he muttered glumly, and shoved himself upright again. His chest only ached. At least he seemed done with the more repulsive aspects of his second infancy. A second adolescence still to come? God forbid. Maybe he could skip over that part. *Why do I dread an adolescence I cannot remember?*

He laughed briefly as she upended the bag and spread about two dozen parts from some disassembled hand weapons across the table. "Test, huh?" He began to pick them up and fit them together. Stunner, nerve disruptor, plasma arc, and a projectile gun . . . slide, twist, click, knock home . . . one, two, three, four, he laid them in a row. "Pow'r cells dea'. Not armin' me, eh? These—extras." He swept half a dozen spare or odd parts aside into a pile. "Ha. Trick." He grinned smugly at her.

"You never pointed those at me or yourself while you were handling them," she observed curiously.

"Mm? Didn' notice." She was right, he realized. He fingered the plasma arc doubtfully.

"Did anything come up for you while you were doing that?" she asked.

He shook his head in renewed frustration, then brightened. " 'Membered som'thin s'mornin, tho'. Inna shar." At speed, his speech slurred into unintelligibility again, a logjam of the lips.

"In the shower," she translated encouragingly. "Tell me. Slow down as much as you need."

"Slow. Is. Death," he enunciated clearly.

She blinked. "Still. Tell me."

"Ah. Well. Think I wuzza boy. Ridin' onna horse. Old man on 'nother horse. Uppa hill. 'S chilly. Horses . . . puffin' lak I 'm." His deep breaths were not deep enough to satisfy. "Trees. Mountain, two, three mountain, covered w' trees, all strung tog'ther wi' new plastic tubes. Runnin' down to a shack a' t' bottom. Gran'da *happy* . . . 'cause tubes are *efficient*." He struggled to get that last word out intact, and succeeded. "Men'r 'appy too."

"What are they doing, in this scene?" she asked, sounding baffled. "These men."

He could see it again in his head, the memory of a memory. "Burnin' wood. Makin' sugar."

"That makes no sense. Sugar comes from biological production vats, not from burning trees," said Rowan.

"Trees," he asserted. "Brown sug'r trees." Another memory wavered up: the old man breaking off a chunk of something that looked like tan sandstone and giving him a taste by popping it in his mouth. The feel of the gnarled old stained fingers cool against his cheek, sweetness tinged with leather and horses. He shivered at the overwhelming sensory blast. *This was real.* But he still could name no names. *Gran'da.*

"Mountains mine," he added. The thought made him sad, and he didn't know why.

"What?"

"Own 'em." He frowned glumly.

"Anything else?"

"No. 'S all there is." His fists clenched. He straightened them, spreading his fingers carefully on the tray table.

"Are you sure this wasn't a dream from last night?"

"*No*. Inna *shar*," he insisted.

"It's very strange. This, I expected," she nodded to the re-assembled weapons, and began putting them back in the cloth bag. "*That*," a toss of her head indicated his little story, "doesn't fit. Trees made out of sugar sound pretty dream-like to me."

Doesn't fit what? A desperate excitement surged through him. He grabbed her around one slim wrist, trapping her hand with a stunner still in it. "Doesn' fi' wha'? *Wha' d' you know?*"

"Nothing."

"Na' nothin'!"

"That hurts," she said levelly.

He let go of her instantly. "Na' nothin'," he insisted again. "*Som'*thin. *Wha'*?"

She sighed, finished bagging the weapons, and sat back and studied him. "It was a true statement that we did not know who you were. It is now a truer statement that we are not sure which *one* you are."

"I gotta choice? Tell me!"

"You are at a . . . tricky stage of your recovery. Cryo-revival amnesics seldom recover all of their memories at once. It comes in little cascades. A typical bell-curve. A few at first, then a growing mass. Then it trails off. A few last holes may linger for years. Since you had no other gross cranial injuries, my prognosis is that you will eventually recover your whole personality. But."

A most sinister *but*. He stared at her beseechingly.

"At this stage, on the verge of cascading, a cryo-amnesic can be so hungry for identity, he'll pick up a mistaken one, and start assembling evidence to support it. It can take weeks or months to get it straightened out again. In your case, for special reasons, I think this is not only more than usually possible, it could be more than usually difficult to detangle again. I have to be very, very careful not to suggest anything to you that I am not absolutely certain about. And it's hard, because I'm theorizing in my head probably just as urgently as you are. I have to be sure that anything you give me really comes from you, and is not a reflection of some suggestion on my part."

"Oh." He sagged back in bed, horribly disappointed.

"There is a possible short-cut," she added.

He surged back up again. "Wha'? Gimme!"

"There is a drug called fast-penta. One of its derivatives is a psychiatric sedative, but its usual use is as an interrogation drug. It's actually a misnomer to call it a truth serum, though laymen insist on doing so."

"I . . . know fas'pent'." His brows drew down. He knew something important about fast-penta. What was it?

"It has some extremely relaxing effects, and sometimes, in cryo-revival patients, it can trigger memory cascades."

"Ah!"

"However, it can also be embarrassing. Under its influence people will happily talk about whatever crosses their minds, even their most intimate and private thoughts. Good medical ethics requires me to warn you about that. Also, some people are allergic to the drug."

"Where'd . . . you learn . . . goo' med'cal ethics?" he asked curiously.

Strangely, she flinched. "Escobar," she said, and eyed him.

"Where we *now*?"

"I'd rather not say, just yet."

"How could that contam'nate m' mem'ry?" he demanded indignantly.

"I can tell you soon, I think," she soothed. "Soon."

"Mm," he growled.

She pulled a little white packet from her coat pocket, opened it, and peeled off a plastic-backed dot. "Hold out your arm." He obeyed, and she pressed the dot against the underside of his forearm. "Patch test," she explained. "Because of what I theorize about your line of work, I think you have a higher than normal chance of allergy. Artificially-induced allergy."

She peeled the dot away again—it prickled—and gazed closely at his arm. A pink spot appeared. She frowned at it. "Does that itch?" she asked suspiciously.

"No," he lied, and clenched his right hand to keep from scratching at the spot. A drug to give him his mind back—he had to have it. *Turn white again, blast you*, he thought to the pink splotch.

"You seem to be a little sensitive," she mused. "Marginally."

"*Pleassse* . . ."

Her lips twisted in doubt. "Well . . . what do we have to lose? I'll be right back."

She exited, and returned shortly with two hyposprays, which she laid on the tray table. "This is the fast-penta," she pointed, "and this is the fast-penta antagonist. You let me know right away if you start to feel strange, itch, tingle, have trouble breathing or swallowing, or if your tongue starts to feel thick."

"Feels th'ck now," he objected, as she pushed up both his sleeves on his thin white arms and pressed the first spray to the inside of his elbow. "How d'I tell?"

"You'll be able to tell. Now just lie back and relax. You should start to feel dreamy, like you're floating, by the time you count backward from ten. Try it."

"Te'. Nan. Ei'. Seben. Si', fav, fo', tree-two-wun." He did not feel dreamy. He felt tense and nervous and miserable. "You sure yo' go' rat one?" His fingers began to drum on the tray table. The sound was unnaturally loud in his ears. Objects in the room were taking on hard, bright outlines with colored fringes. Rowan's face seemed suddenly drained of personality, an ivory mask.

The mask loomed threateningly toward him. "What's your name?" it hissed.

"I . . . I . . . yiyi . . ." His mouth clogged with stutters. He was the invisible eye, nameless. . . .

"Strange," the mask murmured. "Your blood pressure should be going down, not up."

Abruptly, he remembered what was so important about fast-penta. "Fas'pent'—maksmeyper." She shook her head in non-comprehension. "*Yiper*," he reiterated, out of a mouth that seemed to be seizing up in spasms. He wanted to talk. A thousand words rushed to his tongue, a chain-collision along his nerves. "Ya. Ya. *Ya*."

"This isn't usual." She frowned at the hypospray, still in her hand.

"No sh't." His arms and legs drew up like coiled springs. Rowan's face grew charming, like a doll's. His heart raced. The room wavered, as if he were swimming underwater. With an effort, he uncoiled. He had to relax. He had to relax *right now*.

"Do you remember anything?" she asked. Her dark eyes were like pools, liquid and beautiful. He wanted to swim in those eyes, to shine in them. He wanted to please her. He wanted to coax her out of that green cloth armor, to dance naked with him in the starlight, to . . . His mumbles to this effect suddenly found voice in poetry, of a sort. Actually, it was a very dirty limerick playing on some obvious symbolism involving wormholes and jumpships. Fortunately, it came out rather garbled.

To his relief, she smiled. But there was some un-funny association. . . . "Las' time I recited that, som'bod' beat shit outta me. Wuz on fas'pent' then, too."

Alertness coursed through her lovely long body. "You've been given fast-penta before? What else do you remember about it?"

" 'Is name wuz Galen. Angry wi' me. Doan' know why." He remembered a reddening face wavering over him, radiating an implacable, murderous hatred. Blows raining on him. He searched himself for remembered fear, and found it oddly mixed with pity. "I doan' unnerstan'."

"What else did he ask you about?"

"Doan' know. Told 'im 'nother poem."

"You recited poetry at him, under fast-penta interrogation?"

"Fer *hours*. Made 'im mad as hell."

Her brows rose; one finger touched her soft lips, which parted in delight. "You *beat* a fast-penta interrogation? Remarkable! Let's not talk about poetry, then. But you remember Ser Galen. Huh!"

"Galen fit?" He cocked his head anxiously. *Ser* Galen, yes! The name was important; she recognized it. "*Tell me.*"

"I'm . . . not sure. Every time I think I'm taking a step forward with you, we seem to go two sideways and one back."

"Lak to step out wi' *you,*" he confided, and listened to himself in horror as he went on to describe, briefly and crudely, what else he would like to do with her. "Ah. Ah. Sorry, m'lady." He stuffed his fingers into his mouth, and bit them.

"It's all right," she soothed. "It's the fast-penta."

"No—izza *testost'rone.*"

She laughed outright. It was most encouraging, but his momentary elation was drowned again in a new wash of tension. His hands plucked and twisted at his clothing, and his feet twitched.

She frowned at a medical monitor on the wall. "Your blood pressure is still going up. Charming as you are under fast-penta, this is not a normal reaction." She picked up the second hypospray. "I think we'd better stop now."

"M' not a normal man," he said sadly. "Mutant." A wave of anxiety rushed over him. "You gonna tak' my brain out?" he asked in sudden suspicion, eyeing the hypospray. And then, in a mind-blinding blast of realization, "*Hey!* I know where I am! I'm on *Jackson's Whole*!" He stared at her in terror, jumped to his feet, and bolted for the door, dodging her lunge.

"No, wait, wait!" she called, running after him with the glittering hypospray still in her hand. "You're having a drug reaction, stop! Let me get rid of it! Poppy, grab him!"

He dodged the horse-tail-haired Dr. Durona in the lab corridor, and flung himself into the lift tube, boosting himself up with yanks on the safety ladder that sent bolts of searing pain through his half-healed chest muscles. A whirling chaos of corridors and floors, shouts and running footsteps, resolved at last into the lobby he had found before.

He shot past some workmen maneuvering a float-pallet stacked with cases through the transparent doors. No force screen shocked him backward this time. A green-parka'd guard turned in slow motion, drawing a stunner, mouth open on a shout that emerged as thickly as cold oil.

He blinked in blinding grey daylight at a ramp, a paved lot for vehicles, and dirty snow. Ice and gravel bit his bare feet as he ran, gasping, across the lot. A wall enclosed the compound. There was a gate in the wall, open, and more guards in green parkas. "Don't stun him!" a woman yelled from behind him.

He ran into a grimy street, and barely dodged a groundcar. The piercing grey-whiteness alternated with bursts of color in his eyes. A broad open space across the street was dotted with bare black trees with branches like clutching claws, straining at the sky. He glimpsed other buildings, behind walls, farther down the street, looming and strange. Nothing was familiar in this landscape. He made for the open space and the trees. Black and magenta dizziness clouded his eyes. The cold air seared his lungs. He staggered and fell, rolling onto his back, unable to breathe.

Half a dozen Dr. Duronas pounced on him like wolves upon their kill. They took his arms and legs, and pulled him up off the snow. Rowan dashed up, her face strained. A hypospray hissed. They hustled him back across the roadway like a trussed sheep,and hurried him inside the big white building. His head began to clear, but his chest was racked with pain, as if it were clamped in a squeezing vise. By the time they put him back in his bed in the underground clinic, the drug-induced false paranoia had washed out of his system. To be replaced by real paranoia. . . .

"Do you think anyone saw him?" an alto voice asked anxiously.

"Gate guards," another voice bit out. "Delivery crew."

"Anybody else?"

"I don't know," Rowan panted, her hair escaping in snow-dampened wisps. "Half a dozen ground-cars went by while we were chasing him. I didn't see anyone in the park."

"I saw a couple of people walking," volunteered another Dr. Durona. "At a distance, across the pond. They were looking at us, but I doubt they could see much."

"We were a hell of a show, for a few minutes."

"What happened this time, Rowan?" the white-haired alto Dr. Durona demanded wearily. She shuffled closer and stared at him, leaning on a carved walking stick. She did not seem to carry it as an affectation, but as a real prop. All deferred to her. Was this the mysterious Lilly?

"I gave him a dose of fast-penta," Rowan reported stiffly, "to try and jog his memory. It works sometimes, for cryo-revivals. But he had a reaction. His blood pressure shot up, he went paranoid, and he took off like a whippet. We didn't run him down till he collapsed in the park." She was still catching her own breath, he saw as his agony started to recede.

The old Dr. Durona sniffed. "Did it work?"

Rowan hesitated. "Some odd things came up. I need to talk with Lilly."

"Immediately," said the old Dr. Durona—not-Lilly, apparently. "I—" but she was cut off when his shivering, stuttering attempt to talk blended into a convulsion.

The world turned to confetti for a moment. He came back to focus with two of the women holding him down, Rowan hovering over him snapping orders, and the rest of the Duronas scattering. "I'll come up as soon as I can," said Rowan desperately over her shoulder. "I can't leave him now."

The old Dr. Durona nodded understanding, and withdrew. Rowan waved away a proffered hypospray of some anti-convulsant. "I'm writing a standing order. This man gets nothing without a sensitivity scan first." She ran off most of her helpers, and made the room dim and quiet and warm again. Slowly, he recovered the rhythm of his breath, though he was still very sick to his stomach.

"I'm sorry," she told him. "I didn't realize fast-penta could do that to you."

He tried to say, *It's not your fault*, but his powers of speech seemed to have relapsed. "D-d-d-i, diddi, do. Bad. Thing?"

She took far too long to reply. "Maybe it will be all right."

Two hours later, they came with a float-pallet and moved him.

"We're getting some other patients," Dr. Chrys of the wing-hair told him blandly. "We need your room." Lies? Half-truths?

Where they moved him to puzzled him most of all. He had visions of a locked cell, but instead they took him upstairs via a freight lift tube and deposited him on a camp-bed set up in Rowan's personal suite. It was one of a row of similar chambers, presumably the Duronas' residence-floor. Her suite consisted of a sitting room/study and a bedroom, plus a private bath. It was reasonably spacious, though cluttered. He felt less like a prisoner than like a pet, being smuggled against the rules into some women's dormitory. Though he had seen another male-morph Dr. Durona besides Raven, a man of about thirty Dr. Chrys had addressed as "Hawk." Birds and flowers, they were all birds and flowers in this concrete cage.

Later still, a young Durona brought dinner on a tray, and he ate together with Rowan at a little table in her sitting room as the grey day outside faded to dusk. He supposed there was no real change in his prisoner/patient status, but it felt good to be out of the hospital-style room, free of the monitors and sinister medical equipment. To be doing something so prosaic as having dinner with a friend.

He walked around the sitting room, after they ate. "Mind 'f I look at your things?"

"Go ahead. Let me know if anything comes up for you."

She still would not tell him anything directly about himself, but she now seemed willing at least to talk about herself. His internal picture of the world *shifted* as they spoke. *Why do I have wormhole maps in my head?* Maybe he was going to have to recover himself the hard way. Learn everything that existed in the universe, and whatever was left, that dwarfish-man-shaped hole in the center, would be him by process of elimination. A daunting task.

He stared out the polarized window at the faint glitter hanging in the air, as if fairy dust were falling all around. He recognized the force screen for what it was, now, an improvement in cognition over his initial head-first encounter with it. The shield was military-grade, he realized, impermeable down to viruses and gas molecules, and up to . . . what? Projectiles and plasma, certainly. Must be a powerful generator around here somewhere. The protection was a late add-on to the building's ...hitecture, not incorporated into its design. Some history inherent there. . . . "We *are* on Jackson's Whole, aren' we?" he asked.

"Yes. What does that mean to you?"

"Danger. Bad things happenin'. What *is* this pla'?" He waved around.

"The Durona Clinic."

"Ya, so? What you do? Why'm I here?"

"We are the personal clinic of House Fell. We do all sorts of medical tasks for them, as needed."

"House Fell. Weapons." The associations fell into place quite automatically. "Biological weapons." He eyed her accusingly.

"Sometimes," she admitted. "And biological defenses, too."

Was he a House Fell trooper? A captured enemy trooper? Hell, what army would employ a half-crippled dwarf as any kind of trooper? "House Fell give me to you to do?"

"No."

"No? S—why'm I here?"

"That's been a great puzzle for us, too. You arrived frozen in a cryo-chamber, with every sign of having been prepped in great haste. In a crate addressed to me, via common carrier, with no return address. We hoped if we revived you, you could tell us."

" 'S more goin' on than that."

"Yes," she said frankly.

"Bu' you won' tell me."

"Not yet."

"Wha' happens if I walk outta here?"

She looked alarmed. "Please don't. That could get you killed."

"Again."

"Again," she nodded.

"By who?"

"That . . . depends on who you are."

He veered off the subject, then ran the conversation around to it three more times, but could not lull or trick her into telling him any more about himself. Exhausted, he gave up for the night, only to lie awake on his cot worrying the problem as a predator might worry a carcass. But all his bone-tossing did no good but to freeze his mind with frustration. *Sleep on it,* he told himself. Tomorrow must bring him something new. Whatever else this situation was, it wasn't stable. He felt that, felt balanced as though on a knife-edge; below him lay darkness, concealing feathers or sharpened stakes or maybe nothing at all, an endless fall.

He wasn't quite sure of the rationale behind the hot bath and the therapeutic massage. Exercise, now, he could see that; Dr. Chrys had lugged in an exercise bicycle to Rowan's study, and let him sweat himself near to passing out. Anything that painful must be good for him. No push-ups yet, though. He'd tried one, and collapsed with a wide-eyed, muffled squeak of agony, and been yelled at quite firmly by an irate Dr. Chrys for attempting unauthorized bodily motions.

Dr. Chrys had made notes and gone off again, leaving him to Rowan's tenderer mercies. He lay now steaming gently in Rowan's bed, dressed in a towel, while she reviewed skeleto-muscular structure all up and down his back. Dr. Chrys's fingers, doing massage, had been like probes. Rowan's hands caressed. Not anatomically equipped to purr, he did manage a small, encouraging moan of appreciation now and then. She worked down to his feet and toes, and started back up.

Face down, mashed comfortably into her pillows, he became gradually aware that a very important bodily system was reporting for duty, for the first time since his revival. Res-erection indeed. His face flushed in a mixture of embarrassment and delight, and he flung an arm up as-if-casually to conceal his expression. *She's your doctor. She'll want to know.* It wasn't as if she weren't intimately familiar with every part of his body, inside and out, already. She'd been up to her bloody elbows in him, literally. He stayed hidden in his arm-cave anyway.

"Roll over," Rowan said, "and I'll do your other side."

"Er . . . d'rather not," he mumbled into the pillow.

"Why not?"

"Um . . . 'member how you keep askin' if somethin' has come up for me?"

"Yes . . ."

"Well . . . somethin' has."

There was a brief silence, then, "Oh! In that case, definitely roll over. I need to examine you."

He took a breath. "Things we do fer science."

He rolled over, and she took away his towel. "Has this happened before?" she inquired.

"No. Firs' time in my life. This life."

Her long cool fingers probed quickly, medically. "That looks good," she said with enthusiasm.

"*Thank* you," he carolled cheerfully.

She laughed. He didn't need a memory to tell him it was a very good sign when a woman laughed at his jokes at this point. Experimentally, gently, he pulled her down to face him. *Hooray for science. Let's see what happens.* He kissed her. She kissed him back. He melted.

Speech and science were both put aside for a time, after that. Not to mention the green coat and all the layers underneath. Her body was as lovely as he'd imagined, a pure aesthetic of line and curve, softness and floral, hidden places. His own body contrasted vividly, a little rack of bones scored with shocking red scars.

An intense consciousness of his recent death welled up in him, and he found himself kissing her frantically, passionately, as if she were life itself and he could so consume and possess her. He didn't know if she was enemy or friend, if this was a right or wrong thing. But it was warm and liquid and moving, not icy and still, surely the most opposite thing imaginable to cryo-stasis. *Seize the day.* Because the night waited, coldly implacable. This lesson burned from his center outward, like radiation. Her eyes widened. Only his shortness of breath forced him to slow down to a more decorous, reasonable pace.

His ugliness ought to have bothered him, but it didn't, and he wondered why. *We make love with our eyes closed.* Who had told him that? The same woman who'd told him, *It's not the meat, it's the motion*? Opening Rowan's body was like facing that pile of field-stripped weaponry. He knew what to do, what parts counted and which were camouflage, but could not remember how he'd learned it all. The training was there, yet the trainer was erased. It was a more deeply disturbing coupling of the familiar with the strange than any he'd yet experienced here.

She shivered, sighed, and relaxed, and he kissed his way back up her body to murmur in her ear, "Um . . . doan' think I can do push-ups, jus' yet."

"Oh." Her glazed eyes opened, and focused. "My. Yes." A few moments of experiment found a medically-approved position, flat on his back in great comfort with no pressure or strain on his chest, arms, or abdomen, and then it was his turn. That felt right, ladies first and then he wouldn't have pillows thrown at him for falling asleep immediately afterwards. A terribly familiar pattern, with all the details wrong. Rowan had done this before too, he judged, though perhaps not often. But great expertise on her part was scarcely required. His body worked just fine. . . .

"Dr. D," he sighed up at her, "yr a gen'ius. Aes . . . Asku . . . Aesch . . . that Greek guy coul' tak' lessons in resurr'ction from you."

She laughed, and oozed down beside him, body to

body. *My height doesn't matter when we're lying down.* He'd known that, too. They exchanged less-hurried, exploratory kisses, savored slowly like after-dinner mints.

"You're *very* good at that," she murmured wheezily, nibbling on his ear.

"Yea . . ." His grin faded, and he stared at the ceiling, brows drawing down in a combination of gentle, post-coital melancholy, and renewed, if purely mental, frustration. ". . . wonder if I was married?" Her head drew back, and he could have bitten his tongue at her stricken look. "Doan' think so," he added quickly.

"No . . . no," she settled back again. "You're not married."

"Which ever one I am?"

"That's right."

"Huh." He hesitated, winding her long hair in his fingers, spreading it idly out in a fan across the burst of red lines on his torso. "So who d'you think you were makin' love to, jus' now?"

She touched a long index finger gently to his forehead. "You. Just you."

This was most pleasing, but . . . "Wuzzat love, or therapy?"

She smiled quizzically, tracing his face. "A little of both, I think. And curiosity. And opportunity. I've been pretty immersed in you, for the past three months."

It felt like an honest answer. "Seems t'me you made t' opportunity."

A small smirk escaped her lips. "Well . . . maybe."

Three months. Interesting. So he'd been dead a bit over two months. He must have absorbed a lot of the Durona Group's resources, in that time. To begin with, three months of this woman's labor were not cheap.

"Why you doin' this?" he asked, frowning at the ceiling as she snuggled carefully around his shoulder. "I mean t'whole thing. What d'you expect me to do for you?"

Half-crippled, tongue-tied, blank and stupid, not a dollar to his non-existent name. "You're all hangin' on m'recovery like I'm your hope 'f heaven." Even the brutally efficient physical therapist Chrys he'd come to see as pushing him for his good. He almost liked her best, for her merciless drive. He resonated to it. "Who else wants me, tha' you should hide me? Enemies?" *Or friends?*

"Enemies for certain," Rowan sighed.

"Mm." He lay back in lassitude; she dozed, he didn't. He touched her net of hair and wondered. What did she see in him? *I thought of it as the enchanted knight's crystal coffin . . . I picked out enough grenade fragments to be certain you weren't a bystander. . . .*

So, there was work to be done. Nor did the Durona Group want an ordinary mercenary. If this was Jackson's Whole, they could hire ordinary thugs by the boatload.

But then, he'd never thought he was an ordinary man. Not even for a minute.

Oh, milady. Who do you need me to be?

CHAPTER TWENTY-THREE

The re-discovery of sex fairly immobilized him for the next three days, but his instinct for escape surfaced one afternoon when Rowan left him sleeping, but he wasn't. He unlidded his eyes, and traced the pattern of scars on his chest, and thought it over. *Out* was clearly a wrong direction. *In* was one he hadn't tried yet. Everybody here seemed to go to Lilly with their problems. Very well. He would go to Lilly too.

Up, or down? As a Jacksonian leader, she ought traditionally to lodge in either a penthouse or a bunker. Baron Ryoval lived in a bunker, or at least there was a dim image in his head associated with that name, involving shadowy sub-basements. Baron Fell took the penthouse at apogee, looking down on it all from his orbital station. He seemed to have a lot of pictures in his head of Jackson's Whole. Was it his home? The thought confused him. Up. Up and in.

He dressed in his grey knits, borrowed some of Rowan's socks, and slipped into the corridor. He found a lift tube and took it to the top floor, just one above Rowan's. It was another floor of residence suites. At its center he found another lift tube, palm-locked. Any Durona could use it. A spiral staircase wound around it. He climbed the stairs very slowly, and waited, near the top, till he had all his breath back. He knocked on the door.

It slid aside, and a slim Eurasian boy of about ten regarded him gravely. "What do you want?" The boy frowned.

"I want to see your . . . grandmother."

"Bring him in, Robin," a soft voice called.

The boy ducked his head, and motioned him inside. His sock feet trod noiselessly across a deep carpet. The windows were polarized against the dark grey afternoon, and pools of warmer, yellower lamplight fought the gloom. Beyond the window, the force field revealed itself with tiny scintillations, as water droplets or particulate matter were detected and repelled or annihilated.

A shrunken woman sat in a wide chair, and watched him approach her through dark eyes set in a face of old ivory. She wore a high-necked black silk tunic and loose trousers. Her hair was pure white, and very long; a slim girl, most literally twin to the boy, was brushing it over the back of the chair, in long, long strokes. The room was very warm. Regarding her regarding him, he wondered how he could ever have thought that worried old woman with the cane might be Lilly. Hundred-year-old eyes looked at you differently.

"Ma'am," he said. His mouth felt suddenly dry.

"Sit down," she nodded to a short sofa set around the corner of the low table in front of her. "Violet, dear," a thin hand, all white wrinkles and blue ropy veins, touched the girl's hand which had paused protectively on her black silk shoulder. "Bring tea now. Three cups. Robin, please go downstairs and get Rowan."

The girl arranged the hair in a falling fan around the woman's upright torso, and the two children vanished in un-childlike silence. Clearly, the Durona Group did not employ outsiders. No chance of a mole ever penetrating their organization. With equal obedience, he sank into the seat she'd indicated.

Her vowels had a vibrato of age, but her diction, containing them, was perfect. "Have you come to yourself, sir?" she inquired.

"No, ma'am," he said sadly. "Only to you." He thought carefully about how to phrase his question. Lilly would not be any less medically careful than Rowan about yielding him clues. "Why can't you identify me?"

Her white brows rose. "Well put. You are ready for an answer, I think. Ah."

The lift tube hummed, and Rowan's alarmed face appeared. She hurried out. "Lilly, I'm sorry. I thought he was asleep—"

"It's all right, child. Sit down. Pour the tea," for Violet reappeared around the corner bearing a large tray. Lilly whispered to the girl behind a faintly trembling hand, and she nodded and scampered off. Rowan knelt in what appeared to be a precise old ritual—had she once held Violet's place? he rather thought so—and poured green tea into thin white cups, and handed it round. She sat at Lilly's knees, and stole a brief, reassuring touch of the white hair coiled there.

The tea was very hot. Since he'd lately taken a deep dislike to cold, this pleased him, and he sipped carefully. "Answers, ma'am?" he reminded her cautiously.

Rowan's lips parted in a negative, alarmed breath; Lilly crooked up one finger, and quelled her.

"Background," said the old woman. "I believe the time has come to tell you a story."

He nodded, and settled back with his tea.

"Once upon a time," she smiled briefly, "there were three brothers. A proper fairy tale, ai? The eldest and original, and two young clones. The eldest—as happens in these tales—was born to a magnificent patrimony. Title—wealth—comfort—his father, if not exactly a king, commanded more power than any king in pre-Jump history. And thus he became the target of many enemies. Since he was known to dote upon his son, it occurred to more than one of his enemies to try and strike at him through his only child. Hence this peculiar multiplication." She nodded at him. It made his belly shiver. He sipped more tea, to cover his confusion.

She paused. "Can you name any names yet?"

"No, ma'am."

"Mm." She abandoned the fairy tale; her voice grew more clipped. "Lord Miles Vorkosigan of Barrayar was the original. He is now about twenty-eight standard years old. His first clone was made right here on Jackson's Whole, twenty-two years ago, a purchase by a Komarran resistance group from House Bharaputra. We do not know what this clone names himself, but the Komarrans' elaborate substitution plot failed about two years ago, and the clone escaped."

"Galen," he whispered.

She glanced sharply at him. "He was the chief of those Komarrans, yes. The second clone . . . is a puzzle. The best guess is that he was manufactured by the Cetagandans, but no one knows. He first appeared about ten years ago as a full-blown and exceptionally brilliant mercenary commander, claiming the quite legal Betan name of Miles Naismith, in his maternal line. He has shown himself no friend to the Cetagandans, so the theory that he is a Cetagandan renegade has a certain compelling logic. No one knows his age, though obviously he can be no more than twenty-eight." She took a sip of her tea. "It is our belief that you are one of those two clones."

"Shipped to you like a crate of frozen meat? With my chest blown out?"

"Yes."

"So what? Clones—even frozen ones—can't be a novelty here." He glanced at Rowan.

"Let me go on. About three months ago, Bharaputra's manufactured clone returned home—with a crew of mercenary soldiers at his back that he had apparently stolen from the Dendarii Fleet by the simple expedient of pretending to be his clone-twin, Admiral Naismith. He attacked Bharaputra's clone-creche in an attempt to either steal, or possibly free, a group of clones slated to be the bodies for brain transplants, a business which I personally loathe."

He touched his chest. "He . . . failed?"

"No. But Admiral Naismith followed in hot pursuit of his stolen ship and troops. In the melee that ensued downside at Bharaputra's main surgical facilities, one of the two was killed. The other escaped, along with the mercenaries and most of Bharaputra's very valuable clone-cattle. They made a fool of Vasa Luigi—I laughed myself sick when I first heard about it." She sipped tea demurely.

He could actually almost picture her doing so, though it made his eyes cross slightly.

"Before they jumped, the Dendarii Mercenaries posted a reward for the return of a cryo-chamber containing the remains of a man they claim to have been the Bharaputran-made clone."

His eyes widened. "Me?"

She held up a hand. "Vasa Luigi, Baron Bharaputra, is absolutely convinced that they were lying, and that the man in the box was really their Admiral Naismith."

"Me?" he said less certainly.

"Georish Stauber, Baron Fell, refuses to even guess. And Baron Ryoval would tear a town apart for even a fifty percent chance of laying hands on Admiral Naismith, who injured him four years ago as no one has in a century." Her lips curved in a scalpel-smile.

It all made sense, which made no sense at all. It was like a story heard long ago, in childhood, and re-encountered. *In another lifetime.* Familiarity under glass. He touched his head, which ached. Rowan watched the gesture with concern.

"Don't you have medical records? Something?"

"At some risk, we obtained the developmental records of Bharaputra's clone. Unfortunately, they only go up to age fourteen. We have nothing on Admiral

Naismith. Alas, one cannot run a triangulation on one data point."

He turned toward Rowan. "You know me, inside and out. Can't you tell?"

"You're *strange*." Rowan shook her head. "Half your bones are plastic replacement parts, do you know? The real ones that are left show old breaks, old traumas. . . . I'd guess you not only older than Bharaputra's clone ought to be, I'd guess you older than the original Lord Vorkosigan, and that makes no sense. If we could just get one solid, certain clue. The memories you've reported so far are terribly ambiguous. You know weapons, as the Admiral might—but Bharaputra's clone was trained as an assassin. You remember Ser Galen, and only Bharaputra's clone should do that. I found out about those sugar trees. They're called maple trees, and they originate on Earth—where Bharaputra's clone was taken for training. And so on." She flung up her hands in frustration.

"If you're not getting the right answer," he said slowly, "maybe you're not asking the right question."

"So what is the right question?"

He shook his head, mutely. "Why . . ." His hands spread. "Why not turn my frozen body over to the Dendarii and collect the reward? Why not sell me to Baron Ryoval, if he wants me so much? Why revive me?"

"I wouldn't sell a laboratory rat to Baron Ryoval," Lilly stated flatly. She twitched a brief smile. "Old business, between us."

How old? Older than he, whoever he was.

"As for the Dendarii—we may deal with them yet. Depending on who you are."

They were approaching the heart of the matter; he could sense it. "Yes?"

"Four years ago, Admiral Naismith visited Jackson's Whole, and besides counting a most spectacular coup on Ry Ryoval, left with a certain Dr. Hugh Canaba, one of Bharaputra's top genetics people. Now, I knew Canaba. More to the point, I know what Vasa Luigi and Lotus paid to get him here, and how many House secrets he was privy to. They would never have let him go alive. Yet he's gone, and no one on Jackson's Whole has ever been able to trace him."

She leaned forward intently. "Assuming Canaba was not just disposed of out an airlock—Admiral Naismith has shown he can get people out. In fact, it's a speciality he's famous for. *That* is our interest in him."

"You want off-planet?" He glanced around at Lilly Durona's comfortable, self-contained little empire. "Why?"

"I have a Deal with Georish Stauber—Baron Fell. It's a very old Deal, as we are very old dealers. My time is surely running out, and Georish is growing," she grimaced, "unreliable. If I die—or if he dies—or if he succeeds in having his brain transplanted to a younger body, as he has attempted at least once to arrange—our old Deal will be broken. The Durona Group might be offered less admirable deals than the one we have enjoyed so long with House Fell. It might be broken up—sold—weakened so as to invite attack from old enemies like Ry, who remembers an insult or an injury *forever*. It might be forced to work it does not choose. I've been looking for a way out for the last couple of years. Admiral Naismith knows one."

She wanted him to be Admiral Naismith, obviously the most valuable of the two clones. "What if I'm the other one?" He stared at his hands. They were just his hands. No hints there.

"You might be ransomed."

By whom? Was he savior, or commodity? What a choice. Rowan looked uneasy.

"What am I to you if I can't remember who I am?"

"No one at all, little man." Her dark eyes glinted, momentarily, like obsidian chips.

This woman had survived nearly a century on Jackson's Whole. It would not do to underestimate her ruthlessness on the basis of one quirky prejudice about clone-brain transplants.

They finished their tea, and retreated to Rowan's room.

"What in all that seemed familiar to you?" Rowan asked him anxiously when they were alone on her little sofa.

"All of it," he said, in deep perplexity. "And yet—Lilly seems to think I can spirit you all away like some kind of magician. But even if I am Admiral Naismith, I can't remember how I did it!"

"Sh," she tried to calm him. "You're ripe for memory-cascade, I swear. I can almost see it starting. Your speech has improved vastly in just the last few days."

"All that therapeutic kissing," he smiled, a suggestive compliment that won him, as he'd hoped, some more therapy. But when he came up for air he said, "It won't come back to me if I'm the other one. I remember Galen. Earth. A house in London . . . what's the clone's name?"

"We don't know," she said, and at his exasperated grasp of her hands added, "No, we *really* don't."

"Admiral Naismith . . . shouldn't be Miles Naismith. He should be Mark Pierre Vorkosigan." How the hell did he know that? Mark Pierre. *Piotr Pierre. Peter, Peter, pumpkin eater, had a wife and couldn't keep her*, a taunt from out of a crowd that had put an old man into a terrifying murderous rage, he'd had to be restrained by—the image escaped him. *Gran'da?* "If the Bharaputra-made clone is the third son, he could be named anything." Something wasn't right.

He tried to imagine Admiral Naismith's childhood as a Cetagandan secret covert ops project. His childhood?

It must have been extraordinary, if he'd not only escaped at the age of eighteen or less, but evaded Cetagandan Intelligence and established his fortune within a year. But he could think of nothing from such a youth. A complete blank.

"What are you going to do with me if I'm not Naismith? Keep me as a pet? For how long?"

Rowan pursed her lips in worry. "If you are the Bharaputran-made clone—you're going to need to get off Jackson's Whole yourself. The Dendarii raid made an awful mess out of Vasa Luigi's headquarters. He has blood to avenge, as well as property. And pride. If it's the case—I'll try to get you out."

"You? Or you all?"

"I've never gone against the group." She rose, and paced across her sitting room. "Yet I lived a year, on Escobar, alone, when I was taking my cryo-revival training. I've often wondered . . . what it would be like to be half of a couple. Instead of one-fortieth of a group. Would I feel bigger?"

"Were you bigger when you were all of one, on Escobar?"

"I don't know. It's a silly conceit. Still—one can't help thinking of Lotus."

"Lotus. Baronne Bharaputra? The one who left your group?"

"Yes. Lilly's oldest daughter after Rose. Lilly says . . . if we don't hang together, we'll all hang separately. It's a reference to an ancient method of execution that—"

"I know what hanging is," he said hastily, before she could go into the medical details.

Rowan stared out her window. "Jackson's Whole is no place to be alone. You can't trust anybody."

"An interesting paradox. Makes for quite a dilemma."

She searched his face for irony, found it, and frowned. "It's no joke."

Indeed. Even Lilly Durona's self-referential maternal strategy hadn't quite solved the problem, as Lotus had proved.

He eyed her. "Were you ordered to sleep with me?" he asked suddenly.

She flinched. "No." She paced again. "But I did ask permission. Lilly said to go ahead, it might help attach you to our interests." She paused. "Does that seem terribly cold, to you?"

"On Jackson's Whole—merely prudent." And attachments surely ran two ways. Jackson's Whole was no place to be alone. *But you can't trust anyone.*

If anyone was sane here, he swore it was by accident.

Reading, an exercise that had at first given him a stabbing sensation in the eyes and instant excruciating headaches, was getting easier. He could go for up to ten minutes at a time now before it became too blinding to bear. Holed up in Rowan's study, he pushed himself to the limits of pain, an information-bite, a few minutes' rest, and try again. Beginning at the center outward, he read up first on Jackson's Whole, its unique history, non-governmental structure, and the one hundred and sixteen Great Houses and countless Houses Minor, with their interlocking alliances and vendettas, roiling deals and betrayals. The Durona Group was well on its way to growing into a House Minor in its own right, he judged, budding from House Fell like a hydra, also like a hydra reproducing asexually. Mentions of Houses Bharaputra, Hargraves, Dyne, Ryoval and Fell triggered images in his head that did not come from the vid display. A few of them were even starting to cross-connect. Too few. He wondered if it was significant that the Houses that seemed most familiar were also the ones most famous for dealing in off-planet illegalities.

Whoever I am, I know this place. And yet . . . his visions tasted small in scope, too shallow to represent a formative lifetime. Maybe he'd been a small person. Still, it was more than he could dredge up from his subconscious regarding the youth of the putative Admiral Naismith, the Cetagandan-produced clone.

Gran'da. Those had been memories with mass, an almost stunning sensory weight. Who was Gran'da? Jacksonian fosterer? Komarran mentor? Cetagandan trainer? Someone huge and fascinating, mysterious and old and dangerous. Gran'da had no source, he seemed to come with the universe.

Sources. Perhaps a study of his progenitor, the crippled Barrayaran lordling Vorkosigan, might yield up something. He'd been made in Vorkosigan's image, after all, which was a hell of a thing to do to any poor sod. He pulled up a listing of references to Barrayar from Rowan's comconsole library. There were some hundreds of non-fiction books, vids, documents and documentaries. For the sake of a frame, he began with a general history, scanning rapidly. The Fifty-thousand Firsters. Wormhole collapse. The Time of Isolation, the Bloody Centuries . . . the Re-discovery . . . the words blurred. His head felt full to bursting. Familiar, so achingly familiar . . . he had to stop.

Panting, he darkened the room and lay down on the little sofa till his eyes stopped throbbing. But then, if he'd ever been trained to replace Vorkosigan, it all ought to be very familiar indeed. He'd have had to study Barrayar forward and backward. *I have.* He wanted to beg Rowan to shackle him to a wall and give him another dose of fast-penta, regardless of what it did to his blood pressure. The stuff had almost worked. Maybe another try . . .

The door hissed. "Hello?" The lights came up. Rowan stood in the doorway."Are you all right?"

"Headache. Reading."

"You shouldn't try to . . ."

Take it so fast, he supplied silently, Rowan's constant refrain of the last few days, since his interview with Lilly. But this time, she cut herself off. He pushed up; she came and sat by him. "Lilly wants me to bring you upstairs."

"All right—" He made to rise, but she stopped him.

She kissed him. It was a long, long kiss, which at first delighted and then worried him. He broke away to ask, "Rowan, what's the matter?"

". . . I think I love you."

"This is a problem?"

"Only my problem." She managed a brief, unhappy smile. "I'll handle it."

He captured her hands, traced tendon and vein. She had brilliant hands. He did not know what to say.

She drew him to his feet. "Come on." They held hands all the way to the entrance to the penthouse lift-tube. When she disengaged to press the palm lock, she did not take his hand again. They rose together, and exited around the chromium railing into Lilly's living room.

Lilly sat upright and formal in her wide padded chair, her white hair braided today in a single thick rope that wound down over her shoulder to her lap. She was attended by Hawk, who stood silently behind her and to her right. *Not an attendant. A guard.* Three strangers dressed in grey quasi-military uniforms with white trim were ranged around her, two women seated and a man standing. One of the women had dark curls, and brown eyes that turned on him with a gaze that scorched him. The other, older woman had short light-brown hair barely touched with grey. But it was the man who riveted him.

My God. It's the other me.

Or . . . not-me. They stood eye to eye. This one was painfully neat, boots clean, uniform pressed and formal, his mere appearance a salute to Lilly. Insignia glinted on his collar. *Admiral . . . Naismith? Naismith* was the name stitched over the left breast of his officer's pocketed undress jacket. A sharp intake of breath, an electric snap of the grey eyes, and a half-suppressed smile made the short man's face wonderfully alive. But if he was a bony shadow of himself, this one was him doubled. Stocky, squared-off, muscular and intense, heavy-jowled and with a notable gut. He *looked* like a senior officer, body-mass balanced over stout legs spread in an aggressive parade rest like an overweight bulldog. So this was Naismith, the famous rescuer so desired by Lilly. He could believe it.

His utter fascination with his clone-twin was penetrated by a growing, dreadful realization. *I'm the wrong one.* Lilly had just spent a fortune reviving the wrong clone. How angry was she going to be? For a Jacksonian leader, such a vast mistake must feel like counting coup on *yourself*. Indeed, Lilly's face was set and stern, as she glanced toward Rowan.

"It's him, all right," breathed the woman with the burning eyes. Her hands were clenched in tight fists, in her lap.

"Do I . . . know you, ma'am?" he said politely, carefully. Her torch-like heat perturbed him. Half-consciously, he moved closer to Rowan.

Her expression was like marble. Only a slight widening of her eyes, like a woman drilled neatly through the solar plexus by a laser beam, revealed a depth of . . . what feeling? Love, hate? Tension . . . His headache worsened.

"As you see," said Lilly. "Alive and well. Let us return to the discussion of the price." The round table was littered with cups and crumbs—how long had this conference been going on?

"Whatever you want," said Admiral Naismith, breathing heavily. "We pay and go."

"Any price within reason." The brown-haired older

woman gave her commander an oddly quelling look. "We came for a man, not an animated body. A botched revival suggests a discount for damaged goods, to my mind." That voice, that ironic alto voice . . . *I know you.*

"His revival is not botched," said Rowan sharply. "If there was a problem, it was in the prep—"

The hot woman jerked, and frowned fiercely.

"—but in fact, he's making a good recovery. Measurable progress every day. It's just too soon. You're pushing too hard." A glance at Lilly? "The stress and pressure slow down the very results they seek to hurry. He pushes *himself* too hard, he winds himself in knots so bad—"

Lilly held up a placating hand. "So speaks my cryo-revival specialist," she said to the Admiral. "Your clone-brother is in a recovering state, and may be expected to improve. If that is in fact what you desire."

Rowan bit her lip. The hot woman chewed on her fingertip.

"Now we come to what *I* desire," Lilly continued. "And, you may be pleased to learn, it isn't money. Let us discuss a little recent history. Recent in my view, that is."

Admiral Naismith glanced out the big square windows, framing another dark Jacksonian winter afternoon, with low scudding clouds starting to spit snow. The force screen sparkled, silently eating the ice spicules. "Recent history is much on my mind, ma'am," he said to Lilly. "If you know it, you know why I don't wish to linger here. Get to your point."

Not nearly oblique enough for Jacksonian business etiquette, but Lilly nodded. "How is Dr. Canaba these days, Admiral?"

"What?"

Succinctly, for a Jacksonian, Lilly again described her interest in the fate of the absconded geneticist. "Yours is the organization that made Hugh Canaba completely disappear. Yours is the organization that lifted ten thousand Marilacan prisoners of war from under the noses of their Cetagandan captors on Dagoola Four, though I admit they have spectacularly not-disappeared. Somewhere between those two proven extremes lies the fate of my little family. You will pardon my tiny joke if I say you appear to me to be just what the doctor ordered."

Naismith's eyes widened; he rubbed his face, sucked air through his teeth, and managed a strained-looking grin. "I see. Ma'am. Well. In fact, such a project as you suggest might be quite negotiable, particularly if you think you might like to join Dr. Canaba. I'm not prepared to pull it out of my pockets this afternoon, you understand—"

Lilly nodded.

"But as soon as I make contact with my back-up, I think something might be arranged."

"Then as soon as you make contact with your back-up, return to us, Admiral, and your clone-twin will be made available to you."

"No—!" began the hot woman, half-rising; her comrade caught her arm and shook her head, and she sank back into her seat. "Right, Bel," she muttered.

"We'd hoped to take him today," said the mercenary, glancing at him. Their eyes intersected joltingly. The Admiral looked away,as if guarding himself from some too-intense stimulus.

"But as you can see, that would strip me of what seems to be my main bargaining chip," Lilly murmured. "And the usual arrangement of half in advance and half on delivery is obviously impractical. Perhaps a modest monetary retainer would reassure you."

"They seem to have taken good care of him so far," said the brown-haired officer in an uncertain voice.

"But it would also," the Admiral frowned, "give you an opportunity to auction him to other interested parties. I would caution you against starting a bidding war in this matter, ma'am. It could become the real thing."

"Your interests are protected by your uniqueness, Admiral. No one else on Jackson's Whole has what I want. You do. And, I think, vice versa. We are very well suited to deal."

For a Jacksonian, this was bending over backward to encourage. *Take it, close the deal!* he thought, then wondered why. What did these people want him for? Outside, a gust of wind whipped the snowfall to a blinding, whirling curtain. It ticked on the windows.

It ticked on the windows. . . .

Lilly was the next to be aware, her dark eyes widening. No one else had noticed yet, the cessation of that silent glitter. Her startled gaze met his, as his head turned back from his first stare outward, and her lips parted for speech.

The window burst inward.

It was a safety-glass; instead of slicing shards, they were all bombarded by a hail of hot pellets. The two mercenary women shot to their feet, Lilly cried out, and Hawk leaped in front of her, a stunner appearing in his hand. Some kind of big aircar was hovering at the window: one, two . . . three, four huge troopers leaped through. Transparent biotainer gear covered nerve-disruptor shield-suits; their faces were fully hooded and goggled. Hawk's repeated stunner fire crackled harmlessly over them.

You'd get farther if you threw the damned stunner at them! He looked around wildly for a projectile weapon, knife, chair, table-leg, anything to attack with. Over one of the mercenary women's pocket comm links a tinny voice was crying, "Quinn, this is Elena. Something just dropped the building's force screen. I'm reading energy discharges—what the hell is going on in there? You want back-up?"

"Yes!" screamed the hot woman, rolling aside from a stunner beam, which followed her, crackling, across the carpet. *Stunner-tag.* The assault was a snatch, not an assassination, then. Hawk finally recovered the wit to pick up the round table and swing with it. He hit one trooper but was stunner-dropped by another. Lilly stood utterly still, watching grimly. A gust of cold wind fluttered her silk pant legs. Nobody aimed at her.

"Which one's Naismith?" boomed an amplified voice from one of the biotainered troopers. The Dendarii must have disarmed for the parley; the brown-haired merc closed hand-to-hand on an intruder. Not an option open to him. He grabbed Rowan's hand and dodged behind a chair, trying to get a clear run toward the exit tube.

"Take 'em both," the leader shouted over the din. A trooper leaped toward the lift tube to cut them off; the rectangular facet of his stunner discharger winked in the light as he found near-point-blank aim.

"Like hell!" yelled the Admiral, cannoning into the trooper. The trooper stumbled and his aim went wild. The last thing he saw as he and Rowan dove for the lift tube was a stunner beam from the leader taking Naismith in the head. Both the other Dendarii were down.

They descended with agonizing slowness. If he and Rowan could get to the force screen generator, could they get it turned back on and trap the attackers inside? Stunner fire sizzled after them, starry bursts on the walls. They twisted in air, somehow landed on their feet, and stumbled backward into the corridor. No time to explain—he grabbed Rowan's hand and slapped it flat to the Durona-keyed lock-pad, and hit the power-off square with his elbow. The trooper pursuing them yelped and fell three meters, not quite head-first.

He winced at the thud, and towed Rowan down the corridor. "Where are the generators?" he yelled over his shoulder at her. Other Duronas, alarmed, were appearing from all directions. A pair of green-clad Fell guards burst into the corridor's far end and pelted toward the penthouse lift-tube. But what side were they on? He pulled Rowan into the nearest open doorway.

"Lock it!" he gasped. She keyed the door shut. They were in some Durona's residence suite. A cul-de-sac made a poor bolt-hole, but help seemed to be on the way. He just wasn't sure for whom. *Something just dropped your force screen. . . .* From the inside. It could only have been dropped from the inside. He half-bent, mouth wide for air, lungs on fire, heart racing and chest aching, a dizzy darkness clouding his vision. He stumbled to the dangerous window anyway, trying to get a handle on the tactical situation. Muffled shouts and thumps penetrated from the wall by the corridor.

"How t'hell'd those bastards get your screen down?" he wheezed to Rowan, clutching the windowsill. "Didn't hear an explosion—traitor?"

"I don't know," Rowan replied anxiously. "That's outer-perimeter security. Fell's men are supposed to be in charge of it."

He stared out over the icy parking lot of the compound. A couple more green-clad men were running across it, shouting, pointing upward, taking cover behind a parked vehicle, and struggling to get a projectile-weapon aimed. Another guard made urgent negative gestures at them; a miss could take out the penthouse and everyone in it. They nodded and waited.

He craned his neck, face to the glass, trying to see upward and to the left. The armored aircar loomed, still hovering at the penthouse window.

The assailants were withdrawing already. Damn! No chance with the force-screen. *I'm too slow.* The aircar rocked as the troopers hastily re-boarded. Hands flashed, and a thick little grey-clad figure was dragged across the gap, six heart-stopping flights above the concrete. A limp trooper was dragged across too. They were leaving no wounded for questioning. Rowan, teeth clenched, pulled him back. "Get out of the line of fire!"

He resisted her. "They're getting away!" he protested. "We should fight them *now*, on our own turf—"

Another aircar rose from the street, beyond the old and obsolete compound wall. A small civilian model, unarmed and unarmored, it fought for altitude. Through its canopy he could see a blurred grey-clad figure at the controls, a white flash of teeth set in a grimace. The assailants' armored car yawed away from the window. The Dendarii aircar tried to ram it, to force it down. Sparks sprayed, plastic cracked, and metal screeched, but the armored car shook it off; it pinwheeled to the pavement and landed with a terminal crunch.

"Rented, I bet," he groaned, watching. "Gonna have to pay for it. Good try, it almost worked—Rowan! Are any of those aircars down there yours?"

"You mean the group's? Yes, but—"

"Come on. We've got to get down there." But the building was crawling with security by now. They'd be nailing everyone to the wall till identified and cleared. He could scarcely leap out the window and fly down the five flights, though he longed to. Oh, for a cloak of invisibility.

Oh. Yes!

"Carry me! Can you carry me?"

"I suppose, but—"

He raced to the door, and fell backwards into her arms as it opened again.

"Why?" she asked.

"Do it, do it, do it!" he hissed through his teeth. She dragged him back out into the corridor. He studied the chaos through slitted eyes, gasping realistically. Assorted agitated Duronas milled behind a cordon of Fell security now blocking the entry to the penthouse. "Get Dr. Chrys to take my feet," he muttered out of the corner of his mouth.

Temporarily too overwhelmed to argue, Rowan cried, "Chrys, help me! We have to get him downstairs."

"Oh—" Given the impression that this was some kind of medical emergency, Dr. Chrys asked no questions. She grabbed his ankles, and within seconds they were forcing their way through the mob. Two Doctors Durona carrying a white-faced, injured-looking fellow at a run—green-clad armed men stepped hastily aside and waved them on.

As they reached the ground floor Chris tried to gallop toward the clinic area. For a moment he was yanked two ways, then he freed his feet from the astonished Dr. Chrys, and pulled away from Rowan. She gave chase, and they arrived at the outer door together.

The guards' attention was focused on the efforts of the two men with the projectile launcher; his eyes followed their aim to the shadowy form of their retreating target, being swallowed by the snowy clouds. *No, no, don't shoot . . . !* The launcher burped; the bright explosion rocked the car but did not bring it down.

"Take me to the biggest, fastest thing you can make go," he gasped to Rowan. "We can't let them get away." *We can't let Fell's men blow it up, either.* "Hurry!"

"*Why?*"

"Those goons just kidnapped my, my . . . brother," he panted. "Gotta follow. Bring 'em down if we can, follow if we can't. The Dendarii must have reinforcements of some kind, if we don't lose them. Or Fell. Lilly's his, his liegewoman, isn't she? He has to respond. Or *someone* does." He was shivering violently. "Lose 'em and we'll never get 'em back. They're figuring on it."

"What the hell would we do if we caught them?" Rowan

objected. "They just tried to kidnap you, and you want to run after them? That's a job for security!"

"I am—I am . . ." *What? What am I?* His frustrated stutters segued into a confetti-scramble of perception. *No, not again—*

His vision cleared with the hiss of a hypospray, biting cold on his arm. Dr. Chrys was supporting him, and Rowan had one thumb pressed against his eyelid, holding it up while she stared into his eye, while her other hand slipped the hypospray back into her pocket. A kind of glassy bemusement descended upon him, as if he were wrapped in cellophane. "That should help," said Rowan.

"No, it doesn't," he complained, or tried to. His words came out a mumble.

They had dragged him out of the lobby, out of sight near one of the lift tubes to the underground part of the clinic. He had only lost moments to the convulsion, then. There was still a chance—he struggled in Chrys's grip, which tightened.

The snap of women's steps, not a guard's boots, rounded the corner. Lilly appeared, her face set and her nostrils flaring, flanked by Dr. Poppy.

"Rowan. Get him out of here," Lilly said, in a voice dead-level in tone despite its breathlessness. "Georish will be downside himself to investigate this one. *He* has to never have been here. Our attackers seem to have been one of Naismith's enemies. The story will be that the Dendarii came here looking for Naismith's clone, but didn't find him. Chrys, get rid of the physical evidence in Rowan's room, and hide those files. Go!"

Chrys nodded and ran. Rowan took over holding him on his feet. He had an odd tendency to slump, as if he were melting. He blinked against the drug. *No, we have to go after—*

Lilly tossed Rowan a credit chit, and Dr. Poppy handed

her a couple of coats and a medical bag. "Take him out the back door and disappear. Use the evacuation codes. Pick a place at random and go to ground, *not* one of our properties. Report in on a secured line from a separate location. By then I should know what I can salvage from this mess." Her wrinkled lips peeled back on ivory teeth set in anger. "Move, girl."

Rowan nodded obediently, and didn't argue at all, he noticed indignantly. Holding him firmly by the arm, she guided his stumbling feet down a freight lift-tube, through the sub-basement, and into the underground clinic. A concealed doorway on its second level opened onto a narrow tunnel. He felt like a rat scurrying through a maze. Rowan stopped three times to key through some security device.

They came out in some other building's under-level, and the door disappeared behind them, indistinguishable from the wall. They continued on through ordinary utility tunnels. "You use this route often?" he panted.

"No. But every once in a while we want to get something in or out not recorded by our gate guards, who are Baron Fell's men."

They emerged finally in a small underground parking garage. She led him to a little blue lightflyer, elderly and inconspicuous, and bundled him into the passenger seat. "This isn' righ'," he complained, thick-tongued. "Admiral Naismith—someone should go after Admiral Naismith."

"Naismith owns a whole mercenary fleet." Rowan strapped herself into the pilot's seat. "Let them tangle with his enemies. Try to calm down and catch your breath. I don't want to have to dose you again."

The flyer rose into the swirling snow and rocked uncertainly in the gusts. The city sprawling below them disappeared quickly into the murk as Rowan powered them up. She glanced aside at his agitated profile. "Lilly will do something," she reassured him. "She wants Naismith too."

"It's wrong," he muttered. "It's all wrong." He huddled in the jacket Rowan had wrapped around him. She turned up the heat.

I'm the wrong one. It seemed he had no intrinsic value but his mysterious hold on Admiral Naismith. And if Admiral Naismith was removed from the Deal, the only person still interested in him would be Vasa Luigi, wanting vengeance upon him for crimes he couldn't even remember committing. Worthless, unwanted, lonely and scared . . . His stomach churned in pain, and his head throbbed. His muscles ached, tense as wire.

All he had was Rowan. And, apparently, the Admiral, who had come searching for him. Who had very possibly risked his life to recover him. Why? *I have to do . . . something.*

"The Dendarii Mercenaries. Are they all here? Does the Admiral have ships in orbit, or what? How much back-up does he have? He said it would take time for him to contact his back-up. How much time? Where did the Dendarii come in from, a commercial shuttleport? Can they call down air support? How many—how much—where—" His brain tried madly to assemble data that wasn't there into patterns for attack.

"Relax!" Rowan begged. "There's nothing we can do. We're only little people. And you're in no condition. You'll drive yourself into another convulsion if you keep on like this."

"Screw my condition! I have to—I have to—"

Rowan raised wry eyebrows. He lay back in his seat with a sick sigh, drained. *I should have been able to do this . . . to do something. . . .* He listened to nothing, half-hypnotized by the sound of his own shallow breathing. Defeated. Again. He didn't like the taste. He brooded at his pale and distorted reflection on the inside of the canopy. Time seemed to have become viscous.

The lights on the control panel died. They were suddenly weightless. His seat straps bit him. Fog began to stream up around them, faster and faster.

Rowan screamed, fought and banged the control panel. It flickered; momentarily, they had thrust again. Then lost it again. They descended in stutters. "What's wrong with it, damn it!" Rowan cried.

He looked upward. Nothing but icy fog—they dropped below cloud level. Then above them, a dark shape loomed. Big lift van, heavy. . . .

"It's not a systems failure. We're being intermittently field-drained," he said dreamily. "We're being forced down."

Rowan gulped, concentrated, trying to keep the flyer level in the brief bursts of control. "My God, is it them igain?"

"No. I don't know . . . maybe they had some back-ip." With adrenalin and determination, he forced his vits to function through the sedative-haze. "Make a ioise!" he said. "Make a splash!"

"What?"

She didn't understand. She didn't catch it. She should iave—somebody should have—"Crash this sucker!" She lidn't *obey*.

"Are you crazy?" They lurched to ground right-side-p and intact in a barren valley, all snow and crackling crub.

"Somebody wants to make a snatch. We've got to leave mark, or we'll just disappear off the map without a race. No comm link," he nodded toward the dead panel. We have to make footprints, set fire to something, omething!" He fought his seat straps for escape.

Too late. Four or five big men surrounded them in he gloom, stunners at ready. One reached up and unlatched his door, and dragged him out. "Be careful, don't hurt him!" Rowan cried fearfully, and scrambled after. "He's my patient!"

"We won't, ma'am," one of the big parka-clad men nodded politely, "but you mustn't struggle." Rowan stood still.

He stared around wildly. If he made a sprint for their van, could he—? His few steps forward were interrupted when one of the goons grabbed him by his shirt and hoisted him into the air. Pain shot through his scarred torso as the man twisted his hands behind his back. Something coldly metallic clicked around his wrists. They were not the same men who'd broken into the Durona Clinic, no resemblance in features, uniforms, or equipment.

Another big man crunched through the snow. He pushed back his hood, and shone a hand light upon the captives. He appeared about forty-standard, with a craggy face, olive brown skin, and dark hair stripped back in a simple knot. His eyes were bright and very alert. His black brows bent in puzzlement, as he stared at his prey.

"Open his shirt," he told one of the guards.

The guard did so; the craggy man shone the hand-light on the spray of scars. His lips drew back in a white grin. Suddenly, he threw back his head and laughed out loud. The echoes of his voice lost themselves in the empty winter twilight. "Ry, you fool! I wonder how long it will take you to figure it out?"

"Baron Bharaputra," Rowan said in a thin voice. She lifted her chin in a quick defiant jerk of greeting.

"Dr. Durona," said Vasa Luigi in return, polite and amused. "Your patient, is he? Then you won't refuse my invitation to join us. Please be our guest. You'll make it quite the little family reunion."

"What do you want from him? He has no memory."

"The question is not what I want from him. The question is . . . what someone else may want from him. And what I may want from *them*. Ha! Even better!" He motioned to his men, and turned away. They chivvied their captives into the closed lift van.

One of the men split off to pilot the blue lightflyer. "Where should I leave this, sir?"

"Take it back to the city and park it on a side street. Anywhere. See you home."

"Yes, sir."

The van doors closed. The van lifted.

CHAPTER TWENTY-FOUR

Mark groaned. Bright prickles of pain shot through a dark nausea.

"You gonna give him a dose of synergine?" said a voice, surprised. "I didn't get the idea the Baron wanted this one handled gently."

"You want to clean up the flyer if he vomits his breakfast?" rumbled another voice.

"Ah."

"The Baron will do his own handling. He just specified he wanted him alive. Which he is."

A hypospray hissed.

"Poor sod," said the first voice reflectively.

Thanks to the synergine, Mark began to recover from the stunner hit. He didn't know how much time and space lay between him and the Durona Clinic; they'd changed vehicles at least three times after he'd regained consciousness, once to something bigger and faster than an aircar. They stopped at some location, and he and the troopers all went through a decontamination chamber. The anonymously-dressed troopers went their way, and he was given over to two other guards, big flat-faced men in black trousers and red tunics.

House Ryoval's colors. *Oh.*

They laid him facedown, hands and feet bound, in the back of a lightflyer. The gray clouds, darkening toward evening, gave no clue as to the direction they were heading.

Miles is alive. The relief of that fact was so intense,

he smiled in elation even with his face squashed into the sticky plastic seat. What a joyful sight the skinny little bugger had been! Upright and breathing. He'd almost wept. What he'd done, was undone. He could really be Lord Mark, now. *All my sins are taken from me.*

Almost. He prayed that Durona doctor had spoken straight about Miles still recovering. Miles's eyes had been frighteningly bewildered. And he hadn't recognized Quinn, which must have nearly slain her. *You'll get better. We'll get you home, and you'll get better.* He'd haul Miles home and everything would be all right again, better than all right. It would be wonderful.

As soon as that idiot Ryoval had his delusions straightened around. Mark was ready to gut the man outright for screwing up his family reunion. *ImpSec will handle him.*

They entered an underground parking garage without his getting a glimpse of the exterior of their destination. The two guards hauled him roughly to his feet, and released his legs, which twitched and tingled. They passed through an electronic security chamber, after which his clothing was taken from him. They marched him through the . . . facility. It wasn't a prison. It wasn't one of House Ryoval's famous bordellos. The air bore a faint, unsettling medical tang. The place was far too utilitarian to be where surgical body-sculpture was done on patrons. It was too secret and secure to be where slaves were done to order, where humans were made into things not humanly possible. It wasn't very large. There were no windows. Underground? *Where the hell am I?*

He would not panic. He entertained himself with a brief vision of what Ryoval might do to his own troopers, once he discovered they'd snatched the wrong twin. If Ryoval did not realize the mistake at the very first sight of him, he toyed with the idea of concealing his identity for a while. Let Miles and the Dendarii get a bigger head-start. They had not been taken; they were free. *I found him!* They must come for him. And if not them, ImpSec. ImpSec could not be more than a week behind him, and closing fast. *I've won, godammit, I've won!*

His head was still spinning with a bizarre mixture of elation and terror when the guards delivered him to Ryoval's presence. It was a luxurious office, or study; the Baron evidently kept private quarters here, for he glimpsed a living room beyond an archway. Mark had no trouble recognizing Ryoval. He'd seen him in the vid recording from the *Ariel's* first mission here. The conversation where he'd threatened to have Admiral Naismith's severed head encased in plastic for a wall-hanging. In another man, this might be dismissed as hyperbole, but Mark had the uneasy feeling Ryoval had meant it literally. Ryoval was leaning half-seated on his comconsole desk. He had shining dark hair arranged in elaborate bands, a high-bridged nose, and smooth skin. Strong and youthful, for a centenarian.

He's wearing a clone. Mark's smile became vulpine. He hoped Ryoval would not mistake his post-stun tremula for fear.

The guards sat him in a chair and fastened him down with metal bands to his wrists. "Wait outside," the Baron instructed them. "It won't be long." They exited.

Ryoval's hands were trembling slightly. The skin of his bronzed face was faintly moist. When he looked up and smiled back at Mark, his eyes seemed alight with some internal glow, the look of a man so filled with the visions inside his head, he scarcely saw the present reality. Mark was almost too enraged to care. *Clone-consumer!*

"Admiral," Ryoval breathed happily. "I promised you we would meet again. As inevitably as fate." He looked Mark up and down; his dark brows rose. "You've put weight on, the last four years."

"Good living," Mark snarled, uncomfortably reminded of his nakedness. For all he'd loathed the Dendarii uniform, it had actually made him look rather good. Quinn had personally re-tailored it for this masquerade, and he wished for it back. Presumably it had been what had fooled Ryoval's troopers, though, in that moment of heroic temporary insanity.

"I'm so glad you are alive. At first I'd hoped for your unpleasant death in one of your little combats, but upon reflection I actually began to pray for your survival. I've had four years to plan this meeting. Revising and refining. I'd have hated for you to miss your appointment."

Ryoval did not recognize him as not-Naismith. Ryoval was barely seeing him at all. He seemed to be looking through him. The Baron began to stride up and down in front of him, pouring out his plans like a nervous lover, elaborate plans for vengeance that ranged from the obscene to the insane to the impossible.

It could be worse. Ryoval could be making these threats right now to that thin little, vague-eyed, bewildered cryo-amnesic, who would not know even who he was, let alone why these things should be happening to him. The thought sickened Mark. *Yeah. Better me than him, right now. No shit.*

He means to terrorize you. It's only words. What was it the Count had said? *Don't sell yourself to your enemy in advance, in your mind. . . .*

Hell, Ryoval wasn't even *his* enemy. All these gaudy scenarios had been tailored for Miles. No, not even for Miles. For Admiral Naismith, a man who didn't exist. Ryoval chased a ghost, a chimera.

Ryoval stopped beside him, interrupting his whispered tirade. Curiously, he ran a moist hand down Mark's body, fingers curving in precise anatomical tracing of the muscles hidden beneath the layer of fat. "Do you know," he breathed, "I'd planned to have you starved. But I think I've changed my mind. I believe I'll have you force-fed, instead. The results could be even more amusing, in the long run."

Mark shivered sickly for the first time. Ryoval felt it, beneath his probing fingers, and grinned. The man had an appalling instinct for the target. Better he should keep Ryoval focused on the chimera? *Better we should get the hell out of here.*

He took a breath. "I hate to burst your bubble, Baron, but I have some bad news for you."

"Now, did I ask you to speak?" Ryoval's fingers traced back up, to pinch the flesh around his jaw. "This isn't an interrogation. This isn't an inquisition. Confession will gain you nothing. Not even death."

It was that damned contagious hyperactivity. Even Miles's enemies caught it.

"I'm not Admiral Naismith. I'm the clone the Bharaputrans made. Your goons grabbed the wrong guy."

Ryoval merely smiled. "Nice try, Admiral. But we've been watching the Bharaputran clone at the Durona Clinic for days. I knew you would come for him, after what you did to try and get him back the first time. I don't know what passion he inspires in you—were you lovers? You'd be amazed how many people have clones made for that purpose."

So. When Quinn had sworn no one could possibly be following them, she'd been right. Ryoval hadn't been following them. He'd been *waiting* for them. Swell. It had been his actions, not his words or his uniform, which had convicted him of being Naismith.

"But I will obtain him too," Ryoval shrugged. "Very soon."

No, you won't. "Baron, I really am the other clone. Prove it to yourself. Have me examined."

Ryoval chuckled. "What do you suggest? A DNA scan? Even the Duronas couldn't decide." He sighed deeply.

"There's so much I want to do to you, I scarcely know where to begin. I must take it slowly. And in logical order. One cannot torture body parts that have already been removed, for example. I wonder how many years I can make you last? Decades?"

Mark felt his self-control cracking. *"I'm not Naismith,"* he said, his voice going high with strain.

Ryoval grasped Mark's chin and tilted it up, his lips twisting in ironic disbelief. "Then I will practice on you. A dry-run. And Naismith will be along. In time."

You're going to be astonished at what will be along, in time. ImpSec would have no hesitation whatsoever about taking Ryoval's House apart around him, no inhibitions even by Jacksonian standards.

To rescue Miles.

He, of course, wasn't Miles.

He reflected worriedly on that, as the guards entered again at Ryoval's summons.

The first beating was unpleasant enough. It wasn't the pain. It was pain without escape, fear without release, that worked upon the mind, tensed the body. Ryoval watched. Mark screamed without restraint. No silent, suffering, manly pride here, thank you. Maybe that would convince Ryoval he was not Naismith. This was crazy. Still, the guards broke no bones, and ended the exercise perfunctorily. They left him locked naked in a very cold, tiny room or closet, without windows. The air vent was perhaps five centimeters across. He couldn't get his fist, let alone his body, though it.

He tried to prepare, to steel himself. To give himself hope. Time was on his side. Ryoval was a supremely practiced sadist, but of a psychological bent. Ryoval would keep him alive, and relatively undamaged, at least at first. After all, nerves must be intact to report pain. A mind must be relatively unclouded, to experience all the nuances of agony. Elaborate humiliations, rather than immediate flaying to death, must be first on the menu. All he had to do was survive. Later—there wouldn't be a later. The Countess had said Mark's going to Jackson's Whole would force Illyan to assign more agents here whether he wanted to or not, that alone being a sure benefit of Mark's journey even if he accomplished nothing personally at all.

And what, after all, were a few more humiliations to him? Miles's immense pride could be shattered. He had none. Torture was old news to him. *Oh, Ryoval. Have you ever got the wrong man.*

Now, if Ryoval were half the psychologist he clearly imagined himself to be, he would have grabbed a few of Miles's friends, to torment in front of him. That would work beautifully, on Miles. But not, of course, on him. He had no friends. *Hell, Ryoval. I can think of worse things than you can.*

No matter. His friends would rescue him. Any time now.

Now.

He kept up his mental defiance till the technicians came for him.

They returned him to his little cell, afterward, presumably to give him some solitude to think about it. He didn't think for quite some time. He lay on his side breathing in tiny gasps, half-conscious, arms and legs slowly starfishing in rhythm to the pain inside that didn't stop.

At length, the clouds lifted a little from his vision, and the pain eased fractionally, to be replaced by a black, black rage. The techs had secured him, shoved a tube down his throat, and pumped him full of some repulsive high-calorie sludge. Laced with an anti-emetic, they told him, to prevent him getting rid of it later, and a cocktail of metabolic aids to speed digestion and deposition. It was far too subtly complex to have been designed on the spot, it must be something House Ryoval kept in stock. And he'd imagined this was his own private and unique perversion. He thought he'd done himself harm before, but Ryoval's people took it far beyond the limits of merely toying with pain, under the eye of their master, who'd come to watch. And study him, with a growing smile. Ryoval *knew*. He'd seen it in the man's sly, pleased eyes.

Ryoval had stripped his very own rebellion of all its secret pleasure. The one somatic power that had been his call, his control, taken from him. Ryoval had hooked him, gotten under his skin. Way under.

They could do *to* you all day long, and you could just not-be-there, but it was as nothing compared to getting you to do to yourself. The difference between mere torture and true humiliation was in the participation of the victim. Galen, whose torments were physically much milder than anything Ryoval contemplated, had known this; Galen had always had him doing to himself, or thinking he was.

That Ryoval knew this too, he demonstrated later, when he administered a violent aphrodisiac to Mark by hypospray, before giving him to his—guards? or were they employees borrowed from one of the bordellos? So that he became a glazed-eyed participant in his own degradation. It doubtless made a great show for the hovering holovids, recording it all from every angle.

They brought him back to his little cell to digest this new experience much as they'd brought him back to digest the first force-feeding. It took a long time for the shock and drug-fog to clear away. He oscillated slowly between a drained lassitude and horror. Curious. The drug had short-circuited his shock-stick conditioning, reducing it to something like a case of the hiccups, or the show would have been much duller and shorter. Ryoval had watched.

No. Ryoval had *studied*.

His consciousness of the man's eyes had become an obsession. Ryoval's interest had not been erotic. Mark felt the Baron must have become bored with the stereotyped banality of every possible physical act decades ago. Ryoval had been watching him for . . . reflexes? Small betrayals of interest, fear, despair. The exercise had not been arranged for the sake of pain. There had been plenty of pain, but it had been incidental. Discomfort from the force-feeding, and running out of neurotransmitters, mostly.

That wasn't the torture, Mark realized. *That was only the pre-testing. My torture is still being designed.*

Suddenly, he saw what was coming, all whole. First, Ryoval would condition him to this, addict him by repeated doses. Only then would he add pain, and pin him, vibrating, between pain and pleasure; require him to torture himself, to win through to the dark reward. And then he would withdraw the drug and let Mark, conditioned to the scenarios, continue. And he would. And then Ryoval would offer him his freedom. And he would weep and beg to stay, plead to remain a slave. Destruction by seduction. End-game. Revenge complete.

You see me, Ryoval, but I see you. I see you.

The force-feedings turned out to be on a schedule of every three hours. It was the only clock he had, or he would have thought time had stopped. He had surely entered eternity.

He'd always thought being skinned alive was something done with sharp knives. Or dull ones. Ryoval's technicians did it chemically, spraying carefully selected areas of his body with an aerosol. They wore gloves, masks, protective clothing; he tried, but failed, to grab off a mask and let one share what they administered. He cursed his littleness, and cried, and watched his skin bubble up and drip away. The chemical was not a caustic, but rather some strange enzyme; his nerves were left horribly intact, exposed. Touching anything, or being touched, was agony after that, especially the pressure of sitting or lying down. He stood in the little closet-cell, shifting from foot to foot, touching nothing, for hours, till his shaking legs finally gave way.

It was all happening so fast. Where the hell was everybody? How long had he been here? A day?

So. I have survived one day. Therefore, I can survive another one-day. It couldn't be worse. It could only be more.

He sat, and rocked, mind half whited-out with pain. And rage. Especially rage. From the moment of the first force-feeding, it hadn't been Naismith's war any more. This was personal now, between Ryoval and him. But not personal enough. He'd never been alone with Ryoval. He'd always been outnumbered, outweighed, passed from one set of bindings to another. Admiral Naismith was being treated as a fairly dangerous little prick, even now. That wouldn't do.

He would have told them everything, all about Lord Mark, and Miles, and the Count, and the Countess, and Barrayar. And Kareen. But the force-feedings had stopped his mouth, and the drug had stripped him of language, and the other things had kept him too busy screaming. It was all Ryoval's fault. The man watched. But he didn't *listen*.

I wanted to be Lord Mark. I just wanted to be Lord Mark. Was that so bad? He still wanted to be Lord Mark.

He'd almost had it, brushing his grasp. Ripped away. He wept for it, hot tears splashing like molten lead on his not-skin. He could feel Lord Mark slipping from him, racked apart, buried alive. Disintegrating. *I just wanted to be human. Screwed up again.*

CHAPTER TWENTY-FIVE

He circled the room for the hundredth time, tapping on the walls. "If we could figure out which one is the exterior," he said to Rowan, "maybe we could break through it somehow."

"With what, our fingernails? What if we're three floors up? Will you please *sit down*," Rowan gritted. "You're driving me crazy!"

"We have to get out."

"We have to wait. Lilly will miss us. And something will be done."

"By who? And how?" He glared around their little bedroom. It wasn't designed as a prison. It was only a guest room, with its own bath attached. No windows, which suggested it was underground or in an interior section of the house. If it was underground, breaking through a wall might not be much use, but if they could bore into another room, the possibilities bloomed. One door, and two stunner-armed guards outside of it. They'd tried enticing the guards into opening the door last night, once with faked illness, and once for real when his frantic agitation had resulted in another convulsion. The guards had handed in Rowan's medical bag, which was no help, because then the exhausted woman had started responding to his demands for action by threatening to sedate him.

"Survive, escape, sabotage," he recited. It had become a litany, running through his head in an endless loop. "It's a soldier's duty."

"I'm not a soldier," said Rowan, rubbing her dark-ringed eyes. "And Vasa Luigi isn't going to kill me, and if he was going to kill you he'd have done it last night. He doesn't play with his prey like Ryoval does." She bit her lip, perhaps regretting that last sentence. "Or maybe he's going to leave us in here together till *I* kill you." She rolled over in bed, and pulled her pillow over her head.

"You should have crashed that lightflyer."

A noise from under the pillow might have been either a groan or a curse. He had probably mentioned that regret a few too many times.

When the door clicked open he spun as if scalded.

A guard half-saluted, politely. "Baron Bharaputra's compliments, ma'am, sir, and would you prepare to join him and the Baronne for dinner. We will escort you upstairs when you're ready."

The Bharaputras' dining room had large glass doors giving a view onto an enclosed, winter-frosted garden, and a big guard by every exit. The garden glimmered in the gathering gloom; they had been here a full Jacksonian day, then, twenty-six hours and some odd minutes. Vasa Luigi rose at their entry, and at his gesture the guards faded back to positions outside the doors, giving an illusion of privacy.

The dining room was arranged stylishly, with individual couches and little tables set in a tiered semi-circle around the view of the garden. A very familiar-looking woman sat on one of the couches.

Her hair was white streaked with black, and wound up in elaborate braids around her head. Dark eyes, thin ivory skin softening with tiny wrinkles, a high-bridged nose—Dr. Durona. Again. She was dressed in a fine flowing silk shirt in a pale green perhaps accidentally reminiscent of the color of the Durona lab coats, and soft trousers the color of cream. Dr. Lotus Durona,

Baronne Bharaputra, had elegant tastes. And the means to indulge them.

"Rowan, dear," she nodded; she held out a hand as if Rowan might give it a courtier's kiss.

"Lotus," said Rowan flatly, and compressed her lips. Lotus smiled and turned her hand over, converting it into an invitation to sit, which they all did.

Lotus touched a control pad at her place, and a girl wearing Bharaputra brown and pink silks entered, and served drinks, to the Baron first, curtseying with lowered eyes before him. A very familiar-looking girl, tall and willowy, with a high-bridged nose, fine straight black hair bound at her nape and flowing in a horse-tail down her back. . . . When she made her offering to the Baronne, her eyes flicked up, and opened like flowers to the sun, bright with joy. When she bowed before Rowan, her up-turning gaze grew startled, and her dark brows drew down in puzzlement. Rowan gazed back equally startled, a look that changed to dawning horror as the girl turned away.

When she bowed before him, her frown deepened. "You . . . !" she whispered, as if amazed.

"Run along, Lilly dear, don't gawk," said the Baronne kindly.

As she left the room, with a swaying walk, she glanced covertly back over her shoulder at them.

"Lilly?" Rowan choked. "You named her Lilly?"

"A small revenge."

Rowan's hands clenched in deep offense. "How can you? Knowing what you are? Knowing what we are?"

"How can you choose death over life?" The Baronne shrugged. "Or worse—let Lilly choose it for you? Your time of temptation is not yet, Rowan my dear sister. Ask yourself again in twenty or thirty years, when you can feel your body rotting around you, and see if the answer comes so easily then."

"Lilly loved you as a daughter."

"Lilly used me as her servant. Love?" The Baronne chuckled. "It's not love that keeps the Durona herd together. It's predator pressure. If all the exterior economic and other dangers were removed, the far corners of the wormhole nexus would not be far enough for us to get away from our dear sibs. Most families are like that, actually."

Rowan assimilated the point. She looked unhappy. But she didn't disagree.

Vasa Luigi cleared his throat. "Actually, Dr. Durona, you wouldn't have to travel to the far reaches of the galaxy for a place of your own. House Bharaputra could find a use for your talents and training. And perhaps even a little autonomy. Head of a department, for example. And later, who knows?—maybe even a division."

"No. Thank you." Rowan bit out.

The Baron shrugged. Did the Baronne look faintly relieved?

He interrupted urgently, "Baron—was it really Ryoval's squad who took Admiral Naismith? Do you know where?"

"Well, now, that's an interesting question," Vasa Luigi murmured, eyeing him."I've been trying to contact Ry all day, without success. I suspect that wherever Ry is, your clone-twin is also—Admiral."

He took a deep breath. "Why do you think I am the Admiral, sir?"

"Because I met the other one. Under telling circumstances. I don't think the real Admiral Naismith would permit his bodyguard to give him orders—do you?"

His head was aching. "What's Ryoval doing to him?"

"Really, Vasa, this is not dinner-conversation," reproved the Baronne. She glanced curiously at him. "Besides—why should you care?"

" 'Miles, what have you done with your baby brother?' " The quote came from nowhere, fell out of his mouth.

He touched his lips uncertainly. Rowan stared at him. So did Lotus.

Vasa Luigi said, "As to your question, Admiral, it turns on whether Ry has come to the same conclusions as I did. If he has—likely he's not doing much. If he hasn't, his methods will depend upon your clone-twin."

"I . . . don't understand."

"Ryoval will study him. Experiment. His choice of actions will flow from his analysis of his subject's personality."

That didn't sound so bad. He pictured multiple-choice tests. He frowned, bewildered.

"Ry is an artist, in his way," continued the Baron. "He can create the most extraordinary psychological effects. I've seen him turn an enemy into a slave utterly devoted to his person, who will obey any order. The last man who attempted to assassinate him and had the misfortune to live ended up serving drinks at Ryoval's private parties, and begging to offer gratification of any kind to any guest on request."

"What did you ask for?" the Baronne inquired dryly.

"White wine. It was before your time, love. I watched, though. The man had the most haunted eyes."

"Are you considering selling me to Ryoval?" he asked slowly.

"If he's the highest bidder, Admiral. Your and your clone-twin's raid upon my property—and I am still not certain you did not plan it together from first to last—was very costly to my House. And," his eyes glinted, "personally annoying. I'll not bother avenging myself upon a cryo-amnesic, but I do wish to shave my losses. If I sell you to Ry, you'll be better punished than even I care to think about. Ry would be delighted to own a matched pair." Vasa Luigi sighed. "House Ryoval will always be a minor house, I fear, as long as Ry allows his personal gratification to outweigh its profits. It's a shame. I could do so much more with his resources."

The girl returned, served little plates of hors d'oeuvres, refreshed their drinks, some wine-and-fruit concoction, and wafted out again. Slowly. Vasa Luigi's eyes followed her. The Baronne's eyes narrowed, noting his gaze. Her lashes swept down, focusing on her drink, as his head turned back.

"What about . . . the Dendarii Mercenaries, as a bidder?" *Yes!* Just let Bharaputra make that offer, and the Dendarii would come knocking on his door. With a plasma cannon. High bid indeed. This game must be a short one. Bharaputra could not put him up for auction without revealing that he had him, and then, and then . . . *what?* "If nothing else, you could use their competition to force Ryoval's bid up," he added slyly.

"Their resources are too finite, I fear. And not here."

"We saw them. Yesterday."

"A mere covert ops team. No ships. No back-up. I understand they only revealed their identity at all in order to get Lilly to talk with them. But . . . I have reason to believe there is another player in this game. My instincts twitch, looking at you. I have the oddest urge to take a modest middleman's profit, and let the negative bidders apply to House Ryoval." The Baron chuckled.

Negative bidders? Oh. People with plasma cannons. He tried not to react.

Vasa Luigi continued, "Which brings us back to the original question—what *is* Lilly's interest in all this? Why did Lilly set you to revive this man, Rowan? For that matter, how did Lilly obtain him, when some hundreds of other earnest searchers could not?"

"She didn't say," said Rowan blandly. "But I was glad for a chance to sharpen my skills. Thanks to your security guard's excellent aim, he was quite a medical challenge."

The conversation became medical-technical, between

Lotus and Rowan, and then more desultory, as the clone-girl served them an elaborate meal. Rowan evaded as smoothly as the Baron questioned, and no one expected him to know anything. But Baron Bharaputra seemed not to be in a hurry. Clearly, he was setting up to play some kind of waiting game. Afterwards the guards escorted them back to their room, which he realized at last was part of a corridor of identical chambers designed, perhaps, to house the servants of important visitors.

"Where are we?" he hissed at Rowan as soon as the door shut behind them. "Could you tell? Is this Bharaputra's headquarters?"

"No," said Rowan. "His main residence is still under renovation. Something about a commando raid blowing out several rooms," she added snappishly.

He walked slowly around their chamber, but he did not take up banging on the walls again, to Rowan's obvious relief. "It occurs to me . . . that there's another way to escape besides breaking from the inside out. That's to get someone else to break from the outside in. Tell me . . . would it be harder to break in and take someone held prisoner by House Bharaputra, House Fell, or House Ryoval?"

"Well . . . Fell would be the hardest, I suppose. He has more troops and heavy weapons. Ryoval would be the easiest. Ryoval's really a House Minor, except he's so old, he gets the honors of a House Major by habit."

"So . . . if one wanted someone bigger and badder than Bharaputra, one might go to Fell."

"One might."

"And . . . if one knew help were on the way . . . it might be tactically brighter to leave said prisoner at Ryoval's, rather than to have him shifted to some more formidable location."

"It might," she conceded.

"We have to get to Fell."

"How? We can't even get out of this room!"

"Out of the room, yes, we must get out of the room. But we might not have to get out of the house. If one of us could just get to a comconsole for a few uninterrupted minutes. Call Fell, call *someone*, let the world know Vasa Luigi has us. *That* would start things moving."

"Call Lilly," said Rowan sturdily. "Not Fell."

I need Fell. Lilly can't break into Ryoval's. He considered the uneasy possibility that he and the Durona Group might be starting to move at cross-purposes. He wanted a favor from Fell, whom Lilly wished to escape. Still—one would not have to offer very much to interest Fell in a raid on Ryoval. A break-even in materials, and the profit in old hatred. Yeah.

He wandered into the bathroom, and stared at himself in the mirror. *Who am I?* A skinny, haggard, pale, odd-looking little man with desperate eyes and a tendency to convulsions. If he could even decide which one his clone-twin was, glimpsed so painfully yesterday, he could dub himself the other by process of elimination. The fellow had looked like Naismith to him. But Vasa Luigi was no fool, and Vasa Luigi was convinced of the reverse. He had to be one or the other. Why couldn't he decide? *If I am Naismith, why did my brother claim my place?*

At that moment, he discovered why it was called a *cascade*.

The sensation was of being under a waterfall, of some river that emptied a continent, tons of water battering him to his knees. He emitted a tiny mewl, crouching down with his arms wrapping his head, shooting pains behind his eyes and terror locking his throat. He pressed his lips together to prevent any other sound escaping, that would attract Rowan in all her concern. He needed to be alone for this, oh yes.

No wonder I couldn't guess. I was trying to choose

between two wrong answers. Oh, Mother. Oh, Da. Oh, Sergeant. Your boy has screwed up this one, bad. Real bad. Lieutenant Lord Miles Naismith Vorkosigan crawled on the tiled floor and screamed in silence, just a faint hiss. *No, no, no, oh, shit. . . .*

Elli . . .

Bel, Elena, Taura . . .

Mark . . . Mark? That stout, glowering, controlled, determined fellow had been *Mark*?

He could not remember anything about his death. He touched his chest, fearfully, tracing the evidence of . . . what event? He squeezed his eyes shut, trying to remember the last that he could. The raid downside at Bharaputra's surgical facility, yes. Mark had engineered a disaster, Mark and Bel between them, and he'd come flying down to try and pull all their nuts out of the fire. Some megalomanic inspiration to top Mark, show him how the experts did it, to take those clone-children from Vasa Luigi, who had offended him . . . take 'em home to Mother. *Crap, what does my mother know about all this by now?* Nothing, he prayed. They were all still here on Jackson's Whole, somehow. *How* long had he been dead . . . ?

Where the hell is ImpSec?

Besides rolling around here on this bathroom floor, of course.

Ow, ow, ow. . . .

And Elli. *Do I know you, ma'am?* he'd asked. He should have bitten his tongue out.

Rowan . . . Elli. It made sense, in a weird way. His lover was a tall, brown-eyed, dark-haired, tough-minded, smart woman. The first thing presented to his confused awakening senses had been a tall, brown-eyed, dark-haired, tough-minded, smart woman. It was a very natural mistake.

He wondered if Elli was going to buy that explanation.

His taste for heavily-armed girlfriends did have potential drawbacks. He inhaled a hopeless laugh.

It clogged in his throat. *Taura, here?* Did Ryoval know it? Did he know what a lovely big clawed hand she'd had in the destruction of his gene banks, four years ago, or did he just blame "Admiral Naismith"? True, all of Ryoval's bounty hunters he'd encountered subsequently had seemed focused obsessively and exclusively upon himself. But Ryoval's troopers had mistaken Mark for the Admiral; had Ryoval? Surely Mark would tell him he was the clone. *Hell, I'd tell him the same if it were me, on the off-chance of confusing the issue.* What was happening to Mark? Why had Mark offered himself as Miles's . . . ransom? Mark couldn't possibly be cryo-amnesic too, could he? No—Lilly had said the Dendarii, and the clones, and "Admiral Naismith" had all escaped. So how did they come to be *back*?

They came looking for you, Admiral Dipshit.

And had run headlong into Ryoval, looking for the same thing. He was a damned rendezvous.

What a *merciful* state cryo-amnesia was. He wished for it back.

"Are you all right?" Rowan called doubtfully. She stepped to the bathroom door, and saw him on the floor. "Oh, no! Another convulsion?" She dropped to her knees beside him, long fingers checking for damages. "Did you hit yourself on anything?"

"Ah . . . ah . . ." *I'll not bother avenging myself upon a cryo-amnesic*, Vasa Luigi had said. He had better remain a cryo-amnesic then, for the moment, till he had a better grip on things. And on himself. "I think I'm all right."

He suffered her to anxiously put him to bed. She stroked his hair. He stared at her in dismay through half-lidded, pretend-post-convulsion-sleepy eyes. *What have I done?*

What am I going to do?

CHAPTER TWENTY-SIX

He had forgotten why he was here. His skin was beginning to grow back.

He wondered where Mark had gone.

People came, and tormented a nameless thing without boundaries, and went away again. He met them variously. His emerging aspects became personas, and eventually, he named them, as well as he could identify them. There was Gorge, and Grunt, and Howl, and another, quiet one that lurked on the fringes, waiting.

He let Gorge go out to handle the force-feedings, because Gorge was the only one who actually enjoyed them. Gorge, after all, would never have been permitted to do all that Ryoval's techs did. Grunt he sent forth when Ryoval came again with the hypospray of aphrodisiac. Grunt had also been responsible for the attack on Maree, the body-sculptured clone, he rather thought, though Grunt, when not all excited, was very shy and ashamed and didn't talk much.

Howl handled the rest. He began to suspect Howl had been obscurely responsible for delivering them all to Ryoval in the first place. Finally, he'd come to a place where he could be punished *enough. Never give aversion therapy to a masochist. The results are unpredictable.* So Howl deserved what Howl got. The elusive fourth one just waited, and said that someday, they would all love him best.

They did not always stay within their lines. Howl had a tendency to eavesdrop on Gorge's sessions, which came regularly while Howl's did not; and more than once Gorge turned up riding along with Grunt on his adventures, which then became exceptionally peculiar. Nobody joined Howl by choice.

Having named them all, he finally found Mark by process of elimination. Gorge and Grunt and Howl and the Other had sent Lord Mark deep inside, to sleep through it all. Poor, fragile Lord Mark, barely twelve weeks old.

Ryoval could not even see Lord Mark down in there. Could not reach him. Could not touch him. Gorge and Grunt and Howl and the Other were all very careful not to wake the baby. Tender and protective, they defended him. They were *equipped* to. An ugly, grotty, hard-bitten bunch, these psychic mercenaries of his. Unlovely. But they got the job done.

He began to hum little marching tunes to them, from time to time.

CHAPTER TWENTY-SEVEN

Absence makes the heart grow fonder. And, Miles feared, the converse. Rowan had pulled her pillow over her head again. He continued to pace. And talk. He couldn't seem to stop himself. In the time that had passed since his concealed memory cascade, he had evolved a multitude of plans for their escape, all with some fatal flaw. Unable to put any of them into effect, he had re-ordered and refined them out loud. Over and over. Rowan had stopped critiquing them . . . yesterday? In fact, she'd stopped talking to him at all. She'd given up trying to pet him and relax him, and instead tended to stay on the far side of the room, or hide for long periods in the bathroom. He couldn't blame her. His returning nervous energy seemed to be building to something like a frenzy.

This forced confinement was stressing her affection for him to the limit. And, he had to admit, he had not been able to conceal his slight new hesitation toward her. A coolness in his touch, an increased resistance to her medical authority. He loved and admired her, no question, and would be delighted to have her in charge of any sickbay he owned. Under his command. But guilt and the sense of no privacy had combined to cripple his interest in intimacy. He had other passions at the moment. And they were consuming him.

Dinner was due soon. Assuming three meals per long Jacksonian day, they'd been here four days. The Baron had not spoken with them again. What schemes was Vasa Luigi evolving, out there? Had he been auctioned yet?

What if the next person through the door was his buyer? What if nobody bid at all, what if they left him in here forever?

Meals were usually brought on a tray by a servant, under the watchful eye of a couple of stunner-armed guards. He'd tried everything he could think of short of breaking his cover to suborn them, in their brief snatches of conversation. They'd just smiled at him. He was dubious of his ability to outrun a stunner-beam, but at the next opportunity, he resolved to try. He hadn't had a chance to try anything clever. He was ready to try something stupid. Surprise sometimes worked. . . .

The lock clicked. He spun, poised to dart forward. "Rowan, get up!" he hissed. "I'm going to try for it."

"Oh, hell," she moaned, emerging. Without faith, brow-beaten, she rose and trudged around the bed to stand by his side. "Stunning hurts, you know. And then you throw up. *You'll* probably have convulsions."

"Yes. I know."

"But at least it'll shut you up for a while," she muttered under her breath.

He rose on the balls of his feet. Then sank back again as the servant entered. *Oh, my. What's this?* There was suddenly a new player in the game, and his mind locked into over-drive. Rowan, watching him for his announced bolt, looked up too, and her eyes widened.

It was the clone-girl Lilly—Lilly Junior, he supposed he must think of her—in her brown-and-pink silk house-servant's uniform, a long wrap skirt and spangled jacket. Straight-backed, she carried their meal tray, and set it down on the table across the room. Incomprehensibly, the guard nodded at her and withdrew, closing the door behind him.

She began to lay out their meal, servant-fashion; Rowan approached her, lips parted.

He saw a dozen possibilities, instantly; also that this

chance might never come again. There was no way, in his debilitated state, that he could overpower the girl himself. What about that sedative Rowan had threatened him with? Could Rowan get the drop on her? Rowan was not good at catching oblique hints, and terrible at following cryptic orders. She'd want explanations. She'd want to *argue*. He could only try.

"*Goodness* you two look alike," he chirped brightly, glaring at Rowan. She gave him a look of exasperated bafflement, which she converted to a smile as the girl turned toward them. "How is it that we rate, uh, such a high-born servant, milady?"

Lilly's smooth hand touched her chest. "*I* am not my lady," she said, in a tone that suggested he must be a complete fool. Not without reason. "But you . . ." She looked searchingly at Rowan. "I don't understand you."

"Did the Baronne send you?" Miles asked.

"No. But I told the guards your food was drugged, and the Baronne sent me to stay and watch you eat it," she added, somewhat off-the-cuff.

"Is that, uh, true?" he asked.

"No." She tossed her head, making her long hair swing, and dropped him from her attention to focus hungrily upon Rowan. "Who *are* you?"

"She is the Baronne's sister," he said instantly. "Daughter to your lady's mother. Did you know you were named after your, uh, grandmother?"

". . . Grandmother?"

"Tell her about the Durona Group, Rowan," he said urgently.

"Give me a chance to speak, then, why don't you," Rowan said through her teeth, smiling.

"Does she know what she is? Ask her if she knows what she is," he demanded, then stuffed his knuckle into his mouth and bit it. The girl hadn't come for him. She'd come for Rowan. He had to let Rowan take this one.

"Well," Rowan glanced at the closed door, and back to the girl, "The Duronas are a group of thirty-six cloned siblings. We live under the protection of House Fell. Our mother—the first Durona—is named Lilly, too. She was very sad when Lotus—the Baronne—left us. Lotus used to be my . . . older sister, you see. You must be my sister too, then. Has Lotus told you why she had you? Are you to be her daughter? Her heir?"

"I am to be united with my lady," said the girl. There was a faint defiance in her tone, but her fascination with Rowan was obvious. "I wondered . . . if you were to take my place." Jealousy? *Madness.*

Rowan's eyes darkened in muted horror. "Do *you* understand just what that means? What a clone-brain transplant is? She will take your body, Lilly, and you will be nowhere."

"Yes. I know. It's my destiny." She tossed her head again, flipping her hair back from her face. Her tone was one of conviction. But her eyes . . . was there the faintest question, in her eyes?

"So much alike, you two," he murmured, circling them in suppressed anxiety. Smiling. "I'll bet you could exchange clothes with each other, and no one could tell the difference." Rowan's quick glance told him yes, she'd caught it, but thought he was pushing it too hard. "Naw," he went on, pursing his lips and tilting his head, "I don't think so. The girl's too fat. Don't you think she's too fat, Rowan?"

"I am not fat!" said Lilly Junior indignantly.

"Rowan's clothes would never fit you."

"You're wrong," said Rowan, giving up and letting herself be pushed into fast-forward. "He's an idiot. Let's prove it, Lilly." She began to peel out of her jacket, blouse, trousers.

Slowly, very curiously, the girl took off her jacket and skirt, and took up Rowan's outfit. Rowan did not yet touch Lilly's silks, laid out neatly on the bed.

"Oh, that looks nice," said Rowan. She nodded toward the bathroom. "You should go look at yourself."

"I was wrong," Miles admitted nobly, steering the girl toward the bathroom. No time to plot, no way to give orders. He'd have to utterly rely on Rowan's . . . initiative. "Actually, Rowan's clothes look quite good on you. Imagine yourself as a Durona surgeon. They're all doctors there, did you know? You could be a doctor too. . . ." Out of the corner of his eye, he saw Rowan tear the bands from her hair and shake it loose, and grab for the silks. He let the door shut behind him and Lilly, and aimed her at the mirror. He turned on the water, to mask the sound of Rowan's knock on the outer door, of the guard opening it, of her retreat, hair swinging down across her face. . . .

Lilly stared into the long mirror. She glanced at him by her side in it, waving his hand as if to introduce her to herself, then down at the top of his head by her shoulder. He grabbed a cup and took a gulp of water, to clear his throat for action. How long could he keep the girl distracted in here? He didn't think he could successfully sap her on the skull, and he was not completely certain which item in Rowan's medical satchel, sitting on the countertop, was the threatened sedative.

To his surprise, she spoke first. "You're the one who came for me, aren't you. For all us clones."

"Uh . . ." The disastrous Dendarii raid on Bharaputra's? Had she been one of the rescuees? What was she doing back here, then? "Excuse me. I've been dead, lately, and my brain isn't working too well. Cryo-amnesia. It might have been me, but you might have met my clone-twin."

"You have clone-sibs too?"

"At least one. My . . . brother."

"You were really dead?" She sounded faintly disbelieving.

He pulled up his gray knit shirt and displayed his scars.

"Oh," she said, impressed. "I guess you were."

"Rowan put me back together. She's very good." No, don't draw her attention to the missing Rowan. "You could be just as good, I'll bet, if you tried. If you were trained."

"What was it like? Being dead?" Her eyes were suddenly intent upon his face.

He shrugged his shirt back down. "Dull. Really boring. A blank. I don't remember anything. I don't remember dying—" His breath caught. . . . *the projectile weapon's muzzle, bright with flame . . . his chest bursting outward, terrible pain . . .* He inhaled, and leaned against the counter, legs suddenly weak. "Lonely. You wouldn't like it. I guarantee." He took her warm hand. "Being alive is much better. Being alive is, is . . ." He needed something to stand on. He scrambled up on the counter instead, crouching eye to eye with her at last. He twined her hair in his hand, tilted his head, and kissed her, just a brief press of the lips. "You can tell you're alive when somebody touches you back."

She drew back, shocked and interested. "You kiss differently from the Baron."

His brain seemed to hiccup. "The Baron has kissed you?"

"Yes . . ."

Sampling his wife's new body early? How soon was that transplant scheduled? "Have you always lived with, uh, your lady?"

"No. I was brought here after the clone-creche was wrecked. The repairs are almost complete, I'll be moving back soon."

"But . . . not for long."

"No."

The temptations to the Baron must be . . . interesting. After all, she would have her brain destroyed soon, and be unable to accuse. Vasa Luigi could do anything but damage her virginity. What was this doing to her apparent mental conditioning, her allegiance to her destiny? Something, obviously, or she wouldn't be here.

She glanced at the closed door, and her mouth went round in sudden suspicion. She pulled her hand from his grip, and raced back to the empty bedroom. "Oh, no!"

"Sh! Sh!" He ran after her, grabbed her hand again, lunged up to stand on the bed to turn her face to his and regain eye contact. "Don't shout!" he hissed. "If you run out and tell the guards, you'll be in terrible trouble, but if you just wait until she comes back, no one will ever know." He felt quite vile, to be playing so on her obvious panic, but it had to be done. "Be quiet, and no one will ever know." He had no idea if Rowan intended to come back, for that matter. By this point maybe she had just wanted to escape from *him*. None of his plans had assumed a piece of luck like this.

Lilly Junior could physically overpower him with ease, though he was not sure if she realized it. One good punch to his chest would drop him to the floor. She wouldn't even have to hit him very hard.

"Sit down," he told her. "Here, next to me. Don't be afraid. Actually, I can't imagine what you could possibly be afraid of, if your destiny doesn't make you blink. You must be a courageous girl. Woman. Sit . . ." He drew her down; she glanced from him to the door in great uncertainty, but allowed herself to be settled, temporarily. Her muscles were tight as springs. "Tell me . . . tell me about yourself. Tell me about your life. You are a most interesting person, do you know?"

"Me?"

"I can't remember much about my life, right now, which is why I ask. It's a terror to me, not to be able to remember. It's killing me. What's the very earliest thing about yourself that you can remember?"

"Why . . . I suppose . . . the place I lived before I came to the creche. There was a woman who took care of me. I have—this is silly—but I remember she had some purple flowers, as tall as I was, that grew out of this little square of a garden, hardly a meter square, and they smelled like grapes."

"Yes? Tell me more about those flowers . . ."

They were in for a long conversation, he feared. And then what? That Rowan had not yet been *brought* back was a very good sign. That she might not be *coming* back left an unsettling dilemma for Lilly Junior. *So what could the Baron and Baronne possibly do to her?* his mind mocked savagely. *Kill her?*

They talked of her life in the creche. He teased out an account of the Dendarii raid from her point of view. How she had managed to re-join the Baron. Sharp, sharp kid. What a mess for Mark. The pauses grew longer. He was going to end up talking about himself soon, just to keep things going, and that was incredibly dangerous. She was running out of conversation, her eyes turning more and more often toward the door.

"Rowan's not coming back," said Lilly Junior at last. "Is she."

"I think not," he said frankly. "I think she's escaped clean."

"How can you tell?"

"If they had caught her, they would have come for you, even if they didn't bring her back here. From their point of view, Rowan is still in here. It's you who's missing."

"You don't think they could have mistaken her for me, do you?" she gasped in alarm. "Taken her to be united with my lady?"

He wasn't sure if she was afraid for Rowan, or afraid that Rowan would steal her place. What a ghastly, hideous new paranoia. "How soon are you . . . no," he reassured her. Himself. "No. At a glance in the hallway, sure, you'd look quite alike, but someone would have to take a closer look for that. She's years older than you. It's just not possible."

"What should I do?" She tried to get to her feet; he held her arm, pulled her back to his side on the bed.

"Nothing," he advised. "It's all right. Tell them—tell them I made you stay in here."

She looked askance at his littleness. "How?"

"Trickery. Threats. Psychological coercion," he said truthfully. "You can blame it on me."

She looked most dubious.

How old was she? He'd spent the last two hours teasing out her whole life story, and there didn't seem to be very much of it. Her talk was an odd mixture of sharpness and naivete. The greatest adventure of her life had been her brief kidnapping by the Dendarii Mercenaries.

Rowan. *She's made it out. Then what?* Would she come back for him? How? This was Jackson's Whole. You couldn't trust anyone. People were meat, here. Like this girl in front of him. He had a sudden nightmarish picture of her, empty-skulled, blank-eyed.

"I'm sorry," he whispered. "You are so beautiful . . . on the *inside*. You deserve to live. Not be eaten by that old woman."

"My lady is a great woman," she said sturdily. "She deserves to live more."

What kind of twisted ethics drove Lotus Durona, to make of this girl an imitation-willing sacrifice? Who did Lotus think she was fooling? Only herself, apparently.

"Besides," said Lilly Junior. "I thought you liked that fat blonde. You were squirming all over her."

"Who?"

"Oh, that's right. That must have been your clone-twin."

"My brother," he corrected automatically. What was *this* story, Mark?

She was getting relaxed, now, reconciled to her strange captivity. And bored. She looked at him speculatively. "Would you like to kiss me again?" she inquired.

It was his height. It brought out the beast in women. Unthreatened, they became bold. He normally considered it a quite delightful effect, but this girl worried him. She was not his . . . equal. But he had to kill time, keep her in here, keep her entertained for as long as possible. "Well . . . all right. . . ."

After about twenty minutes of tame and decorous necking, she drew back and remarked, "That's not the way the Baron does it."

"What do you do for Vasa Luigi?"

She unfastened his trouser-strings and started to show him. After about a minute, he choked, "Stop!"

"Don't you like it? The Baron does."

"I'm sure." Dreadfully aroused, he fled to the chair by the little dining table, and scrunched himself up in it. "That's, um, very nice, Lilly, but it's too serious for you and me."

"I don't understand."

"Just exactly so." She was a *child*, despite her grown-up body, he was increasingly certain of it. "When you are older . . . you will find your own boundaries. And you can invite people across them as you choose. Right now you scarcely know where you leave off and the world begins. Desire should flow from within, not be imposed from without." He tried to choke off his own flow by sheer will-power, half-successfully. *Vasa Luigi, you scum.*

She frowned thoughtfully. "I'm not going to be older."

He wrapped his arms around his drawn-up knees, and shuddered. *Hell.*

He suddenly remembered how he'd met Sergeant Taura. How they had become lovers, in that desperate hour. Ah, ambushed again by the pot-holes in his memory. There were certain obvious parallels with his current situation, it must be why his subconscious was trying to apply the old successful solution. But Taura was a bioengineered mutation, short-lived. The Dendarii medicos had stolen her a little more time with metabolic adjustments, but not much. Every day was a gift, each year a miracle. She was living her whole life as a smash-and-grab, and he heartily approved. Lilly Junior could live a century, if she wasn't . . . cannibalized. She needed to be seduced to life, not sex.

Like integrity, love of life was not a subject to be studied, it was a contagion to be caught. And you had to catch it from someone who had it. "Don't you want to live?" he asked her.

"I . . . don't know."

"I do. I want to live. And believe me, I have considered the alternative*deeply*."

"You are . . . a funny, little, ugly man. What can you get from life?"

"*Everything*. And I mean to get more." *I want, I want.* Wealth, power, love. Victories, splendid, brilliant victories, shining reflected in the eyes of comrades. Someday, a wife, children. A herd of children, tall and healthy, to rock those who whispered *Mutant!* right back on their heels and over on their pointed heads. *And I mean to have a brother.*

Mark. Yeah. The surly little fellow that Baron Ryoval was, quite possibly, taking apart strand by strand right now. In Miles's place. His nerves stretched to the screaming point, with no release. *I've got to make time.*

He finally persuaded Lilly Junior to go to sleep, wrapped up in the covers on Rowan's side of the bed. Chivalrously, he took the chair. A couple of hours into the night and he was in agony. He tried the floor. It was cold. His chest ached. He dreaded the thought of waking with a cough. He finally crept into the bed on top of the covers, and curled up facing away from her.

He was intensely conscious of her body. The reverse was obviously not so. His anxiety was the more enormous for being so formless. He didn't have control of *anything*. Near morning, he at last warmed up enough to doze.

"Rowan, m'love," he muttered muzzily, nuzzling into her scented hair and wrapping himself around her warm, long body. "M'lady." A Barrayaran turn of phrase; he knew where that *milady* came from, at long last. She flinched; he recoiled. Consciousness returned. "Ak! Sorry."

Lilly Junior sat up, shaking off his ugly-little-man grasp. Grope, actually. "I am not my lady!"

"Sorry, wrong referent. I think of Rowan as milady, inside my head. She is milady, and I'm her . . ." *court fool* "knight. I really am a soldier, you know. Despite being short."

At the second knock on the door, he realized what had awakened him. "Breakfast. Quick! Into the bathroom. Rattle around in there. I swear we can keep this going another round."

For once he did not try to engage the guards in conversation leading to bribery. Lilly Junior came back out when the door closed again behind the servant. She ate slowly, dubiously, as if she doubted her right to food. He watched her, increasingly fascinated. "Here. Have this other roll. You can put sugar on it, you know."

"I'm not allowed to eat sugar."

"You should have sugar." He paused. "You should have everything. You should have friends. You should have . . . sisters. You should have education to the limits of your mind's powers, and work to challenge your spirit. Work makes you bigger. More real. You eat it up, and grow. You should have love. A knight of your own. Much taller. You should have . . . ice cream."

"I mustn't get fat. My lady is my destiny."

"Destiny! What do you know about destiny?" He rose, and began to pace, zig-zagging around bed and table. "I'm a frigging *expert* on destiny. Your lady is a false destiny, and do you know how I know? She takes everything, but she doesn't give anything back.

"*Real* destiny takes everything—the last drop of blood, and strip out your veins to be sure—and gives it back doubled. Quadrupled. A thousand-fold! But you can't give halves. You have to give it all. I *know*. I *swear*. I've come back from the dead to speak the truth to you. Real destiny gives you a *mountain* of life, and puts you on top of it."

His conviction felt utterly megalomanic. He adored moments like this.

"You're insane," she said, staring at him warily.

"How would you know? You've never met a sane person in your life. *Have you?* Think about it."

Her rising interest fell. "It's no use. I'm a prisoner anyway. Where would I go?"

"Lilly Durona would take you in," he said promptly. "The Durona Group is under House Fell's protection, you know. If you could get to your grandmother, you'd be safe."

Her brows drew down just like Rowan's had, when she was knocking holes in his escape plans. "How?"

"They can't leave us in here forever. Suppose . . ." he walked behind her, gathered up her hair, and held it in a messy wad on the back of her head. "I didn't get the impression Vasa Luigi meant to keep Rowan past the point of need for secrecy. When I go, so should she. If they thought you were Rowan, I bet you could just walk right out."

"What . . . would I say?"

"As little as possible. Hello, Dr. Durona, your ride is here. Pick up your bag, and go."

"I couldn't."

"You could try. If you fail, you'll lose nothing. If you win,you'll win *everything*. And—if you got away—you could tell people where I've gone. Who took me, and when. All it takes is a few minutes of nerve, and that's free. We make it ourselves, out of ourselves. Nerve can't be taken away from you like a purse or something. Hell, why am I telling you that? You escaped the Dendarii Mercenaries on nerve and wit alone."

She looked utterly boggled. "I was doing it for my lady. I've never done anything for . . . for *myself*."

He felt like crying, strung up to the point of pure nervous collapse. This was the sort of all-out exalted eloquence he usually reserved for persuading people to *risk* their lives, not save them. He leaned across to whisper demonically in her ear. "Do it for yourself. The universe will be around to collect its cut later."

After breakfast, he tried to help her fix her hair Rowan-fashion. He was terrible at hair. Since Rowan was too, the final result was quite convincing, he fancied. They survived the delivery and removal of lunch.

He knew it wasn't dinner when they didn't knock before entering.

There were three guards, and a man in House livery. Two of the guards took him, wordlessly, and fastened his hands in front of him. He was grateful for that small favor. Behind his back would have been excruciating, after the first half-hour. They prodded him into the hall. No sign of Vasa and Lotus. Out looking for their lost clone, he hoped? He glanced back over his shoulder.

"Dr. Durona," the House man nodded at Lilly Junior. "I am to be your driver. Where to?"

She brushed a loose wisp of hair from her eyes, picked up Rowan's bag, stepped forward, and said, "Home."

"Rowan," Miles said. She turned.

"Take all, for it will all be taken back in time. That's a grave truth." He moistened dry lips. "Kiss me goodbye?"

She tilted her head, wheeled, bent. Pressed her lips to his, briefly. Followed the driver.

Well, it was enough to impress the guards. "How'd you rate that?" one inquired, amiably amused, as he was led in the opposite direction.

"I'm an acquired taste," he informed them smugly.

"Cut the chat," sighed the senior man.

He made two attempted breaks on the way to the groundcar; after the second, the biggest guard simply slung him over his shoulder, head-down, and threatened to drop him if he wriggled. They'd used enough force tackling him the second time that Miles didn't think he was joking. They bundled him into the back of the vehicle between two of them.

"Where are you taking me?"

"To a transfer point," one said.

"What transfer point?"

"That's all you need to know."

He kept up a steady stream of commentary, bribes, threats, insults, and at last, invective, but they never rose to the bait again. He wondered if any of them could be the man who'd killed him. No. No one involved in that mess at the surgical facility could be so calm about it all. These guys had been far away, that day. His voice went hoarse. It was a long ride. Groundcars were hardly used outside the cities, the roads were so bad. And they were far outside any city. It was past dusk when they pulled over beside a lonely intersection.

They handed him off to two humorless, flat-faced men in red and black House livery, who were waiting patiently as oxen. Ryoval's colors. These men fastened his hands behind his back, and his ankles too, before slinging him into the back of a lightflyer. It rose silently into darkness.

Looks like Vasa Luigi got his price.

Rowan, if she'd made it, must send anyone looking for him to Bharaputra's. Where Miles would not be. Not that he was so sure Vasa Luigi wouldn't just cheerfully sic them right on to Ryoval.

But if Ryoval's location was easy to find, they would have found it by now.

By God. I could be the first ImpSec agent on-site. He'd have to be sure and point that out, in his report to Illyan. He had looked forward to making posthumous reports to Illyan. Now he wondered if he was going to live long enough.

CHAPTER TWENTY-EIGHT

"I hate to be the one to tell you this, Baron," said the technician, "but your torture victim appears to be having a wonderful time."

Gorge grinned around the tube gagging his mouth as Baron Ryoval walked around him and stared. Admiring his amazing stomach, perhaps.

"There are a number of possible psychological defenses in these situations," Ryoval said. "Split personalities and identification with the captor included. I expected Naismith to work through them all, eventually, but—so soon?"

"I didn't believe it either, sir, so I took a series of brain scans. The results were unusual."

"If his personality is indeed splitting, it should show up on the scan."

"*Something* shows up on the scan. He seems to be shielding portions of his mind from our stimuli, and his surface responses certainly suggest a split, but . . . the pattern is abnormally abnormal, if that makes sense, sir."

"Not really." Ryoval pursed his lips with interest. "I'll take a look at them."

"Whatever is going on, he's not faking it. That I am sure of."

"So impossibly fast . . ." murmured Ryoval. "When do you think he snapped? How could I have missed it?"

"I'm not sure. Early. The first day—maybe the first hour. But if he keeps it up, he's going to be very elusive, to bring much force to bear upon. He can keep . . . changing shifts."

"So can I," stated Ryoval coldly.

The pressure in his stomach was growing into pain. Howl prodded anxiously, but Gorge would not give way. It was still his turn. The Other listened attentively. The fourth one always listened, when Baron Ryoval was present. Rarely slept, almost never spoke.

"I didn't expect him to reach this stage of disintegration for months. It throws off my time-table," the Baron complained.

Yes, Baron. Aren't we fascinating? Don't we intrigue you?

"I must consider how best to re-focus him," Ryoval mused."Bring him to my quarters later. I'll see what a little quiet conversation and a few experiments will yield, in the way of new directions."

Beneath his flattened affect, the Other shivered in anticipation.

Two guards delivered him/them to Baron Ryoval's pleasant living room. There were no windows, though a large holovid display took up most of one wall, presently running a view of some tropical beach. But Ryoval's quarters were surely underground. Nobody would break through windows here.

His skin was still patchy. The techs had sprayed the raw areas with some kind of coating, to keep him from oozing on Ryoval's fine furniture, and dressed the other wounds with plastic bandage, so they wouldn't break open and bleed and stain.

"Think this'll do any good?" the tech with the sprayer had asked.

"Probably not," his comrade had sighed. "I suppose I'd better go ahead and put a cleaning crew on call. Wish he'd put down a tarp or something."

The guards sat him now in a low, wide chair. It was just a chair, no spikes or razors or impalements. His hands were fastened behind him, which meant he could not settle back. He spread his knees and sat uncomfortably upright, panting.

The senior guard asked Ryoval, "Do you wish us to secure him, sir?"

Ryoval raised an eyebrow. "Can he stand up without help?"

"Not readily, from that position."

Ryoval's lips crooked up in amused contempt, as he gazed down at his prisoner. "Ah, we're getting there. Slowly. Leave us. I'll call you. Don't interrupt. It may become noisy."

"Your soundproofing is very effective, sir." The flat-faced guards saluted and withdrew. There was something wrong with those guards. When not following orders, they tended to just sit, or stand, wordless and blank. Constructed that way, no doubt.

Gorge and Grunt and Howl and the Other stared around with interest, wondering whose turn it was going to be next.

You just had your turn, said Howl to Gorge. *It'll be me.*

Don't bet on it, said Grunt. *Could be me.*

If it weren't for Gorge, said the Other, grimly, *I'd take my turn right now. Now I have to wait.*

You've never taken a turn, said Gorge curiously. But the Other was silent again.

"Let's watch a show," said Ryoval, and touched a remote. The tropic display changed to a life-sized vid recording of one of Grunt's sessions with the . . . creatures, from the bordello. Grunt watched himself with great interest and delight, from all these new angles. Gorge's work was gradually threatening to put many interesting events out of sight, below his equator.

"I am thinking of sending a copy of this to the Dendarii mercenary fleet," Ryoval murmured, watching him.

"Imagine all your senior staff officers, viewing this. I think it would fetch a few to me, no?"

No. Ryoval was lying. His presence here was still secret, or he wouldn't *be* present here. And Ryoval could be in no rush to give that secret away. The Other muttered dryly, *Send a copy to Simon Illyan, why don't you, and see what that fetches you.* But Illyan belonged to Lord Mark, and Mark wasn't here, and anyway, the Other never, ever, ever spoke aloud.

"Imagine that pretty bodyguard of yours, joining you here . . ." Ryoval went on, in detail. Grunt was perfectly willing to imagine some parts of it, though other parts offended even him. *Howl?*

Not me! said Howl. *That's not my job.*

We'll just have to make a new recruit, they all said. He could make a thousand of them, at need. He was an army, flowing like water, parting around obstacles,impossible to destroy with any one cut.

The vid display changed to one of Howl's finest moments, the one which had given him his name. Shortly after he'd been chemically skinned, the techs had painted sticky stuff on him that made him itch unbearably. The techs hadn't had to touch him. He'd almost killed himself. They'd given him a transfusion afterwards, to replace the blood lost in the raking wounds.

He stared impassively at the convulsing creature in the vid. The show that Ryoval wanted to see was himself. Looking at him right now must have all the drama and excitement of watching a test-pattern. Boring. Ryoval looked like he wanted to aim the remote at him, and switch programs.

The Other waited with growing impatience. He was beginning to get his breath back, but there was still the damned low chair to contend with. It had to be tonight. By the next opportunity, if any ever came, Gorge might have immobilized them all. Yes. He waited.

Ryoval's lips puffed with disappointment, watching his serene profile. He shut the vid off and rose, and walked around the chair, studying him through narrowed eyes. "You're not even with me, are you? You've gone up around some bend. I must think what will bring you back to me. Or should I say, you all."

Ryoval was much too perceptive.

I don't trust you, said Gorge to the Other, doubtfully. *What will happen to me, after?*

And me, added Grunt. Only Howl said nothing. Howl was very tired.

I promise Mark will still feed you, Gorge, the Other whispered, from deep inside. *At least now and then. And Grunt. Mark could take you to Beta Colony. There are people there who could help you clean up enough to come out in the daylight, I think. You wouldn't need Ryoval's hypospray. Poor Howl is all exhausted anyway, he's worked the hardest, covering for the rest of you lot. Anyway, Grunt, what if Ryoval decides on castration next? Maybe you and Howl can get together, and Mark could rent you a squad of beautiful women—wouldn't women be a lovely change?—with whips and chains. This is Jackson's Whole, I bet you could find some in the vid directory. You don't need Ryoval. We save Mark, and he'll save us. I promise.*

Who are you, to pledge Mark's word? said Gorge grumpily.

I am the closest to him.

You've certainly hidden out the best, said Howl, with a hint of resentment.

It was necessary. But we will all perish, one by one, as Ryoval hunts us down. He's terribly sharp. We are the originals. The new recruits would only be distorted shadows of us anyway.

This was true, they all could see.

"I'm bringing you a friend to play with," Ryoval commented, walking around him. Having Ryoval behind him had some odd effects on his internal topography. Gorge flattened, Howl emerged, then sank again as Ryoval came back in view. Grunt watched alertly for his cues, rocking just slightly. "Your clone-twin. The one my stupid squad failed to take along."

Deep down inside, Lord Mark came wide awake, screaming. The Other smothered him up. *He lies. He lies.*

"Their fumble proved to be a costly error, for which they will pay. Your double vanished, then somehow turned up with Vasa Luigi. A typically smooth bit of sleight of hand on Vasa's part. I'm still not convinced dear Lotus doesn't have a private line of some kind into the Durona Group."

Ryoval circled him again. It was very disorienting. "Vasa is quite convinced his twin is the Admiral, and you are the clone. He has infected me with his doubts, though if as he claims the man is indeed cryo-amnesic, it could prove most disappointing even if he's right. But it doesn't matter now. I have you both. Just as I predicted. Can you guess what is the first thing I shall have you two do to each other?"

Grunt could. Spot-on, though not with the whispered refinements Ryoval added.

Lord Mark raged, wept with terror and dismay. Not a vibration rippled Grunt's slack-mouthed surface, nor marred the flat glisten of his eyes with any inner purpose. *Wait*, begged the Other.

The Baron walked to a counter or bar, made of some zebra-grained, polished wood, and unwrapped an array of glittering tools, which no one could quite see, though Howl stretched his neck. Meditatively, Ryoval looked his kit over.

You have to stay out of my way. And not sabotage me, said the Other. *I know Ryoval gives you what you hunger for—but it's a trick.*

Ryoval doesn't feed you, said Gorge.

Ryoval is my food, whispered the Other.

You'll only get one chance, said Howl nervously. *And then they'll come after me.*

I only need one chance.

Ryoval turned back. A surgical hand-tractor gleamed in his grip. Grunt, frightened, gave way to the Other.

"I believe," said Ryoval, "that I will pull out one of your eyes, next. Just one. That should have some interesting psychological focusing effects, when I threaten the remaining one."

Smoothly, Howl gave way. Last of all, reluctantly, Gorge gave way, as Ryoval walked toward them.

Killer's first attempt to struggle to his feet failed, and he fell back. *Damn you, Gorge.* He tried again, shifted his weight forward, heaved up, stepped once, half-unbalanced without the use of his arms to save himself. Ryoval watched, highly amused, unalarmed by the waddling little monster he doubtless thought he had created.

Trying to work around Gorge's new belly was something like being the Blind Zen Archer. But his alignment was absolute.

His first kick took Ryoval in the crotch. This folded him neatly over, and put his upper body within practical range. He flowed instantly into the second kick, striking Ryoval squarely in the throat. He could feel cartilage and tissue crunch all the way back to Ryoval's spine. Since he was not wearing steel-capped boots this time, it also broke several of his toes, smashed up and down at right angles. He felt no pain. That was Howl's job.

He fell over. Getting up again wasn't easy, with his hands still shackled behind him. Wallowing around on the floor trying to get his legs under himself, he saw with disappointment that Ryoval wasn't dead yet. The man writhed and gurgled and clutched his throat, on the carpet next to him. But the room's computer control did not recognize the Baron's voice commands now. They had a little time yet.

He rolled near to Ryoval's ear. "I am *too* a Vorkosigan. The one who was trained as a deep-penetration mole and assassin. It really pisses me off when people underestimate me, y'know?"

He managed to get back on his feet, and studied the problem, which was, Ryoval was still alive. He sighed, swallowed, stepped forward, and pounded the man with repeated blows of his feet till Ryoval stopped vomiting blood, convulsing, and breathing. It was a nauseating process, but in all, he was very relieved that there seemed no part of himself who actually enjoyed it. Even Killer had to muster a determined professionalism, to see it through to the end.

He considered the Other, whom he now recognized as Killer. *Galen made you, mostly, didn't he?*

Yes. But he didn't make me out of nothing.

You did very well. Hiding out. Stalking. I'd wondered if any of us possessed any sense of timing at all. I'm glad at least one of us does.

It was what the Count our Father said, Killer admitted, pleased and embarrassed to be praised. *That people would give themselves to you, if you waited them out, and didn't rush to give yourself to them. And I did. And Ryoval did.* He added shyly, *The Count's a killer too, you know. Like me.*

Hm.

He pulled his wrists against the shackles, and limped over to the zebra-wood counter to study Ryoval's kit. The selection included a laser-drill, as well as a sickening assortment of knives, scalpels, tongs, and probes. The drill was a short-focal-range surgical type suitable for cutting bone, a dubious weapon, but a most suitable tool.

He wobbled around and tried to pick it up, behind his back. He almost wept when he dropped it. He was going to have to get down on the floor again. Awkwardly, he did so, and lumbered around till he managed to grub up the drill. It took many minutes of fiddling, but at last he got it turned around and aimed in such a way as to cut through his shackles without either slicing his hand off, or burning himself in the butt. Released, he flung his arms around his swollen torso, and rocked himself like someone rocking a weary child. His foot was starting to throb. The assorted mass vectors had apparently also combined to wrench his back, when he'd kicked Ryoval in the throat.

He stared, aside, at his victim/tormentor/prey. *Clone-consumer.* He felt apologetic toward the body he had pummeled underfoot. *It wasn't your fault. You died, what, ten years ago?* It was the one up top, inside the skull, who had been his enemy.

An illogical fear possessed him that Ryoval's guards would break in, and save their master even in death. He crawled over, much easier now that he had his hands free, took the laser-drill, and made certain that no one would be transplanting that brain again, ever. No one, no way.

He sagged back into the low chair, and sat in utter exhaustion, waiting to die. Ryoval's men surely had orders to avenge their fallen lord.

No one came.

. . . Right. The boss had locked himself in his quarters with a prisoner and a surgical kit, and told his goons not to bother him. How long before one worked up the courage to interrupt his little hobby? Could be . . . quite a long time.

The weight of hope returning was an almost intolerable burden, like walking on a broken bone. *I don't want to move.* He was very angry with ImpSec for abandoning him here, but thought he might forgive them everything if only they would charge in *now*, and waft him away without any further exertion or effort on his part. *Haven't I earned a break?* The room grew very silent.

That was over-kill, he thought, staring down at Ryoval's body. *A trifle unbalanced, that. And you've made a mess on the carpet.*

I don't know what to do next.

Who was speaking? Killer? Gorge, Grunt? Howl? All of them?

You're good troops, and loyal, but not too bright.

Bright is not our job.

It was time for Lord Mark to wake up. Had he ever really been asleep?

"All right, gang," he muttered aloud, unfolding himself. "Everybody up." The low chair was a torture-device in its own right. Ryoval's last snide dig. With a groan, he regained his feet.

It was impossible that an old fox like Ryoval would have only one entrance to his den. He poked around the underground suite. Office, living room, small kitchen, big bedroom, and a rather oddly equipped bathroom. He gazed longingly at the shower. He had not been allowed to bathe since he'd been brought here. But he was afraid it might wash off the plastic skin. He did brush his teeth. His gums were bleeding, but that was all right. He drank a little cold water. *At least I'm not hungry.* He vented a small cackle.

He found the emergency exit at last in the back of the bedroom closet.

If it's not guarded, stated Killer, *it must be booby-trapped.*

Ryoval's main defenses will work from the outside in, said Lord Mark slowly. *From the inside out, it will be set up to facilitate a quick escape. For Ryoval. And Ryoval alone.*

It was palm-locked. Palm-lock pads read pulse, temperature, and the electrical conductivity of the skin, as well as the whorls of fingerprints and grooves of life-lines. Dead hands didn't open palm-locks.

There are ways around palm locks, murmured Killer. Killer had been trained in such things once, in a previous incarnation. Lord Mark let go, and floated, watching.

The surgical array was almost as useful as an electronics kit, in Killer's hands. Given abundant time, and as long as the palm lock was never going to be required to work again. Lord Mark gazed dreamily as Killer loosened the sensor-pad from the wall, touched here, cut there.

The control virtual on the wall lit at last. *Ah*, murmured Killer proudly.

Oh, said the rest. The display projected a small glowing square.

It wants a code-key, said Killer in dismay. His panic at being trapped quickened their heart rate. Howl's tenuous containment loosened, and electrical twinges of pain coursed through them.

Wait, said Lord Mark. If they needed a code-key, so must Ryoval.

Baron Ryoval has no successor. Ryoval had no second-in-command, no trained replacement. He kept all his oppressed subordinates in separate channels of communication. House Ryoval consisted of Baron Ryoval, and slaves, period. That's why House Ryoval failed to grow. Ryoval didn't delegate authority, ever.

Therefore, Ryoval had no place nor trusted subordinates with whom to leave his private code-keys. He had to carry them on his person. At all times.

The black-gang whimpered as Lord Mark turned around and returned to the living room. Mark ignored them. *This is my job, now.*

He turned Ryoval's body over on its back, and searched it methodically from head to toe, down to the skin and farther. He missed no possibility, not even hollow teeth. He sat back uncomfortably, distended belly aching, sprained back on fire. His level of pain was rising as he re-integrated, which made it a very tentative process. *It has to be here. It has to be here somewhere.*

Run, run, run, the black-gang gibbered, in a remarkably unified chorus.

Shut up and let me think. He turned Ryoval's right hand over in his own. A ring with a flat black stone gleamed in the light. . . .

He laughed out loud.

He swallowed the laugh fearfully, looking around. The Baron's soundproofing held, apparently. The ring would not slide off. Stuck? Riveted to the bone? He cut off Ryoval's right hand with the laser drill. The laser also cauterized the wrist, so it wasn't too drippy. Nice. He limped slowly and painfully back to the bedroom closet, and stared at the little glowing square, just the size of the ring's stone.

Which way up? Would the wrong rotation trigger an alarm?

Lord Mark pantomimed Baron Ryoval in a hurry. Slap the palm lock, turn his hand over and jam the ring into the code slot—"This way," he whispered.

The door slid open on a personal lift tube. It extended upward some twenty meters. Its antigrav control pads glowed, green for up, red for down. Lord Mark and Killer gazed around. No obvious defenses, such as a tanglefield generator. . . .

A faint draft brought a scent of fresh air from above. *Let's go!* screamed Gorge and Grunt and Howl.

Lord Mark stood spraddle-legged and stodgy, staring, refusing to be rushed. *It has no safety ladder,* he said at last.

So what?

So. What?

Killer sagged back, and muffled the rest of them, and waited respectfully.

I want a safety ladder, muttered Lord Mark querulously. He turned away, and wandered back through Ryoval's quarters. While he was at it, he looked for clothes. There wasn't much to choose from; this clearly was not Ryoval's main residence. Just a private suite. The garments were all too long and not wide enough. The trousers were impossible. A soft knit shirt stretched over his raw skin, though. A loose jacket, left open, provided some more protection. A Betan-style sarong, bath-wear, wrapped his loins. A pair of slippers were sloppy on his left foot, tight on his swollen, broken right foot. He searched for cash, keys, anything else of use. But there was no handy climbing gear.

I'll just have to make my own safety ladder. He hung the laser drill around his neck on a tie made from a couple of Ryoval's belts, stepped into the bottom of the lift tube, and systematically began to burn holes in the plastic side.

Too slow! the black gang wailed. Howl howled inside, and even Killer screamed, *Run, dammit!*

Lord Mark ignored them. He turned on the "up" field, but did not let it take them. Clinging to his hot hand and foot holds, he pocked his way upward. It was not difficult to climb, buoyed in the flowing grav field, only hard to remember to keep his three points of contact. His right foot was nearly useless. The black gang gibbered in fear. Mulish and methodical, Mark ascended. Melt a hole. Wait. Move a hand, foot, hand, foot. Melt another hole. Wait. . . .

Three meters from the top, his head came level with a small audio pick-up, flush to the wall, and a shielded motion sensor.

I imagine it wants a code word. In Ryoval's voice, Lord Mark remarked blandly, observing. *Can't oblige.*

It doesn't have to be what you guess, Killer said. *It could be anything. Plasma arcs. Poison gas.*

No. Ryoval saw me, but I saw Ryoval. It will be simple. And elegant. And you will do it to yourself. Watch.

He gripped his handhold, and extended the laser drill up past the motion sensor for the next burn.

The lift tube's grav field switched off.

Even half-expecting it, he was nearly ripped from his perch by his own weight. Howl could not contain it all. Mark screamed silently, flooded in pain. But he clung, and did not let them fall.

The last three meters of ascent could have been called a nightmare, but he had new standards for nightmares now. It was merely tedious.

There was a tanglefield trap at the top entrance, but it faced outward. The laser drill disarmed its controls. He managed a crippled, shuffling, crabwise walk into a private underground garage. It contained the Baron's lightflyer. The canopy opened at the touch of Ryoval's ring.

He slid into the lightflyer, adjusted the seat and controls as best he could around his distorted and aching contours, powered it up, eased it forward. That button on the control panel—there? The garage door slid aside. Once through, he shot up, and up, and up, through the dark, the acceleration pummeling him. Nobody even fired on him. There were no lights below. A rocky winter waste. The whole little installation must be underground.

He checked the flyer's map display, and picked his direction—*East.* Toward the light. That seemed right.

He kept accelerating.

CHAPTER TWENTY-NINE

The lightflyer banked. Miles craned his neck, and caught a glimpse of what was below. Or what wasn't below. Dawn was creeping over a wintry desert. There appeared to be nothing of interest for kilometers around.

" 'S funny," said the guard who was piloting the lightflyer. "Door's open." He touched his comm, and transmitted some sort of code-burst. The other guard shifted uneasily, watching his comrade. Miles twisted around, trying to watch them both.

They descended. Rocks rose around them, then a concrete shaft. Ah. Concealed entrance. They came to the bottom, and moved forward into an underground garage.

"Huh," said the other guard. "Where's all the vehicles?"

The flyer came to rest, and the bigger guard dragged Miles out of the backseat, and unfastened his ankles, and stood him upright. He almost fell down again. The scars on his chest ached with the strain from his hands bound behind his back. He got his feet under himself, and stared around much as the guards were doing. Just a utilitarian garage, badly-lit, echoing and cavernous. And empty.

The guards marched him toward an entrance. They coded through some automatic doors, and walked to an electronic security chamber. It was up and running, humming blankly. "Vaj?" one guard called. "We're here. Scan us."

No answer. One of the guards went forward, looked around. Tapped a code into a wall pad. "Bring him through anyway."

The security chamber passed him. He was still wearing the grey knits the Duronas had given him; no interesting devices woven into the fabric, it seemed, alas.

The senior guard tried an intercom. Several times. "Nobody answers."

"What should we do?" asked his comrade.

The senior man frowned. "Strip him and take him to the boss, I guess. Those were the orders."

They pulled his ship-knits off him; he was far too outmassed to fight them, but he regretted the loss deeply. It was too damned cold. Even the ox-like guards stared a moment at his raked and scored chest. They re-fastened his hands behind him, and marched him through the facility, their eyes shifting warily at every intersection.

It was very quiet. Lights burned, but no people appeared anywhere. A strange structure, not very large, plain and—he sniffed—decidedly medical in odor. Research, he decided. Ryoval's private biological research facility. Evidently, after the Dendarii raid of four years ago, Ryoval had decided his main facility wasn't secure enough. Miles could see that. This place did not have the business-air of the other locale. It felt military-paranoid. The sort of place where if you went there to work, you didn't come out again for years at a time. Or, considering Ryoval, ever. He glimpsed a few lab-like rooms, in passing. But no techs. The guards called out, a couple of times. No one answered.

They came to an open door, beyond which lay some sort of study or office. "Baron, sir?" the senior guard ventured. "We have your prisoner."

The other guard rubbed his neck. "If he's not here, should we go ahead and work him like the other one?"

"He hasn't ordered it yet. Better wait."

Quite. Ryoval was not the sort to reward initiative in subordinates, Miles suspected.

With a deep, nervous sigh, the senior man stepped

across the threshold, and looked around. The junior man prodded Miles forward in his wake. The study was finely furnished, with a real wood desk, and an odd chair in front of it with metal wrist-locks for the person who sat in it. Nobody ran out on a conversation with Baron Ryoval till Baron Ryoval was ready, apparently. They waited.

"What do we do now?"

"Don't know. This is as far as my orders went." The senior man paused. "Could be a test. . . ."

They waited about five more minutes.

"If you don't want to look around," said Miles brightly, "I will."

They looked at each other. The senior man, his forehead creased, drew a stunner and sidled cautiously through an archway into the next room. His voice came back after a moment. *"Shit."* And, after another moment, an odd mewling wail, cut off and swallowed.

This was too much even for the dim bulb who held Miles. With his ham hand still locked firmly around Miles's upper arm, the second guard followed the first into a large chamber arranged as a living room. A wall-sized holovid was blank and silent. A zebra-grained wood bar divided the room. An extremely low chair faced an open area. Baron Ryoval's very dead body lay there face-up, naked, staring at the ceiling with dry eyes.

There were no obvious signs of a struggle—no overturned furniture, nor plasma arc burns in the walls—except upon the body. There the marks of violence were focused, utterly concentrated: throat crushed, torso pulped, dried blood smeared around his mouth. A double line of fingertip-sized black dots were stitched neatly across the Baron's forehead. They looked like burns. His right hand was missing, cut away, the wrist a cauterized stump.

The guards twitched in something like horror, an all-too-temporary paralysis of astonishment. "What happened?" whispered the junior man.

Which way will they jump?

How did Ryoval control his employee/slaves, anyway? The lesser folk, through terror, of course; the middle-management and tech layer, through some subtle combination of fear and self-interest. But these, his personal bodyguards, must be the innermost cadre, the ultimate instrument by which their master's will was forced upon all the rest.

They could not be as mentally stunted as their stolidity suggested, or they would be useless in an emergency. But if their narrow minds were intact, it followed that they must be controlled through their emotions. Men whom Ryoval let stand behind him with activated weapons must be programmed to the max, probably from birth. Ryoval must be father, mother, family and all to them. Ryoval must be their god.

But now their god was dead.

What would they do? Was *I am free* even an intelligible concept to them? Without its focal object, how fast would their programming start to break down? *Not fast enough.* An ugly light, compounded of rage and fear, was growing in their eyes.

"I didn't do it," Miles pointed out with quick prudence. "I was with you."

"Stay here," growled the senior man. "I'll reconnoiter." He loped off through the Baron's apartment, to return in a few minutes with a laconic, "His flyer's gone. Lift tube defenses buggered all to hell, too."

They hesitated. Ah, the downside of perfect obedience: crippled initiative.

"Hadn't you better check around the facility?" Miles suggested. "There might be survivors. Witnesses. Maybe . . . maybe the assassin is still hiding somewhere." *Where is Mark?*

"What do we do with *him*?" asked the junior man, with a jerk of his head at Miles.

The senior man scowled in indecision. "Take him along. Or lock him up. Or kill him."

"You don't know what the Baron wanted me for," Miles interrupted instantly. "Better take me along till you find out."

"He wanted you for the other one," said the senior man, with an indifferent glance down at him. Little, naked, half-healed, with his hands bound behind him, the guards clearly did not perceive him as a threat. *Too right. Hell.*

After a brief muttered conference, the junior man pushed him along, and they began as rapid and methodical a tour of the facility as Miles would have wished to make himself. They found two of their red-and-black uniformed comrades, dead. A mysterious pool of blood snaked across a corridor from wall to wall. They found another body, fully dressed as a senior tech, in a shower, the back of his head crushed with some blunt object. On descending levels they found more signs of struggle, of looting, and of by-no-means-random destruction, comconsoles and equipment smashed.

Had it been a slave revolt? Some power struggle among factions? Revenge? All three simultaneously? Was the murder of Ryoval its cause, or its goal? Had there been a mass evacuation, or a mass killing? At every corner, Miles braced himself for a scene of carnage.

The lowest level had a laboratory with half a dozen glass-walled cells lining one end. From the smell, some experiment had been left cooking far too long. He glanced into the cells, and swallowed.

They had been human, once, those lumps of flesh, scar tissue, and growths. They were now . . . culture-dishes of some kind. Four had been female, two male. Some departing tech, as an act of mercy, had neatly cut each one's throat. He eyed them desperately, his face pressed to the glass. Surely they were all too large to have been Mark. Surely such effects could not have been achieved in a mere five days. Surely. He did not want to enter the cells for a closer examination.

At least it explained why more of Ryoval's slaves did not try to resist. There was an air of awful economy about it. Don't like your work in the bordello, girl? Sick of the boredom and brutality of being a guard, man? How would you like to go into scientific research? The last stop for any would-be Spartacus among Ryoval's human possessions. *Bel was right. We should have nuked this place the last time we were here.*

The guards gave the cells a brief glance, and pressed on. Miles hung back, seized by inspiration. It was worth a try. . . .

"Shit!" Miles hissed, and jumped.

The guards spun around.

"That . . . that man in there. He moved. I think I'm going to vomit."

"Can't have." The senior guard stared through the transparent wall at a body which lay with its back to them.

"He couldn't possibly have witnessed anything from in there, could he?" said Miles. "For God's sake, don't open the door."

"Shut up." The senior guard chewed his lip, stared at the control virtual, and after an irresolute moment, coded open the door and trod cautiously within.

"Gah!" said Miles.

"What?" snapped the junior guard.

"He moved again. He, he, sort of spasmed."

The junior man drew his stunner and followed his comrade inside, covering him. The senior man extended his hand, faltered, and on second thought pulled his shock stick from his belt and prodded it warily toward the body.

Miles smacked the door control with a duck of his forehead. The glass seal slid shut, barely in time. The guards smashed into the door and up it like rabid dogs. It barely transmitted the vibration. Their mouths were open, howling curses and threats at him, but no sound passed. The transparent walls must be space-grade material; it stopped stunner fire, too.

The senior man pulled out a plasma arc and began burning. The wall started to glow slightly. Not good. Miles studied the control panel . . . there. He pushed at menu blocks with his tongue till it brought up *oxygen*, and re-set it down as far as it would go. Would the guards pass out before the wall gave way to the plasma arc?

Yes. Good environmental system, that. Ryoval's dogs crumpled against the glass, clawed hands relaxing in unconsciousness. The plasma arc fell from nerveless fingers, and shut off.

Miles left them sealed in their victim's tomb.

It was a lab. There had to be cutters, and tools of all sorts . . . right. It took several minutes of contortions, working behind his back, during which he nearly passed out, but his shackles gave way at last. He whimpered with relief as his hands came free.

Weapons? All weapons *per se* had been taken, apparently, by the departing inhabitants, and without a biotainer suit he was disinclined to re-open the glass cell and retrieve the guards' gear. But a laser-scalpel from the lab made him feel less vulnerable.

He wanted his clothing. Shivering from the cold, he trotted back through the eerie corridors to the security entrance, and donned his knits again. He turned back into the facility, and began to seriously search. He tried every comconsole he came to that wasn't smashed. All were internally dedicated, no way to tap an outside channel.

Where is Mark? It occurred to him suddenly that if there could be anything worse than being held prisoner in some cell here, waiting for his tormentors to come again, it would be to be locked in a cell here waiting for tormentors who *never* came again. In what was perhaps the most frantic half-hour he'd ever experienced in his life, he opened or broke open every door in the facility. Behind every one he expected to find a sodden little body, its throat mercifully cut . . . He was wheezing and fearing another convulsion when, with great relief, he found the cell—closet—near Ryoval's quarters. Empty. It stank of recent occupation, though. And the bloodstains and other stains on the walls and floor turned his stomach cold and sick. But wherever Mark was, and in whatever condition, he was not here. He had to get out of here too.

He caught his breath, and found a plastic basket, and went shopping in the labs for useful electronic equipment. Cutters and wires, circuit-diagnostics, readers and relays, whatever he could find. When he thought he had enough, he returned to the Baron's study, and proceeded to dissect the damaged comconsole. He finally managed to jump the palm-lock, only to have a little bright square patch come up on-view and demand, *Insert code-key*. He cursed, and stretched his aching back, and sat again. This was going to be tedious.

It took another pass through the facility for equipment before he was able to jump the code-key block. And the comconsole would never be the same. But at last, finally, he punched through to the planetary communications net. There was another short glitch while he figured out how to charge the call to House Ryoval's account; all fees were collected in advance, here on Jackson's Whole.

He paused a moment, wondering who to call. Barrayar kept a consulate on the Hargraves-Dyne Consortium Station. Some of the staff were actually diplomatic and/or economic personnel, but even they doubled as ImpSec analysts. The rest were agents-proper, running a thin network of informants scattered across the planet and its satellites and stations. Admiral Naismith had a contact there. But had ImpSec been here already? Was this their work, rescuing Mark? No, he decided. It was ruthless, but not nearly methodical enough. In fact, it was utter chaos.

So why didn't you guys come looking for Mark? A bothersome question, and one to which he had no answer. He punched through the consulate's code. *Let the circus begin.*

They were down on him in half an hour, a tense ImpSec lieutenant named Iverson with a rented squad of local muscle from House Dyne in paramilitary uniforms and with decent military equipment. They'd dropped straight from orbit in a shuttle; heat wavered off its skin in the watery morning light. Miles sat on a rock outside the pedestrian entrance, or more properly speaking, emergency exit he'd found, and watched sardonically as they all galloped out, weapons at the ready, and spread out as if to take the installation by assault.

The officer hurried up to him, and half-saluted. "Admiral Naismith?"

Iverson was no one he knew; at this level of the echelon the man must take him for a valued, but non-Barrayaran, ImpSec hireling. "The one and only. You can tell your men to relax. The installation is secured."

"You secured it yourself?" Iverson asked in faint disbelief.

"More or less."

"We've been looking for this place for two years!"

Miles suppressed an irate remark about people who couldn't find their own prick with a map and a hand-light. "Where is, ah, Mark? The other clone. My double."

"We don't know, sir. Acting on a tip from an informant, we were about to make an assault on a House Bharaputra location to retrieve you, when you called."

"I was there last night. Your informant did not know I was moved." Had to be Rowan—she'd got out, hooray! "You would have been embarrassingly late."

Iverson's lips thinned. "This has been an incredibly fouled-up operation from first to last. The orders kept changing."

"Tell me," Miles sighed. "Have you heard anything from the Dendarii Mercenaries?"

"A covert ops team from your outfit is supposed to be on its way, sir." Iverson's "sirs" were tinged with uncertainty, the dubious regard of a Barrayaran regular for a self-promoted mercenary. "I . . . wish to ascertain for myself if the installation is fully secure, if you don't mind."

"Go ahead," Miles said. "You'll find it an interesting tour. If you have a strong stomach." Iverson marched his troopers indoors. Miles would have laughed, if he weren't screaming inside. He sighed, slipped from his perch, and followed them.

Miles's people came in a small personnel shuttle, swooping right into the concealed garage. He watched them on the monitor from Ryoval's study, and gave them directions how to find him. Quinn, Elena, Taura and Bel, all in half-armor. They came clanking into the study double-time, almost as impressively useless as the ImpSec crowd.

"Why the party clothes?" was his first weary question as they heaved into view. He should stand, and receive and return salutes and things, but Ryoval's station chair was incredibly comfortable and he was incredibly tired.

"Miles!" Quinn cried passionately.

With the sight of her concerned face he realized just how very angry he was, and guilty for it. Furiously angry because furiously afraid. *Where is Mark, damn you all?* "Captain Quinn," he put her on notice that this was duty-time before she could fling herself on him. She skidded to a halt in mid-fling, and came to a species of attention. The others piled up behind her.

"We were just coordinating with ImpSec for a raid on House Bharaputra," Quinn said breathlessly. "You've come back to yourself! You were cryo-amnesic—have you recovered? That Durona doctor said you would—"

"About ninety percent, I think. I'm still finding holes in my memory. Quinn—what *happened*?"

She looked slightly overwhelmed. "Since when? When you were killed—"

"Start from five days ago. When you came to the Durona Group."

"We came looking for you. *Found* you, after nearly four bleeding months!"

"You were stunned, Mark was taken, and Lilly Durona hustled me and my surgeon off to what she thought was going to be safety," Miles cued her to the focus he wanted.

"Oh, she was your *doctor*. I thought—never mind." Quinn bit back her emotions, pulled off her helmet and pushed back her hood, raked red-tipped fingers through her smashed curls, and began organizing the information into its essentials, combat-style. "We lost hours at the start. By the time Elena and Taura got another aircar, the snatchers were long gone. They searched, but no luck. When they got back to the Durona Group, Bel and I were just waking up. Lilly Durona insisted you were safe. I didn't believe her. We pulled out, and I contacted ImpSec. They started to pull in their people, who were scattered all over the planet looking for clues as to your whereabouts, and sent them to focus on Mark. More delays, while they worked through their pet theory that the kidnappers were Cetagandan bounty-hunters. And House Ryoval had about fifty different sites and facilities to check on, not including this one, which really was secret.

"Then Lilly Durona decided you were missing after all. Since it seemed more important to find you, we diverted all available forces to that. But we had fewer leads. We didn't even find the abandoned lightflyer for two days. And it yielded up *no* clues."

"Right. But you suspected Ryoval had Mark."

"But Ryoval wanted Admiral Naismith. We thought Ryoval would figure out he had the wrong man."

He ran his hands over his face. His head was aching. And so was his stomach. "Did you ever figure that Ryoval wouldn't *care*? In a few minutes, I want you to go down the corridor and look at the cell they kept him in. And smell it. I want you to look *closely*. In fact, go now. Sergeant Taura, stay."

Reluctantly, Quinn led Elena and Bel out. Miles leaned forward; Taura bent to hear.

"Taura, what happened? You're a Jacksonian. You know what Ryoval is, what this place is. How did you all lose sight of that?"

She shook her big head. "Captain Quinn thought Mark was a complete screw-up. After your death, she was so angry she could barely give him the time of day. And at first I agreed with her. But . . . I don't know. He tried so hard. The creche raid only failed by a hair. If we'd been faster, or if the shuttle defense perimeter had done their job, we would have brought it off, I think."

He grimaced in agreement. "There's no mercy for failures of timing in no-margin operations like that one was. Commanders can have no mercy either, or you might as well stay in orbit and feed your troops directly into the ship's waste disintegrators, and save steps." He paused. "Quinn will be a good commander someday."

"I think so, sir." Taura pulled off her helmet and hood, and stared around. "I kind of came to like the little schmuck,though. He *tried*. He tried and failed, but no one else tried at all. And he was so alone."

"Alone. Yes. Here. For five days."

"We really did think Ryoval would figure out he wasn't you."

"Maybe . . . maybe so." Some part of his mind clung to that hope himself. Maybe it hadn't been as bad as it looked, as bad as his galloping imagination supplied.

Quinn and company returned, looking universally grim.

"So," he said, "you've found me. Now maybe we can all focus on Mark. I've been all over this place in the last hours, and I haven't found a clue. Did the absconding staff take him along? Is he out wandering around in the desert somewhere, freezing? I've got six of Iverson's men looking outside with 'scopes, and another one checking the facility's disintegration records for fifty-plus kilo lumps of protein. And other bright ideas, folks?"

Elena came back from a peek in the next room. "Who do you figure did the honors on Ryoval?"

Miles opened his hands. "Don't know. He had hundreds of mortal enemies, after his career."

"He was killed by an unarmed person. A kick to the throat, then beaten to death somehow after he was down."

"I noticed that."

"You notice the tool kit?"

"Yeah."

"Miles, it was Mark."

"How could it have been? It had to have happened sometime last night. After what, five days of being worked over—and Mark's a little guy like me. I don't think it's physically possible."

"Mark's a little guy, but not like you," said Elena. "And he almost killed a man in Vorbarr Sultana with a kick to the throat."

"What?"

"He was *trained*, Miles. He was trained to take out your father, who is an even bigger man than Ryoval, and has years of combat experience."

"Yes, but I never believed—*when* was Mark in Vorbarr Sultana?"*Amazing, how being dead for two or three months will put you out of touch.* For the first time, his impulse to fling himself directly back into active-duty command status was checked. *A maniac with three-quarters of a memory and a habit of going into convulsions is just what we want in charge, sure. Not to mention the shortness of breath.*

"Oh, and about your father, I should mention—no, maybe that had better wait." Elena eyed him in worry.

"What about—" He was interrupted by a buzz from the comm link Iverson had given him as a courtesy. "Yes, Lieutenant?"

"Admiral Naismith, Baron Fell is here at the entrance. With a double-squad. He, ah . . . says he's here to collect his deceased half-brother's body, as next-of-kin."

Miles whistled soundlessly, and grinned. "Is he, now? Well. Tell you what. Let him come inside, with one bodyguard. And we'll talk. He may know something. Don't let his squad in yet, though."

"Do you think that's wise?"

How the hell should I know? "Sure."

In a few minutes, Baron Fell himself puffed in, escorted by one of Iverson's rental troopers and flanked by a big green-clad guard. Baron's Fell's round face was slightly pinker than usual with the exertion, otherwise he was the same plump, grandfatherly figure as ever, exuding the usual dangerously deceptive good cheer.

"Baron Fell," Miles nodded. "How good to see you again."

Fell nodded back. "Admiral. Yes, I imagine everything looks good to you just now. So, it really was you the Bharaputran sniper shot. Your clone-twin did an excellent job of pretending to be you, afterward, I must say, much to the confusion of an already very confused situation."

Argh! "Yes. And, ah, what brings you here?"

"Trade," stated Fell, Jacksonian short-hand for, *You first.*

Miles nodded. "The late Baron Ryoval had me brought me here in a lightflyer by two of his erstwhile bodyguards. We found things much as you see them. I, um, neutralized them at my first opportunity. How I came to be in their hands is a more complicated story." Meaning, *That's all you get till I get some.*

"There are some extraordinary rumors starting to circulate about my dear departed—he is departed, I trust?"

"Oh, yes. You can see in a moment."

"Thank you. My dear departed half-brother's death. I had one first-hand."

A former Ryoval employee from here fled directly to him as an informant. Right. "I hope his virtue was rewarded."

"It will be, as soon as I ascertain he was telling the truth."

"Well. Why don't you come look." He had to get up out of the station chair. He marshalled the effort with difficulty, and led the Baron into the living room, the House Fell bodyguard and the Dendarii following.

The big bodyguard shot a worried glance at Sergeant Taura, looming over him; she smiled back, her fangs gleaming. "Hi, there. You're kinda cute, you know?" she told him. He recoiled, and sidled closer to his master.

Fell hurried to the body, knelt by its right side, and held up the severed wrist. He hissed with disappointment. "Who has done this?"

"We don't know yet," said Miles. "That's how I found him."

"Exactly?" Fell shot him a sharp glance.

"Yes."

Fell traced the black holes across the corpse's forehead. "Whoever did this, knew what he was doing. I want to find the assassin."

"To . . . avenge your brother's death?" Elena asked cautiously.

"No. To offer him a *job*!" Fell laughed, a booming, jolly sound. "Do you realize how many people have been trying, for how many years, to accomplish this?"

"I've an idea," said Miles. "If you can help—"

In the next room, Ryoval's half-butchered comconsole chimed.

Fell looked up, eyes intent. "No one can call in here without the code-key," he stated, and heaved to his feet. Miles barely beat him back into the study, and slid into the station chair.

He activated the vid plate. "Yes?" And almost fell out of his seat again.

Mark's puffy face formed above the vid plate. He looked like he'd just come out of a shower, face scrubbed, hair wet and slicked back. He was wearing grey knits like Miles's. Blue bruises, going greenish-yellow around the edges, made what skin Miles could see look like a patchwork quilt, but both eyes were open and very bright. His ears were still on. "Ah," he said cheerfully, "there you are. I thought you might be. Have you figured out who you are yet?"

"Mark!" Miles almost tried to crawl through the vid image. "Are you all right? *Where are you?*"

"You have, I see. Good. I'm at Lilly Durona's. God, Miles. What a place. What a woman. She let me have a *bath*. She put my *skin* back on. She fixed my foot. She gave me a hypo of muscle-relaxant for my back. With her own hands, she performed medical services too intimate and disgusting to describe, but very badly needed, I assure you, and held my head while I screamed. Did I mention the bath? I love her, and I want to marry her."

All this was delivered with such deadpan enthusiasm, Miles could not tell if Mark was joking. "What are you *on*?" he asked suspiciously.

"Pain killers. Lots and lots of pain killers. Oh, it's wonderful!" He favored Miles with a weird broad grin. "But don't worry, my head is perfectly clear. It's just the bath. I was holding it together till she gave me the bath. It unmanned me. Do you know what a wonderful thing a bath is, when you're washing off—never mind."

"How did you get out of here, and back to the Durona Clinic?" Miles asked urgently.

"In Ryoval's lightflyer, of course. The code-key worked."

Behind Miles, Baron Fell drew in his breath. "Mark," he leaned into the vid pick up with a smile. "Would you put Lilly on a moment, please?"

"Ah, Baron Fell!" said Mark. "Good. I was going to call you next. I want to invite you to tea, here at Lilly's. We have a lot to talk about. You too, Miles. And bring *all* your friends." Mark gave him a sharply meaningful glance.

Quietly, Miles reached down and pressed the "alert" button on Iverson's comm link. "Why, Mark?"

"Because I need them. My own troops are much too tired for any more work today."

"Your troops?"

"Please do as I ask. Because I ask it. Because you *owe* me," Mark added, in a voice so low Miles had to strain to hear. Mark's eyes burned, a brief spark.

Fell muttered, "He used it. He has to know—" He leaned in again, and said to Mark, "Do you know what you have in ah, hand, Mark?"

"Oh, Baron. I know what I'm doing. I don't know why so many people have so much trouble believing that," Mark added in a tone of hurt complaint. "I know *exactly* what I'm doing." Then he laughed. It was a very disturbing laugh, edgy and too loud.

"Let me talk to Lilly," said Fell.

"No. You come here and talk to Lilly," said Mark petulantly. "Anyway, you want to talk to me." He nailed

Fell's eye with a direct look. "I promise you will find it profitable."

"I believe I do want to talk with you," murmured Fell. "Very well."

"Miles. You're there in Ryoval's study, where I was." Mark searched his face,for what Miles could not guess, but then Mark nodded quietly to himself, as if satisfied. "Is Elena there?"

"Yes . . ."

Elena leaned forward on Miles's other side. "What do you need, Mark?"

"I want to talk to you a moment. Armswoman. Privately. Would you clear the room of everyone else, please? Everyone."

"You can't," Miles began. ". . . Armswoman? Not—not liege-sworn? You can't be."

"Technically, I suppose she's not, now that you're alive again," said Mark. He smiled sadly. "But I want a service. My first and last request, Elena. *Privately.*"

Elena looked around. "Everybody out. Please, Miles. This is between Mark and me."

"Armswoman?" Miles muttered, allowing himself to be thrust back out into the corridor. "How can—" Elena shut the door on them all. Miles called Iverson to arrange transport, and other things. It was still a polite race with Fell, but it was clearly a race.

Elena emerged after a few minutes. Her face was strained. "You go on to Durona's. Mark has asked me to find something for him here. I'll catch up."

"Collect all the data you can for ImpSec while you're at it, then," said Miles, feeling bewildered by the pace of events. Somehow, he seemed not to be in charge here. "I'll tell Iverson to give you a free hand. But—Armswoman? Does that mean what I think it does? How can—"

"It means nothing, now. But I owe Mark. We all do. He killed Ryoval, you know."

"I was beginning to realize it had to be so. I just didn't see how."

"With both hands tied behind his back, he says. I believe him." She turned again toward Ryoval's suite.

"That was Mark?" Miles muttered, heading reluctantly in the opposite direction. He couldn't have acquired some other clone-brother while he was dead, could he? "It didn't sound like Mark. For one thing, he sounded like he was glad to see me. That's *Mark*?"

"Oh, yes," said Quinn. "That was Mark all right."

He quickened his pace. Even Taura had to lengthen her stride to keep up.

CHAPTER THIRTY

The Dendarii's little personnel shuttle kept pace with Baron Fell's larger drop shuttle; they arrived at the Durona Group's clinic almost simultaneously. A House Dyne shuttle belonging temporarily to ImpSec was waiting politely across the street from the entrance, by the little park. Just waiting.

As they were circling for a landing, Miles asked Quinn, who was piloting, "Elli—if we were flying along, in a lightflyer or an aircar or something, and I suddenly ordered you to crash it, would you?"

"Now?" asked Quinn, startled. The shuttle lurched.

"No! Not now. I mean theoretically. Obey, instantly, no questions asked."

"Well, sure, I suppose so. I'd ask questions afterward though. Probably with my hands wrapped around your neck."

"That's what I thought." Miles sat back, satisfied.

They rendezvoused with Baron Fell at the front entrance, where the gate guards prepared to code open a portal in the force screen. Fell frowned at the three Dendarii in their half-armor, Quinn and Bel and Taura, trailing Miles in his grey knits.

"This is my facility," Fell pointed out. His own pair of green-clad men eyed them without favor.

"These are my bodyguards," said Miles, "for whom I have a demonstrated need. Your force screen appears to have a malfunction."

"*He* was taken care of," said Fell grimly. "That won't happen again."

"Nevertheless." By way of concession, Miles jerked his thumb at the shuttle by the park. "My other friends can wait outside."

Fell frowned, thinking it over. "All right," he said at last. They followed him inside. Hawk met them, bowed to the Baron, and escorted them formally up through the series of lift tubes to Lilly Durona's penthouse.

The word for it, Miles thought, rising past the chromium railing, was "tableau." It was all arranged as perfectly as any stage setting.

Mark was the centerpiece. He sat back comfortably in Lilly Durona's own chair, his bandaged right foot propped on a silk pillow on the low round tea table. Surrounded by Duronas. Lilly herself, her white hair braided today like a crown wreathing her head, stood at Mark's right hand, leaning bemusedly on the upholstered chair back, smiling down beneficently upon the top of his head. Hawk took up position on Mark's left side. Dr. Chrys, Dr. Poppy, and Dr. Rose clustered admiringly around them. Dr. Chrys had a large fire-extinguisher by her knee. Rowan was not here. The window had been repaired.

On the center of the table sat a transparent cold-box. Within it lay a severed hand wearing a big silver ring set with what appeared to be a square black onyx.

Mark's physical appearance disturbed Miles. He had been braced to witness traumas of unnamed tortures, but Mark was covered neck to ankle in concealing grey knits like his own. Only the bruises on his face and the bandage on his foot hinted at the past five days' activities. But his face and body were strangely and unhealthily bloated, his stomach shockingly so, more than the stoutly-balanced figure he'd seen here in Dendarii uniform just a few days ago, and far beyond the almost-duplicate of himself he'd tried to rescue from the raid on the clone creche four months ago. In another person, Baron Fell for example, the near-obesity wouldn't have made him even blink, but Mark . . . could this be Miles himself, someday, if he slowed down? He had a sudden urge to swear off desserts. Elli was frankly staring, horrified and repelled.

Mark was smiling. A little control box lay under his right hand. His index finger kept pressure on a button.

Baron Fell saw the cold-box containing the hand, and started for it, crying, "Ah!"

"Stop," said Mark.

The Baron stopped, and cocked his head at him. "Yes?" he said warily.

"The object you are interested in is sitting in that sealed box on top of a small thermal grenade. Controlled," he lifted his hand with the remote in it, "by this dead-man switch. There is a second, positive-control switch in the hands of another person, outside of this room. Stun me or jump me, and it will go off. Frighten me, and my hand might slip. Tire me out, and my finger might give way. Annoy me enough, and I might just let go for the hell of it."

"The fact that you have made such an arrangement," said Fell slowly, "tells me you know the value of what you hold. You wouldn't. You're bluffing." He stared piercingly at Lilly.

"Don't try me," said Mark, still smiling. "After five days of your half-brother's hospitality, I'm in a *real* hostile mood. What's in that box is valuable to you. Not to me. However," he took a breath, "you do have some things that are valuable to me. Baron, let's Deal."

Fell sucked on his lower lip, and stared into Mark's glittering eyes. "I'll listen," he said at last.

Mark nodded. A couple of Duronas hurried to bring chairs for Baron Fell and Miles; the bodyguards arranged themselves standing. Fell's guards looked like they were thinking hard, watching the box and their master; the

Dendarii watched the green-clad guards in turn. Fell settled himself with a formal air, half-smiling, eyes intent.

"Tea?" inquired Lilly.

"Thank you," said the Baron. The two Durona children hurried out at her nod. The ritual was begun. Miles sat gingerly, and clamped his teeth together, hard. Whatever was going on here, he hadn't been briefed. It was clearly Mark's show. But he wasn't entirely sure Mark was sane, right now. Smart, yes. Sane, no. Baron Fell looked like he might be coming to the same conclusion, staring across the tea table at his self-appointed host.

The two opponents waited in silence for the tea to arrive, sizing each other up the while. The boy brought in the tray, and set it beside the gruesome box. The girl poured just two cups, Lilly's finest imported Japan Green, for Mark and the Baron, and offered tea cookies with them.

"No," said Mark to the cookies in a tone of loathing, "thank you." The Baron took two, and nibbled one. Mark started to lift his tea cup left-handed, but his hand was shaking too badly, and he set it hastily back in its saucer on the arm of Lilly's chair before it could spill and scald. The girl slipped silently up to him, and lifted it to his lips; he sipped and nodded gratefully, and she settled down with the cup by his left knee to serve again at his word. *He's hurt one hell of a lot worse than he's managing to look right now,* Miles realized, his stomach cold. The Baron looked at Mark's trembling left hand, and more dubiously at his right, and shifted uneasily.

"Baron Fell," Mark said, "I think you will agree with me that time is of the essence. Shall I begin?"

"Please do."

"In that cold-box," Mark nodded toward the severed hand, "is the key to House Ryoval. Ry Ryoval's, ah, secret decoder ring." Mark cackled loudly, bit back the laugh, and nodded to the girl for another sip of tea. He regained control of his voice and continued. "Embedded in the ring's crystal are all of the late Baron Ryoval's personal code-keys. Now, House Ryoval has a peculiar administrative structure. To say that Ry Ryoval was a paranoid control freak would be a gross understatement. But Ryoval is dead, leaving his scattered subordinates at scattered locations without their accustomed direction. When the rumors of his death reach them, who knows what they will do? You've seen one example.

"And a day or two from now, the vultures will be flying in from all over to tear at the carcass of House Ryoval. Possession is rather more than nine points of the non-existent law around here. House Bharaputra alone has obvious congruent interests in House Ryoval's wares. I'm sure you can think of others, Baron."

Fell nodded.

"But a man who had Ryoval's own code-keys in his hand *today* could be at a considerable advantage," Mark went on. "Particularly if he was well-supplied with personnel to provide material back-up. Without the tedious delays of cracking Ryoval's codes one by one, he could put himself in position to take immediate control of most or all of House Ryoval's current assets, from the top down instead of piecemeal. Add to that a well-known tie of blood to lend legitimacy to his claims, and I think most of the competition would sheer off without need for any expensive confrontation at all."

"My half-brother's code-key ring is not yours to trade," said Fell coldly.

"Oh, yes it is," said Mark. "I won it. I control it. I can destroy it. And," he licked his lips; the girl raised the teacup again, "I paid for it. You would not now be offered this exclusive—and it is still exclusive—opportunity if not for me."

The Baron gave a very tiny nod of concession. "Go on."

"What would you say the value of the Durona Group is, compared to the value of House Ryoval's current assets? Proportionally."

The Baron frowned. "One-twentieth. One-thirtieth, perhaps. House Ryoval has far more real estate. The, er, intellectual property value is harder to calculate. They specialize in rather different biological tasks."

"Leaving aside—or leaving behind—the real estate. House Ryoval is clearly enormously more valuable. Facilities, techs, slaves. Client list. Surgeons. Geneticists."

"I would have to say so."

"All right. Let's trade. I will give you House Ryoval in exchange for the Durona Group, plus value in a bearer-paid credit chit equal to ten percent of the assets of House Ryoval."

"Ten percent. An agent's fee," said Fell, looking at Lilly. Lilly smiled and said nothing.

"A mere agent's fee," Mark agreed. "Cheap at twice the price, which not-coincidentally is at least what you will lose without the advantages of Ry Ryoval's code-keys."

"And what would you do with all these ladies if you had them, ah, Mark?"

"What I wist. Wist, from *wistful.* I think I like the verb form better."

"Thinking of setting up in business here yourself? Baron Mark?"

Miles froze, appalled at this new vision.

"No," sighed Mark. "I wist to go home, Baron. I wist it real bad. I will give the Durona Group—to themselves. And you will let them go, free and unmolested and without pursuit, to wherever they—wist. Escobar, was it, Lilly?" He looked up at Lilly, who looked down at him and smiled, and nodded slightly.

"How very bizarre," murmured the Baron. "I think you are mad."

"Oh, Baron. You have no idea." A weird chuckle escaped Mark. If he was acting, it was the best acting job Miles had ever seen, not excluding his own wildest flights of scam.

The Baron sat back, and crossed his arms. His face grew stony with thought. Would he decide to try to jump them? Frantically, Miles began trying to calculate the military options of a sudden fire-fight, Dendarii on deck, ImpSec in orbit, himself and Mark at risk, *the sudden bright muzzle-flare of a projectile weapon*—oh God, what a mess—

"Ten percent," said the Baron at last, "*less* the value of the Durona Group."

"Who calculates the value of that intellectual property, Baron?"

"I do. And they evacuate immediately. All property, notes, files, and experiments in progress to be left intact."

Mark glanced up at Lilly: she bent and whispered in his ear. "The Durona Group shall have the right to duplicate technical files. And have the right to carry away personal items such as clothing and books."

The Baron stared thoughtfully at the ceiling. "They may carry away—what each one may carry. No more. They may *not* duplicate technical files. And their credit account remains, as it has always been, mine."

Lilly's brows drew down; another whispered conference behind her hand with Mark. He waved away some objection, and pointed orbit-ward. She finally nodded.

"Baron Fell," Mark took a deep breath, "it's a Deal."

"It's a Deal," Fell confirmed, watching him with a slight smile.

"My hand on it," Mark intoned. He snickered, turned his control box over, and twisted a knob on the underside. He set it back down on his chair-arm, and shook out his trembling fingers.

Fell stretched in his chair, shaking off the tension.

The guards relaxed. Miles almost fell into a puddle. *Cripes, what have we done?* At Lilly's direction, assorted Duronas scattered in a hurry.

"It's been very entertaining, doing business with you, Mark." Fell rose. "I don't know where home is for you, but if you ever decide you want a job, come see me again. I could use an agent like you, in my galactic affairs. Your sense of timing is . . . viciously elegant."

"Thank you, Baron," Mark nodded. "I'll keep it in mind, should some of my other options not work out."

"Your brother, too," Fell added as an afterthought. "Assuming his full recovery, of course. My troops could use a more active combat commander."

Miles cleared his throat. "House Fell's needs are mainly defensive. I prefer the Dendarii's more aggressive type of assignments," he said.

"There may be more assault work, upcoming," said Fell, his eyes going slightly distant.

"Thinking of conquering the world?" Miles inquired. *The Fell Empire?*

"The acquisition of House Ryoval will put House Fell in an interestingly unbalanced position," said Fell. "It would not be worthwhile to pursue a policy of unlimited expansion, and cope with all the opposition that must result, for a mere five or so years of rule. But if one were to live for another fifty years, say, one might find some most absorbing work for a military officer of capacity. . . ." Fell raised an inquiring brow at Miles.

"No. Thank you." *And I wish you all joy of each other.*

Mark gave Miles a slit-eyed, feline glance of amusement.

What an extraordinary solution Mark had wrought, Miles thought. What a Deal. Did a Jacksonian defy his upbringing by joining the side of the angels, rebel by becoming incorruptible? So it appeared. *I think my brother is more Jacksonian than he realizes. A renegade Jacksonian. The mind boggles.*

At Fell's gesture, one of his bodyguards carefully picked up the transparent box. Fell turned to Lilly.

"Well, old sister. You've had an interesting life."

"I still have it," smiled Lilly.

"For a while."

"Long enough for me, greedy little boy. So this is the end of the road. The last of our blood-pact. Who would have imagined it, all those years ago, when we were climbing out of Ryoval's sewers together?"

"Not I," said Fell. They embraced each other. "Goodbye, Lilly."

"Goodbye, Georie."

Fell turned to Mark. "The Deal is the Deal, and for my House. This is for me. For old times' sake." He stuck out a thick hand. "May I shake your hand, sir?"

Mark looked bewildered and suspicious; but Lilly nodded to him. He allowed his hand to be engulfed by Fell's.

"Thank you," said Georish Stauber sincerely. He jerked his chin at his guards, and vanished down the lift tube in their company.

"Do you think this Deal will hold?" Mark asked Lilly in a thin, worried voice.

"Long enough. For the next few days, Georish will be much too busy assimilating his new acquisition. It will absorb all his resources and then some. And after that, it will be too late. Regret, later, yes. Pursuit and vengeance, no. It's enough. It's all we need."

She stroked his hair fondly. "You just rest now. Have some more tea. We're going to be very busy for a while." She turned to gather up the young Duronas, "Robin! Violet! Come along quickly—" She hurried them into the interior of her quarters.

Mark slumped, looking very tired. He grimaced in bemusement at the teacup, switched it to his right hand, and swirled it thoughtfully before drinking.

Elli touched her half-armor helmet, listened, and vented a sudden bitter bark of laughter. "The ImpSec commander at Hargraves-Dyne Station is on the line. He says his reinforcements have arrived, and where should he send them?"

Miles and Mark looked at each other. Miles didn't know what Mark was thinking, but most of the responses that were leaping to his mind were violently obscene.

"Home," said Mark at last. "And they can give us a ride while they're at it."

"I have to get back to the Dendarii fleet," said Miles urgently. "Ah . . . where are they, Elli?"

"On their way from Illyrica to rendezvous off Escobar, but you, sir, are going nowhere near them till ImpSec Medical has cleared you for active duty," she said firmly. "The fleet is fine. You're not. Illyan would pin my ears back if I sent you anywhere but home right now. And then there's your father."

"What about my father?" Miles asked. Elena had started to say something—icy terror seized his chest. A kaleidoscopic vision of assassinations, mortal illnesses, and political plots all rolled together spun through his mind. Not to mention aircar accidents.

"He had a major coronary failure while I was there," said Mark. "They had him tied to a bed in ImpMil waiting for a heart transplant at the time I left. Actually, they should be doing the surgery right about now."

"You were there?" *What did you do to him?* Miles felt like he'd just had his magnetic poles reversed. "I have to get home!"

"That's what I just said," said Mark wearily. "Why d'you think we trooped all the way back here, but to drag you home? It wasn't for the free holiday at Ry Ryoval's health spa, let me tell you. Mother thinks I'm the next Vorkosigan heir. I can deal with Barrayar, I think, but I sure as hell can't deal with *that.*"

It was all too much, too fast. He sat down and tried to calm himself again, before he triggered another convulsion. That was just the sort of little physical weakness that could win one an immediate medical discharge from the Imperial Service, if one wasn't careful about who witnessed it. He had assumed the convulsions were a temporary snag in his recovery. What if they were a permanent effect? Oh, God. . . .

"I am going to lend Lilly my ship," said Mark, "since Baron Fell so-thoughtfully has stripped her of sufficient funds to buy thirty-six passages to Escobar."

"What ship?" asked Miles. *Not one of mine . . . !*

"The one Mother gave me. Lilly ought to be able to sell it at Escobar orbit for a tidy profit. I can pay back Mother and get Vorkosigan Surleau out of hock, and still have an impressive amount of pocket-change. I'd *like* to have my own yacht, someday, but I really couldn't use this one for a while."

What? What? What?

"I was just thinking," Mark went on, "that the Dendarii here could ride along with Lilly. Provide her with a little military protection in exchange for a free and fast ride back to the fleet. Save ImpSec the price of four commercial passages, too."

Four? Miles glanced at Bel, so very silent throughout, who met his eyes bleakly.

"And get everybody the hell out of here, as fast as possible," added Mark. "Before something else goes wrong."

"Amen!" muttered Quinn.

Rowan and Elli, on the same ship? Not to mention Taura. What if they all got together and compared notes? What if they fell into a feud? Worse, what if they struck up an alliance and colluded to partition him by treaty? North Miles and South Miles. . . . It wasn't, he swore, that he picked up so many women. Compared to Ivan, he was practically celibate. It was just that he never put any *down*. The accumulation could become downright embarrassing, over a long enough time-span. He needed . . . Lady Vorkosigan, to put an end to this nonsense. But even Elli the bold refused to volunteer for that duty.

"Yes," said Miles, "that works. Home. Captain Quinn, arrange Mark's and my transport with ImpSec. Sergeant Taura, would you please put yourself at Lilly Durona's disposal? The sooner we evacuate from here the better, I agree. And, um, Bel . . . would you stay and talk with me, please."

Quinn and Taura took the hint, and made themselves scarce. Mark . . . Mark was in on this, Miles decided. And anyway, he was a little afraid to ask Mark to get up. Afraid of what his movements would reveal. That flip phrase about Ry Ryoval's health spa was entirely too obvious an attempt to conceal . . . what?

"Sit, Bel," Miles nodded to Baron Fell's vacated chair. It put them in an equilateral triangle, he and Mark and Bel. Bel nodded and settled, its helmet in its lap and its hood pushed back. Miles thought of how he'd perceived Bel as a female in this room five days ago, prior to his memory cascade. His eye had always conveniently interpreted Bel as male, before, for some reason. Strange. There was a brief, uneasy silence.

Miles swallowed, and broke it. "I can't let you go back to command of the *Ariel*," he said.

"I know," said Bel.

"It would be bad for fleet discipline."

"I know," said Bel.

"It's . . . not just. If you had been a dishonest herm, and kept your mouth shut, and kept on pretending to have been fooled by Mark, no one would ever have known."

"I know," said Bel. It added after a moment, "I had to get my command back, in the emergency. I didn't think I could let Mark go on giving orders. Too dangerous."

"To those who'd followed you."

"Yes. And . . . I would have known," added Bel.

"Captain Thorne," Admiral Naismith sighed, "I must request your resignation."

"You have it, sir."

"Thank you." And that was done. So fast. He thought back over the scattered pictures in his head of Mark's raid. There were still pieces missing, he was pretty sure. But there had been deaths, too many deaths had made it irredeemable. "Do you know . . . what happened to Phillipi? She'd had a chance, I thought."

Mark and Bel exchanged a look. Bel answered. "She didn't make it."

"Oh. I'm sorry to hear that."

"Cryo-revival is a chancy business," sighed Bel. "We all undertake the risks, when we sign on."

Mark frowned. "It doesn't seem fair. Bel loses its career, and I get off free."

Bel stared a moment at Mark's beaten, bloated body, huddled down in Lilly's big chair; its brows rose slightly.

"What do you plan to do, Bel?" asked Miles carefully. "Go home to Beta Colony? You've talked about it."

"I don't know," said Bel. "It's not for lack of thinking. I've been thinking for weeks. I'm not sure I'd fit in at home anymore."

"I've been thinking myself," said Miles. "A prudent thought. It strikes me that certain parties on my side would be less paranoid about the idea of you running around the wormhole nexus with a head full of Barrayaran classified secrets if you were still on Illyan's payroll. An informant—perhaps an agent?"

"I don't have Elli Quinn's talents for scam," Bel said. "I was a shipmaster."

"Shipmasters get to some interesting places. They are in position to pick up all kinds of information."

Bel tilted its head. "I will . . . seriously consider it."

"I assume you don't want to cash out here on Jackson's Whole?"

Bel laughed outright. "No shit."

"Think about it, then, on the way back to Escobar. Talk to Quinn. Decide by the time you get there, and let her know."

Bel nodded, rose, and looked around Lilly Durona's quiet living room. "I'm not altogether sorry, you know," it said to Mark. "One way or another, we've pulled almost ninety people out of this stinking gravity well. Out of certain death or Jacksonian slavery. Not a bad score, for an aging Betan. You can bet I'll remember them, too, when I remember this."

"Thank you," whispered Mark.

Bel eyed Miles. "Do you remember the first time we ever saw each other?" it asked.

"Yes. I stunned you."

"You surely did." It walked over to his chair, and bent, and took his chin in its hand. "Hold still. I've been wanting to do this for years." It kissed him, long and quite thoroughly. Miles thought about appearances, thought about the ambiguity of it, thought about sudden death, thought the hell with it all, and kissed Bel back. Straightening again, Bel smiled.

Voices floated from the lift tube, some Durona directing, "Right upstairs, ma'am."

Elena Bothari-Jesek rose behind the chromium railing, and swept the room with her gaze. "Hello, Miles, I have to talk with Mark," she said, all in a breath. Her eyes were dark and worried. "Can we go somewhere?" she asked Mark.

" 'D rather not get up," Mark said. His voice was so tired it slurred.

"Quite. Miles, Bel, please go away," she said straightly.

Puzzled, Miles rose to his feet. He gave her a look of inquiry; her return look said, *Not now. Later.* He shrugged. "Come on, Bel. Let's go see if we can lend anyone a hand." He wanted to find Rowan. He watched them as he descended the lift tube with Bel. Elena pulled a chair around and sat across it backwards, her hands already opening in urgent remonstration. Mark was looking extremely saturnine.

Miles turned Bel over to Dr. Poppy, for liaison duty, and sought Rowan's suite. As he'd hoped, she was there, packing. Another young Durona sat and watched, looking a little bewildered. Miles recognized her at once.

"Lilly Junior! You made it. Rowan!"

Rowan's face lit with delight, and she hurried to embrace him. "Miles! Your name *is* Miles Naismith. I thought so! You've cascaded. When?"

"Well," he cleared his throat, "actually, it was back at Bharaputra's."

Her smile went a little flat. "Before I left. And you didn't tell me."

"Security," he offered warily.

"You didn't trust me."

This is Jackson's Whole. You said it yourself. "I was more worried about Vasa Luigi."

"I can see that, I suppose," Rowan sighed.

"When did you each get in?"

"I made it yesterday morning. Lilly came in last night. Smooth! I never dreamed you could get her out too!"

"The one escape was lock-and-key to the other. You got yourself out, which enabled Lilly to get herself out." He flashed a smile at Lilly Junior, who was watching them curiously. "I did nothing. That seems to be the story of my life, lately. But I do believe you'll all make it off-planet before Vasa Luigi and Lotus figure it out."

"We'll all have lifted before dusk. Listen!" She led him to her window. The Dendarii personnel shuttle, with Sergeant Taura piloting and about eight Duronas aboard, was lifting heavily from the courtyard of the walled compound. Point-women, going up to prepare the ship for the others to come.

"Escobar, Miles!" Rowan said enthusiastically. "We're all going to Escobar. Oh, Lilly, you're going to love it there!"

"Will you stay in a group when you get there?" Miles asked.

"At first, I think. Till it gets less strange for the others. Lilly will release us at her death. Baron Fell anticipates that, I think. Less competition for him, in the long run. I expect he'll have the top people stripped from House Ryoval and installed here by tomorrow morning."

Miles walked around the room, and noticed a familiar little remote box on the sofa-arm. "Ah! It was you who had the other control to the thermal grenade! I might have known. So you were listening in. I wasn't sure if Mark was bluffing."

"Mark wasn't bluffing about anything," she stated with certainty.

"Were you here, when he came in?"

"Yes. It was a little before dawn this morning. He came staggering in from a lightflyer wearing the most *peculiar* costume, and demanding to speak with Lilly."

Miles raised his brows at the image. "What did the gate guards say?"

"They said *Yes, sir.* He had an aura . . . I don't know how to describe it. Except . . . I could picture large thugs in dark alleyways scrambling to get out of his way. Your clone-twin is a *formidable* young man."

Miles blinked.

"Lilly and Chrys took him off to the clinic on a float-pallet, and I didn't see him after that. Then the orders started flying." She paused. "So. Will you be going back to your Dendarii Mercenaries, then?"

"Yes. After some R&R, I guess."

"Not . . . settling down. After that close call."

"I confess, the sight of projectile-weapons gives me a new and unpleasant twitch, but—I hope I won't be cashing out of the Dendarii for a long time yet. Um . . . these convulsions I've been having. Will they go away?"

"They should. Cryo-revival is always chancy. So, you . . . don't picture yourself retiring. To Escobar, say."

"We visit Escobar now and then, for fleet repairs. And personnel repairs. It's a major nexus intersection. We may cross paths again."

"Not the same way we first met, I trust." Rowan smiled.

"Let me tell you, if I ever *do* need cryo-revival again, I'll leave orders to look you up." He hesitated. *I need my Lady Vorkosigan, to put an end to this wandering. . . .* Could Rowan be it? The thirty-five sisters-in-law would be a distant drawback, safely far away on Escobar. "What would you think of the planet Barrayar, as a place to live and work?" he inquired cautiously.

Her nose wrinkled. "That backward pit? Why?"

"I . . . have some interests there. In fact, it's where I'm planning to retire. It's a very beautiful place, really. And underpopulated. They encourage, um . . . children." He was skirting dangerously close to breaking his cover, the strained identity he'd risked so much lately to retain. "And there'd be lots of work for a galactic-trained physician."

"I'll bet. But I've been a slave all my life. Why would I choose to be a subject, when I could choose to be a *citizen*?" She smiled wryly, and came to him, and twined her arms around his shoulders. "Those five days we were locked up together at Vasa Luigi's—that wasn't an effect of the imprisonment, was it. That's the way you really *are*, when you're well."

"Pretty much," he admitted.

"I'd always wondered what adult hyperactives did for a living. Running several thousand troops would just about absorb your energies, wouldn't it?"

"Yes," he sighed.

"I think I'll always love you, some. But living with you full-time would drive me crazy. You are the most incredibly domineering person I think I've ever met."

"You're supposed to fight back," he explained. "I rely on—" he couldn't say *Elli*, or worse, *all my women*, "my partner fighting back. Otherwise, I couldn't relax and be myself."

Right. Too much togetherness *had* destroyed their love, or at least her illusions. The Barrayaran system of using go-betweens to make marital arrangements was beginning to look better all the time. Maybe it would be best to get safely married first, and then get to know each other. By the time his bride figured him out, it would be too late for her to back out. He sighed, and smiled, and gave Rowan an exaggerated, courtly bow. "I shall be pleased to visit you on Escobar, milady."

"That would be joust perfect, sir," she returned, deadpan.

"Ow!" Dammit, she could be the one, she underestimated herself—

Lilly Junior, sitting on the sofa watching all this with fascination, coughed. Miles glanced at her, and thought about her account of her time with the Dendarii.

"Does Mark know you're here, Lilly?" he asked.

"I don't know. I've been with Rowan."

"The last time Mark saw you, you were going back with Vasa Luigi. I . . . think he'd like to know you changed your mind."

"He tried to talk me into staying on the ship. He didn't talk so well as you," she admitted.

"He made this all happen. He bought your passage out of here." And Miles wasn't sure he wanted to think about the coin. "I just trailed along. Come on. At least say hello, goodbye, and thank you. It will cost you nothing, and I suspect it would mean something to him."

Reluctantly, she rose, and allowed him to tow her out. Rowan gave them a nod of approval, and returned to her hasty packing.

CHAPTER THIRTY-ONE

"Did you find them?" Lord Mark asked.

"Yes," said Bothari-Jesek tightly.

"Did you destroy them?"

"Yes."

Mark flushed, and leaned his head back against Lilly's chair, feeling the weight of gravity. He sighed. "You looked at them. I told you not to."

"I had to, to be sure I was getting the right ones."

"No, you didn't. You could simply have destroyed them all."

"That's what I finally did. I started to look. Then I turned off the sound. Then I put them on fast-forward. Then I started just spot-checking."

"I wish you hadn't."

"*I* wish I hadn't. Mark, there were hundreds of hours of those holovids. I couldn't believe there was so much."

"Actually, there were only about fifty hours. Or maybe it was fifty years. But there were multiple simultaneous recordings. I could always see a holovid pick-up hovering, out of the corner of my eye, no matter what was going on. I don't know if Ryoval made them to study and analyze, or just to enjoy. A bit of both, I guess. His powers of analysis were appalling."

"I . . . don't understand some of what I saw."

"Would you like me to explain it to you?"

"No."

"Good."

"I can understand why you'd want them destroyed. Out of context . . . they would have been a horrible lever for blackmail. If you want to swear me to secrecy, I'll vow anything."

"That's not why. I have no intention of keeping any of this a secret. Nobody is ever going to get a handle on me again. Pull my secret strings ever again. In general outline, you can tell the whole wormhole nexus, for all I care. But—if ImpSec got hold of those holovid recordings, they would end up in Illyan's hands. And he would not be able to keep them from the Count, or the Countess either, though I'm sure he'd try. Or, eventually, Miles. Can you imagine the Count or the Countess or Miles watching that shit?"

She drew in her breath between her teeth. "I begin to see."

"Think about it. I have."

"Lieutenant Iverson was furious, when he broke in and found the melted casings. He's going to send complaints up through channels."

"Let him. If ImpSec cares to air any complaints about me or mine, I will air my complaints about them. Like, where the hell were they for the last five days. I will have no compunction nor mercy about calling in that debt on anyone from Illyan down. Cross *me*, will they . . ." He trailed off in a hostile mutter.

Her face was greenish-white. "I'm . . . so sorry, Mark." Her hand touched his, hesitantly.

He seized her wrist, held it hard. Her nostrils flared, but she did not wince. He sat up, or tried to. "Don't you *dare* pity me. I *won*. Save your sympathy for Baron Ryoval, if you must. I took him. Suckered him. I beat him at his own game, on his own ground. I will not allow you to turn my victory into defeat for the sake of your damned . . . *feelings*." He released her wrist; she rubbed it, watching him levelly. "That's the thing of it. I can shed Ryoval, if they'll let me. But if they know too much—if they had those damned vids—they'd never be able to leave it alone, ever. Their guilt would keep them coming back to it, and they would keep *me* coming back to it. I don't want to have to fight Ry Ryoval in my head, or in their heads, for the rest of my life. He's dead, I'm not, it's enough."

He paused, snorted. "And you have to admit, it would be particularly bad for Miles."

"Oh, yes," Bothari-Jesek breathed agreement.

Outside, the Dendarii personnel shuttle, with Sergeant Taura piloting, lifted the first load of Duronas to Mark's yacht in orbit. He paused to watch it rise from sight. *Yes. Go, go, go. Get out of this hole, you, me, all of us clones. Forever. Go be human too, if you can. If I can.*

Bothari-Jesek looked back at him and said, "They'll insist on a physical exam, you know."

"Yeah, they'll see some. I can't conceal the beatings, and God knows I can't conceal the force-feedings—grotesque, weren't they?"

She swallowed, and nodded. "I thought you were going to—oh, never mind."

"Right. I told you not to look. But the longer I can avoid examination by a competent ImpSec doctor, the vaguer I can be about all the rest."

"You have to be treated, surely."

"Lilly Durona has done an excellent job. And by my request, the only record is in her head. I should be able to slide right by."

"Don't try to avoid it altogether," Bothari-Jesek advised. "The Countess would spot that even if no one else did. And I can't believe you don't need . . . something more. Not physically."

"Oh, Elena. If there's one thing I've learned in the past week, it's just how badly cross-wired I really am, down in the bottom of my brain. The worst thing I met in Ryoval's basement was the monster in the mirror, Ryoval's psychic mirror. My pet monster, the four-headed one. Demonstrably, worse even than Ryoval himself. Stronger. Quicker. Slyer." He bit his tongue, aware that he was starting to say far too much, aware that he sounded like he was edging into dementia. He didn't think he was edging into dementia. He suspected he was edging into sanity, the long way around. The hard way. "I know what I'm doing. On some level, I know exactly what I'm doing."

"In a couple of the vids—you seemed to be fooling Ryoval with a fake split personality. Talking to yourself . . . ?"

"I could never have fooled Ryoval with a fake anything. He was in this trade for decades, mucking about in the bottoms of people's brains. But my personality didn't exactly split. More like it . . . inverted." Nothing could be called split, that felt so profoundly whole. "It wasn't something I decided to do. It was just something I *did*."

She was looking at him with extreme worry. He had to laugh out loud. But the effect of his good cheer was apparently not so reassuring to her as he might have desired.

"You have to understand," he told her. "Sometimes, insanity is not a tragedy. Sometimes, it's a strategy for survival. Sometimes . . . it's a triumph." He hesitated. "Do you know what a black-gang is?"

Mutely, she shook her head.

"Something I picked up in a museum in London, once. Way back in the Nineteenth and Twentieth Centuries, on Earth, they used to have ships that sailed across the tops of the oceans, that were powered by steam engines. The heat for the steam engines came from great coal fires in the bellies of the ships. And they had to have these suckers down there to stoke the coal into the furnaces. Down in the filth and the heat and the sweat and the stink. The coal made them black, so they were called the black-gang. And the officers and fine ladies up above would have nothing to do with these poor grotty thugs, socially. But without them, nothing moved. Nothing burned. Nothing lived. No steam. The black-gang. Unsung heroes. Ugly lower-class fellows."

Now she thought he was babbling for sure. The panegyric of fierce loyalty for his black gang that he wanted to sing into her ear was . . . probably not a good idea, just now. *Yeah, and nobody loves me,* Gorge whispered plaintively. *You'd better get used to it.*

"Never mind." He smiled instead. "But I can tell you, Galen looks . . . pretty small, after Ryoval. And Ryoval, I *beat.* In a strange sense, I feel very free, right now. And I intend to stay that way."

"You appear to me to be . . . excuse me . . . a little manic, right now, Mark. In Miles, this would be normal. Well, usual. But eventually, he tops out, and finally he bottoms out. I think you need to watch out for this pattern, you may share it with him."

"Are you saying it's a mood swing on a bungee cord?"

A short laugh puffed from her lips despite herself. "Yes."

"I'll beware of the perigee."

"Hm, yes. Though it's the apogee where everybody else has to duck and run, usually."

"I'm also on, well, several painkillers and stimulants, right now," he mentioned. "Or I would never have made it through the last couple of hours. I'm afraid some of them are starting to wear off." Good. That would account to her for some of his babble, perhaps, and had the advantage of being true.

"Do you want me to get Lilly Durona?"

"No. I just want to sit here. And not move."

"I think that might be a good idea." Elena swung out of her chair, and picked up her helmet.

"I know what I want to be when I grow up, now, though," he offered to her suddenly. She paused, and raised her brows.

"I want to be an ImpSec analyst. Civilian. One who doesn't send his people to the wrong place, or five days late. Or improperly prepared. I want to sit in a cubicle all day long, surrounded by a fortress, and get it *right.*" He waited for her to laugh at him.

Instead, to his surprise, she nodded seriously. "Speaking as the one out on the sharp end of the ImpSec stick, I would be delighted."

She gave him a half-salute, and turned away. He puzzled over the look in her eyes, as she descended out of sight down the lift-tube. It wasn't love. It wasn't fear.

Oh. So that's what respect looks like. Oh.

I could get used to that.

As Mark had declared to Elena, he just sat for a time, staring out the window. He was going to have to move sooner or later. Maybe he could use the excuse of his broken foot to inveigle a float-chair. Lilly had promised him that her stimulants would buy him six hours of coherence, after which the metabolic bill would be delivered by hulking bio-thugs with spiked clubs, virtual repo-men for his neurotransmitter debt. He wondered if the absurd dreamy image was the first sign of the approaching biochemical breakdown. He prayed he'd hold out at least till he was safely in the ImpSec shuttle. *Oh, Brother. Carry me home.*

Voices echoed up the lift tube. Miles appeared, with a Durona trailing along after him. He was skeletally thin and ghostly pale, in his Durona-issued grey suit. The two of them seemed to be on some kind of growth-reciprocal. If he could magically transfer all the kilos Ryoval had foisted on him the last week directly to Miles, they would both look much better, Mark decided. But if he kept growing fatter, would Miles attenuate altogether, and vanish? Unsettling vision. *It's the drugs, boy, it's the drugs.*

"Oh, good," said Miles, "Elena said you were still up

here." With the cheerful air of a magician presenting a particularly good trick, he urged the young woman to step forward. "Do you recognize her?"

"It's a Durona, Miles," said Mark, in a gentle, weary tone. "I'm going to see them in my dreams." He paused. "Is this a trick question?" Then he sat up, shocked by recognition. You *could* tell clones apart—"It's her!"

"Just so," smiled Miles, pleased. "We smuggled her out from Bharaputra's, Rowan and I. She's going to go to Escobar with her sisters."

"Ah!" Mark settled back. "Ah. Oh. Good." Hesitantly, he rubbed his forehead. *Take back your coup, Vasa Luigi!* "I didn't think you were interested in rescuing clones, Miles."

Miles winced visibly. "You inspired me."

Er. He hadn't meant that as a reference to Ryoval's. Clearly, Miles had dragged the reluctant girl up here in a bid to make Mark feel better. Less clearly to Miles, though like crystal to himself, was an element of subtle rivalry. For the first time in his life, Miles was feeling the hot breath of fraternal competition on the back of his neck. *Do I make you uneasy? Ha! Get used to it, boy. I've lived with it for twenty-two years.* Miles had spoken of Mark as "my brother" in the same tone he'd use for "my boots," or maybe, "my horse." Or—give credit, now—"my child." A certain smug paternalism. Miles hadn't been expecting an equal with an agenda of his own. Suddenly, Mark realized he had a delightful new hobby, one that would provide entertainment for years to come. *God, I'm going to enjoy being your brother.*

"Yes," Mark said cheerily, "you can do it too. I knew you could, if you only tried." He laughed. To his dismay, it turned into a sob in his throat. He choked off both. He didn't dare laugh, or express any other emotion, right now. His control was much too thin. "I'm very glad," he stated, as neutrally as he could.

Miles, whose eye had caught the whole play, nodded. "Good," he stated, equally neutrally.

Bless you, Brother. Miles understood this, at least, what it was like to teeter on the raw edge.

They both glanced at the Durona girl. She moved uneasily, under the weight of this double expectation. She flipped back her hair, mustered words. "When I first saw you," she said to Mark, "I didn't like you much."

When you first saw me, I didn't like me much either. "Yes?" he encouraged.

"I still think you're funny-looking. Even funnier-looking than the other one," she nodded at Miles, who smiled blandly. "But . . . but . . ." Words failed her. As cautiously and hesitantly as a wild bird at a feeder, she ventured nearer to him, bent, and kissed him on one puffy cheek. Then like a bird, she fled.

"Hm," said Miles, watching her swoop back down the lift-tube. "I was hoping for a little more enthusiastic a demonstration of gratitude."

"You'll learn," said Mark equably. He touched his cheek, and smiled.

"If you think that's ingratitude, try ImpSec," Miles advised glumly. " 'You lost *how much* equipment?' "

Mark cocked an eyebrow. "An Illyan-quote?"

"Oh, you've met him?"

"Oh, yes."

"I wish I could have been there."

"I wish you could have been there too," said Mark sincerely. "He was . . . acerb."

"I'll bet. He does acerb almost better than anyone I know, except for my mother when she's lost her temper, which thank God is not very often."

"You should have seen her annihilate him, then," said Mark. "Clash of the titans. I think you'd have enjoyed it. I did."

"Oh? We have a lot to talk about, it seems—"

For the first time, Mark realized, they did. His heart lifted. Unfortunately, so did another interruption, via the tube. A man in House Fell livery looked over the chromium railing, saw him, and gave him a semi-salute. "I have a courier delivery for an individual named Mark," he said.

"I'm Mark."

The courier trod over to him, flashed a confirming scanner over his face, opened a thin case chained to his wrist, and handed him a card in an unmarked envelope. "Baron Fell's compliments, sir, and he trusts this will help speed you on your way."

The credit chit. Ah, ha! And a very broad hint along with it. "My compliments to Baron Fell, and . . . and . . . what do we want to say to Baron Fell, Miles?"

"I'd keep it down to *Thank you*, I think," Miles advised. "At least till we're far, far away."

"Tell him thank you," Mark told the courier, who nodded and marched out again the way he had come in.

Mark eyed Lilly's comconsole, in the corner of the room. It seemed a very long way off. He pointed. "Could you, um, bring me the remote-reader off that comconsole over there, Miles?"

"Sure." Miles retrieved and handed him the board.

"I predict," said Mark, waving the card around, "that I will be seriously short-changed, but not quite enough so that I would risk going back to Fell and arguing about it." He inserted the card into the read-slot, and smiled. "Spot-on."

"What did you get?" asked Miles, craning his neck.

"Well, that's a very personal question," said Mark. Miles uncraned guiltily. "Trade. Were you sleeping with that surgeon?"

Miles bit his lip, curiosity obviously struggling with his gentlemanly manners. Mark watched with interest to see how it would come out. Personally, he'd bet on curiosity.

Miles took a rather deep breath. "Yes," he said at last.

Thought so. Their good fortune, Mark decided, was divided exactly fifty-fifty; Miles got the good luck, and he got the rest. But not this time. "Two million."

Miles whistled. "Two million Imperial marks? Impressive!"

"No, no. Two million Betan dollars. What, about eight million marks, I guess, isn't it? Or is it closer to ten. Depends on the current exchange rate, I guess. It's not nearly ten percent of the value of House Ryoval, anyway. More like two percent," Mark calculated aloud. And had the rare and utter joy of rendering Miles Vorkosigan speechless.

"What are you going to do with it all?" Miles whispered, after about a minute.

"Invest," said Mark fiercely. "Barrayar has an expanding economy, doesn't it?" He paused. "First, though, I'm going to kick back one million to ImpSec, for their services the last four months."

"Nobody *gives* money to ImpSec!"

"Why not? Look at your mercenary operations, for instance. Isn't being a mercenary supposed to be profitable? The Dendarii Fleet could be a veritable cash cow for ImpSec, if it were run right."

"They take out their profit in political consequences," said Miles firmly. "Though—if you really do it, I want to be there. To see the look on Illyan's face."

"If you're good, I'll let you come along. Oh, I'm really going to do it, all right. There are some debts I cannot ever repay," he thought of Phillipi, and the others. "But I intend to pay the ones I can, in their honor. Though you can bet I'll keep the rest. I should be able to double it again in about six years, and be back to where I started. Or better. It's a lot easier to make two million out of one million than it is to make two out of one, if I understand the game correctly. I'll study up."

Miles stared at him in fascination. "I bet you will."

"Do you have any idea how desperate I was, when I started on that raid? How scared? I intend to have a value no one can ignore again, even if it's only measured in money. Money is a kind of power almost anyone can have. You don't even need a Vor in front of your name." He smiled faintly. "Maybe, after a while, I'll get a place of my own. Like Ivan's. After all, it would look funny if I was still living in my parents' house at the age of, say, twenty-eight."

And that was probably enough Miles-baiting for one day. Miles would, demonstrably, lay down his life for his brother, but he did have a notable tendency to try to subsume the people around him into extensions of his own personality. *I am not your annex. I am your brother.* Yes. Mark rather fancied they were both going to be able to keep track of that, now. He slumped wearily, but happily.

"I do believe," said Miles, still looking nicely stunned, "you are the first Vorkosigan to make a profit in a business venture for five generations. Welcome to the family."

Mark nodded. They were both silent for a time.

"It's not the answer," Mark sighed finally. He nodded around at the Durona Group's clinic, and by implication to all of Jackson's Whole. "This piecemeal clone-rescue business. Even if I blew Vasa Luigi entirely away, someone else would just take up where House Bharaputra left off."

"Yes," Miles agreed. "The true answer has to be medical-technical. Somebody has to come up with a better, safer life-extension trick. Which I believe somebody will. A lot of people have to be working on it, in a lot of places. The brain-transplant technique is too risky to compete. It must end, someday soon."

"I . . . don't have any talents in the medical-technical direction," said Mark. "In the meantime, the butchery goes on. I have to take another pass at the problem before someday. Somehow."

"But not today," Miles said firmly.

"No." Out the window, he saw a personnel shuttle descending into the Duronas' compound. But it wasn't the Dendarii one returning, yet. He nodded. "Is that by chance our transport?"

"I believe so," said Miles, going to the window and looking down. "Yes."

And then there was no more time. While Miles was gone checking on the shuttle, and couldn't watch, Mark rounded up half a dozen Duronas to help pry his stiff, bent, half-paralyzed body out of Lilly's chair and lay him on a float-pallet. His crooked hands shook uncontrollably, till Lilly pursed her lips and gave him another hypospray of something wonderful. He was perfectly content to be carried out horizontally. His broken foot was a socially acceptable reason not to be able to walk. He looked nicely invalidish, with his leg propped up conspicuously, the better to persuade the ImpSec fellows to carry him to his bunk, when they arrived topside.

For the first time in his life, he was going home.

CHAPTER THIRTY-TWO

Miles eyed the old mirror in the antechamber to the library of Vorkosigan House, the one that had been brought into the family by General Count Piotr's mother as part of her dowry, its frame ornately carved by some Vorrutyer family retainer. He was alone in the room, with no one to observe him. He slipped up to the glass, and stared uneasily at his own reflection.

The scarlet tunic of the Imperial parade red-and-blues did not exactly flatter his too-pale complexion at the best of times. He preferred the more austere elegance of dress greens. The gold-encrusted high collar was not, unfortunately, quite high enough to hide the twin red scars on either side of his neck. The cuts would turn white and recede eventually, but in the meantime they drew the eye. He considered how he was going to explain them. *Dueling scars. I lost.* Or maybe, *Love bites.* That was closer. He traced them with a fingertip, turning his head from side to side. Unlike the terrible memory of the needle-grenade, he did not remember acquiring these. That was far more disturbing than the vision of his death, that such important things could happen to him and he didn't, couldn't, remember.

Well, he was known to have medical problems, and the scars were almost neat enough to look medical. Maybe people would let them pass without comment. He stepped back from the mirror to take in the general look. His uniform still had a tendency to hang on him, despite his mother's valiant attempts to make him eat more these last few weeks since they'd arrived home. She'd finally turned the problem over to Mark, as if yielding to superior expertise. Mark had grinned with amusement, and then he had proceeded to harass Miles without mercy. Actually, the attentions were working. Miles did feel better. Stronger.

The Winterfair Ball was sufficiently social, without formal governmental or military obligation, that he was able to leave the dual dress sword set at home. Ivan would be wearing his, but Ivan had the altitude to carry it off. At Miles's height, the long sword of the pair looked damned silly, practically dragging on the ground, not to mention the problem of tripping over it or banging his dance partner in the shins.

Footsteps sounded in the archway; Miles turned quickly, and swung one booted leg up and leaned against a chair-arm, pretending to have been ignoring the narcissistic attractions of his reflection.

"Ah, there you are." Mark wandered in to join him, pausing to study himself briefly in the mirror, turning to check the fit of his clothing. His clothing fit very well indeed. Mark had acquired the name of Gregor's tailor, a closely-guarded ImpSec secret, by the simple expedient of calling Gregor and asking him. The boxy loose cut of the jacket and trousers was aggressively civilian, but somehow very sharp. The colors honored Winterfair, sort of; a green so dark as to be almost black was trimmed with a red so dark as to be almost black. The effect was somewhere between festive and sinister, like a small, cheerful bomb.

Miles thought of that very odd moment in Rowan's lightflyer, when he'd been temporarily convinced he was Mark. How terrifying it had been to be Mark, how utterly isolated. The memory of that desolation made him shiver. *Is that how he feels all the time?*

Well, no more. Not if I have anything to say about it.

"Looks good," Miles offered.

"Yeah." Mark grinned. "You're not so bad yourself. Not as cadaverous, quite."

"You're improving too. Slowly." Actually, Mark was, Miles thought. The most alarming distortions of whatever horrors Ryoval had inflicted upon Mark, and which he resolutely refused to talk about, had gradually passed off. A solid residue of flesh yet lingered, however. "What weight are you finally going to choose?" Miles asked curiously.

"You're looking at it. Or I wouldn't have invested the fortune in the wardrobe."

"Er. Are you comfortable?" Miles inquired uncomfortably.

Mark's eyes glinted. "Yes, thank you. The thought that a one-eyed sniper, at a range of two kilometers at midnight in a thunderstorm, could not *possibly* mistake me for you, is very comfortable indeed."

"Oh. Well. Yes, there is that, I suppose."

"Keep exercising," Mark advised him cordially. "It's good for you." Mark sat down and put his feet up.

"Mark?" the Countess's voice called from the foyer. "Miles?"

"In here," said Miles.

"Ah," she said, sweeping into the antechamber. "There you both are." She smiled at them with a greedy maternal gloat, looking most satisfied. Miles could not help feeling warmed, as if some last lingering ice chip inside from the cryo-freezing finally thawed, steaming gently. The Countess wore a new dress, more ornate than her usual style, in green and silver, with ruffs and tucks and a train, a celebration of fabric. It did not make her stiff, though—it wouldn't dare. The Countess was never intimidated by her clothing. Quite the reverse. Her eyes outshone the silver embroidery.

"Father waiting on us?" Miles inquired.

"He'll be down momentarily. I'm insisting we leave

promptly at midnight. You two can stay longer if you wish, of course. He'll overdo, I predict, proving to the hyenas he's too tough for them to jump, even when the hyenas aren't circling any more. A lifetime of reflex. Try and focus his attention on the District, Miles. It will drive poor Prime Minister Racozy to distraction to feel Aral is looking over his shoulder. We really need to get out of the capital, down to Hassadar, after Winterfair."

Miles, who had a very clear idea just how much recovery chest surgery took, said, "I think you'll be able to persuade him."

"Please throw your vote in. I know he can't fool you, and he knows it too. Ah—just what can I expect tonight, medically speaking?"

"He'll dance twice, once to prove he can do it, and the second time to prove the first wasn't a fluke. After that you'll have no trouble at all persuading him to sit down," Miles predicted with confidence. "Go ahead and play mother hen, and he can pretend he's stopping to please you, and not because he's about to fall over. Hassadar strikes me as a very good plan."

"Yes. Barrayar does not quite know what to do with *retired* strong men. Traditionally, they are decently deceased, and not hanging around to pass comments on their successors. Aral may be something of a first. Though Gregor has had the most horrifying idea."

"Oh?"

"He's muttering about the Vice-royalty of Sergyar, as a post for Aral, when he is fully recovered. The present viceroy has been begging to come home, it seems. Whining, actually. A more thankless task than colonial governor I cannot imagine. An honest man gets ground to powder, trying to play interface between two sets of conflicting needs, the home government above and the colonists below. Anything you can do to disabuse Gregor of this notion, I would greatly appreciate."

"Oh, I don't know," Miles's brows rose thoughtfully. "I mean—what a retirement project. A whole planet to play with. Sergyar. And didn't you discover it yourself, back when you were a Betan Astronomical Survey captain?"

"Indeed. If the Barrayaran military expedition hadn't been ahead of us, Sergyar would be a Betan daughter-colony right now. And much better managed, believe me. It really needs someone to take it in hand. The ecological issues alone are crying for an injection of intelligence—I mean, take that worm plague. A little Betan-style prudence could have . . . well. They figured it out eventually, I guess."

Miles and Mark looked at each other. It wasn't telepathy. But the thought that perhaps Aral Vorkosigan wasn't the only over-energetic aging expert Gregor might be glad to export from his capital was surely being shared between them, right this second.

Mark's brows drew down. "How soon might this be, ma'am?"

"Oh, not for at least a year."

"Ah." Mark brightened.

Armsman Pym stuck his head around the archway. "Ready, milady," he reported.

They all herded into the black-and-white paved hall, to find the Count standing at the foot of the curved stairs. He watched them with delight as they trooped into his view. The Count had lost weight in his medical ordeal too, but it only made him look more fit, in his red-and-blues. He managed uniform and sword-set with unconscious ease. In three hours, he'd be drooping, Miles gauged, but by then he'd have made a lasting first impression on his many observers, on this his first formal outing with his new heart. His color was excellent, his gaze as knife-sharp as ever. But there was no dark at all in his hair anymore. Aside from that, you really might think he could live forever.

Except Miles didn't think that anymore. It had scared the hell out of him, retroactively, this whole cardiac episode. Not that his father must die someday, perhaps before him—that was the proper order of things, and Miles could not wish it upon the Count for it to be the other way around—but that Miles might not be here when it happened. When he was needed. Might be off indulging himself with the Dendarii Mercenaries, say, and not get the word for weeks. *Too late.*

Being both in uniform, the Lieutenant saluted his father the Admiral now with the usual tinge of irony with which they commonly exchanged such military courtesies. Miles would rather have embraced him, but it would look odd.

To hell with what it looked like. He walked over and hugged his father.

"Hey, boy, hey," said the Count, surprised and pleased. "It's not that bad, really." He embraced Miles in return. The Count stood back and looked them all over, his elegant wife, his—two, now—sons. Smiling as smugly as any rich man could, he opened his arms as if to embrace them all, briefly and almost shyly. "Are the Vorkosigans ready to storm the Winterfair Ball, then? Dear Captain, I predict they will surrender to you in droves. How's your foot, Mark?"

Mark stuck out his right shoe, and wriggled it. "Fit to be trod upon by any Vor maiden up a hundred kilos, sir. Steel toe caps, underneath," he added to Miles, aside. "I'm taking no chances."

The Countess attached herself to her husband's arm. "Lead on, love. Vorkosigans Victorious."

Vorkosigans Convalescent, was more like it, Miles reflected, following. *But you should see what the other guys look like.*

Not to Miles's surprise, practically the first person the Vorkosigans' party met upon entering the Imperial

Residence was Simon Illyan. Illyan was dressed as usual for these functions, parade red-and-blues concealing a multitude of comm links.

"Ah, he's here in person tonight," the Count murmured, spotting his old Security chief across the vestibule. "There must be no major messes going on elsewhere, then. Good."

They divested their snow-spangled wraps to Gregor's household staff. Miles was shivering. He decided his timing had been skewed by this last adventure. Usually, he managed to arrange an off-planet assignment during winter in the capital. Illyan nodded, and came over to them.

"Good evening, Simon," said the Count.

"Good evening, sir. All calm and quiet, so far tonight."

"That's nice." The Count raised a dryly amused eyebrow at him. "I'm sure Prime Minister Racozy will be delighted to hear it."

Illyan opened his mouth, and closed it. "Er. Habit," he said in embarrassment. He stared at Count Vorkosigan with a look almost of frustration. As if the only way he knew how to relate to his commander of thirty years was by making reports; but Admiral Count Vorkosigan was no longer receiving them. "This feels very strange," he admitted.

"You'll get used to it, Simon," Countess Vorkosigan assured him. And towed her husband determinedly out of Illyan's orbit. The Count gave him a parting half-salute, seconding the Countess's words.

Illyan's eye fell on Miles and Mark, instead. "Hm," he said, in the tone of a man who had just come out second-best in some horse-trade.

Miles stood up straighter. The ImpSec medicos had cleared him to return to duty in two months, pending a final physical exam. He had not bothered mentioning the little problem with the convulsions to them. Perhaps the first one had just been an idiosyncratic effect of the fast-penta. Sure, and the second and third ones, drug flashbacks. But he hadn't had any more, after that. Miles smiled diffidently, trying to look very healthy. Illyan just shook his head, looking at him.

"Good evening, sir," Mark said to Illyan in turn. "Was ImpSec able to deliver my Winterfair gift to my clones all right?"

Illyan nodded. "Five hundred marks each, individually addressed and on time, yes, my lord."

"Good." Mark gave one of his sharper-edged smiles, the sort that made one wonder what he was thinking. The clones had been the pretext Mark had given Illyan for handing over to ImpSec the million Betan dollars he'd sworn he would; the funds were now in escrow for their needs, among other things paying for their place in that exclusive school. Illyan had been so boggled he'd gone absolutely robotic, an effect Miles had watched with great fascination. By the time the clones were out on their own the million would be about used up, Mark had figured. But the Winterfair gifts had been personal and separate.

Mark did not ask how his gift had been received, though Miles was dying to know; but rather, drifted on with another polite nod, as if Illyan were a clerk with whom he had just concluded some minor business. Miles saluted and caught up. Mark was suppressing a deep grin, resulting in a smirk-like look.

"All this time," Mark confided to Miles in a low voice, "I was worried about never having received a present. It never even crossed my mind to worry about never having *given* one. Winterfair is an entrancing holiday, y'know?" He sighed. "I wish I'd known those clone-kids well enough to pick something right for each. But at least this way, they have a gift of choice. It's like giving them two presents in one. How the devil do you folks give anything to, say, Gregor, though?"

"We fall back on tradition. Two hundred liters of

Dendarii mountain maple syrup, delivered annually to his household. Takes care of it. If you think Gregor's bad, think about our father, though. It's like trying to give a Winterfair gift to Father Frost himself."

"Yes, I've been puzzling over that one."

"Sometimes you can't give back. You just have to give on. Did you, ah . . . sign those credit chits to the clones?"

"Sort of. Actually, I signed them 'Father Frost.' " Mark cleared his throat. "That's the purpose of Winterfair, I think. To teach you how to . . . give on. Being Father Frost is the end-game, isn't it?"

"I think so."

"I'm getting it figured out," Mark nodded in determination.

They walked on together into the upstairs reception hall, and snagged drinks. They were collecting a lot of attention, Miles noted with amusement, covert stares from the flower of the Vor assembled there. *Oh, Barrayar. Do we have a surprise for you.*

He sure surprised me.

It was going to be huge fun, having Mark for a brother. *An ally at last! I think. . . .* Miles wondered if he could ever draw Mark on to love Barrayar as he did. The thought made him strangely nervous. Best not to love too much. Barrayar could be lethal, to take for one's lady. Still . . . a challenge. Enough challenges to go around, no artificial shortages of those here.

Miles would have to be careful about anything Mark might interpret as an attempt to dominate him, though. Mark's violent allergy to the least hint of control was perfectly understandable, Miles thought, but it made mentoring him a task of some delicacy.

Better not do too good a job, big brother. You're expendable now, y'know. He ran a hand down the bright uniform cloth of his jacket, coolly conscious of just what *expendable* meant. Yet being beaten by your student was the ultimate victory, for a teacher. *An enchanting paradox. I can't lose.*

Miles grinned. *Yeah, Mark. Catch me if you can. If you can.*

"Ah," Mark nodded to a man in a wine-red Vor House uniform, across the room. "Isn't that Lord Vorsmythe, the industrialist?"

"Yes."

"I'd love to talk with him. Do you know him? Can you introduce me?"

"Sure. Thinking of more investing, are you?"

"Yes, I've decided to diversify. Two-thirds Barrayaran investments, one-third galactic."

"Galactic?"

"I'm putting some into Escobaran medical technology, if you must know."

"Lilly?"

"Yep. She needs the set-up capital. I'm going to be a silent partner." Mark hesitated. "The solution has to be medical, you know. And . . . do you want to bet she won't return a profit?"

"Nope. In fact, I'd be very leery of laying any bet against you."

Mark smiled his sharpest. "Good. You're learning too."

Miles led Mark over and performed the requested introduction. Vorsmythe was delighted to find someone who actually wanted to talk about his work *here*, the bored look pasted on his face evaporating with Mark's first probing question; Miles turned Mark loose with a wave. Vorsmythe was gesturing expansively. Mark was listening as though he had a recorder whirring in his head. Miles left them to it.

He spied Delia Koudelka across the chamber, and made for her, to claim a dance later, and possibly cut out Ivan. If he was lucky, she might offer him a chance to use that line about the dueling scars, too.

CHAPTER THIRTY-THREE

After a most fascinating chat on the topic of Barrayaran high-growth economic sectors, Vorsmythe was reclaimed by his wife for some escort purpose, and dragged out of the window embrasure he and Mark had taken over; he parted with Mark reluctantly, promising to send him some prospectuses. Mark looked around for Miles again. The Count was not the only Vorkosigan in danger of over-doing it tonight while trying to prove his health to assorted observers, Mark had realized.

Mark had, by default, become Miles's confidant for self-tests he didn't want to share with his ImpSec superiors, checking knowledge bases, going over old material ranging from Service regs to five-space math. Mark had made a joke about it exactly once, before he realized the depth of terror that was driving Miles's obsessive probing. Particularly when they actually found some hole or another in Miles's memory. It bothered Mark deeply, this new hesitation, this desperate diffidence in his big brother. He hoped Miles's obnoxious self-confidence would return soon. It was another strange reciprocity, that Miles should have things he wanted to remember, and couldn't, while Mark had things he wanted to forget. And couldn't.

He would have to encourage Miles to show him around some more. Miles enjoyed playing the expert, it put him automatically in the one-up position to which he was addicted. Yeah, let Miles expand his highly-inflatable ego a bit. Mark could afford it, now. He'd give Miles a run for it some other time, when Miles was up to speed again. When it was more sporting.

Finally, by hopping up on a chair and craning his neck, Mark spotted his brother just leaving the reception chamber, in the company of a blonde woman in blue velvet—Delia Koudelka, Kareen's tallest sister. *They're here. Oh, God.* He abandoned the chair and went on a fast search for the Countess. He finally ran her to ground in a third floor lounge, chatting with some older women,obviously cronies. She took one look at his anxious smile, and excused herself to join him in a nook in the carpeted corridor.

"Have you run into a problem, Mark?" she asked, arranging her skirts on the little settee. He perched gingerly on the opposite end.

"I don't know. The Koudelkas are here. I promised back at the Emperor's Birthday to dance with Kareen, if I made it home in time. And . . . I'd asked her to talk with you. About me. Did she?"

"Yes."

"What did you tell her?"

"Well, it was a long conversation . . . ."

Oh, shit.

"But the gist of it was that I judged you an intelligent young man who had had some very unpleasant experiences, but if you could be persuaded to use that intelligence to get your problems straightened out, I could support your suit."

"Betan therapy?"

"Something like that."

"I've been thinking about Betan therapy. A lot. But I dread the thought of my therapist's notes all ending up in some ImpSec analyst's report. I don't want to be a damned show." *Again.*

"I think I could do something about that."

"Could you?" He looked up, shaken with hope. "Even though you wouldn't get to see the reports either?"

"Yes."

"I . . . would appreciate that, ma'am."

"Consider it a promise. My word as a Vorkosigan."

An adopted Vorkosigan, even more so than he. But he did not doubt her word. *Mother, with you all things seem possible.*

"I don't know what details you told Kareen—"

"Very few. She's only eighteen, after all. Barely assimilating her own new adulthood. More, hm, advanced matters could wait, I judged. She has to get through school, first, before undertaking any long-term commitment," she added pointedly.

"Oh. Um." He wasn't sure if he was relieved, or not. "It's all out of date anyway. I've acquired . . . a whole new set of problems, since. Much worse ones."

"I don't sense that, Mark. To me, you have appeared much more centered and relaxed, since you and Miles got back from Jackson's Whole. Even though you won't talk about it."

"I don't regret knowing myself, ma'am. I don't even regret . . . *being* myself." *Me and the black gang.* "But I do regret . . . being so far from Kareen. I believe I am a monster, of some sort. And in the play, Caliban does not marry Prospero's daughter. In fact, he gets stomped for trying, as I recall." Yes, how could he possibly explain Gorge and Grunt and Howl and Killer to someone like Kareen, without frightening or disgusting her? How could he ask her to feed his abnormal appetites, even in some dream or fantasy play? It was hopeless. Better not to try.

The Countess smiled wryly. "There are several things wrong with your analogy, Mark. In the first place, I can guarantee you are not subhuman, whatever you think you are. And Kareen is not superhuman, either. Though if you insist on treating her as a prize and not as a person, I can also guarantee you will run yourself into another kind of trouble." Her raised brows punctuated the point.

"I added, as condition to my blessing on your suit, the suggestion that she take the opportunity during her schooling on Beta Colony next year for some extra tutoring. A little Betan education in certain personal matters could go a long way, I think, to widening her perceptions enough to admit, um, complexities without choking. A certain liberality of view an eighteen-year-old simply cannot acquire on Barrayar."

"Oh." That was an idea which had never even crossed his mind, tackling the problem from Kareen's end. It made . . . so much sense. "I'd . . . thought about school on Beta Colony for myself, next year. Some galactic education would look good on my record, when I apply here for the job I have in mind. I don't want to leave it all to pure nepotism."

The Countess tilted her head in bemusement. "Good. It seems to me as though you have a sound set of long-range plans, well-coordinated to advance all your goals. You have only to carry them through. I entirely approve."

"Long-range. But . . . tonight is right now."

"And what were you planning to do tonight, Mark?"

"Dance with Kareen."

"I don't see the problem with that. You're allowed to dance. Whatever you are. This is not the play, Mark, and old Prospero has many daughters. One may even have a low taste for fishy fellows."

"How low?"

"Oh . . ." The Countess held out her hand at a level about equal to Mark's standing height. "At least that low. Go dance with the girl, Mark. She thinks you're interesting. Mother Nature gives a sense of romance to young people, in place of prudence, to advance the species. It's a trick—that makes us grow."

Walking across the Residence ballroom to greet Kareen Koudelka felt like the most terrifying thing Mark had ever voluntarily done, not excepting the first Dendarii combat drop onto Jackson's Whole. There the resemblance ended, for after that, things *improved.*

"Lord Mark!" she said happily. "They told me you were here."

You asked? "I've come to redeem my word and my dance, milady." He managed a Vorish bow.

"Good! It's about time. I've saved out all the mirror dances and the called reels."

All the simple dances he could be expected to do. "I had Miles teach me the steps to Mazeppa's Minuet last week," he added hopefully.

"Perfect. Oh, the music's starting—" She hauled him onto the inlaid floor.

She wore a swirling dark green dress with red trim, that set off her ash-blonde curls. In a sort of positive paranoia, he wondered if her outfit could possibly have been deliberately color-coordinated with his own clothes. Surely it must be a coincidence. How—? *My tailor to my mother to her mother to her. Hell, any ImpSec analyst ought to be able to figure out that data trail.*

Grunt, alas, had a distracting and distressing tendency to mentally undress her, and worse. But Grunt was not going to be permitted to speak tonight. *This one is Lord Mark's job. And he isn't going to screw it up this time.* Grunt could just lurk down in there and build up steam. Lord Mark would find a use for the power. Starting with keeping the beat. There was even a dance—Mazeppa's Minuet, as it happened—where the two partners touched each other, holding the hand or the waist, for almost the entire pattern.

All true wealth is biological, the Count had said. Mark finally saw exactly what he meant. For all his million Betan dollars, he could not buy this, the light in Kareen's eyes. Though it couldn't hurt . . . what was that damned

Earth bird or other, that built wildly elaborate nests to attract a mate?

They were in the middle of a mirror dance. "So, Kareen—you're a girl. I, uh, had this argument with Ivan. What do you think is the most attractive thing a fellow can have? A lightflyer, wealth . . . rank?" He hoped his tone suggested he was running some sort of scientific survey. Nothing personal, ma'am.

She pursed her lips. "Wit," she said at last.

Yeah. And what store are you going to buy that in, with all your Betan dollars, boy?

"Mirror dance, my turn," said Kareen. "What's the most important thing a woman can have?"

"Trust," he answered without thinking, and then thought about it to the point of almost losing his step. He was going to need a mountain of trust, no lie. *So, start building it tonight, Lord Mark old boy. Hauling one bloody basket load at a time, if you have to.*

He managed to make her laugh out loud four times, after that. He kept count.

He ate too much (even Gorge was sneakily sated), drank too much, talked too much, and danced *far* too much, and generally had a hell of a good time. The dancing was a little unexpected. Kareen reluctantly lent him to a string of several curious girlfriends. He was interesting to them only as a novelty, he judged, but he wasn't inclined to be picky. By two hours after midnight he was stimulated to the point of babbling, and starting to limp. Better to call it quits before Howl had to come out and take charge of his burnt-out remains. Besides, Miles had been sitting quietly in a corner for the last hour, looking uncharacteristically wilted.

A word passed to an Imperial household servant brought the Count's groundcar back for them, driven by the ubiquitous Pym, who had taken the Count and Countess home earlier. Miles and Mark took over the rear compartment, both sagging into their seats. Pym pulled out past the Residence's guarded gates and into the winter streets, grown as night-quiet as the capital's streets ever did, only a few other vehicles prowling past. Miles turned the heat up high, and settled back with his eyes half-closed.

Mark and his brother were alone in the compartment. Mark counted the number of people present. One, two. Three, four, five, six, seven. Lord Miles Vorkosigan and Admiral Naismith. Lord Mark Vorkosigan and Gorge, Grunt, Howl, and Killer.

Admiral Naismith was a *much* classier creation, Mark thought with a silent sigh of envy. Miles could take the Admiral out to parties, introduce him to women, parade him in public almost anywhere but Barrayar itself. *I suppose what my black gang lacks in savoir faire, we make up in numbers. . . .*

But they all ran together, he and the black gang, on the deepest level. No part could be excised without butchering the whole. *So, I'll just have to look after you all. Somehow. You just live, down there in the dark. Because someday, in some desperate hour, I may need you again. You took care of me. I'll take care of you.*

Mark wondered what Admiral Naismith took care of, for Miles. Something subtle but important—the Countess even saw it. What was it she had said? *I won't seriously fear for Miles's sanity till he's cut off from the little Admiral.* Hence the desperate edge in Miles's drive to reclaim his health. His job with ImpSec was his lifeline to Admiral Naismith.

I think I understand that. Oh, yes.

"Did I ever apologize, for getting you killed?" Mark asked aloud.

"Not that I recall. . . . It wasn't altogether your fault. I had no business mounting that drop mission. Should have taken Vasa Luigi up on his ransom offer. Except . . ."

"Except what?"

"He wouldn't sell you to me. I suspect he was already planning to get a higher bid from Ryoval, even then."

"That would be my guess. Ah . . . thank you."

"I'm not sure it made a difference, in the end," Miles said apologetically. "Since Ryoval just tried again."

"Oh, yes. It made a huge difference, in the end. All the difference in the world." Mark smiled slightly, in the dark. Vorbarr Sultana's wildly assorted architecture passed by outside the canopy, snow-softened to a kind of unity.

"What do we do tomorrow?" Mark asked.

"Sleep in," murmured Miles, oozing down a little further in his stiff uniform collar, rather like paste being sucked back into a tube.

"After that."

"The party season ends here in three days, with the Winterfair bonfires. If my—our parents really go down to the District, I suppose I'll divide my time between Hassadar and here, till ImpSec lets me come back to work. Hassadar is slightly warmer than Vorbarr Sultana, this time of year. Ah—you're invited to come along with me, if you like."

"Thank you. I accept."

"What do you plan to do?"

"After your medical leave is over, I think I'll sign up for one of your schools."

"Which one?"

"If the Count and Countess are going to be mainly residing in Hassadar, maybe the District college there."

"Hm. I should warn you, you'll find a more, um, rural crowd there than you would in Vorbarr Sultana. You'll run into more Barrayaran old-style thinking."

"Good. That's exactly what I want. I need to learn how to handle those hassles without accidentally killing people."

"Er," said Miles, "true. What are you going to study?"

"It almost doesn't matter. It will give me an official status—student—and a chance to study the *people.* Data I can get off a machine. But I'm weak on people. There's so much to learn. I need to know . . . everything."

It was another kind of hunger, this insatiable gluttony for knowledge. An ImpSec analyst must surely possess the hugest possible data-base. The fellows he'd met at the coffee dispenser in ImpSec HQ had conducted flashing conversations with each other over the most appalling range and depth of subjects. He was going to have to hustle, if he wanted to compete in that crowd. *To win.*

Miles laughed.

"What's funny?"

"I'm just wondering what Hassadar is going to learn from *you.*"

The ground car turned in at the gates of Vorkosigan House, and slowed. "Maybe I'll get up early," said Mark. "There's a lot to do."

Miles grinned sleepily, puddled down in his uniform. "Welcome to the beginning."

Miles Vorkosigan/Naismith: His Universe and Times

Chronology	Events	Chronicle
Approx. 200 years before Miles's birth	Quaddies are created by genetic engineering.	*Falling Free*
During Beta-Barrayaran War	Cordelia Naismith meets Lord Aral Vorkosigan while on opposite sides of a war. Despite difficulties, they fall in love and are married.	*Shards of Honor*
The Vordarian Pretendership	While Cordelia is pregnant, an attempt to assassinate Aral by poison gas fails, but Cordelia is affected; Miles Vorkosigan is born with bones that will always be brittle and other medical problems. His growth will be stunted.	*Barrayar*
Miles is 17	Miles fails to pass physical test to get into the Service Academy. On a trip, necessities force him to improvise the Free Dendarii Mercenaries into existence; he has	*The Warrior's Apprentice*

Chronology	Events	Chronicle
	unintended but unavoidable adventures for four months. Leaves the Dendarii in Ky Tung's competent hands and takes Elli Quinn to Beta for rebuilding of her damaged face; returns to Barrayar to thwart plot against his father. Emperor pulls strings to get Miles into the Academy.	
Miles is 20	Ensign Miles graduates and immediately has to take on one of the duties of the Barrayaran nobility and act as detective and judge in a murder case. Shortly afterwards, his first military assignment ends with his arrest. Miles has to rejoin the Dendarii to rescue the young Barrayaran emperor. Emperor accepts Dendarii as his personal secret service force.	"The Mountains of Mourning" in *Borders of Infinity* *The Vor Game*
Miles is 22	Miles and his cousin Ivan attend a Cetagandan state funeral and are caught up in Cetagandan internal politics.	*Cetaganda*

Chronology	Events	Chronicle
	Miles sends Commander Elli Quinn, who's been given a new face on Beta, on a solo mission to Kline Station.	*Ethan of Athos*
Miles is 23	Now a Barrayaran Lieutenant, Miles goes with the Dendarii to smuggle a scientist out of Jackson's Whole. Miles's fragile leg bones have been replaced by synthetics.	"Labyrinth" in *Borders of Infinity*
Miles is 24	Miles plots from within a Cetagandan prison camp on Dagoola IV to free the prisoners. The Dendarii fleet is pursued by the Cetagandans and finally reaches Earth for repairs. Miles has to juggle both his identities at once, raise money for repairs, and defeat a plot to replace him with a double. Ky Tung stays on Earth. Commander Elli Quinn is now Miles's right-hand officer. Miles and the Dendarii depart for Sector IV on a rescue mission.	"The Borders of Infinity" in *Borders of Infinity* *Brothers in Arms*

Chronology	Events	Chronicle
Miles is 25	Hospitalized after previous mission, Miles's broken arms are replaced by synthetic bones. With Simon Illyan, Miles undoes yet another plot against his father while flat on his back.	*Borders of Infinity*
Miles is 28	Miles meets his clone brother Mark again, this time on Jackson's Whole.	*Mirror Dance*
Miles is 29	Miles hits thirty; thirty hits back.	*Memory*
Miles is 30	Emperor Gregor dispatches Miles to Komarr to investigate a space accident, where he finds old politics and new technology make a deadly mix.	*Komarr*
Miles is 31	The Emperor's wedding sparks romance and intrigue on Barrayar, and Miles plunges up to his neck in both.	*A Civil Campaign*

Miles Had a Cunning Plan...

A CIVIL CAMPAIGN

by Lois McMaster Bujold

The following is an excerpt from the latest novel in the Hugo-winning Vorkosigan series, available in paperback from Baen Books.

0-671-57885-5
$7.99

CHAPTER ONE

The big groundcar jerked to a stop centimeters fromthe vehicle ahead of it, and Armsman Pym, driving, swore under his breath. Miles settled back again in his seat beside him, wincing at a vision of the acrimonious street scene from which Pym's reflexes had delivered them. Miles wondered if he could have persuaded the feckless prole in front of them that being rear-ended by an Imperial Auditor was a privilege to be treasured. Likely not. The Vorbarr Sultana University student darting across the boulevard on foot, who had been the cause of the quick stop, scampered off through the jam without a backward glance. The line of groundcars started up once more.

"Have you heard if the municipal traffic control system will be coming on line soon?" Pym asked, apropos of what Miles counted as their third near-miss this week.

"Nope. Delayed in development again, Lord Vorbohn the Younger reports. Due to the increase in fatal lightflyer incidents, they're concentrating on getting the automated air system up first."

Pym nodded, and returned his attention to the crowded road. The Armsman was a habitually fit man, his graying temples seeming merely an accent to his brown-and-silver uniform. He'd served the Vorkosigans as a liege-sworn guard since Miles had been an Academy cadet, and would doubtless go on doing so till either he died of old age, or they were all killed in traffic.

So much for short cuts. Next time they'd go around the campus. Miles watched through the canopy as the taller new buildings of the University fell behind, and they passed through its spiked iron gates into the pleasant old residential streets favored by the families of senior professors and staff. The distinctive architecture dated from the last un-electrified decade before the end of the Time of Isolation. This area had been reclaimed from decay in the past generation, and now featured shady green Earth trees, and bright flower boxes under the tall narrow windows of the tall narrow houses. Miles rebalanced the flower arrangement between his feet. Would it be seen as redundant by its intended recipient?

Pym glanced aside at his slight movement, following his eye to the foliage on the floor. "The lady you met on Komarr seems to have made a strong impression on you, m'lord . . ." He trailed off invitingly.

"Yes," said Miles, uninvitingly.

"Your lady mother had high hopes of that very attractive Miss Captain Quinn you brought home those times." Was that a wistful note in Pym's voice?

"Miss Admiral Quinn, now," Miles corrected with a sigh. "So had I. But she made the right choice for her." He grimaced out the canopy. "I've sworn off falling in love with galactic women and then trying to persuade them to immigrate to Barrayar. I've concluded my only hope is to find a woman who can already stand Barrayar, and persuade her to like me."

"And does Madame Vorsoisson like Barrayar?"

"About as well as I do." He smiled grimly.

"And, ah . . . the second part?"

"We'll see, Pym." *Or not, as the case may be.* At least the spectacle of a man of thirty-plus, going courting seriously for the first time in his life—the first time in the Barrayaran style, anyway—promised to provide hours of entertainment for his interested staff.

Miles let his breath and his nervous irritation trickle out through his nostrils as Pym found a place to park near Lord

Auditor Vorthys's doorstep, and expertly wedged the polished old armored groundcar into the inadequate space. Pym popped the canopy; Miles climbed out, and stared up at the three-story patterned tile front of his colleague's home.

Georg Vorthys had been a professor of engineering failure analysis at the Imperial University for thirty years. He and his wife had lived in this house for most of their married life, raising three children and two academic careers, before Emperor Gregor had appointed Vorthys as one of his hand-picked Imperial Auditors. Neither of the Professors Vorthys had seen any reason to change their comfortable lifestyle merely because the awesome powers of an Emperor's Voice had been conferred upon the retired engineer; Madame Dr. Vorthys still walked every day to her classes. *Dear no, Miles!* the Professora had said to him, when he'd once wondered aloud at their passing up this opportunity for social display. *Can you imagine moving all those books?* Not to mention the laboratory and workshop jamming the entire basement.

Their cheery inertia proved a happy chance, when they invited their recently-widowed niece and her young son to live with them while she completed her own education. Plenty of room, the Professor had boomed jovially, the top floor is so empty since the children left. So close to classes, the Professora had pointed out practically. *Less than six kilometers from Vorkosigan House!* Miles had exulted in his mind, adding a polite murmur of encouragement aloud. And so Ekaterin Nile Vorvayne Vorsoisson had arrived. *She's here, she's here!* Might she be looking down at him from the shadows of some upstairs window even now?

Miles glanced anxiously down the all-too-short length of his body. If his dwarfish stature bothered her, she'd shown no signs of it so far. Well and good. Going on to the aspects of his appearance he could control: no food stains spattered his plain gray tunic, no unfortunate street detritus clung to the soles of his polished half-boots. He checked his distorted reflection in the groundcar's rear canopy. Its convex mirroring widened his lean, if slightly hunched, body to something resembling his obese clone-brother Mark, a comparison he primly ignored. Mark was, thank God, not here. He essayed a smile, for practice; in the canopy, it came out twisted and repellent. No dark hair sticking out in odd directions, anyway.

"You look just fine, my lord," Pym said in a bracing tone from the front compartment. Miles's face heated, and he flinched away from his reflection. He recovered himself enough to take the flower arrangement and rolled-up flimsy Pym handed out to him with, he hoped, a tolerably bland expression. He balanced the load in his arms, turned to face the front steps, and took a deep breath.

After about a minute, Pym inquired helpfully from behind him, "Would you like me to carry anything?"

"No. Thank you." Miles trod up the steps and wiggled a finger free to press the chime-pad. Pym pulled out a reader, and settled comfortably in the groundcar to await his lord's pleasure.

Footsteps sounded from within, and the door swung open on the smiling pink face of the Professora. Her gray hair was wound up on her head in her usual style. She wore a dark rose dress with a light rose bolero, embroidered with green vines in the manner of her home District. This somewhat formal Vor mode, which suggested she was just on her way either in or out, was belied by the soft buskins on her feet. "Hello, Miles. Goodness, you're prompt."

"Professora." Miles ducked a nod to her, and smiled in turn. "Is she here? Is she in? Is she well? You said this would be a good time. I'm not too early, am I? I thought I'd be late. The traffic was miserable. You're going to be around, aren't you? I brought these. Do you think she'll like them?" The sticking-up red flowers tickled his nose as he displayed his gift while still clutching the rolled-up flimsy, which had a tendency to try to unroll and escape whenever his grip loosened.

"Come in, yes, all's well. She's here, she's fine, and the flowers are very nice—" The Professora rescued the bouquet and ushered him into her tiled hallway, closing the door firmly behind them with her foot. The house was dim and cool after the spring sunshine outside, and had a fine aroma of wood wax, old books, and a touch of academic dust.

"She looked pretty pale and fatigued at Tien's funeral. Surrounded by all those relatives. We really didn't get a chance to say more than two words each." *I'm sorry* and *Thank you*, to be precise. Not that he'd wanted to talk much to the late Tien Vorsoisson's family.

"It was an immense strain for her, I think," said the Professora judiciously. "She'd been through so much horror, and except for Georg and myself—and you—there wasn't a soul there to whom she could talk truth about it. Of course, her first concern was getting Nikki through it all. But she held together without a crack from first to last. I was very proud of her."

"Indeed. And she is . . . ?" Miles craned his neck, glancing into the rooms off the entry hall: a cluttered study lined with bookshelves, and a cluttered parlor lined with bookshelves. No young widows.

"Right this way." The Professora conducted him down the hall and out through her kitchen to the little urban back garden. A couple of tall trees and a brick wall made a private nook of it. Beyond a tiny circle of green grass, at a table in the shade, a woman sat with flimsies and a reader spread before her. She was chewing gently on the end of a stylus, and her dark brows were drawn down in her absorption. She wore a calf-length dress in much the same style as the Professora's, but solid black, with the high collar buttoned up to her neck. Her bolero was gray, trimmed with simple black braid running around its edge. Her dark hair was drawn back to a thick braided knot at the nape of her neck. She looked up at the sound of the door opening; her brows flew up and her lips parted in a flashing smile that made Miles blink. *Ekaterin.*

"Mil—my Lord Auditor!" She rose in a flare of skirt; he bowed over her hand.

"Madame Vorsoisson. You look well." She looked wonderful, if still much too pale. Part of that might be the effect of all that severe black, which also made her eyes show a brilliant blue-gray. "Welcome to Vorbarr Sultana. I brought these . . ." He gestured, and the Professora set the flower arrangement down on the table. "Though they hardly seem needed, out here."

"They're lovely," Ekaterin assured him, sniffing them in approval. "I'll take them up to my room later, where they will be very welcome. Since the weather has brightened up, I find I spend as much time as possible out here, under the real sky."

She'd spent nearly a year sealed in a Komarran dome. "I can understand that," Miles said. The conversation hiccuped to a brief stop, while they smiled at each other.

Ekaterin recovered first. "Thank you for coming to Tien's funeral. It meant so much to me."

"It was the least I could do, under the circumstances. I'm only sorry I couldn't do more."

"But you've already done so much for me and Nikki— " She broke off at his gesture of embarrassed denial and instead said, "But won't you sit down? Aunt Vorthys—?" She drew back one of the spindly garden chairs.

The Professora shook her head. "I have a few things to attend to inside. Carry on." She added a little cryptically, "You'll do fine."

She went back into her house, and Miles sat across from Ekaterin, placing his flimsy on the table to await its strategic moment. It half-unrolled, eagerly.

"Is your case all wound up?" she asked.

"That case will have ramifications for years to come, but I'm done with it for now," Miles replied. "I just turned in my last reports yesterday, or I would have been here to welcome you earlier." Well, that and a vestigial sense that he'd ought to let the poor woman at least get her bags unpacked, before descending in force.

"Will you be sent out on another assignment now?"

"I don't think Gregor will let me risk getting tied up elsewhere till after his marriage. For the next couple of months, I'm afraid all my duties will be social ones."

"I'm sure you'll do them with your usual flair."

God, I hope not. "I don't think flair is exactly what my Aunt Vorpatril—she's in charge of all the Emperor's wedding arrangements—would wish from me. More like, shut up and do what you're told, Miles. But speaking of paperwork, how's your own? Is Tien's estate settled? Did you manage to recapture Nikki's guardianship from that cousin of his?"

"Vassily Vorsoisson? Yes, thank heavens, there was no problem with that part."

"So, ah, what's all this, then?" Miles nodded at the cluttered table.

"I'm planning my course work for the next session at university. I was too late to start this summer, so I'll begin in the fall. There's so much to choose from. I feel so ignorant."

"Educated is what you aim to be coming out, not going in."

"I suppose so."

"And what will you choose?"

"Oh, I'll start with basics—biology, chemistry . . ." She brightened. "One real horticulture course." She gestured at her flimsies. "For the rest of the season, I'm trying to find some sort of paying work. I'd like to feel I'm not totally dependent on the charity of my relatives, even if it's only my pocket money."

That seemed almost the opening he was looking for, but Miles's eye caught sight of a red ceramic basin, sitting on the wooden planks forming a seat bordering a raised garden bed. In the middle of the pot a red-brown blob, with a fuzzy fringe like a rooster's crest growing out of it, pushed up through the dirt. If it was what he thought . . . He pointed to the basin. "Is that by chance your old bonsai'd skellytum? Is it going to live?"

She smiled. "Well, at least it's the start of a new skellytum. Most of the fragments of the old one died on the way home from Komarr, but that one took."

"You have a—for native Barrayaran plants, I don't suppose you can call it a green thumb, can you?"

"Not unless they're suffering from some pretty serious plant diseases, no."

"Speaking of gardens." Now, how to do this without jamming his foot in his mouth too deeply. "I don't think, in all the other uproar, I ever had a chance to tell you how impressed I was with your garden designs that I saw on your comconsole."

"Oh." Her smile fled, and she shrugged. "They were no great thing. Just twiddling."

Right. Let them not bring up any more of the recent past than absolutely necessary, till time had a chance to blunt memory's razor edges. "It was your Barrayaran garden, the one with all the native species, which caught my eye. I'd never seen anything like it."

"There are a dozen of them around. Several of the District universities keep them, as living libraries for their biology students. It's not really an original idea."

"Well," he persevered, feeling like a fish swimming upstream against this current of self-deprecation, "*I* thought it was very fine, and deserved better than just being a ghost garden on the holovid. I have this spare lot, you see . . ."

He flattened out his flimsy, which was a ground plot of the block occupied by Vorkosigan House. He tapped his finger on the bare square at the end. "There used to be another great house, next to ours, which was torn down during the Regency. ImpSec wouldn't let us build anything else—they wanted it as a security zone. There's nothing there but some scraggly grass, and a couple of trees that somehow survived ImpSec's enthusiasm for clear lines of fire. And a criss-cross of walks, where people made mud paths by taking short cuts, and they finally gave up and put some gravel down. It's an extremely boring piece of ground." So boring he had completely ignored it, till now.

She tilted her head, to follow his hand as it blocked out the space on the ground plan. Her own long finger made to trace a delicate curve, but then shyly withdrew. He wondered what possibility her mind's eye had just seen, there.

"Now, *I* think," he went on valiantly, "that it would be a splendid thing to install a Barrayaran garden—all native species—open to the public, in this space. A sort of gift from the Vorkosigan family to the city of Vorbarr Sultana. With running water, like in your design, and walks and benches and all those civilized things. And those discreet little name tags on all the plants, so more people could learn about the old ecology and all that." There: art, public service, education—was there any bait he'd left off his hook? Oh yes, money. "It's a happy chance that you're looking for a summer job," *chance, hah, watch and see if I leave anything to chance,* "because I think you'd be the ideal person to take this on. Design and oversee the installation of the thing. I could give you an unlimited, um, generous budget, and a salary, of course. You could hire workmen, bring in whatever you needed."

And she would have to visit Vorkosigan House practically *every day*, and consult *frequently* with its resident lord. And by the time the shock of her husband's death had worn away, and she was ready to put off her forbidding formal mourning garb, and every unattached Vor bachelor in the capital showed up on her doorstep, Miles could have a lock on her affections that would permit him to fend off the most glittering competition. It was too soon, wildly too soon, to suggest courtship to her crippled heart; he had that clear in his head, even if his own heart howled in frustration. But a straightforward business friendship just might get past her guard. . . .

Her eyebrows had flown up; she touched an uncertain finger to those exquisite, pale unpainted lips. "This is exactly the sort of thing I wish to train to do. I don't know how to do it *yet*."

"On-the-job training," Miles responded instantly. "Apprenticeship. Learning by doing. You have to start sometime. You can't start sooner than now."

"But what if I make some dreadful mistake?"

"I do intend this be an *ongoing* project. People who are enthusiasts about this sort of thing always seem to be changing their gardens around. They get bored with the same view all the time, I guess. If you come up with better ideas later, you can always revise the plan. It will provide variety."

"I don't want to waste your money."

If she ever became Lady Vorkosigan, she would have to get over that quirk, Miles decided firmly.

"You don't have to decide here on the spot," he purred, and cleared his throat. *Watch that tone, boy. Business.*

"Why don't you come to Vorkosigan House tomorrow, and walk over the site in person, and see what ideas it stirs up in your mind. You really can't tell anything by looking at a flimsy. We can have lunch, afterward, and talk about what you see as the problems and possibilities then. Logical?"

She blinked. "Yes, very." Her hand crept back curiously toward the flimsy.

"What time may I pick you up?"

"Whatever is convenient for you, Lord Vorkosigan. Oh, I take that back. If it's after twelve hundred, my aunt will be back from her morning class, and Nikki can stay with her."

"Excellent!" Yes, much as he liked Ekaterin's son, Miles thought he could do without the assistance of an active nine-year-old in this delicate dance. "Twelve hundred it will be. Consider it a deal." Only a little belatedly, he added, "And how does Nikki like Vorbarr Sultana, so far?"

"He seems to like his room, and this house. I think he's going to get a little bored, if he has to wait until his school starts to locate boys his own age."

It would not do to leave Nikolai Vorsoisson out of his calculations. "I gather then that the retro-genes took, and he's in no more danger of developing the symptoms of Vorzohn's Dystrophy?"

A smile of deep maternal satisfaction softened her face. "That's right. I'm so pleased. The doctors in the clinic here in Vorbarr Sultana report he had a very clean and complete cellular uptake. Developmentally, it should be just as if he'd never inherited the mutation at all." She glanced across at him. "It's as if I'd had a five-hundred-kilo weight lifted from me. I could fly, I think."

So you should.

Nikki himself emerged from the house at this moment, carrying a plate of cookies with an air of consequence, followed by the Professora with a tea tray and cups. Miles and Ekaterin hastened to clear a place on the table.

"Hello, Nikki," said Miles.

"Hi, Lord Vorkosigan. Is that your groundcar out front?"

"Yes."

"It's a barge." This observation was delivered without scorn, as a point of interest.

"I know. It's a relic of my father's time as Regent. It's armored, in fact—has a massive momentum."

"Oh yeah?" Nikki's interest soared. "Did it ever get shot at?"

"I don't believe that particular car ever did, no."

"Huh."

When Miles had last seen Nikki, the boy had been wooden-faced and pale with concentration, carrying the taper to light his father's funeral offering, obviously anxious to get his part of the ceremony right. He looked much better now, his brown eyes quick and his face mobile again. The Professora settled and poured tea, and the conversation became general for a time.

It became clear shortly that Nikki's interest was more in the food than in his mother's visitor; he declined a flatteringly grownup offer of tea, and with his great-aunt's permission snagged several cookies and dodged back indoors to whatever he'd been occupying himself with before. Miles tried to remember what age he'd been when his own parents' friends had stopped seeming part of the furniture. Well, except for the military men in his father's train, of course, who'd always riveted his attention. But then, Miles had been military-mad from the time he could walk. Nikki was jump-ship mad, and would probably light up for a jump pilot. Perhaps Miles could provide one sometime, for Nikki's delectation. A happily married one, he corrected this thought.

He'd laid his bait on the table, Ekaterin had taken it; it was time to quit while he was winning. But he knew for a fact that she'd already turned down one premature offer of remarriage from a completely unexpected quarter. *Had* any of Vorbarr Sultana's excess Vor males found her yet? The capital was crawling with young officers, rising bureaucrats, aggressive entrepreneurs, men of ambition and wealth and rank drawn to the empire's heart. But not, by a ratio of almost five to three, with their sisters. The parents of the preceding generation had taken galactic sex-selection technologies much too far in their foolish passion for male heirs, and the very sons they'd so cherished—Miles's contemporaries—had inherited the resulting mating mess. Go to any formal party in Vorbarr Sultana these days, and you could practically taste the damned testosterone in the air, volatilized by the alcohol no doubt.

"So, ah . . . have you had any other callers yet, Ekaterin?"

"I only arrived a week ago."

That was neither yes nor no. "I'd think you'd have the bachelors out in force in no time." Wait, he hadn't meant to point that out . . .

"Surely," she gestured down her black dress, "this will keep them away. If they have any manners at all."

"Mm, I'm not so sure. The social scene is pretty intense just now."

She shook her head and smiled bleakly. "It makes no difference to me. I had a decade of . . . of marriage. I don't need to repeat the experience. The other women are welcome to the bachelors; they can have my share, in fact." The conviction in her face was backed by an uncharacteristic hint of steel in her voice. "That's one mistake I don't have to make twice. I'll never remarry."

Miles controlled his flinch, and managed a sympathetic, interested smile at this confidence. *We're just friends. I'm not hustling you, no, no. No need to fling up your defenses, milady, not for me.*

He couldn't make this go faster by pushing harder; all he could do was screw it up worse. Forced to be satisfied with his one day's progress, Miles finished his tea, exchanged a few more pleasantries with the two women, and took his leave.

Pym hurried to open the groundcar door as Miles skipped down the last three steps in one jump. He flung himself into the passenger seat, and as Pym slipped back into the driver's side and closed the canopy, waved grandly. "Home, Pym."

Pym eased the groundcar into the street, and inquired mildly, "Go well, did it, m'lord?"

"Just exactly as I had planned. She's coming to Vorkosigan House tomorrow for lunch. As soon as we get home, I want you to call that gardening service—get them to get a crew out tonight and give the grounds an extra going-over. And talk to—no, *I'll* talk to Ma Kosti. Lunch must be . . . exquisite, yes. Ivan always says women like food. But not too heavy. Wine—does she drink wine in the daytime, I wonder? I'll offer it, anyway. Something from the estate. And tea if she doesn't choose the wine, I know she drinks tea. Scratch the wine. And get the house cleaning crew in, get all those covers off the first floor furniture—off all the furniture. I want to give her a tour of the house while she still doesn't realize . . . No, wait. I wonder . . . if the place was a dreadful bachelor mess, perhaps it would stir up her pity. Maybe instead I ought to clutter it up some more, used glasses strategically piled up, the odd fruit peel under the sofa—a silent appeal, *Help us! Move in and straighten this poor fellow out*—or would that be more likely to frighten her off? What do you think, Pym?"

Pym pursed his lips judiciously, as if considering whether it was within his Armsman's duties to spike his lord's taste for street theater. He finally said in a cautious tone, "If I may presume to speak for the household, I *think* we should prefer to put our best foot forward. Under the circumstances."

"Oh. All right."

Miles fell silent for a few moments, staring out the canopy as they threaded through the crowded city streets, out of the University district and across a mazelike corner of the Old Town, angling back toward Vorkosigan House. When he spoke again, the manic humor had drained from his voice, leaving it cooler and bleaker.

"We'll be picking her up tomorrow at twelve hundred. You'll drive. You will always drive, when Madame Vorsoisson or her son are aboard. Figure it in to your duty schedule from now on."

"Yes, m'lord." Pym added a carefully laconic, "My pleasure."

The seizure disorder was the last souvenir that ImpSec Captain Miles Vorkosigan had brought home from his decade of military missions. He'd been lucky to get out of the cryo-chamber alive and with his mind intact; Miles was fully aware that many did not fare nearly so well. Lucky to be merely medically discharged from the Emperor's Service, not buried with honors, the last of his glorious line, or reduced to some animal or vegetative existence. The seizure-stimulator the military doctors had issued him to bleed off his convulsions was very far from being a cure, though it was supposed to keep them from happening at random times. Miles drove, and flew his lightflyer—but only alone. He never took passengers anymore. Pym's batman's duties had been expanded to include medical assistance; he had by now witnessed enough of Miles's disturbing seizures to be grateful for this unusual burst of level-headedness.

One corner of Miles's mouth crooked up. After a moment, he asked, "And how did you ever capture Ma Pym, back in the old days, Pym? Did you put your best foot forward?"

"It's been almost eighteen years ago. The details have gone a bit fuzzy." Pym smiled a little. "I was a senior sergeant at the time. I'd taken the ImpSec advanced course, and was assigned to security duty at Vorhartung Castle. She had a clerk's job in the archives there. I thought, I wasn't some boy anymore, it was time I got serious . . . though I'm not just sure that wasn't an idea she put into my head, because she claims she spotted me first."

"Ah, a handsome fellow in uniform, I see. Does it every time. So why'd you decide to quit the Imperial Service and apply to the Count-my-father?"

"Eh, it seemed the right progression. Our little daughter'd come along by then, I was just finishing my twenty-years hitch, and I was facing whether or not to continue my enlistment. My wife's family was here, and her roots, and she didn't particularly fancy following the flag with children in tow. Captain Illyan, who knew I was District-born, was kind enough to give me a tip, that your father had a place open in his Armsmen's score. And a recommendation, when I nerved up to apply. I figured a Count's Armsman would be a more settled job, for a family man."

The groundcar arrived at Vorkosigan House; the ImpSec

corporal on duty opened the gates for them, and Pym pulled around to the porte cochère and popped the canopy.

"Thank you, Pym," Miles said, and hesitated. "A word in your ear. Two words."

Pym made to look attentive.

"When you chance to socialize with the Armsmen of other Houses . . . I'd appreciate it if you wouldn't mention Madame Vorsoisson. I wouldn't want her to be the subject of invasive gossip, and, um . . . she's no business of everyone and his younger brother anyway, eh?"

"A loyal Armsman does not gossip, m'lord," said Pym stiffly.

"No, of course not. Sorry, I didn't mean to imply . . . um, sorry. Anyway. The other thing. I'm maybe guilty of saying a little too much myself, you see. I'm not actually courting Madame Vorsoisson."

Pym tried to look properly blank, but a confused expression leaked into his face. Miles added hastily, "I mean, not *formally*. Not *yet*. She's . . . she's had a difficult time, recently, and she's a touch . . . skittish. Any premature declaration on my part is likely to be disastrous, I'm afraid. It's a timing problem. Discreet is the watchword, if you see what I mean?"

Pym attempted a discreet but supportive-looking smile.

"We're just good friends," Miles reiterated. "Anyway, we're going to be."

"Yes, m'lord. I understand."

"Ah. Good. Thank you." Miles climbed out of the groundcar, and added over his shoulder as he headed into the house, "Find me in the kitchen when you've put the car away."

(the above was an excerpt from A Civil Campaign, *by Lois McMaster Bujold, available from Baen Books, ISBN 0-671-57885-5, $7.99, paperback)*

PRAISE FOR *LOIS McMASTER BUJOLD*

What the critics say:

The Warrior's Apprentice: "Now here's a fun romp through the spaceways—not so much a space opera as space ballet. . . . it has all the 'right stuff.' A lot of thought and thoughtfulness stand behind the all-too-human characters. Enjoy this one, and look forward to the next." —Dean Lambe, *SF Reviews*

"The pace is breathless, the characterization thoughtful and emotionally powerful, and the author's narrative technique and command of language compelling. Highly recommended."
—*Booklist*

Brothers in Arms: ". . . she gives it a genuine depth of character, while reveling in the wild turnings of her tale. . . . Bujold is as audacious as her favorite hero, and as brilliantly (if sneakily) successful." —*Locus*

"Miles Vorkosigan is such a great character that I'll read anything Lois wants to write about him. . . . a book to re-read on cold rainy days." —Robert Coulson, *Comic Buyer's Guide*

Borders of Infinity: "Bujold's series hero Miles Vorkosigan may be a lord by birth and an admiral by rank, but a bone disease that has left him hobbled and in frequent pain has sensitized him to the suffering of outcasts in his very hierarchical era. . . . Playing off Miles's reserve and cleverness, Bujold draws outrageous and outlandish foils to color her high-minded adventures." —*Publishers Weekly*

Falling Free: "In *Falling Free* Lois McMaster Bujold has written her fourth straight superb novel. . . . How to break down a talent like Bujold's into analyzable components? Best not to try. Best to say: 'Read, or you will be missing something extraordinary.'" —Roland Green, *Chicago Sun-Times*

The Vor Game: "The chronicles of Miles Vorkosigan are far too witty to be literary junk food, but they rouse the kind of craving that makes popcorn magically vanish during a double feature." —Faren Miller, *Locus*

MORE PRAISE FOR LOIS McMASTER BUJOLD

What the readers say:

"My copy of *Shards of Honor* is falling apart I've reread it so often. . . . I'll read whatever you write. You've certainly proved yourself a grand storyteller."

—Lisa Kolbe, Colorado Springs, CO

"I experience the stories of Miles Vorkosigan as almost viscerally uplifting. . . . But certainly, even the weightiest theme would have less impact than a cinder on snow were it not for a rousing good story, and good story-telling with it. This is the second thing I want to thank you for. . . . I suppose if you boiled down all I've said to its simplest expression, it would be that I immensely enjoy and admire your work. I submit that, as literature, your work raises the overall level of the science fiction genre, and spiritually, your work cannot avoid positively influencing all who read it."

—Glen Stonebraker, Gaithersburg, MD

" 'The Mountains of Mourning' [in *Borders of Infinity*] was one of the best-crafted, and simply best, works I'd ever read. When I finished it, I immediately turned back to the beginning and read it again, and I can't remember the last time I did that."

—Betsy Bizot, Lisle, IL

"I can only hope that you will continue to write, so that I can continue to read (and of course buy) your books, for they make me laugh and cry and think . . . rare indeed."

—Steven Knott, Major, USAF